TRIAL & TRIUMPH

A NOVEL ABOUT MAIMONIDES

OTHER BOOKS BY RICHARD G. HUBLER

Fiction:

I'VE GOT MINE
THE QUIET KINGDOM
THE BRASS GOD
THE CHASE
IN DARKEST CHILDHOOD
THE PASS
MAN IN THE SKY
THE SHATTERING OF THE IMAGE
TRUE LOVE, TRUE LOVE
BLUE-AND-GOLD MAN
WORLD'S SHORTEST STORIES (editor)

Nonfiction:

LOU GEHRIG
I FLEW FOR CHINA (with Royal Leonard)
FLYING LEATHERNECKS (with John DeChant)
SAC: STRATEGIC AIR COMMAND
ST. LOUIS WOMAN (with Helen Traubel)
BIG EIGHT
STRAIGHT UP
WHERE'S THE REST OF ME? (with Ronald Reagan)

TRIAL & TRIUMPH

A NOVEL ABOUT MAIMONIDES

BY LESTER M. MORRISON & RICHARD G. HUBLER

CROWN PUBLISHERS, INC., NEW YORK

The authors wish to acknowledge their appreciation of the valuable assistance and expert knowledge of Millen Brand and Naomi Rosenbach.

L.M.
R.G.H.

CONTENTS

TRIAL & TRIUMPH

A NOVEL ABOUT MAIMONIDES

BOOK I

MAIMON BEN JOSEPH SPEAKS

CHAPTER 1

When Moses was thirteen years old—I mean, of course, my own son Moses ben Maimon, not the Moses ben Amram (peace unto him) who spoke directly to God Himself, though I suspect my son means to do the same before he dies—he entered into manhood.

At that age he came to the crossing of the roads. He stood with me at the side of his mother Naomi as she died and suffered the anguish of not being recognized by her in her delirium. The next night he and I, as most of the Jews of Cordova were to do, left the city. We began the long journey that was eventually to take us out of Spain forever. How deeply this struck into his heart can be known by the fact that never afterward did he sign his name without affixing the words "the Sephardi," that is to say, "the Spaniard."

Today I, Maimon ben Joseph, his father, sit in the shadows of his fame. I am content. I am a man of seventy years, bowed with sorrow and exile, but in my time I have been a well-known rabbi and dayyan. I know what it is to have been a teacher and preacher, guide, judge, and healer for my people. A good son who honors his father is doubly blessed when he follows in his footsteps. Moses has gladdened my heart beyond what I dared hope.

Yet I do not understand him. He is far from the perfect man many people believe him to be. I have spent these years in study of him and his ways. He has virtues and faults which few realize. You may be sure that what I write about him is the truth.

At this moment, Moses, or Maimonides, "Son of Maimon," as he is called, sits across the courtyard from me in a little arbor sacred to him alone. These early morning hours are best for writing. The angle of the Egyptian sun is not so steeply hot, the tiny flies of the Nile not so numerous. Maimonides and I take advantage of the quiet and the cool to

3

collect our thoughts for the day. In the unearthly green light which filters through the grape leaves and tinges his gown and turban, my son writes those Arabic characters he prefers, script like the marks made by skaters on the ice in Madrid in a hard winter. I myself prefer to write—as I do this— in our ancient Hebrew.

Maimonides is a man of more than ordinary stature, with broad shoulders and narrow hips, more gaunt than I would like. He has a lean face, swarthy complexion, a crisp tawny beard, and the eagle aspect of our family. His mother bequeathed him his large liquid black eyes which seem so hypnotic when he is lecturing or conversing. He has a low soothing voice capable of the greatest expression; I have rarely heard him raise it, however, in either anger or joy. Once in a great while he may laugh but even his smiles are unusual. His expression has settled into something like lively melancholy.

In this respect we are not at all alike. I enjoy a good joke, a glass or two of sweet wine, and I have a respectable paunch to prove my appetite. I confess I am in awe of the insatiate desire of my son for knowledge, his remorseless pursuit of God. No one, not even myself, can see more than a corner of that enormous room which is his mind, heaped with theory and idea, piled with facts and quotations from the Greek, Arab, and Jew. I am bewildered by the breadth of his extraordinary memory that can glimpse the columns of a scroll of split sheepskin and instantly print them word-perfect inside his head, even to the shape and size of the letters and the thickness of the strokes.

Most of all, my son—nicknamed "The Rambam" by our anagrammatic friends in Cairo from his designation, Rabbi Moses ben Maimon—has a passion for order in the universe. He hates confusion or waste. He would arrange everything like dishes in a cupboard, from God down to the latchet of his shoe, in such a way that the most hidden mysteries can be grasped by the simplest mind. Again, here we disagree: I think a little confusion, something secret, an air of the inscrutable, is necessary to religion, and that formality and rules are more often than not a cage for the spirit.

What Maimonides is writing about so earnestly now, I have no idea. I suspect he is taking up some cause or other, probably that of the Jews in Yemen. That, I must add, is another of his characteristics. Somewhere there is always a forgotten tribe of Jews no one ever heard of or cared about, yet *he* cares.

4

He is always denouncing tyranny and persecution and fighting against them.

This is the last and greatest difference between father and son: I long ago got used to the ways of the world and the Jews in it. I accept our lot and go on living, but Maimonides will not have it so. He insists on writing letters and treatises and making himself conspicuous. I am not in favor of this fashion of life; many of our friends have criticized my son privately to me. He makes too much trouble and, at my time of life, one chooses to avoid trouble.

But I find myself digressing, this pleasant morning in Fostat. Here, a three-mile journey from the city of Cairo in the caliphate of Egypt, our family has been comfortable. We live peacefully under our own vine and fig tree and I trust Maimonides does nothing to get us into disfavor with the authorities. He is very highly regarded, but people often find themselves deceived (as was I) by those in power who profess to be their friends.

Let us begin, then, back in the golden age of Spain, in the days in glorious Cordova. Each morning began as sparkling bright as if it had been newly coined by the Creator; the birds sang for sheer joy, the fragrance of oranges and roses drifted through the windows, the ranks of olive trees danced in silver robes with the wind. On such a day I sat in my library like a king in a castle, surrounded by the fort of my palimpsests and manuscripts, cased and rolled and stacked, thinking what I should say that evening in the solemn service of our faith.

Entered my young Maimonides without a word. He turned and faced my shelves, slowly falling on his knees as if in prayer. He was fond of games and he knew they irritated me at such a time.

"What sort of nonsense is this?" I asked.

Maimonides rose and considered me with his dark enveloping gaze. "My father," he said softly, "I come here to worship knowledge."

"It is right to worship only our God, blessed be His Name, and to Him alone is it right to pray," I replied sternly.

His eyes moved from my face to the books along the walls and traveled back to meet my stare of reproof. "Do you truly believe that?" he asked.

My hand lifted as if to strike him before I knew it. Restraining myself, I said only: "With all my heart and soul."

After a moment Maimonides asked permission to read the

5

treatises of the Greek philosopher Aristotle. I nodded and he took the thick roll tenderly, leaving me with no more than a bow. It was only after he had gone that I remembered how he carried Aristotle—with the reverent care of a mother for a baby or of a dayyan with the sacred Torah.

It is difficult to describe the love between a father and his son. It is like the wind, invisible but strong, angry and caressing, destructive and life-giving, moving and shaking the world. Often, in the long blue evenings of Fostat, I ask myself: If we are the children of God, does not this account for our sufferings as well as our rejoicings? I do not know if Maimonides hates or loves me but I find comfort in his illimitable gift of memory. Occasionally, when he is free, he will sit beside me and recite, word for word, the contents of the books I once reluctantly allowed him to borrow. Is this love—or subtle hatred?

As for myself, I have seen the struggle in the soul of my son between knowledge of the world and love of God. Solomon in his wisdom was right: Increase of knowledge is increase of sorrow. I have tried to spare Maimonides this sorrow, but without success.

First, the legends about my son. My own ancestry is distinguished in Israel, passing back through Judah the Patriarch, who compiled the great Mishnah, to the royal house of David, blessed be he. I am the son of Joseph, son of Isaac, son of Joseph, son of Obadiah, son of Solomon, son of Obadiah—all of whom were dayyanim, leaders of our people, except Solomon, who threw away his substance in riot and women.

Maimonides is blood of my blood, yet the foolish persist in believing that I was told in a vision to marry the daughter of a butcher of Cordova. Those in this trade are respectable and prosperous, but the tale is false—as false as it is to say that the father of Saadiah Gaon, the great rabbi of Sura, was a butcher, barber, leech, even a Moslem muezzin! I have worked with my hands—since it is forbidden for a rabbi to earn his living by merely instructing his people—but my wife Naomi could trace her own lineage as far back as my own. It is truly written that a man should sell all that he has in order to take to wife the daughter of a scholar; if he find not such, let him marry the daughter of a great one; if none can be his, let him marry a daughter of the chiefs of the synagogue; if not, let him marry a daughter of those who distribute charity; if all these are lacking, let him marry the daughter of a teacher

6

of children—but it is loathsome to marry the daughter of an ignorant man.

There is the story, as well, that the birth of Maimonides killed Naomi, but that is not true; those circumstances I shall relate in their place. Nor did I, as the gossips say now, marry again. I have been told by those who should know better that I was forced to send my son off to school because of his unruly nature, and that when he returned to Cordova on the Sabbath, he went into the synagogue and delivered a learned lecture on the Talmud at the age of ten. Even if such had been permitted, Maimonides would never have been so brash.

Finally, there is the story that Maimonides was a child who was so little inclined to study that I committed him to the tutorship of the eminent Joseph ben Migash to be disciplined. It is true that I myself studied under this great teacher and that my son also studied his philosophy—but when that ancient died, Maimonides was barely seven years old. Whatever the gain or blame may be, I must take it on my shoulders. It was I who taught my son the truths of religion; as for the sciences, a half-dozen learned Moorish scholars showed him the light in mathematics, logic, and the use of the alembic at the Academy of Cordova. In astronomy and medicine, myself and others were his teachers; and in the latter I suffered my first disappointment in his talents.

Despite my denials, however, where there is so much of rumor there are certain facts. My son, when young, was filled with what seemed at times the energy of Satan, the Adversary. This appeared to me on the fatal day when he quarreled with young Samuel ben Ali Halevi over the girl Zamira.

Since they had been children scuffling in the dust and wiping the purple juice and seeds of stolen pomegranates from their lips, Maimonides and Zamira had been playmates. There was nothing, I thought, between them, nor any common link of belief and heritage. He was my son; she was the daughter of a high official in the autumn court of Cordova in which I myself held office and favor. The high-walled garden of our house just outside the city walls, with its orange trees and wide gray gravel walks, was a favored meeting-spot for the two. I welcomed their vague chatter as I meditated, walking behind the marbled lattices of the covered way adjoining. With them this day, as he had been more than once, was Samuel, son of Ali Halevi, brother to Judah, the noted physician-poet of Toledo.

I saw their childish tableau in the rays of the late after-

7

noon sun and paused to watch. They were, I guessed, engaged in the business of childhood which no elder understands. My eyes turned to the small form of Zamira.

A child in age she was, certainly, but a woman in her heart. What her flushed round face concealed was betrayed by her eyes of dark blue; mischievous, full of the guile of a sex still unknown to her. Most astonishing of all for a Moorish girl, her hair was gold, so bright as to be almost white, escaping under her fringed kaffiyeh, shaken loose by the quick graceful movements of her body. She stood between the two boys in their tunics and tiny black skullcaps.

Young Samuel was one of those virile children of our race that I love to see but whose future I dread. Hair black and curled, precocious enough to have a slight beard, with a sharp, dominating face, flashing eyes and a vehement, arrogant way of speaking. I feared him. He was blameless in the Law but hard and unforgiving, used to having his own way, without understanding for the softer human needs. His mind already showed signs of an intellect as penetrating as that of my son.

Maimonides stood a little apart from both Zamira and Samuel, as if unwanted. His severe narrow face was intent upon them both, as if his stare might break the intangible bond which bound the golden girl and the dark proud boy together. At that moment, as they stood under the spined branches of the trees bent by the bright fruit, I felt a sudden strange heaviness in my heart. I knew God had matched these two against each other in this life, locked them in a rivalry which could be ended solely by death and decided by the Judge of all judges.

"See," Samuel said. With the toe of his soft boot he marked out a square in the gravel. "This is where you must stand, Zamira."

Zamira laughed, a light trill of amusement. She stepped inside the lines as Maimonides watched silently.

"Here?" she asked teasingly. "Am I your faithful slave?"

"No," Samuel said, smiling boldly, "this is our housetop. In Cordova the housetops belong to the wives."

Zamira's laughter ceased. "I am not your wife, I shall never be your wife," she whispered and sprang swiftly outside the square.

"No, no!" cried Samuel. He flung his arms around her and lifted her back within the square; she was half-afraid, half-pleased.

8

"Let her go," said Maimonides in his low even voice. "She is not yours, she belongs to herself and to God."

Samuel stepped back, his face impassive. He laughed with a different sound. He watched Zamira escape again from the prison he had made, without an effort to stop her.

"It is only a game," he said softly, but his tone made my blood run cold. Zamira went to Maimonides and stood close beside him; he made no motion toward her. Samuel approached and stood with his fists tight on his hips.

"You must give me a love token," he said teasingly, "as a ransom for your flight."

Zamira smiled shyly and patted his knuckles. "There," she said, "that is my tribute to my conqueror."

"No," persisted Samuel, leaning toward her and ignoring Maimonides, "that is nothing of value." He looked at my son. "Is a pat on the hand like that to a dog, even from Zamira, worth anything?" he demanded. Maimonides did not answer, his brows knotted together.

"What do you mean?" Zamira asked, her light trill mingling with the sound of the fountain near them. "I have nothing else to give you except a song. Would you like to hear me sing?"

"That, and more, too," Samuel said ardently. He reached out and took her hand. She glanced at Maimonides. I was surprised at his silence, for he did not lack words and the knowledge of how to use them.

"I cannot give you something for nothing," Zamira faltered.

"Here, I shall give you this," Samuel told her, reaching inside his girdle. "Here is a scored gold dinar. I break it in half." He pressed half into her hand. "Give me a kiss and the rest shall be yours."

Zamira shook her head. "I do not sell my kisses," she said faintly.

"Give me back my own gift to you!" commanded Maimonides.

"Gift?" said Samuel ben Ali, pretending ignorance. "What are you talking about?"

"We once pledged each other's friendship and exchanged gifts," Maimonides said sternly. "Now that pledge is broken. I shall return your ivory box if you return my dagger."

"The dagger of steel, with the brass handle, with the serpent entwined, with the garnet in its mouth?"

"Yes."

9

The other boy shrugged. "It is a pity," he said, "but I have lost it."

"A kiss!" cried young Samuel, turning again to Zamira.

Maimonides spoke. "What is a kiss?" he asked harshly, his voice trembling. "It is nothing, is it not? A payment on an old debt owed by all women to all men, is it not?"

"Wisdom, wisdom!" cried Samuel mockingly. "Muni is a sage already!"

Zamira was angry. "Do you believe that?" she demanded of my son. He did not reply.

She glanced at Samuel. Her eyes fluttered and lowered. "Perhaps," she said, so low I could scarcely hear, "if Muni says so. Maybe I should pay a little on the debt. If Muni believes it, you may kiss me."

She raised her tiny veil and presented her cheek to Samuel. Maimonides started, his face contorted in anger, but it was too late. Samuel took her in his arms, his mouth against her flesh.

Zamira cried out in pain and wrenched away. I saw the mark of Samuel's teeth in her cheek, the slow blood oozing. Zamira cried out in wild weeping: "You have bitten me!" Samuel nodded in satisfaction, licking his lips like a beast. "I have marked you as my own," he said. "Now you will never find another."

He turned not a moment too soon. Maimonides charged him, driving him back, clipping his feet out from under. In an instant they were struggling on the ground, pummeling each other, Samuel shouting in rage and my son growling in an incoherent voice. I watched him as he clutched Samuel's throat and only when he was rolled underneath did I step out to command them to halt. Yom Kippur was beginning.

Samuel sprang up and stood erect. Maimonides came erect and continued to flail at him and Samuel did nothing to prevent him. My son saw me and stopped, stumbling back, sucking in deep breaths.

"Shalom," Samuel said to me and bowed.

"Shalom aleichem," I said mechanically.

Samuel turned and went out the gate. Zamira, still sobbing, her hand clutched to her cheek, fled in another direction. Maimonides went slowly past me, his eyes straight ahead, his expression fixed, not bothering to beat the dust from his dress.

I halted him with an outstretched hand. "You will come with me to the synagogue when you have cleansed yourself," I said. "Your mother is not well. But she insists on going tonight. You must help your father now."

10

I swayed on my feet. The heat of our synagogue was intolerable, reflected back from the blue-and-white tiles. My tallit seemed burning cloth. Though the sun had set long ago, shimmers of heat rose from the congregation before me, a visible greasy layer over their bowed heads. Odors of sweat and incense mingled, sweet to sickening. My beard seemed to drag down my voice as I intoned the opening prayer: "Praised be Thou, O Lord our God . . ."

The words came without thought, recited by me a thousand times before, but for the first time they were without meaning. On this Eve of the Day of Atonement, in this year of 1148 as the Christians reckoned it from the death of their rabbi of Nazareth, groveling for sins committed more than three thousand years ago seemed an empty ceremony: " '. . . do all My commandments and be holy unto your God.' "

I turned unsteadily. The two elders opened the shining doors of the Ark of the Covenant. Beside me I heard Maimonides take up the service: "The Lord is my shepherd, I shall not want . . ." I lifted the Scrolls of the Torah like a great weight and descended among the people to consecrate again the pact between God and His own. I scarcely heard the low chanting, hardly saw the people as they kissed the holy object or touched it with their fingertips.

My thoughts were with a white-faced figure in the rear, a slight erect form, holding herself upright only by what I knew was a blind, inexplicable strength; the fit had been coming upon her all day and she would not yield to my pleas or commands to stay home. I paced toward Naomi in inward terror, extending the Torah. She touched it, her fingers sliding over the exquisitely engraved silver. As she did, she gave a low moan. Her head went back and she crumpled where she stood.

Before I could think clearly, I had turned and thrust the Torah into the hands of the attending hazzan behind me. I knelt beside my wife and, instantly strong, lifted her unconscious form, breaking my way through the sound and crush of the roused congregation. Out of the pattern of gaping faces a small, muscular man joined me, gray bearded, with compassionate eyes: I recognized him with a surge of hope, Judah ben Samuel Halevi, the poet, physician of Toledo. I had not known he was at the service nor did I know why he had come to Cordova but I rejoiced in his presence. He tapped my hand with his cool fingers and nodded toward the door.

Outside in the courtyard, we hurried under the shivering canopy of a huge olive tree; there a basined well reflected the

11

flickering light of the torches behind us. Judah flung off his cloak and I laid Naomi gently down on it. We soaked our linen kerchiefs in the water and laid them on her face and hands. "Muni," said Judah urgently to my pale son beside us, "my cloak. Quickly, quickly!"

Naomi stirred and moaned again. Suddenly she cried out, as if she were singing; her voice rose to a piercing shriek, a hoarse shout that ended as she sat up and fell back, her spine curved, her eyes wide and rolled upward. She twisted madly within the tight embrace of Judah and myself. Spit and foam, pale green in color and mingled with blood, came from her open mouth. Judah snapped off a branch of the olive tree and thrust it across her mouth, between her teeth. His hand went out in a swift, practiced gesture, rummaging in the cloak Muni had brought. He handed me a clay phial. Uncorking it, I held it under Naomi's nostrils and slowly, gradually, her racking convulsions ceased. Softly, Judah placed her back upon the cloak. As he did, the ululations from the crowd commenced to soften.

Maimonides stood upright, eyes wild, his face working and ashen, both hands over his mouth. Half-rising, I butted him in the chest with my head, shoving him backward as hard as I could. The boy staggered, tripped, and tumbled head over heels into the cold water of the basin.

No one moved as he thrashed about and regained the brim. I knelt once more beside Naomi. Judah and I looked at each other, tears brimming my eyes and rolling down my cheeks in spite of myself. Judah, a gentle man with a genius for herbs and love poetry, also wept. He beckoned two of the nearest men. They took Naomi up like a pearl of price, bearing her away with Judah in attendance.

Miserable and weak, I watched them go. The dripping Maimonides, shivering from his immersion, clambered out and stood beside me. His voice wavered as he spoke. "I am sorry, my father," he managed to say, "I could not help myself. I was sick, about to faint."

"I know, my son."

"Will you forgive me?"

"There is nothing to forgive."

Maimonides moved closer to me. His voice was fearful, a whisper. "Was—was that the falling sickness?" he asked.

I nodded, turning back inside to finish the service, to disrobe and hurry back to be at her bedside with Judah. Maimonides had never known that his mother suffered from epi-

12

lepsy, next to leprosy the most dreaded and inexplicable disease of all. He had thought she was weak, that she fainted often; I had carefully concealed the nature of her illness from him, excluding him from her bedroom, sending him out to play or study. The futility of hiding the truth was apparent. I had once hoped he would take my place or that of Judah as the chief healer of his race, but that illusion now vanished. The first qualification of a physician was to be able to control his own feelings in the face of disease or injury—and this, I thought, Maimonides would never be able to do.

But there was one service at least he could do for me. Before the still-murmuring congregation, I took my tallit from my shoulders and draped it over his. I turned and addressed the people: "Through a gift of God, my son has been able to commit to memory each word of the Holy Scriptures and the Holy Day services. I now command him to commence the closing prayers." As I hurried from the synagogue, behind me I heard the low voice of Maimonides, trembling, then growing stronger as he began the last recitation from the ancient holy writings.

That night, hour after hour, I sat by the cool blue linen couch of Naomi. The great white candles on either side stood with unflickering flames, their stalactites of wax growing. Judah sat helplessly in the corner. We had done all we could, all that medicine knew, for Naomi, but the damage to her brain (as we guessed) had taken its toll. She was dying.

I brought my leather stool close. She held my hand with fingers like steel clamps. I could feel the pounding pulse in her wrist leaping higher and higher, as if to escape the vein. It surged, leaped, mingled with my own; it fluttered and paused, renewing its desperate effort like a bird beating its wings. I had ceased to weep. Now the sweat coursed silently, unceasingly down my body, down my face, burning and blinding my eyes. I blinked incessantly, seeing Naomi's body twist and turn; I felt myself pulled in response to the ghastly rhythm, my blood receding into the depths of my body as her life vanished. I smelled the acrid odor of death mixing with the scent of orange blossoms just outside the window.

Beside me stood Maimonides, motionless, his face darkened. Judah rose and knelt beside Naomi. He shook his head. I offered him from my medical kit what he and I knew was needed, the last service we could do. Staring at Naomi's face I understood how others could believe in Azrael, the Angel

13

of Death. The struggle between life and death was so ferocious that it seemed as if an actual foe were in the room, grappling with the dying soul. Our prayers and sighs flew like arrows at this invisible enemy as he muffled her breath with his huge black wings.

From the other side of the couch, Judah bent over Naomi and gently opened her stiffened lips, pouring in a dark, brewed potion of opium. Almost immediately it seemed to relieve her. Her clenched fists relaxed and I withdrew my numbed hand. Naomi slowly opened her eyes: They were drowsy with a sleep from which I knew she would not waken, pupils gray, the white around them like a pool. I seized Judah's rock-steady shoulder and managed to stand; I saw Naomi's lips move and bent to them.

"Maimon," I heard her whisper, as if she were already far away, "you will be all right?"

I nodded and heard her again: "Muni—will Muni be all right?"

"Yes, yes," I sighed and the tears, the drops that scald the dead, that form the iron river of Hell, flowed again from my eyes into my beard.

"He is such a strange child and I love him so much."

"I will take care of him."

"Love him more, try to understand him."

"Yes."

"And David—where is David?"

"He is not here," I said. I had told the servants not to admit either of the other two children into the chamber.

"He is our wild one, Maimon. You and Muni must take care of him."

"Yes."

"Yaltah—she will miss me so much. And she needs me."

"Naomi, Naomi!"

"And you, Maimon. You have loved God better than you loved me. But I—I have loved you better than I have God. Is that a great sin, Rabbi?"

My head fell on my breast and my body shook with sobs. I could feel only the torture of bottomless grief, my fingers tearing at my breast. It was Judah who took me by the shoulders and raised me, looked into my eyes, my tears reflected on his face, shaking his head. I turned away; for the moment, I could face nothing living.

The tall nail-studded door burst open with a hammering of small fists. David ben Maimon, not yet six years old but

14

brawny and muscular far beyond his years, with black hair and dark eyes, burst into the room still wearing his sleeping loincloth.

"I don't want to sleep," he announced, "it's too hot."

No one answered him. He peered suspiciously about the dim room, rubbing his eyes against the light of the candles. Behind him in the corridor stood his nurse Ramah, silently crying, holding the wide-eyed Yaltah in her arms. It was Maimonides who closed the door and went to David. "David," he said, holding his voice steady, "you must go back to bed."

"I said I didn't want to."

"You must, David."

"I want to stay here with the grownups."

"David, come into the garden," Maimonides said earnestly.

"What's the matter with Mother?" asked David, his attention riveted on the bed.

"She's resting. There's nothing the matter."

"Is she sick?"

"David, if you won't go back to sleep, come into the garden with me."

"Why don't *you* go to bed? What are you doing up late?"

Unable to hear any more, I wheeled about. "David, go with Muni!" I had never before spoken harshly to him and his surprise shone in his eyes.

"Are you crying?" he asked me. Maimonides pulled at his bare bronzed arm but the boy resisted. He watched Judah bending over the bed.

"You're shutting my mother's eyes," David said.

"Yes," Maimonides told him, swallowing with an effort. "She's very tired."

"Is she too tired to shut them herself?"

"We want her to sleep."

"She doesn't look sleepy," David said, avoiding the grip of Maimonides and trying to move closer to the couch.

"Don't you understand?" exclaimed Maimonides, his voice breaking. David glanced sharply at him.

"She does look tired," he said judicially, moving back a step. "When she's tired, her nose gets sharp and her nose is very sharp."

"Don't wake her up."

"I'll be very quiet. Can I go and kiss her?"

"No, no," Maimonides sighed as if in pain. "David, we must go out in the garden now."

"Why?"

15

"Because I tell you to, because she's asleep, because we should never stay here, because you should!" cried Maimonides to the child's bewilderment. He grasped David by the shoulders, turned him around and marched him out the door. For no reason, David commenced to cry and in the hall Yaltah echoed his sobs.

I felt faint. Judah offered me an unstoppered bottle; I pushed it away, refusing to smell it. I looked at him, drew a deep breath, and stood erect. Together, as if with one thought, we began to intone the Kaddish, the prayer for the dead.

The stars burned out with the candles. The room and the sky filled with the sickly gray of false dawn. Judah and I sat with glazed and unseeing eyes opposite each other across the body of Naomi. At last Judah rose, came round the couch, and, taking me by the shoulders, shook the blood back into my head. I stood heavily and followed him out into the lessening darkness that hung over the deserted garden like a ceiling-sheet, wall to wall. We paced the gravel, crunching it under our feet, feeling the bite of sharp edges through our slippers. Judah turned, looking up at me, his face lined with concern. I shook my head.

"Judah, old friend," I said, "I have no wish to talk."

"I must speak to you."

"There is nothing you can say."

"You are wrong, Maimon."

"Naomi is dead," I said wearily. "I have wept until I am dry, until my soul is withered."

"I shall not speak of her. But I must tell you news, Maimon."

My throat rasped in a mirthless laugh. "I cannot sleep nor rest but there is news. What news could there be, Judah, that keeps you from your bed?"

"I am wretched indeed to add more grief to your loss, Maimon, but it is God's will."

"Tell me what you want," I said, hardly hearing him. "What is it?"

Judah came closer. His voice changed. "Did you see my brother Ali at the synagogue, Maimon?"

I tried to think. Vague faces flitted through my memory but none of Ali. "No," I said. "He was not there. But I know the reason. This afternoon his son and Muni quarreled here in this garden over a Moorish girl. He thinks his family wronged and perhaps it is true. If you like, I shall see him and settle it."

16

"Was it not strange he was not there?"

"Strange?" I paused and considered. "As I think of it, it was strange. Ali is one of the most devout of men; so, too, his son Samuel. He would not miss a service on the Day of Atonement unless—unless—"

Judah eagerly took me up. "Unless what, Maimon?"

"Unless," I said slowly, "the world were about to be turned upside down and the Day of Judgment at hand."

"Yes," Judah replied simply.

My torpid brain stirred angrily. "What do you mean, Judah?" I demanded. "Must you talk in parables, in riddles?"

Judah gave me a tired smile and I regretted my words as soon as they were spoken. He was as exhausted as I. "I am a poet and a physician," he said. "You can answer yourself. Do we ever talk any other way, for the good of the patient?"

"But I am lost," I said, as petulantly as a child. "I wander in darkness and sorrow—and you talk of Ali."

"You said he would not miss a Yom Kippur service unless the world was about to come to an end. Maimon, your world, his world, my world have all come to an end."

"What foolishness is this?" I flared. I strode down the path and felt him tug at my sleeve.

"I came south to attend the services in Cordova rather than in Toledo because I came to warn you," Judah said quietly. "Ali and his family are no longer in the city. They have set out for the coast to take ship to Beyrouth, overland to Bagdad, to establish themselves under the good Moslem caliph there."

I peered down into his face. He had a vestige of a smile in the glimmering light. "But why?" I stammered.

Judah looked around him like a hunted man. Coming close to my ear, he put his mouth to it and whispered briefly. I drew away, shaking my head in disbelief. "Never!" I said. "Even if it is true, my friends will save me!"

"Poor Maimon," Judah said compassionately, "your power and influence have vanished like night into dawn." He pointed to the colored east. "Now you have no friends except Jews. How will we, condemned ourselves, save you?"

"I am an official of the court, a physician, a chief justice, a rabbi—"

Judah broke into my tirade. "Save your breath. Will you go?"

"I am tired of life," I said spiritlessly. "I will stay."

"Are you also tired of the lives of Muni, of David and Yaltah?"

17

"Go, go!" I cried. "Leave me!"

Judah's face shifted like clay under the fingers. "Let us go together," he said breathlessly. "You are rich, Maimon, you can hire guards and mules."

"And your family in Toledo?"

Judah shrugged. "If I could, I would return," he said. "But the roads, they say, may be already blocked. I am desperate."

"You are a weakling, Judah," I said contemptuously. "You tell me of my family and you are willing to desert your own."

"My wife, light of my heart, is dead," Judah said bitterly.

"And your children?"

"Yes, they live and are cared for. I love them. But I love the heavenly light and the City more."

"Pfaugh!" I said contemptuously.

He caught me by the lappets. "Each man to his own loves," he said intensely. "Yours are of the flesh, mine are of the heavenly verses. Jerusalem is a fount of living waters to me!"

Almost as if he were speaking of his family, he whispered softly:

> "City of the world most fair, most chaste,
> I, in the West—see how I weep for thee!
> Oh, had I eagle wings to lift, to fly
> To thee and with my tears make moist thy waste!
> My heart soars east of me, yet here I lie.
> How can the sweetest food taste sweet to me?
> How can the object of my vows be gained,
> With thee and me alike by distance chained?
> To leave the joys of Spain were joys to be;
> To see thy desolation, ecstasy."

Affected in spite of myself, I said slowly: "Judah, I should drive you out with whips. But you have been close to me tonight. Your fingers closed the eyes of Naomi."

I stopped. I could say no more. Judah's eyes flickered, his mouth worked and hardened. He put his hands together and bowed his head almost as if in mockery. "Shalom," he said calmly and turned toward the gate.

"We shall meet again," I said after him, "whether in this world or the World-to-Come, God knows." Judah gave no sign that he heard me; his form disappeared behind the wall without a glance behind. I knew then that he was irrevocably committed to a wandering life, that he had abandoned his profession, not even taking with him his kit of medicines.

The click of the gate was still in my ears when I saw another figure in the garden, that of Maimonides, rigid as a judge. He came toward me with a queer dragging step like an injured creature. His face was stiff.

"I heard what my mother said to you," he murmured. I bowed my head. Maimonides cleared his throat. "Once you told me we should worship only God, not the ten dilemmas of Aristotle, not the logic of the Greeks."

"Yes," I said.

His eyes flamed; he came nearer. "I do not know enough of our God," he said.

"This is not the time nor place for such talk," I told him. "You may have guessed, too, what Judah Halevi said."

"Yes," Maimonides replied. His mouth twisted into a caricature of a smile. "He is a fool. Why should we run like whipped dogs from Cordova?"

"What else can we do?" I demanded.

"Stay!"

"To be butchered like sheep!"

"Who would dare butcher us? What do you mean?"

I sighed, shutting my eyes and shaking my head. "You must have faith in your father," I said wearily. "What more can I tell you?"

Maimonides moved to confront me. "My father," he said slowly, "you must tell me more of God." I saw the sun glow red behind the head of this questioner like the halo of a demon. "Is God—our God—merciful?" he asked.

"Yes," I sobbed.

"Is our God compassionate, pitying us?"

"Yes, yes."

"Is the God of the Jews powerful?"

"He has all powers, bless His Name."

"Does He know all that was, that is, that will be?"

"Yes."

"Does He always do what is right and good?"

"That is what I have taught you from your cradle."

"Is it true?"

"Yes!" I exclaimed desperately. "What you have said is true, as true as it is that I live and you live and God Himself lives!"

"Is it as true," cried Maimonides in a terrible voice, "as it is that my mother Naomi lives?"

The spear of his sorrow pierced my belly. I could no longer stand; I fell to the gravel, weeping and rolling, tearing my

19

dress. I felt his contempt pour on me as he stooped and helped me to my feet.

"Is that the answer to my question, my father?" he asked with irony.

"The wisdom of God is not for fools such as you and I," I whispered. "His knowledge is inscrutable."

"Is it not the knowledge He has given us?"

"I do not know. We must warn the others, we must leave this dreadful place!"

Maimonides was silent, brooding, regarding me. "Are you, as well, a coward, my father?" he said.

"Yes!" I shouted. "I am a Jew and a Jew is a coward, all Jews are cowards! What else could we be in this world of hell!"

I paused. "And you," I said, breathing painfully, "are you to come with me and with David and Yaltah wherever we may go?"

Maimonides raised his head, its eagle profile sharp in the first rays of the sunlight. "I shall not go unless you tell me why Cordova is a dreadful place."

"Our days of exile have come at last," I said slowly, the truth tearing at my lips. "The wild Almohades from the mountains of Morocco have launched a holy jihad against their Moorish brethren. They have crossed the sea. More than one city of Spain has been taken. Judah has told me that in three days they will be at the gates of Cordova; in a week, at Toledo. They will give me and mine no choice except to be true converts to Mohammed. Or be slaughtered."

CHAPTER 2

Here it is fitting that I write about the times in which we live. Those who read this will find it difficult to understand the reasons for our actions without knowledge of the age we inhabit. Understanding comes with information: I shall do the best with what I myself know to be true.

We Jews in the West had never seen great Jerusalem, the city of our fathers. We knew of it only in its desolation, from the tales of travelers, from rumors that came back to us with the merchants who had observed the ungodly and savage Christians in their "crusades." Though they professed to worship their Prince of Peace (himself a rabbi who turned against our faith), their desire to shed blood—even amongst themselves—seemed incredible. In my father's day the gossip was not much more than the tales of such cruelties and barbarisms done in the name of God. But we secretly blessed such expeditions because thereby, at least in some degree, the Jews in the isolated kingdom of Spain were spared persecutions.

In truth, if—in those days—a Jew could live anywhere in peace, it was in Moslem Cordova. We were proud to give our labor, our science and discoveries to make it one of the three queen cities of the world. Such enchanted years were singularly free from the general terror and superstition. For upwards of six generations unto Maimonides, we had lived in quiet and prosperity. We felt admonished by God, praised be He, to save and improve what we could of the best of man's genius and learning.

Cordova seemed the calm center of a whirlwind of war and pomp, lust and luxury. The Jews existed with the gigantic figures of their enemies revolving about them like the shadows of a magic lantern. God had seen fit to raise up three great nations against each other—the Franks, the Moslems, and the Greeks—across Asia and Europe. From none could the Jew expect mercy; of them all, only the Moslems allowed us to live unharmed on the exaction of yearly tribute.

In those times Cordova was reckoned the most charming city in all the world. At least ten miles in length, filled with rare flowers and trees, with houses and places of worship like jewels, interlaced with the shining threads of life-giving water, it was a wonder to every visitor—and none was forbidden entrance in the gates. According to the Moslems, it numbered 600 mosques, 900 baths, and 200,000 dwelling places— but I do not believe this. Knowing the extravagances of the chroniclers, I would guess they exalted the facts ten times their worth—a calculation which might give a more reasonable estimate.

The same caution must apply to their description of the state of learning in Cordova, even down to my own time. The declaration that the royal library, eminent as it was, had a total of 600,000 volumes (of which 44 were used as the catalogue alone) may be fact. But I have never seen a tenth of this number nor any place which might be used to house them; and the rumor that a doctor, like myself, needed a train of one hundred camels to transport his personal library, is pure fiction.

Nevertheless, the magnificence of our city surpassed that of all others, even of Bagdad, in taste and quality. One might arise in the morning to be refreshed by the sight of the spires and minarets gilded by the sun, the parks planted with exotic shrubs, the pleasure domes and groves and fruiting gardens—all of which still existed when Maimonides was a boy. So, too, did the passion of the Moslem still exist for the investigation of knowledge, a yearning that can be too much applauded.

Much was written. The annals of Cordova tell of more than three hundred prominent scriveners, but all of them suffered from childish qualities of extravagance and flattery. Rarely could a fact be found in a column of their fanciful nonsense. It was this, I think, which swung Maimonides in the opposite direction. He went so far as to say, "It is a sin to write or speak one more word than is necessary."

The Moslem Almoravides, the fanatic horde from the desert, had found Cordova a soft and willing mistress for four centuries. In her perfumed arms, they relaxed both their fierceness and their creed in the delights of art and science. As they grew weaker, the Christian strength again increased; two years before Maimonides was born, Alfonso the Battler burned the very suburbs of Cordova, including two villas which belonged to me.

These events affected the Jews scarcely at all. The tides of the first crusade of the Christians passed us by. The reputation of Cordova in learning and authority increased until it outstripped that of the Babylonian cities of Sura and Pumbeditha, going far beyond that of Bagdad. It was only when the second fanatic wave from across the Mediterranean came—a people from the Atlas mountains, the Almohades—that the era of light and culture was succeeded by the darkness of piety. Once again the terrible cry resounded through the land: "The Book or the Sword!" It was the Koran or death. Christian, Jew, and apostatizing Moor alike were to flee before the pitiless persecution of the Almohades.

The final hours of that most sorrowful Day of Atonement had come at last. Since sunrise the nursemaid Ramah and I, with the aid of Maimonides—and before the frightened eyes

22

of Yaltah and the helplessly weeping David—had prepared the body of my own Naomi for burial. Together we bore her to a secret grave, a rock-sealed granite tomb in a nearby hillside. It was past sunset when we returned, weak from our lamentations and the hunger from the holy fast day, but we could not stop to eat. The warning of Judah rang in my ears; too much remained to be done. We did not even commence the ordained thirty days of mourning, praying God to forgive us.

Instead, under the cover of early darkness, we put into effect the plan of escape which is always as much a part of the life of the Jew as his religion. Mules and litters were brought up on the riverside to the small hidden postern door in the walls. One by one, in procession, we labored to carry out the possessions of my house.

After no more than an hour, we found our strength had ebbed beyond endurance. Food had become essential: We sat down to a silent meal of bread and water and cold meats. I could eat little, despite my gnawing stomach, and stood up from the table; more than meat to me was my desire for a last walk in my cherished garden. There was, I thought, time enough; our duty had been done, I had sent Maimonides to warn the rest of the Jewish community of Judah's information.

Under the pale sliver of the new moon, breathing for the last time the fragrance of the blossoms in the heaviness of the night air, I had only bitter meditations—those of a man about to leave heaven for an eternity of wandering in the depths. With quick apprehension I heard the gate open; I wheeled to see the bright presence of Zamira in the dusk.

Her mare whinnied outside as she came straight to me with a respectful greeting. "I have come to you, Cadi Maimon," she said with her small sweet smile and lilting voice, "because I have a cut on my cheek. My father asks you to cure it."

"All cures are in the hands of God," I replied, bowing, "but we may assist the healing. Let me see, my daughter." I removed the poultice and dirty cloth. With dismay I saw that the bite of Samuel had indeed swollen and festered. As the boy had boasted, she would bear his mark for the rest of her life, a senseless brand. As I examined it, I became aware of the quiet presence of Maimonides. He had returned and was behind me.

"I have a sovereign balm," I assured Zamira, "that will give it soothing and promote healing in a day or two. Cleanliness also will help it." I turned to Maimonides and told him to bring my medicines. He hesitated and I frowned; behind him,

Ramah nodded tiredly and hastened off to obey my command. I bit my lip but did not interfere.

Zamira looked shyly at my son. He returned her glance with one of his rare warm smiles. I saw what was happening and determined to shatter their mood. I took Zamira's hand. "Tell me, my child," I said softly, "how was it that your cheek was injured? Did you fall—or were you wounded?"

Zamira blushed painfully; Maimonides looked away. Neither answered. At that moment Ramah returned with the medicine pouch and I, inwardly amused, secured the salve and applied it to her tender cheek. As I finished and pressed the little box of salve into her hand for future use, I raised my head sharply. I imagined I had heard the sound of a troop of horsemen in the distance. It reminded me of our danger.

"You must return home this moment," I said rapidly to Zamira. "Your father would not be willing for you to be here a second longer than needed. This is the house of a Jew; there will be ugly rumors."

Proudly, she drew herself up. "No one will speak against you," she said. "You are a counselor for my uncle, and his will in Cordova is law."

"My father thinks that there may come another law in the city," Maimonides said calmly. Zamira's eyes went wide; she looked at me questioningly. I hushed my son and spread my fingers to placate the girl. "I have heard stories only," I said, "and I am sure your father has heard them before."

My words were suddenly drowned in the drumming of hoofs outside. I smelled the dry choking odor of rising dust. I cried out over the creak of leather and rattle of steel. Ramah was already running toward the house. I thrust the two children after her. I was too late.

As I moved, the gate crashed back. Through the same entrance where for many years only friends and guests had come, poured silently a black irresistible flood. The Almohades, cloaked and hooded, had come to Cordova.

Years afterward I realized that this troop of small wiry riders was not the army of the lieutenants of Abdullah ibn Tumart. Rather they were a column of Almohades horsemen sent more than a day ahead, according to the Moslem custom, for the purposes of scouting and forage. Surrounding us, they made no more sound than they had at their arrival, as if they were phantoms summoned up from Gehenna. They knew their work well. As we stood paralyzed by their appearance, a few lounged about us as guards with bared scimitars, plucking oranges and crushing flowers under their boots. The remainder had moved quickly on, into the house. I could hear them roving at will, breaking and destroying. I had some small hosanna in my heart: The sacred articles had been taken by me in the first packet to the mules outside the walls—and I knew the first care of Ramah must have been to take David and Yaltah there to await the event.

The clang of silver vessels being flung into sacks, the crashing of furniture and glass, the destruction of all that was most precious to me made a din of madness. I turned away; I pressed the palms of my hands over my ears. If it was God's will, we might escape or bribe our way free, but there was something next to my life which could not escape. I thought of my library and cried aloud in anguish.

I became aware of one of the Almohades peering at me from under his mask. He saw the direction of the single glance I flung at the house and summoned two of his fellows with a gesture. I was pinioned between them. They forced me to go with them, stumbling along the passage, into my library. Here they confronted me.

"Is this your treasure?" demanded their leader, his eyes glittering with contempt. He spoke in the lingua franca and I answered him in the same. "It is my treasure, indeed," I said.

His eyes narrowed with the glare of a demon. "You are one of the damned," he said and spat on the polished tiles. "Lost to the true religion, relapsed from faith, fallen from the holy words of the Prophet! Worse than a Jew, you should be slaughtered on the spot!"

Hope leaped in my bosom. He had mistaken me, with Moorish dress and fluent Arabic, for one of their own misbegotten tribe. I bowed my head to conceal my expression of rejoicing. "I plead for mercy and forgiveness," I said humbly.

"Death to the Christians, hold the Jews for ransom," he said harshly, "and for such as you, your fate hangs upon the grace of one who comes tomorrow, sent of Allah!" He stared about him in growing disgust.

"Is there no end to these books?" he wondered.

"There is nothing else but these herein, be assured."

"These are your riches?"

"These are the riches of all the world."

One of his companions extended his spear tentatively and stirred the manuscripts with its point. I uttered an involuntary

25

cry of pain, as if it had touched my own body. "Desist, I beg you," I muttered, "you break the peaceful rest of the sages."

"Tear them down!" ordered their leader, convinced that my concern was for some hidden gold. In an instant, to my horror, the room was heaped with the rarest of vellum and parchment in an ever growing heap. When they were halfway through their task, a sharp order came. They halted, knee-deep in the world's knowledge, coughing in the dust their sacrilege had raised. Their leader shrugged and turned to me.

"There is an antidote for this thrice-distilled poison," he said in a careless tone. "If these are copies of the Koran, they are holy. Are they so?"

"Not so," I admitted. "The Koran of the Prophet is at the great mosque."

"So nothing is lost."

As I saw their intent, I uttered a shriek. Two caught me and whirled me away to the wall, stifling my cries. One of them took his torch and applied its flame to the pile of books in each corner of the room. He stepped back as the dry stuff took the flame at a touch and roared upward. My library ignited like the tinder of a Greek firebox, mounting up to the ceiling, sparks and flame, illuminating the body instead of the soul. Like children around a winter bonfire, the Moslems watched in pleasure. I took advantage of the moment to break free, dashing frantically about, vainly attempting to quell the flames with my skirts. It was useless. They laughed at me, lit like devils by the flames. I shrank away from the scorching holocaust.

"Let us go," said their leader at last, flinging open the door. "Let the deceiving dog die here if he wishes. What we have not burned, we shall take with us."

"Shall we not take this one, too?" asked his companion, prodding me with his spear shaft.

"He is too old, too full of vile humors; he is worthless for ransom. He will die too quickly as a slave to be a bargain."

They laughed and passed out, leaving me on my knees in prayer. The fire mounted wildly, higher and higher about me. For a moment I entertained a wild wish to die as a martyr with my manuscripts. Then I renounced it; I could endure the heat of the room no longer. I leaped over the flames, burst through the door in a cloud of smoke, slamming it behind me. I spied about me, seeing no one, and ran down the passage, slipping outside into the latticed way, fearful for Maimonides and Zamira. I had heard no cries from Yaltah or David; I felt sure they had been rescued in time by Ramah.

Peering upward through the lattice, I saw with the joy of desperation that the flames and smoke mounted in billows into the night sky. They took with them my life, my learning, my reputation as a man of science and wisdom—but the fire was a signal, as well, to the loyal troops in the city. God willing, we should be revenged at the least!

A smothered cry came from the garden. I wheeled, gripping the lattice, scarcely daring to breathe. It was a sight calculated to freeze the blood, more so because I understood their vile dialect. Maimonides, standing erect, was held by one of the Almohades. Two other horsemen held Zamira, each grasping one slender arm. They spoke to each other jestingly over her golden head.

"What shall we do with this yellow-hair?"

"Tie her in a sack with a quintal of unslaked lime. Drop her in the river from the seventeen-arched bridge. Then she will both burn and drown as befits one seduced by luxury from the true belief."

"Shall she have a hundred bastinadoes on the back, a hundred on her breasts?"

"Anoint her with honey and tie her naked to an anthill!"

"Ah, no," said the first, playfully swinging Zamira's rigid form off the ground. "In this country the ants do not obey the will of the Prophet as well as in Morocco. This little one shall sit on the seat of the mighty!"

A murmur of unholy pleasure arose. To my horror, one of the invaders seized his javelin and planted the shaft in the soft earth of the garden, the iron point slanting upward. Two took the tight-lipped, tearless Zamira by arms and legs and swung her shamelessly aloft, her brilliant hair tossed and floating out from under her hood, her slender white legs naked and shining to the thighs and loincloth in the brazen light of the torches and the fire beyond. Even now I can recall the sight of her expression in the glare, her eyes wide with fear, convulsed with the knowledge of what they intended. They were about to impale her on the javelin point.

Their first swing of her body upward seemed only a feint, perhaps designed to increase her fears, to make her cry out for the increased pleasure of her torturers. Its purpose failed: Highborn girl that she was, she uttered no sound. As her feet struck the ground and the howling Berbers prepared to swing her up again, Maimonides uttered a long shout like the scream

27

of an animal in pain. He managed to break loose from the grip of his captor and rushed at the men in the black burnooses.

One of them whirled and brought the hilt of his scimitar heavily down on the head of my son. He groaned and fell. I, in my sanctuary, felt the blow as if it were to my own head but I was too paralyzed to move. Maimonides writhed on the ground. The others paused with Zamira, waiting to observe this new amusement. The Almohade kicked at my son: I gasped but could not take my eyes away. Maimonides jerked back and the foot barely missed his head. The Moslem staggered, off-balance. Maimonides shot out his hand, catching the other by the heel. He jerked with all his might.

The man reeled, lost equilibrium. Before my eyes, he toppled backward, then fell sideways on the point of the javelin, spitting himself like an ox on the instrument he had intended for an innocent one. As he bawled out in pain, flopping about like a black beetle with a pin through it, his arms and legs aimlessly thrashing, the air was heavy with suspense, with rage, with the devil's emotions.

Through this miasma cut the bray of trumpets outside the walls, the thunder of horses, the familiar rallying cry of the Cordovan troops. The Almohades knew, with the instinct of cornered rats, that they were next to being caught in the cul-de-sac of my garden. Their shouts of rage were cut short. A flood of dark forms burst from my house, dashing toward the gate with all possible speed. The panic spread. The others joined them in jostling melee, leaves blown before the wind of terror.

As they went, indeed, two vengeful javelins were directed at my son. He rolled out of the way of one; the other pinned him to the ground. I uttered a cry of anguish that was lost in the universal shout of defiance. The Almohades mounted their horses and clattered off, hotly pursued by the cavalry from the city.

I ran to Maimonides, already grieving for a son lost. I found, thanks be to God, that the second javelin had only scratched his side, piercing his clothing so that he was caught to the earth. He tore himself free with my fumbling help. He sprang up. I gripped his arm only just in time to prevent him from lunging at the gate in chase.

"Have you lost your mind?" I shouted.

"Zamira! She is gone! Zamira has been taken by the Almohades!"

28

It was the truth: The small girl had vanished with the raiders. I tightened my hold on Maimonides' arm. "It is the will of God!" I said sternly. "She is not one of the elect; she is no more than a Moorish girl!"

I had said more than I meant to in the stress of the moment and Maimonides turned his fury against me. I let him go, drawing back in fear that he would commit the deadly sin of striking his father. Instead, he turned again for the outer gate. I disgraced myself by flinging my body at his feet and bringing him down sprawling on the gravel.

"We must go!" I panted in his ear. I rose, dragging him across toward the river gate hidden behind the trees on the other side. "I am your father and I command you to come!" Maimonides did not reply but his body ceased to be tense. It became a limp dead weight that I was forced to drag to safety without his help.

Ramah, with the laden mules, David, and Yaltah, greeted us. Maimonides stood up, brushing the dust hopelessly from his robes and refraining from looking at me. David flung himself upon his brother, crying out: "What happened, Muni, what was it? Did you kill anybody?"

"Hush, my son," I said sternly. I shuddered: I still felt the slubbering of my feet through the sticky blood of the dead Almohade. I could not get out of my mind the fixed, hideous stare on his face as, mask awry, his pocked countenance stared sightlessly upward.

"Nothing happened," Maimonides said. He glanced briefly at me. I could not tell the meaning of his look. "Nothing happened except the will of God, aided by my father."

A mule is a cursed animal with a skin that shivers and shifts like the tides, bags for a belly and sticks for legs, with the sharpest rib of Satan for a backbone. He that rides him for long must have thighs of leather and the balance of an acrobat. Mile after mile across the plain that night I rode with that edged rod of iron between my legs, berating the animal with all the names (in alphabetical order) of all the fiends I could summon to memory—and Maimonides remembered more than I. Yet the mule took its own time, huge ears falling back and forth in rhythm to its disjointed gait. Behind me on another mule followed Ramah, with Yaltah on her knees, and after her, David. Two more mules carried what goods we had been spared. Maimonides, silent and lowering, brought up the rear of our tiny caravan.

So much we had rescued from ruin. From the days of Moses in Egypt, our race had learned how to be ready to depart from the happiest of dwellings: In a niche, at all times, stood sealed bags filled with food and clothing, ready for the inevitable moment of exile. God had given us Cordova and God had taken it away, praised be He. It was small comfort to remember that Job had suffered such woes on the prompting of the Adversary and had at the last become more blessed than before with riches, wives, and sons, for Job had not lived in marvelous Cordova.

We headed toward the mountains of the south and the sea. My instinct was to skirt the path of the invaders, but beyond this I saw no other refuge in my bewildered mind that night. Every hand seemed turned against our kind. We wore Moslem garb and spoke the idiom as well as any native—but when Moslem slew Moslem, who would be safe?

Following the stars by the astronomical calculations I had studied and taught, we knew our direction. The spring air had a sweet savor to it. My spirits might have risen except that I had a heavier weight upon my mind. Once, as we paused for rest, Maimonides came beside me. I looked at my son and groaned. He questioned me with a glance.

"You have killed a man," I said.

"It was by accident," he returned, "yet I admit the intention of his death was with me."

"Murder is a sin," I said, "by the commandments of Moses."

"Not in such a case."

"And so soon after the close of the Day of Atonement," I said with heat.

Maimonides shook his head. "No," he replied calmly, "for the Rabbi Eleazar has said that it is permissible to cut down such a man on the Day of Atonement, even if it fall on the Sabbath."

"Such wisdom will not wash the conscience clean," I said angrily and rode out ahead. Only at the crimson warning of dawn did I stop, my path crossed by a stray Barbary ape, scuttling from the side of a hill next to our path. I turned in. I discovered, as I had guessed, a spring bubbling under the shade of three low-branched ilexes. Here we dismounted, washed our hands and faces, gave thanks in prayer, and took time for food.

Maimonides came and stood beside me until I gave him permission to sit. "My father," he said submissively, "let us not be at cross purposes."

"I am your father," I said, "and you are a thirteen-year-old boy. Do not forget that."

He bowed his head. "I yield with all my heart," he said, "but I am puzzled. What is the reason for our exile?"

"In the mind of God or the mind of man?"

Maimonides shrugged. "The mind of God is unknowable," he admitted. "In the mind of man, then."

I gazed into the clefts of the rock for inspiration. As I stared, a hare leaped out in fright and scuttled away. I pointed after him.

"Once," I said to Maimonides, "there was a hare that fled from all the world because they pursued and persecuted him unto death. He fretted and pined about mankind hating him, not comprehending his soul, wanting only his skin and flesh. He wept tears of fat and blood and his form became thin, shrinking to the size of a mouse. In such a condition, he crept out of his pleasant hole in the ground and sought another. He discovered a small burrow at the base of a wall and entered. He found himself in a garden full of choice fruits and delightful food and drink. Here he stayed for a time and began to believe he existed in an eternity of bliss where he could fill his belly as full as he wanted. As he devoured the substance of the garden, he grew fat and sleek once more.

"One day he knew the bellowing of the hounds outside, he heard their sniffing along the wall. He realized they had found his haven and that their masters could not be far behind. He attempted, in his fear, to escape through the same hole through which he had entered; it was not to be. The hole had remained as small as ever, but he had grown fat. Again he sweated beads of fat and blood and again his shape became small, even to mouse-size. Sorrowfully yet joyfully he squeezed through the hole and escaped the fate designed for him. Yet, even as he set out to seek another garden, he regretted all he had left behind that had made him so happy.

"Was the hare wise or foolish, my son?"

"He was wise to go," Maimonides said slowly, "and he was foolish to regret."

"No," I said, "he was wise both to escape and to remember. Memory is the single treasure from the past that one may keep with him to the grave."

Two days after, approaching Granada with sore bones and weary flesh, we endured a strange encounter. It proved to me that my son had more knowledge of the world than I, wisdom

31

which I had disdained in my pride. If it had not been for his skill in interpretation—but this is the tale.

We had seen no human faces except our own during this time. We had entered the first of the saw-edged, tumbled hills which mark the beginning of the coastal range of mountains, dark with low forests, white with cliffs of limestone. It was early afternoon. I drowsed on my mule. A loud hail from the slopes above wakened me: A man on a nag came sliding down in a storm of rocks, crunching them to powder under the hoofs of his mount. He raised a hand in the sign of peace and paced slowly toward us.

"Do you go to Granada?" he asked. I surveyed him carefully. He was a short, broad-shouldered man with a red face and twinkling eyes; his hair was short and black and his beard cropped. He rode easily but his mangy horse bowed under his weight. "I am for the city," he added, "and company shortens a journey." His eyes twinkled under their bushy brows. He laughed a hearty laugh. I could not keep from smiling and motioned him to join us.

He was a Christian and a miller, he said, bound for Granada on affairs of business. He inquired our names. I allowed it to appear that we were Moslems intending to stop in the Rabad al Bayazin, the Falconers' Quarter of the city, to visit friends. "Well and good," he said, slapping his thigh. "Do you know riddles?"

"I have heard a few," I replied cautiously.

"Then tell me," he said, urging his horse closer, "what three things weary a man?"

"An unlit lamp, a late messenger, and a table set without guests," said Maimonides from behind me. I turned irritably.

"Allow your father to answer," I instructed him.

"Your pardon," he said meekly.

I looked at our companion. "Tell me," I said cunningly, "by what three marks is a reputable man known?"

"By pardoning quickly, dealing honestly, and loving his fellow men," said Maimonides behind him. I wheeled, in a rage.

"Allah choke your throat!" I cried. "Have I not told you to keep silence?"

"He seems an apt boy," said the stranger.

"Far too clever," I said, fuming.

"Perhaps he can tell us what three things mark a fool?"

Maimonides was silent. "Well," I said scathingly, "inform

32

our friends once more. Share with us your immense knowledge of riddles."

"My father," Maimonides said humbly, "I do not know."

"Then I shall reply," I told him. "A fool is known by quickness in answering, in much speaking—and in faith in all men." I turned triumphantly to the newcomer. The burly man said nothing, smiling slightly, his right hand thrust into the bosom of his gown. He gazed around him and at the mountains ahead, then broke his silence unexpectedly.

"The snow is on the mountain tops," he said.

I strained my eyes in that direction but I could see no sign of white. I shook my head, saying nothing out of courtesy "This is barren land," I ventured, looking about me.

He laughed, a rich echoing sound that made my heart glad. "Aye," he said, "but soon I shall pull the plow through the gray stubble."

"Is this domain yours, then?" I asked out of puzzled curiosity.

"Not yet, but soon."

Again he laughed. A feeling of unease crept into my soul, I knew not why.

"If water could be brought here," I remarked, "land such as this would blossom like the rose of Sharon."

He looked sharply at me. His thick nose quivered like that of a dog on the scent. "Nay," he replied, "it needs nothing. The harvest is at hand."

"Selah, enough," hissed Maimonides behind us. He spoke into the very ear of the stranger. "Stop your horse, take your hand from your bosom. Dismount!"

I reined up in astonishment. My son had drawn a long knife from under his cloak. He held it with the point digging into the man's back. The other's jolly face lost its color; feeling the threat, he had become pale.

"Put that away!" I commanded. "What sort of fellowship is this?"

"My father," Maimonides said softly, "tell him to remove his hand from his bosom with what it holds." Slowly the stranger moved his hand, then whirled.

I saw the flash of a blade in his fist, I saw him strike toward my son. But Maimonides was as quick; his own knife leaped up to meet the other. A clash, light against the early shadows of the valley. Next moment the knives were still, one blade against the other, striving for mastery. David whooped with

33

excitement and urged his mule forward as if to help, despite Yaltah's scream.

The angle of the knives, crossed on high, shifted. The superior strength of the stranger, man against boy, began to tell. The blade of Maimonides slipped down along the other's, to his hilt. With a grunt of triumph, he twisted his knife with all his might. Maimonides' blade, caught in a cunning slit in the guard, snapped at the handle. The stranger knocked the hilt from his hand. He drew back his blade for a final thrust.

Almost without knowing it, I had dismounted, and was scrabbling on the ground, feeling a stone in my fingers. Madly I flung it with both hands and God guided it to the mark. It thudded against the man's head; he swayed, reeled in his saddle and fell headlong, unconscious, his knife dropping from his fingers. Maimonides leaped upon it and picked it up as I found another rock, larger and heavier. I staggered forward with it and poised it over the man's head as he tried to rise. To my chagrin, it was my son who kept me back, who forbade my vengeance.

"What do you do?" I exclaimed to Maimonides as the stranger stood uncertainly upright, blood streaming from his head. Maimonides did not reply; instead, he kicked the other's ungainly nag in its hollow ribs. It cried out, tossing its head and heels, racing away over the hill. Maimonides pushed me atop my mule, picked up the knife and remounted. He slapped the flanks and kicked his own beast. The others followed, leaving the stocky black-haired man staring murderously after us. "You condemn me to die here," he shouted in a reedy voice, totally unlike his tones of a moment before.

"You have condemned yourself," Maimonides flung over his shoulder. "Your journey is no longer ours. Eat your black heart, drink your own blood, not ours."

"You are the bloodsuckers who devour Spain!" cried the man wildly. "I know you for lying Jews! I shall remember you and you will remember Brujo the Black!" His rage was so great that his lips showed foam.

Maimonides lashed my mule and the others to a swifter pace. We went on, leaving our erstwhile friend on the path to shake his fists and lift his voice in imprecations. Out of sight and earshot at last, I twisted toward my son. "How did you know of his treachery?" I demanded.

Maimonides shook his head. I suspected that his eyes gleamed with a humor I had not detected in him before. "You have lived too long with books, too little in the world," he told me. "This fellow chose to speak in a language he did not think you knew, the riddling of thieves in the markets of Cordova."

"Is that where you have spent the days of your youth?"

"Will you say they were misspent? He meant to kill and rob all of us in this lonely spot. When he spoke of snow on the mountains, he meant you were old and weak. When he spoke of pulling the plow through the stubble, he meant your nose through your beard. And when he said the harvest was at hand, it was the moment to act."

"Where did you get that hidden knife?"

"I have—or once I had—friends among the Moors."

"Why did you not let me kill the man?" My voice was harsh. Maimonides shook his head and tucked the man's treacherous knife away in his bosom. I was on the point of commanding him to throw it away but he kept shaking his head. I knew it was no use either to ask an answer to my question or to deprive him of his weapon.

In my turn I kept a furious silence. My face was set forward: I recalled with shame the three marks of the fool in the riddle I had propounded. But no more than a mile further, it was Maimonides who rode beside me to say words of comfort.

"My father," he said gently, "is not the faith of a fool truly the love of the wise man for all men? Are they not one and the same?"

CHAPTER 3

The Moslems have a saying which runs: "Every journey and every change causes blessing and brings salvation." If any show of their damnation were needed, this would prove the point. For the man who wanders at pleasure, it may be a joy; for him who travels at need, it is a curse and abomination. To him, all places at last become one and the same place, each with its frown for the stranger and suspicion at his arrival. The wandering Jew has nowhere to put his head, no familiarity with anything on earth. And it is the familiar which makes life bearable: old friends, the accustomed taste of wine and food, the well-known view from the window, words in old books—even the familiar hardness of a couch or the poverty of home.

Anything is endurable at home, but the smallest trifles confront a stranger as the Red Sea did the Egyptians. My family and I, driftage on the beach of the world, were to ebb and flow with the succeeding waves of Moslem invaders from across the sea. As Jews we had no choice. As men of peace, of meditation and scholarship, of finance and commerce, unused to weapons of hand but superior to our foes in idea and invention, we served their ends. Having used us, they thrust us out again into the chill world, our brains and purses picked.

So it was on our weary journey through the south of Spain. We huddled at night around the fire, the teeth of the mountains black around us like the crenelations of a prison. By day we trudged on, over desert flatlands, through valleys thick with crowds of oaks. We climbed crags on paths a goat would disdain; we picked wild berries and dug roots, stopped at huts and purchased coarse wheat and corn flour. We grew lean and acid and haggard from hunger, but not one among the herds of wild pigs did we kill for food. And, if the truth be known, we learned many curious and useful things in our wanderings.

"Angels eat only once a day," I told Maimonides, "and men twice. Beasts eat three times."

He patted his sunken stomach. "Today," he said in one of his unaccustomed jests, "I am an angel. And I am light enough in the head to fly this moment."

He could not understand why I would not enter the nigh city of Granada, nor could I tell him. Again I anticipated one of those wretched arguments in which he always made me feel a simpleton.

"Why should we not stop at Granada?" he demanded. "You were there many times as a young man. You have told me that our family has good friends there."

"That is true," I said, my lips closing on the words. I thought of the lofty citadel of the town and the bright green of the pomegranate groves like a belt of velvet around the hill. My memories of years gone stung my eyes with tears.

"Why can't we go there?" asked David plaintively. I looked at his dark-curled head and the eyes that were a reminder of his mother's and shook my head. "Because I choose not to," I said miserably.

36

"I choose we should go," David replied promptly.

"It doesn't seem right nor logical," Maimonides joined in reproachfully.

"What do you know of logic?" I flared at him.

"Are you afraid of that man with the prickly hair?" David piped.

"Perhaps. Yes, that is it," I said. I felt a twinge in my breast and rose convulsively. Maimonides came to his feet, his face concerned in the firelight.

"If it is your heart that pains you, we should seek a doctor in Granada," he said. "It is not wise to treat yourself."

"My heart," I said slowly, "tells me not to go to Granada. Where the heart is sound, the body is sound; where the heart is corrupt, the body is corrupt."

"God has made the heart master over all the members of the body," Maimonides replied promptly, "and the veins are its agents, watchers over all. Therefore, when a healer feels the throbbing of the veins, he understands a man's whole nature."

"This is a child's share of medical learning," I said suspiciously, squatting on my heels.

"Let me feel the beat of your wrist-vein," Maimonides said softly beside me.

Reluctantly I extended my left arm. Maimonides put his fingers lightly on my wrist. He cocked his head at me.

"Is it a vegetable reason you will not go to Granada?" he whispered. I deigned no reply.

"Is it mineral?" Again I was silent.

"Is it animal?" I wrenched my wrist from his light grasp and frowned. Quietly Maimonides reached for it once more and I submitted.

"Is it fear?" I looked away from him.

"Of a man?" I compressed my lips and wondered what this mummery meant, not without uneasiness.

"Is it love?" My heart beat faster and I closed my eyes.

"Of a woman?"

I stood up abruptly. As I did, Ramah uttered a wail. I strode to her side and she looked up at me in pain, fearfully holding her stomach. "Give me medicine, Rabbi," she murmured. "I have eaten too much leavened bread. My stomach hurts."

I took a jar and poured water in my palm. Sprinkling a little salt in it, I knelt beside her. I held her head and let the lotion trickle into her eyes, brushed my hands and got up. Ramah stared at me with bleared astonishment.

37

"How can that cure the pain?" she asked faintly.

"It will clear your vision so that you will see better and not make a pig of yourself about food," I said shortly. I knew now what Maimonides had done: His fingers had read my pulse and ascertained my secret but I had no intention of allowing him to be indiscreet.

"My son," I said grimly, "you are fond of Aristotle. Perhaps you do not yet know as much about his works as you think. Do you recall those five things he says are wasted, availing nothing?"

"No, I cannot remember," he said and averted his eyes.

"I will tell you. Rain upon an ass's back, a lamp burning in the sun of noonday, a virgin wed to a man who is without manhood, a savory dish put before him who is drunk—and a kindness done to him who does not realize it. I have been kind to you. Some day you will know it."

As I said, Maimonides made me feel like a fool. For only afterward did I think upon his fabulous memory that never failed to recall the smallest word. He had lied to me, for what reason I could not tell.

Our journey fell just short of nine days before we came through the pass and saw the slow-winding river and the city of white called Almería, with its four towers spread out on the rich plain in the cup of the mountains. The vineyards flickered in the autumn's afternoon sun. We could smell the acrid odor of grape-pressings, the exhalation of the fermenting vats. Beyond spread the dark blue of the sea, with the quays of wood and stone, fingers clutching the shore. The harbor lay filled with a thicket of masts, the slanting lateen sails reefed. It was a welcome sight. Though the town had been taken (so I had been told) the year before by the Christian warriors of Alfonso from Castile, aided by Genoese troops, it had been recaptured soon after. Now, I felt, it was a proper refuge for us.

By twilight we had passed through the walls, under the portcullis—"Lift up your heads, O ye gates," I murmured as we plodded past the casual glances of the burnoosed sentries. We entered the still-humming tented bazaar, passed through its round purple shadows, around its bales of cordage and piles of fruit. I halted at a booth and inquired after the house of Isaac the Blind. We were directed to the east side of the throng, through a gate in a wall to the Place of Fishsellers, over a ruined Roman bridge which spanned the river, along a winding silent street of blackness overhung with buildings.

At last we arrived at what could only be called a shape in the night. It was a house indeed; but I shuddered when I compared the dark-gray stone pile, shapeless and hideous with lichen and stinking moss in every cranny, to the wide airy pleasant dwellings of Cordova. I would not have imagined anyone lived inside.

We found the gate into the pitch black of the courtyard by sheer good fortune. I ordered the others to wait. I abandoned them, stumbling through the filth to where the door might be. My fingers slipped along the wall to a deep reveal; I diagnosed the slick-wet obstacle as a door and hammered on it with both fists. After long minutes and harder hammering, a barred peephole opened. A scowling face looked out. It listened mutely as I explained our presence. The hole clapped to and I waited again; at last I heard the sound of bars and chains heaved aside and the door slowly creaked open. The servant, a squat unkempt fellow, slipped out without a word to herd our beasts and baggage into some unknown stable.

I, with the children following and Ramah in the rear, made uncertain progress through an unending clammy passage lit by a single guttering candle. We found a staircase at the end by the simple expedient of barking our shins. Feeling our way up and up, we gained the next floor. Without warning I bruised my nose upon a door studded with bolts, crisscrossed by iron straps. "In the name of Asmodeus," I muttered disgustedly, "what kind of a den does Isaac the Blind keep?"

As if in answer to my question, the door swung wide. We gaped and blinked at the sight of blazing light and luxury. The decayed ruin of the exterior was totally rejected by the room we entered. It was a wide apartment, filled with costly and colorful furniture. Thick rugs overspread the floor, the walls were hung with rich tapestries. Flowers and lamps were everywhere, glare in the eyes, scent in the nostrils. There was a wall paneled with fragrant cedar, lavishly decorated with intertwined Hebrew symbols in gilt. In the middle stood a large round table, a flame-red cloth flung over it, gilt legs showing beneath. Directly above it hung a seven-armed lamp of Israel in shining brass.

"You are late, Maimon ben Joseph," came a deep voice from the other side of the room. "We had expected you before this." Automatically my fingers went to my lips and my breast as I bowed. I could not yet see the speaker but I realized he must be lord of the house. "We have been a long time on the road," I said. "I beg for hospitality."

39

"My house is yours as long as you care to stay," came the formal reply, "even as your house would be mine."

"Alas," I said, "my humble home no longer exists." I raised my head and noted that already Maimonides was peering keenly about. I followed his gaze and saw the speaker. He sat beside a long table of dark polished wood, in an upholstered armchair, one hand on the table and the other on a small stand of ivory, engraved and illuminated by tracings and color until it seemed that its fragile form could not endure the weight of such decoration. He was a man younger than I by ten years or more, thin and erect in his seat; his face massive, with a high forehead and prominent bones. The flesh was white except for two spots of pink at the cheekbones. The eyes were closed. I knew he was none other than the notorious Isaac the Blind.

Yet more curious than Isaac himself (who seemed like some exotic indoor plant) were two figures behind him. They were identical in height and coloring; even their expressions were the same. White-faced as the man in the chair, with dusty yellow hair and dull blue eyes, they seemed no more than twelve years old, rigid as statues and watching us unblinkingly.

"I have, of course, heard of the famous Cordova doctor," said Isaac in his sonorous voice, "and of his remarkable son, Moses; but my poor reputation, I fear, has not reached your ears."

"Nay, but it has, learned Isaac," I hastened to say. "Your devotion to the holy works of our fathers and the words of our God has long been a byword among us."

"Perhaps it will become even better known," said the blind man. His expression shifted into a smile, delicate and ingenuous. "I have been host to a friend of yours until three days gone. Had you arrived then, I might have enjoyed the pleasures of all my honored visitors together."

"May I inquire his name?"

"Judah ben Samuel Halevi," returned Isaac the Blind. I said nothing.

"Before he took ship," Isaac said, his blind face again expressionless, "he left a message for you."

I felt my muscles tighten in distaste and regret. Isaac reached out to the ivory table next to him, his hand as sure as that directed by the keenest vision. He picked up a small scroll on a blue spindle and handed it to me. I accepted it and reluctantly unrolled the parchment, holding it up to the light. I recognized Judah's spidery Arabic script.

"Since I am Chief Rabbi in Almería," came Isaac's silky

voice, "Judah was sure you would come here eventually in your travels. He left this for you. Will you read it to me if it is not a personal affair? I am fond of his writings."

"It was unsealed, good Isaac," I said, "and it is nothing close to me." I commenced to read aloud:

"TO MAIMON BEN JOSEPH: FAREWELL!

"Dear God, put not Thy hand upon the sea
  To still its rolling waves,
Nor give commands for such depths not to be;
  Spare them as Thy slaves,
Until their lowly task for me is done:
  To take me with my Lord
From ravaged Spain to fair Jerusalem,
  Far from the Arab horde.

"And if Thou question, do I courage lack for sailing?
Thou knowest I am pledged to Thee, the Never-failing."

In spite of myself, my eyes moistened. Judah had served the rich and poor in his capacity of physician at Toledo, the good and bad; he had done a long task well, treating all and gaining little that his soul really desired. Second only to his heavenly fountain of verse, he had, from a child, been enamored of the land of our fathers which he had never seen. I could not forgive his cowardly abandonment of his small daughter and his son, Judah. But I could feel at this moment a little of the yearning in his verses for the fulfillment of another, perhaps greater, love.

"He is a charming poet, if not always philosophically sound," remarked Isaac. For the first time, he stirred in his chair. "But I have bad manners. These, respected Maimon, are my friends and disciples, Ezra and Azriel, from Gerona in the north, brothers in the faith and twins in blood." The two young men bowed simultaneously with puppet-like gestures. I frowned. "Disciples?" I inquired. "Do you mean they are pupils, studying with you?"

Isaac the Blind waved his long thin hand lightly. "I have made many secret discoveries in the Bible and the Talmud," he declared, "and I find echoes in the Koran. It is an entirely new knowledge, though entirely traditional. I call it the Kabbala. If you like, if you wish to devote seven years to it, I shall teach it to you or your son."

"There is nothing hidden in the Talmud," I protested.

41

"Indeed there is, my father," broke in Maimonides, excitedly stepping past my chair, his face alight. "What Judah of our own family did needs to be done again, to make the Oral Law, the Mishnah, understandable to the people. It is not a Mishnah now but a mess."

I was astounded. "For a child, you seem to be developing mighty ambitions," I managed to say. "Such a part of the Talmud as the great Babylonian collection must remain chiefly a mystery."

"It need not be so," Maimonides exclaimed. He was interrupted by the laugh of Isaac the Blind.

"Will you deny the works of the blessed martyr Rabbi Akiba, more than a thousand years ago?" he asked of me.

Again I felt bewilderment. "What has he to do with it?" I inquired.

"Four entered the mystic Garden of Life—Ben Zoma, Ben Azzai, Aher, and the mighty Rabbi Akiba. Ben Zoma looked and died. Ben Azzai looked and went mad. Aher looked and lost his faith. Rabbi Akiba entered in peace and went forth in peace."

Maimonides came closer to the figure of the blind man in the chair. Ezra and Azriel took a step forward as if to protect their master. "Tell me what you have found, Rabbi Isaac," Maimonides said intently.

Isaac the Blind hesitated. "Come closer," he said at length. Maimonides advanced to the side of his armchair; I held my breath, without knowing why. The hands of Isaac touched his form, fingered his dress, ran up his figure like mice, molding themselves around his face and head in the fashion of a blind man recognizing another person. Isaac nodded to himself. "You have the bones and flesh of a wise youth," he murmured. He dropped his hands and leaned forward.

"Will you understand this, young Maimonides?" he asked in a tone that sent a quiver of fear into my heart. "Listen well. As you say, the wisdom of the Babylonian Oral Law has never been organized for understanding by the common people. But should it be so? Is there not all mystery therein? Pay attention: There are the Names. The Letters arise from the Names; the Numbers arise from the Letters. The Ideas emerge from the Numbers and from the Ideas come the Forces. And the Forces give birth to the Shema."

He ceased and after a moment Maimonides shook his head. "I do not understand," he said.

"Then listen once more. The Shema is one, its Columns are

42

two, its Powers are three; its Reflection in holiness produces eight, which, multiplied once more by the mystic three, offers us the Twenty-four Thrones of Wisdom. Do you comprehend?"

My heart stirred with joy. Maimonides had stepped back, his face white, his expression hostile. "I understand that this is the thought of the Greek Pythagoras, the philosopher in numbers. I know the two Talmuds, of Palestine and of Babylon, and I can think of nothing in them like it."

Isaac the Blind straightened up suddenly. "It is not a matter of thought," he said austerely. "It is a reflection of the soul." He clapped his hands. His disciples moved to his side in quick obedience.

"But we are true rabbis, all," he said with a mirthless smile. "Here we are, splitting hairs between us while you are still travel-stained and worn. I have been remiss in my duties as a host. Ezra, Azriel, conduct them to their chambers and see that they have warm water to bathe. Shalom, my friends! Food awaits you upon your return."

With protestations and thanks we turned to follow our guides. As we did, the voice of Isaac the Blind broke in again. "A moment," he said. "You may be interested to know that Judah, our poetic friend, sailed for Alexandria. He intends, so he told me, to visit the Jewish communities at Cairo, to go on to that of Damascus before he enters the Holy Land."

"It is a long journey," I murmured, not knowing what else to say.

"I might add," Isaac said with a touch of malice, "that his departure crossed just behind the path of another illustrious person of our race, Ali Halevi. Judah had no desire to see his brother; in truth, he avoided him. But I noted a curious thing, Maimon."

I waited without replying, Maimonides at my elbow. Isaac went smoothly on: "Ali speaks highly of you but he and his son, Samuel, bear you hatred."

"A childish thing that will pass," I said wearily. "As children do, the boys quarreled, but it is nothing."

"I trust you are right. But Samuel is an overproud boy. He does not easily forget what he conceives to be an injury. He spoke of blows by the hand of your son."

I bowed silently. Isaac the Blind waved his hand and we followed his disciples out of the room into the chill of the corridor.

43

That night after the meal we sat late at table over carobs and honey spiced with ginger, with a wine so strong its surface could be lighted by a wax taper. I forced myself to dilute it more than half with water; even then I felt its dizzying influence. Ramah had tucked David and Yaltah into bed. I allowed Maimonides to sit with myself and our host and his followers: in truth I did not feel secure alone under the sway of this strange man.

But Isaac talked no more of the mysterious Kabbala nor of his many visitors. Rather, our speech ranged across the multitudinous bits of news and gossip from Jewry in the world. Isaac, who was in constant touch with his father, Rabbi Abraham ben David of Posquieres in France, told us stories that Abraham had received from Germany of the horrible cruelty of the first crusaders. In France they had done little more than drive the Jews into churches at swordspoint and demand death or baptism—a choice quickly made and recanted next day. In Germany, however, William the Carpenter led a plundering horde of Christians. At their bloodstained approach—some actually painted the crosses on their dress with Jewish gore—the women and girls became so frantic that they loaded themselves with stones and threw themselves into the river. In Worms, this band murdered eight hundred of our faith.

But by far the most diabolic plot was that hatched by one Count Emmerich in Mayence. He and his relative, Archbishop Ruthard, devised a scheme for the ruthless extermination of the Jews. The churchman proclaimed his sympathy for the Jews and offered them protection in the cellar of his palace. More than thirteen hundred Jews accepted his mercy. Next daybreak the mob came and stormed the place without resistance, killing all. Ruthard and Emmerich divided the possessions of the dead between them.

"It was a poor return for that suffering," Isaac said reflectively, "but it was God's judgment that all two hundred thousand of those crusaders perished miserably in Hungary when the peasants rose in anger against their looting and murdering."

"And those Jews who apostatized?" asked Maimonides. "What happened to them?"

Isaac held up his wine that he could not see. "It was the good Rabbi Solomon ben Isaac of Troyes who declared—and I agree: 'Far be it from us to reject those who have returned;

they acted from fear of the sword and lost no time in coming back to the faith of their fathers.' "

"But they denied their faith when they swore to that of the Christians," I said indignantly.

"Are they better off dead than alive?" asked Isaac. "I tell you, more than twelve thousand Jews were killed in two months! Can we build on such a foundation of corpses?"

"It is better to die than renounce," I said.

"I do not believe that," Maimonides muttered at my side. Isaac's keen ears heard his dissent; he looked in his direction and gave him a thin-lipped smile of approval. I stood up and thumped down my glass, about to begin a denunciation of such weak-willed heresy. I never spoke a word; I was interrupted by a thunder of blows on the doors below.

Isaac the Blind started in his place. It was plain he was expecting no one. The squat serving-man vanished at his gesture to see who it might be. Maimonides and I looked at each other.

We had not long to wait. Up the stairs, in a fury of resentful fear, tumbled the servant; behind him, striding into the room as if it were their own, came two Moslems, scimitars bared, giving their escort a last prick with the points. They halted as he scuttled away; they surveyed the room with a cold stare. Isaac rose and turned his face toward them without a word.

"Are you Isaac the Blind?" the first rasped. His face was drawn, burned black by the sun; his tone was a sneer.

"I am."

"Do you house one Maimon ben Joseph, lately arrived in the city? Do not deny it. We have been informed well by the men of the bazaar who spoke with him. They have sworn they directed him here."

"There is no need to lie," Isaac said with dignity. "He is the honored guest of my house."

I rose, "I am he whom you seek," I said, with a tardy obeisance. "What is your wish?"

"You are the Jew physician, Chief Rabbi of Cordova? We want no mistake."

"I am he."

The older man next to him, seemingly his superior, moved a leisurely step forward. "We come most urgently," he said courteously. "We are bid here to fetch you to the governor, His Excellency, Mohammed ibn Abdul, at the palace. He has been ill, in great pain, for a week or more past. By the favor of Allah, he must be cured. He requests that you come as soon as possible; none of the healers in the city of Almería has been able to relieve him."

I shook my head free of the fumes of wine and then, as his face darkened, said hastily: "I am prepared to go with you immediately," I said, "and I am honored by His Excellency's request." I felt Maimonides move closer to me and glanced down at his pleading face. I divined what he desired. "Sir," I said to the older man, "may I bring my son, who is my assistant? It is possible that he will be of use and he may be able to learn something into the bargain."

The Moslem shrugged. "Take whom you need," he agreed.

In a second, Maimonides had raced off and secured my medicinal pouch. By the time he returned I had put on my caftan and head-covering under the scornful eyes of the younger Moslem guard. I announced that we were ready. We proceeded down the stairs, followed by the murmured farewell of Isaac. We followed a torch held by the sullen servant; he lighted us out the door to the courtyard where two lightly saddled mares waited. I looked at them with apprehension.

"Behind me," said the younger guard briefly to Maimonides. He sprang upward and the older man nodded to me. I stuck my foot into the stirrup and heaved myself up behind his wooden saddle. Instantly the horses broke into a headlong gallop out of the courtyard. As I held on for my life I looked behind and saw the face of Isaac's servant convulse as he spat contemptuously on the stones.

We rode on the wind. I had only my faith to uphold me that these wild soldiers knew their way. I clung to the rider like a drowning man, imagining what a sight I must be with my black robes intermingled with the white cloak of the Moslem. Half-hidden before us, I could see Maimonides clutching the medicine pouch with one hand, waving the other in high excitement, holding to his seat only by the grip of his knees on the flank of the horse. I held the rider before me as I saw a dim obstacle loom up in front of us. Before I knew it we were in the air; it was a rickety cart. Both horsemen leaped over it. We thundered on down the street, scattering the few late passers-by with their lantern-boys like hens before a rooster. Striking sparks, we dashed around a turn, across a wide tree-studded square, and through the gracefully pinched arch of the Moslem gates of the palace. We veered to the left. Beyond us I saw the ghostly white outline of an exquisitely fashioned mosque, its needle towers rising like fingers pointing to God.

We jarred to a halt. Our Moslem escort flung themselves from their steaming horses, Maimonides after them. I descended more painfully, holding my aching back, unused to such horsemanship. We were hurried into the inner courtyard around the sedately splashing fountains, the flowerbeds. At a torchlit entrance we were surrendered to a pair of eunuch slaves. They led us through a maze of passages that resembled a puzzle-garden, up a long flight of stairs, and into the private quarters of the governor of Almería.

He was a large man, too fat for health. He lay under a silk quilt of crimson, propped up on white pillows; between the drawn curtains of his couch, I could see he wore a thin gown through which his pink flesh was visible. His chest heaved with pain, his head rolled restlessly back and forth. It was bare and bald; a pale scar ran across his forehead.

I signaled to Maimonides to put down the medicine pouch. As I advanced, I felt at home in this large chamber with a cool breeze blowing through the lattices of the tall windows. I stood at his bedside between the two large oil lamps on either side of the couch.

Mohammed cocked his ear and ceased to rock his head and moan. Instinctively I salaamed; Maimonides followed. One of the slaves bent over the bed and whispered in the sick man's ear. As he turned his face toward me, I could see his eyes were horribly red and swollen.

"Shalom," I said quickly. "May the blessing of the prophets Abraham and Mohammed protect Your Excellency."

Mohammed moaned again and gave a loud belch. "You are the Jew doctor with magic powers?" he inquired in a peculiarly high voice.

"I have no magic, Excellency," I said, "and I do only what skill and medicines can do."

"See that you do well."

"Is it your eyes, Excellency?"

"What else, you fool?"

"Pardon: I was not informed." I gestured to one of his attendants. He understood me and unhooked one of the lamps. I carried its yellow flame close to the head of the stricken man.

"If Your Excellency would honor me by opening his eyes so that I can examine them?"

"Idiot! If I could open them, would I call for you?"

"Allow me, then, honored sir." As he moaned again from

47

the pain, I handed the lamp to Maimonides and bent over him, gently prying the lids apart. I placed my fingertips lightly on the upper lids of the closed eyes, feeling with alarm the pressure behind the eyeballs.

"Unbelieving Jew," said the sick governor, "you must relieve my agony. I cannot see, I cannot stand this torture. If you cure me, name your own fee; if not, your eyes will suffer the same pain, I promise you."

Slowly I drew back, dreading what I had to say. I shook my head. "Well," demanded the governor impatiently, "why do you delay?" He turned his bulging tight-lidded eyes on me. "Are you prepared to work your magic?"

"Excellency," I said, swallowing hard, "it is difficult for me to tell you what is the fact."

"You mean you do not know?"

"Alas, I know well enough. You are afflicted—I cannot believe by the will of God—with what the Greeks call *glaukoma*."

"What does that mean?"

"In Greek, it means 'light-gray eyes.'"

"My eyes are black!"

"Not so, Excellency. The disease has changed their color."

"Then I am blind!" he wailed, putting his hands to his eyes as if he would tear them out. I restrained him.

"No, no, Excellency," I said soothingly. "It is a disease only. And like all diseases, it has its cure."

"Ah!" Mohammed expelled his breath and sank back on his pillows. "Then to work, Jew, to work!"

"Let me explain further, honored sir. There is a pressure of liquid behind your eyes that strives against the eyeball, that causes it to cry out in pain. Allow me to aid you."

"Why do you keep talking? What will you do?"

"With your permission, I wish you to drink the juice of one of your native flowers, the poppy. This will relieve the pain for a time. In addition, I will also apply a healing ointment of Calabar seed. Every half hour you should command your attendants to place hot wet cloths over your eyes.

"So be it. And this will cure me?"

I could not help heaving a sigh. Mohammed's ears caught the sound. "Seize the Jew!" he cried. In an instant I was pinioned by one of the eunuchs; the other grasped Maimonides. I made no resistance. "I can only tell you the truth, Excellency," I said. "But for your own sake, I can quiet your pain before you condemn me."

48

Mohammed gave a grudging signal to my captor. I opened the medicine kit and secured two vials, making sure of their contents by odor and taste. I gave the governor a draught of the opium juice. I applied the Calabar balm to a soft linen bandage and pressed it lightly over his eyes. With the feral gaze of the eunuchs on me, I waited a few minutes; soon the lines of suffering in the governor's face faded. The color commenced to return to the gray flesh. I stooped over him. "Is the pain less, Excellency?" I asked.

Mohammed nodded drowsily. "Praise be to Allah and yourself, Jew, the pain is much less."

I gave Maimonides a swift glance, nerved myself, and went on: "Your Excellency, though I have the knowledge to diagnose your illness, I do not have the skill nor the instruments to do what must be done."

"I am content," the governor said.

"But this is only for a time, what I have done. The cause must be attacked, not the symptoms."

"What nonsense is this? What do you wish to do?"

I bit my lips. "I wish to call upon another healer for aid in this case."

Mohammed turned his bandaged face toward me again. I could see his forehead furrow in a frown. He realized as well as I that this was an extraordinary proposal. To call in another doctor to treat my patient was tantamount to admitting failure. "Know, Your Excellency," I said, "that such a consultation is favored by tradition. The first and greatest physician of all, Hippocrates of Greece, declared that it was wise and right for one to call in another healer who has devoted his life to the study of special afflictions."

"Then, in the name of Allah, summon the man!"

I drew a deep breath. "Excellency, it is not a man. It is a woman."

"A woman!"

"And of my own race!" My voice rang out louder than I intended.

Mohammed bolted upright on his couch. He clapped his hands to his eyes and sank back, groaning softly in pain. He licked his dry lips and nodded. "As you wish, Jew," he articulated. "I am your slave as long as I am blind. Do as you wish." He raised his voice to the eunuchs. "I command you to obey his orders as if they were my own!" The eunuchs bowed and muttered their acknowledgments of his decree.

"One thing only," the governor said, sinking deeper into his

49

pillows and preparing for sleep. "The Jew will stay under guard here in the palace until such time as I am better. If I am blind or die—a red-hot sword blade or a needle through his own eyes so that I may have a companion in misery."

"As you will, Excellency. Do I have permission to send for her?"

"Who is this paragon of women? Where does she dwell?"

"Her name is Rachel bat Abor," I said, speaking a name I had banned from my lips for many years, tasting its forbidden sweetness with all the more delight. "She is of Toledo, a famous healer of eyes."

"Toledo! I shall die with pain before she will arrive!"

"Nay," I said. I hesitated, my eyes roving momentarily to the tense form of Maimonides. "I have information that she has lived in Granada these past months. It is her second home."

"Is this an excuse to gain time for a scheme to save your life?"

"Excellency, the one God in His wisdom has seen fit to give a few of His children great gifts. Who are we to question Him? This woman has cured many sicknesses of the eye in all the countries of Europe. I pray she has not already departed for France; I have heard that the Frankish king has sent emissaries from Paris to seek her and ask for her aid for his blindness—and her fee is to be the whole of a year's taxes from a principality."

Mohammed turned his head slowly toward his slaves. "Dispatch me two couriers immediately to Granada. Instruct them not to return without this woman, even though she be on the road to France. By force or bribe or free will, on their heads be it!"

One of the eunuchs patted his hands together, bowed over them, and left at a jog trot. Mohammed fell back exhausted, his senses overcome by the sleeping-draught. I did not look at Maimonides; I could not look at him; I felt he knew the secrets of my inmost self, his dark eyes boring into my bosom like twin bowed-drills into stone. Turning away, I addressed the air over the head of the sleeping governor.

"Maimonides, return to the house of Isaac. Tell him, tell Ramah, I shall stay here tonight in accordance with His Excellency's invitation. I shall renew his comfort tomorrow and expect the healer from Granada by the following evening. Then I shall again be the guest of our friend."

As Maimonides moved toward the outer door, the second

50

slave returned from his mission. He beckoned me in another direction. I followed him willingly. I was shaking and weak—from our journey, from my meeting with Isaac, from the encounter with the governor. Most of all, from the unseen expression of my son that I could not face for the first time in my life.

Large and comfortable and ornate was the room assigned to me. The divan was the best by far that I had rested on since Cordova and my own couch. But I could not sleep. Perhaps it was the night, the odor of strange trees outside, the rattling of vines along the wall. I crossed to the window and looked out on the slumbering citadel of Almería. I heard the distant talk of sentries in the stillness, the occasional sonority of a single bell-clang possibly marking the time. The moon, not yet in her full orb, rested on the sea horizon like a maiden reclining.

From below, rising as all sounds rise, I heard voices in the night. The two guards of the governor, squatting on either side of the door with their scimitars across their knees, talked to each other across the intervening space.

"They are dogs, cunning dogs," said the younger. "I say, Musef, they are a danger to the true belief. They steal our arts and sciences, they take our bread and our very religion."

"And you speak like a fool," returned the older man. "Ahmed, Ahmed, when will you remember that the Sent of Allah sought their communion and, even when basely spurned, still taught love and tolerance for all creatures of Allah."

"They mock the Prophet, as do the Christians. Put them to the Formula or the Sword, I care not which."

"I do not say we disagree, I say you are impatient, Ahmed. As they learn from us, we from them. We accept their arts as gifts from Allah and increase our own strength. They have skill in trade and, as you have seen tonight, in the healing arts; they counsel wisely and, when they have sworn by their God, they can be trusted. Kill the Christians if you will; but for every Jew you slay, you take some splendor from the jewel of Islam."

"Say on," replied Ahmed in a disgruntled voice, "and your head will grin from the highest spire of the gates."

Musef chuckled. There was a pause and, after a moment, he continued cautiously: "What would you say if you knew I spoke with the young Jew before he left?"

"What could pass between you?"

"He knows the Koran better than the most devout. He speaks with the wisdom of the sages. Such a one cannot fail to come to the bosom of Mohammed. Shall I declare what he said?"

"Say on."

"He averred that Allah and his own God are one."

Ahmed stirred in amazement. "Then he is one of us!"

"He said also that the God of the Christians may be the same."

"The foul young dog!"

"A dog that may grow up to be big enough to bring both you and me to heel. This land reels with conflict; last year we repulsed the Christians but next year? Moslem fights against Moslem and who is victor? Must we waste our force in these endless arguments, Ahmed, or shall we find one ground of salvation?"

I fell back from my eavesdropping at the window. I had heard enough. In my bosom a queer hard ache commenced to throb. I thought of my son and his misguided charity that came close to apostasy. I stifled a cry: How had he strayed so far? I flung myself face downward on my couch. Half-wretched for Maimonides, half-rejoicing at seeing Rachel again on the day after the morrow, I fell asleep.

CHAPTER 4

With the composure of a goddess, Rachel sat down on a cordwain stool placed for her by the small table. She opened her case of stiff, tooled red leather. She took out her instrument packets one by one. She unrolled them deftly from the lamb's wool in which they were bedded and placed them in exactly parallel rows, a fingertip apart.

Though I had long known her professional aplomb, I was amazed at her care. Inwardly I approved wholly of the way she made everything ready for instant use. All the more, I thought, because behind her—like watchful mastiffs—stood two ornately dressed Moorish doctors.

"Two lamps, well trimmed," Rachel murmured to the attendant assigned to her side. The hulking Negro jumped to obey, bringing in two brass saucers with blazing wicks. Rachel herself arranged them at either side of the bed, as close as possible to the scarred bald head of the suffering Mohammed. She beckoned to me.

"Take this, Maimon," she said in a low voice. She handed me a burning glass fixed in a frame with a wooden handle. "Hold it so the light is concentrated into his eyes."

I had never seen such a device before but I obeyed her instructions. A brilliant circle of light appeared on the governor's face, outshining the sunlight through the windows. He moved restlessly.

"Excellency," Rachel said soothingly, "I must ask you to drink another potion. It will make you sleepy and remove most of the pain." She held a cup to his lips, tasting it first herself, as was the custom, administering it with her slender fingers. Mohammed sank back. His breathing became slow and stertorous.

Rachel turned her dark eyes to me enigmatically. "Now we shall wait a few moments," she said. She took her seat once again on the stool. I sank down upon the leather-covered X-chair behind me, still holding the burning glass, my gaze on the floor. I reflected upon my position.

Not out of pride but to praise God, I may declare that my profession is favored above all others in material gain. In Cordova, as well as in the other cities of the Moslems, honors are not lacking for wisdom nor wealth for medicine. Those who sell herbs and drugs become rich, and the physician is not far behind. My grandfather often related to me how Ibra'il ibn Bukht-Yishu, a famous Persian doctor, acquired extraordinary wealth. He was of such high repute that he received 120,000 dirhams yearly from the government of his country; from his king, 50,000 dirhams; from the Persian nobles and their families, 400,000 dirhams. Each year, when he had twice bled and purged the caliph Haroun al Raschid, he accepted 200,000 dirhams; the Barmecides of the caliph—who acted as his ministers—paid him 1,400,000 annually for his treatments.

Thus Ibra'il received an income of 2,170,000 dirhams a year for his services, and they continued without cease for twenty-three years. The treasure of Ibra'il mounted beyond counting; in all but blood he became the equal of the monarch of Persia. His gold-and-silver embroidered turban, said my grandfather, rose as high as an ordinary ceiling and his sleeves, trailing the floor, were so heavy with precious gems as to prevent him from lifting his hands without two assistants.

Even allowing for the Moslem exaggeration to the tenth place, it must be admitted that such reward for physicians is munificent. But it must not be thought that such art could be unattended by the most terrible dangers. Nothing is more hazardous than to have the life of a king in one's hands. The wisest of us collect whatever fees we can in advance, hide them well, bless our family as if for the last time, and go forth in trepidation to try our skills and potions. If an eminent patient gets well (and indeed nature often does as much as we), we are secure until the next illness. But if he dies—or continues the same—or takes a turn for the worse, then our state is pitiful. Our rewards in such a case are at the least to be stripped of all wealth and position; beyond that, to be tortured by drinking our own medicine or undergoing the same treatment by slaves; or to be imprisoned for long years, or whipped to a whimpering bloody heap or even maimed or put to death on the spot. And as Jews, we know our recompense will be much less than that given to one of Moslem faith—and our punishment much more terrible.

Occasionally, though our healing may be irreproachable, our tact may fail us. In the story of one of the most famous of our clan, the great Rhazes, another Persian, failed to carry out some trivial chemistry experiments for the ruler of Bokhara. He was condemned to be beaten over the head with his own huge medical compilation, *Al Hawi*, until either his head or the book was broken. As a result, he lost his sight.

What laws exist governing the practice of medicine are so strict, they almost forbid treatment. Most of them deal with the abnormal fear of these times about the chastity of all women. Touching the hand, arm, or breast of a maiden is punishable by fine or castration. No physician can bleed a woman in the absence of relatives "because occasionally some advantage may be taken with the opportunity," says the law.

Not unnaturally, this produces woman healers such as Rachel. Few they are, but needed and necessarily talented. Since the day that the foolish Christians outlawed the practice of medicine by their priests, we especially encouraged female students in Cordova. In some cities, societies of such women were formed but became discredited because of loose talk and lascivious acts. Some female doctors pay much attention to poisoning, I might add. I need give only a single example of their hideous prescriptions to reveal their wickedness: a compound of ground bones in the earth seven years mixed with menstrual discharge at the dark of the moon. This vilest concoction is believed to decay the gums and teeth, dispose of hair and beard, and dry up the body unto death within a year without remedy.

Rachel had arrived early that morning with the governor's escort. They had gone immediately to the palace; a messenger had been sent to Isaac's for Maimonides. He had hurried to the bedside with all speed only to find Rachel completing her preparations for immediate operation.

"Maimon, we are ready," Rachel said calmly to me. She took a last look at her table and the lamps. She propped up Mohammed's head dexterously with a pillow. I moved at her side, steadying the glass. The Moorish doctors crowded close.

"Open his eyes," Rachel said to me. I gave the burning glass to Maimonides at my side. Leaning over, I parted the eyelids of the unconscious man. The gray film showed clearly. I shuddered; the eyes seemed to be those of a dead man.

Undisturbed, Rachel took a tiny vial from the table. Rapidly, she placed three drops in the corner of each eye. There came a rasping sound from the governor's lungs. The Moorish physicians grinned and looked at each other like vultures. Rachel palpated the eyelids, feeling as I had, the ball of the eye—as hard as an agate pebble. She nodded to herself. I risked a look at Maimonides. He held the burning glass absolutely steady, his eyes wide. His face was pale. He swallowed slowly.

Rachel turned to wash her hands in a basin filled with yellow pungent liquor. She dried each finger with care on a fine linen cloth. Then she unrolled her last and smallest nest of wool. It displayed the tiniest, most remarkable knife I had ever seen. It was made of gold, with what must have been a tip of steel out of Damascus, no bigger than an edged needle. Rachel swirled it briefly in the liquor of the basin, holding it between thumb and forefinger. With her left hand she took what seemed a shining flat tweezers from the table, reversed in action. She gently spread back the eyelids of the right eye. Her glance flicked at me. I hastened to hold them open.

She bent down, almost touching the purple face of Mohammed. We all bent with her, Maimonides excepted. He stood tall, holding the glass exactly as needed. Rachel poised the knife in her hand. With a motion infinitely careful but fast as a darting insect, she punctured the edge of the pupil between light and dark. A thin watery fluid spurted out, bathing the eye. Rachel took a bit of linen held out to her by Maimonides and lightly dried the eye. She pointed to a jar. Maimonides instantly passed it to her. She palpated the eyeball again, expressing more liquid, and gently applied the balsam.

Again she retracted the eyelids of the left eye and allowed me to hold the instrument. She performed the same incredibly delicate operation. At the very moment of the spurting of the same colorless liquid, I heard a smothered exclamation from Maimonides. I spared one upward glance just in time to see the smaller of the two Moorish doctors sway against one of the standing oil lamps. (Whether from accident or design or a sheer faint, I never discovered.)

I kept my eyes steadily before me, holding the eyelids apart, determined I should burn to cinders before the patient under my hands should suffer. Rachel seemed in another world, aloof, unhearing, totally concentrated on the operation. Out of the corner of my eye I saw the lamp sway away on its pedestal. It slowly commenced to topple, directly toward Rachel and myself, toward the unconscious governor.

Just before it slid from the polished top of its pedestal, Maimonides dropped the burning glass. He seized the slipper-shaped container. Burning, bubbling oil slopped over its side. Drops fell upon the bedside, flaring up and going out in brown spottings. But none came near myself or Rachel; it was Maimonides who suffered, lighted oil splashing on his sandals and gown.

I was aware that he did not cry out. Instead, steady as a soldier, holding the flaming pot in front of him, he marched to a table on the bare stone floor beyond. He deposited his searing burden. Only then did he utter a long exhalation of pain. Nor did he stop there: He seized one of the heap of spare quilts at the foot of the governor's bed and flung it over lamp and table, effectively smothering the fire in a burst of black smoke.

It had happened so quickly that the Moorish doctors still stood like children beside the bed, wringing their hands, uttering moaning little cries, half-paralyzed, their turbans askew on their shaved heads at absurd angles. Having applied the balm carefully to the left eye of the patient, Rachel deigned to look up at them. With an expression of impatience, she turned to me. "Go to the boy," she said.

56

I plunged into my kit of medicines and snatched out a box of unguent. I leaped to the side of Maimonides, who stood swaying in pain, his mouth opening and closing in spasmodic breaths. I picked him up and placed him on a couch, tearing away his clothing. His burns, I found—by the will of God, praised be He—were only on hands and feet; a few drops on his robe, but they did not penetrate to the skin. I bathed his hands and feet with massive doses of the soothing oil, feeling his bowstring-tight muscles relax under my fingers.

"Are you all right, my son?" I whispered.

He opened his eyes and stared at me. "That is not the correct question for a physician," he murmured. "I am not all right, as you can see, but I am feeling better."

I almost laughed aloud to hear his voice again, calm and gentle. "Then you are better?" I demanded.

"Much better," he said and closed his eyes once more.

A succession of screams came to my ears. I looked over my shoulder. The tall eunuchs had the pair of Moorish doctors before them, arms twisted up their backs to the napes of their necks, walking them along tiptoe. It must have been painful but it was nothing compared to the terror in their eyes. Nothing could be done about it; it was their fee for misfeasance. They were thrust roughly out the door and vanished from our knowledge forever.

Only one clue to their disappearance came to that center of gossip, the house of Isaac the Blind, three days later. It told of two high members of the governor's court being executed by cremation, alive, in burning naphtha.

Rachel was oblivious of their shrieking forced departure. She had soaked a pad of linen with a strong-smelling decoction and placed it on Mohammed's chest, directly under his nostrils. She turned back to the task of sedulously packing away her instruments, waving off the burly Negro attendant. She had barely finished when the governor awoke suddenly. He gave a gasping snort. I whisked away the pad from his nose. He tried to lift his head, falling back with a bitter moan. "Blind, blind, blind!" he exclaimed.

Rachel moved to his side and took his head in her hands. "I do not think so, Excellency," she said in her cool, caressing voice. "I have relieved the pressure within your eyes and the nerves of vision have been released. Allow me to remove the cloths."

She lifted them free. Mohammed's bloodshot eyes stared into the room. Light dawned in them, as if he had seen a miracle. "I see!" he shouted in ecstasy. "I see again! I am raised from the blind, nay, from the dead! This is my room, these are my windows, those my gardens! Praised be Allah!"

"Praised be God," said Rachel softly.

"And your God, too," agreed the governor. He sat upright. Rachel pushed him back. "You must rest awhile," she warned him. "The bandages must be placed over your eyes again lest the light renew your suffering." So saying, she reapplied them. Mohammed's face was masked except for his beatific smile.

"Name your fee, miracle-worker, name your fee," he murmured.

"Later," Rachel said. The governor gave a faint chuckle. "Whatever you ask, I shall give double," he said, "if only to have heard a doctor—and a Jew at that—ask that the fee be paid later." His head rolled to one side; he had passed into a natural slumber.

"Rachel," I said in a hoarse whisper, "I yearned for you as I yearn now for Paradise. But even though I won you, I was not able to keep you. You were sworn to your profession, not to love. Heaven is held on high like a balloon by the blasts of heat from Hell below; when those cease to rise, Heaven falls. The sea of my tears extinguished those flames at last and I am fallen into the depths."

"By dawn," Rachel said thoughtfully, "we shall be able to remove the bandages on the eyes of the governor. Then we shall be able to tell of our success."

I stood up abruptly and she regarded me with amusement. "Did you wish to speak of love or medicine?" she asked. I turned away, going to the window of my apartment in the palace to feel the cool breeze of night on my forehead. A bird chirped impudently on the sill; I banged the lattice to put it to flight. The feast in honor of the governor's successful operation, lasting as it did from noon to twilight, had not improved my temper.

I sensed the presence of Rachel behind me. "You are sorry for the sin of loving me, Maimon," she said gently.

"I don't know."

"As one grows older, one grows sorrier."

I wheeled to face her. "I don't believe that," I said violently. "Have you suffered?"

She laughed, her low musical laugh I could not forget. "What a pair we are, Maimon, probing each other's conscience," she said. "No, I regret nothing because regret is useless—and only the useful has meaning for me. I cherish what was: all the more now that I have seen Maimonides."

I paced moodily away from her presence. I could not think clearly when she stood so close. "He is a son to be proud of," I admitted, "but he is different."

"Did you expect him to be the same?"

"He is very strange, sometimes."

"Yet you love him as you loved me, almost against your will."

I gave her stare for stare, challenging her to drop her extraordinary dark eyes with their thick fringes of eyelash. I could not imagine what she saw in me now, an elderly Jewish healer, exiled from his home; but I saw in her still that which had swept me into the most terrible chasms of youthful love.

Rachel was a large woman, yet so perfectly proportioned that she seemed an enlargement of one of the little terra-cotta statues I had purchased in Cordova, brought from the plow-turned soil near Athens. Her dusky red hair, long enough to be plaited and wound around her head, glinted like a crown. Her skin was like fine porcelain from the East, translucent to the light, blue veins glistening.

Her red full-lipped mouth with its slight confident smile told me she was, as ever, aware of her breath-taking beauty. My gaze wandered boldly over her full breasts barely hidden under the sheerness of her gown, down her thighs and tapering legs, and once again back to her steady amused eyes. She shrugged her bare shoulders, broad as a man's, and looked out the window.

"The nightingales sing in the gardens here, Maimon," she murmured, "as they sing in Toledo."

"They have not sung for me in long years."

"You are married; you are happy."

"Naomi is dead," I said roughly. "Peace to her soul, she died in my arms."

A frown of pain crossed Rachel's faultless face. She made an involuntary gesture toward me. "Maimon, I know," she said. "Forgive me for pretending. Judah Halevi sent the news back to Toledo with his message that bade good-by to his family."

In that moment I felt a twinge of envy for the small gray poet on his lonely pilgrimage to Jerusalem. "He did something I never had the courage to do," I said bitterly.

Rachel became remote. "You had the courage to leave me, to marry Naomi," she said.

"I was lonely," I replied desperately.

"Were you lonely because you loved me?"

"You could not be loved!" I cried. "No more than the snow-covered peaks, so cold, so distant!"

"You did not think so in other days," she said slowly.

I took a pleading step toward her. "Rachel," I said, "in the lodestone there is an attraction which pulls all that is different to it. Those who are unlike have the strongest and most lasting bond between them. Naomi and I were alike; you and I, we were always strangers."

"But the bond is still there, Maimon?" she said carelessly. I could smell the odor of her body heightened by the fragrance of perfume like unknown blossoms. I drew back.

"I have two sons and a daughter," I said defiantly, a man raising a shield between himself and temptation.

"Only one son, when we talk together," she murmured.

"Even now we talk about different things."

"I see," Rachel returned. "I cannot speak of Maimonides."

"No," I said almost inaudibly.

She smiled and I felt my head whirling. I looked away. "It was you who taught me medicine, Maimon," she said in a low voice.

"But it was you who learned it so well that now you far surpass me in knowledge and skill—and in fame, as well."

"Are you angry?"

"No. I have cause to bless your coming." The tension between us had lessened; I believed the moment of stress was past and took a pace or two away from her.

"Knowledge is not all, Maimon."

"I have not said it was," I returned, astonished. "It is certain many things are meant by God to be mysteries for all time."

"That is not what I mean," Rachel said, her enchanting eyes gazing far away. "I look for the day when our Messiah shall come and bring us deliverance."

My nerves tightened. "No one knows the day nor the hour, the year nor the century," I ventured. "It has been long since this was prophesied. It may be longer still, beyond our lifetime."

"Such a man would compel the love of every woman," Rachel murmured.

"Not such a woman as you."

"Do you mean a woman who has a mind of her own, a certain training, an ability to think like a man?"

60

"Yes."

"Ah, Maimon, how little you know about us! It is just such a woman as myself who would fall into the Messiah's arms!"

I felt offended. "You bring a mission of the spirit down to the level of the flesh," I said stiffly. "If the Messiah comes, he will not want such followers."

Rachel glanced at me, almost mischievously. "Think well, Maimon," she said. "What if the Messiah were a woman like myself?"

I was aghast at her words, though I knew she meant them for mere nonsense. "I will not hear such abomination," I replied.

Rachel laughed, her delightful trill of amusement. "You see," she said. "A woman, even one like myself, must have someone in whom she believes even unto salvation—body as well as soul—or she is damned."

"Rachel, Rachel—"

She sighed and took a step away from me. "I have wasted no time like yourself with the Law or the Prophets—or with the worship of any other gods than those of Galen and Avicenna."

I approached her. "Was Avicenna only a drunken, lecherous fool?" I demanded.

"He was a great genius."

"Perhaps, perhaps. But his genius for things other than medicine—his love of wine and women—these killed him."

"Look at my hands, Maimon." Rachel extended them to me. I saw once more the tapering slender fingers, white as alabaster, which had once entranced me. "Averroës, who studied him, showed me how to use them. Feel their strength, Maimon."

Trembling, I took them into my own. They lay lax, then folded themselves into mine, nesting in my palm. I could not help myself; I gripped them and drew her to me. My mouth met hers in a hard bruising kiss. We gasped in the flood of emotion that swept us away.

"My father," said Maimonides' quiet voice behind me, "do I come at an unwelcome time?"

Rachel and I parted. I swung round in a fury of frustration and despair. "Unnatural son!" I cried. "Do you creep up on your father in this way?"

Maimonides said nothing. Instead, he dropped his eyes to his bandaged hands, to his feet where the rolls of linen had muffled his approach. In revulsion against myself, I dropped to my knees and stretched out my arms to him. He came to me, step by step, but his gaze was intent over my head, directed to Rachel.

I rose and stood aside, watching him as he and Rachel faced each other. Beyond my shame, I was conscious of an extraordinary feeling pulsing in the room.

"I came to see my father," said Maimonides evenly, "but it was only to talk of you." He paused slightly. "To praise you," he said.

"Thank you," Rachel said, her hand at her breast.

"It is rare to see such skill as yours."

"You are very generous, Maimonides."

"And to see it in a woman."

Rachel's face shifted. "Thank you."

"Most of all, to see it in a beautiful red-haired woman."

"I am very grateful for your compliments, Maimonides," Rachel said. She gave a short, embarrassed laugh. I felt nonplused. My son was actually dominating this self-possessed woman. Though he appeared to be lauding her, his tone was measured and aloof; her replies were those of an unwilling slave to her master.

"If it were not for those hands of yours," Maimonides said, "my father and I should now be in the dungeons underneath."

"When you caught the flaming lamp," Rachel said, regaining her poise, "you paid all such debts."

"So," Maimonides said flatly, "our lives have become dependent, one on the other, now?"

"Yes, yes!" Rachel replied eagerly, almost too quickly. Maimonides searched her face; his own did not change its austere expression. He moved backward with a slight bow, toward the door.

"My son," I told him, "now that you have come, remain with us for a time. I have not shown you my ring, have I, eh?"

"What ring is that?" asked Rachel.

"The ring from the middle finger of an ancient king," I responded cuttingly. "It is graved with this motto: THOU ART A BORE! DEPART!"

"If you wish it, I will stay," Maimonides said defiantly.

"I wish it, too," Rachel added. "Come, sit by me." She indicated a divan. Maimonides seemed deaf. He sat down carefully on a small chair in the middle of the room and solemnly surveyed Rachel. An exasperated expression flitted across her face. "You are strange," she said.

"Yes," Maimonides replied. "I think I am the only one in the realm of Spain with freshly burned feet and hands."

I cleared my throat. "Maimonides," I said, "you should know more of our visitor. She is not only famous in her own name, she descends from an illustrious line. Her father was Abi-Abor, rabbi of Lerida. He operated with success upon King Juan of Aragon, to remove cataracts from both eyes. Her great-grandfather, Yochanan ben Mesue, was the most famous healer of eyes in the world, curing two caliphs and instructing a hundred pupils. He wrote ten books of medicine on his art and founded the famous medical school at Rheims in France."

Maimonides nodded, as if it were of no consequence. With a note of pride, he said: "My father, I came also to tell you that today I did not tremble nor grow faint. This art I have seen for the first time in its true light. I think that the—the *other* case"—he gave the ambiguous phrase an odd emphasis —"affected me because it was too close to my heart. Is that understandable?"

"What was the other occasion?" Rachel asked interestedly.

"Nothing," Maimonides said. Rachel directed her inquiring gaze at me. I took a deep breath.

"His mother died of the falling sickness the night before we left Cordova," I told her in a low voice.

Rachel's countenance became as expressionless as marble. After a time she spoke again: "Maimonides, if you like medicine, would you like to study it?"

"Perhaps," he said. "But there are so many things to know."

"The finest place in all the world to study the profession of healing is in Toledo."

"I cannot go there."

"That is my home," protested Rachel. "I am known and respected. I could take you there with me."

Maimonides stood up painfully. "With all my thanks, no," he returned courteously, "but I am grateful." He turned and left the apartment, carefully closing the door behind him.

I crossed to a sideboard in the corner covered with gilded Arabic scribblings. "Their praises of Allah are even in their decorations," I said, rubbing my fingers over the inlay. I took up the bottle of Shiraz wine—the best in the palace, brought by order of the eunuchs—and poured a half-glass, diluting the sweet red stuff with water.

"Maimon," said Rachel behind me, in a tense voice, "what did you tell the child about us?"

"Nothing. And he is far from a child."

"He suspects. He knows!"

"He knows nothing," said I, sipping the wine, "except that his father, wretched soul, embraces strange, divinely beautiful women in the dead of night, in the palace of a heathen governor."

"He knows much more. I can read it in his eyes!"

I finished the glass and poured another. "If you can read anything there, Rachel," I told her, "you are the first to do it."

She paid no attention to me. Her eyes had a faraway expression, as if she were peering into the future. "Perhaps our child will be the Messiah of whom the sages speak," she murmured, "the one who will deliver our race and make it triumphant."

"Nonsense," I said. "We must wait for the will of God, not anticipate it."

"Do you think so, Maimon?" Rachel said. Her lips smiled as she took the wine but her eyes were veiled. On another night like this, in another land, I was to remember her expression with terror.

Hours after Maimonides' dignified departure, we still sat and talked. We had descended to the governor's chamber and examined his eyes once more; the improvement we had noted had continued. Now, back in my apartment, we renewed our old debate, one I thought had been settled once for all.

"Maimon," said Rachel from the divan, "who knew of our marriage?"

"Only the rabbi, Judah Halevi, and he is gone on his wanderings, like Mohammed on his Hegira."

"Did he tell anyone else?"

"None that I know," I said. A mood of melancholy settled over me.

"Does Maimonides know anything of it? That you gave me the bill of divorcement I asked."

"No."

"Then why does he act so?"

"Rachel, if I knew the soul of my son, I would not need one of my own. He keeps his thoughts to himself."

The statuesque redheaded woman seemed more agitated than I had ever seen her. "What shall we do?" she wailed.

"There is nothing to be done."

"He thinks I am a harlot, a woman of the street!"

My long-repressed rancor came uppermost. "That is possible," I said.

64

Rachel's beautiful palm shot out, catching me on the cheek. I staggered, my sight darkened by the violence of the blow. I put up my hands to keep her off. She blazed at me indignantly: "You! Of all the people in the world, you to say that!" She wrung her fingers painfully. Wonder of wonders, I saw tears creeping down her face.

"Rachel," I began penitently.

She shook her head. She held out her hand, reddened and twisted. "See what you have done," she said. "I shall not be able to operate for days."

I took the fingers in both my hands, rubbing them gently, lovingly. "Rachel," I murmured, "there must be an end to this. We shall do no good, you and I, abusing each other for what is past. What Maimonides knows, he knows, and I care not. What he supposes, that is beyond our knowledge or control. Let us live in this world as if we would live forever."

"No," Rachel said, her face set. She withdrew her hand. "I shall tell him everything."

"Rachel! The mother of Maimonides was most truly Naomi," I said sternly. "He was rejected and she accepted him. He has no other parent beyond myself."

"What do you mean?" cried Rachel.

"I mean that the true mother of a child is not always the one who bears him. I mean, she is the woman who rears, who nurtures and trains him. There is flesh of one's flesh—but there is a higher, holier flesh, too."

Rachel had become completely calm. She stepped back regally and observed me, her magnificent head at a provoking tilt. "Maimon," she declared, "you are a better philosopher than you are a doctor."

"Some have not thought so," I replied, stung at her meaning, trapped no matter how I chose to answer.

"You have forgotten those lessons you gave me about human reproduction."

"I have not forgotten about human love," I said angrily.

Rachel sighed and my heart melted toward her. "Once," she said vaguely, "I thought that like Sarah's, Rachel's children were promised by God that they would inherit the land of Canaan."

"Still, Moses saw the Promised Land only from afar."

Rachel straightened her body. Her face became animated, her tones crisp and alert. I recognized her change of mood: now she was the woman professional.

"Maimon," she said, her gaze level, "these are dangerous

times. The Jews are the black goats, first to be slaughtered for the sins of others. What good did your high position in Cordova do you? Coming here as I have has endangered my own influence. When the riders of Mohammed found me, I was setting out with a Frankish escort to Paris. Their king, Louis, had offered me escort and safe-conduct through France to come to his court, where he lodges three hundred ransomed knights of the first crusade, blind from years of imprisonment in Palestine cells. He paid for them; he wants them cured. And I am not there. The king's knights could easily have done away with the Moslem couriers. I forbade them," she remarked simply.

"Do you regret coming here?" I demanded.

She laughed. "Never, not after having seen Maimonides," she said.

"And me?" I asked jealously.

"And you, too, Maimon," she answered, touching my hand briefly. She swept past me toward the door. "I must go to my own apartment and try to sleep before I examine His Excellency at dawn," she said. "Shalom." Before I could reply, she had vanished down the corridor.

I have heard it said that a strong man may endure nine hours on the cross and that weaker men succumb after less than three hours. Tossing on my bed during the endless darkness of early morning, I found a like torture of mind without rest. In my memory I reviewed the days Rachel and I had to ourselves in the gray granite rock-city of Toledo, in the pleasant gardens of Seville and Granada. I relived my years with Naomi; I saw again our fiery expulsion from Cordova. In the catacombs of my head, filled with the skeletons of joys past, I felt an urgency of warning. Rachel had left with a scheme in her head. I did not know what it was; I had to find out, for I was sure it concerned Maimonides.

Just before dawn, I must have fallen into a light doze. I was wakened by the brightening through the windows, by a tapping at the door. I yawned, wrinkled my nose at the odor of sour spilled wine and answered. I got up slowly. I donned my outer garments, washing my face and hands in order to attend the governor's sickbed.

I proceeded down the stairs to his second-story chamber and received a surprise: I was forbidden entrance by the governor's personal guards. The elder of the two, Musef (as I knew), looked at me inquiringly. I felt a quiver of alarm in

66

my breast. The second man, young Ahmed, smiled openly.

"Old man," he said, "Your good fortune has run out like sands in an hourglass."

"What do you mean?" I asked. "Has the governor's condition become worse?"

"Not at all. He is recovering rapidly. At this moment, he is sleeping again."

"But he was to be examined this morning," I protested.

"True. He has already been examined by your female colleague and pronounced very well. You and she have his permission to depart."

Musef broke in sympathetically. "Honored Maimon," he said to me, "look well to your son."

Filled with dread, I rushed down the staircase to the gate outside. At the bottom of the broad flight, I ran full tilt into Maimonides himself. I drew back. His feet and hands were still muffled in bandages but now they were covered with tough cordovan leather. He was dressed for travel. A short distance behind him stood Rachel, her musk-scented, rose-colored traveling gown billowing about her. Her face was inscrutable.

"What is this?" I burst out. "What are you doing? Why are you dressed so?"

"I would not have gone without your permission, my father," Maimonides said quietly. "We were coming to your apartment. You have said that I am old enough and wise enough to make my own decisions."

"You have made a decision?"

"We talked for a long time last night," Rachel interjected.

I struck my hands together once, twice, three times. Curses, names like "Jezebel," flitted through my mind as it went awash with agony; but I said not a word. I could not quarrel here, not with the guards lounging and looking down at us from the balcony. Nor could I meet Rachel's wiles except by the most reasonable attitude. I sucked in a deep breath and straightened up.

"Maimonides," I said calmly, "you are right, of course. It is your decision to make. But what is it?"

"With your permission, I shall go to Toledo with your friend, Rachel."

"No friend of mine!" I cried. Quieting myself by an effort of will, I asked: "Last night you refused the same offer. What brought about your change of mind?"

67

"It was what you yourself said," Rachel declared. "I told him."

Her words dazed me. "That I said? What did I say?"

"That we should live in this world as if we were to live forever," Maimonides replied. I rapped my forehead and remembered dimly.

"True," I nodded.

"But that is not the spiritual world in which I desire to live. In that world, we must live today as if we would die tomorrow."

"And this," I said in amazement, "this drives you away from your father and to Toledo?"

"My father, there is so much to be known, so much to be studied. So much to be found out—astronomy, logic, metaphysics, medicine, sciences of all sorts. Toledo, Rachel has told me, is the chief city for this knowledge in all the world."

"In that, at least, she has not lied," I said, striving for calm. "But while you are pursuing these marvelous studies and stuffing them into your head—what of your father in Almería?"

Maimonides hesitated; his face contracted. "You have David and Yaltah," he said at last. "You are high in the respect of the governor; you have friends and protectors here."

"I see you have learned your arguments well," I said, unable to help myself, "and that you have already acquired a protector."

For the first—and almost the last—time in Maimonides' life I saw him blush. The telltale rise of the blood in his cheeks made his tawny hair and dark eyes seem like those of a woman. He did not say a word; it was Rachel who broke the silence. "That was unworthy of you, Maimon," she said in dull reproof.

"In making war, there is strategy," I said shamefacedly. "In making peace between a man and his neighbor, there is exaggeration; in quarreling with a woman, there is every sin in the world."

"My father," Maimonides said in a low voice. He stopped and said again: "My father."

"What is it?" I mumbled.

"I will not go unless you bless me," he said with exquisite sincerity.

My anger and disappointment crumbled. I knew that a mightier force than Rachel's blandishments or my own displeasure held my son, to lift him into far places. I bowed my head.

"I give you permission to go," I said, "and I give you my blessing as well. Nay, I will say further: I shall go part of the way with you."

It was a large passenger-cart, two-wheeled, roofed in bent wood and white leather. The sides were white woven leather strips, an opening in the middle of each side. The big wheels were single-spoked with spiled rims of metal. The whole was drawn by two mules; it was upholstered inside with red cloth and cushions. Such a luxurious conveyance (despite the constant screaming of the ungreased wheels) would take no more than a few days to reach Toledo. Such carts, on urgent errands, had covered more than fifty miles in twenty hours, and it was as easy to sleep in them as ride. With the escort which Mohammed ibn Abdul had promised would join them at the north gate, the safety and speed of the trip was assured.

According to my promise, I traveled with them, pacing by their side. The Moorish driver handled his team expertly through the crowded streets of the city. As we turned into the square of the bazaar, we were still silent. Not one of us had uttered a word over the cacophony of wheels. Next to me, Rachel gazed straight ahead. Next to her, on the far side, Maimonides looked solemnly out on the world from the governor's personal vehicle of state, assigned to Rachel by his grateful Excellency. She had reassured him of my competence to take care of his eyes; she had divided a fee of one hundred and twenty-five thousand dirhams among herself, Maimonides, and myself. The guard and the passenger-cart had been parting gifts.

As I walked with a hand on the cart-side, my chance medley of thoughts commenced to clear and take on significance. If I had been the victim of a plot, perhaps it had turned out for the best. Like the Moslems, almost, I had begun to believe in the superstitious rumors of Rachel's magic-working. Had she not enchained me as a young man? Now, years later, had she not stolen Maimonides from my side by the only sort of bribe he could not resist?

Yet I knew in my heart that despite her female sorcery, her success with two Maimon generations was no more than her beauty and her devotion to medicine. Such dedication had a pure attraction of its own beyond her womanhood. It was this, surely, which had brought my son to her side. As I considered, my comfort grew: Maimonides was old enough to meet the world, and at her side—just as he sat in the cart—he would have a friend of power, of riches, of influence with kings such as few men had. My bosom swelled with pride in the thought that Maimonides would one day surpass his father; this was his first step to such eminence.

I heard a cry. I turned; I halted in surprise. I heard Rachel command the driver to stop a few paces beyond. Through the throng of colored robes and turbans in the bazaar, a burly man elbowed his way. Bareheaded, his red face screwed up with rage, his short black hair and brows bristling like those of a boar rampaging, I could not help recognizing him. It was Brujo the Black. The same man who had tried to rob and murder us on the trail to Almería.

No thought of what to do came to me. His ugly mouth, his ferocious gaze, seemed to suck strength from my muscles and melt my marrow. His eyes were transfixed; his epithets befouled the air. He sprang out of the crowd like an acrobat, landing just before me.

Panting, his breath foul with venom, he threw back his head and deliberately spat in my face. With a howl of glee, he crowed like a cock, shouting: "Filthy Jew, cursed by Allah and by God alike, death is your fate!"

With his left hand, undoubtedly used to wipe his rear, he made the most insulting gesture he could make—he snatched at my beard. I started back from this insult, galvanized into reflex. Brujo cursed me in a slaver. He reached out both clawed fists. As he did, a thick-thewed black arm cut down across his forearms, like an executioner's ax. I heard the bones of the man crack on impact; his face went wide, vacant with pain, his eyes bulging and unseeing like a man in a fit. The same arm, a pendulum of flesh, swung up and out, shoving him back.

A cudgel of tough thorn whistled over my head. It crashed into his face. Three blows, so rapid that the cry of Rachel from behind me came only with the last shattering impact. Brujo fell, his face a mass of battered pulp, his mouth a gaping hole without teeth, bones broken, flesh crushed. I dropped to my knees beside him. Rachel sprang out of her cart and knelt beside me, careless of her gown.

I looked up at our deliverer. It was the same hulking Negro assistant who had aided Rachel in her operation on the governor. He scowled at me, bowed low to her, and made his stained cudgel twirl in the air. The crowding people of the bazaar fell back in fear.

"Do—do you come from His Excellency?" I faltered, trying to hold my voice level.

The Negro nodded. He opened his mouth and pointed within. A tremor ran through me. The purple-red cavern of his gullet appeared huge, lined by striations of white tendons. Nothing there, except a hollow. His tongue had been cut out. Clenching my teeth, I turned my attention to the stricken Brujo.

The enormous strength of the blackamoor had done its work. Brujo was unconscious, covered with blood, lying in a slimy pool of sewage from the market place. Rachel and I looked at each other. She shook her head as diagnosis. I noted Maimonides had hobbled out of the cart to stand beside her. I rose to my feet and motioned to the Negro to pick up Brujo. To my surprise, he shook his head, pointing to Rachel. We understood his gesture: he had been given to Rachel as a present by the governor. He was her slave; thus, he had followed us.

"See!" Rachel said aloud. "These people are witnesses! I give you to this man!" She pointed to me. The Negro bowed. Instantly he followed my order, standing with the man dripping blood in his arms. I told him to carry him to the house of Isaac the Blind and he set out in obedience.

"You had better be gone," I said to Rachel and Maimonides. "This is the commencement of my medical work in Almería. I have my first patient. These are injuries that I understand very well."

Without a word, before them all, Rachel kissed me on the forehead. Maimonides took my hand and caressed it lightly. Both climbed back into the cart. It began its rocking pace toward the north gate.

I did not stay to watch them depart. All my skill was needed desperately at the house of Isaac the Blind.

CHAPTER 5

To Rabbi Maimon ben Joseph, may God protect
him, greetings:

My respected father, since I arrived here, I have found
the city of Toledo a place of wonder, a palace of learning.
It is not like our beloved Cordova. The streets are narrow and gloomy, parks and flowers and trees are not
everywhere. But the very air is exhilarating. The company of so many scholars and teachers is not to be
matched in the world. I am very happy. I hope and trust
you are the same.

My classes every day (except the Sabbath) are filled
with students as eager as myself. In truth, the most infectious disease of all is the thirst for knowledge, of whatever sort, that I see about me every hour. We have strict
discipline as we squat around our master in the hall. No
one is allowed to converse or even whisper on pain of
expulsion. The lectures, free to all, consist of a reading
from the masterworks, followed by comment and demon-
stration (if he chooses) by the teacher. No one is allowed
to take notes, all must be memorized. Arabic alone is used
and diagrams are drawn with a burned stick on the floor.
Discussion is permitted at stated times. Questions may be
asked, though the teacher is not obliged to answer unless
he wishes. If anyone, of any age, completes the course of
lectures he is given coffee of honor and a certificate of
attendance; he may even request a permit to disseminate
his knowledge at another college, either in practice or
teaching. Thus does learning flourish like the green bay
tree.

Toledo is remarkable chiefly for its College of Transla-
tors, their books, and its teachers and hospitals. I shall tell
about the first two here; that is all I wish to say in this
letter.

It is a miracle such a group as the College exists at all,
since it is wholly the work of the intolerant Christians,

most intolerant of each other. It is the inspiration of the good and scholarly Archbishop Raymund. Eighteen years ago, he appointed his archdeacon, Dominicus Gundisalvi —a man of more energy than learning—to collect a hundred noted men of language and hire them to translate all Moslem works of science into Latin.

As you know, such labor is needless to me. You taught me to regard Arabic as my mother tongue next to Hebrew —I find I much prefer to read and write it—but their diligence has brought together an enormous number of texts from all over the world.

This corps of linguists do their work in a literal fashion, for fear of making mistakes. By that same token, they compound errors. Over each word of the original (already badly translated from the Greek, for example) they simply write the same word in Latin. Or, if such a synonym is nonexistent, they ink in the identical Moslem term—as in the cases of such words as *alcohol, alembic, cipher,* and others.

I suspect this to be quite wrong. Whoever is a slave to literal meanings, to the original order of words and sentences in another tongue, will make an untrustworthy— even dangerous—translation. In my own readings, I find I must first try to grasp the sense of the whole passage (by this I mean what the author is trying to convey). Then I state the original content as clearly and briefly as I can. This is easiest in mathematics and most difficult in philosophy. It means, of course, changing the order, substituting words, adding and taking away—but I do not see how it can be done otherwise.

These so-called Saracenic translations include some of the earliest Hebrew scrolls, such as one by Asaf Judaeus, who wrote his *Remedies* more than six hundred years ago, and those by Jew John of Toledo, an apostate from our race, who composed a manuscript on Aristotle and a book called *How to Keep One's Health.* (I do not agree with his religion but his writings are excellent.) There are ancient Christian treatises, such as those composed by the Bishop Isodore of Seville. Even rare are some permitted to be read in the original only by the chosen. These are by Donnolo, who claimed to know "all the lore of the Greeks, Arabs, Babylonians, and Indians." Their total wisdom must have been small indeed; his works consist of two short manuscripts only. One is a ridiculous thing on astrology; the other, the *Antidotarium,* a mere collection of 120 remedies in Hebrew. The records of the College also show that knowledge among other peoples, especially in medicine, is very small. Such things as the leech-books of the Anglo-Saxons are worthless to the scholar. They are repetitions of the same simples as Ramah, our nursemaid, has known all her life.

But there is an abundance of copies of Hippocrates, Galen, and Ptolemy's *Almagest,* as well as any desired book of Aristotle. The works of Rhazes, Serapion, and Constantine the African (who was everywhere accused of sorcery because of his unusual successes) are here. So are the works of Ibn Galib (who, by the way, is a Christian) and even the works of Abulcasis on the cutting and mending of flesh and bones and teeth. Greatest of all, as you know, are the gigantic writings of Avicenna, collected in his *Canon,* even though he has been ridiculed by Avenzoar, who praises Galen. I must add that the respected Averroës, pupil of Avenzoar—I am proud to say I am the pupil of Averroës—does not share Avenzoar's opinions.

I suppose what I am writing is confusing to you. Indeed it is to me also: I sometimes spend all night (the Moslem idea of the cool, quiet, dark hours for study is good, I think) pondering and classifying the ideas thrown at me each day like a hail of stones at an adulterer. The work is made easier by the fact that Jews and Moslems help each other, jokingly calling themselves "Mozarabes." As for the Christians, they do not even help each other; they are simply Christians. As a result, they fall far behind in comprehension.

This letter is already much too long. You must forgive the enthusiasm which prompts me to write so much. Still, I am not seduced by medicine. I shall describe in another letter what has ravished my imagination. Let God in His mercy strengthen you and lengthen your days. Such is the wish of your son,

MOSES BEN MAIMON THE SEPHARDI.

Post scriptum: My father, yet one more request: How are David and Yaltah and Ramah, and our friend, Isaac the Blind? Rachel bat Abor is very well and sends greetings.

I rerolled the parchment of the letter. Slowly, filled with thoughts, I put it down on the table beside me. I was roused from my meditation by a voice. "What does it say?" demanded David.

I looked down, recollected myself and looked up into his

face. At well past seven years, David was growing with the insensate energy of the wild sorrel. He was a tall boy with the promised shoulders of a bull, a face as sharp and handsome as those stamped on old Greek coins. He grinned under his black curly mop and held out his hand. "It's from Muni, isn't it?" he asked.

"Yes," I said somberly.

"It's about time we heard from him. It's been more than a year. This is his first letter."

"It arrived two weeks ago by the Toledo city messenger," I said, "and I have just read it again."

David did not hear me. He was absorbed in spelling out the characters, bobbing his head and moving his lips as he wandered in the labyrinth of Arabic lettering. At last he gave up. He pushed it back to me. "You read it," he said. "It makes me tired."

"You are not the scholar your brother is," I told him, unrolling the script. "At five, he could read both Arabic and Hebrew and at your age, he had memorized the Torah."

"I never pretended to be Muni," David said. "I'm only David, remember? And he can't pretend to be me. Has he a collection of rocks like mine?"

"At least he didn't spend his time roaming the hills with a slave and a copper maul," I said irritably. "Pay attention. Listen to what your brother writes."

To my disappointment, David seemed bored by the letter. He yawned openly halfway through my reading. At the end, he turned away without comment. I stopped him. "Is nothing at all what you have to say?" I inquired.

"All he talks about is books, study, teachers—things like that," complained David.

"What else would you have him talk about?" I demanded, my heart swelling.

David kicked the toe of his sandal into the thick rug. He considered. "Well," he said, "he could have said something about the horses and the warriors and the parades—they must have military parades. At least something about those swords they make there."

He looked at me out of the corner of his eye and braced himself for an outburst. I felt it was useless. I nodded. He bowed, his white smile flashing from his small bronzed face, and went outside.

I sat alone in the twilight and brooded, as I had been doing for a fortnight, over the news from Toledo. I felt helpless and weary. My thoughts seemed at odds; I could form no clear conclusion. I had been thinking about a letter to Maimonides. As yet, I had nothing to say.

My eyes wandered out to the mountains beyond the window. I stood and bathed my head in the warm breeze, staring out at the hills, hoping for strength. It had been just this season a year ago that Maimonides had left with Rachel for Toledo. I knew it was difficult to communicate place to place, what with the roving bands of marauders and broken knights, thieves and beggars, the ever increasing bands of plundering pilgrims heading east for Palestine. Still, most of the synagogues and monasteries and the city governments had their own messengers for post. They could cover as much as forty miles a day. In ancient Persia, the riders on the King's Highway had been able to do twice that speed.

Yet perhaps Maimonides had written before and the letter had been captured and destroyed. I had no way of knowing. And I, in my pride, had never thought of writing him first.

"David and Yaltah are very well," I said to the early autumn sunset, answering Maimonides as if my whisper would carry to his ear in high Toledo. "David is growing up to be a strong, handsome, arrogant youth who thinks he will live forever. Yaltah is patient and pretty. She is already looking for a husband, though at her age she dare mention it only to her dolls." I hesitated. "As for Ramah and me," I said, "we are merely growing old and lonely."

Standing in the rosy reflections, I strained my ears. Perhaps I hoped to hear an answer from my son, so far away in Toledo: I missed his youthful wisdom and presence more than I cared to admit. But there was only the sigh of the trees outside, the susurration of the winds. Oddly disappointed, I turned back into my room and sank into a chair.

This was a pleasant house, airy and cool, near the west wall of Almería. It had been given to me by Mohammed ibn Abdul —apparently as a pledge of his favor as long as I continued to be his physician. Truly Moslem in situation and gardens, it was well furnished with purchases from the bazaar. We had not been entirely penniless when we arrived (I had had the foresight to carry with us a sufficient purse). This, with my share of Rachel's fee from the governor, had been more than enough to renew housekeeping—on a scale less than that of Cordova, certainly, but still entirely comfortable. I closed my eyes. After all, with such good fortune, I was ungrateful to God to regret Maimonides' absence.

"Master Maimon," said a hoarse voice, "shall I enter?"

"I give you leave," I said. I raised my head to see Brujo the Black in the doorway. "Come in, come in," I said impatiently.

By this time Brujo was quite healed of the wounds given by the hulking Negro—whose name, we had learned, was Zayd. I had managed to cure him almost wholly, following the instructions of the manual of Albucasis, the Moslem surgeon with whom Maimonides was even now studying. I had fitted together his broken bones and healed his flesh. His face turned out quite presentable after a few months, except for his lost teeth. Here, praise to Albucasis, I was also able to be instructed.

The cudgel blows had knocked out all but three molars in the left lower jaw and two in the upper; four remained on the right lower side, three above. It presented a unique problem; I like to think I solved it well. I knew iron would rust. Copper and brass would taste like garlic; silver would corrode from acid saliva. Thus I procured gold from the governor's personal smith (at a very reasonable price) and molded it into a pair of upper and lower half-circles. Taking impressions of Brujo's gum ridges with wax, I used this to insure the tightness of the fit. At each end of the two half-moons, set with carved ivory teeth in cement of oxide, I placed rings of annealed gold.

These rings I clamped around Brujo's remaining rear teeth. After many trials, they fitted as exactly as possible. I may add that all would have failed if Brujo had not been endowed with an unusually large mouth.

My work was a spectacular success. Brujo became proud of his appearance, unduly so. If he smiled against the sun on a bright day, the ivory-and-gold effect was dazzling. He learned to use this explosion of a smile—contrasting well with his swarthiness and stiff black hair—with the skill of a consummate actor. He was known no longer as Brujo the Black but as Brujo Chrysostom, "the Golden-mouthed." It increased his fame; it made men envious, and the women, behind their ever present veils, were visibly adoring. For the most part, however, he kept his jaws shut, lips clamped over his pet possession—possibly to keep some thief from seizing his precious decoration. Whatever the reason, it worked wonders on his disposition; from a garrulous, boisterous man, he became dignified and taciturn.

I should mention that Brujo's splendor influenced Zayd. The

Negro came to me. He indicated by signs that he would knock out all his own teeth if I would create another set like those in the mouth of Brujo. I managed to dissuade him only by having the goldsmith beat out a thin strip of gold and bending it tightly over three of his upper incisors. This influenced his disposition, too, in a remarkable fashion. Previously Zayd had been dour, smiling only rarely; now his continual smiling (for purposes of exhibition) transformed him into the most cheerful member of my household.

"Master," Brujo said, "I have a request to make of Your Honor."

"Ask what you wish," I told him.

Brujo hesitated. "It will seem strange to you," he said diffidently, wholly changed from his usual bravado.

"What is it?" I asked, more sharply than I intended. Brujo ducked his bristling head; I was surprised to see it graying, like the pelt of a wolf. He looked at me with a serious expression. "I wish to become a Jew," he said with a slight whistle through his gold teeth.

"A Jew is born," I said.

"Is it forbidden to become one of the children of God?"

"No," I said. "It is all the more meritorious. The great-grandmother of King David, blessed be she, was not one of us. But when one has not known the laws and customs from childhood, it is hard to be one of us. There are many laws. In the Torah alone there are six hundred thirteen ordinances to be observed."

"You could tell me of them and I would follow you," Brujo said humbly.

"There are other things," I said doubtfully.

Brujo grinned. His teeth flashed in the sun, blinding me momentarily. "If you mean circumcision," he said, "there is no need to worry." He undid the sash of his breeches, unlaced his soft leather underclothing and dropped both around his feet. I stared in horror. It was true that he had been circumcised; but his sacrifice amounted to more than the foreskin. A dark red irregular half-closed orifice, covered with hair soft as that of a woman, showed between his thighs. His genitals had been torn out; almost, it seemed, by the roots. I looked away in revulsion.

"No one ever saw that but myself and yourself," Brujo said, hastily lacing himself up. "See, I am part Jew already."

"Who were the fiends who did it?" I asked, my head still averted.

78

"Out of hunger I stole some bread in Marseilles," Brujo said simply. "The Crusaders, those of the Most Blessed and Merciful Virgin, caught me. Special orders had been issued to prevent looting. It was all right; the punishment was correct."

"You're lucky to be alive."

"It was very painful but one can survive. Can you teach me your religion?"

"You will have to give up eating pork," I said slyly, knowing he loved it. Brujo grimaced. "If one must, one must," he said simply. "Giving up one meat is an easy price to pay for heaven."

"Don't be too sure of that," I warned.

"Aren't you sure?" Brujo was astonished.

"That's enough," I said sharply. "Don't you want the houris and the wine and the gardens of the Prophet?"

Brujo gave me his golden smile again with a wry expression. He gestured at his crotch. "What good would it do me?" he asked.

I saw it was useless to go into philosophical discussion of the future, in the body or out of the body. "All right." I dismissed him. "I shall instruct you."

Yet it was this renegade Christian Brujo that instructed me in my distress. My worries about Maimonides could not be downed. At night I often started awake with a vision of his being consigned to eternal exile from the World-to-Come and lay awake in the sweatings of my fears. One humid morning after such a night, I summoned Brujo to recite to him our faith. "Hear, O Israel," I said, beginning the Shema in a voice I could barely control, "the Lord our God, the Lord is One." I hesitated. "Our God requires," I said to the attentive Brujo, "that we fear Him, that we walk in all His ways, that we love Him and serve Him with all our heart and soul." As I said it, I could not refrain from weeping; the tears rolled down my cheeks unchecked.

Brujo stood in astonishment. "What disturbs you, Rabbi?" he asked.

"My son," I said with difficulty. "While you, born outside the faith, have come to me for instruction, Maimonides has wandered from the fold."

Brujo frowned and shook his head. "Do you know this?" he inquired. I sighed and grew calmer. "He has the seeking heart," I said.

"This is very worthy," Brujo said. "He fights for virtue as he once fought with me, with cleverness and skill."

"Aye," I said gloomily, "with too much cleverness, too much skill. The two gates of Hell are designated ENTER, YE WHO ARE TOO CLEVER! and ENTER, YE WHO ARE TOO SKILL-FUL!"

Even after the first letter, we heard from Maimonides only rarely. Once we received a brief message from Seville by a courier. He was a cripple, legs drawn up around his torso, quivering momently, possibly from a brain injury at birth. He had ridden all the way in a side hamper of a mule because he had heard from my son that I was an eminent doctor and might be able to help him. He surrendered the note and asked for aid. When I admitted I could do nothing for him, he cursed me for a charlatan Jew, crawling away like a frog.

Maimonides had sent me news that he was studying at an academy in that city. I returned a curt message instructing him not to raise the hopes of those whom God had afflicted beyond powers of human help. Perhaps he was offended. At any rate, his next letter did not come until more than a year afterward. He had returned to Toledo. It ran as follows:

To Rabbi Maimon ben Joseph, may God enrich his days, in Almería, quickly, greetings:

My respected father, I have been busy at my studies in Toledo but I fear I shall be a disappointment to you, even as I have been to Rachel bat Abor. The art of healing and medicine, though a great one, seems much less than the light which has dawned in my study of philosophy. I have become more and more drawn to such thinking. The darkness of my mind grows less.

I have learned to turn my thoughts from all else when I read the Shema, to keep my heart and soul occupied only with understanding it. I seem to think of philosophy alone, that love of wisdom, even when I engage in experiments or idle conversation.

This does not please Rachel. She is a practical person, not given to theories. She does not understand why I do not get enough sleep. It is difficult to explain that, alone and on my couch at night, I lie awake and meditate on the worship of God. A curious thing happens to one during such meditations. Sometimes the truth shines into the brain like a flash of lightning. But it illuminates only to bring a blacker darkness than before. Yet I see there is a kind of understanding that glows like the cold fire of phosphorus, small but steady, once in a long while emitting flashes of understanding. One must be prepared to see them or else lose them forever.

More and more I recognize the God-given function of the Jew—to be the builder-of-bridges, *pontifex maximus,* as the Romans called their priest. We are the true link of knowledge, of learning and faith, of civilization itself, between the East and the West. We love truth for its own sake. In this way alone can man be free in these times which grow darker every day.

The studies of medicine (which I continue but with much less enthusiasm) seem to extend endlessly, in every direction, like the corridors of a caliph's palace. There are so many diseases to be identified and understood. One from Germany rots the limbs so they drop off one by one; another from France is known by extremes of cold and heat in the flesh, the legs and arms becoming blistered and blue. Following this, they seem deprived of blood, and gangrene sets in. There is the sweating sickness of weakness; the dancing sickness of madness; the disease that corrupts the gums and causes the teeth to fall, the pustulant decay of the genitals (brought, I hear, from the East); and, above all, that incurable and horrible disease of leprosy that strikes where it will.

Most of my fellow students believe such afflictions are God's vengeance against mankind for its sins. I cannot believe they are all generated thus. They also come from superstition and filth, from being crowded without air or sun into the walled towns, from being as bestial and immoral as animals. Many times such ailments are aggravated by cheats who pose as healers, who look for nothing but money. These cursed individuals actually send their servants before them into a town with trumpets, drums, and banners to spread false gossip about their miracle-working.

In truth, my father, I have discovered there are no miracles in medicine. Nature works in her own ways. Much of the time our efforts are simply to give her what she needs. The quacks and itinerant healers, without books, with no knowledge of symptoms, have no cures beyond tricks. Most cannot even read or write. They are incredibly evil in their greed for money. Nearly all of them are barbers or runaway slaves or bath-keepers. I have heard that Duke Roger in Sicily has decreed that all such must apply to the judges for licenses. They avoid that island as they would death itself.

Avenzoar has denounced such false healers with all his strength, and he is a learned man of authority and standing, but he is quite old. Among my teachers, I admire Averroës, with his stately presence and graying beard, the most. He has a great talent for logical thinking. He is devoted to Aristotle, chief of all philosophers. Though he does not know Greek and must refer to Arabic translations, his knowledge is very full and he meditates day and night. He agrees with Protagoras that man is the measure of all things. He disregards theological creeds, saying that not such knowledge but individual truth, an inward power directed toward unity with God, is the real goal. He sees that God is eternal and that the world is in God and is, therefore, eternal itself. All these ideas I can comprehend, but I cannot agree with his reverence for astrologers. It seems to me that being "an observer of times," as they call themselves—doing nothing except as they interpret the stars for good or bad—is nonsense. It is a deception practiced upon the common people, and, worse, it detracts from astronomy, one of the most precise of sciences.

Here, my honored father, you may see the direction of my thoughts. I am no longer as much concerned with medicine as you might have hoped. I despair of ever being a physician. My inclinations are toward the soul, not the body. I long to reach God, not to restore man to health. Of what use is a strong body if the soul is sick?

It is possible that we left Cordova in too much panic. Some Jews, I hear, have returned there and become prosperous merely by the empty recitation of the Moslem creed at intervals. Is this too much of a price to pay for knowledge such as only that city or faraway Bagdad possesses? My Moorish friends here, who have spoken with the Almohades now in Cordova bring back fantastic reports of their beliefs. Here is what their leader, Ibn Tumart, said:

"God is one in His kingdom; He is the creator of the whole universe, the heights and the depths, the throne, the heavens, the earth, and all that is in them. All creation is subject to His power. Not a mote is moved without His permission. He is living and ever existing; to Him appertains neither slumber nor sleep. He knows that which is hidden, that which is seen; nothing in earth or heaven is hidden from Him. He knows that which is on the dry land and that in the sea. Not a leaf falls unless He knows it—not a single grain in the darkest part of earth, neither a green thing nor a dry thing that is not written in His

82

clear book. He comprehends all things with His knowledge, He counts all things according to their number. He does all He desires, He has power over all He wishes to perform.

"To Him is the kingdom, to Him belongs wealth; to Him is power and might; to Him is eternity; to Him belongs judgment. He makes decrees and none can hinder them. He hopes for no reward and fears no punishment, subject to no judgment. All His favors to us are acts of grace, and every punishment He inflicts is just.

"He was before all creation and He is nowhere in space, not above nor below, not at the right hand nor at the left, not before nor behind. It cannot be said whence He came or where He goes or how He exists. He is the maker of space and ordainer of time, but time does not hold Him nor space contain Him.

"No intelligence can grasp or comprehend Him; no imagination can configure Him; no soul can form His likeness. Nothing is like to Him. But still He hears and sees, the tenderest of rulers, the most loving of helpers. Those who know Him know Him through His works but deny all limit to His greatness. And however our thought may conceive of God, He is different."

Ponder this well, as I have, my father. Is it not a noble and exact description of the God of Israel? Is it not possible that the triune god of which the Christians boast may be the God of the Jew, the Moslem, and the Christian in One?

I read no more. I clapped the scroll together convulsively. Under my calash, the hair of my head rose in horror. Shadows jigged madly in my brain like the great cruel three-armed idols of the East, all reaching with their clawed hands for the soul of my son. I sat upright, recalling the fatal conversation I had overheard between Ahmed and Musef years before, the night before Rachel's arrival in Almería. All my suspicions of Maimonides' apostasy rose before me once more.

I sprang to my writing case. I searched with shaking hands for the necessary materials. As fast as I could scribble, I indited a script to Maimonides. It commanded him, by all authority of a father, to return from Toledo to Almería at once. I sealed it with my own seal. I inscribed it: QUICKLY QUICKLY QUICKLY. I called Zayd and gave it into his big plum-colored hands, heaping money atop to hire a Moslem courier from the governor's retinue.

I sat back full of my grim energy, bursting out against time and space. In my mind I saw Zayd jogging down the path toward the town, the gold jingling in the pouch on his girdle, seeking to do my will toward Maimonides. I saw the messenger ride out on his horse, cantering easily through the miles, slowing to halt at the post-houses, sunrises and sunsets coloring him like a picture as he went on, a blank figure, into the distance. I flung my thoughts before him. I envisioned the bleak gates of Toledo rising, the winding mole-runs of streets and the chattering schools. The messenger came in through the gates, holding the words I had written so wildly, looking about him (carefully, for he was a Moslem in Christian domain) and asking directions. At last, in my imagination, he met Maimonides.

To my dismay, I could not recognize my son. His face had become strange to me, no more than a charcoal cartoon of shadow and light. It was the face of a stranger: erect, waiting, part of the scenery of Toledo I had glimpsed so distortedly when I was with Rachel. Maimonides blended into the background, something I had never thought could happen in this woeful life.

The image in my head grew painful, etching into my consciousness. I rose from my seat in the padded klismos. I took a turn around the room, rapping fretfully upon the tortoise inlay with its light gay echo. Perhaps it was I who had changed, not Maimonides. Possibly there was no change at all in either of us and I had conceived a fantasy. I approached his screed on my desk as if it were a live thing. I took it up in my fingertips. For a moment I was undecided—whether to read it, to finish it, to possibly discover some circumstance in the concluding lines that would shift my mind into more peaceful imaginings. Then, almost as if directed by another force than my own will, I crossed the room. I dropped Maimonides' words into the glowing brazier opposite the window. As they blazed up, I uttered a cry of pain I could not stifle.

Less than a month later, the messenger returned to Almería. Zayd met him and came back to report to me. By unmistakable signs, interpreted again and again by myself and Brujo, he told us what had happened. The courier had come alone. Nor was there a message with him. (It sent my thoughts into dull torment, for it confirmed what I had imagined.) My epistle had been delivered faithfully into the hands of Rachel herself, at the door of her house. The courier had been thanked, fed, and housed for two days. Yet he had not seen Maimonides nor had there been any response.

84

Out of the ashes of my despair rose stubbornness. If my son would not come to me, if he would not reply, I would not change. I had bowed down far enough in my role as parent. I would not go to him nor would I write again. If another year passed without a response, I thought, I would assume the dreaded responsibility that must be met. Despite myself, I would at last pronounce the Kaddish over Maimonides, dead to blood, faith, and heritage. Solemnly I walked out to the entrance of my house. I touched the tiny mezuzah with my fingers and repeated softly: "A Jew I am, and a Jew I shall be to the end of this world and the next!"

CHAPTER 6

Brujo thrust the scroll at me with the gesture of a man getting rid of a scorpion. "Here, Rabbi Maimon," he said, "I beg you, take this. I have held it long enough."

"What is it?" I asked with irritation, interrupted in my evening meditations.

"A message for you."

"Undoubtedly. I did not believe it was a copy of the Torah." Brujo dropped it on my desk. He ignored my sarcasm and ostentatiously wiped his hand on his faded linen breeches. "Who gave it to you?" I asked.

"I was marketing in the Place of the Fishsellers. The servant, I think it was, gave it to me."

"What servant?" I demanded, tired of question and answer. "Tell me, fool!"

"The servant that looks like a toad," Brujo said injuredly. "The slave of Isaac the Blind."

Without another word, he rolled out of my room, his bottom a study in insulted dignity. I sat frowning across the room at the tortoise-shell-inlaid ambry which held my tiny library. Oddly enough, to most of my friends, I found the goyim acceptable more on a basis of friendship than as servant and master. The idea of such a relationship is not generally taken kindly among my people. But I confess Brujo inspired me with far less terror after I had healed him than before. But he was often incomprehensible. I debated with myself if I should forbid him from his growing intimacy with Ramah. He was not yet a Jew; and, even if he became one, there was a question as to his suitability as a husband. The first commandment of God was to be fruitful and multiply; the first question to be asked of a man on the Day of Judgment, said the Talmud, would be: "Have you married and founded a family?"

I shook my head and regarded the script on the polished Spanish oak before me. I turned the scroll over and thumbed it idly, speculating what it might contain. Somehow, I entertained much the same suspicions of it that had seemed to animate Brujo. I tried to think of the last time I had heard from Isaac the Blind. My memory failed me.

Knowing fish and visitors stink after too long a time, I had not stayed more than two or three months at his house, no more than the time it took for Brujo to be partially healed. My unreasoning dislike of his house, ornate within and filthy without, added to the munificence of the governor, had prompted me to surrender his hospitality within a week after receiving the villa.

Despite the fact that Zayd, the Negro, and Brujo often quarreled with his slaves—and once even with his disciples—Isaac had not been gracious about the departure of my household. He was proud of his hospitality. He felt I had rejected it in some degree. More than that, like many blind, especially those who pride themselves on their intellect, he had relished our long conversations. A split hair was his idea of a triumph; a hidden contradiction in the Talmud, his delight. He appeared to have been particularly put out by the abrupt departure of Maimonides with Rachel for Toledo.

"Swords and false witness," he had sneered to me, "what else do they forge in that city of Christians and fools?"

"Yet Alfonso has been as tolerant as the Moors with our race," I replied. "He has encouraged learning without inquiring into religion."

"The greater fool, he," Isaac replied. "It would not be so if I were king."

I vouchsafed no reply. Staring sightlessly past me, Isaac opened his hand buddingly like a flower. "They say," he murmured, "that in that city they have our sacred Book of Psalms written in a book of gold pages, in the ink of melted rubies. Do you believe it is so?"

"Not I," I told him. "If such a treasure exists, then Musa the Conqueror sent it to Damascus long ago with the emerald tables. But I may add that gold is most difficult to write upon and, in my estimation, it is impossible to reduce rubies to ink."

Isaac sighed. "Yet it may be possible with magic," he said softly. "I have felt the velvet smoothness of gold and the dark sharpness of the edges of rubies." He leaned forward to me. "Tell me, Maimon," he said with sudden eagerness, "what is the color of gold? What is the color of rubies?"

I commenced to speak but the words stuck in my throat. I realized how foolish it was to attempt to tell of color to a man blind from birth. "Good Isaac," I mumbled regretfully, "it is a question that only God Himself, blessed be He, can answer for you in the World-to-Come."

As if offended, Isaac drew himself back. "You see, then," he remarked coldly, "how my mind is freed for thoughts on things more rare and difficult than the most precious gems."

He waved his two pupils, Ezra and Azriel, forward to sit at either knee and hear him expound his doctrines. I took his gesture as one of dismissal. I wanted to hear nothing of his twisted philosophy. I rose and left as they began their esoteric schooling.

After that day I saw Isaac less often, the last time only to say ceremonious thanks and farewell before leaving for my villa on the hills near the sea. He bade me speed and blessings in his rich voice, nothing more. His ugly servant watched sullenly as we filed out of the muddy courtyard into the busy street. I found myself sucking in deep breaths as we went, as if I had emerged from a cloud of ill-smelling vapor.

In three years of living in the villa, I had seen Isaac only on holy days and festivals—sometimes not then, depending on his frail health. We sent greetings and I begged his forgiveness and he begged mine, as was customary on Yom Kippur, but this was mere formality. Ministering to the scar-headed Mohammed for exorbitant fees and to the poor for naught, assisting with the services at the pitiful synagogue, busy with my studies and my longing for Maimonides, instructing David and Brujo together in the faith, amusing Yaltah—my days were full indeed.

Now, this message. I picked it up gingerly. As I did, a second, smaller scroll tumbled out. Alive with curiosity, I unrolled it. The writing of Judah Halevi sprang out at me, as if animated by its message.

87

FROM ALEXANDRIA

Within the depths of the sea,
The stars shine, like a crowd
Of wanderers, carelessly
Caught in a watery shroud.
They give the deeps a show
Of fire within the weather;
Sea above and sea below
Grow calm and join together
And, in the dark, they grow
One spangled sea. But now a third I see,
Invisible, my heart adoring Thee,
Its rhythm in a holy fall and rising
Offering Thee eternal love and praising.

For long moments I stood motionless. I suffered the same
waves of emotion which must have prompted Judah to write
so. It was a wrench of agony—after these long years—to hear
an echo from him, rousing memories of that last night in Cordova. I had heard rumors of his travels inland in Egypt to the
Jewish communities scattered throughout that mysterious land.
With an effort that seemed to tear my inmost soul, I detached
my attention from the little scroll. It curled back into itself
like the balling up of a hand. Fumblingly I unrolled the other
which had enclosed it. It proved to be a script in the childish
scrawl of Ezra, the disciple of Isaac the Blind.

To beloved Rabbi Maimon ben Joseph, greetings:

Herein is a verse from our friend Judah, pleasing enough
in its fashion. I send it to you, knowing how you enjoy
his poetry. I have also news to tell you that will delight
your heart. Tonight, at my home, near the twelfth hour,
I am expecting a visit from your own son, Moses ben
Maimon. I respectfully ask that you honor us both by
greeting him. Love and obedience,

Isaac ben Abraham

My senses whirled like a compass at the approach of iron.
Then they steadied, quivering in one direction, that of anger
and humiliation. My pride choked me but I swallowed it down
with the draught of a father's love. I had no choice: If Maimonides preferred to come to the house of Isaac the Blind

88

rather than mine, I must endure it. My yearning to see him conquered every other emotion; a thousand conjectures turned in my head—if he were ill; if he had not known where to find me; if he were wounded; at the gates of death, perhaps!

I hastened out of the room to change into more suitable garb. "Brujo!" I cried. "Bring torches to escort me down to the town! Hurry, hurry!"

In order that none may misunderstand my dislike for going to the house of Isaac the Blind, it is here I must explain some of his strange doctrines on the misnamed Kabbala. In the months I had spent in his house, he had managed to tell me much about his secret meditations. Indeed, as I grew to comprehend, it might have been my inner dismay at recognizing such a poisonous growth in our faith that influenced my hasty letter to Maimonides. In those days the serpent spawned by Isaac the Blind writhed itself about our Tree of Life, as it does still today. What Isaac told me, in essence, was this.

God is above all, above everything, above Himself. None can say that He speaks or acts, that He thinks or wills; these are human attributes, limited in space and time. God, being perfect, is unlimited everywhere and beyond time: thus He may take the name *En Sof,* that is to say, "Without End."

But because of His very essence, this Eternal is inconceivable to man. Existence everywhere is the same as existence nowhere, at least to human thought. En Sof is really *Ein,* that is to say, Non-existence.

In order to make Himself known to man, the En Sof became active and creative in the human sense.

"But by this wish and act, did He not limit Himself?" I inquired uncomfortably one evening.

"Attend to me," said Isaac sternly. His disciples stirred at his feet like dogs in sleep. His blind white face went on, its mouth opening and shutting like the gill of a fish.

"In its sinful state, the world could not have been created by the En Sof. Perfection cannot create imperfection; the infinite cannot create the finite. Therefore, the prime radiation from the En Sof, partaking of His perfection and infinity, had to take on some finite earthly qualities. This was called the *Sephira.*"

"But is not the Sephira an imperfect creation of the perfect, precisely what you said it could not be?"

"Listen and be enlightened.

"This same first Sephira radiated once more and produced a

second force, a second Sephira. This again reproduced itself until there were ten mystic Sephirot. As sparks are different from fire and yet the same, so were the Sephirot different from the En Sof, yet the same: like a bit of triangular glass splitting sunlight into ten colors, yet all from the same light.

"These Sephirot are the ten attributes of En Sof. The three highest are named Wisdom, Reason, and Knowledge, comprising the Crown; the seven lower Sephirot are as yet unnamed. Together they may form the unspeakable Name, the Tetragrammaton. In the Book of Formation by that blessed martyr, Rabbi Akiba, these are united with the Twenty-two Letters to form the Thirty-two Paths of Wisdom by which En Sof shapes the world. The Sephirot are also six directions in space, two in time, and the two extremes of good and evil. The last of the seven lower Sephirot is *Adam Kadmon,* the heavenly archetype of man.

"The universe may be likened to a giant tree with an ever increasing number of branches, twigs, and leaves, bearing both good and bad fruit; its roots are the Sephirot. It may be likened to a closely wrought endless chain binding earth to heaven; its last ten links are the Sephirot. Or a sea continually filled from a series of sources, each flowing into the other; these are the Sephirot."

"Then what is good and what is evil?"

"What is good is what is nourished by the roots," intoned Isaac. "What is good is a strong link in the chain or an unsullied spring of ever living water. Evil is the lack of good, the blocking of the flow from heaven to us.

"So the ten Sephirot match the Ten Commandments, the ten Declarations, the ten Spheres, the ten Forces, the ten Numbers. From this comes the meaning of the ten-fingered blessing. All power is in the bosom of the Sephirot, either emanating from them or roused against them by demons. By them is created the material world in their own image; by them it is supported and given divine life. Through them the En Sof may give himself a visible human form, and by their resistance to them, the powers of darkness are made more damned.

"The souls of men created, destined for earth, are dropped like chips into this ever flowing stream. If they remain pure, they return to the spirit; if tainted, they are compelled to return to earth again and again (though I have heard some say, no more than three times), for purification in other bodies."

90

"But this is, as Maimonides has said, the Greek theory of Pythagoras!"

"Hearken and comprehend," Isaac told me.

"So few are holy that most souls are returned to a new earthly existence. But the Messiah cannot come except as the last soul of all. Therefore the hastening of the coming of the Millennium depends upon the wise and righteous being translated to make room for the untried souls to come."

With a shudder I thought of these things recited to me by Isaac the Blind, as I walked through the dark streets of Almería, Brujo and his two pine torches before me. These theories seemed to make up a world as dark and threatening as the shadows that rose before us and fell behind us. But no terror could be great enough to keep me from Maimonides' homecoming.

I turned into the courtyard of the hideous place of scarred stone with revulsion. I bid the scowling Brujo wait with the squat servant he despised. I half-ran through the nauseous corridor, up the stairs, and beat upon the door. It opened to me. I stepped into what seemed the room of a stranger. It was bare of furniture and rugs, lighted only by the seven-branched candlestick. Isaac, in curiously worked robes, sat upright in his chair in the center. He was alone. A stool stood at his feet.

"Where is my son?" I gasped. "Where is Muni?"

Isaac made no reply, his hand indicating the stool. I sank upon it, repeating my question.

"In good time you shall see him," Isaac said sonorously. I glanced about me with agitation. "Why have you prepared this room so?" I asked. "Is this the way you live now?"

"We are ready to greet your son," Isaac announced. "I shall bring him to you so that you will know him in truth." His tone puzzled me in its measured, priestly cadence. I assumed he had prepared a feast elsewhere, that this was to be a celebration of a strange sort. How strange I did not know until a moment later.

Isaac leaned forward toward me, his blind eyes searching the vacancy which contained me. "Maimon," he said, "what is the proof of the divine?"

"Shall we not keep such a discussion until later?"

"Tell me!"

"That which is immortal," I said, humoring him.

"Precisely. Each body has its immortal part—the soul, which lives after death, which lives before and beyond life."

"Such a question has never been decided by the Talmud," I said judiciously.

"There are many interpretations of the Talmud," Isaac replied. "Your own forefather, Judah the Prince, made the first and greatest—and there have been others."

"And you have made your own, good Isaac?"

"In my fashion."

I stood up. "I have come here to greet my son," I said, more sharply than I intended. "Is he here?"

"Sit," Isaac bade me. "He has not yet arrived, but be assured his guides will bring him soon."

"When?"

"In a moment," Isaac replied. "We are ready for his reception."

Isaac the Blind clapped his hands slowly three times. Raising his voice, he cried: "Bring in the sword, the bowl, and the crown!"

From the shadows, noiseless as phantoms, clothed in samite, came the erect figures of Ezra and Azriel, their faces pale and long hair flowing. Ezra stood by the left side of Isaac's chair. Azriel took the sword. Using its point, he swiftly drew Solomon's seal, its six points surrounding us. Within it again, he inscribed a circle, keeping us well within it. In the space between star and circle, he wrote characters in Arabic and Hebrew with red chalk, and I felt my blood chill. He added figures whose significance I could not understand, underlining them twice, five times, seven times.

At the six corners, Ezra placed small heaps of gray powder in crystal saucers. These he lit ceremoniously with a taper from the candelabra. They burned with hissing, varicolored flames that gave off odors of incense. Azriel placed a small circlet of gold studded with opals on the head of the immobile Isaac. Into Isaac's left hand he put the sword, point upright; on his right palm, he balanced the bowl filled with a substance that shimmered like quicksilver. Though the bowl must have been heavy, Isaac's hand held it rigidly before him. Locked in my place by wonder, I felt the first crawlings of fear.

"Come close to me, Maimon," Isaac said in an unnatural whisper.

"Why must this be?" I said hoarsely.

"For your salvation. Bring those you would save, leave those you would destroy."

"I want nothing of this, Isaac," I said more loudly. "What do you intend to do?"

92

"No more than was done by the familiar of the woman of En-dor who called upon Samuel for the sake of Saul."

"You work magic!" I cried, starting up.

Isaac lifted his head; the sword trembled. "I have the power to call upon the souls that choose to respond to my knowledge," he declared.

"My son will not attend a ceremony such as this!" I exclaimed. I saw a slight grimace pass across Isaac's face. More from that than from any other indication, I sank back upon the stool. Azriel stepped forward. From his hand dangled a chain of gold, at its end a polished silver disk reflecting the light as it turned.

"Observe the disk," murmured Isaac. In truth, I could not take my eyes from it. The multi-colored hues from the saucers of burning powder shone back into my face. Somewhere in the distance I heard Isaac the Blind commence a chant.

"By the powers of the Mercaba, which Ezekiel knew how to invoke, I urge the messenger.

"By the Paradise located in the four ends of heaven, which only the great Akiba, of the Four That Entered, went into and came out of in peace, I adjure the messenger.

"By the hidden secrets of the Midrash, I summon the messenger.

"By the Four Worlds, of Formation and Creation, of Deed and Uplifting; by the ten Sephirot, by the Crown of the Three Essences of En Sof, by the names of Abraham, Isaac, and Jacob, I call the messenger!

"By the Five Stages of the human spirit, by the Seven Souls, by the Forty-nine Days and the Seventy-two Names; by the Thirty-two Paths, by the Six Directions, by the virtues of Adam Kadmon, I say, Arise!

"By the *Shechina,* the ghost of the En Sof, by the symbols and powers of the Six-winged Seraphim of Isaiah, the Beasts and Wheels of Ezekiel, the Angel of Zerubbabel, the Cherubim and Seraphim, the *Hayot* and *Ofannim,* I address you!

"By *El Chai,* by Shaddai, by Adonai Melech, by *Eheieh Asher Eheieh,* by Tetragrammaton Adonai, come!"

The room dimmed, clouding my vision in the silver disk. Except for the face of Isaac and the flames growing brighter, turning toward him as if in obedience, all else faded. A gust from nowhere extinguished the seven flames of the candles above.

The room grew and grew. It lost all feeling of confinement, it took on the quality of vast space; sounds in the lost air commenced to rise. Sparks danced upon the tip of the sword; the quicksilver churned in the bowl.

The silver disk before my eyes turned faster, flickering in the red and blue, in the yellow and orange flames from the points of the star. In its reflection I saw dim faces pressing against the bars of light, as if they were peering longingly back into life from the exile of Gehenna: some desperate; some writhing in pain; some staring with ferocity; some struggling with unknown and hideous emotions. I heard the trample of hoofs, the sound of rasping whispers magnified in my ears. There was the padding of paws, the rustle of garments, a sniffing like that of dogs at an unopened door.

"Come," Isaac said in an indistinguishable voice. He held out the bowl of quicksilver. I rose, like a man summoned from a sickbed, my feet dragging painfully. I came to his side and saw sweat pouring down his sunken face. He lifted the sword. A dark star coruscated at its point. "Look!" commanded Isaac. I peered into the reflecting surface of the bowl.

"My son, my son," I whispered. I swear the face of Maimonides looked back at me, the same tawny hair that I loved, the same calm enigmatic face, the dark eyes. I stretched out my arms to encompass him. They were stayed by an invisible force. I heard his voice whispering in my ear; I strained to hear the words.

Suddenly his voice came to me, loudly and clearly, echoing in the vastness that was the dark room about me. I heard Maimonides as if he were no more than outside the door. "Isaac!" he shouted. "Isaac the Blind! Open up!"

There was a thunder of knocks on the outer door. The flames from the saucers wavered and commenced to die. Isaac dropped the sword. The bowl fell, the quicksilver escaping, pelleting away to hide in the corners. The two disciples, garments disarrayed, ran wildly about lighting candles at random, flames that glowed and grew straight and healthy. Isaac sat on his chair in a blind daze, his crown slipping from his head. From somewhere the air blew clean and wholesome, driving away the odors of thick incense.

Again the tattoo of knocks beating against the door. Repeated shouts, this time other voices than that of Maimonides. I saw where the entrance was through eyes clearing themselves of mist; I stumbled toward it, got my hands on the chains and bolts, and shakily undid them one by one. The door swung open. Red torchlight blazed through.

Maimonides, straighter and taller than I had ever seen him,

94

stood there. He flung his arms out wide to hold me, his face under his turban filled with gladness. Tears burst from my eyes. The hot flow washed me into sanity again. I fell forward into Maimonides' arms as he took me to his breast, never a more welcome moment in my life. He said nothing; his embrace was enough.

Beyond him I heard voices in strange accents, talking casually to each other. Through my sobs, their words came distinctly, a broken French I had never before experienced. But I understood perfectly what they said.

"What a woeful place, by the faith of my body," said a voice in an idle accent, a rasp to its edge. "I should smite the men and destroy it, lock and stone, with my own hands."

"Forbear," said the other, a deeper tone. "This our young and noble companion has found friends. Doubtless he would not thank you halfheartedly if you should break the covenant, even for such a foul kennel. But let us go down to the court and cleanse it of the daffish servants."

The clink of iron and the rattle of harness retreated and died away. I raised my head and stepped back from Maimonides, brushing by eyes and beard. "Thanks be to the God of Israel and to our friend, Isaac the Blind," I said unsteadily, "that brought you back."

"Isaac the Blind?" demanded Maimonides, peering at me, then past me. "What has he done for thanks?"

"Has he not summoned you?" I quavered, as he swung me about.

Maimonides allowed one of his unaccustomed smiles to transform his face. "My father," he told me, "I have not seen nor heard of this man since the day I left Almería. I came to you of my own free will. I have been two weeks on the road. Nothing except my love has brought me. And the hope that what I tell you will bring you back to Toledo with me."

Somehow we struggled out of the door, tripping down the steps, laughing, arguing, kissing, seizing each other to make sure of reality, catching and supporting, pushing in delight, losing balance and recovering, a little demented by the moment.

From the upper chamber behind us came a different, frightening sound. I heard the voice of Isaac the Blind in a shrill keening, as if some alien being inhabited his body. "True!" he cried in a shriek. "True! True! Here is the heart I have dragged bleeding out of eternal mystery! I have power! I summon, and the princes of air and darkness bring me the one I command to be brought! At last, I am their master!"

I shut my ears to his piercing cries that seemed more pain than joy. The hysterical blind man, the rustle of the robes of his silent worried disciples hovering about him, faded behind us. I slammed the door and felt the cool breath of night.

You may imagine the happiness and the dancing that exploded in my villa when we entered. Maimonides was caught in a tender ring of flesh, the joined hands of David and Yaltah as they danced around him, singing, laughing, rejoicing. In the door stood Ramah, gently weeping for joy, Brujo's protective arm around her shoulders. In a corner was Zayd, grinning uncertainly, his teeth flashing in the light of the oil lamps. He looked now and then with a scowl of puzzlement at our two guests, tall bearded men in rusty armor. They stood near the door and leaned on their scabbarded swords. Their countenances showed interest and, I thought, amusement; but they remained silent, waiting for another will than their own to instruct them.

As I watched the spontaneous rejoicing, my thoughts unaccountably flew back to the city. I recalled the moment when we emerged from the house of Isaac the Blind, into his foul courtyard. It was lit by torches, sputtering orange in sconces alongside the house; it was filled with the cries of Isaac's servant that Brujo had described as resembling a toad. In the lurid illumination, he ran about the place like a cornered thing, weaving, sobbing, in a figure-of-eight, near exhaustion, scuttling as fast as he could go. Urging him on, the two stranger knights stood like pillars of steel at either end of the courtyard, whacking him on the rear with the flat of their swords as he went by.

One side of the courtyard was avoided by the fellow as if it were guarded by dragons. In truth, it held two of the most fabulous animals I had ever seen: two of what I later learned were the famous Fleming horses. Like their masters, they seemed creations out of another substance than flesh, patterned out of another world: immense, great chests bulging with hillocks of muscle, heads of granite—yet with shining kindly eyes—legs that were like palisades thrust into the ground. They stood immobile, draped with leather-lined steel plates. I was to learn that my first impression was correct: Here were animal forts, capable of incredible endurance, even short bursts of furious gallop, with hundreds of pounds of man and armor and equipment on their backs.

Holding the bridles of these horses (as well as of their own), two sergeant men-at-arms stood by. They approved their masters' amusement with loud guffaws. Short and solid, they resembled the horses; indeed, they were so bulged with sinew, their arms hung out from their bodies. When they walked, they straddled their legs to prevent painful friction. Thus, I guessed rightly, they spent most of their time in the saddle. Such massive strength came from a life of daily exercise with lance and truncheon, with mace, battle-ax, and sword. Maimonides told me afterward most of the Franks were like this, bulls in strength and lions in courage.

I concluded long ago that his description was accurate but I feel, as a physician, that their bravery (deservedly famous as it is) came from a natural insensitivity. I suspect that the Franks—and others like them—simply do not feel pain as quickly or deeply as most. Natural stubbornness and lack of ability to move quickly, perhaps because of their layers of muscle, hold them to a single spot until death. I have had reports of a few of their battles; they came down to much the same: single men, swinging swords, armor shorn away, bleeding from a dozen wounds, surrounded like a stag by hounds, finally going down knee by knee, dying with an incomprehensible grin. These men, I feel, love fighting for its own sake, accepting only death or victory as alternatives.

The painted stirrups of their massive mounts held pennons with the flamboyant gold fleur-de-lis crest of the French king, Louis. Lances, extra swords, and massive Danish battle-axes were strapped to the flanks of the horses. Behind them, two bony mules stood loaded with baggage.

As we came into view, the knights ceased their horseplay. Still squalling from fright and pain, their victim ran into Isaac's house. The knights and men-at-arms mounted. Myself and Maimonides climbed into half-saddles behind them. I was still dazed by this apparition of my son from nowhere, half-believing it was the magic of the debased Kabbala which had induced it. We pounded off, following my directions, to the villa.

Now, deeming the celebration had been carried far enough for the moment, I stepped forward. I clapped my hands again and again to overcome the din. At last, my eyes more than moist, I broke up the dance around my son and made myself heard.

"Let us have an end!" I cried over the subsiding tumult. "Tomorrow will come! Then we shall have our own Hanukkah. Meantime, we have guests to serve and gratify, who have come many leagues to visit us!"

I gestured to Brujo. "Take the men-at-arms to their quarters; see that they lack nothing," I ordered. "Put up their beasts, Zayd." Zayd bowed. Brujo smiled brightly, though briefly. With Zayd and the sniffling Ramah, he went to obey my commands. I turned to David, whose handsome young face puckered with disappointment. "My boy," I said to him, "you will be able to greet your brother properly tomorrow. Now it is late; your couch is lonely for you." Obediently, without a word, he kissed Maimonides and myself and made his way out of the room. "You, too, my daughter," I said to Yaltah, as she lingered. She had noticed Maimonides less—after the first raptures—than she had the knights, enthralled by their powerful appearance.

When they had all gone, I salaamed to the knights. I bade them take seats and remove their armor. They acknowledged my courtesy and sat down heavily; with clumsy fingers unused to the offices of war, I helped them unlace their corselets, revealing stained leather jerkins underneath. I hastened to serve them with wine and offered them some pipes with rare tobacco. They drank eagerly, stoup after stoup, until they belched in satiation. The pipes they handled gingerly, looking at them with hesitation; then shook their heads and handed them back. "From the East," I explained. "These contain a soothing herb. When fired and inhaled in smoke, it calms the heart."

"Nay," said the first man in a gravelly voice, "it is a mystery we know naught of, and we trust no strange Jew."

"I am sorry," I said. "In my house you may feel at ease. You will find no treachery nor discourtesy."

The knight nodded briefly, dismissing my words. "I am Marquis Armand du Bois," he said brusquely. "My companion is no less noble, Sieur Guilbert de Bayonne. We have sworn a vow on behalf of yourself and your son. This is our devoir."

I blinked in astonishment. "A vow in my behalf?" I inquired.

"Because of the healing miracle of the Jewess Rachel," said De Bayonne in a high carrying voice. "Thus far we have completed the half. God willing, we shall do the rest."

"Rachel?" I demanded.

Maimonides had stood silent in a corner of the room. He broke into my perplexity by coming beside my chair. "Here," he said, proffering me a scroll, "here is a letter from Rachel bat Abor. Perhaps it will explain." He bent over and whispered quickly in my ear: "Do not take offense at these men, my father. They are truly gentle men, rough of tongue, but honorable and true."

I nodded to indicate I had heard, though not agreeing. I shook my head at the fatness of the scroll I held: indeed a weighty note. I broke the seal, not without a pang at seeing Rachel's bold scarab signet impressed on the wax. I unrolled it and scanned the first columns.

To the Well-loved Rabbi Maimon ben Joseph, may God increase his health and wealth, greeting:

Knowing you for a stubborn and wise man, dear Maimon—demanding all facts before decision—I must write a long letter. I must explain many things.

Believe then, that this country of France (from which I write) is prosperous and wretched, ignorant and valiant and divided, corrupt and divine. You know that I was here once before. The reason for my present visit stems from the disastrous Battle of Damascus, reports of which rang through the world. There the caliph took hundreds of Frankish knights prisoner, stripped them, and plunged them all instantly into the darkest dungeons. They remained there for years, in unspeakable dirt and disease, fed only bread and water. Most of them died; about 300 survived, a tribute to their ruggedness.

Well, the good King Louis having returned, the families, liege lords, and priests managed to get about 5,000,-000 dinars together to ransom them. The Moslems packed them home like cattle. They sent back no bargain: All were totally blind. Louis quartered them here in the Hôtel de Dieu.

On my arrival, I examined these helpless, hopeless men. Blindness had reduced the great warriors to whimpering children or grim lost souls. Even the king's command barely sufficed for them to let me touch them; I did it finally by wearing sweet perfumes (which I abhor) and allowing them to feel my face and hands and gown.

I discovered none had suffered destruction. I had feared that scarring of the eyes, the *trachoma,* as the

Greeks call it. As you know, this is an ancient disease of Palestine. Nothing can be done about it, so infectious is this inflammation which sears the eye. My inquiries brought out that their blindness had developed first at night, then during the day, finally becoming a settled condition. For lack of any other idea, I guessed it must have been the bread-and-water diet. I ransacked the libraries (sending to Toledo, since there were only twenty books in the library of Paris) and reread the writings of Asaf Judaeus.

Here I must make my first confession. It was Maimonides who did the research which confirmed my guess. He provided copies of Philo, who had investigated ancient Egyptian scrolls describing the same state. It was Maimonides who pointed out that Hippocrates had seen it over a thousand years ago, calling it *xerophthalmia,* and recognizing it as an affliction caused by diet. It was Maimonides who told me the Egyptians had cured it as long as three thousand years prior to that, by feeding the patient on lamb's liver.

I decided to try his suggestion (such faith I have in your son!) on one or two of the knights. Of course I disguised what I gave them, grinding up the meat secretly, changing color and odor with a few other harmless ingredients. The results were almost beyond belief. Within a few weeks, my first knights were actually able to see.

I placed all of them on the same diet, blessing Maimonides. One by one they recovered—virtually completely. Then my true troubles commenced. First, I was deemed a miracle-worker; then I was adored as Jewess Mary, mother of their god, come back to earth. You have no conception of the city's hysteria. I was worshiped, mobbed, my clothing torn for sacred relics, kissed and slobbered over. More than a hundred people were crushed or died in fits. It was claimed I had walked over the sea from Jerusalem to Paris; at one point, I was seriously requested to lead another crusade. My denials were taken for heavenly modesty; my anger was seen as divine ecstasy. I never felt more helpless in my life.

The priests and healers of Paris rose and cursed me. Naturally the church people were horrified. The doctors —who practice hideous black arts merely to line their purses—demanded that I be burned at the stake as a witch. Possibly there is not much difference between a witch and a saint, after all, but I was relieved when Louis put a guard about my house.

Third—perhaps you will not believe this, Maimon—
seventy-three of the knights fell in love with me. They
demanded a tournament with me as the prize, either as
mistress or wife, I know not. Imagine my bewilderment
as I became, in such swift succession, the mother of God,
a witch, and the consort of mortal knights! It all ended
happily by the command of Louis. He made me his
personal ward.

I did receive one offer which intrigued me. It came
from Henri de Bouillon. A small man, though surprisingly muscular, noble in thought and appearance, he is
one of the exponents of the spreading way of life known
as "chivalry." This appears to be a good system, Maimon: it refers to men who ride horses, nobles or knights,
who take solemn oaths to respect women as jewels of
price. They are supposed to be good, generous, kind,
honorable, noble, pious—you know the rest of this list
of good intentions. Plundering and murder are allowed
only against Jews like ourselves or Moslems and Greeks.

At any rate, Henri took me to his city of Montpellier—
in which, by the way, there is a large group of our faith—
and told me he would build the greatest hospital and
school in the world if I would accept him and his religion. Both seemed attractive (I like men and loathe
gods). But I refused, saying I was dedicated to my healing arts.

I come to the meat of the egg. During some love-play
while I visited Henri, I discovered that a third crusade is
planned in a few years. As ever, there will be knights and
rabble, though far less of the former. It will be heavily
financed—and not by the Christians. They will use Jewish and Moslem riches for their treasury. You and Maimonides must seek protection. Of all places, I believe
that Toledo is the most tolerant and sheltering.

I realize you will not want to see me again after the
circumstances of our parting—even less when you finish
this letter—but this is no obstacle. I intend to stay in
France under the protection of my high sponsors—the
king and Henri.

I want to work among the peasants and in the cities.
The people are an unbelievable mass of ignorance, stupidity, and fear. Both the priests and doctors have now
been subdued; I see a great opportunity for my work. I
intend to seize it.

Thus, you will not meet me in Toledo for a long time.
I offer my house to Maimonides and yourself.

I come to my final confession. I know of your letters

and pleadings to Maimonides. My servants had instructions to surrender them to me. I opened, read them, and cast them into the fire. He never received one—though I allowed his to be sent to you to allay your fears. I was afraid he would be too dutiful, that you would woo him back to Almería before his studies in Toledo were sufficient. I knew your nature: I knew you would attempt to end his one chance for freedom of knowledge, to confine him within the crib of your faith. I counted on your pride and his stubbornness (he was homesick many times) to sustain the masquerade. It succeeded. I am happy. Maimonides has had the whole world spread out before him and my task is done. He will be a great man, Maimon. I had no intention of letting anyone interfere with his career.

So he has not heard from you at all. But he has written you, despite his disappointment, which, I must say, made him study all the harder. He has become filled with the delights of learning and will never abandon them.

I give him back to you to add his plea to mine for your coming to Toledo. I have sent with him two of my knights, sworn to his protection and yours. They carry the seal of Louis and his safe-conduct—with their own swords, the best guarantee of your safety.

Forgive me for my womanly plots, if you can. What I have done, I have done; it is for love of Maimonides and, in a corner of my heart, my affection for you. Shalom.

RACHEL BAT ABOR

" 'Shalom,' she says!" I cried, crushing the parchment. "She dares to say 'peace' to me!"

"What has she written, my father, that disturbs you?" asked Maimonides in a troubled voice.

Hardly daring, yet drawn to it, I looked up at Maimonides' face, with its light growth of reddish beard. It showed concern but betrayed no recognition of the shame I felt. I got slowly to my feet, salaaming to the two knights who watched with hostile, curious expressions.

"Good knights," I said, clearing my throat, "I have been too much taken up with my own affairs. I beg of you to rest here tonight. Tomorrow we shall talk."

Du Bois and his companion stood upright with curt nods. I implored Maimonides with a glance. "Find Ramah," I said to him, "since you do not know my house. Tell her these friends are weary. I would give them the best rooms and whatever food they require."

"Nay," Du Bois said briskly, "we sleep hard and, if need be, in harness. So much is not necessary."

"Honor a poor man," I said. "I ask no more."

"Upon my faith," De Bayonne said in his penetrating tones, "this Jew has excellent manners. I think we would be churls to refuse."

"As you will," Du Bois said carelessly. He fixed Maimonides with a stare. "But tell him of the news given you by the divine Rachel," he said. Maimonides bowed assent and led them out of the room. I sank back into my chair, deep in a chaos of agonizing thoughts. Long moments must have passed unknown to me; I was roused out of my reverie by the touch of Maimonides' hand on my shoulder.

"You are in pain," he said gently.

"In my heart," I assented. I sighed and dropped my head. "Did you never wonder when you did not hear from your father?" I asked.

"Look at me," Maimonides said. I raised my head. "You are my father, dear to me. What you decide is not for me to question."

"You have changed," I said in astonishment.

"If you did not choose to write, there were reasons. There is no need to explain."

"Indeed there is!" I cried. I thrust the letter into his hands. "Rachel, curse her lovely head of flame, took my letters to you and destroyed them! She excuses herself herein, saying that I would have dragged you back to Almería by the hair of your head!"

There was a glint of amusement in Maimonides' eyes. "And would you not?" he asked. I stared at him. Suddenly my grief vanished; my heart overflowed. I commenced to laugh. Maimonides joined me in my hilarity.

"You are home," I said, wiping my eyes. "The prodigal son has returned. I shall kill the fatted calf, if I can find one in the market place. Now you are home and here you shall remain."

Maimonides became sober. "No, my father," he said earnestly, "we must return."

"You may continue your studies here!"

"That is not the reason."

"Not the reason?" My tongue stumbled. "Is it that you must see Rachel again?" I asked fearfully.

"Nor that, though I love her," he said simply.

"You do not wish to stay with David and Yaltah and myself?"

"I want nothing in heaven or earth more."

"Then?"

"There is the new crusade, the new persecution."

"Tchah!" I said. I slapped the letter in his fist contemptuously. "Such things have happened before and we have avoided them. Have you forgotten that?"

"No, my father," Maimonides said seriously. "It is none of these things. There is the news my Christian friends told me to give you."

Instantly my suspicions grew within me. "What?" I demanded.

Maimonides took my hand. "Do you remember that night when certain evil strangers sailed up the Guadalquivir and broke into our garden in Cordova?"

"As if it were only yesterday."

"Such evil has come again. The crusades, the rise of Saladin, the growing strength of Alfonso, the river of men and blood that flows to and fro across the land—it is rising. Each side, Christian and Moslem, believes itself challenged. Each will meet the challenge, to what end, God knows."

"Say what you mean, my son," I told him somberly.

"The Almohades have risen again. On our way, we had sure information of their landing. In a week, they will be in Almería as they were in Cordova."

I sank back in thought. Oddly enough, the images were pleasant, soothing as I had not imagined they could be. Maimonides frowned at me in bewilderment.

"Tonight," I said, rising, "tonight I shall write a letter to Rachel in Paris. Do you know what I will say, my son?"

"No."

"I shall say only this: 'The nightingales sing forever in the gardens of Toledo.' "

CHAPTER 7

I know Maimonides derides the calculations of the astrologers as foolish nonsense—has he not said that "Whoever says one time is favorable, another unfavorable, by the stars, speaks lies which fools imagine to be words of truth"?—but I am not altogether convinced. Surely, from the time we set out on the long journey to Toledo, there were opposing influences in the very air. It was a desperate journey, one that left me feeling as if I had passed through death in life. It marked the beginning of the most unhappy times of my life, all the more in remembering glorious Cordova and peaceful Almería.

Perhaps one should be ashamed to say it, but the grim air of the knights, our protectors, disheartened me from the first. I have no doubt that the Marquis Armand du Bois and his companion, Sieur Guilbert de Bayonne, were both noble and honorable. But their silent fanaticism to an ideal I could not understand frightened me.

It was my first encounter with a new order, one I was to hear much about. A word about these wild, yet dedicated men will not be amiss. Known commonly as Knights Templar (or, as Brujo properly described them, the Poor Knights of Christ and the Temple of Solomon, a fearful mixture of blasphemy and simplicity), they were to become more powerful than kings, richer than empires, more feared than any other power on earth. This band of devoted knights—and others like the Teutonic Order and the Hospitalers—soon became a military order, then a mighty and secret force. It grew in strength and opulence, in discipline and influence. In later days the Templars had a Grand Master of supreme authority in their own Temple of Jerusalem. Only in a few cases, such as those of declaring war or peace, was he bound to consult the majority of his thousands of chosen fellows.

Each Templar swore lifelong allegiance and obedience, "as if commanded by God," as their oath ran. They decided the fate of principalities and thrones in secret conclave. They were forbidden to hawk or hunt (except the lion, symbol of Satan), and all display of pride in manner or dress was forbidden. Their meals were simple, their couches strips of carpet on the floor, their clothes wool or linen—the world and its pleasures wiped out even in memory. They could accept no gifts even from their own kin. Women were anathema; even the kiss of courtesy was frowned upon.

They presented themselves even as did our guides—short hair and rough beards, soiled white mantles embroidered with a red cross. Rarely defeated in battle (though they had been repelled from the walls of Damascus—some said by treachery or bribery) they achieved the height of fame. Yet somehow, though they had the approval of their pope in Rome and were even elevated above the Christian church itself, few trusted them. Worthy as they were, there was that about the Templars—a ruthless, fanatic ambition, though in the name of God—which inspired fear and hatred.

I remember Maimonides questioning them as we rode along the broken pavement of the old Roman highway toward Toledo. They had told him, in their characteristic French jargon, of some of their doings. He expressed wonder. "With only your weapons and faith," Maimonides said tentatively, "how may the Templars achieve such great things?"

"Well said," replied the marquis. "Young one, know then that we are amassing treasure. Gold may do what steel cannot, to bring about Christ's kingdom on earth. Who else but our Order made a loan of fifty thousand soldi to the empty chests of Louis of France?"

"So much?" I blurted out in amazement.

Sieur Guilbert glanced contemptuously at me over his shoulder. "Gold is much, but the sword and force of arms are more," he said shortly. "The opinion of others is not mine."

"Does King Louis himself hold your band in high regard?" asked Maimonides.

"We are his good right arm," the marquis replied. "Even now, as we ride, he remakes his own army under our supervision, by our disciplines. We direct his mind."

"Will not your success create envy in the court?"

"Perhaps, perhaps," the marquis replied carelessly. "But when God has raised up such as we from the very dust, who among men shall put us down?"

There seemed to be no answer to such a misguided question. I allowed my mule to drop behind in response to a quick look from Maimonides. He followed suit, allowing the two knights to ride ahead. No more was spoken as we trotted leisurely around one of the rocky jags of the road between the mountains. We entered a defile already shadowed by twilight. Directly beside the road, as we passed over an ancient humped bridge, we saw a crouched white figure in Moslem dress. We drew abreast and shuddered: As the thing raised its head, we saw that it was nearly faceless. Its nose and cheeks were eaten away by the horrid disease of leprosy, a running sore, yellow and black. The beggar held up a wooden bowl. Between teeth exposed in a lipless mouth, he whined: "Alms! Alms, for the love of God!"

The marquis snarled at the apparition, his huge horse shying off. Just behind him, Sieur Guilbert rasped out his sword in a motion quicker than my eye could see. The blade gleamed in the rays of the sun—if their armor was rusty, the Templars' blades were always greased and polished. The blade whirled downward. I gasped. The hand of the beggar seemed to leap into the air. The bowl clattered to the ground. From the stump of the wrist, twin jets of blood spurted like miniature fountains. Sieur Guilbert gave his whinnying laugh and snicked home his sword into his scabbard.

Maimonides uttered a cry of anguish, as if the deed had been done to him. He flung himself down from his mule, tearing loose his girdle. He knelt beside the prostrate moaning thing in its burnoose, tenderly holding its arm and winding it tightly to stop the deadly bleeding. I was amazed to see my son so changed that blood no longer daunted him. As astonishing was his reverence for life, no matter whose, always venerated as the manifestation of God and His divine works. Before I realized it, I was beside him.

Next moment I straightened up with a gasp. I felt a stabbing, unbearable pain in my back, in my ribs. From behind came the warning hollo of Brujo, the shouts of the squires, a stifled cry from Ramah echoed by Yaltah, sitting before her in the saddle. Zayd pounded past me on his sway-backed mount, hoofs brushing my robe. Maimonides, absorbed in his task, did not look up but I rose to my feet, swaying in agony.

What I saw banished my pain in a greater agony: fear of sudden death. Outlined in the sunlight of the dying day I saw once more that onslaught of strange men that had haunted my dreams since Cordova. Down the hillside, like a flow of dark evening mist, careened a half-dozen Moslem horsemen, their black robes flying behind them, riding like demons, as if they were part of the bodies of their slim-legged mounts. Never a cry nor a signal, only the clicking of hoofs on the rocks and the whuffled snorts of the horses. Above each one gleamed a silver halo, the circle of a brandished scimitar.

Before I realized it, a shower of stones, like hail driven horizontal to the ground, fell about us. I knew they were the rounded pebble-flints of slingers. It was one of these which had caught me so shrewd a blow in the side, expelling my breath, that for days I could only gasp painfully. I heard their whirring next to my ear and stooped low, but I could see whence they came. A trio of slingers stood silhouetted against the sky at the top of the hill. The blur of their whirling strips of leather was interrupted only by the rhythmic movement of their left hands into their pouches to secure new stones.

To my surprise, the marquis and Sieur Guilbert did not hesitate a moment. I heard the clash of visors flung down, the skreen of swords from their scabbards. The squires fewtered their lances and bowed for shelter behind their horses' necks, driving forward. Their masters jammed their reins in their visors, brandishing their great two-handed swords about their heads, urging their mounts with knee and spur into an uphill gallop, dead against the oncoming riders.

"Deus le vult!" they cried as one man. "God wills it! *Deus le vult!"* The squires echoed their cries. A moment later the issue was joined before my staring eyes.

As the knights encountered the first of the Moslem horsemen, the latter slipped aside with a deft movement of their bodies instantly obeyed by their chargers. As they did, Sieur Guilbert uttered a hoarse cry: "To the point! To the point!" His words rose above the rattle of the stones that jolted off their armor. The marquis appeared to understand. For the first time, I witnessed the extraordinary method of fighting ("foining," they call it) which was to become the secret *botte* of the Templars. Their big double-edged swords were not squared or blunt at the end, as was customary; they were lengthened to a long point. Their swinging about their heads was only a feint: Not once did they use the edge of their blades. Instead, with wondrous horsemanship which excelled that of the Moslems, they leaned far to one side of their fearless giant horses. With all the strength of their sinewy arms, they thrust home. Before I recognized what had happened, three of the Moslems—breasts gaping and flowing—writhed on the ground; the others turned and galloped away in the direction from which they had come.

The squires had not bothered to aid their masters—as if

they foreknew the outcome of the encounter. Instead, they had clambered directly up the side of the hill toward the slingers. Before their assault, the hail of stones ceased. The slingers melted in flight over the crest.

The ambush was done as quickly as it had begun. Suddenly, more shocking than the fight itself, stillness descended. The squires and knights held their places a moment, as if in tableau, then turned and came back to the path.

"My father," Maimonides said in a low, stricken voice, "this man is dead."

He had not risen. I doubt if he had seen anything of the fray; at least, in later years he avowed that he could not recall it. Despite my aching ribs, I knelt beside him. Maimonides was right. The pulse of the beggar had ceased to beat. His hideous flesh was cooling, his breath was still. He was now no more than a crumpled heap of stinking clothes and foulness. I rose slowly, Maimonides beside me; I scrubbed my hands with a handful of sand and motioned to him to do the same.

As I looked toward the knights, I swallowed hard. The marquis had dismounted. He methodically thrust his sword twice through the breast of each fallen Moslem. Then he turned and strode toward us, the squires sliding down beside him. He raised his maculated sword in both hands over the breast of the dead beggar.

"No," Maimonides said in a strangled voice. He flung up both hands in appeal. "He is dead, I swear it! Do not tear his body like a wild beast's! He has suffered enough in life; in death, let him be."

"He must not live!" cried the marquis in fury.

"He is dead!"

"I, too, will swear it," I said.

The marquis shook his head, his bony unhandsome face still twisted in the grimace of battle, his beard sprinkled with sweat. "I shall make sure," he grunted. Again he raised his sword for its downward stroke.

"Then know this, Marquis Armand," Maimonides said quickly. I gave a start at his commanding voice. "If you pierce the breast of this one, your sword will be fouled with the deadly curse of leprosy; you will carry the sickness in your scabbard. You will be a plague to your companions—and how will you swear and kiss your sword, how will you present it to your Order for blessing?"

Arrested in mid-stroke, the marquis looked up at Sieur Guilbert, who sat frowning in his chaired saddle. He gave a barely distinguishable shake of his head. Slowly the face of the marquis lost its ferocity. It reassumed its habitual frown. He sheathed his sword. "You say well," he said at last. He signaled for his mount and clumsily swung onto its back, gazing about him in a last stern reconnoiter.

"Zayd!" said Maimonides. "Where is Zayd?"

"And Brujo?" I added.

I glanced about, seeing that David sat transfixed where he had been at the commencement of the brief struggle. Behind him I saw Ramah and Yaltah, their faces shining with tears of apprehension. I opened my mouth to shout. As I did, a familiar bristling head popped up from behind a boulder, six cubits off. It was Brujo.

This apparition from nowhere, in the midst of the bloody field, momentarily deprived us of speech. Brujo came slowly forward, his uneasy rictus fading as he saw our faces.

"In the fray," I demanded, my voice shaking, "where were you?"

His eyes refused to meet mine. "Seeking help," he muttered.

"Behind the rock?" I said with fierce sarcasm.

"The One is our refuge in time of trouble," he dared to reply. "I was praying for your success."

"You are a knave, unfit to live," rasped the Marquis Armand suddenly in his harsh French. Fear in his face, Brujo twisted, turned about by the words. He sank to his knees, as if his legs had melted. Behind the marquis, Sieur Guilbert nodded to one of the squires. "We will not foul our swords," he said dryly. "Kill the dog with your dagger!"

Brujo uttered the moan of an abandoned animal. But I could not find it in myself to succor him who had deserted us in our hour of most need. I held my peace.

It was Maimonides who sprang between the advancing squire and Brujo. He spread his arms in a gesture of protection. "True," he said, "this one is a knave and a man whose bowels turn to water at a fight. But, sirs, so am I. It is a fault that a man cannot change without long endeavor, if he is born a craven."

"But you," said the marquis sternly, "even though you are a Jew and no man of war, you conducted yourself nobly."

"I am a Jew!" cried Brujo, sobbing uncontrollably. "I am a Jew!"

With disbelief in his face, the marquis glanced at me. "Is it true?"

110

I nodded slowly. "I have instructed him and he has accepted our faith," I said with difficulty.

"Do you wish him spared, young Maimonides?" demanded the marquis, already impatient with a task he deemed unimportant. "I warn you, he will be nothing to you but trouble. Better to leave his carcass to rot."

"I wish what I know my father wishes," Maimonides said. "I implore your clemency."

The marquis shrugged. He waved off the squire and his bared dagger, turning away with an air of inexpressible contempt. As he did, there was a totally unexpected interruption. Without warning, David flung himself from his mule. He sprang upon Brujo, beating him to the ground with his fists. "I shall kill him!" he shouted breathlessly. "Give me the dagger, I shall let his blood, the traitor!"

Before I could move, Maimonides, with that extraordinary strength he sometimes exhibited, seized David by the shoulders and thrust him aside. "Do not be a fool," he said coldly.

"He betrayed us!"

"He did no more than his fears drove him to do."

David faced Maimonides resolutely. "You shall not always have your way," he said bitterly.

Maimonides nodded calmly. "We shall see," he said. David turned away sullenly and remounted. Trembling, Brujo rose and sidled off to his own mule. For the rest of the journey, face sunken and eyes turning constantly in apprehension, he rode three lengths behind the party.

One more surprise still was destined to us. As we came to the next turn of the road, a tall dark figure appeared in our path. It was the Negro slave, Zayd. He held before him at arm's length a slighter figure, dangling like a plucked chicken, one of the Moslem slingers.

Zayd did not look at us at all. Instead, his gaze was directed toward the rigid face of Sieur Guilbert in an unspoken question. The knight nodded slightly. Zayd closed his enormous grip. With a shudder I heard the faint sickening snap as the neckbones broke. Zayd tossed the lifeless corpse aside. He calmly straddled his mule, which Brujo led; but he refused to ride beside him as he had before.

We had not bothered to bury the dead. I thought of demurring—not because of pity but because of disease such rotting flesh might spread—but I knew that our escorts would not permit it. Night was coming; there was always the possibility of another ambush or a raid of revenge. Somberly, we went on our way.

I write of this incident on our way to Toledo only because it bore evil fruit in the days to come. Evil, and good: for who can say what time and the will of God will not change as the years pass? I truly believe that the enmity of Sieur Guilbert to my son was born on that day, implacable to the end; then, too, perhaps the curious change in David. For on that occasion of slaughter, I realized his face shone like a light. The muscles of his body moved in rhythm with those of the striking Templars, his mouth curved about the same war cry, his frown and grimaces were the same. I observed this and said nothing to him; I did not want him to know what I had seen. It was later, that same night, that he came beside me as we rode onward and murmured ecstatically: "What great men these knights are, my father!"

"If you deem killing your fellows a great feat, they are indeed," I answered in a low voice. "But the evil eye, the evil principle, and hatred of mankind drive men out of the world, as the Rabbi Joshua has said."

"Was it not chivalrous of them to protect us?" he protested indignantly.

"That is so," I admitted.

"We should have been able to protect ourselves," David said, half to himself. I looked closely at him, feeling fingers of coldness creep into my bosom.

"What do you mean?" I demanded, kicking my mule closer to his.

"I am strong," he said. "My shoulders are broad. I also can carry armor and swing a sword, one day."

"You have not been taught to be a killer of men," I said sharply. David lowered his head. He rode for long moments in silence. Then he murmured, so that I could barely hear him:

"If one must kill or be killed," he said, "in such a case, is it not better to remain alive? How may one live a life worthy of God and man—if he is dead?"

"This is not the place nor the time to argue," I snapped at him and rode ahead.

If I had known that starlit night what I know now of his nature, I might have spoken to him more understandingly. But it was not to be. I was foolish and stupid, in pain with my swelling bruise, unable to see my son's iron fancy, which was to be tempered into reality. Indeed, that journey to Toledo changed our lives as they were not to be changed again for a long time.

Now that I look back on the seven years we spent in Toledo (as long as Jacob served for his Rachel), I have the uneasiness of a man recalling a bad dream. I am torn. I had no real love for that dark and solemn city, whose gates we entered a few days after the ambush of the leper. It seemed to me a place as stark and uncompromising as the granite rock on which it was founded. Currents of new and untried thought—of ideas that clawed the mind—flowed through its narrow streets like the icy, foaming Tagus River which flows around its base, waters in which the famous steel blades are quenched. In such a place the most fiery faith may be quenched as well. My fears for Maimonides multiplied.

Possibly because of this, Toledo for me had an air of unreality. It stalked the hours of my days. Life became distorted, like storm shadows at evening or morning. The people of the city seemed hunted things, devoured, prey to their own mad theories. I could not rid myself of the conviction that we labored in vain, nay, more, to our own destruction, in such a place. If Rachel bat Abor had been there, she might have reassured me; but, then, she was in Paris, as far away for all of me as if she were a woman in the moon.

If these thoughts disturbed me and darkened even the sunniest days, they had no such effect upon Maimonides. For him it seemed each dawn was a plunge into purest pleasure. But knowledge gnawed at his vitals; his liver grew pale even while he reveled in his books and lectures. His face became hollow and narrow, his nose thin and prominent. His chin jutted and his eyes took on an inward stare, dark and brooding. His figure seemed stooped from an invisible burden. For him, though he was courteous and affectionate, Yaltah and David and myself hardly existed; his mind seemed leagues away. He rarely slept except for a nap at the hot midday. He ate sparingly, his gaze always buried in one of the new codices which were taking the place of the old manuscripts and scrolls that I loved.

For me it was difficult to practice medicine in such an atmosphere. Many others did, but simply to satisfy an overwhelming, almost obscene curiosity, I felt, rather than to alleviate the ills of humanity. Kindness and good will somehow took second place to a great impersonal, merciless investigation of everything from fingernails to excrement. I commenced to feel the same weariness with my religion as with my pro-

113

fession. Perhaps Judah Halevi had felt this in Toledo too. I visited his family but was received coldly; they felt somehow that I had a share in the blame—blame which they justly threw upon his head for abandoning them to the charity of our Jewish community and setting out on his fantastic pilgrimage to Jerusalem. But perhaps Judah had gone to find again the true source of faith, the wellhead of Jerusalem, to renew his devotion.

Meanwhile, I discovered that the quantity of information and the eagerness of my people to be the first to absorb it submerged even their everyday duties. The congregations in the synagogues grew thin, the members secretly studying on the Sabbath. Appeals for justice often went beyond our local rabbis to the constituted authorities of the Moslems. More than the Koran, more than the holy Torah itself, it seemed, the works of a famous Moslem healer, Avicenna, were worshiped. The monstrous production of this dissolute genius—he was said to have dictated his monumental work, *The Canon*, to a half-dozen secretaries while caressing a prostitute and consuming a dozen bottles of unqualified wine—daunted me by its very existence, despite Rachel's admiration for him.

Be it said to the credit of Maimonides, he realized my dilemma in this strange city ruled by Christians yet tolerant of Jews and Moslems. He must have pitied me as I sought duties in the community of Jews or wandered in the small parks of Toledo. It was because of this feeling, I am sure, that he one day brought into my room—a luxurious apartment in the ornate Moorish style—a board composed of red and white squares, together with a handful of small ivory and ebony figures.

"My father," he said, "would this amuse you?"

"I do not seek amusement," I said stiffly. Maimonides paid no attention to my querulousness. He placed the board on a table and commenced to arrange the figures in two opposing files. "You have heard of this game," he told me, "but have you played it?"

"I do not know it."

"It is called chess."

"I have heard of it only as a waste of time."

"I confess it may seem so but it is at once a relaxation and an exercise for the mind."

"I seek diversion for the soul."

Maimonides went on as if he had not heard me: "Here are

114

twenty-four figures—kings and peasants, castles and knights, even priests."

"Could there not be rabbis?" I asked.

Maimonides gave me a half-smile. "Perhaps," he admitted. "But this is a game of Persian invention, played according to the rules of war."

"I do not care for war."

"This is more merciful. See, the object is not to slay the king but to force him into a corner, to render him impotent."

"That is what you have tried to do to your father," I said wearily.

Maimonides shot me an indescribable look, then resumed arranging the pieces. "Thus it is played," he pointed out. "Women of our own race played it first—never on the Sabbath, of course. Now men play it without reproach, though there is the danger of becoming so interested in the game that one might wager on the outcome."

"It will never enchant my mind to that degree."

"Let me at least explain the way the pieces move," Maimonides murmured. He demonstrated and, in spite of myself, my interest grew. I could see the application of its rules forming in my mind, even to the unusual hop-and-skip movement of the knight. But I refused to admit it. "I shall not play," I said decisively. "Still, leave the board and the men. The carving is admirable."

Maimonides bowed and left me. I contemplated the tiny figures. After a long moment, my fingers reached out and I made my first tentative move. My son had been right; it was a game worthy of the keenest mind.

As a matter of fact, I was indulging in a match with my own wits on the same board on an afternoon a week later when Maimonides reappeared. He saw my occupation (which I vainly tried to conceal) and laughed aloud, his rare mirth which I loved to hear. "I see you are a convert to the wicked ways of the heathen," he said.

"It is a child's game," I said pettishly, "and I prove nothing except my own childishness when I play."

"Then this may interest you more," Maimonides said, placing a scroll before me. "If you will grant me a request, my father, read this. A small composition of my own."

Not without qualms, I unrolled the parchment. I scanned the first lines. They gave me startled pause and I reread them aloud: " 'An eminent person, a chief judge who writes clearly and eloquently in Arabic, once asked a youth who had studied

115

the arts of logic to explain the language and meaning of the terms—and to do it as briefly as possible.' "

I looked up from the manuscript to the expectant face of Maimonides. I found myself envying his youthful tuft of reddish beard. I shook my head. "Who," I asked, "is this 'eminent person' who asked for this to be done?"

"You," Maimonides said, without moving a muscle.

"I?"

"Yes."

"I have no memory of asking you anything of the sort."

"It was a long time ago. Do you recall the night of our journey to Almería when you demanded what I knew of logic?"

I sighed. His words brought back piercing memories. I weighed the scroll in my fingers. "It is rather light for so weighty a subject," I said.

"Logic is not difficult."

"All this time, you have remembered my idle remark?"

"Yes."

"How many grudges you must hold against your old father!"

Maimonides said nothing. I sighed again. "This is my answer from a sixteen-year-old boy?"

"You have not read it, my father," Maimonides pointed out.

I felt put upon. I nodded. "Very well," I said coldly, "I shall read it when I have time. I am close upon an *eschec mat* in the chess game you so thoughtfully showed me." I put the scroll down beside my worn vellum copies of the Gemara and Mishnah that lay beside the chessboard. Maimonides' expression darkened and grew inscrutable. He bowed, leaving the room silently.

As soon as he had gone, I picked up the spindles of the script and spun it open. I read the first column eagerly: "The Art of Logic," indeed! I began to peruse it and almost instantly became enthralled. Fourteen chapters of what Judah might have called the purest river of living waters in prose. I was both delighted and confounded. It was short, simple, directly to the point—a very model of clarity but perhaps too condensed to be properly appreciated. I myself possess a flowing style of which I am proud. I feel it is not only appropriate but necessary, now and then, to let one's self go with a few ornate figures of speech. But here was natural writing, cut to the bare essentials, like the naked body of a child about to plunge into the cool waters of a hammadan.

" 'Zayd stands or does not stand, that is all. . . . Let us consider Zayd of Basra, residing in the house of 'Amr, who killed his son, Abu-Bekr of Egypt.' " I frowned. Why had Maimonides used the name of our slave, the Negro Zayd? But I read on, chapter after chapter, finding it a treatise that could be digested in an afternoon. At the end of each chapter Maimonides had noted the terms he explained—as few as four in the first, as many as twenty-five in the last, a hundred and seventy-five in all. Out of curiosity, I counted the words he had used in his remarkable economy: They amounted to less than a thousand to explain the whole art of thought.

Almost without my realizing, some of Maimonides' matter-of-fact statements settled deep into my mind:

"Self-government is acquiring good habits and removing evil ones."

"Habits are characteristics of the soul that show themselves in actions; then they are called vices or virtues."

"Household government is knowing how the members of the family should help each other so as to bring about the best possible improvement of their mutual condition."

"City government is the science of imparting to the citizens a knowledge of true happiness, showing them how to obtain it and how to avoid its opposite."

I rolled the manuscript together thoughtfully, one phrase ringing in my ears, filling my heart: "In these times we do not need the laws of old; for divine laws govern human conduct."

"Ah, my son, my son," I said aloud, "how little you know of the human animal and his ways! How he would rather wallow in the dung of his own bowels than stand clean and upright in the sight of God!"

"But this I do know," Maimonides' calm voice broke in. He had returned, a shadow in the doorway. I caught on his face another of those smiles I yearned to glimpse. "This is what I thought fit to discuss and perhaps, God willing, my work will fulfill its purpose."

"And its purpose?"

"To force those who read it to think well and deeply."

"How will you force them to read it at all?" I inquired.

Maimonides allowed himself the ghost of a smile. "There are ways," he said enigmatically. "I have used the name of Zayd as an example, as a reward for his loyalty. He cannot read except for that one word. He will think it magic to see his name on parchment and he will teach himself to read my book on logic to see what is written about him."

I cannot say with justice that Maimonides did not learn many precepts and habits useful to our way of life. I had already observed with pleasure that the sight of blood no longer turned his stomach. He persisted in his love for philosophy, however, despite what I believed to be an appetite for medicine in him. He was barred from the dissection of animals by our faith, since only the entrails of swine were used. He disliked the lectures where one professor read, another—or a barber-surgeon—cut up an animal, and a third held up the inner organs as the lecturer droned. He felt the need to see more, to ask questions, to be a participant in the discoveries.

He roamed the shops in search of natural remedies, dissatisfied that man should have to maim man in order to effect cures. He believed that health might be restored by herbs and simples. Often I accompanied him to the apothecary's shops where the jowled proprietor sat cross-legged in the midst of his curious odors, surrounded by jars filled with wormwood, cardamon, hemlock, costus, castoreum, antimony, agaric, henna, bugloss, cinnamon, borage, acanthus, and like mixtures —perhaps even a clear glass jar of the brown mummy-juice which was so expensive, used to stanch severe bleeding. Often Maimonides tried his own hand at mixing small quantities of various concoctions. He sometimes tested them himself and would be pale and nauseated for a day or two. Occasionally I was persuaded, out of sheer boredom, to join him, in such an experiment. I can testify personally to his failure to produce anything but the most horrific smells and stomach-turning messes: the taste of some of his mixtures remains alive on my tongue at this very moment.

At last, in the sixth year of our stay, he disappeared altogether from the house for three days. I grew frantic with the thought that he had fallen into harm. But he reappeared, filled with enthusiasm, thinner than ever—with a glowing eye and bubbling with a new ambition. He dragged me out into the streets.

"Where are we going?" I demanded, resisting his strength.

"I shall show you," he replied, "if you keep silent. It will be an experience you shall never forget. But you must not be seen nor heard."

"I refuse!" I cried—but I was still protesting when he hauled me around a corner and into a small marble archway next to a mosque. Passing through a hallway decorated with gilt scribblings in Arabic, we came to a screened passage. Here I was stationed by Maimonides. "Be quiet and watch," he whispered in my ear. "You shall see a miracle wrought."

He vanished. I, my curiosity piqued, peered through the interstices of the screen to the other room. It was a small place, bare and swept, possibly an anteroom to the mosque. It contained no furniture except a single bare table with a shining white marble top.

I had not long to wait. From an opposite door came a tall elderly man, apparently a Moslem, with a handsome face and long white beard. Stooped in the shoulders, he walked with an air of unmistakable command. His gown was white, plain, without decoration. Directly behind him, with all the signs of reverence, came Maimonides.

"You realize, my young friend," said the stately old man, tying back his long beard as he addressed my son, "that there is considerable danger in this?"

"I understand," Maimonides said. "But I have faith in you."

The other made a clucking irritable noise. "Of course," he told him. "There is nothing new here, I have completed similar tasks a dozen times. The danger is from the relatives. If anything goes wrong—and this, my boy, is a gambler's life— I fear the relatives and the law."

"We can only do our best."

"Yes. We must for the sake of the woman, for the sake of my profession. All the same, my first order to you as assistant is to have a pair of litters, with fast-paced slaves, at the rear door, ready to leave at a moment's notice."

Maimonides hesitated, then bowed and turned away. Muttering, the man examined the room closely, moving from corner to corner. He was still occupied with this minute scrutiny when Maimonides returned. "It is done," he said.

"Good. Is everything prepared? Instruments, linen, the oil lamps?"

"I will have them brought in."

"Touch nothing except with the scorched cloths."

"I shall see to it. I have also had drawings made of the Greek and Roman way of stopping the flow of blood and sewing up the wounds made by the knife."

"So much was not necessary," responded the elder man. "I have those engraved in the very stuff of my brain."

I thought him highly irritable but my interest was high. I held my peace and watched. In a moment, four men carried in an obscenely fat woman, already asleep and snoring with

119

loud, sluggish sounds. They stretched her supine on the marble table.

"Filthy, filthy," said the older man disgustedly. He motioned them out abruptly and beckoned to Maimonides. My son and he went to a basin brought by a fifth man and washed their hands with powder and water. They took off their robes and slaves replaced them with white linen tunics. A smaller table, covered with unusual instruments, was brought in. Maimonides approached the woman, felt her wrist-beat, opened her eyelids and peered at them for a few moments as his mentor grunted approval. Then Maimonides carefully parted her dress and exposed the belly of the woman, showing a huge whitened abdominal swelling with a reddish rim, like some strange awful egg.

"Now," said the older man. He took up a knife from the smaller table, dipped it in a blue liquid, and made a deft sweeping stroke across the bulge on her stomach. The skin split back; he made a following series of small but extremely precise cuts. The whole mass was laid bare. I was amazed not to see blood come until Maimonides murmured: "The drugs in the potion worked very well."

"Do not speak again," his companion said curtly. The patient stirred. Maimonides seized her, pinning her to the table. In response to a gesture from the older man, he whipped off his sash, tying her hands. The elderly man himself sprang to hold down her feet.

Before my eyes, the monstrous mass in the woman's belly seemed to be moving, swelling up like yeast in a trough. Delivered from its sac of skin, it now sought to escape entirely. "Observe," the older man said hoarsely, "it is attached to the uterus. Have you studied this?"

"We shall have to call for aid," Maimonides said, his face white.

The other nodded. Maimonides gave a sharp cry. Through the door waddled a disheveled old hag. She started for the basin but Maimonides called her back. "There is no time to wash," he said tensely. The midwife wambled across to the old surgeon, mopping his face and eyes with a cloth. As he re-examined the patient, she climbed up and lay face-down across the patient's feet, holding her rigid.

"We shall clamp off the tubes, cut the sinews, and remove all," the older man said decisively. "There is no other way." His eyes flicked at Maimonides. "These are decisions that we physicians must make at a moment like this. For good or ill."

He commenced to work with a delicacy like that of the finest jewel-carver. I concentrated on his work with such intensity that I could not believe more than seconds had gone by when he finally straightened up with a mock groan. All had been cut free; the blood vessels had been tied, the wound sutured with the split catgut of which Albucasis had spoken. The snoring woman, except for a great red scar down her belly, looked human once more.

"Do you know," said the man, undoing the knot of his beard behind his neck and pulling it forward, "what I have found the weakest part of a good surgeon to be?"

Maimonides, checking the pulse and the eyes of the sick woman, shook his head. His companion smiled. "His back," he said; rubbing it, he moved slowly across to the basin to wash his hands once more. Maimonides nodded to himself. His color was returning as he carefully dropped a cloth across the woman's abdomen; her breathing was easier, I realized, now that the massive impediment to the action of her lungs and blood flow had been removed.

Wiping his hands, the older doctor returned. He smiled sardonically at Maimonides. "Will she live?" he inquired. "Or shall we mount the litters in haste?"

"She will live," Maimonides said in a small shaky voice.

The other man nodded. He put his hand on my son's shoulder. "Then I shall confess to you," he said, "that this is the first time I have ever done such an operation. How shall we name it?"

"The first time!" cried Maimonides. In my screened niche, I silently echoed his words of amazement.

The surgeon nodded. "That is not the question," he said peevishly. "What shall we call the operation for future generations, eh?"

Maimonides controlled himself. He cast about in thought. "Let us credit the Greeks," he said at last. "Since you have removed her womb to save her life, let it be known as a *hysterectomy*."

The elder physician nodded with gravity. "So be it," he said. "This is as much the work of heaven as mine. It was ordained that she should live, that we should be the tools of a higher power."

Cramped from my long wait, I rose as best I could. I could hold back no longer. I emerged and made my way across the room. I salaamed to the bearded man, who regarded me with

121

surprise. "I am eternally grateful to you," I said, "now that I have seen a miracle of surgery."

"Who is this man?" he demanded of Maimonides. Maimonides flushed; behind him the four men had re-entered at the signal of the midwife and were removing the still-snoring woman.

"He is my father, Maimon ben Joseph," Maimonides said. He turned to me. "My father, this is the famous Avenzoar, one of my teachers."

Sparks of anger seemed to fly from the older man's eyes. "Did you dare," he sputtered to Maimonides, "to bring a stranger to spy upon such a delicate affair as this?"

"But I have heard of you," I interposed. "Great Avenzoar, you are a Jew and I am a Jew. I know that you were born in Cordova, where I was born. I know your fame and I—I am a physician myself."

My boldness took him aback. His face changed, shifted, from doubt to interest and then to amusement. He laughed without warning, his high-pitched mirth rattling in the room as the slaves behind carried out the tables and removed all traces of the operation.

"I must charge you a fee for your education," he said, wiping his eyes with his robe.

"I should be glad to pay it."

"No, no, it is only a jest! Between healers, there is no thought of charge. Was it interesting to you?"

"I thought it was magnificent!"

"You should have brought your father closer to the table," Avenzoar said to Maimonides in grave reproof. Maimonides bowed silently. Avenzoar chuckled, his good humor entirely restored. Suddenly he thrust out a long bony finger and poked my middle. He pursed his lips and shook his head. "My friend," he said to me, "we of the profession find it hard to diagnose ourselves. But let me warn you, a young concubine and a clever cook are the greatest dangers to men of our age."

Before I could protest that I had neither, he had begun his rising giggle of laughter and turned to go out, still chortling as I heard him make his way down the corridor.

Even this happy encounter—and I had the delight of meeting and talking to Avenzoar many times before his death two years later—did not serve to disperse my melancholy as Maimonides had hoped. He offered no reproof for my brashness in entering the room—but he knew I was no surgeon such as this man, merely a simple adviser of remedies. My thoughts

122

upon my own inadequacies depressed me further; I determined to engage in some vocation which would busy my hands and tire my brain.

So it was that in Toledo I turned to the education of David as I once had devoted myself to that of Maimonides. I was determined that if one son had made his way out of the fold, the second should not. Using the remnants of the treasure we had brought from Cordova and Almería, David and I found a common interest in a small business of buying and selling precious stones.

To speak the truth, it was a trade which had always fascinated me. I had ridiculed David's hobby of collecting rare stones from the rocky Spanish landscape, but secretly I had envied him. It may be that he had inherited a love for the glinting colored light caught in polished hardness. For my own part I had a very small (as was fitting for a rabbi) but excellent (as was fitting for a man of taste) collection of the queer old cylinders from Babylon with their angular stooklike figures, some from Assyria and Persia with winged lions, palms, chariots, and high-crowned figures. Rarest of all, and most cherished, were the delicate Greek seals in jasper, obsidian, and crystal.

I consoled myself with the sensuous pleasure of rubbing their smooth surfaces, with watching the infinitely varied play of light from the gravings and the depths of the stones. Had not the elders of my own race proved their appreciation of such things? Was not the breastplate of the high priest at beloved Jerusalem—before the Ark, the seven-branched candelabra, and shewtable—composed of twelve varieties of precious stone? I could call them off from memory: sardonyx, topaz, and emerald; carbuncle, sapphire, and jasper; ligure, agate, and amethyst; chrysolite, beryl, and onyx. Was not the sin of Judah written with the point of a diamond? Did not Daniel and Joseph carry the signet rings of the greatest monarchs of the known world of their day?

Yet, through this sheen of romance, I also knew the practical side of the business. I had the art of testing the hardness of a gem by drawing a sharp edge across quartz, then topaz, and finally diamond, to see which it would scratch. The clearness of pure water was familiar to me as a mark of excellence; so, too, the brilliancy achieved by the careful splitting and polishing of small faces on selected stones to reflect the inner fire. I knew that the judicious application of flame to dark yellow topaz would turn it pink and to blue quartz would turn it yellow.

And—perhaps most important of all in selling such stones —I was acquainted with all their qualities in the minds of the superstitious. Rubies were supposed to stop bleeding, green jasper guaranteed fertility, the purple of amethyst was a preventive of drunkenness, to mention only a few. Never did I propose that such gems actually possessed such magical properties—nay, I denied it to such as would listen—but it was an aid, all the same.

Finally, I knew how to cut by cleavage, how to grind by water and quartz-sand taken from a river, how to detect cheats made by dyeing the back of a stone set in a ring; I knew the many ways to create the masculine dark color from the light feminine; I could easily spy out (with the aid of a Moslem enlarging glass) the double and triple frauds concocted by cementing stones together with clear hoof-glue. Thus I was not unprepared to enter upon such an association nor to tutor David in what I knew.

In our sixth year at Toledo, I hired a small shop in the Court of Jewelers and laid in a stock of stones. MAIMON & SON read our sign under the device of a huge painted diamond. David and I went to work there daily, polishing and grinding, setting and cleaving, bargaining and chaffering.

At first David appeared wholly devoted to the work. I rejoiced that I had discovered his inclination. I had visions of his becoming the most famous dealer in precious gems that the world would know. I laid plans for the future. Even Toledo commenced to seem rosy, as if seen through the glass of a fine feminine ruby.

Then, even as Maimonides had done, David disappeared for nearly a week. Heart heavy, I kept the shop and looked for his return as I had hoped for that of Maimonides. At last he came back, without a word as to where he had spent his days. Nor did my pride allow me to ask him. A few days and he disappeared again. It was only after a fortnight more that I discovered the shocking truth about his absences.

CHAPTER 8

Quintains high, quintains low, all planted in procession for men to practice killing one another. These scare-battle posts of the Templars stood rotted in a wide, barepacked clay field near their priory inside the north wall of Toledo. Here every day one could see tilting and jousting, swordplay and lance-work, by these men with faces of granite and thonged muscles.

In my walks about the city by night and day, I occasionally passed by this famous field. The urchins of the city—Moslem and Christian alike—gathered at dawn after the first prayers of the Templars to stare wide-eyed at these champions hacking away at wood instead of flesh. Posts sunk into the ground with boards pegged to them, daubed with figures of enemies —sometimes Moslems, sometimes caricatures of savages or members of other orders—the quintains held a fascination for children and knights. Bright reds and blues predominated in the painted faces. Some of these wooden warriors extended lath swords; others held out pole lances. Each concealed a secret penalty for misstrokes. If the mock blow strayed from the mid-line of the figure, forehead to crotch, the blow itself made the board revolve. A bag of water doused the unlucky man, or a flat paddle whacked him on the rump, or a swing-ing sack of sand hurtled round and thumped him on the back of the neck.

Such a show provided entertainment daily, all day, bringing cheers and laughter from the crowds which squatted around the boundaries until the sharp black shadows of the wall above indicated it was time to quit. I wondered why the Templars did not perform their practice inside the priory walls—until I saw the savage dexterity of their strokes. Often this ferocity hewed down a post as thick as my leg in a half-dozen blows without quintain penalty. I knew then that this was a necessary part of their program: Their exercise within view of others was simply to awe the onlookers with their prowess. Their reputation alone was to win many a battle.

For most, perhaps, it was the finest show in Toledo. Not to one who, like myself, had seen the Templars and their ruthless ways of fighting. When I passed their exercise grounds, I hurried my walk, averting my eyes. It is not pleasant to think that man prepares so deliberately to kill other men.

Yet shortly after David had disappeared, I found myself aimlessly roaming the streets to look for him. I stopped at this very spot. It was a hot afternoon. I moved under the shade of a gigantic spreading ilex gnarl-rooted in the rocks and soil. I had heard a voice I recognized, the high shrill sibilants of Sieur Guilbert de Bayonne, long since freed from his vow to escort us to Toledo. I squinted against the sunlight. Across the grounds, I could see the same brawny man in leather undress, soaked with dark patches of sweat. He exhorted a young man whose face I could not see. Bare to the waist, his sinews coiling like serpents, the pupil thrust and cut and lunged.

"Coupez, coupez!" Sieur Guilbert cried in his penetrating tone. "Slash, slash!" His pupil obediently followed orders. The splinters flew like snow.

"Featly foined!" he exclaimed as his protégé thrust into the soft pine, wrenching out his point again without apparent effort.

"En reverso!" Sieur Guilbert cried. "The other edge!"

The shoulders of the youth heaved. He halted the swing of his blade in mid-stroke and directed a powerful backhand blow at the quintain. Unhappily, his aim this time was less accurate than it had been previously. The painted scowl of the Moslem figure vanished. The quintain swung about with a shriek of rusty iron. A sack of sand from nowhere dealt a stunning blow to the nape of the youngster's neck. He stumbled forward. He sprawled prone at full length. He lay inert while Sieur Guilbert straddled him, holding his sides, throwing back his head to bray with laughter.

At last the fallen youth recovered from the stunning blow. He stirred and rolled over. He pushed himself up to sitting position, a slight dazed smile on his handsome bloodless face. With a deathly chill I recognized him: I had come to the end of my search. The tilter at the quintain was no other than my own son, David.

Slowly, as if drunken, I turned away, slinking behind the hooting, laughing crowd to hide myself and my disgrace. I had no desire to acknowledge kinship with David in such a place. A vast emptiness, such as I had not endured since the

126

death of Naomi, filled me. My inner emotions mingled painfully—disgust, perhaps pride and fear, filled me; for the first
time my soul could not comprehend my own flesh and blood.
Truly Maimonides and myself had often argued, used hard
words, even parted in anger, but we had always known that at
heart we were one, on common ground. If our fashion was
not the same, if youth and age did not agree, still we were not
different in our goals. And a man, as the Talmud says, may
approach his vision of paradise by many paths, though there is
only one gate. And, as Nahum said, if a man does not judge
himself, all things will judge him.

But here—before my eyes—I had seen David using the
great sword of the Templars, under the instructions of a
knight whose heart I knew was as adamant. Heavier and
heavier became my meditations. I know not when I reached
Rachel's house and stumbled up to my room. The shock had
left me trembling; I huddled in a corner of my apartment. If
I had been afraid of the heretical studies of Maimonides, how
much more had I to fear in the activities of David which he
had deliberately concealed from my knowledge!

Nor could I, through a perverse loyalty to my younger son,
tell Maimonides aught of what had happened. At the evening meal, and again for the whole of the next day, I felt his
eyes constantly upon me, striving to strike through my silence
and downcast face. I could not stir my tongue to betray (and
I thought it no less) his brother. Once and again Maimonides
inquired if I were ill; I dismissed him with an abrupt word,
returning to my room to lie awake as I had the night before.
I contemplated the shifting stars through the window, remembering the constellations themselves were in the figures of
Greek warriors.

David returned on the third day. He accompanied me to
our stall. He was uncommunicative beyond his wont, looking
at me now and then as if he suspected me of knowing the
truth. But I paid him little attention. I asked no questions and
conducted myself gaily—enough so that I sold a gem sapphire
for less than half its cost to a rejoicing Moslem merchant.
I was exhausted by the end of the day. I went homeward
through the dying colors of sunset with David at my side, as
if I were with a stranger.

The meal was plain, without garnish: fruit, bread, meat, and
wine. Brujo served us without a word. The night darkened
outside and the moon rose behind the witchlike towers of
Toledo. I sat where I was. I determined not to rise before

David spoke, knowing that he could not leave until I gave permission. He fumbled the crumbs of his loaf between his fingers, rolling them into balls, flipping them into his mouth. At last he said: "Have I your leave to go, my father?"

"No," I said.

"We have been lonely without you," Maimonides said.

"And have you always been seated here, every night, with our father?" inquired David bitingly.

"No," Maimonides returned. "But my hours, day and night, were devoted to learning."

"As are mine," David said abruptly. He seemed to make up his mind. He swung about on his stool to face me. "My father," he said determinedly, "I have a confession to make."

"I am ready to listen, my son," I told him.

He hesitated. In the distance I heard one of those lugubrious chants which the Christians raised in their ceremonies. I shuddered. But what I heard was not what I expected. Surprising as it was, I consider that I met it with equanimity.

"I wish to marry," David told me abruptly.

I stiffened, then relaxed and shrugged, lifting my eyes to his. "It is a holy ambition," I said, "but you are very young."

David flushed. "Many have been married younger than I," he protested, "and our people are scattered. If not now, I shall never marry!"

"According to the Talmud, a man first learns the Torah and then marries," Maimonides said. "It is written that a girl must be past twenty and say 'I love you' before it is right to betroth her."

David paid no attention to his brother. He kept his eyes riveted on me. "You yourself have been watching for a husband for Yaltah and she is not yet twelve," he accused me.

"That is true. But she is a girl. The persecution of our race is more frequent every day. It may be that the portion of our goods I have reserved for her dowry will be dissipated, and she may remain forever unmarried."

"Is it not true that the laws of the Torah were made for the times?" demanded David. "Are we to be broken by their weight?"

"It is said that it is good to be married before eighteen," Maimonides interposed.

David turned on him. "Will you keep silent with your droning of laws and sayings? You speak on both sides of a question, quote equal authorities, and expect others to make up their minds while you smugly sit back and fold your hands!

128

You—you who are now twenty-two! You who are without wife or family, as is commanded! You—you who are without anything but a musty mind filled like an attic with forgotten books and stupid quotations!"

Maimonides' face grew pale. I hastened to speak. "You have no right to address your elder brother in such a fashion," I said. "He is doing his best to aid you."

"If he is, it's not much," David muttered.

"Whom do you wish to marry?" I inquired.

David lifted his face, his features shining as if the lamplight daubed them with gold. His eyes glistened, the lines of his cheeks and mouth turned upward. I felt my heart melt and flow toward him.

"My father," he said softly, "do you recall a girl who came to our stall in the Court of Jewelers six months and four days ago?"

"No."

"You must!"

"We have had many clients, David," I told him reasonably. "How should I recall one from another? Did she make a large purchase?"

"She made none at all."

"But she returned many times?"

"She never came back."

I made a gesture of impatience. "Then how should I know anything at all of her?" I demanded.

"You should," David said, "for she will be my wife."

I glanced at the impassive Maimonides. "Why are you so sure?" I asked David.

"My heart will admit no one else."

"Tell us," Maimonides said gently, "how she looks."

David turned to him, glowing ecstatically. "Muni," he said, "she is an angel on earth!"

"Seraph or cherub?" asked Maimonides politely.

David slammed his hand angrily down upon the table and stood up. "Sit," I said. He seated himself again, breathing hard. I tried to restrain my own resentment but I had no success. "Your brother means nothing but pleasantry," I told him. "You are the one to blame for your neglect of your family. How can I tell you the hours I have wept over you and your absence? You leave our house and our business without a word of explanation—then come home to tell us your desire to marry! Is this the proper conduct for a younger son?"

David looked straight ahead. "I wish to marry," he said levelly. "Her name is noble. She is hight Demoiselle Madeleine de Lys."

" 'Hight'?" inquired Maimonides. "Is that the word?"

"It is the knightly word!" David cried.

This news rendered me speechless. Before I could utter a syllable, David had gone on. "She has eyes as dark as night, as pools with the stars shining on them," he said rapturously, his anger vanished. "Her hair is the color of a raven, with tiny blue lights in lamplight. Her figure is ravishing, her body moving as if it knew a secret dance. Her throat is like snow, her bosom is as full as—"

"Stop, stop!" Maimonides said, raising his hands. "So far it is the custom to go but no farther. We wish to know nothing of these detailed, intimate lover's rhapsodies."

"Her feet are so tiny I can hold them both in one hand," David said sullenly.

"She is not a maiden like the one before the king in the Song of Songs," I said, steadying my voice. "With a name like that."

"Her name is divine!"

"Of what family is she?"

"She is one of the noble De Lys."

"She is a Christian," Maimonides said, "and a Frank."

"I love her," David said. He rose again slowly and looked around him, challenging Maimonides and myself, defying us.

"This is the talk of folly!" I burst out.

"My father," Maimonides said, "there is nothing in our faith to forbid marriage with another race. The great-grandmother of King David, blessed be he, was such."

"I did not know that," David said. "But it is she I will marry. No one else, though I die as I am."

"Will she turn to the true faith?" I inquired anxiously.

"In time perhaps. But I shall not persuade her against her will."

"My father—" Maimonides began.

I cut him short: "Keep your peace! David, that is not enough. You will have children, you have the most ancient lineage of our kind."

"For the time it must be enough," David responded. "It will be hard enough to win her as it is."

"What do you mean?" Maimonides asked.

David sat down again, his fist on his chin, his eyes with a hidden fire. "I have deceived you," he said quietly.

"I know."

"What do you know?" David roused himself to stare at me.

"I have seen you in the field, quarreling madly with those wooden dolls that are so chivalrously hacked," I said contemptuously.

"I had no thought you would spy on me," David said.

"It was chance, no more!" I shouted. "If anyone had told me of these heathen doings of my son, I should have cursed him with the curse of all curses! But I saw it as I passed, and came home in my disgrace! What have I done to serve God so badly as to deserve such a son?"

"David," Maimonides said, "our father has asked the same question of heaven about me many times."

"Know then," David said, a slight quiver in his voice, "that the exercises you condemn so loudly are what must be done to win the glory of her hand. And, I shall not lie, they are pleasant to me. Sieur Guilbert is willing, out of chivalry, to instruct me."

"Aye," I muttered, "willing to do it to put me to shame."

"Why must you pass through such an ordeal?" inquired Maimonides of David. Of the three of us, Maimonides alone appeared to be thoughtful, collected, in his mood.

"There are others who love her," David said heavily. "Others who can no more resist her beauty, her lips, her cheeks and her grace, than can I."

"But you are the favored?"

"Not so. There is a Christian also, a squire two years my senior, Noel de Rivière."

"You hope to win her love by your gallant exhibitions?" I demanded.

"I shall fight for her!" David cried. "I shall take her over his dead body!" He struck the table once more and strode from the room without my permission. I sat stunned in my place, blinking dazedly at Maimonides.

My elder son looked long at his fingers spread upon the polished oak; reflectively, he cracked his knuckles one by one. At last he spoke: "There is more to this than David realizes," he said.

"I know," I returned, "but we must hope that it is but the whim of a boy, that he will recover his senses."

Maimonides shook his head. "No, his mind is set," he responded. "He will not change. He spoke the truth to us—but he does not see far enough."

Such was David's cunning with his concubine, that there was no hope—and I hoped there never would be—of meeting her. Still, as it happened, I encountered her in no other place than the upper chamber of Rachel's home.

The meeting was by chance, in my favorite room in this fragile dwelling which, outside, exhibited the ornate carving, delicate arches and pillars, all the types of lightly rising architecture the Moslems had introduced into Spain. Inside, in the upper room, the atmosphere and furnishings were as I knew them from years before, comfortable, with all possible color and dignity. A portrait of Rachel stood against the wall, a crude mural done in fixed chalks; flowers in water were everywhere, though, usually, Jews plucked them only for the Sabbath. A bronze clock with the steady drip of watered time was there; so, too, candlesticks of brass and silver, gold and silver ornaments, painted platters of wood and clay, table covers worked with golden birds and fishes, wall inscriptions in gilt of holy words from the Torah, couches of leather and cloth, chairs of carved wood and ivory, rugs of wool.

Next to this room was Rachel's library, in which I browsed for pleasurable hours, reveling in her scrolls and tablets. It was in her room that I read; it was here, as both Maimonides and David knew, I spent my leisure hours.

One day, to my amazement, I found my lair already occupied. I was forewarned by the buzz of voices I heard, one raised in anger. But all sound ceased when I entered. Three figures—robed Maimonides, David in his leather cotehardie, and a young woman just under medium height—turned to me as I entered. The tableau poised itself in time, as if I were a magician who had turned them to stone. I realized instantly that the girl could be no other than David's love.

She was, as David had said, an enchanting girl. Her hair was long and black to her shoulders, uncovered except by a gold-spotted veil. Her face round, the cheeks flushed high, eyes large and dark; her forehead high and white, yet her nose short, the one feature I deplored. Her skin was flawless. She knew it well, wearing a low-cut, tight-laced scarlet bodice to draw up her young breasts. Her full white skirt fell to the ground, but her long draped sleeves were knotted to keep them from the mud. Her small feet, in red pointed boots, moved restlessly. Her air was both haughty and uneasy. I noted that she wore brooches and rings and necklaces of gold as if they were of little worth.

"Demoiselle de Lys," David said uncomfortably, "this is

132

my father." He made a ceremonious bow. I clasped my hands across my breast and bowed my head. For her part, she did not move except to lower her eyelids. David saw her embarrassment.

"We must go," he said to me. "Have we permission?"

Silently, I nodded. Without a word, she swept past me. David followed, carefully shutting the door behind them. I turned to Maimonides.

"I heard your voices raised in contention," I said cautiously.

"Not mine," Maimonides said briefly.

"Then David's?"

"I was doing my duty as his brother. I spoke to him of the unsuitableness of his passion."

"Praise to God, blessed be He!" I ejaculated.

"He refused to be convinced," Maimonides said ironically. "He has become a gentle Jewish knight."

"Would he marry her as he said?" I asked incredulously.

Maimonides nodded. "I have done nothing but settle him in his purpose," he told me, "but I am not sure she herself will be his, as he thinks."

"It is impossible!"

"Remember," Maimonides said, "that marriage of your sons is not a sin, my father. As many go to the sea and face its dangers, coming back alive and full of spirit and wealth, so do many adventure on the sea of marriage. Most of them prosper; only a few are lost."

"Once I was wrecked," I said meaningfully.

Maimonides nodded. "It was the same with the son of our ancestor, Judah the Prince, may his memory live."

"I do not recall it."

"When he returned from a long absence he found his wife aged and desired to take another. His father spoke against the divorce and ordered him to pray. By divine intervention, the youth of his first spouse was restored."

"Alas, such happy days are gone!" I said bitterly. I spoke the words of the Talmud: " 'When a man's wife dies, a man's world is darkened, his step is slow, his mind is heavy: She dies in him, he in her.' I have died a long death since that night in Cordova."

"Yet Rachel has lightened it for you, has she not?" Maimonides inquired. I raised my head only in time to see him softly exit from the room; he had learned the trick of a pert answer and absenting himself to avoid a reply. Yet, had he stayed, I am not sure that I could have replied honestly.

Two scrolls lay open upon the reading mat. I knelt to see what they were. To my surprise, one was that supreme verse from the lyre of King David, singing of his woman:

> Arise, my love, my fair one, and come away:
> O my dove, thou art in the clefts of the rock, in the
> secret places of the stairs,
> Let me see they countenance, let me hear thy voice;
> For sweet is thy voice and thy countenance is comely:
> My beloved is mine and I am hers:
> She feedeth her flock among the lilies,
> Until the day break and the shadows flee away.

I can never read such verses unmoved. Now, in my condition of hope and fear, they affected me strongly. I turned quickly to the other manuscript and found that the moisture in my eyes dried as I read. It was the code of laws common to the famous Courts of Love of the Christians, full of abominations:

> Marriage is not a justifiable excuse for refusing love.

> He who cannot keep a secret does not know how to love.

> A true love longs for the embraces of the loved one only.

> Too easy a success in love loses its charm; difficulties make it precious.

> Dreaming on his love robs the lover both of appetite and sleep.

> A true love is haunted by the image of the loved one forever.

> A lover finds no pleasure except in that which pleases the loved one.

> Love can deny love nothing.

My breath stopped in shock. The first scroll was from Rachel's collection, one of the few not devoted to the study of medicine. The other—and I could not mistake it—was copied in David's childish backward scrawl. If indeed his soul and mind were those of a Jew, his heart was entirely Christian.

My anguished meditation was disturbed by the sound of footfalls behind me. I turned, anticipating the newcomer. I

134

was not mistaken. David had returned; he stood before me. I offered him the bit of parchment with the code of love.

"This is yours," I said caustically. "You should not be careless with the rituals of the small gods you worship."

He merely nodded and accepted the scroll. "Yes," he said, "it is mine." He regarded me with a look full of meaning.

"They are both mine," he said. "There is no man who does not worship, openly or secretly, at the shrine of some woman; is that not so, my father?"

I had no answer for him. David confronted me.

"Do you believe I am wrong to marry her?"

"Will she have you?" I muttered.

"Yes. She has sworn it."

"There is much against it. You endanger us, the whole community of the Jews, by such a marriage."

"The son of Count Berenger was the lover of a Narbonnese Jewess! Even now, Alfonso, the king, is so infatuated with his Jewish mistress—mark this, my father!—that he is accused of neglecting all his kingly duties!"

"These are lovers and mistresses, not wives—and these are Christians wooing Jewesses. You are a Jew wooing a Christian woman."

"I do not see your point," David said stubbornly.

"You will," I sighed, "you will."

"You do not object beyond this? You have not spoken of children."

I shook my head. "It is written, even more charitably, that 'the offspring of a Jew who marries a wife not of the Jewish race but who is a woman of good heart and modesty and charity, must be preferred to the children of a Jewess by birth who lacks those qualities.'"

I appeared to have confirmed his decision. David nodded as if he had heard an unspoken word. He said, "In four days, at dawn, I am to meet the squire, Noel de Rivière, at the tilting-grounds. Sieur Guilbert is to be marshal of the lists. We are to prove on each other's bodies which is the better man for love of the Demoiselle de Lys."

As David said, so it was. In those times—though it is interdicted now—there was no restriction, no difference, between Christians and Jews in battle. Jews could carry arms and use them, nay, became famous at the art; their right to trial by combat was recognized as readily as that of any other human being. And in the depths of my heart I wished that it had

135

never been so. The duel for the fair was a mad superstition, derived from the belief of the German barbarians that there exists an appeal from common sense to God, that the brave not only will win, but alone deserve to win, the prize. Even the Christian church had declared it just and legal for hundreds of years. I thought of it as no more than detestable, an invention of the devil himself to bring about the destruction of a young soul together with the bloody death of a young body.

In the dawn of that cursed day, Maimonides and I sat shivering under the same oak from which I had first seen David at practice. The evening before—weeks after his first confession—David had told me what he had learned of the art of being an idiot at arms. Tilting astride a great horse, lance in right hand, shield on the left to defend against an opponent who must come from that direction, spear fewtered under the neck of the horse, avoiding the humble sweeping blow, directing the point toward the helmet visor-bars of a foe. "If you yourself engage in such an affair," he had told me with his faint inimitable smile, "do not forget to ride loosely with lance easy and balanced. The second before you strike home, squeeze the flanks with your knees, brace the lance, rise forward in your seat whilst you hug your elbow to your side. And trust your aim may be true and his go astray." He had shown me a heap of borrowed armor, convex on the breastplate to allow the spear to glance aside; the shield, concave in the center to hold and toss over the other's spear.

Nor was this all. David declared he had learned the use of the sword, both blade and point; he had become an expert in archery, always a passion with our race. My heart swelled to hear it. Had not Nimrod and Esau been mighty hunters; had not Herod, the king of the Jews, once slain forty wild beasts in a day with lance and bow? I comforted myself with thinking I had heard of English Jews with rank of knights, that the Jews of such cities as Worms and Prague had taken up arms. I knew that in Portugal there were Jews who outshone the Christians as cavaliers, with richly caparisoned horses, fine cloaks, silk doublets, and gilt swords. There was no reason why David should not succeed. Yet I had my moments of dark despair. "We shall not fight with boiled leather helmets nor with swords of bone but with bare steel; the right shall prevail," David had told me proudly with a glittering glance.

It inspired me with a wild thought that might prevent the

136

contest of death. "I know the Templar order is forbidden to have to do with women," I said eagerly. "How, then, may this fellow engage in such a duel?"

David gave me a pitying glance. "He is not a squire of the Temple," he said. "Even if he were, there are things which pass behind the walls of their priory that you do not know, my father. Feats of chivalry and *outrance* such as you could not imagine—and the names of the fair are often used as war cries."

There was nothing for me to say after. I was reduced to a spluttering silence. My protests, even to my own ears, sounded silly and fatuous. So now Maimonides and I sat, circled by the misty wreaths of early morning, anticipating nothing but a dull ache in my posterior for having haunched so long on a root of the oak.

The place of the rencontre, as it was called, was narrow, two lanes filled with rust-colored rotten bark from the cork-oak to soften falls and soak up spilled blood. Between the lanes was a low barrier of split dried saplings, painted with tar and whitewash in alternate stripings. The whole was surrounded by a line drawn in lime, a long narrow rectangle. The quarrel would take place within these boundaries, David had explained to me; to step outside or across the barrier was disgrace. It was praise to fight as close as possible to the barrier.

To me, such laws of combat were ridiculous, but I said nothing. Peace, peace, I kept saying to myself; first to him who is far off, then to him who is near, peace!

I saw my son dressed and mounted in dueling armor—helmet and breastplate, gorget, epauliere, brassart, cubitiere, and gauntlets with a curious rim of iron—the tasses and tuilles spread out to protect bare unarmored legs from a chance stroke. They spread out at the waist like the skirt of a dancer, reminding those who fought that a stroke below the navel was unchivalrous. David climbed—as if he were ascending a mountain—from a small ladder up onto the saddle of an enormous white horse. He couched his lance, a dozen feet in length, upon the stirrup. He smiled briefly at myself and Maimonides and shut his visor. Instantly he was anonymous in steel.

We turned and saw the young squire Noel at the farther end, undergoing the same preparations. I had not seen him before. His bulk and bone startled me: He seemed to be as burly as the gray horse upon which he was climbing. I clasped my hands and began to repeat the Shema under my breath.

137

Maimonides said nothing. Nor did he move: His eyes darkened a shade and he kept his gaze upon his brother at the far end of the lists.

Few people were about, praise be to God! Though Noel claimed not to be a squire of the Templar order, a few of the knights were watching. It was too early yet for the people of the town. I turned my head in time to see Sieur Guilbert, clad in a blue robe, step out with a white baton in his hand, the marshal's truncheon. He held it at waist-level. When he lowered his arm or dropped the baton, a trumpet would sound, and the fighting would cease under pain of disgrace and loss of honor. He raised it high: It was the signal to commence combat.

I heard the muffled cries of my son and the squire urging their mounts—from both sides of my vision, the horses broke into a trot, then a canter. The spears swung out, under the necks of the horses, held with point upward. The two towers of metal careened toward each other. They were within a horse's length. Suddenly they crouched forward, spears became rigid, points rose toward the helmets.

I shouted despite myself: A fair hit, a fair hit for both! The points took the bars of the visors. The heads of the combatants jerked back as if God had taken them by the hair. I was glad our David had such a thick neck, so many muscles in his shoulders. It was Noel who lost his seat first, tumbling down over the crupper of his gray mount, who turned aside to graze. David was unlucky; his seat was lost, he struggled too long to recover it. He was precipitated to the ground by a shrug of the massive shoulders of his horse. It stumbled. As he fell, his foot caught. I cried out, and ceased as Maimonides' hand gripped my arm painfully.

"My father," Maimonides said softly, "be strong and of good courage. Let not the mighty hand of the enemy and our own weakness frighten you. Such events as these are only trial and proof of our faith and love." Before I could ascertain whether he offered me words of comfort or words of mockery, the battle was joined again.

David struggled free of his horse. He limped as he dragged himself up, pulling his sword from its scabbard. He leaped back at the same moment to avoid the stroke of the squire. His own blade hissed in a whirl but failed to find a mark. As his body turned with the force of his stroke, the squire aimed a shrewd half-lunge and it rang off David's breastplate. I heaved a sigh of excitement despite myself. David retreated

138

a pace from the barrier. Noel pressed him, raining blow after blow upon his helmet. David sagged under the stunning strokes and his heels came treacherously near the line of lime. I felt pain in my head and discovered that my fists were pulling at my hair.

Suddenly David seemed to revive. His limp vanished. He ducked aside and Noel's last stroke missed, the blade burying itself deep in the logs between them. David waited an instant; I screamed aloud. As the squire pulled out his blade, David lunged with the point, penetrating the cubitiere of the other at the elbow. I saw the seep of bright blood. Noel's big body staggered but his strength appeared unimpaired. He raised his sword in both hands, high above his head, for a mighty stroke. At that moment, disregarding the threat as he put the bare back of his neck under its menace, David lunged a second time. His point, moving upward, found the unprotected leather joint of the armpit under the plate. It went home. The squire twisted in agony, the sword fell from his nerveless hands.

The marshal's baton dropped. With it the squire came tumbling down like a massy trunk of a tree, shuddering in pain but without a cry or a yielding. David stepped back, leaning on his sword as Noel's seconds hurried to their champion. I, too, directed by sheer instinct toward the hurt, hastened to his side. I pushed my way through the little crowd; I thrust aside one who was weeping, continually crying: "Will he live, will he live?" A gray hood was thrown back. The face which confronted me was the pale passionate flesh of Demoiselle de Lys, her eyes wide with shock and grief. I looked at her for only a moment—perhaps my own eyes reflected surprise and triumph, perhaps grief as well—then I shook my head and pushed past the girl.

"I am a physician," I said loudly as I gained the side of the prostrate squire. "Stand back, allow him to breathe! I must see his wound!"

They parted with scowling looks, without a word. I bent and examined young Noel: The gash my son had inflicted gaped wide, blood bubbling out thickly, bright, then dark. "The sinews are torn," I said, rising abruptly, "and the large vessel which carries blood from the heart is severed. He must be taken this moment to the only man who can help him. To the physician Avenzoar."

"Where can he be found?" demanded Sieur Guilbert roughly.

I gave them swift directions to Avenzoar's house. The litter was brought, the fainting squire lifted upon it and hastened away between two horses. "Gently, gently!" I cried after them. "Do not disturb the clotting of the blood!"

I felt the gimlet eyes of Sieur Guilbert on me and raised my head to meet a black gaze. His face set itself in bitterness. "That was a felon stroke of your kin," he said between clenched teeth. "Look to yourselves, Jews!"

He turned on his heel and strode away, his sollerets crunching the cork-bark as he went. He walked heavily to the other end of the lists. David, waiting there according to custom, greeted him eagerly and with respect. A little behind, Maimonides and I listened.

"Is my comrade Noel in a way to recover?" he demanded. "I had not meant so much to wound him."

"Nay," Sieur Guilbert said, "it is the fortune of combat."

David's face enlarged and shone. "Have I done well, then?" he asked of Sieur Guilbert.

A grim smile parted the knight's thin lips. "You have done more than you were trained to do," he said enigmatically. "Bow down, young David, and receive your reward." He wrenched out his sword and stood expectant. David's pale face brightened still more. With slow ceremony, he bowed. "Lower, lower," said Sieur Guilbert. David obeyed. The knight took a single step to the side and whirled his sword in a blow. The flat of his blade caught David across the rear.

David leaped upright, his face blazing with fury. He sprang toward Sieur Guilbert, who waited his coming, point ready; a dagger had appeared in the knight's left hand. "Do you dare, Jew?" he snarled at him.

Anger and humiliation in David's eyes changed to bewilderment; he seemed to reel in his place. Maimonides and I caught him by the shoulders as he fainted and fell. But it was I who supported him. Maimonides, his face colder and more severe than I had ever seen it, stepped fearlessly forward, unweaponed, to the knight. His eyes burned with contempt.

"We thank you for your great kindness and your surpassing courtesy," he said. Each word stabbed the knight, who crouched like a beast. "We know you now. A gentle perfect Christian knight."

The words, clear and distinct, dripped like acid in an open wound. With an inarticulate cry, Sieur Guilbert jerked up his sword. Maimonides nodded, as if it was what he had expected. "You are very chivalrous," he said quietly. "You may slay me, an unarmed Jew. Will that fulfill the code of the Templars?"

He turned from the baffled knight and walked to my side. Together, without a backward look, we raised up the unconscious body of our brother and son and took him away. I knew, as we proceeded with our unconscious burden, that this farce had been proposed not in fairness nor in chivalry nor in challenge—but in revenge. My son had lent himself unwittingly to a scheme to dishonor himself and his family. All of us had been the target of their hatred—possibly since they had been induced by illness to take their vow to Rachel—and because of David's skill they had been foiled. I felt a surge of dark rejoicing at what had happened—but only for a moment.

Within my brain I experienced the same wave of warning which had swept my feelings once before; the tide of imminent danger which washed upon me at that moment in Cordova when Judah warned me of the coming of the Almohades. Here I heard tolling the signal to depart. We were no longer welcome, nor even safe, in Toledo under Alfonso. It was time to steal away like hunted animals, to seek another refuge.

That night we sat late at our meal. In the rear of the house, under the directions of Ramah, Brujo packed together household goods that might go with us. Yaltah, prattling and playing, watched and helped when she could. Her sweet voice came clearly to us. Zayd was without, gathering the mules and packs for our trip to nowhere.

I sat at table, legs crossed, and looked from David on my left to Maimonides on my right. Maimonides shook his head. "It is our destiny," he said, "to move like shadows from city to city in search of peace."

"I shall not leave Toledo," David said listlessly. He had eaten nothing and drunk only sips of watered wine. His face was splotched with color, his breathing irregular. He did not seem master of himself.

"It is necessary we go," I said urgently. "It is a question whether or not Noel will live. If he dies, you may be accused of murder at the most; at the least, the maiming or attacking of a Christian warrior, an arm of the king himself."

"I must talk with her. I do not believe what you have told me you saw."

"Do you say that your father lies?" I cried.

"I only say you may have been mistaken," David replied

slowly. "What you read in her countenance, you may have misread. I shall not be satisfied until I hear it from her own lips."

"But she was there, at Noel's side, not yours!"

"He was a noble youth. Why should she not attend the wounded, even as you did?"

I opened my mouth and closed it again without a sound. There was no point to discussion with David at such a moment. I looked to Maimonides for help. "Do you," I implored him, "judge between us."

Maimonides shook his head. "A judge must think of a sword over his head and hell under his feet," he responded. "Nor can one judge between a father and a brother, if he is related —for that is like taking a bribe from each and giving neither satisfaction."

"Nor is a woman a true witness for the facts," David said suddenly.

"That is so," Maimonides admitted. "We will be spattered by the dust from evil tongues and must endure it. Evil speaking is worse than idolatry, incest, and murder together. Therefore we must not revile the Christians."

"Then we shall stay in Toledo?" inquired David with animation.

"Drink your wine," Maimonides said to him in a kindly tone. David seized his goblet and emptied it at a draught. He coughed, the tears coming into his eyes.

"Why do the Templars hate Jews?" he asked naïvely.

Maimonides smiled in spite of his brother's woebegone face. "Have you never looked at the carvings of our synagogues?" he asked.

"Of course."

"What do they represent, David?"

David thought dully a moment. "Mostly flowers and animals, I think. I remember the lion best."

"Yes. The Lion of Judah. But do you also know that the lion is the only beast the Templars are allowed to hunt—and that because the beast represents Satan, the great Adversary? Now do you understand?"

Eyes straight ahead, David nodded very slowly. "Say you will stay here with me, Muni," he begged.

Maimonides shook his head. "There is a time to remain and a time to depart," he said. "Our father knows this well and I am beginning to learn. The Jew was not meant to rest from his wanderings but to leaven the world with his presence. We shall go, according to the command of our father, David."

David got to his feet. He swayed a little, his tongue thick. "I shall stay, no matter what happens," he announced. Without warning, he fell headlong like a log to the floor. I sprang up in terror. "He is dead!" I cried.

"No, my father," Maimonides returned calmly. "I placed a drug in his wine. I knew David would not go willingly. Now we may take him while he sleeps. When he recovers, we shall be far enough away so that he cannot return."

"You are wise," I said with a sigh, relaxing with his words.

"Am I wise enough?" Maimonides said. He shook his head. "Whether I am or not, the time has come when my education in Toledo is over. I hope Rachel bat Abor will not suffer because of David's foolishness and our flight."

At dawn the next day, I heard years afterward, a messenger from the king arrived. He knocked at the door with a writ for the appearance of David at the court. He found the house empty and the cupboards clean of food and clothing. Even the stall in the Court of Jewelers had yielded its whole stock for our small purse, to carry us on our way. Maimonides had shown me the law he later enunciated: to abhor myself and repent, to do everything out of love and rejoice in afflictions —for they are milestones on the long highway to the presence of God.

CHAPTER 9

Lest anyone think the Jew an outcast in our generation, I must declare otherwise. Of all the peoples in the world, none was more closely knit in blood, in religion and heritage. True, among ourselves we were vastly different in occupation and fortune in this world, but we looked toward the World-to-Come, a congregation of the blessed, faces turned upward, through the dark mists of persecution, toward Heaven.

Jews lived everywhere in the known world—like fleas in the folds of an old patched cloak, as Maimonides jokingly

143

remarked. Where one was, there was another welcome. They formed a vast nassa whose meshes caught news and gossip, business information, messages of government and castle throughout Europe and Asia and Africa, even in England and the cold North countries. Not all Jews lived in congregations; and the largest of these numbered only a few hundred. Most were families or even individuals, eking out sustenance in hostile lands, bowing to the yoke and rising to the necessity even like ourselves. But we were joined in the only real community, that of the soul, by what we believed and taught, the same from age to age, from birth to death.

Many times during our wanderings after we had departed from Toledo we slept in local synagogues, tumble-down and drafty, fed by kindly, new-made friends. Again and again, after these small meals, we bowed our heads over candles wavering in the wind, to recite words which were a reminder of the generosity of our people: "I have been young and now am old; yet have I not seen the righteous forsaken nor his seed begging bread."

Never did we go hungry or uninformed, answer harsh questions, or sleep without a roof. If we had known we were snared in this world-wide cordage of kindness, how much easier our escape from Cordova to Almería might have been! We touched the mezuzah at the threshold of Jews where there existed only man and wife, or of groups where there were less than the required ten men to make up a minyan. We huddled around their dying fires, shared their blankets, listened to their tales: fashioners of silk and glass, painters, artisans in gold and silver, brewers and vintners, beggars and peddlers. We laughed a hundred times at the same joke—for only our humor, in company with our faith, was universal.

> Save me from Christian *koach*;
> Save me from Jewish *moach*.

Christian bullying and Jewish cunning: our path to salvation lay straight between them. Though we did not wander as far as the famed Abraham ben Ezra, who crossed and recrossed Europe, twice visiting faraway England—still we discovered we could devour the dust of the miles and find it nearly nourishing.

We left Toledo in the dead of night through the south gate, a sleepy sentinel allowing us to pass *cuevrefu* as physicians with a patient sick of brain-fever. Miles on our way by the time the sun rose, we doubled back, in case of search, along the road to the east, the sleeping David in a litter borne by Zayd and Brujo. It was past noon of the first day before my younger son awoke, so potent was Maimonides' brew. To our surprise, David said little; he neither complained, inquired, nor attempted to return. He obediently mounted a led mule. Later, he spent his hours in what appeared to be a sullen despondency, riding ahead a few paces—a Jewish knight *desdichado* of his lady-love.

Our travels were like passing over a great black-and-white chessboard, Moslem and Christian citadels alternating in this strange age and, in most places, only the Jew—though observed with suspicion and hatred—allowed to go his way. We traveled on to Barcelona, the tiny but beautiful city by the sea. Here lived such men as the wise rabbis Shesheth, Solomon, and Abraham, reputed masters of trading on better-than-equal terms with the sharpest wits from Greece and Genoa, from Alexandria, Palestine, and Africa. Much news was to be got. Unexpectedly, through the good Rabbi Shealtiel (bowed with years but bearing a mind untouched by time), I received a message from an old friend.

The moment came after an excellent meal: fowl in garlic sauce diluted with wine; flat fish cooked in wine and water with a savory of sage, dittany, thyme, pepper, and salt; our bellies restored by raisin wine, unclouded to the bottom of the cup. "Here," said the eminent Shealtiel, handing me a sealed tablet, "this was directed to the house of Isaac the Blind in Almería, but that worthy refused to send it on. He returned it to me. I was on the point of forwarding it, when lo! you arrived."

"My gratitude," I said, bowing, "for your kindness."

Shealtiel regarded me with his narrow blue eyes. "Has Isaac placed the sword of disputation between you in the bed of friendship?" he inquired.

"It is difficult to keep the Talmud and the Torah unspotted from the world," I said evasively.

Shealtiel's face twisted in a smile. "I understand," he said over his shoulder as he departed. "Your feelings do you much credit."

I unsealed the tablet and found within another of Judah Halevi's verses, simple and unadorned, without title or greeting, soft as his voice.

Say, who shall touch my hand
And lead me to that land
Where, long ago, the heavenly
Angels blessed a chosen band
With prophet ecstasy?

Say, who shall give me wings
To end my wanderings
With pain and sorrow overpassed—
To where the choir of Zion sings
And I can rest at last?

I passed the rectangles of boxwood to Maimonides and bowed my head. When I lifted it, Maimonides was still silently reading the verses; I could feel the lines burning themselves into his memory. He gave it to David, who passed his eyes indifferently over the tablets, handing them almost immediately to the others. Ramah wept, and Yaltah, in sympathy with her; Zayd inspected the wood, and Brujo, who saw nothing but the overlaid beeswax scored with stylus markings—such is the hidden magic of words—grimaced and gave it back to me.

Next day we went on to Gerona (a second reminder of Isaac, the birthplace of his disciples). It was a journey of a day and a half, but we did not linger. Midway on our three-day trip to Narbonne, we passed by the seaward shoulder of the Pyrenees, bristling with epaulettes of pine and oak, dark and forbidding. It was the border between Spain and Provence. Though I did not know it then, myself and all the Maimon household were leaving our motherland of Spain for all time.

Something of the pain of the unknown moment entered into me. I stopped the mules. I gazed up at the massive mountains. "From whence cometh my help," the Psalm so reads; but to me they seemed only a barrier to what I had dearly loved. With this thought I suddenly realized my little band was trending toward a mysterious destination. Metal to the lodestone: Paris, where lived Rachel bat Abor. For seven long years in Toledo I had not heard a word of her by messenger nor by post, not even if she was still alive. Like myself, Maimonides seemed to sense an irresistible urge toward the city, the country where she must be. "Does happiness for us lie this way?" he said, pointing to the north. "Or does it lie here?"

"Nowhere, nowhere," I answered roughly, guessing he divined my thoughts. "But we shall not go in that direction."

To my surprise, Maimonides nodded. "We must discover

146

ourselves before we seek to find another," he said simply. He cocked his eyes at the cloudless sky above that rounded off the land. "At night," he added, "I have thought of writing about the stars. I watch them from my bed. They are what I would like to be: far-off, bright, revolving immortally in their courses through eternity."

In due time we came to Marseilles, three days' journey from Arles. Here lived four hundred Jews divided into two congregations, one in the castle enclosure on the heights, and the other on the seashore. We settled in the latter, in the coils of the labyrinth of dark, twisting streets. I attempted to bury myself in study and meditation. For a time, my spirit knew peace. We might have remained there for the rest of our lives except for Maimonides.

It was a turgid night, lost in one of the heavy fogs that hold the commerce of Marseilles in a soft gray grip impossible to lift until sunrise. Though a sea-coal fire blazed on the hearth in my rooms, it burned low, its crackle subdued. I supported my head in my hands over the books of the Talmud which had been lent me, concentrating on them without success; my attention kept being drawn to the slow drip of the tiles outside, the suppuration of the night. At last I rose to go to my private pouch, which held most of our wealth. I took out a single stone and returned to the table to contemplate its beauty.

It was a rough diamond, polished clear on two sides, as large as a small bird's egg. It had the clear luminosity of water seen by moonlight, a faint bluish tinge. At times like these it comforted me to stare into its depths, to let my thoughts pour into the unfeeling substance as if it were the eye of a friend, steady and sympathetic. It was a great treasure—one I could not bear to part with, I knew, except in the most extreme emergency. I had bought it in Toledo, during David's absence, from a traveling Indian merchant. The price had been exorbitant. No one else knew of its existence.

In the midst of my reverie, I heard a double knock on the door. Hastily, I slipped the stone into the chamois pouch and went to loose the chain. I frowned as Maimonides entered, but my displeasure melted instantly. His perturbation of spirit was apparent in his pale face, his involuntary movements, his shuffling step. He sank onto a stool beside the table. His head drooped. I touched his hand. "What ails you, Muni?" I asked, in affectionate diminutive.

He looked up at me through heavy-lidded eyes. "Weariness,

nothing but weariness," he murmured in a voice so low I could scarce distinguish the syllables.

"So are we all weary," I said, sitting beside him. "Body and soul we are drained by this endless wandering from place to place, driven like thistledown before a wind."

"My weariness is neither of these. If it were only the body, I might go on forever. If it were the soul, I might fall on my knees and address myself to God."

"What do you mean?"

Maimonides turned to me with a singular intensity. His expression changed and hardened, the light shining from the stretched skin over his cheekbones and nose, his thick brows shadowing his eyes. "In the depths of my mind, as in the depths of clear water," he said slowly, "I see the manuscripts of Cordova, the books of Toledo, turning and sinking. A gray film issues from nowhere as I watch. It obscures the pages, the letters, the illuminations."

"You need rest, my son," I said.

Maimonides shook his head. "There is no rest which will cure this dreadful inner vision," he affirmed. "It is the fading of memory, my father, set upon by the gray disease of forgetfulness." His voice rose and quickened. He grasped convulsively at a paper in his sash. "But I have tried to rescue as much as possible, night and day! See, here I have written a thing of no worth on the calendar of the Jews!"

Again I put my hand on his arm to quiet him. I spread the parchment on my knee. It was a hastily inscribed series of suggestions for a revision of the Jewish system of recording months and years. I could see it was ingenious but wholly unacceptable, even contradictory to tradition.

"It is excellent," I said, hiding my true sentiments. Maimonides was not deceived. "It is dreadful, my father," he returned. "There are ideas there, that is so; but they are weak or inadequate, not founded on logic and reason. I have not done what I intended." He looked at me with eyes of anguish. "It is the first time in my life that such has happened!" he cried. "I have never attempted anything of the mind before that I have not been able to do, clearly and well, better than any before me!"

"So it will be again," I soothed him. "You must rest."

He shook me off as if he had not heard, as if my fingers were an intolerable weight. He went on, talking feverishly, almost to himself. "I have written more besides—these unfinished theses on the Talmud, explaining and interpreting as

148

best I might—but it has come to nothing." He flung the sheets to the floor. "There is nothing left to draw up from the dry well of consciousness! The cord is cut, the wheel broken at the cistern, the golden bowl of memory cast away!"

I picked up his commentaries from where they lay on the floor and gave them a swift scanning in the lamplight. I was surprised: I had no need to lie about the excellence of these. "These are remarkable," I said with enthusiasm. "Unfinished perhaps, but full of meat and perception. They must be finished."

"No. I shall attempt no more. These are only fragments of a great work I had intended. Now I shall never accomplish it."

"You must not despair," I said sharply, attempting to prod him out of his discouragement. "That is for children or fools."

"No. It is, for me, a decision long denied."

"Think no more!" I exclaimed.

Maimonides returned his gaze to mine, a tired sardonicism hidden deep in its wavering fire. He allowed a tiny smile to appear above his thickened beard, a sign not of mirth but of sorrow so heavy it seemed his lips could scarcely bear it. "This is not the worst, my father," he said, dragging out the syllables of Arabic, "there is more. You know that once I studied with the Moslem philosopher, Abu Bekr ibn Alzaig—the sons of Ibn Afla of Seville and I used to argue night into dawn with our sophistries from Zeno to Aristotle."

I heaved a sigh. "I remember, I remember Cordova," I replied in a strangled voice.

"I commenced to dream of a great work, one which would explain to Jew and Moslem alike—perhaps some day to the Christians—the true meaning of our religion. Those arguments planted the seed from which the present disaster has sprung."

"I do not understand."

"I am twenty-three. I have begun such a great work. But I stand paralyzed, my face fixed against a wall of glass. Beyond I can glimpse the gardens of Paradise but I am barred from them. I press my face against the cold invisible barrier, I implore the wall to dissolve but it stands firm. I am lost, lost!"

He commenced to wail and turn away. I gripped him by the shoulder to divert him from his maunderings. "Tell me," I commanded him, "what have you called this work?"

"I call it *Siraj*."

I nodded: "In our Hebrew, that is *Meor*."

"Yes. Light. I meant it to light the path of all Jews, to be a commentary on the Mishnah of the Talmud—to explain the word as well as the spirit, to be a guide to the wise and to the student. I had proposed to speak concerning all the Oral Laws, to say which are true, which arguable, which in dispute."

Astonished in spite of myself, I could not help shaking my head. "You attempt too much," I said gravely. "I cannot say it is wrong nor that it is evil—I only say it is impossible."

"Yet I must try it—or go mad. As you see, I am going mad."

"You must cease to talk nonsense!"

With a trembling hand that I grieved to see in one so young, Maimonides reached into his gown and secured a larger scroll. He handed it to me. I unrolled it slowly. As it crackled between my fingers, he spoke: "Here are thirteen articles of faith for our religion."

"What do you mean by that?"

"They are proposals only. It seems to me that they are rocks on which we stand; we must believe these or be damned to Gehenna forever."

"What do you dare to say?" I demanded.

"Read them."

"This is sacrilege for you, a youth, to make such a statement!"

Maimonides for the first time gave me a true smile, as if I amused him. "You were young once," he said gently, "but time amended the fault. What does it matter, young or old, if the truth appears? Perhaps I am right, perhaps wrong; my father, you will never know unless you read."

I bent my eyes to the parchment reluctantly, as if I were reading a document from the Adversary. But Maimonides' clear style worked its charm. My eyes roved freely, quickly, right to left. The Arabic words jumped into meaning. "What I want this to mean is much what our endless journeys have meant," Maimonides murmured. "There is a purpose in our departures. We are free to stay and be destroyed; we are also free to travel under compulsion and be saved. Our faith is a religion, but one cannot indulge himself, once it has been accepted. Too many Jews think they can call themselves such without believing in our precepts."

Much as I felt he was right, more I was daunted by his austere enumeration of these precepts in this introduction to his *Abot*. According to my son, a true Jew must believe in the existence of God and His Oneness, His Ghostliness, and His Eternity—in God, who knows the thoughts and deeds of all men and will reward and punish them at the coming of the Messiah; in Moses, greatest of all prophets, who on Sinai revealed the Torah which cannot be changed; in the resurrection of the dead; and in the conviction that all worship is due God alone.

"I remember one discussion on that," I said, placing a finger on the last precept. "Did not a certain pert youngster come into a certain library?"

"Of a certain learned man in a certain city in Spain," Maimonides said. "But when we say 'certain' we mean in our hearts 'uncertain.' Yes, my father, we know better: it was I and it was you, in Cordova."

"These are what all Jews should believe," I said thoughtfully, "except that I am not sure of resurrection."

"Perhaps that remains to be proved."

"Is there not here some echo of the Moslem and the Christian creeds?"

"It is possible these are echoes of the One Religion."

"Is not our life best when it is holy conduct, not merely reciting a set of such beliefs?"

"Is not every word of the Torah a dogma in itself?"

"But," I said defensively, "this is very far from the Torah, the revealed word of God. There is no way to enforce these beliefs of yours."

"If they are true, God will raise up authority to defend them," Maimonides said cryptically. "If they are false, He will obliterate them."

His face had fallen into its old lines. His weariness, indeed, was unutterable. For a moment, in the excitement of dialectic, he had regained color and vivacity; now he was sunk once more into pale lassitude. I got to my feet. I seized his shoulders, raising him from his seat. "Think no more of these things," I reiterated. "I shall read them and we will talk of them another day. Now get to rest. No one shall disturb you in the morning."

A wraith of an expression crossed Maimonides' face. "I must tell you, my father," he said, "that Zayd is spelling out my treatise on logic—he wants to discover what I said of him."

Before I could answer, Maimonides made his way out of my chamber. The susurration of his slippers died away. I was left alone with the sounds of the dripping fog and its hollow echoes on the tiles. I slumped once more beside the table and

151

took from my girdle the rough, partly polished diamond. I rolled it out before me, between the manuscripts: wealth and wisdom, wealth and wisdom, symbolized on the boards. Both gave comfort and position in this world—but did either serve in the World-to-Come?

How long I meditated, I do not know. What roused me was a sound at the door—still unlatched, unbarred after the exit of Maimonides. I lifted my eyes heavily, aware of the diamond on the table whose gleam had transfixed my gaze. Almost in the same motion, I stood up and peered into the shadow.

Brujo stood there. I experienced a moment of uneasiness, then forgot about it. I signaled him to come forward. "What do you desire at this hour of the night?" I demanded.

He had been looking at the table and now he swung his lidded gaze toward me. "Rabbi Maimon," he said slowly, "I have come to ask you a great favor."

"What is it?"

"Ramah and I—we wish to be married. We wish you to marry us."

I stared incredulously at him as he stood half in shadow. "You!" I exclaimed. "You are not a man!"

Brujo drew himself up. His face turned red and angry, as I had not seen it before. "You do not dare talk to me like that!" he challenged.

"Were you a man in the ambush on the road to Toledo?" I asked him. "And is your body fit to bear children?"

His cheeks lost some of their color at my cruel questions. I regretted them on the spot. But it was too late: an arrow sped, a word spoken, they cannot return.

"I was afraid on the road," he said simply. "But I have paid for that many times over in your neglect and Zayd's contempt. Only Master Muni has been kind to me."

I said nothing, deserving the rebuke. Brujo went on in an unnaturally calm voice: "As for children, we may adopt a babe-in-arms. I know I have been deprived of my manliness —but is that a fault that can be laid to my account?"

"No," I said humbly.

"I am a Jew, I have come into your race, I accept the same contumely, the same abuse," Brujo said more loudly. "I do not ask more than you can do or are allowed to do."

"And Ramah?"

"She loves me for what I am. I love her. She has forgiven

152

me for my weaknesses as others have not." His words bit into my soul. I bowed my head.

"Let her come in," I said. "I shall marry you tonight, this instant."

"But I wish the full ritual for her, all of the ceremonies."

"Very well," I said. I spoke gruffly, hiding the quick lift of my heart. I would be performing once again the ceremony I loved most of all, the union of two souls in faith and happiness.

It was dawn on a fair warm morning of early summer, a Friday in the new moon. I rose and dressed myself carefully, with attention to each detail of my costume. I hurried out to drink some hot water with the juice of an orange, a habit I had contracted to aid my stomach in digestion. Maimonides, equally excited over the event, came clattering down the flight of stone stairs. It was his task to escort Brujo to the synagogue for the wedding.

"Where is the bridegroom?" he demanded.

I shrugged. "Perhaps he is still in his room," I suggested. Maimonides shook his head. "I have only just come from there," he replied. "I shall look in the courtyard."

He hurried out and I sighed. I had to ascend the stairs once more: I had forgotten my best tallit. Slowly I went above and thrust open the door of my chamber. I entered and halted in surprise. Brujo was there, in his best garments, huddled over the manuscripts on my table. As he heard me enter, he gave a convulsive start and twisted about. His face seemed pale, his eyes staring.

"Did I interrupt your studies?" I said jestingly, taking my tallit from its peg on the wall, draping it over my shoulders.

"No," Brujo said in a strained voice. "I was curious."

"Come, come!" I cried, finishing the arrangement of my tallit. "Maimonides waits for you below, the people wait for us all in the synagogue!"

Brujo left the table, holding his hands stiffly at his sides. "Hebrew is a difficult language to read," he said in the same reedy voice.

"For you," I told him, "it is impossible. But this is a waste of time. Let us go immediately!"

I led the way out of the room. As I preceded him, he bent, his customary bow as I passed; out of the corner of my eye I caught a slight gesture, hand to mouth. He straightened instantly, following me without a word. I thought nothing more of it.

153

As I made my way through the twisting streets of Marseilles, up the hill to the synagogue in the fortress, I mused upon what had happened, not without a smile. Unwittingly I had become the shadchan, a matchmaker between two servants—and I had charged no fee. But I did not regret my charity.

There had been a feast the night before, the shidduchin—at my expense, instead of Brujo's, which was proper. I had presented Ramah with an illuminated Haggadah, the ritual for Passover; girdles and ornaments for her hair had been given by Maimonides and David; even Yaltah had timidly (perhaps hopefully, dreaming of her own wedding) added a brooch. To Brujo I had given a box of sweetmeats and added the betrothal ring, a hoop with a turreted temple and a spinning weathercock atop, wrought in the best gold. It was Maimonides who had insisted on presenting the plain ring with *mazal tov,* "good luck," engraved within. What was missing, I thought with a twinge of regret, was that Judah might have blessed the whole with an ode.

As we proceeded through the lifting gray of the dawn, a dozen of the members of the congregation followed with torches and music and singing. I confess I was taken aback to see Maimonides among them, twanging a gittern. It was he who returned and brought Ramah in her simple finery from our house, her face rosy, glowing with happiness.

She wore a white veil of sarcenet and a fur robe. Brujo stood in a cowled garment, worn in memory of the destruction of the temple. I placed him on the north side of the Ark as the people chanted a hymn; then Ramah came in, David escorting her with garlands. I waited, facing them all, as he brought her to me, then turned and put her to the right of her future husband. Ramah's mouth formed a word or two: I bent my head.

"If I set my left foot over his right, will I be able to rule him all our days?" she whispered.

"Mere superstition," I muttered—but I noted her left slipper stealing out toward his right foot.

I omitted the techina and strewed ashes on the heads of both as a token of our long exile, turning their faces to the east. Maimonides took the corner of Brujo's hood and draped it over both their heads.

I sang the blessings of the marriage and turned to David and Maimonides. I took Ramah's hand and showed the ring. According to ritual, I demanded: "Is this the proper ring?"

154

"Yes," Brujo said.

"Is it of value?"

"Yes."

I closed her hand on it. "Repeat after me," I said. I commenced to intone, and Brujo obediently followed my words.

"Be thou consecrated to me by this ring, according to the laws of Moses and of Israel!"

He put the ring on her finger. The *ketubah*—the marriage contract—was given them, and I continued with the Seven Blessed Blessings and ended: "Oh, make these loved ones greatly to rejoice, even as of old Thou didst gladden Thy creatures in the Garden of Eden!"

I turned to them both and said in a loud voice: "Thou, O Lord, didst create joy and gladness, bridegroom and bride, mirth and exaltation, pleasure and delight, love, comradeship, peace and fellowship. Soon may there be heard in the cities of Judah and the streets of Jerusalem the voice of joy and gladness, the voice of the bridegroom and the voice of the bride, the jubilant notes of the bridegrooms from their canopies and of youths from their seats of song. Blessed art Thou, O Lord, who makest the bridegroom to rejoice with the bride!"

I took their hands and clasped them together. There was a shout and others about them threw wheat over their heads and shoulders. I bent my own head and—instead of whispering the usual words, "Be fruitful and multiply," which in conscience and honesty I could not say—I merely murmured: "Be happy, be happy."

Then I extended the wineglass to Ramah, to Brujo, allowing each to take a sip. When they had touched it with their lips, I gave the glass to Brujo. He grinned and took it, ceremoniously turning and flinging it with a crash against the wall, signifying the completion of the ritual. The congregation shouted again, clamoring forward to surround the pair.

Weary and yet refreshed, I entered my chamber and took the tallit from my shoulders. I sank down at the table. Suddenly, I stiffened. I remembered what I had been doing the night before: I had been examining again, with loving care, the diamond that the Indian merchant had called the Closed Eye of Siva. I looked for it. It was not there. I scrabbled frantically among the papyrus and tablets; it was not there. I flung myself on my knees and searched the floor in the long rays of morning sunlight. The diamond was gone. I fumbled

155

myself erect, feeling the blood drain from my head, dizziness growing before my eyes. I took my head in my hands.

I know not how much time passed nor what thoughts raced through my mind. My hands and feet felt clammy-cold. I held my hair at the temples, tugging at it vainly to make myself feel pain, to rouse my stunned mind into logical thinking. I cried aloud at the pain and sat myself down on a stool.

Maimonides? Impossible. But Yaltah might have borrowed it for a toy, not knowing its value. Ramah? No, many such things had passed through her hands before and she was scrupulously honest—yet this might have tempted her. Zayd? There, indeed, was a character of suspicion, if even only for the fact that he never could speak. David? Nonsense: son of my heart, heart of my soul, he was beyond reproach. Yet perhaps he had found another maiden among the goyim who might have driven him to it. Even Maimonides might have been tempted, to buy books and manuscripts; I knew the temptations of the scholarly, the fierce desire for possession of a parchment that might make the most honest sage covet it for his own.

And I, myself. Was I truly clear of all suspicion? Careless and heedless, I had thrown away our treasure. But perhaps, I repeated frantically within, I had only lost it, put it somewhere that thought could not recall.

Brujo? Brujo! The bridegroom? But certainly not, I thought indignantly. He—but wait! That night when he may have seen the gem. The wedding morning, only today, when I had happened upon him in my room; his turning away, his hand to his mouth, his quick swallowing. None of it made sense unless he was the culprit. I struck the brass summoner on my table, hearing its clashing sound almost with relief.

The door swung noiselessly open and shut. Brujo, like a phantom, stood before me. "You called me," he said.

"Yes," I told him. I found it difficult to begin.

"Ramah waits for me," Brujo said in a tone of reproof.

"You have nothing to offer her," I said brutally.

I watched him carefully. For the first time, my suspicions blossomed. Instead of resenting what I said, as he had before, he remained silent and pale.

"I had a diamond," I said. "It was a very valuable stone."

"I did not know that."

"Did you not see it the other night?"

"What night?"

156

"A night some while before this one," I said thickly. Brujo shook his head. "It has been stolen!" I shouted.

"Perhaps it has been misplaced," he suggested wanly.

I struck the table with my palm, feeling the room fill and become warm at the height of my quick rage. I leaned forward and spat at him through my teeth. "Did you take that stone?" I cried. Brujo shook his head again.

"Confess!"

"What should I confess?"

"You stole it!"

"What did I steal?"

"You know what it is!"

"How should I know, master?"

I heaved a sigh. Brujo blinked innocently at me. "You answer every demand with a question," I said.

"How else should I answer?"

I struck my leg with my fist in fury. "You stole the diamond! Where is it?"

"What diamond, Rabbi Maimon?"

The question enraged me until suddenly I realized it did not come from Brujo. I wheeled and saw Maimonides standing inside the room. "Did you have my permission to enter?" I said.

"I beg you to excuse me," he said and turned to go but I halted him. "Wait," I said. "This fellow of ours, this Brujo, has stolen the most precious gem in our purse, a diamond."

Maimonides surveyed both of us with his calm dark eyes. "How do you know that he stole it?" he asked.

"You talk as he does," I said, exasperated. "I know it because he was the only one to see it."

"When did I see it?" protested Brujo. "Where did I see it?"

"May weeds grow from your filthy head and wither!" I cried. "You saw it that night, in my chamber!"

"Wait," Maimonides said, raising his hand. "This man is one of us, my father, by profession of faith. He cannot even light fires or toil on the Sabbath, as we cannot; such work must be done by Zayd. If you accuse him, it must be done in due course."

"I shall do it," I said grimly, seating myself. "I declare that this is a rabbinical court."

"Very well," Maimonides said, ranging himself beside Brujo. I glanced at him in surprise. "I do not need your help," I told him, "I can prosecute my own case and it is allowed by the Law."

157

"I know that very well," Maimonides said, "but who will defend one of our faith as the Law provides? I shall do that office."

"Against your own father?"

"Does justice recognize father or son?"

I flapped my hands on my knee, unable to reply to this paragon of Talmudic knowledge. He was right; yet he was wrong, and the knowledge of it defeated me.

Gradually an inspiration came to me. I peered at Brujo closely in the lamplight and saw him slowly swallowing, regularly, one gulp after another. I recalled that when Brujo and I had left my room he had bowed and clapped one hand to his mouth. At that moment I was sure of my accusation.

"What do you accuse him of, my father?"

"Of the theft of a diamond belonging to me, polished on two faces."

"When was it stolen?"

"This very morning! But enough of this foolishness. I shall rest my case on a single experiment."

I beckoned to Maimonides and he came to me. I whispered in his ear and, looking over his shoulder, I was pleased to see Brujo grow pale as he leaned forward in an attempt to hear our whispers. Maimonides nodded and turned to him.

"It is very reasonable," he assured Brujo. "My father says he is willing to drop the accusation against your honesty, if only you will consent to a simple act."

"What is it?" Brujo asked fearfully.

"It is to swallow a half-handful of the ground cascara seed in olive oil—and remain in this apartment for six hours."

Brujo's face brightened. I could see he had no idea of the medicinal qualities of cascara. "Nothing else?" he inquired cautiously.

"Nothing."

"Then I agree."

"As his agent, my father, I agree." Solemnly we clasped hands. Maimonides went to prepare the dose. Brujo and I remained in silence, he standing, while I sat in meditation. Maimonides returned. Brujo willingly took the medicine, washing it down with a bowl of wine. Significantly, I rose and with slow steps went to a corner of the room. I returned with a large clay slop-basin. I placed it ceremoniously in the middle of the floor. Brujo looked at me with uncomprehending eyes in which there was beginning to be a hint of returning fear. "What is that for?" he asked. "You said there would be nothing more."

"Nothing that you will not do yourself," I said soothingly. "You may have some use for this before the day is gone. Let us go, Maimonides; leave him to his wretched thoughts."

Maimonides bowed and left with me behind him. We closed the door and fastened the latch. I smiled at my son. "You do not know everything, Muni," I said. "I can read character with my old, experienced eye better than you with the blindness of youth."

"We shall see," Maimonides replied. Both of us squatted down in the corridor outside, prepared to doze. We were interrupted by David bounding breathlessly up the stairs. "Ramah has asked for her husband," he said reprovingly. "She expects him."

"He will be yet a little while," Maimonides told him.

"We are conducting an experiment," I said grandly, "and Brujo is aiding us." The whole affair—were it not for the price of the gem—seemed now almost comic.

"Experiment?" inquired David with a puzzled face.

"In good and evil," Maimonides said.

"Of the movements of good and evil which some sages suppose are located in the stomach," I said. I laughed aloud. David gave me a bewildered smile as he departed, but the expression of patient waiting on Maimonides' face did not change.

We had not long to wait. An hour or two and we commenced to hear groans and heavy breathing inside; then retching and the sighing of relief. At this we hurriedly opened the door. I saw the pale convulsed Brujo seated over the clay pot, his pantaloons crumpled on the floor. As we entered, he attempted to rise; he was too weak. I allowed him to finish his convulsion, then I swept the clay pot from under him and took it to the window. Holding it there, as the wind blew the stink away, I rinsed it out with an amphora of water, swirling it to settle whatever objects might be inside.

I gave a shout of joy. Tipping the pot, I emptied most of its foul contents, then reached within with the most delicate fingertip touch. I held up my prize: the diamond. "Here it is!" I cried triumphantly. "Deny, you rascal, that you stole it!"

"I did nothing but yield to temptation," Brujo said sullenly. He trembled as he jerked up his breeches, still weak from purging. "I have nothing, you have everything. You tricked me into this today."

Washing the stone carefully in a basin, I flung over my shoulder: "Do you hear the fellow, Muni? He has the face to brazen it out!"

Brujo shrank away from my anger. "Once you would have killed me," he said, his voice shaking. "I remember well the road to Almería. Except for your son, I would be dead."

"And good riddance!" I burst out. "Are you still the knave —have you learned nothing from our holy precepts?"

Brujo drew himself up. "I have learned that anger is unseemly," he said. "That the hasty tongue and the hard heart are sins against the Most High."

I felt a strangling in my throat to have my own words thrown back at me in this fashion, corrupted by him.

Maimonides said nothing. I glanced in his direction and saw, to my surprise, that he was preparing a soothing potion for Brujo. He gave it to him: The man's color commenced to creep back into his face. Maimonides watched him pensively. "What are your thoughts?" I demanded, polishing the diamond with a cloth.

"I do not ask forgiveness," Brujo broke in.

"Do you refuse even to repent?" I asked sardonically.

"I repent that you were clever enough to know what I had done."

"He who has done wrong must ask pardon," said Maimonides, "but equally, he who has been offended must be easily pacified and forget his anger."

"I shall turn him into the streets," I said.

"I shall be happy to go!"

"You are sinners both in the eyes of God," Maimonides said imperturbably.

I stared at him. "I demand justice and punishment and I am a sinner?" I asked in astonishment.

"And I, do I sin because I take from those who have much, for myself who has nothing?" asked Brujo in an injured voice.

Maimonides looked at him. "Do you truly abandon the sin of theft, cast it from your thoughts and resolve in your heart never to repeat it?" he asked.

"Yes," grumbled Brujo. He looked up defiantly, seemingly himself again though somewhat shrunken. "You are too clever for me. I shall not try again."

To my renewed surprise, Maimonides suddenly chuckled. "That is enough," he said, "and reason enough. And you, my father?"

"Are you to act as judge?"

"There is no one else."

"Then," I said grudgingly, "I suppose I must forgive him since he admits he is too stupid to do it again. But I demand penance."

"You have humiliated him with his bride," Maimonides said. "Do you ask more?"

I remained silent. "Has Ramah also sinned?" Maimonides persisted. To my dismay I saw Brujo's eyes glisten: His love for her was indeed real, his humiliation complete. To cover my discomfiture, I tossed the diamond to Maimonides. I took a turn up and down the chamber, peering covertly at my son. I noted a change in his expression as he examined the diamond.

"What, then, shall we do with this one?" I asked at last.

Maimonides did not reply at once. He held up the diamond, so that its varicolored lights in the afternoon sun sparkled in every corner of the room. It cast a pale brief reflection over the drawn face of Brujo huddled in the corner. I repeated my question.

"Nothing," Maimonides said abruptly. "Let him go."

"What do you say?" I demanded incredulously.

"Ramah, his bride, awaits him."

"But he is a thief!"

"He has yielded once to temptation. That is true."

"I do not think he swallowed the diamond because he believed it a ripe olive," I said sarcastically.

Maimonides ignored my bitterness. "There is no one of us but that shall sin before he dies," he said obliquely. "I think Brujo is right to rebuke us."

"He is a schnorrer of religion!" I said violently.

"Go," Maimonides said to Brujo. "When my father is angry, he is becoming compassionate. He has forgiven you. In this, your day and night of joy, we do not wish to blacken your bridal bed with evil memories. Tonight, it is yours without a thought of sin. But tomorrow, Brujo, think and repent."

Casting a look of unutterable gratitude at Maimonides, Brujo sidled out of the room. I shook my head at my son. He sat down at my feet. "If he does no more than steal a diamond, he will be among the elect in the World-to-Come," Maimonides declared. "But he has done a great deal for us today."

"Your prophetic vision extends farther than mine," I responded sourly. The taste of what Brujo had done to us still stuck to my tongue, the odor of it in my nostrils.

"He will not steal again," Maimonides averred. "He has felt the lash of his own conscience. Remember how many opportunities he must have had to steal before and resisted? How much have you trusted him?"

"Much," I agreed reluctantly.

"Now he is grateful. He is sealed to our tribe. He knows the penalties he carries within himself."

"Is this what he has done for the family of Maimon?"

Maimonides shook his head. He sprang to his feet, his face alight. "No," he said energetically. "But I know that you do not wish to remain here in Marseilles—yet you do not know where to go."

"I have not said so."

"Your every expression, your gestures, your silences, have said so."

"Do you have a place for refuge?"

"I have," Maimonides said. His voice dropped but still held its eagerness. "It may be that my memory fails but books are the most lasting memories of all. The great library at Cordova that we possessed is gone—but there is another."

"Where?"

"It belongs to Joseph ben Shoshan, the great rabbi of Fez."

"Fez!" I bounded to my feet, as alarmed as Maimonides had been pleased. "It is the capital of Morocco, a land over-run by the enemy Almohades! Would you take your father and his family into the very jaws of the beast?"

"Where better can we hide?"

"Anywhere!"

"If one is in the jaws of the beast, he looks for other prey. Where else can I secure the sources I need for my commentary on the Mishnah?"

I sank back into my seat, speechless. I shook my head. "You are the one who wrote a treatise on logic," I marveled.

"Believe me, my father, human nature is not modeled after the laws of the mind. And here we have the treasure that shall take us there." He held up the diamond.

I snatched it from him. "You will never sell this beautiful stone!" I cried. "We shall never go to Fez!"

Maimonides bowed. When he lifted his head his face was grave and inscrutable. "Today it is yours without a thought of sin," he said. "Tomorrow, you will think and repent."

It was only after he left that I realized he had quoted the same words to me that he had spoken to Brujo, the thief.

Nevertheless, I nodded to myself with secret satisfaction. I had baffled my son's omniscience. He would not know until the proper moment that I, too—despite my fears—wanted to visit Fez to greet an old friend.

CHAPTER 10

As she bent over me, I felt the warm tears of Naomi—or was it Rachel?—fall softly on my face. I started awake. I lay on my back on my sleeping mat, on the roof of our small stone dwelling in Fez. It was almost dawn. One of the rare showers from the sea had visited inland to sprinkle the town in the valley.

It vanished as unexpectedly as it had come, the clouds breaking into ghosts of gray vapor above me. I remained a moment in contemplation. Mindful that God had again snatched my soul from the region of dreams, I put down the rebellious thought that another day of mitzvot, of good deeds, seemed more of a burden than a blessing. Almost without knowing it, I murmured: "Yet I thank Thee because Thou hast restored me; great is Thy love, great my unworthiness."

Over the eastern hills, the light brightened. A certain whiteness from my breast caught my eyes. I peered down at its source and lo! it was my beard. It was white; I was old.

I sighed at the swift flight of time. Man, I said to myself, is the shimmer of wind on water, here a moment and gone; flourishing as the sweet grass and flowers of the field, next moment devoured by the grave, good for nothing except as fodder for the earth. To my memory came the solemn words of King David, peace unto him, sung to his palace harp when the Jews were a power in this world: "What is man that Thou art mindful of him, the son of man that Thou thinkest of him? Yet Thou hast made him little less than divine, crowning him with glory and honor."

I rose and slipped on my outer garments, rolling up my mat into its corner. I stretched; my sloth after sleep vanished. Against the darkness of the west, born in the rays of the still-hidden sun, there appeared the bridge to Paradise—a rainbow, overarching the valley in colors like those of a maiden's veil. I raised my hands and called down the five blessings that sanctify the smell of fragrant plants, the sight of lofty mountains, the blossoms of flowers and trees, the wonder of the rainbow, the vision of the sea. Truly, though the sea lay twenty-five parasangs to the north, I could still see its blue bosom breathing with the wind.

All the sweetnesses of life were with me in the sacred moment of waking, even the dream-memory of women's tears. It was little more than a year after our arrival in Morocco; I felt at home for the first time since our departure from Spain.

As I finished my prayers, the sun broke over the crest of the mountains before me. It laid a flat crimson blade like an accolade across the land. From a tower spiring upward through the greenery of the city of Fez, I heard the thin wail of the muezzin on his balcony, calling the Moslem faithful to prayers of their own: "Allah is great, there is no god but Allah and Mohammed is his prophet! It is better to pray than to sleep!"

I dropped to my knees, not in reverent prostration. I crawled toward the square opening between the beams of the roof, to the ladder whereby I might descend. In Fez it was not safe to be seen on one's feet at dawn prayers.

As I placed my feet on the rungs bound by strips of raw goathide, my mood of rejoicing disappeared. I wondered if we would be forced again to depart in search of another refuge, like hares hunted to their hole. Like so many towns of the world, then and now, Fez was a mixture of hatred and tolerance, of open piety and secret abominations, full of contradictions, of hidden, treacherous currents. Years before, the raging Berbers from the hills had laid it waste, venting their fanaticism against synagogue and church. Only mosques had been rebuilt. Intolerance had died down, flame into embers, but the red glow still existed under the ashes, ready to flare up at a breath of provocation.

Despite my own inward fears, we had come to Fez with renewed hope. Though I was his father and he my son (though I bowed under more than twice his age of twenty-five years), Maimonides once more had exercised his influence over me. Quoting the good Hillel, "More flesh, more worms; more wealth, more care," he had broken my will. I had sold the diamond of my bosom, in Marseilles, to Rabbi Isaac ben Abba Mari—not without haggling, since he said he would have to deal with the Genoese who would have to sell it to the Christian nobles of wealthy Pisa; besides, he argued, it would interfere with his preparation of his lifework, the *Baal Haittur*. The proceeds had been more than enough to ship us aboard a galeasse for Morocco, on a sea so calm we seemed to sail on silk, so windless we were forced to use oars for more than half the three-day journey.

I was amazed to see, for the first time, fear in my son's eyes. Not of man nor of any of man's works, but of the sea, the elemental creation of God. David and Yaltah, Ramah and Brujo, Zayd standing motionless at the prow like a black figurehead, enjoyed it thoroughly. Maimonides became pale and emaciated from an illness I could not diagnose. He huddled near the bulwarks day and night, refusing to eat and taking little to drink.

At last we came to the coast of Africa and rowed along beside the rugged cliffs, seeing a few sandy beaches, marshes, finally the green-and-blue valley of Alhucemas. Here we disembarked, to the undisguised relief of the sailors. The fools considered it had been our magic which had provided such a smooth passage, yet they believed the presence of a family of Jews aboard was an omen of future ill-luck.

As we mounted mules, bought in the village for the long overland climb to Fez, I saw that Maimonides had miraculously revived. I twitted him about his weakness.

"You seem to be quite well again," I said dryly, watching him devour dried meat and hard bread from the pannier at his side.

"I am ravenous," he admitted. "The sickness of the sea has left me the appetite of a beast."

"Why should you be ill upon such a soft sailing? The voyage was a delight to me and to the others—you, who were so insistent about coming, grew shaken and thin."

Maimonides spoke from a full heart as well as a full mouth: "The sea is not a place proper for our people. I suffer from the time I set foot on the evil-smelling deck until I feel the earth under me again."

"Yet there have been Jewish pirates and famous navigators," I said with asperity.

"I am neither one nor the other," Maimonides replied with as much dignity as he could summon up with crumbs falling from the corners of his crammed mouth. "I am à scholar."

I kicked my mule ahead in exasperation. I sensed—as I hunched my *haique* against the searing *sharki* wind from the desert—that despite the fact that I had acceded to his wishes

165

in coming, there remained a conflict, unresolved, between our souls. I felt forewarned it might be here that our differences would come to defiance.

At the end of our road—much of the four days' travel was through desolate country, along trails frowned down upon by rocks, half-blocked by slides where a misstep of our mounts would plunge us into mist-lined gorges—we had a pleasant surprise on seeing Fez. It lay on the right bank of the muddy Wad Fas, stretching out between low hills, among turreted ruins of Empire forts, groves of oranges, brilliant pomegranate clumps, lines of silver-skirted olives. The foliage of gardens and fall of fountains interspersed with mosque towers brought memories of Cordova.

My illusions were rudely dispelled as our small caravan entered the ancient gates. The streets twisted about with hardly a level spot to rest. Narrow and sunless, overhung with buildings, they ran with water which cleansed them of offal but left dampness which presaged sickness of the lungs. Maimonides brightened with interest at the sight of three large libraries; I frowned upon seeing the famous Karueein mosque, largest in all Africa.

We had little difficulty in finding temporary lodging, going directly to the Jewish quarter. The friends we found here used their good offices further in succeeding days to find a house on the outskirts of their settlement. It pleased me. I knew the wood for the roof of the Cordova synagogue had come from Fez, a certain hard, well-grained cypress. Our family established itself near such a grove, near fields where I might walk and meditate. I came to love the slinking yellow fox, the geometrical boundings of the gray antelope, the swarms of fearful rabbits, the small charming bird that Brujo called *tabib*, the doctor, because of its judicious air and pompous walk.

Oaks with the bark that floats, trunks a dozen feet thick, grew on the nearby hills. For miles and miles there lay hills seemingly covered with straw in summer, then, in the rains of winter, blazing up in color: masses of pink lilies, white heather, thyme, purple thistle and lavender, slopes of poppies and marigold, acres of enormous daisies, whole beds of delicate mignonette. The hues were overpowering: I commenced to understand the fierce coloring Moslems used in their paintings. And the mingled odors seemed at night to recall the incense of the mosques.

Maimonides did not share my love of nature. His love was

166

of men and learning. He went in search of the sages in religion, in philosophy and astronomy. Only in the bazaars where they sold the famous golden leather slippers, sashes of embroidered silk and wool, pottery and brass trays and the small Fez caps dyed dull crimson from the juice of a native berry gathered on the far side of the river—only here did our tastes coincide.

"What shall we do in the place you have chosen?" I demanded a week after our arrival. "I cannot stroll in the fields and market place day after day."

"Myself, I have begun to write as I study," Maimonides responded placidly. "My work on the Mishnah goes well. I have accumulated the names of forty fathers in direct lineage to David as my authorities."

"That is well for you," I snapped, "but there are others of the family who are not as blessed."

"We shall live as we have always lived."

"There is little liking for Jews here. The quarter pays a yearly tribute of thirty thousand dinars. Six thousand of our people were killed here four generations ago, and only fourteen years past the Almohades again massacred the Jews."

"Yet we live in peace and religious freedom."

"With deception at our right hand."

"Yet we live. Others have lived here much longer. Are you once more afraid, my father? I have said before, we left Cordova too soon, in a panic of fear. Will you allow it to overwhelm our days once again? We must learn to abide, to grin at fright when it moves its fleshless jaws at us."

"Muni, I cannot think of myself, I must think of all," I returned earnestly. "You may be blithe but, tell us, how shall we survive?"

"As Jews," Maimonides said instantly. "You must know by now that the Jew is as indestructible as the world itself."

He looked up at the small bronze water-clock glowing in the rays of the afternoon sun. He rose to his feet and held out his hand. "Where are we going?" I asked. Maimonides looked solemnly at me. "To pay our respects to a man you should have visited before," he replied. "To meet Rabbi Joseph ben Shoshan, leader of the Jews in Fez."

I raised my hand to hide my smile; my complaints had worked well. For one of the few times since our arrival, my son was about to do what I wanted him to do—without his knowledge.

167

It warmed my heart to see my old friend. He was not one of those thin vinegary Jews, but plump and rosy, almost illuminated in the darkness of his house. Ben Shoshan was garbed as we, in Moslem dress, but his manners were distinctly of the synagogue. As soon as we came in, I folded him in my arms with a hearty kiss that he returned smackingly, his beard sparkling whiter than my own. Maimonides stared at us in surprise.

"Have you known each other before?" he demanded.

My friend laughed, throwing back his head. "You do not know everything yet, my son," I said, joining Ben Shoshan in his merriment. "You do not think I came to Fez only to forward your studies, no, indeed!"

"Your eminent father helped me build the first great synagogue in Toledo," gurgled Ben Shoshan.

"And this more eminent man aided me in building ours in Cordova," I added. I grew sober. "But why did you come to Fez, Joseph?" I asked. "I know they loved you in Toledo."

"To aid my fellow Jews," he said simply, "in danger of persecution." His eyes twinkled. "And there was the matter of the excellent schools and libraries for one's use—if one could successfully assume the outward guise of a Moslem."

When we embraced, I had noted a pleasant smoky odor like burning cedar bark on his clothes. As we sat down beside the fire, I knew the source: the twisted burning boughs on the hearth.

"I am honored you have come," he said, his genial countenance beaming. He waved me to the wine and cakes.

"We are honored to be here," I said, helping myself generously inasmuch as Maimonides made no move to join me.

"Who has not heard of the eminent Maimon family, its healing father and its wise son?"

"Many thanks," I said, sipping and gazing at the well-lined walls around me with envy. "You have a full library here."

"I collect my poor best. It is at your service."

"I have been working here for days," Maimonides explained. He turned to Ben Shoshan. "It was your knowledge of the Talmud and the Mishnah which brought us here."

"That and the sale of a prized diamond," I muttered.

"Knowledge is always more precious than wealth," Shoshan said.

"Sometimes it is less salable," I returned.

"Your son has a mighty mind. He and I have talked many hours away."

"He talks and writes like an angel. But can he earn enough for a family?"

"He is a scholar," Shoshan said in surprise. "You must provide his keep."

"I shall do what the fathers of old have instructed," I said without relish.

"The good Rabbi Shoshan has been a help in time of trouble," Maimonides broke in hurriedly. "As I speak with him, my memory clears miraculously."

Shoshan shook his head generously. "A word here, a hint there," he declared. "The rest is yours."

"You will read what I write and give me the benefit of your wisdom?" Maimonides asked eagerly, his eyes shining.

"Certainly, my son."

There was more talk but it escapes my memory. When finally we rose to go, however, the rabbi of Fez touched my arm. His expression was serious. "A word before you go," he said in a low tone. "Here we live like the king of old, sitting over a pit, on rotten planks, with a sword hanging above. As long as we pay lip service to the Moslem creed, we are not persecuted."

"Have no fear," I said shortly, "I shall do nothing."

"That is most dangerous of all."

"I shall not tempt God's wrath by agreeing to their will."

Our friend shook his head slightly. "It is best to bow to the wind and rise again, rather than be broken."

"Have you become one of the Anusim?" I asked bitterly. "A half-Jew?"

"If you choose. What I do, I do to preserve our faith in an unhappy time."

"He is right," Maimonides said solemnly.

"I do not agree," I exclaimed. "How many have been martyrs like Akiba?"

"How many more have been saved by pretended conversion like Meir and Eleazar?" asked Ben Shoshan.

I bowed. "We part friends, honored sir," I said stubbornly. Joseph ben Shoshan sighed and bowed. "For these many years I have remained alive to assist such friends as you," he replied. "God will preserve us. Tomorrow I shall have Maimonides meet a dear friend of mine who will assist him in his studies."

As I feared, my son met the friend of Rabbi ben Shoshan—and, as I had suspected, he was a Moslem. A poet and theologian, a tall, dark, and intense-looking man, he showed the strong curved nose and prominent cheekbones that indicate the artistic soul. His name was Abdul ibn Mosa, of a famous Arab family. Maimonides brought him to our house a week after our meeting with Rabbi ben Shoshan, and, I thought, showed more trepidation than usual. Both David and I had questioned him about this Moslem acquaintance and he had been either evasive or silent.

It appeared, when I insisted on meeting Ibn Mosa, that there was more to their friendship than even I guessed. Sitting by lamplight in our raftered stone room, we exchanged the customary amenities and Ibn Mosa launched into fervent praises of Maimonides.

"Rabbi Maimon," he announced, "your son is a great man."

"Your tongue bears honey," I said apologetically.

"He will be an ornament in the crown of the belief of the Surrendered," he said emphatically. My head jerked up: I knew that in Arabic this was Islam. I looked at Maimonides; his gaze encountered mine with what I interpreted as a defiant stare.

Before I could utter a word, Ibn Mosa went on in his rattling manner: "I know Mohammed has said that Jews are a 'sect who twist their tongues concerning the Book that ye may reckon it to be from the Book but it is not from the Book,' and that he, Allah be praised for his message, has added, 'How the Jews lie, God quarrel with them!' but I do not believe this of your son."

"He is an honest child," I murmured.

"He knows the Koran as he does your own Torah," Ibn Mosa went on enthusiastically. "You are to be congratulated as a father who is not intolerant of other beliefs."

"What he has learned of others is his own doing."

"He has a great dream of bringing the Moslems and the Jews together into one religion," Abdul ibn Mosa said. "This was the dream of the Prophet as well."

I could not answer. I fixed my eyes on Maimonides' expressionless face and tried to find some sign of what he had told our visitor. I could discover no clue to his feelings. The volley of Arabic from Ibn Mosa sounded far away in my ears, unreal and blasphemous.

Suddenly I roused myself as Maimonides got up from his stool. "Come," he said to Ibn Mosa, "we shall be late for our studies." I rose with him as did the Moslem, and bowing with bewilderment, I bade them both farewell. I turned to meet

David's frown as the door closed behind the pair. "What was the man talking of?" demanded my other son. He stood, his big body dominating the room. I laid my hand affectionately on his shoulder and shook my head. "Be patient," I said. "Maimonides shall tell us himself when he comes home."

But neither I nor David examined Maimonides, partly from fear of what we might discover, partly because he had resumed his old ways, studying and writing at night, sleeping during the day. I knew there was no hope of gaining anything but a quarrel with him in which I would lose my temper and he would remain serene and impregnable. Being silenced on my part did not mean I had been convinced; doubts roused in Almería and Toledo were again revived. To avoid a possible schism in the family, I turned my efforts to what might prove more fruitful and less argumentative—gaining a livelihood for all of us. I summoned David. I explained to him what I had discovered in the market: There was an increasing demand for jewels in such countries as Spain and Algarve, in the land of the Franks, and, most especially, in Italy. I suggested we return to the occupation we had shared in Toledo, our trade in precious stones.

David made no protest. He had become quiet and reserved in his manner since his affair in Toledo, aloof from all. He was a different person from the enthusiastic, energetic boy I had known: a young man turned inward, his very flesh drawn in and lean, his muscles corded. I wondered what worm ate at his vitals; more than once I tried to draw him out, without success. Never discourteous nor without respect, he countered my questions with what I styled the "Muni manner," using monosyllables and vague speech. Twice I came upon him talking to Yaltah with passion, once with Brujo. But I asked no questions and no one confided in me.

I lost no time in visiting the main bazaar. There I bargained for the lease of a stall where David and I might renew our activities. Maimonides, walking and discussing matters with Ibn Mosa, came upon us there. He was less than helpful. He desired me to give without question the price asked—when I knew, as did its proprietor, that its proper rent was half of what he demanded. It was Ibn Mosa who finally determined the bargain in my favor, God spare his soul from Hell.

On the matter of the two letters which have now become so famous—fame which I could have dispensed with—this is

171

the true tale. Near the end of our first year in Fez, still fretting about the silences of my sons and the problem of the marriage of Yaltah, I received a communication which demanded a Responsum, a determination of the law, from me.

The communication came from a friend in a city on the coast of Morocco, to the east. It detailed the difficulties of Jews in the Maghreb, our West Land. It described an opinion asked of a rabbi in Spain as to the status of those who had saved their lives and those of their children by uttering the formula of the Moslems: *"La ilaha illa Allah, wa-Mohammed rasul Allah"* ("There is no god but Allah and Mohammed is his Prophet"). The stern reply had been that any Jew who publicly confessed belief in Mohammed had thereby denied God. His prayers would find no acceptance; his secret performance of all the Jewish rites was to no avail; he could no longer be regarded as a member of our faith. It was tantamount to ordering a man to martyrdom.

The appeal to my own thought on the subject came like an explosion of one of those mangonel fire-pots used by the Greeks. Smoke, noise, a strangling sensation, the feeling of numbness and bewilderment. Abruptly, my own vision opened to a larger view than that of my own family: I saw the Jews of all the world, weary and driven, an endless procession of homeless and abandoned, some so scourged by the wretchedness of this world that they had lost the vision of the World-to-Come. Some, I had heard, had embraced the faith of the Moslems with fervor, in the belief that Mohammed, too, had been sent to earth by God as a prophet like Moses.

Long I sat and pondered. I had never swerved from my feeling that acknowledgment of any part of another belief was mortal sin. I had told this to Maimonides again and again. The dreadful riddle was not a matter of theory or discussion now; it was one of torture, of life and death. Could I abandon my fellows to such a fate?

Busily composing my reply one night, I became aware of Maimonides entering, pausing at my elbow. I looked up. He stood beside my table, looking down with knotted brows. "Welcome home," I said. "We have not seen you all day."

"We have been delving in difficult fields, Ibn Mosa, Ben Shoshan, and myself," he responded. Then, without preamble, he said: "I give nothing, earn nothing for the support of our house. Am I wrong to do so?"

I dropped my pen and massaged my fingers. My head ached. "So many questions," I said, but I felt secretly pleased that this weighed on his conscience. "If you were guilty, I would have said so. You are a scholar, as Ben Shoshan has said. The words of the Fathers adjure us to keep and cherish scholars, giving all that is needful for them to pursue their studies."

"You are a scholar."

"I am old; you are young. That is the difference between us—a life running out, a life flowing in."

"I know all this," Maimonides replied brusquely. "I endure feelings of remorse, nevertheless. Should I not aid you and David?"

"No," I said.

"Should I not aid you in the work you do here?"

"No," I repeated shortly, feeling the rise of an emotion next to jealousy. "This is my duty, that of none other."

Before I could clap my palms atop the parchment, Maimonides had cast his quick glance over it, his memory inscribing in an instant what I had written. "What is this you write?" he asked aggressively.

My face flushed. Startled by his question, I reared back, a horse reined in at full career. "I do what I do to comfort a few of our people," I said. "It is none of your affair."

"You have not written a Responsum for a long time."

"Then it is all the more proper that I write at this time."

Maimonides gazed at me, his eyes smoldering. "How can you comfort the tortured and the dying?" he demanded. "I know of their sufferings."

"God has not abandoned them."

"For one who sees his house looted, his servants carried away, his wife raped, his children impaled, who feels his own lifeblood seeping through his fingers, comfort is a cold word. A man without life is a man without belief, just as surely as if he had not been born."

I swallowed convulsively. "I can do no more than I do," I said, "no more than I know, for one who is perplexed at the ways of God."

"I, too, am perplexed at His ways," Maimonides returned gravely. He folded his legs and sat down, his chin in his hands. "I sit at your feet," he said. "Read to me what you have written."

I hesitated, then cleared my throat in a whisper:

" 'It is clear from the writings of the Prophets and the Fathers that God is true, His messages are true, and that these have been truly handed down to us. These things have no

173

flaw, no deception. God never changes; He does not choose and then reject; only man wants a thing and, when it comes, rejects it. How can He—who knows all before it happens, Who causes all as He wills it—come to hate that which He loves?' "

"This is not an argument of logic but one of the heart," Maimonides interjected.

"To you be the head, to me the heart," I said. Maimonides did not reply.

" 'We must lean upon God, believe Him and bless Him. We cannot doubt His promises any more than we can doubt that He lives. He has promised to draw us near Him; He will not cast us off. Other nations prosper but we must not fear. In spite of their rage at us, their victory over us, our slavery to them, we trust in God and His promises.' "

"This is not what they should hear," Maimonides said. I paid no heed to his comment, reading on.

" 'We must hold to the Law and not relinquish it. We, who are underlings, are like those drowning. We sink in a pool of calamity, the waters pass over our heads; but the rope of our salvation hangs suspended between heaven and earth. Whoever lays hold of it has hope; he who lets go will surely perish. Let no man mistake—he who grips the rope of God with all his strength will be saved sooner than he who touches it with his fingertips, but even he has more hope than he who lets it go.

" 'The Law is our rope. We must cling to it, obey it, think upon it. What we can do, we must do. Prayer is permitted everywhere; if you do not know the whole prayer, say part; keep those rituals that you may, and remember the others for happier days. If things go well, be not elated; if they go badly, do not be depressed. He who loves this world more, loves God the less.' "

I could not contain myself. I read in a loud voice, with a passion I could not resist:

" 'When misfortune comes, when no ruler gives law, no counselor advises, when there is nowhere to flee, no army for defense—yea, when we are denied everything but death—then we may flee to God as our eternal refuge. We will call and He will answer; we will cry out and He will give help. O Lord, our strength and our refuge!' "

Maimonides clapped his hands twice: slowly, sardonically. He rose to his feet. "It is a triumph of sentiment, not of sense," he said crisply. "This is a foe we must fight with more than emotion. What authorities have you, what rulings, what words that cut like swords?"

"Few or none at all. This is my own heart speaking."

A week later Maimonides sought me out in my room. He presented me with a codex scrawled in Arabic. "Written in a mosque," he said, "but I have addressed this to those same sufferers to whom you wrote. Will you approve it?"

I glanced over page after page of what he had inscribed. Despite myself, I thrilled, as always, to his passionate pleading, to his array of authorities and references to holy works. I could not help feeling, nonetheless, that he was wrong in saying apostate Jews should be welcomed back into the faith.

"We must distinguish between those who are forced to recant," he wrote, "and those who do so wickedly. To judge them by one standard is against Scripture and the witnesses of the past."

As for breaking the law under duress, Maimonides went on to cite the examples of Meir and Eleazar, who had saved their lives by pretending to other beliefs (though he did not mention the martyrs Akiba or Gamaliel). He admitted such men as the former acted badly but added:

"This persecution differs from the others because formerly Jews have been called upon to break the law by acts. Here they are asked only to recite an empty formula which the Moslems themselves know we utter insincerely to escape the bigot. Any Jew who wants to observe the whole of the six hundred thirteen precepts in his home may do so safely. If any Jew wishes to be a martyr, he has done nobly and his reward is great before the Lord. But if a man asks me, 'Shall I be slain or utter the formula of Islam?' I answer, 'Utter the formula and live.'"

I shook my head. "This I deny," I said, pointing. "We cannot survive in sin."

"You have not finished," Maimonides said calmly. "If you read on, you will see I advise that if we cannot perform our duties to God in safety, we should leave the land, even homes and children, to find a place where we can observe the law without compulsion or fear."

"The logic of the mind is not enough," I said, "this needs also the touch of the heart."

"Perhaps," Maimonides said. "Let yours be sent first and mine later. We shall see which shall do more."

"And prove ourselves hypocrites and liars?"

Maimonides' face broke into anguish. I was astonished to

175

see his tears flow. "As God is my witness," he cried, "we must defend others, not ourselves! If such a reproach as this were brought against me alone, I should not have sought help for myself, knowing my sin of pretense. I should have said, 'Let me lie in my shame, let my confusion cover me, I have sinned against the Lord our God. I know, O God, I have done wickedly.' If it had not been so sorely insisted upon—in the letter sent you, my father—that those who pray, after such a public lie, are committing a transgression, I should have been silent." He wrung his hands. "But what of all Israel? Will not all our people forsake their faith? If they feel that praying is a sin in such a case, will they not stop praying altogether?"

His voice rose, his tears choked him into silence. I drew him to me and we wept together. When he rose once more, he had reassumed his grim expression. "I shall ask them," he said, "to send a copy of both of these to every community, city, and village, to strengthen faith; to have them read publicly and in private—only taking precautions that the message be not divulged to the heathen by an evil person."

"No," I said, my head bowed. "Mine must be read only to those who wish encouragement."

"As you will, my father," Maimonides agreed submissively. His voice hardened. "But if my epistle is sent, I shall so instruct those who receive it." He turned, hesitating at the door. "Tell me," he said, "if the choice were forced upon you, yourself—would you choose to lie about your belief in God? Or would you endure torture and death?"

"I don't know," I said very slowly, "I don't know."

In due time my letter was posted by secret courier. It achieved some good, in its fashion, but before it could reach most of the far-flung Jewish communities, another incident occurred. A second zealot rabbi, in another city, declared in Responsum an even stricter code: If any Jew repeated the Moslem confession, even without believing in it, or if he entered a Moslem place of worship, he was thenceforth outcast from all Jewry. After knowledge of this, I could no longer restrain Maimonides. Nor did I have the will to attempt it. His letter went out, a ringing defense of the Anusim.

As I had foreseen, these communications brought us much unhappiness. It was to be endured only if our scripts were instrumental in saving for future repentance those who had sinned in forced conversion. Praise be to God, we remained unknown for years as the authors, anonymous enough to take

176

respite in Fez. But other elements of danger, gathering as a pillar of cloud in the west, forced us to live in a weird twilight of apostasy.

Signs of the evil change in our happier condition came in the fourth year. We were well established, known in the city as jewel merchants; Maimonides stood highly respected for his learning; and I, even in my humble station, renewed again some practice of rabbi and physician. We had prospered in gem-trading; and Maimonides reported himself more than halfway through his gigantic review of the Mishnah, his effort to simplify it for the common, unlearned people. The good Ibn Mosa (whom I had gradually come to trust implicitly, despite my early doubts) was often at our house. Less frequent but even more welcome were the visits of Joseph ben Shoshan, a comfort to the mind and heart.

My worries centered themselves about Yaltah and David. The girl had grown up: At the age of sixteen, she was lovely and demure, with a slight, full-bosomed figure, an oval-shaped face, with long dark hair and the glowing eyes of the family. As her father, I said she was beautiful; the least a passer-by might have said was that she was charming.

She felt increasingly restless, more dissatisfied than I knew. Five years above the age for marriage, she found none of the Jewish youths in the Fez quarter interested her. I promised her I would not marry her off against her will. I had preserved her dowry, and her whim, I believed, was only a passing one; I was sure time would cure it.

From day to day, David had changed. No longer aloof was he, nor as he had been, eager and curious. Instead, he appeared to have acquired a certain arrogance, a hard shell like that of a sea-animal. He wanted neither advice nor aid; he demonstrated an increasing contempt for shopkeeper's work. The same untoward absences which had plagued me in Toledo again became habitual. Long hours of most of the days of the week I was forced to substitute for him in the stall. I did not know where he went nor why, and I feared to be alone. Certain pricklings in my chest, once a fit of giddiness, warned me I was not as robust as I had been.

Both David's situation and Yaltah's were to undergo a dreadful change. By fate, they were to be interlocked with mine, even more so in my weakness than in my strength. Maimonides, on the other hand, as his research lessened and writing increased, became a constant companion on my walks, replacing Brujo or Yaltah. It was on one of these occasions that my hopes for David were rudely dispelled.

On a blue spring day, with so bright and cloudless a sky that rocks and dry hills took on the sheen of good turquoise by reflection, Maimonides and I strolled on the dusty road. It ran as a narrowing path between the patterns of the flower-decked hills. Suddenly the air behind us shook; the thunder of horses ridden at full speed echoed around us. Maimonides raced for shelter, knowing the wild ways of the Berber horsemen: They stopped for no obstacle, human or otherwise. He gained a small niche in the hillside, scrambling to safety, looking back in horror.

Screams that thinned the blood, shouts and cries, the increasing beat of hoofs: three horses side by side around the curve, the riders streaked with mud and foam, standing in their stirrups with their robes flying back, their burnooses loosed, their long hair streaming, handling the slim Arab horses as if they were part of their own bodies. It was a sight engraved indelibly into my mind—struck as a coin is minted from a blow struck by a hammer: the cords bursting from the flesh of the animals, their bloody eyes starting from their sockets; the mad riders in their career, half in air and half on earth, in a single massive rhythm that made the ground quiver.

Helpless, dazed, I stood in the middle of the road, in the path of the riders. I waved my arms, collapsing into a supine heap. Maimonides, secure on the face of the rock, whirled and flung himself back, across my cowering body. Next instant, they were upon us. The middle horseman lashed his horse frantically, pulled back on the reins. His mount seemed to take wings, soaring over me as I, on the back of a similar horse, had soared over a cart one night long ago in Almería. I stared upward at the wagging phallus of a stallion. Then all were gone, down the road, leaving us to cough and sneeze in a cloud of settling dust.

Maimonides helped me solicitously to my feet. I leaned heavily on his shoulder, my heart pounding wildly. I fumbled for his hand. A quick sweat ran down my body; the peace of the morning was gone.

Maimonides stood beside me. He shaded his eyes to peer after the riders, who had not turned their heads to see what had happened. I balanced shakily on my feet, my head whirling with what I had seen—not because death had passed so near, nor from fright nor awe, but I had seen the face and

178

form of the middle rider of the three horsemen, the one who had vaulted over us.

"Muni," I said hoarsely, "did you see him?"

Maimonides remained rigid. I thrust him around, forcing him to confront me, my curls dusty and disarranged, clothes filthy. I peered up into his iron face. "Did you see him?" I shouted again, frantically.

"Yes."

"Tell me it was not he!"

"I cannot," Maimonides said. "It was David himself."

A sharp pain pierced my left side. The world turned about me, its colors blurring. I felt my legs melt to water; I sank helplessly to the ground. Faintly, far away, I heard the bitter voice of my son: "The riders of the devil, bound for hell! David, my brother!"

I heard no more. My senses failed. A surge of darkness overcame my sight and mind. I swooned, stretched out like a Canaanite beggar on the road.

CHAPTER 11

"How else can we gain back our Holy Land?" David demanded in exasperation. "Must we always be driven like sheep? Shall we not some time turn on our persecutors and rend them like wolves?"

"My son, fighting and killing are not for us. We are forbidden by the Torah, by the laws under which we live, by every instinct of our people."

"We have been robbed by every nation on earth," David said grimly. "First, the Moslems, then the Christians. The land of our forefathers is desolate, the battleground of all nations, held as a heathen kingdom by the crusaders!"

I raised myself on an elbow, anger animating my weak body. "You prate so bravely of what must be done," I said, "tell me how you will deliver Zion. By the might of your own fist?"

David looked reflectively at his right hand and curled it

up slowly. He gave me a tight-lipped smile. "It is not a weak one," he replied. "We have had heroes before—the Maccabees, Saul and David, Samson. We have conquered the armies of Antiochus of Syria, as well as the Philistines. You, my father, speak of things of the heart; my brother speaks of ideas of the head. I have neither of these: I have only a strong body—but with this, one can do much."

"You can destroy us all, if you are known. Jews will despise you as a renegade, Moslems will loathe you as a Jew."

"A mighty man of arms is of as much value as one who deals in books. He is the only one who can save the Jews."

"I shall rejoice to see Jerusalem free, to see the Temple rise again," Maimonides said. He passed a wet cloth over my forehead as I sank back on my bed. His tone was cold as he addressed his brother. "You desire to become a dealer of death, a gladiator." He looked at David ironically. "You do not hope to oppose the Christians and the Moslems by yourself, I think?"

"No," David said sullenly.

"Then how will you redeem Zion?"

David's eyes brightened. "We must bring together all our people, throughout the world!"

"I have thought of that," Maimonides said.

"We must organize them into an army, bring them to Palestine! Conquer it once more as Moses' successors did!"

"Where will you find the money for such a world-shaking enterprise?"

"Not all Jews are poor."

"Perhaps. But they will not contribute for a dream and this is no more. Further, if there is any sign of such an organization, your life will be forfeit for it."

David beat his hands together in a gesture of despair. "I shall join the Moslems, we shall see!"

"Don't talk nonsense," Maimonides told him sharply. His tone softened. "David, two things are needed. There is, first, the need to bring all Jews together in belief, to end the schisms and feuds which plague us. The next is to gain enough influence and wealth to compass such a wish as yours. Then, I will guarantee its success. All will flock to the starred standard of Israel."

"In a thousand years," I muttered, "in a thousand years."

They paid no attention to me. "Will you help me, Muni?" David asked eagerly.

Maimonides nodded. "It shall be my task to unite our

brethren, to save them from despair, give them hope," he said.

"And mine?"

"There is wealth to be gained. You must devote yourself to the business of acquiring it. Not to the useless riding and swordsmanship you have practiced."

David's face became clouded. His inward sun was obscured and lost. He looked away. Maimonides and I watched him, our breathing bated. "I will do what I can," he said at last, his voice breaking. "Do not ask me now what my decision is."

"And I?" I inquired petulantly. "Am I to have no part in this great design?"

David's smile irradiated his face again; he squeezed my hand so mightily that he seemed to crush the bones. I uttered a smothered yelp. Maimonides patted my forehead with his vile-smelling cloth that would have resuscitated a corpse. "You must get well first," he said soothingly to me, as if he, not I, were the elder physician. "We shall assign you the deserved role of elder general, with robes and badges of honor."

"Get out, get out, both of you," I said gruffly, exercising my bruised hand under the cloak. "We have talked enough foolishness. You shall argue David from his folly, Muni, or else beat him."

David laughed aloud, patting his brother on the head—he towered over him. He led the way from the room. He and Maimonides realized I was exhausted. Also, I needed to be alone to assess my condition. My fainting-fit on the road, I thought now, had been occasioned not so much by the unexpected sight of David with a party of mamelukes as by my irregular diet, my lack of exercise, and—very possibly—my continued exasperation and anxiety. Maimonides said it was a weakness of the heart: not fatal, but a warning that one could not disregard. I bore his diagnosis without visible irritation, but it is always difficult to be treated by a son. He suspected my exaggerated acquiescence. I nodded too rapidly when he advised keeping the head warm and the feet cool; I was too ready to accept the small dry sponge he gave me, saturated with a rare and reviving clove scent, to be dampened and inhaled in case of another seizure.

David's withheld penitence for his actions I could not condemn. I had deplored too little his return to participation in sham battles: He confessed to duels with wooden spears, lances and swords, on the mock fortalices and barricades of the exercise grounds near the guard barracks of the University of the Caliphate. There was something martial in his nature which needed expression; time alone could soften his spirit. And, I thought secretly, it might be that his valor would set an example to all Jews, if God so willed it. Thus, though I had censured him for his renewal of those same activities which had driven us from Toledo, my rebukes were half-hearted. All the more perhaps because I feared his long silence about what we had done to him in Toledo: drugging him and taking him away against his desires. His strange, self-imposed lack of complaint—for we never dared mention it—was in itself a warning.

Eight months marched slowly by in comparative peace. David tended the stall in the bazaar dutifully, but at home I could sense his chafing against the bonds of daily business. I chafed as well at my enforced seclusion. To a limited extent I continued my work in medicine, tending the poor, poring over the old manuscripts of the Arabs in search of forgotten remedies, blending and brewing potions in the rude clay alembics of the town, resuming my daily walks in the fields to gather herbs and roots. On these expeditions a stout cypress-bough staff and Brujo were my companions. Amazingly enough, Brujo had become as stiff-necked, in his observances of the Law, as the most Pharisaical of Jews. Maimonides and I often were amused at it. "How do you like being one of us?" I inquired of him during an afternoon excursion. He shrugged: "I have found a loving wife and the love of God," he said with his golden-gummed smile. "I have been forgiven sins enough—and Paradise is at least as possible for the Jew as it is for Moslem or Christian."

"You do not regret your conversion?"

"Once a Christian, always a Jew," Brujo said. I laughed for the first time since my illness.

Not long after this conversation, we were interrupted early one morning in our wanderings by the arrival of Maimonides. He came up mounted on a mule, leading another. "We are summoned!" he cried excitedly. "To the quarters of the chamberlain Ibn Harout in the palace of the emir! He is ill, he wishes us to attend him."

"How does he know our name?" I demanded in alarm, visions of unknown ordeals flashing through my mind.

Maimonides shrugged. "I have no idea," he acknowledged, "but we must obey the command, must we not?"

I nodded, frowning. I had heard of Ibn Harout's sickness.

182

I dreaded to be his physician. "This man has been sick a long time," I reminded Maimonides.

"So much the more credit to you for his cure," my son remarked airily. I waved my cudgel at him. "You have more faith in your father than he deserves," I said. "There are some diseases only a miracle can cure. I suspect this may be one of them."

"Are you diagnosing his ailment from such a distance?" Maimonides asked innocently. I sighed. I beckoned Brujo to assist me atop the cursed mule.

Laden with what small supplies of medicine we had managed to accumulate during our years in Fez, we came into the courts of the palace. My eyes were dazzled. My heart bounded like a deer in the meadows. I had not been granted admission to these grounds before and I discovered they were another reminder of dear Cordova.

A hundred gilt-and-marble columns and pillars of exquisitely inlaid mosaic upheld scores of arches. These, in turn, framed a multitude of sweeping vistas of gardens and groves, traceries and fountains which surrounded the palace. In the brilliant summer sun of Morocco, the iridescent tiles blazed in fantastic variations of colors that hurt the eye—like nothing so much as the tapestries of the hills in the spring, like the palaces of the djinni in Arabian tales.

Maimonides and I, two men in a dream, spellbound by the beauty of the place, entered after examination by the guard. We were taken in tow by a gnarled black slave. With many suspicious looks, he led us at a limping pace up to the second story of the east wing, into the spacious, sparsely furnished bedchamber of the emir's chief official.

Again, the room forced me to gasp with pure pleasure. It was a room that seemed filled with coruscations of jeweled light, from the polished tiled floor to the light-vaulted roof that surely must have been erected by angels; slender pillars, bright colors that swooned in the eye, silks and stuffs everywhere that Moslem rulers love so well. On the customary dais in the middle, a mass of red and yellow cushions upon a divan caught our attention immediately.

To my surprise, I glimpsed five figures on it. The central one barely nodded at the eunuch's announcement. We salaamed deeply. I straightened up—to remain rooted to the spot in a species of indescribable emotion. Here was a man who, I had been told, was old and sick unto death. Yet he sat naked

183

in the warmth of the sun, in the midst of four stark-nude young Nubian dancing girls.

If the chamberlain appeared to be an angular stick of pale ivory, the girls were figures carved out of ebony, delicate features in silhouette. All sat cross-legged, surrounding their master. What made my eyes bulge was the fact that their hair, the glory of womankind, had been taken from them. Heads, arms, legs, even their shamelessly exposed pink crotches, had been shaved to the quick.

Before each girl spread a chessboard, filled with intricately carved figures of ivory: green and white, black and white, red and white, blue and white. The slaves stared straight down at them with extraordinary concentration, seemingly without knowledge of anyone else's presence in the chamber. Maimonides and I (my own senses titillated as well as horrified, I was exasperated to observe Maimonides with a gleam of more than interest on his face) stood where we were, hardly daring to breathe. As we watched, Ibn Harout reached out a withered hand. One after the other, he moved a chessman at each board. He sighed with satisfaction. At last he looked at us.

"You are the honored Maimon ben Joseph and his son, Maimonides," came a reedy voice that must once have been a bellow. "Learn from what you see. If you want sport at chess, play for high stakes. I have taught these girls the art of the game; now, if they give me *eschec mat* but once, I have promised them liberty. They make their moves with the patience and subtlety of Iblis himself—but I am, thus far, more than a match for my old Adversary."

He snapped his fingers in command. As one, the girls promptly rose. Gracefully and carefully they lifted the boards so as not to disturb the pieces, placing a colored counter on each to indicate the coming turn was theirs. They moved in undulating procession from the room without a word; I perceived Maimonides' eyes following them as if attached to their behinds. I sighed gustily for my own youth.

"Sometimes they attempt to cheat me by moving men without my knowledge," remarked Ibn Harout. "But they have learned to reckon with my memory. If they are caught, they are executed." He spoke pure Arabic, totally unlike the execrable Berber jargon.

In truth, I thought the man himself was worth more study than the figures of his women. Tall, cadaverous in the extreme, he resembled a living corpse. His skin was the gray of parch-

184

ment, his face a graven, sharp-angled mask at the cheekbones and nose and chin, the flesh sunken elsewhere. The eyes dominated his expression. They resembled two coals burning without flame, flickering in deep sockets. Whatever emotion he felt was registered here, just beneath his white-turbaned shaven head.

"Approach, healer of the Jews," said his voice in a whisper of amusement. "Be not alarmed by my methods of healing. The touch of young flesh is warming, reviving, so I believe. Did not your own King David have Abishag to sleep with him, to warm his old age? Thus I have four fires in my bed at night, four pleasures by day."

His eyes moved to Maimonides. "This is your famous son, Maimonides? He is better known than he imagines. I may have use for his spiritual talents. But it is to you, Maimon, that I come first to heal the body. Advance, as befits my guests; sit."

"You deign to honor us," I stammered.

"I disarray your senses as well," came the barely audible answer. "What do you think of my medication?"

"It is a worthy prescription," said Maimonides unexpectedly. I ground my teeth in despair at his insolence.

The great eyes of Ibn Harout turned slowly to him. "You have more courage than sense, young one, great though your sense is reputed to be."

"He meant nothing," I said hastily. "Pardon a father for having such a son."

The chamberlain nodded slightly, swiveling his look back to me. "I have taken potions of Moslem physicians, Maimon ben Joseph. They have done me good; they keep me free from pain, thanks to Allah; yet my mind remains clear. I am enabled to enjoy women and the noble game of chess. Next to war, these have delighted me most. Now, however, I am tired of being death in life. I wish to know the truth, whether I shall live or die."

"Perhaps that is beyond my skills," I murmured.

"Perhaps. I do not think so. Do not fear for what you say; it may be that my own feelings have anticipated you— But we must have music."

He snapped his fingers twice. Trotting into the room came three gaudily robed musicians: a lutist, a reed-player, a plucker of the five-stringed rebub. They took their places at the corner of the dais, playing and singing softly the peculiar plaintive melodies that delight the Moslem ear.

185

The sick man closed his eyes as if to enjoy the moment, then inclined his head for us to come closer. "This morning I shall not see my stallions nor my harem from the window," he said. "Truth is the greatest pleasure. It is my wish today to enjoy it, bitter or sweet. Do you wish to examine my body, physician?"

I nodded respectfully. I assumed a kneeling position next to him. My fingers felt his pulse and his head, tapped his chest lightly; my nose smelled his breath, the odor of his urine and sweat. I ran my hands over his scaly dead skin, feeling the edged bones, observing the color and coldness of hands and feet. My hands dwelt long upon a round lump under his right armpit, a second one on his belly.

I was careful and precise with this powerful old man. I did not wish to appear haughty nor overzealous but thorough and dutiful. As the code for healers advised, I was humble yet firm, asking only one or two questions, dealing with time and diet and fomentations, with appearance and odor of excrement. I knew that such sicknesses increase the sensitivity of the patient. I governed myself accordingly. I knew what all the signals of the body silently shouted to me. "That is sufficient," I said unsteadily. I drew back.

The chamberlain, who had remained rigid, with closed eyes, relaxed and opened his dark eyes upon me. To my amazement, they held nothing but humor. "What is it, Maimon ben Joseph, that makes your voice quiver?" came the thin voice from nowhere.

I shook my head. Maimonides had a perturbed expression as did I; he was versed enough in medicine to recognize symptoms.

"Are you loath to tell me the truth?" asked Ibn Harout. "Is it poison?"

I hesitated, not unwilling but unable to speak of the terrible death which God had assigned to this evil man: His blood devoured itself within his body, turning the stuff of life to poison. It was not administered by others but by his own wicked life.

Then, to my dumbfounding, Ibn Harout himself made a correct and fearless diagnosis. "Are you afraid to tell me still?" he asked, languid among the pillows. "If so, I shall tell you. I have a rat in my body that devours me daily; nothing can be done for me. Yet I have no fear, no more than in battle. I have done holy battle for the Prophet, I have conquered my foes in the jihad, I have finished my pilgrimage to Mecca.

So death will be a release, from the tediousness of life to eternal bliss amongst flowers and wine, music and running water, with crystal colors and houris." He sighed. "Will they match those I have loved and fondled on earth?"

"You may recover," Maimonides said earnestly. "I have seen others with the disease in Toledo. It is will and spirit which are the best medicines."

"Young men like yourself may think this is desirable," Ibn Harout said drowsily. "As for me, I no longer think life delectable." He paused, breathing slowly within his almost transparent chest. "I have faced death many times; I made the Black Angel fly to do my bidding. Now he believes he commands. But I shall make him my servant, to carry me off—not as a slave, as an old friend. I shall welcome him with a kiss."

He lay back, partly supported by the pillows. "Let me sleep," he whispered. I knew what he wanted. Taking an ornate wine jar, I mixed a sleeping powder in a cup and held it to his lips. He drained it and was silent a long time, eyes closed. I thought him asleep. I touched Maimonides. We rose and, as we did, his eyes flickered open, impaling us.

"Tell me," he said, "are you truly Jews or truly Moslems?"

The question was a thunderbolt. My jaw fell, my mind teetered. Maimonides stood silent. I cleared my throat and gave the only answer I could, expecting the worst: "We are Jews."

The old man twitched with soundless laughter. "I have slain hundreds like you with my good Damascus scimitar," he wheezed, "but now that is over. Did you expect arrest and torture? No—such as I, dying, do not derive pleasure any longer from the bastinado or the rack. You will go to your destined place, I to mine."

"You are very wise."

"Only old and ill. A word of warning to you. I say this because of the reason I heard your name and summoned you. You and a woman healer cured my father's cousin, Mohammed, of blindness in Almería. He remains grateful."

"We were fortunate and he is kind."

Ibn Harout waved a claw. "The storm of the fanatics will come again, one like that of which I once was the van and terror. Were I younger, healthier, I might take part. But I am denied this."

I said nothing and he went on. "Healer Maimon, the people are not as sophisticated, as knowledgeable as I or as yourself. They believe with all the madness of the ignorant."

187

"I know."

"If their feelings rise, if the shouts of 'Death to the Jews and Christians' come, I shall not stifle them. The life of not one soldier shall be wasted. You can see how I, with so little of my own treasure left, value life."

"I understand."

The chamberlain coughed. "You must look to yourselves for protection," he said. He peered at Maimonides. "Your letter to your fellow Jews—I have read it. Your Jewish courier rots in his grave. I quote your words: 'We are asked only to recite an empty formula, which the Moslems themselves know we say without believing it, in order to fool the fanatic.' That you wrote. You are right; you are wrong. The Christians tighten their net about us each month—and we shall tighten our noose about the neck of the Jew. It amused me to send your letter on, written as it was in fair Arabic. I cannot read your vile Hebrew."

"It was a good deed," Maimonides said slowly.

The head of Ibn Harout nodded. He sank back, still nodding.

"I have said more than my strength allows. You have done well to me and my relatives with your arts." He paused. "In the days to come, remember that I have been a friend to you."

We stood immobile and silent as he gasped for breath. The sick man shook his head feebly. "If your doctrine of Paradise is right—if mine is wrong—I shall ask you to remember Ibn Harout as a friend and plead for his soul to be lifted from the fires of Hell."

He fell back, snapping his fingers thrice. The humped slave came with his sliding gait and reluctantly handed me a purse of a hundred gold dinars. He escorted us to the door, watching us depart from the wondrous palace, a demon at the portals of paradise.

The words of the dying chamberlain were harbingers of disasters that followed us in Fez from that day forward. The jewelry trade languished: black silences in the bazaar. We heard mutterings about evil magic practiced by Jews. And, finally, at the end of the hot African summer, the locusts came.

They came in a dark-green cloud rising from the desert, obscuring the sun, bodies of insects descending on the city like rain. For miles about, the fertile river valley was blanketed. The crops vanished overnight. The locusts attacked the hills in rows, like troops, advancing in irregular lines; flying with a whir, devouring with a rustling sound—and leaving nothing but bare ground behind. Trees, fields, gardens, even solid wood, were gnawed and ruined. Nothing was left after this terrible visitation.

We and the rest of the inhabitants of Fez fought them by fire, water, by crushing them until the soil beneath was slippery with their juices. Nothing availed. They came on by millions. Maimonides was seized by the neighbors and forced into the fields to chant what the fools believed were incantations against the plague. He merely invoked Hebrew curses on insects and superstition. He wrote nonsense on slips of parchment and burned them as charms, with ironic ceremony, under the threat of clubs, even as the insect bodies pelted him. Released he was, but only under imprecations and mutterings of hysteria.

Our last resource was to retreat into our homes, to barricade doors and screen windows. There we remained for two days. At length, at some appointed sign, there was a great whirring of wings. The locusts took flight once more.

They left nothing behind. All had disappeared. There was no food. The reserves of grain and oil and wine in the huge underground jars (stored against just such a time) were soon devoured by the hungry people, as if they themselves were scavengers. In a week, rain came. Soon after, an act of God's mercy, the ground gave birth. We mouth-cropped the green shoots in the field and quarreled about the weeds, even as had Nebuchadnezzar in his idiocy.

Our family sought any employment, even the lowliest. Every day David and I, Brujo, Zayd, and Ramah, even Maimonides, ground grain with our two hands at the homes of wealthy Moslems. In return we received a tiny sliver of bread, thin as a wafer, hardly fit for dogs. During the nights, as we painfully joked, our stomachs sagged to the ground like an old woman's breasts. My swollen wind-paunch was my nightly pillow.

Because of the intense cold, many of the poorer Jews burrowed into steaming dungheaps and rubbish piles for shelter. No firewood was to be had except at great cost. We invited all to huddle in our house, keeping each other warm by the bodies' heat, night after night.

Help came in a fortnight from other cities of Morocco but the Jews were the last to profit by it. Worst of all, we received news that Ibn Harout was at the point of death. The Moslem doctors, who had avoided us, pointed the finger of reproach in our direction. We did not know whether or not they had the ear of the emir, and we grew fearful.

"Be not afraid," counseled Ibn Mosa, who had come each day to console us, often with hidden gifts of food. "I have some influence at the court. I shall do all I can. If you flee, you are sure to be pursued; and if you are found out and caught, that will be taken as admission of guilt. Better, wait for the event."

His advice was good. We were too weak to go far, and many of the pack animals had been slaughtered for food. As we delayed, we gained courage. Our bodies put on flesh; our determination grew, not to be ousted by false fears. Rewarding it was that we came to this decision, for one afternoon we welcomed an unexpected visitor: Benjamin of Tudela, well known for his travels in the far parts of the earth. He had come to Fez on a special errand, he said, to visit the colony of Jews and to bring the Maimon family gifts.

"Gifts?" I said wonderingly. "Have you been to Spain?"

"No," Benjamin returned. He smiled, showing his yellow snaggled teeth between beard and mustachio. He was a gangling, stooped man with roving eyes and an evil breath, nearly bald; but he possessed infinite energy and endurance and his mind was stocked with news of other places, something which never fails to please a Jew. He was of good character and respected in the synagogues. We were pleased to have him honor our house.

"I have come from the East," he told us in his rusty voice. "Let me tell you that I have seen a friend of yours elevated to the highest position possible for a Jew in this world."

"To the top óf a cross, perhaps?" inquired Maimonides.

"Be still!" I cried. "Your wit has no place here tonight. Tell us more, Benjamin."

"To put it plainly, he is Samuel ben Ali. He is now Gaon, the Excellency of Bagdad."

Maimonides and I looked at each other in astonishment. Samuel ben Ali! The child I had last seen in our garden in Cordova, now head of the great Bagdad congregation of Jews, the man who gave law and judgment to by far the greater part of our people! This was news, indeed!

"He is head of the Gaon Jacob Academy, greatest of them all," Benjamin said, satisfied with his sensation. "On the death of Daniel ben Hisdai a year ago, Samuel succeeded to the office which is styled 'Our Lord the Head of the Captivity of All Israel.' He wields great power."

"This is interesting," Maimonides said, struggling to regain his calm.

"He spoke very kindly of you."

"What of his father, Ali?" I asked.

"Alas, he is dead."

Benjamin fumbled in his pack and brought out a shining black glass bottle. He handed it to Maimonides with a flourish. "Samuel sends you a gift of the most choice wine," he told us. "See his seal." Indeed, the mouth of the bottle was sealed in black wax, stamped with the open-mouthed lion of the Babylonians, backed with the six-pointed star of Solomon.

"We shall drink to his friendship," Maimonides said. He handed the bottle to the grinning Zayd behind him. The big Negro licked his lips and carried it to one side to open it.

"And yet another present," Benjamin said. "As I passed through Alexandria on my way hither, I met another of our faith, a second friend of yours." He gave me one of the familiar scrolls of Judah Halevi and my fingers trembled as I unrolled it.

I read it with eyes filled with tears, seeing in it a relic of the buried past. I passed it on to Maimonides, who shaped the phrases aloud, caressingly:

> "Thou livest far above the sky;
>   How canst Thou be within an ark?
> Thy throne is far beyond our eye—
>   But still within our humble mark:
> Who can say he has not seen Thee?
> Heaven and earth reflect Thee meanly,
>   Witnessing day and dark."

"Very moving and somewhat heretical," Benjamin said. "I am not a man who loves poetry, however."

Maimonides tucked the scroll away. "I am not a man who loves Samuel ben Ali," he said briefly and coldly.

Benjamin wagged his head disapprovingly, his sunken cheeks fluttering. He caught his long lower lip with his teeth, gnawing at his beard with an air of exasperation. Maimonides sat quietly, his hands in his lap, his glowing dark eyes watching our visitor.

"Samuel ben Ali," Benjamin muttered. He shook his head. "You will gain nothing by opposing him, Moses ben Maimon. He is a great man, not only in our nation but among the nations of the earth."

"I oppose no one," Maimonides said calmly. "I am at peace with the world, God be praised."

"Amen," Benjamin replied testily. "You may say so, but your very nature opposes him. As well you might say that the cliff does not quarrel with the sea. Your position, his position—these make the conflict."

"Do you say that Maimonides should yield to him?" I interposed.

Benjamin shot me a glance of irritation. "I say no such thing," he returned with the diplomatic say-nothing which he had undoubtedly learned in his travels. "I do not say that one should yield, another stand firm. I say only that there is danger here."

"Between the cliff and the sea?" I pressed him.

"Aye," Benjamin caught me up. "We Jews are between them. Crushed by one, drowned by the other. Here are two authorities, two guides for our distressed people, two forces that rise above our heads, yes, our knowledge. What shall we do?"

"There is the Torah," Maimonides said. "There is the unchanging Law and the Talmud to shed light on it."

"But who of us truly understands the Talmud?" cried Benjamin. "The Talmud contradicts itself. Every rabbi has his own meaning for every word. Only you and Samuel speak with the voices of truth."

"And we two are opposed?" asked Maimonides, almost as if he were amused.

"Yes. You know that very well."

"Then one of us is wrong?"

"Cursed be your logic, that Greek beast which devours our thought!"

"I can only say what I believe to be right," Maimonides said. "I cannot say what Samuel thinks nor control what he says. Nor even say if he says what he thinks."

Benjamin sighed. "Well," he replied, "it is better then that I remind you he is very powerful."

"Powerful in the ways of the world?"

"What better way is there?" demanded Benjamin. "Every fifth day he goes to pay a visit to the caliph. Now mark this as evidence. As he rides, in robes of silk embroidered with precious metals, a huge turban of gems on his head—and on a stallion allotted to him by the caliph, mind you—he has both Jew and Christian and Moslem horsemen at his beck. They ride before him, shouting."

192

"Shouting?" I asked.

" 'Make way before our lord,' they cry again and again. 'Make way for Samuel, son of Ali, as is his due!' "

"He boasts of his ancestry," I said. "We may do as much."

"You must understand," Benjamin protested. "Behind him floats a long white cloth and on it are engraved the symbols of Mohammed, their Prophet."

"Then he profanes his own faith," I said.

"Not at all, not at all. It is his duty to the One to protect our people. You must know that more than forty thousand Jews live in Bagdad, in peace and friendship with all, because of Samuel."

"That is good," Maimonides said.

"They have twenty-eight synagogues there, all filled on the Holy Days."

"Samuel could not do otherwise," Maimonides agreed.

"He will permit no opposition to his power," Benjamin continued eagerly. "The caliph alone can make him bow. Even the Moslems give him great power. Mohammed, the former caliph, commanded that he and all his descendants should have the chain and seal of office over all the congregations of Jews. Even if any should fail merely to salute him, the offender will receive a hundred stripes on his back. Myself, I have seen it."

Maimonides was pensive. "And if he goes before the caliph, does that worthy rise and salute him, too?" he asked.

"This is the talk of a madman!" stormed Benjamin. "Know, then, that he appears and kisses the hand of the caliph and pays the tribute of our people in gold and silver, then mounts a throne—imagine this for a Jew—and all the Moslem princes themselves salute him."

"Do they salute him for his worth in the eyes of Heaven or do they salute him for the tribute paid into their coffers?"

"A throne?" I demanded. "A throne for a rabbi?"

"But he is a great and proud rabbi. Do you know what is engraved upon the back of his throne for all eyes to see?"

"A verse from the Torah, no doubt?" I had not thought Maimonides' voice could be so stinging.

"I will tell you. 'The sceptre shall not depart from Judah nor a lawgiver from between his feet until he come to Shiloh; and to him shall the gathering of the people be.' "

"Then it *is* such a saying from the Book." Maimonides nodded as if to himself. "That is well. Tell me, does he judge wisely? Does he administer the laws of our people well?"

"Exceedingly well," Benjamin replied almost defiantly.

"Tell me of it."

"In his hands is the giving or taking away of office for all rabbis. They bring him offerings from Samarkand and India, from Shinar and Khurasan."

"Then he must be very rich."

"He is rich beyond all belief," exclaimed Benjamin with fervor. "He owns houses of resort, gardens, plantations flowing with water and loaded with fruit and flowers, and much land—so much that it would take the whole of a night merely to mention those in the name of Samuel."

"But he is persecuted, even as we are?" Maimonides said this with a peculiar intonation.

Benjamin flung back his head, as proud as if he were Samuel himself on his throne in Bagdad. "It is decreed by the caliph that no one, under pain of death, can take a grain of dust from him by force, blessed be the Name of the One."

"Then he is the only one of our race who is so blessed and so secure," I interposed.

"Yes, yes," Benjamin assented eagerly. "He receives tribute from taverns, from the merchants and markets."

"What does he give to the poor?"

"I know not. But he dines many Jews at his table every day and explains the Talmud to them as they feast."

"It is a new way of explaining the words of our fathers," Maimonides said slowly. "If he is allowed all this, the Moslems themselves must be fond of his presence."

"He brings much to the caliphate; they are no more than grateful. If you could have seen what I saw! Each year on the day when he is confirmed in office, he rides in splendor behind only the caliph. With him go timbrels and fifes."

The picture of the magnificence of Samuel, whom I could imagine as no more than the little boy in the dim far-off garden of Cordova so many years ago, was overwhelming. I bowed my head. Maimonides himself was silent for a long moment. Benjamin's face was ecstatic: At last he had made us understand the power and fame of Samuel ben Ali.

"And his synagogue—is it in accordance with all this?" Maimonides asked at length in a low voice.

"In truth it is the whole reflection of his glory," said Benjamin. "The columns are of marble, in curious shapes, each of a different color, overlaced with gold and silver. The words of the Psalms are everywhere inlaid in solid gold. Before the Ark there are ten steps of solid marble that—"

"Enough! Cease!" Maimonides flung himself upright. His face was alive with anger, flushed with passion.

Benjamin got to his feet. His face was puzzled and resentful. "I came here in peace and joy," he said. "Have I offended?"

A gurgle of pain, a slithering thud. Our nerves leaped, tingling the skin as we jerked about. Behind us lay Zayd, writhing on the floor, his eyes uprolled in agony, fingers scrabbling in pain on the dirt floor between the carpets. I stooped over him as Benjamin and Maimonides attempted to hold his flailing limbs. I could make no guess as to his ailment—until my eyes fell upon the black bottle of wine from Samuel ben Ali. It lay open on the ground beside Zayd, its contents flowing out.

As if a light had dazzled me, I understood: he had drunk some of it. I passed my fingers over the Negro's thick purplish lips. He gave a great exhalation. His body stretched out limply. I smelled my fingers and detected the odor of wine and of another vaguely familiar substance. I touched my lips and they tingled warningly. My fingers had a burning sensation. Under my other hand, the heart of Zayd commenced to slow; he breathed as one being strangled. Aconite, the swift deadly poison distilled from the flowers of nightshade.

I got up numbly, my hands shaking. I looked from Benjamin to Maimonides, down to Zayd's convulsed dark face as its muscles loosened. "Where," I said fearfully, "is Yaltah? Where are Brujo and Ramah?"

As if in answer to my question, a figure clambered down the ladder from the roof, springing lightly to the floor: it was David. I repeated my question as he stared blankly at the poisoned Zayd. "They are in the city at the bazaar," he said in a strangled voice.

I told Maimonides: "If we are discovered with the dead body of a Moslem slave, we shall ourselves suffer death. He must be buried instantly. Here, beneath the roof of our house; secretly, without knowledge of anyone. It must be done before their return."

The glowing sun, coal in the brazier of the sky, was low before we had finished. We lowered Zayd's cooling body into the pit, dug mostly by David's muscles. We heaped earth over it, dampening it with water and tramping it down, dampening and tramping ceaselessly. Our drained bodies felt crazily light and drunken, weighed down only by the heaviness of hearts and heads. Back and forth we went in procession, Maimonides, David, Benjamin, and I, a treadmill over the grave of our faithful slave.

"Poison," Maimonides said in a strange hushed voice, "sent as a gift by Samuel."

"I cannot believe it," Benjamin panted.

"You have seen it."

"But the Head of the Captivity!"

"Perhaps a mistake," I said painfully.

Suddenly, from without, I heard the sound of madness. I cannot describe it otherwise: the sound of a crowd running in fury that communicated itself like a fever, one to the other, until all were lost in universal mindlessness.

We ceased our activities; David climbed rapidly up the ladder to the roof; Maimonides followed him, agile as a monkey. I labored after them. Benjamin, wringing his hands, was still under the shock of what his gift had brought. He sank onto a stool, rocking from side to side, head in his hands in sorrow.

On the roof: Those who have seen the bore-tides of rivers in France will know what I mean when I say that a mob is like such a tide. A wave of humanity, tumbling with sticks and stones, advancing with fearful rapidity; a tide of people with shouts and curses; foam, waving of hands and clothing, flotsam; an animal howling that has nothing human in it.

I saw Yaltah running down the narrow street, her feet flying absurdly behind her; her hair streaming out like a shadow; her mouth stretched into an ugly scream that could not be uttered. Behind her, like dogs after a fawn, baying curses and threats, flecked with their own spittle, came the mob of Moslems, fiends set loose. They closed in upon her, clutching her garments.

I cried out; my heart bubbled up into my mouth, choking me. Next to me David shouted a furious wordless cry into the air. He tumbled down the ladder, into the house. I could not stir. My eyes fixed themselves upon the dreadful scene; I felt them straining at the sockets. My fingers ached from their grip upon the clay tiles of the parapet.

Almost before our door, Yaltah stumbled. She sprawled as if thrown, lying there a moment stunned, too long, too late. Her hands spasmodically clutched the dust as if to urge her forward to sanctuary. The leader of the crowd—a short-bearded, howling Moslem, flung himself upon her, sprawling between her legs that were bolsters of helpless naked flesh.

She lay open before him. He heaved her legs aside, thrusting himself up by his grip upon her thighs. With a swift movement he ripped away her garments. He fumbled a moment. Seizing her, he pulled her to him. He threw back his head in a shriek of triumph, his pointed beard skyward, his throat distended, corded in spasm. I heard a shriek of pain and terror, a scream of agony from my daughter.

David hurtled from the door, an arrow of vengeance. A knife stretched before him; shaft of flesh, steel at its head. It pierced the upturned throat of the Moslem. Blood spurted. I wailed in thanksgiving at the foul sacrifice on the altar of my child. The man fell backward, gurgling in a drench of his own blood, drowning in his iniquity.

The Moslem mob, maddened by blood, by fanatic lunacy, by lust and their own mouthings, fell upon David. He was lost to my sight in a cloud of dust, in a mass of bodies flailing and kicking. A high ululation from an animal with a thousand heads and limbs came from the heap. Out from under it all, crawling and filthy, emerged the shape of Yaltah with agonized, disfigured face, on hands and knees. She gained our house and vanished as I sank in prayer.

Next moment, I was transfixed anew. From the door beneath, pacing in silence, robed in pure white, came Maimonides. His face was set as rock in a mountain. His arms were outstretched. His appearance was like a vision. In an instant, the mob was quieted with fear.

I heard the penetrating voice of my son, the voice I had heard so often in prayer, in the readings of the Torah. It was raised in a new chant, one I could not believe.

"La ilaha illa Allah, wa-Mohammed rasul Allah! La ilaha illa Allah, wa-Mohammed, rasul Allah!"

The sprawling mob assumed individual forms. It broke and dissolved, drawing back in the frustrated, growling manner of a pack of jackals interrupted at a feast. Maimonides, without a sign of dismay, walked slowly into their midst. He raised David's battered and bleeding form.

A cry broke loose. It was repeated, a wild eerie threat of death. The mob, a wave in motion, moved forward a step. Maimonides supported his brother with one hand and extended the other. Again I heard his voice.

"Will you slay one who is your fellow? Will you put to death a brother Moslem? Is it not said in the Koran by the holy Prophet Mohammed that 'He who slays a True Believer will live forever in the bottomless pit of a thousand hells, that he shall have no scent of Paradise, even though that scent were strong enough to carry forty days' journey'? Woe to you who raise your voice and will against that of the Prophet! It is He who will appear at the Day of Judgment to testify against you!"

Without a glance backward, as he had walked from the Christian knight in Toledo, Maimonides turned and carried David's body back into the house. A moment later I heard the sound of the door barred and chained; a rising moan of anger came from the crowd but I saw them commence to disperse and even run from the spot.

I rose, trembling, trying to find my way. I fell to the floor with a pain in my side too great to endure. I floundered about helplessly into darkness.

When I regained my senses, I was in the darkened room beneath. I felt the presence of Maimonides near me. I tried to reach his hand. My left arm refused to obey my will.

"Why am I tied?" I demanded querulously.

"You are not tied, my father," came Maimonides' soothing voice. "It is your affliction. Have no fear, all will be as you desire."

"Maimonides," I said breathlessly, "Moses, son of Maimon ben Joseph: If it is true I am paralyzed, I hereby transfer to you the authority of a father, admonishing all to look upon you, to respect you, as they would myself."

"I have already assumed this," he responded, "knowing and believing you would consent. Much has had to be done in the past hours."

"Is it late?"

"Very late."

"Is there danger?"

"Much danger—but we shall soon be free of it."

"We are leaving Fez, are we not?"

"Tonight, my father."

I roused myself, swinging my right arm across to caress his face in the gloom. "Where do we go, head of the family?" I asked him fondly. "Let us return to Spain, to Cordova, and die there."

"No more of us shall die," Maimonides said.

"No more?" I whimpered. "Have some died?"

"Zayd is dead, as you know. And Brujo and Ramah—they are dead."

"Dead!" My voice rose in anguish. Maimonides clapped his palm over my mouth.

"The mob of beasts, God grind their bones to dust," Maimonides said in a low tense tone. "They tore them to bits in the market place. Only Yaltah escaped. They tore Brujo's golden teeth from his clenched jaws."

"Ah," I said in agony, "the advice of our friend, Ibn Mosa, was not enough. Did he escape?"

"I did not see him."

I moaned under his restraining fingers and he removed them. "David and Yaltah?" I asked thickly.

"David is better, he is able to travel," Maimonides said somberly. "As for Yaltah—she is speechless and silent, weeping without tears. I do not know."

"Where shall we go? Where shall we go?" I could not keep back my sobs any longer. "Where shall we dwell that we will not dwell with death and torture, with animals instead of men, with fury and desolation rather than peace and plenty?"

"Not in Spain," Maimonides said firmly. "To return there means enduring the rule of the Almohades again. This I cannot do."

"Where?"

"To the Promised Land!" Maimonides' voice had a ring of exultation in it that made my heart leap. I felt my left arm stir, the fingers move: I deemed it a miracle.

"To Palestine itself!" he repeated.

"The Christians are there!"

"So are our hopes, the bones of our ancestors, the soul of our race! What shall avail against the might of the Lord, who is ever with us? We shall take the ship that waits at the roadstead for Benjamin," Maimonides breathed.

"Where does it sail?"

"To the East."

"To the East!" I cried in horror, my mind still full of the dreadful face of Zayd. "To Bagdad?"

I felt Maimonides' finger on my lips. "No," he said. "But if we are to die by the will of God, let us at least die in Palestine, the land of our fathers."

My throat swelled with emotion. I clasped his hand in mine and carried it to my cheek.

"And Joseph ben Shoshan," I said feebly, not willing to argue with such conviction. "Will he go with us?"

"He is dead," Maimonides said, his voice colorless now. "The same uprising that slew Brujo and Ramah also murdered him." Sharply into my brain came the remembered pungence of cedar burning, the incense of memory for me of that good man.

"Come," said the anxious voice of Benjamin out of the darkness. "It is late. The ship will not wait in the bay forever. We have days of hiding and nights of journeying to get to the sea."

I raised myself painfully. "Muni," I said.

Maimonides came closer to my side; I felt him looking down at me.

"Muni," I said, "I, too, have studied the Koran of the Moslems. I have never read that passage which you quoted, which saved David's life. From which sura did it come?"

"My father," Maimonides said in a low voice, "the language of the Koran is easy to imitate, the sentiments are simple."

I felt a flood of uneasy surprise. I imagined the ghost of a smile on my son's face. "What do you mean?" I stammered.

"No such passage exists," Maimonides said. "Consider me now one of the prophets of the Moslems. I invented the thing —to save David."

CHAPTER 12

As Benjamin had promised, his ship lay at anchor in the very bay where we had landed. We had pressed on hard during the night and all the next day, careless of the poor beasts under us, fearing capture at any moment. But there was no fateful cloud of dust on the horizon. We came onto the shore without incident. Just at sunset we were taken aboard.

To my surprise, the captain was a Jew. He stood bowlegged and freckled, with a head of thin black hair and a scanty beard, at the bulwarks as we lifted ourselves aboard. He helped me a bit, noting the helplessness of my left arm. But he was adamant about his payment: two hundred dinars for what was left of our ill-fated family—David, Maimonides, Yaltah, and myself. Nor would Benjamin aid our purse; he said he needed his own funds for further travel. I was forced to pay the whole amount, leaving us little for our hoped-for debarkation at Palestine.

As soon as we stepped on deck, fare paid and our poor packets stowed, the captain, who called himself "rabbi of the ship," ordered the anchor up. His rowers picked up the beat to windward so that he might take advantage of the nightly offshore breeze.

Weary from the long jolting journey to the coast, I fell into instant slumber. When I woke, to the rhythmic creak of timber and rush of water, bright sunlight filtered through the cracks. I observed Maimonides and David standing on the deck above. Laboriously, I got to my feet to join them. To my delight, I perceived the paralysis of my left arm had worn off; save for a slight stiffness, it was perfectly well. I clambered onto the half-decking. I found myself in the midst of a blue day: blue waters, blue sky, the distant blue shore of Africa. The waters spread calm, ruffled only slightly by a breeze driving us toward the East; the oarsmen were resting, silent and sullen, at their oars. The drum which guided the tempo of their strokes was silent as well.

I beckoned to Maimonides. He came to my side with glad surprise. "Your arm is better," he said, as David joined him.

"It is well," I said with some asperity. I included them both in my gaze. "We are alone now. We are four against the world. Remember that. Remember also we must fulfill our duties to the dead."

"Is it permissible on the sea?" asked Maimonides.

I scowled in doubt. "Let us remember it when we come to Palestine," I said at last. My reply was dictated less by the Torah than by the sight of Yaltah seated near the prow, pale, motionless as a figurehead.

"Has she spoken?" I asked in a low voice.

Maimonides shook his head. "She seems like one dead," David said. His face altered, his jaws tightening; I knew his violent thoughts. "We must be kind to her," I said rapidly. "It is the shock of outrage, no bodily ill. She will mend."

"A blow to the mind is sometimes worse than one to the body," Maimonides said.

"Will you teach me medicine?" I demanded sardonically.

Maimonides said nothing. I went forward to touch Yaltah, to speak to her. She was as cold and still as a statue, damp with the spray from the cleaving bow. I sighed and desisted, turning to look at the ship.

A wooden, strongly built affair, perhaps one hundred fifty

feet long from stem to stern, its ribs covered by planking secured by wooden pegs. It boasted three sharply raked masts, the ones before and behind being square for running before the wind; the middle one was a slanted lateen which, so they said, was magic enough to make the pilot's will the wind's will when running close-hauled. At bow and stern stood two high buildings, for defense against raiders and passenger quarters. At the prow stood a beak in the form of a roc's head, near what appeared to be a small birdhouse.

"That," said the captain's garlic breath at my ear, "is the shrine for the ship's god. I keep my cheese in it. High like that, it keeps out the mold."

"What god do you believe in?" I asked stiffly.

He looked at me with surprise. "I'm a Jew, you're a Jew," he said. "So what god do you believe in?"

I shook my head resignedly.

"I'm as good a Jew as you are," he complained. "If I weren't, I wouldn't have waited. I have plenty of cargo business without worrying about passengers."

"If you were as good a Jew as you say," I told him pointedly, "you wouldn't have sailed yesterday anyway. It was the Sabbath."

He shrugged, jerking his thumb overside. "Look down there," he advised me, "this is a good ship you're in. Lead sheathing with bronze studs. Against the worms."

"Worms?"

He laughed raucously as he moved forward. "There are worms in the sea, Rabbi, that devour wood like dirt."

I could hardly believe his tale. But I was intrigued by the number of oarsmen on his roster: I knew they were expensive, that merchantmen usually depended upon sail. When I looked at their backs, I saw the crimson letters GAL branded; I knew they were slaves.

The captain came back down the raised way of planks toward me with his peculiar rolling gait. He bobbed his head and grinned, exposing a lamentable lack of teeth.

"You use slaves to row," I said. "You should set them free, if they desire it."

"Excuse me," he replied. "A poor man like myself cannot afford it. Perhaps a rich man like yourself."

"Rich! I gave you our last dinars to pay for our passage aboard this hulk!"

"Then you could not afford it either," he said blandly.

"It is written," I said with dignity, "that 'You shall pay them their wages.' "

"It is also written," the captain said, "that 'Wherever there is justice, there is peace.' "

"That does not apply," I said irritably. "The blessed Hisdai said, 'The man who is arrogant cannot dwell with me in this world.' "

"I agree," said the captain equably, "and Ishmael ben Joseph pointed out, 'He who is haughty is foolish and wicked.' "

"It is written that 'Evil eye, evil principle, and hatred drive a man out of this world,' " I exclaimed.

"Ah," replied the captain, "it was the good Levitas who said: 'Be exceedingly humble, for the hope of mortal man is the worm.' "

"Do not the Fathers say that 'even the fleas and gnats are part of the world'?" I demanded sarcastically.

"Aye, and the blessed Raba declared that you 'should not set foot on one who is greater in wisdom and years.' "

"It is written, 'Be not a tail to the lion nor yet the head of a fox.' "

The captain shrugged at my anger. "Simeon ben Eleazar said, 'Do not soothe thy associate in his hour of anger.' "

His answer made me furious. It was impossible that I, a rabbi for so many years in Cordova, one of the greatest congregations in the world, should be confuted by an ordinary sea captain!

"Ben Azzai has said," I shouted, "that 'Transgression is the reward for transgression'!"

The captain chuckled. I broke in again: "And no less than Akiba, blessed be he, has declared: 'Laughter and levity lead to hell'!"

"To 'sin,' isn't it?" said the captain.

At this moment, I heard Maimonides' voice behind me.

"It was Ben Azzai who said that 'No man is insignificant,' " he murmured quietly, "and Joshua ben Levi pointed out that 'Peace is to the earth what yeast is to the dough.' Moreover, Hananiah ben Teradion has said: 'When two have not between them the words of the Torah, lo, this is the seat of the scornful.' "

The captain looked at my son in admiration. "So young and so learned," he said appreciatively.

"His name is Maimonides," I said with assurance.

The captain bowed. "And mine is Jacob ben Cohen," he returned politely.

I found nothing to reply to his ignorance of my son's importance. I expected Maimonides to answer but his face was pale and his gullet working; I knew the sickness of the sea had overtaken him once again. He left us hurriedly to lean over the side of the ship.

"Where did you learn your Talmud?" I asked of the captain as he strolled off for the bow. He paused, replying over his shoulder: "A seaman has little to do on long voyages, except to read. You should try it."

Out of sight of land, the irregular coast of Morocco gradually fading, I experienced an easing of the heart. Jews were not important enough to be pursued this far, though the emir's war galleys could certainly catch up with us within days. I knew the pride of the Berber, and to turn out a royal ship for a parcel of bankrupts: impossible!

Therefore I breathed the soothing salt air and felt the velvet of the wind on my face with pleasure. Jacob had informed us that our first port would be Palermo, in Sicily. There he intended to take on provisions and water with cargo destined for the Kingdom of Jerusalem. Thenceforth, there would be no ports of call. He intended to sail south, then east, directly down the middle of the sea by the stars; when I suggested to him that both Maimonides and myself were learned in scanning the sky, I received a look of tolerant contempt. I fled before a text from the Talmud could be flung at me.

For nearly a month the weather was pleasant. But south of Cyprus, just when we had expected a voyage of unexampled peace, we encountered the storm. It struck us so fiercely that momentarily we expected to be overset. For days we scudded before the wind with bare poles, seeing in the far south-distance at night a weird glow from the famous pharos of Alexandria. Up and down monstrous blue hills, momently changing into valleys, winds howling like Moslem dervishes; the passengers locked by muscle and tied by rope within the hull; the ship dragging a sea-anchor made of sail and oars (the others having been long ago drawn inward and braced for shelter).

I remember how the water spurted between the planks of this galeasse trading-ship, pouring down into the hull from above. The drench cold on lips and flesh, tasting like a bitter salt spring, kept me in continual ague. Without, the sea roared, a den of angry lions. Blows of giants could be felt, making

204

the ship shudder throughout its whole length. I could hear, above the tumult of the storm, hoarse shouts from the captain, the cries of the rowers, thudding of the crew's feet as they tried to shift sails or change cargo.

Within a dozen feet of us, three of the men bailed frantically. The whipping, singing wind, exulting in triumph, constantly fretted our ears like the whine of a gigantic dog. Before long I gave up the family of Maimon for lost.

Worst of all were the pitching and rolling of the ship. The motions, unexpected and violent, kept my stomach in a turmoil. The stink of the bilge, as they bailed, did nothing to calm my bile. David rolled from side to side under the decking, his face green, his eyes closed, giving no heed to his battering from the sea. Yaltah sat stiff and braced against a rib of the ship, her eyes staring wide, straight ahead. Ever since that terrible moment in the streets of Fez, she had been like one in a dream: not speaking, moving only at command, unseeing, and scarcely taking food or drink. As for myself, having vomited my very guts upon the floor, surrounded by my own thin yellow slime, I waited for the end.

What surprised me—even arousing a feeble indignation— was the attitude of Maimonides. He sat upright, arms and legs spread out to balance, eyes closed, and his face a healthy color. I managed to crawl to his side. I put my lips to his ear: "My son, you who are so frightened of the sea, what makes you calm? Do you have so much faith in God?"

"My father," came the low response, "I am thinking. I have unraveled the meaning of thirteen Halachot on this voyage, and I shall write them down when we land."

"Are you so sure of our landing?" I upbraided him.

"God will not abandon us."

I dry-retched, then replied: "But God may have abandoned the captain, and our lives depend upon him."

The wind shrieked. A wave towered. It toppled over onto us, but we were past caring. The ship lurched and creaked and sobbed in the clutches of the elements. I repeated the Shema and tried to think other thoughts.

But thought could not quiet the sea. Its rut ran higher, the northwest wind whistled and roared in contempt of the sailors' feeble efforts. The boisterous water swept through the ship, driven by scuds of wind; heaven above crashed with thunder and showed its teeth with lightning flashes; we rose to the top and descended, it seemed, into the bowels of earth simultaneously; and I, without strength, bent formlessly into a heap, lifted my eyes and saw a foot dangling before me.

I looked upward weakly. I saw it was the captain—of all persons—munching on a bit of cheese. My stomach revolted. My acid rose to my teeth. "What's the matter?" he asked with a crunch of his jaws.

"Stop eating!" I groaned. "Get some sense, save this ship from certain wreck!"

"It's nothing," he said airily, swinging his feet, "except that the sail's split, the masts are sprung, the keel is turned upward, and the rigging is blown away. Is that enough?"

"Can you do nothing, nothing at all?" I entreated with the last breath in my body.

He considered gravely. "Except that today is the Sabbath," he admitted, "something might be done."

"Sabbath! Our lives are in hazard! I beg you, I command you, do something about it!"

"And who are you to command me? Know that the Cohanim were high priests in the Temple."

"I am a rabbi of Cordova."

His eyes twinkled at me. I saw a slight smile on his face. "In that case, then," he said, "we must certainly take steps to quiet the sea."

It was this storm that demonstrated to me my own bodily weakness, just when I had come to consider myself a sailor. David, too, was afflicted, but Maimonides showed, by sheer concentration of thought, that he was able to conquer the elements. Still, it wrought on him as well, more than I thought. When at last we limped into the harbor at Acre, he showed me what he had written in his daybook:

"On the evening of the first of the month of September of the year 1165, we went to sea. On the first Sabbath in October, we had a dreadful storm. The sea was in a cold fury. We were in danger of perishing. Then I vowed to keep these two days always as days of total fasting for myself and the household and all those related to me; to command my children to do the same throughout all their generations. They should also give to charity according to their ability. For myself, I further vowed to remain apart from human intercourse on those anniversaries, to speak to none, to pray and study only. On the day of the storm I saw no one on the sea except the Holy One, praised be His Name. So will I see no one, stay with no one, on that day in years to come."

206

That vow, I may add, he has kept religiously ever since. But his daybook writings made me curious. As we advanced slowly toward the dock, warping ourselves in by ropes alongside the giant rocks of the breakwater, I addressed him.

"But you have no children, Maimonides."

He made no answer, his face averted.

"Did you truly see God upon the waters?" I asked, curious.

"He is everywhere. He does not desert us even in the midst of watery desolation."

I took a deep breath. "You speak of yourself as if you are alone," I said.

He nodded, his eyes straining toward the shore of the Holy Land. "A month ago, you gave me the headship of the Maimon family," he said. "Do you rescind that gift?"

I hesitated. "No," I said strongly. "No, my son, I say it again with all my soul." From that moment to this, Maimonides has been chief of our household.

Off the ship, we kissed the ground and stared about us at the frowning walls, the white houses, the evidences of the Christian occupation begun thirty-one years before Maimonides was born. So this was the target of all those bands of Christians which had moved across the face of Europe toward the East during so many years. We hired mules at an exorbitant price and picked our way up from the waterside, not without hearing a final farewell from the captain of our ship: "Remember, Ishmael said: 'Be submissive to the ruler, patient under oppression, and receive everyone with cheerfulness.' Shalom!" To this day I do not know if it was encouragement or jeer.

Acre (or Acco or Ptolemais, whatever one wanted to call it), was built on a low rocky promontory south of Tyre. Its streets were filled with people; none looked like those we had seen in Spain. The dwellings were not castles but spacious Moslem houses; the mosaics and tiles, Persian rugs and silk hangings, copper and silver utensils, which we glimpsed within, were all Moslem. So, too, were the men dressed in flowing silk robes and turbans and the women in oriental gauzes with sequins. Even music that we heard was thin and twanging, with none of the martial flair we thought we might encounter. "The Franks have conquered and lost," muttered David, close behind me.

All that was familiar showed in the hard, half-shaven faces

of the men, the swagger of the Christian monks who walked like soldiers, the empty scheming faces of the women. Now I believed what I had been told: The scum of the West had flowed east for gain and ease. Under the pretext of regaining what they called the Holy Sepulchre, the most dreadful war of deceit and treachery ever waged had been won.

We did not stay long at Acre. That very afternoon, after rest and refreshment in a hostelry near the waterfront, we mounted again. We set out on what Maimonides insisted was our only purpose: to seek Jerusalem. And, indeed, as we went on the road, I noted his very features seemed to soften and glow with an inward light. It made him almost unrecognizable. He pressed on without a sign of fatigue.

Heading south, Jerusalem eighty miles away, we traveled a sandy road to Haifa, at the foot of Mount Carmel. Here the stream of Kishon flowed, and on either bank were many Jewish graves; the mountain itself was pocked with caves occupied by incredibly hairy Christian hermits who spent most of their time singing doleful songs and beating each other with whips.

Along the coast to Caesarea we wended for three days, then to Samaria, where lay the ruins of the palace of mighty Ahab —a land of brooks, gardens, orchards, and vineyards intermingled with olive groves. Two parasangs beyond lived abominable Jews who observed the written Torah alone without regard to the Law, claiming that they were of the seed of Aaron and that their Mount Gerizim was the true side of the Temple. They were wholly without the fold—without dignity, kindliness, and humility. Our stay was short and unpleasant.

Thence we proceeded with growing happiness to the city of Shechem, and onward finally, into the holy city of Jerusalem itself, at the end of five days. Though its sacred qualities were undiminished, the city itself was a disappointment beyond words. In all the ruins of the place—protected by only three walls—there were only four pitiable Jews. The rest were Jacobites, Syrians, Greeks, Georgians, and Franks, a conglomeration of people goodhearted enough but with a confusion of tongues such as Babel might have known. The Jews here were dyers, a low occupation. Visiting and encouraging them was Japhet ben Eliahu, a leading Jew of Acre. He was a small man, withered but active, versed in the Talmud in a practical way but somewhat opinionated. He told us that the few Jews here paid tribute to the Christian king Amalric (his brother Baldwin had died three years before) on condition that none others could take up their noisome trade. They lived in one corner, under the Tower of David, the largest and strongest structure of all, built partly by our ancestors, and partly restored by the Moslems.

As for the Christians, we found they existed in constant expectation of fighting once more for the land. They knew not how to live, being riotous and licentious, but they were bound by vows each year to protect what they had won. They did some good: A hospital, maintained by the Knights of St. John and the rude Templars, welcomed all the sick, of whatever belief. But it was also a barracks which lodged four hundred knights who rushed out every morning to indulge in battle exercises with trumpets and clanging and much shouting.

The only other great building was blasphemously called "the Temple." It was truly the great palace originally built by King Solomon; here too were quartered three hundred knights. Their chief occupation, other than brawling, drinking, and women, was to devoutly attend services at the great church called the Sepulchre.

We had entered Jerusalem by the immemorial Gate of Abraham. We discovered the other three—those of David, of Zion, and of Jehoshaphat, the last facing an ancient temple called Templum Domini by the Latins. Nearby was the Western Wall, once one of the walls of the Holy of Holies, inner sanctum of our God. Thither came Jews continuously to bewail the destruction of the Temple.

Here in Jerusalem, in the midst of the most incredible desolation, we stayed for three days, worshiping at the broken shrines of our ancestors. Maimonides went on to Hebron to enter the caves below the ground through a very old gate of iron. He wished to see the tombs of Abraham, Isaac, Jacob, of Sarah, Rebecca, and Leah. As for me, not filled with such fierce desire, I journeyed two parasangs with David, along the sea of Sodom to view the pillar of salt into which Lot's wife had been transformed. Flocks of sheep lick it continually. It is said to change back into female shape by magic—but I noted well that the tongues of the animals unseal salt springs below, which again renew their flow and deposit.

We waited for Maimonides until evening of the second day, beneath the Tower of David, in a hut thatched with straw, the floor covered with chaff. We ate our simple supper— barley bread with gruel of cabbage and turnip—and scratched our simple fleas. David and I and Yaltah—still withdrawn and silent as marble—sat in this half-stone, half-brick enclosure, which lacked windows and had only a low-linteled door with a worn mezuzah; we squatted under its ceiling of billowing smoke raised from the fire of cattle chips and waited. Hanukkah will soon come, I thought irrelevantly: What a queer place in which to celebrate eight days of rejoicing for freedom in our faith, to kindle candles for the "strong delivered into the hands of the weak." Instantly I reproached myself. I had thought of the feasting and gifts and games, and not of the spiritual meaning. I bent my head and prayed for forgiveness. As I did, Maimonides entered the hut.

One look at his downcast face and I knew his mood. It was one with mine. I moved to take his hands, to sit by his side. After a long while, refusing to take food, he spoke to us as one who had only lately emerged from an evil dream.

"A mournful sight, this Jerusalem of ours," Maimonides said despondently. "Only one Jew did I find near the site of our forefathers' greatness, a simple dyer, and he persecuted, poor, oppressed, despised. I offered to relieve his wants with all of my purse but he refused it; I placed it on his doorstep and fled. Here—here in such an humble dwelling—gather less than the minyan of ten, wretched folk, beggars whose very eyes reflect their destitution. And all this in a land that is still wonderful for beauty." His eyes kindled and he raised his head. "Truly," he said, "it is a land that after centuries may still flow with milk and honey as it did in the days of greatness."

He knelt between David and myself, taking our hands. "My father, my brother," he said in the melting accents which always took my soul by the nearest way, "we, too, are people who have seen affliction and known desperate times. We have triumphed through faith, in the hope of the future. For the time, for the time only, the destiny of the Jews lies in other lands. We are banished from the tables of Spain and Morocco, removed from friends and kin, too far for them to meet us or for us to go to them—but this we must reconcile ourselves to accept. We must not be weak; we must be strong. We are not alone, we have each other. We have our belief that has lasted for ages before us and will continue past our death."

He paused, for David and I were weeping, and releasing our hands, stood up; his eyes took on the far-off, veiled glance of the Prophets. "But the loss of all—" he declared in a ringing voice, "of all the glories that the world can offer—all these are nothing now for the joy of being a day in the desolate courts of Jerusalem, seeing the ruins of the Temple and tombs, weeping over the abandoned sanctuary now the home of wild dogs and weeds. I caress the stones, sift the dust between reverent fingers, weep over what remains. My tears are bitter but sweet; my fingers, tearing at my garments, also tear away my sorrow."

He clasped his hands in an agony of expectation as he peered into the future. "I see our Jerusalem rising as a shining phantom from the past, regaining outline and substance, turning again to her youth and glory, becoming once more the altar and sacred center of the Jew. Nowhere else can this be. Nowhere else can the smell of destruction turn to sweet incense in our nostrils. Here, sanctified by the blood and tears of those who visit such a spot, we find surcease for all our troubles, and lay ourselves to rest!"

He knelt again and took my hand. "Now," he said humbly, "I understand what I did not know before. I understand what drove the spirit of Judah Halevi here, the search of his soul for that comfort which can rise only like mists of morning from the scattered and broken stones of Jerusalem. His love was more than mortal, more than human. His desire was for things gone, things risen to a paradise from which, God willing, they will return to earth at their appointed time. And I, my father, if I cannot live here now, when I die, I will be buried here. I shall add to this whatever of holiness I may achieve in this life, to be part of the blessed band who watch over it still and drop the dew of their tears from heaven nightly upon what has been, and their assurance to us from God Himself of what will be!"

Unknown to us, our attention centered wholly on Maimonides' passionate declaration, Japhet ben Eliahu had entered. He squatted near the dying fire and looked up at us as Maimonides finished. He spoke softly, in contrast to the ringing voice of my son.

"All that you say is true," he murmured, "but it is untrue."

"How?" demanded Maimonides almost angrily.

"What can I say to you of our country? Held by idolaters and heathen, abandoned sometimes it seems even by God. Great is the solitude and great is the waste here. The more sacred the shrine, the greater the desolation and the loss of hope. Judea is worse than wretched Galilee; and Jerusalem is more desolate than all the rest. Jews? There are no Jews here. Many fled when the Moslems came; the rest, when the Christians came. I alone am left with my tiny following."

211

He was right, I felt in my soul; there was nothing here for a Jew. Another time, perhaps; but my heart revolted against making our home in another country where the very soil had become infertile from its blood-soaking from the veins of my fathers. "This is not the place," I said, "this is not the place."

Maimonides did not respond. His body slumped, his eyes stared blankly across the fire into those of Yaltah. Slowly he rose and went to her, folding her into his arms. "My sister," he said, rocking her to and fro, "my dearest sister, my blessed sister!" To the astonishment of us all, Yaltah gave a wailing cry. Her tears came as out of a fountain.

How untenable were our hopes of staying in Jerusalem was soon to be shown us. Maimonides was inexorable in his inner determination to stay until some sign of heaven could be vouchsafed. He had seemingly abandoned all his work on the *Mishneh Torah;* it lay gathering dust in a corner of the humble house of Japhet where we had taken up our abode. Every day we made a pilgrimage to the Wailing Wall; every day we repaired to the other various holy places. Each fortnight we went on foot, a long road, to Hebron to pray at the tombs of our ancestors.

I grew weary of it. It seemed to me that we lived with the dead, inhaled their dust, knelt in their darkness and loneliness. Surely, I thought, the blessed are at rest in Abraham's bosom; they care nothing for the relics of bones left behind. Why, then, do we reverence them so? Is it not better to live well during our own lives here? But when I put such questions to Maimonides, my son compressed his lips. His face took on the haughty-eagle look which indicated he did not wish to talk about it.

Nor was I the only one with such secret misgivings. David became restless again. His big fingers closed and opened whenever he saw a Gentile sword, his eyes danced and gleamed as he was forced to take to the ditch to let a crusader by. I feared lest his unruly temper would again get the best of him. As for Yaltah, however, she became ethereal in her ways, light and dainty; not quite knowing where she was or what she was doing, happy as a child is happy, with very small things.

At last Japhet made his feelings known in plain terms to Maimonides and myself. Crouched over his fire one night after prayers and the evening meal, he turned to Maimonides without prelude.

"This is no resting-place for you," said the little wizened

rabbi bluntly. "As long as my congregation of three remain, I shall remain, but it is no place for you. You are a famous man, suspected by Moslems, without recourse to the Christians."

Maimonides cocked his head, his intense eyes fixed upon the face of Japhet. Japhet went on sadly: "We must pay tribute humbly, entertain all Moslems who come for three days, keep our voices low, swear not to shelter spies nor to build or repair synagogues, not to learn the Koran or teach it or try to prevent our own people from apostatizing. We must keep apart in such things as saddles, seals, and language, stand up when they sit, honor and respect them." His voice took on a shade of bitterness. "We must not make our houses higher, must not keep weapons of any kind at home or on journeys even to protect ourselves, must not sell wine nor display it. A thousand prohibitions hang about us like chains; we scarce breathe but it violates one of them."

"Do they force you to repeat the Moslem or the Christian formula?" asked Maimonides.

"The letter you wrote to the others has no effect here," Japhet replied. "The Christians, violent men all, kill without a question. The Moslems are more lenient. They ask for the recital. If we refuse, they force us to lie down upon a plank and ask again; if we again refuse, they put a spear at our breast and ask once more; if we refuse then, they thrust it through our bodies. They have a saying: 'A Jew is never near a Moslem but he plots to kill him.' "

"This is monstrous," I muttered.

"That is true."

"Can you not merely repeat their empty blasphemies and practice our own precepts at home?" said Maimonides.

Japhet shook his head wryly. "I have said your letter is of no use to us," he declared. "They force us to take an oath, as well, since they saw it."

"They have seen my letter?"

"Jews have traitors, as well as others."

"Well?" I demanded. "Of what use is an oath?" Japhet shivered. "I have not told you what it is," he responded.

"Tell us," requested Maimonides.

"They make us, stripped naked, gird ourselves with brambles about our middle and take the holy Torah in our hands. Then we must say: 'In the name of the blessed Lord, the God of our fathers, who made heaven and earth and led us on dry land across the Red Sea, I do not lie. If I be found a perjurer, may the Lord God afflict me with the leprosy of Gehazi and Naaman and with the punishment of Eli the priest; and may the earth open up and swallow me alive, even as Dathan and Abiram.' "

Even Maimonides could not repress his revulsion at such an awful oath. I nodded in sympathy with Japhet ben Eliahu. "I understand," I murmured.

"We shall stay," Maimonides said between his teeth, snarling like a lion. Japhet made a hopeless movement of his shoulders. He peered into the dying red depths of the fire as if to seek the answer to a riddle there.

How right was Japhet and how wrong was my son was shown within less than ten days. The terror of the truth came to lodge with us like some unclean bird of prey on our shoulders. It happened very early on a cool morning when the four of us—Maimonides, Japhet, David and myself—passed outside the city on a stroll before returning to spend the forenoon praying at the ruins of the Temple. Almost, I had got used to this life and forgotten the luxury of blessed Cordova, but it was not to be.

We stood outside the Gate of Abraham, whence we had entered, and looked at the bare hills about Jerusalem, the weary disjointed gait of an overburdened camel that passed, a woman with amphorae, two pilgrims with their unutterable diseases and whining pleas for alms.

But the rising sun was sweet and the air fresh; the breeze from Galilee ruffled our hair. Imagine the vast empty country, a yellowing carpet unrolling down to the unseen sea beyond, lonely beyond thought. Now the people had vanished as we slowly walked down the road. We were alone except for a single bareheaded pilgrim coming toward us in the distance and a horsed knight in the brown mantle of the Templars, sauntering on his morning ride.

It happened suddenly, almost like the whim of some senseless being; we seemed to be both spectators and participators in an event which we could not control.

With a steel-muffled view-halloo, as if on the hunt, the knight pricked his horse into an easy canter. He rode upright, like one on parade. He slowed slightly before the diminutive pilgrim. As the knight came near, the pilgrim stretched his arms wide. His voice rose in a full-throated chant. I could almost hear the words. Suddenly I realized David had stopped stock-still, his face paling. "I know that man," he said in a stifled tone. And I; I mistook what he meant. I, too, had recognized someone—but we did not mean the same person. Maimonides and Japhet halted.

The knight rode easily until he was five paces ahead of the pilgrim. Then quickly, rising in his stirrups, he plucked a javelin from the sheath at the bow of his saddle, twisted and stretched back his arm in an almost leisurely fashion.

I could not believe what happened before my eyes. The javelin drove forward with a smooth easy motion. He meant to frighten him, my thoughts flashed. It was not so: The javelin flew straight to its mark. The breast of the pilgrim was pierced through, high on the right side. His voice faltered, ended. He stumbled forward in his dusty sandals and lay prone on the road, his body twitching.

The knight turned about. I half-saw his mustachioed face, twisted into a smile. He slapped his horse and approached at a walk, ready to pull out his javelin. I stood unable to move in my growing fear.

David, at my side, whipped off his girdle. He stooped like lightning, seizing a round stone from the roadside. Slipping it into the girdle, gripping both ends, he whirled it around his head with all his might, as he used to hunt birds on the wing in Spain. The knight saw him. His first instinctive motion was to lower his visor. It was too late; he could not duck his head at the same time. David's stone, flung from his improvised sling with all his strength, clanged like the doom of God upon his helmet. The knight reeled in his saddle, his legs went limp. He fell forward, his weight sagging sideways, slipping head-down onto the road, one solleret fixed in the stirrup. His horse, in half-panic, trotted away, dragging the body in its clashing armor behind it.

We found our scattered senses again. David and Japhet rushed for the knight, Maimonides and I for the pilgrim. Maimonides knelt beside him, turning him over. His gray-bearded face, fouled with dust, rolled upward toward the sun. Maimonides stiffened with shock, his expression contracting. I dropped beside him, shaken with dry astonishment, then torn by a storm of sobs. I gave vent to all I had felt during those unhappy days.

It was the familiar face of Judah Halevi, worn and aged, as parchment left too long in the sun. His deep-set sightless eyes met mine uncomprehendingly. They moved to those of Maimonides. I saw the return of his vision, an effort at a smile.

215

"Maimon, Muni—old friends."

"Judah, Judah!" I articulated.

"So," he whispered faintly, blood in the bubbling of his voice, staining the breast of Maimonides, "I die before I have reached the city of my dreams, beloved Jerusalem. Too much time I spent wandering, visiting friends in Egypt, too long I delayed ecstasy like a bridegroom with his bride. Muni was right, we should not return to the place of slavery and flesh-pots. And now I die, before I see the glories of the City of God."

"You will never die, Judah," Maimonides said through pale lips.

I could not tell him the glories of Jerusalem had long since vanished except in the minds of the exalted few. I bent my head, no longer able to look on his face. Held to the bosom of Maimonides, Judah spoke in a surprisingly loud voice, one that forced bubbles of froth and blood out of the hole in his bosom. He spoke words that have echoed in my ears ever since:

"O Zion, wilt thou not say shalom to us? We
Who seek from distant lands to say shalom to thee?
Captives in the east, the north and west and south,
Dost thou not hear shalom to thee from every mouth?"

His head fell back, his lips moved in indistinct phrases. He wished to tell us more but he could not. A slight glaze appeared on his wise, tired eyes as he closed them. The wound bubbled frantically. Judah was dying.

As his eyes closed, he received, from some supernal source, a new strength. I bent to his mouth, to hear what he said, to drink in the unfaltering accents I knew so well. I heard a whisper:

"Oh, God, when from Thy love I flee,
In life, I find my death;
But when I die, in love with Thee,
I draw eternal breath."

Judah's whole body leaped in Maimonides' arms. The blood spurted out, thickened, then failed for a moment. He was dead. Maimonides caught him again to his breast, uttering incoherent cries, rocking him like a child, back and forth in his shattering sorrow.

216

"Come," David said behind me at that moment. His voice was that of a stranger. "See what the Lord hath wrought."

"My friend, the friend of your youth is dead!"

David's hands literally dragged me to my feet. We roused Maimonides and departed, bearing the body of Judah.

At the insistence of Maimonides, we buried Judah at Tiberias, the burying ground of our own revered ancestors. We laid him in the graveyard which holds Judah the Prince, who edited the Mishnah, and near the great rabbi, Ben Zakkui. "Judah was a martyr, even as Akiba," Maimonides said, "and Akiba is here, as well as our own patriarch."

This was true although I did not know it then. I took him to task for his resolution to remain in Palestine. "Was not the death of Judah the sign from heaven for us to depart?" I asked. Maimonides shook his head. "A coincidence is not a sign, in heaven or on earth," he said quietly. "In relation to the stars, they call it astrology; here you call it the will of God. But neither is true."

"David," I said, "you thought you knew that murderous knight. Who was he?"

"A ghost," he said harshly, "a ghost in armor." He would say no more, no matter how I pressed him.

So we chanted the Kaddish and bewailed the parting of the true poet. Abraham, a local rabbi, wished to discuss his favorite study of astronomy with Maimonides afterward, but my son refused. He was anxious to return to Jerusalem to resume his prayers and meditations. Yet this, according to the will of God, was not to be: How it came about that we left Palestine, its sacred deserts and alien Christians, will be told.

After all the rest had departed, I alone stood at the side of Judah's grave. I mourned inwardly for the friend of my boyhood. "Truly," I thought bitterly, "Maimonides is right. Judah is dead and yet the heavens have not fallen. God has not spoken—the Messiah has not yet come."

CHAPTER 13

The truth about the Jews is that every day we expect the Messiah to come and the world to end. As Maimonides is fond of repeating, "Even if the Messiah be delayed, I shall live every day as if I expect him to come each moment." When He does come, the tradition says all Jews will be transported to Heaven (except for those who may have to suffer a short time in Gehenna for extraordinary sins). The rest of the world—except for those like the Moslems, who have paralleled the Jewish faith—will be hurled into Hell, especially the idol-worshiping Christians with their triple god.

I am old and melancholy enough to doubt this. A good man, it seems to me, is a good man, no matter what his beliefs. In the last days, his actions shall speak loudest. I am convinced all Jews shall be in Abraham's bosom at the last because it is written, "All Thy people shall be righteous at the last." But I am sure also that others will accompany them to everlasting bliss.

For those who read this and doubt the possibility of such deliverance, I must repeat that it is one of the duties of all Jews to look for signs of the coming of the Messiah. I have often told Maimonides that the Messiah's rule of the world, under the love of God, is the great hope of our people. My son has come to believe implicitly in our oldest Messianic vision, handed down from our ancestors' exile from Jerusalem eleven hundred years ago. This declares the most likely date for fulfillment of the prophecy of the Messiah's coming to be in the year which, according to the Christian calendar, is 1210. Maimonides expects to live to see the glorious hour.

I regret I cannot be as sure as he is about the event. Like poverty and persecution, the problem of identifying the true Messiah always has been with the Jews. Bar Kochba fought the Roman troops with the blessings of Akiba and was proved false. Then came Moses of Crete, three centuries after; subsequently a Syrian Jew named Serene and a Persian Jew named Abu-Isa Obadia rose, each claiming the cloak of the true Messiah. None of these—and there were a dozen others —was our savior. Sometimes I feel these hints of his coming in the sacred writings may be merely legends; bait for the ignorant, as we draw the hearts of children to learn the Torah during the week by giving them nuts and cakes on the Sabbath.

However, it must be hoped for. As Maimonides has written, "At that time there will be neither famine nor war, neither jealousy nor rivalry. There will be an abundance of all good things, as plentiful as the dust. The whole world will be dedicated solely to the knowledge of God."

Even Maimonides does not believe in a world remade in the twinkling of an eye. Such superstitions annoy him. He states that we do not long "so ardently for the days of the Messiah because of their plentiful crops and riches nor that we may drink wine to music," but rather because "the pious will gather and there will be a reign of goodness and wisdom." In his thought, the world will continue much as it is, "the Messiah neither adding to nor subtracting from it."

There may be those not of our faith who will not understand how this hope has been our buttress for thousands of years. It is part of our very soul. It is expressed in the mystic prophecies of Elijah and Daniel; it is found in the profound utterances of Simon ben Yohai after his escape from the Romans and his twelve-year meditation in a cave; in the strange ecstatic recitals of Ishmael ben Elisha. There are many versions of how it will come about but this one is the most generally accepted.

The special guardian of our fate, assigned by God to care for us, the Archangel Michael, called Metraton, is given the overseership of the Messiah's coming. At this very moment, his seraphim with six wings and sixteen faces aid us in our hardships of exile. Each day, before the exalted Throne, they burn the ledgers of Satan on which he totals up the sins of the Jews.

Before Michael can make the will of God known, ten signs must precede the coming of the Messiah. The first is to be the rise of three kings. These will pretend to be converted to our faith but in reality they will be black goats to lead our people to despair and slaughter. Their treachery, according to Ben Elisha, will cause many Jews to abandon the truths of our fathers and "the gates of Heaven will be closed." Taxes will increase tenfold, persecutions will multiply, and a decree will be sent forth that all Jews must deny the Temple, the Torah, and the Lord.

At the same time, a race from the farthest ends of the earth will appear. Their faces will be so hideous—with two skulls and seven eyes—that their fiery glances will kill others by a single look. The second sign will destroy them, a season of unbearable heat which will bring a multitude of pestilences to slay myriads; only the pious will be saved by their prayers. Third of the signs will be a bloody dew falling on the world, to drink of which will be certain death. Fourth, a healing dew will descend to comfort those who still survive. The fifth sign will consist of the disappearance of the sun for thirty days, during which time many of the heathen will secretly become Jews.

The sixth sign will give power to one city in all the world. It will be called "Edom" (once thought to be Rome, but that has proved mistaken). It will rule all mankind for nine months, destroying other cities and peculiarly afflicting the Jews. At this time there will apear the first Messiah, called Nehemiah, son of Hushiel. He will assemble an army recruited from the tribes of Ephraim, Gad, Manasseh, and Benjamin. He will also kill the king of Edom, lay waste the city, restore the sacred utensils to the Temple, make a peace with Egypt, and slay all idolaters about Jerusalem.

The appearance of Armilius, the antichrist, will be the seventh sign. Born of the union of a demon and the marble statue of a woman, he will be "thirty-six feet high, six feet wide, with slanted red eyes, golden hair, two skulls, and green footsteps behind him." The children of Esau will cleave to him. He will demand godlike homage from Nehemiah and Nehemiah will refuse. Thereupon they will battle. Nehemiah will be killed, but his corpse will be preserved and hidden by angels. Following this Armageddon, there will come a period of Jewish suffering the like of which has not been since the beginning of time. Its severity will alienate all weak or doubting Jews. A faithful remnant will be saved; protected by Michael, they will gather in the desert for forty-five days.

The eighth sign will be heralded by three blasts from the trumpet of Michael. The surviving Jews of the desert will be led back to Jerusalem by the true Messiah—unnamed, but of the lineage of David and Elijah. As Isaiah declares, "With the breath of his lips shall he slay the wicked," and Armilius is doomed.

At the next sign—a prolonged trumpeting from Michael

which will shake the poles of the earth—God will collect the ten lost tribes from their exile; the Messiah will send messengers to all lands to bring the faithful home; and the graves of the blessed, first in Palestine, will open and their occupants rise.

Then the Temple shall be rebuilt, according to Ben Yohai, with seventy-two huge pearls atop to "shine from one end of the world to the other" and Israel will live in peace for two thousand years. Some say the Temple will be destroyed then and rebuilt again; others claim men shall feast on the flesh of the behemoths and shall be threatened by the leviathan of the sea and the gigantic bird of the air called Ziv. But the Ziv shall tear the leviathan to pieces with its claws and beak and Moses himself, blessed be he, shall reappear to slay the Ziv.

At the end of the two thousand years, according to the holy Rashi, "The Holy One, blessed be He, will sit on the throne of justice in the Valley of Jehoshaphat. Heaven and earth will fall apart, the moon be confounded, the sun ashamed, the mountains dissolve, and the hills be removed." The gates of Hell will yawn at the brook of Joshua and, in three days, the gates of the Garden of Eden will again be flung wide, to remain so forever.

The date of these happenings is not predicted. It was once widely believed they would come one thousand years to the day after the destruction of the Temple. It did not so happen. Maimonides once wrote an inquirer, Joseph ben Jabir of Bagdad, that it was not proper to speculate upon the time. Perhaps he felt, as do many of us, that the sins of the Jews are so manifold that the time of the Messiah has been put off.

If this hope has been our hearts' ease, it has also given inspiration to charlatans and cunning men. There is a curious exaltation connected with the Messianic feeling; it appears to inspire hopes of flying through the air. Severus, a Jew in Spain, promised to enable his disciples to fly to Palestine; he was taken and scourged in the midst of the synagogue for his blasphemy. In the heart of the Frankish kingdom, Maimonides told me, a false messiah gained many followers by some sort of trick, gliding from tree to tree like a bird. The Franks justly executed him; all his arts did not enable him to escape.

Not infrequently, even the learned and holy are deceived. Such a one was Moses al-Dar'i, who appeared in Fez shortly after our sojourn there. He told of a bloody dew on a Friday and the coming of the Messiah on Passover eve. A red rain

221

did appear—Maimonides described it scornfully as "red mud," possibly from a high desert storm meeting the clouds. Thereby many Jews were seduced and Al-Dar'i was disgraced.

I say all this by way of prelude to one of the most fearful sights of my life. I saw it in Acre and still, when I think of it, my limbs tremble and my heart is racked. It is the story of that wretch, David al-Ro'i, and his presumptions, which God at last revenged for blasphemy against the Highest.

Judah had been buried in Tiberias, graced by a plank from the table of the Jews in Jerusalem, carved by David in the sign of the Cohanim, two open hands of benediction. His place in the House of Life, as we called the burying-place, was secure for eternity. We, his stricken mourners, returned slowly to Jerusalem, wailing and tearing our garments and scattering dust on our heads for our souls' relief. Maimonides again visited the caves of the Patriarchs at Machpelah. We waited three miserable days for his return. Haggard and worn, he came back, seemingly exhausted. He did not object when Japhet suggested we return to his home in Acre. We retraced our steps to that city on the flatlands, now being fortified in mad haste by the slaves of the crusaders heaving huge ashlars into place in a double wall to protect them against possible attack from land or sea. Occupied with our sorrows, we endured their jeers and insults, even their spittle, without return, David alone daring to raise his head to glare defiance. Japhet quieted him. He led us through the gates and across the city, through its narrow twisting streets, between the houses which nearly leaned together over our heads.

To my surprise I discovered the Jewish quarter in Acre was not devoted to the scurrying business of the docks. It lay open and quiet, filled with peace. Japhet lived in an enclosure which held several houses, built of both wood and stone, with overhanging eaves, high narrow windows and doors fitted with many nailheads and bars, though they opened easily on the latch. About these houses lay small gravel courtyards, running with water from a nearby spring. These in turn were surrounded by carefully tended fruit-bearing trees, rows of garden culture, even beds of brilliant flowers. It was a pretty sight, one I had not seen since the palaces of Morocco and Spain. I bent and plucked a flower, murmuring a blessing.

"All of the Jews in Acre live here," Japhet said. "There are four families—with many young men and women—who tend these plots with me. We carry on a trade in grape-growing and the manufacture of wine. Since we are forbidden to drink wine made by others, we make a virtue of necessity. Many of the Christian knights come here to buy—and at least one was impressed enough by the quality of our wares to believe it came from magic. He begged me to give him the charm."

"What did you tell him?"

"I presented him with an old mezuzah and the advice of washing his feet when he trampled the grapes."

He chuckled and led the way within. Here were two rooms —the outer for summer heat, the inner for winter cold— decorated with taste and, to my envy, with some costliness. "You make your home a palace," Maimonides said, echoing my mind.

"We have been fortunate," Japhet admitted. "All roads lead to Jerusalem in these troubled times. The pilgrims often arrive without more than their gold. This they are willing to pay for what we grow here."

I looked around me with an exhalation of appreciation. The floor was earth, close-packed and oiled, scrupulously clean. The table, white-scrubbed, was set with bright-painted pottery, partly covered with a linen cloth. There was a polished brass goblet for the master of the house, flowers in the jugs, even a cushion or two on the leather-stripped chairs and stools. In the air, like incense, hung the odor of good food simmering in the pot.

Japhet clapped his hands. From without bustled a plump sunburned woman, beaming with pleasure at seeing guests. He introduced her as Rebecca, his wife; a girl, possibly seventeen, with dark eyes and curling hair, stood behind her and gazed intently at David, who did not return her glance. Thereupon she smiled at Maimonides. He promptly averted his eyes, staring upward at the two bronze lamps that swung from the low ceiling. This annoyed me: an excellent Jewish girl making eyes at my son and he ignored her. It was time for him to get married; yet even his brother had attempted romance before him.

"Speak to the girl," I said, nudging him.

"I am the head of the family," he returned in a low voice. "Speak to her yourself."

I was speechless for a moment at his impudence but before I could say a word, Japhet broke in: "My daughter, Naomi, good dayyan Maimon."

Naomi! My eyes filled with tears and I looked away out of shame. The girl retired. I made apology for all of us to Japhet. He waved it aside and invited us to bathe our hands and face before we sat down to a supper of seethed lamb and wine with bread and fruit.

Before we could rise, there was a heavy portentous knock at the door. We looked at each other apprehensively: Had we been seen in our encounter with the murdering wanton knight on the road outside the wall of Jerusalem? We drew back into the shadows of the corner farthest from the door and waited, David alone maintaining his place without change of countenance.

As it happened, there was no need to fear. Japhet returned. Behind him came a man so tall he was forced to stoop under the lintel. He was young in face but his hair was a premature silvery white. He had eyes of deep fire under his shaggy brows; his dress was a simple white tunic and sandals. Japhet turned to bring us together in greeting, but before he could utter a word, Naomi sprang into the circle, her eyes fixed devoutly on the newcomer. He halted her with a gesture, raising his hands. She imitated him.

"Whence comest thou, O pilgrim?" he demanded in a deep harsh voice.

"From Egypt," Naomi said in her girlish accents.

"Art thou delivered from bondage?" inquired the man in severe accents.

"Yes," she said eagerly, "I am free."

"Whither goest thou?"

"To Jerusalem!"

"Yea!" cried the stranger, flinging his arms wide, his immensely tall figure towering over us all. "Yea! That is the place where we shall at last be truly free, the place from whence the world shall be ruled!"

I was aghast at this parody of a Passover ceremony, but the moment had a weird solemnity I could not interrupt. I did indeed wait for the voice of Maimonides but, to my faint disappointment, it did not come. He stood motionless at my side, his arms folded, watching all from under his dusty, lightly folded turban.

It was Japhet who stepped forward. I was astonished to hear his voice, quavering in a sort of semireverence and fear. "She will not go to Jerusalem," he said.

"Will she not?" asked the man sardonically.

"She will not disobey her father," Japhet returned defiantly, giving back a step.

Suddenly the newcomer threw back his head and let loose a shout of laughter. He turned and lumbered out of the room, still giving vent to his fiendish glee. We heard it down the street long after he had slammed the outer door behind him. I wheeled and looked at Japhet; his face was white and his flesh shook on his bones. He sank to the table and put his head in his hands. I hesitated, noting that not only Naomi but also Rebecca stood still as images, their faces rapt as if in a trance. I sank to the side of Japhet and hugged his shoulders.

"Who is that visitor?" I said, forcing my voice to keep level.

Japhet raised his head. He wore an expression of unspeakable sorrow. "He," he whispered, "is David al-Ro'i."

We sat long at the table but few of us ate well. Above our heads the lamps guttered and flared, throwing fantastic shadows about. Japhet commenced to tell us the story of David al-Ro'i.

Fifteen years before, he had appeared from the city of Amadia in Kurdistan. His towering form, his flaming glance, his abrupt way of speaking had won him notice long before he finished his studies under Hisdai, then Head of the Captivity. Before he passed through the Academy Gaon Jacob in Bagdad, he was famous for his knowledge of the Torah, the Halachah, and the Talmud, as well as the Koran. More, he was versed in the secret lore of the magicians and soothsayers.

He returned home and roused the Jews of Persia to rebellion against the king by showing them miracles. "He passed a slender sword through his body without drawing more than drops of blood," Japhet said mournfully, "and it stood out from his back two hands-breadths." I looked at Maimonides: We knew from our studies of the body in Toledo that certain spots were without large blood vessels or vital organs— and that a careful man, schooled against pain, could do such a trick with ease.

Al-Ro'i declared he was king of the Jews, sent by the Blessed One to take Jerusalem and free the land from the Gentiles. Captured and thrown into prison by the king of the Persians, he escaped within three days and came again of his free will to the court. According to the witnesses, he defied the king, Japhet said, but he could not be seized because he was invisible. He crossed the river outside the city by sailing over it on his shabby cloak. Thenceforth he had appeared in many cities at many times, apparently with the speed of the wind, inciting the Jews to rise against their rulers.

"Because of this," Japhet said, shivering openly, "the Emir al-Muminin at Bagdad has said that if this one is not taken and slain, the Moslems will execute all the Jews in his empire."

"Why do you not take him?" asked David abruptly.

"He is stronger than we," Japhet said simply. "Not in the body but out of it. No one dares forbid him entrance nor betray him nor in any way hinder him."

He went on to say Al-Ro'i had been excommunicated from the Jewish community by Samuel ben Ali, both by word of mouth and by letter to all the Jews of the East. But he recked nothing of this ban. Many believed on him, if not as the Messiah himself, certainly as Nehemiah, the herald. Nor did Al-Ro'i divest himself of such titles.

"Not only the men," said Japhet mournfully, "but the women follow him and idolize him as the Christians do their images."

"Are there many such?" asked Maimonides.

"There are many. Some of them are Gentiles who believe he is their Christ come again. Chief among them all is his concubine. A woman fit to match him in height, and as beautiful as he is hateful, with hair as flaming as fire itself."

I felt a cold gripe close itself around my heart. I drew back a little, as if I dreaded his answer. "How is she named?" I faltered. I felt the body of Maimonides next to me grow tense as a drawn bow.

"She came to Palestine with the accursed family of De Bouillon as a physician. Once here, she changed her nature and ran wild like a bitch set loose, corrupting men and women alike. She was the beloved of many men, disdaining them all until she fell under the foul enchantments of Al-Ro'i."

"Her name!"

Japhet looked curiously at me. "She calls herself Hephzibah," he returned. "That is the mysterious consort who is prophesied as the right hand of the Messiah. Her lineage is directly from David."

I sank back, shuddering with relief. Maimonides passed his hand around my waist to support me. "Are you ill?" Japhet inquired solicitously. I wiped the sweat from my forehead. I managed to shake my head.

"A cup of wine," Japhet announced. He stood up and went to the rude sideboard with his own goblet. He returned and set down both bottle and goblet. As he poured, I received another shock. I restrained his hand and examined the bottle

226

with a growing sense of uneasiness and dread. There was no mistaking it: It was the same or a twin. Six-sided, of black glass, with the molded forms of the menorah, the palm tree, the grape cluster, with the same wide-funnel mouth. Even the remains of the black seal could be seen on its side. I thrust it away as if it were a scorpion.

"I am sorry you reject my wine," said Japhet with cold formality. "It was a gift to me, the best I have."

"From whom was it a gift?" Maimonides asked slowly.

"Every year," Japhet responded, "the heads of the Jewish community throughout the world receive such bottles of rare wine as gifts for the feast before Passover."

"From whom?" I asked unsteadily.

"From whom should it be except from the head of the Jews in exile? From the Head of the Captivity, Samuel ben Ali himself."

I twisted about, was caught full in the dark stare of the eyes of Maimonides. "Is this the sign of heaven for you?" I said hoarsely.

He shook his head. With a quick gesture, he reached out and snatched up the bottle. He drank two deep gulps from it and put it down before David or I could raise a hand.

"It is very good," Japhet said, his humor restored by Maimonides' action. "I regret I drank half of it or more shortly after it came from Bagdad."

Our eyes met and instantly, foolishly, we commenced to laugh shamefacedly. I took the bottle and poured myself a glass and drank gratefully. Whatever had been in the glass when Zayd had drunk in Morocco was missing: It was an excellent wine of the Bagdad vintage but it still gave me an ache within to feel it trickling down. I remembered Zayd's flaccid eyes too well. Nevertheless, I finished half the draught and put the goblet down firmly before me. I looked up to see Japhet's face abstracted as he poured a libation for himself.

"Concerning Al-Ro'i's woman, however," he murmured, "I have heard disturbing rumors. That she spoke falsely, taking the name of Hephzibah to fulfill what had been written. According to the Gentiles, she is called rightfully Rachel bat Abor."

The spasmodic jerk of my hand flung the cup on its side. The metal rattled, the dark wine flowed. Careless of all, I lowered my head, beating it against the wooden planks.

How long I lay there in stupor, I do not know. What roused me was a long trumpet-call, thrice repeated, reminding me of the shofar; but it was long after sunset and the Sabbath was two days off. I lifted my head in weary wonder.

It was Japhet who sprang from his seat beside me, where he had been uttering soothing words to comfort my fit, which he did not understand. "The signal!" he cried. "Then this is the night!"

"What night?" asked Maimonides.

Japhet paid no attention. He rushed outside. We heard his cries for his wife and daughter. A moment later he burst inside, panting and distraught.

"Gone!" he shouted, his face contorted in an indescribable expression. "Both Rebecca and Naomi! Gone after that cursed magician!"

Dizziness swept through my head; my body shook uncontrollably. As Maimonides and David sprang to their feet, I tried to imitate them and almost fell. My right leg seemed paralyzed. They tried to help me. Angrily I waved them back and followed them as best I could into the night.

It was a tall building, one of the tallest in Acre, I afterwards discovered. It loomed over us like some square white ghost. Before me, Japhet, Maimonides, and David leaped up the stairs that angled in a zigzag on the outside of the walls. I was forced to follow like a cripple, sobbing at every breath, dragging myself upward. At last I gained the top of the three stories. I found myself on an open flat roof of poles and earth. Maimonides and David stood at one side, as if restrained by an invisible barrier; with them was Japhet, unaccountably balked. At the far side huddled a group of women, most of them hooded and veiled beyond recognition. Among them rose the menacing figure of Al-Ro'i.

So Japhet was right, I thought to myself as I hobbled forward; this was the place. But what will happen here tonight in this dreadful calm before the deed? As if in response to my mind, a figure detached itself from the women and came swiftly to Al-Ro'i. "When is the moment, master?" she asked.

I started with pain. It was the remembered voice of Rachel. I could not resist a cry.

"Rachel!" I said.

She did not look at me. But her face dilated and she spoke to the tall form of Al-Ro'i. "May I speak to this one, master?" she asked pleadingly.

Al-Ro'i jerked his head in reluctant assent. He shambled away to the other side of the roof. I was left alone to face the one I had known as Rachel bat Abor, as lovely as ever but far more distant.

"Well, Maimon?" she challenged me. I hobbled a little closer to her.

"You are not the Rachel I knew."

"Did you ever know me, Maimon?"

"Yes. I am bold to say it but, yes, I knew you!"

"Perhaps in the flesh. But not as a redeemed spirit."

I clasped my hands in pain. "Rachel, do you know what you say?"

She smiled at me, a vague misty smile, her eyes looking beyond me. "I know it very well."

I could not help remembering that faraway night in Almería when Rachel had first astonished me by declaring so mystically in favor of some messiah for our race. Of all persons, I had not expected it of her; now I knew her rigorous scientific temperament must have had a flaw of the wild and romantic in it that had led her to her fate.

"You are strange on this strange night," I said.

She roused herself in a gust of passion. "Look at me, Maimon! Do I look like yourself? Am I, like you, ready to die?"

Her words were acid cast upon my flesh; I recoiled from them because I could not deny them. She went on, regal in her demands, looking, in her simple white gown, younger than I had ever seen her.

"Truly," I said humbly, "you are more glorious than I have ever seen you."

"I am prepared to live forever," she said, suddenly calm again.

"Do you truly believe that this man Al-Ro'i is the Messiah?"

"He is my Messiah, Maimon, he and none other. I shall enter the World-to-Come or the hell-to-come, whatever may befall, at his side."

Her words seemed to me to savor more of earthly love than of heavenly bliss. I changed my tone, hoping to turn her from this miserable obsession. "Do you never think of Cordova, Rachel? Or of Toledo or Almería? Of nightingales and roses?"

Her smile was one of utter contempt. "I have given away all my possessions, Maimon; I have deserted my friends; I have abandoned the world. When the end of all things is at hand, when Heaven itself is to be rolled up like a scroll, does one think of the beauties of this world?"

229

"Are you so sure?" I cried.

"Tonight, Maimon," Rachel said rapidly, "we shall fly from the roof here in Acre to the holy city of Jerusalem. There before our eyes, the Temple shall rise again in the wink of an eye, built by angels, decorated by God!"

"Rachel!" I exclaimed in anguish. "You are mad, mad beyond redemption!"

She took no offense at my words, almost as if she had expected them. "Am I mad, Maimon, because of the words of Elijah and Daniel, because I believe in their prophecies?"

"No, no! But is Al-Ro'i the One they promised?"

"They have said what they have said."

"And doubtless he has said what he has said," I returned in my bitter wildness. "You know all this for truth?"

"Has not David himself told me?"

"The devil is the father of all lies," I groaned.

Rachel shook her head in aloof pity. "Maimon," she said, "how shall we know the truth except by revelation? Who can prove the word of God and His messenger by anything other than faith? How did the children of Israel prove the mission of Moses except by faith?"

"That is blasphemy, sacrilege!"

"To you, perhaps. What disagrees with your own disbelief is always blasphemy. To me it is the highest truth. I know, I know! Nothing else is true!"

I endeavored to calm my beating heart, to activate my useless leg. I gripped the flesh of my thigh until the pain made my head spin. "Rachel," I said, "there has been much doubt, in the writings of the Fathers, about the coming of the Messiah. They have set no date, no time of his arrival in our midst."

"He has come. The time is now. And we waste it unnecessarily, Maimon. Come with me, join the miracle with your own body, see God with your own eyes!"

She held out her hand to me but I resisted an almost overpowering impulse to take it. "Rachel," I said urgently, "have you forgotten your own great mission, that of healing?"

She hesitated. "No," she said slowly, as if the words were pulled out of her throat, "but of what use is it to heal the bodies of men endlessly when their souls are sick to all eternity?"

I drew a deep breath. I made my last cast of the twin dice of reason and emotion. "And Maimonides?" I said boldly. "Have you forgotten the child of our bodies?"

230

Rachel's dark eyes clouded uncertainly in the starlight. She moved her head from side to side, as if shaking off an invisible halter, almost turning her gaze to one side to see Maimonides but at the last minute turning back to me. For the first time Rachel seemed unsure of herself. I advanced, eager to press my advantage; before I could say a word, she whirled and ran lightly across the roof to the other side. Cursing my impotence, I followed her and was forced to halt. The figure of David al-Ro'i came between us.

"No," he said heavily. "She is pledged to me."

I wheeled and cried: "David! Maimonides! Help me!" Not one of them moved; they stood like phantoms in the shadows. David indeed started a step but Maimonides' arm thrust out, pushing him back. Japhet wrung his hands but he did not move. I was defeated and alone.

"Come, Rachel!" boomed the voice of Al-Ro'i, staring up at the stars. "It is the moment! You shall be the first! We shall fly like the sacred cranes of Egypt, a van of glory across the night! Come!"

As he spoke, the women formed themselves into angled lines; I was horrified even more to see Naomi and Rebecca as the second pair to follow Rachel, one on either hand.

With the pale staring face of a somnambulist, Rachel turned, walked with her light tread toward the parapet. I could not believe she would attempt it; yet I shamed myself when I admitted that for a heart-stopping moment I imagined it was possible. I saw her mount in one lithe movement to the top. As she did, all the others, the chosen, waited just below. They stood, a row of statues in the night, white and immobile, their robes fluttering about them as if they were already in flight.

I cried out but nothing came from my throat. I started forward but I could not move. I was caught in the jaws of a trap: my own disbelief in the thing, my own hope it would be true. I saw Rachel shimmering against the blackness of night wherein the stars blinked with blinding radiance, outlining her divine form. I stretched my hands to her in wordless appeal, to come back to me if she could not come back to the world. I was too late.

"Depart!" It was the harsh voice of Al-Ro'i. She heard it. She stretched out her arms over the abyss of the street below. In a single motion, as if all her muscles were attached to a string, she launched herself into space like a swan. Instantly she disappeared. The air did not buoy her up, the angels of the Lord did not come to succor her with their wings, the heavens did not open to save her. In the distance, the stars winked as inscrutable and as cold as ever.

My body bathed itself in sweat. The moment was so long that it was intolerable. I heard nothing; an insane hope loosed itself in my breast. Perhaps, after all, it was true: Perhaps Rachel had swooped to another eyrie, to the stars, saved by a miracle.

Then I heard a single shriek, cut short by a sickening thud. There was a long groan and silence. David al-Ro'i uttered a curse so terrible that even now I cannot repeat it; he threw himself over the parapet onto the stairs, precipitating himself headlong to the lower levels, tumbling and rolling, shouting all the while. The rest of us stood paralyzed but not for long.

While we remained rooted, two other women, walking in the same dreamy fashion as Rachel, approached the edge of the roof. Instantly David and Japhet threw themselves forward. They bore them down to the room beneath them. In my moment of surprise, I saw Japhet was struggling with his wife and David had Naomi in his arms—and, greater surprise, I saw his lips pressed to hers.

Maimonides remained where he had been, motionless as a judge. I crossed to him. Together we made our way to the edge of the roof, slowly, as if to a funeral. Looking over into the darkness below, we could see the white form of Rachel stretched out, another gaunt white form bent over it. As we watched, the figure of Al-Ro'i rose. Scrambling away, howling like a wild beast, running like one in fear of more than the loss of his life, he vanished down an alley.

"My son," I said, my voice quivering, "you did not come to my aid."

"It would have been to save that woman," Maimonides said.

I made no answer. After a moment, Maimonides said: "In the words of the blessed Akiba, 'The judgment is a judgment of truth.' God is not mocked."

"She was a worthy woman but she was deceived," I managed to say.

"As it is written: 'As a jewel of gold in the snout of a swine, so is a fair woman without sense.' "

"She was deceived!"

"I find comfort in Hillel: 'Because she died, they killed her; in the end they that killed her shall be killed.' " His voice broke on the last words. I peered closely at his face. To my astonishment, for the first and last time, I saw my son silently weeping.

Thus died Rachel bat Abor, in her ageless glory, uselessly, foolishly, wickedly. It is not worthwhile to tell more except to say that her crushed body in the street caused a superstitious seven-days' wonder in Acre, her death being attributed to her having been a sorceress who was carried up to a great height by rebellious demons and dashed down to the earth. Nor is it much to boot to add that less than a year later the prediction of Maimonides came true: David al-Ro'i had a price of ten thousand gold pieces set upon his head by Samuel ben Ali in Bagdad. He was murdered in his sleep by his own father, crazed by lust for gold.

Nor is it of warrant to describe how we gathered Yaltah again to our bosom, took farewell of Japhet, and set sail secretly the next night for Alexandria. Maimonides had always said that it was forbidden for Jews to settle in Egypt, but on this occasion—one of few—he reversed his judgment. And, indeed, we had nowhere else to go. Much more might be said of how Naomi came to Alexandria two months later and was wedded happily there to David, my son.

As for Maimonides, sequestered more than ever with his books, he enjoyed increasing fame among the world of Jews. With it, he endured the penalties of the great. His rooms became so thronged by petitioners for advice and admonition, his desk heaped so high with Responsa demanded from all corners of the earth, that finally—after two years—we left Alexandria. We sailed more than one hundred thirty miles up the Nile beyond Cairo to the small, peaceful village of Fostat. Here we have lived ever since.

Though the conflicts between us have become less during the years and our thoughts harmonized—has not Sota said that a father should sympathize with his son?—we are not yet reconciled in all our beliefs. Two days ago Maimonides brought me the letter he had been writing. As I suspected, it was in reply to Jacob ben Natanel of Yemen. Since it concerned the rise of false messiahs in that land as in Palestine, I am of the opinion Maimonides was more caustic than is his wont in his denunciations of such pretenders. The memory of what happened in Acre is still fresh in his mind; the memories of the old—as Judah ben Tema says—are prone to fade at my age.

I read what he had written, sighed, and gathered the pages of the codex together. Maimonides leaned toward me, intently watching my expression. "You do not approve," he said.

"You have advanced far along the road to righteousness," I said.

"There is something you do not approve."

"You have not yet won to the greatest virtue of all," I said slowly.

He considered me. "What is this greatest virtue?" he demanded.

"Tolerance of others," I said. "All the Law of Israel may be taught you while you stand on one foot and it is this: Do nothing to anyone that you would hate to be done to you. If we Jews expect others to cease hating us, we must cease despising them."

Maimonides combed his beard with his fingers, deep in thought. "I know the passage you mean," he said at length. "It is the one where I speak of those who call themselves Christians. Read it aloud to me."

I opened the thick book again, found my place, and began: " 'There arose a new sect which combined conquest and controversy because it believed this procedure would be best to wipe out every trace of the Jews and their religion. It resolved to claim prophetic visions and to found a new faith contrary to our divine religion, to contend it was equally God-given. It hoped to rouse doubts and create confusion. Such is the remarkable plan contrived by any man who is envious and complaining: He will strive to kill his enemy and to save his own life, but when he finds it impossible, he devises a scheme whereby both will be slain.' "

"I see nothing objectionable there," Maimonides said abruptly.

"Let me go on," I remonstrated. I continued: " 'The first to have adopted this plan was Jesus, the Nazarene, may God forgive him for his blindness. He impelled people to believe he was a prophet sent by God to clarify perplexities in the Torah and that he was the Messiah that was predicted by each and every seer. He interpreted the Torah in such a way as to lead to its total annulment, to the abolition of all its commandments and to the violation of its prohibitions.' " I closed the codex and looked at the hawklike face of my son, haggard and sunken from his long studies. "Even this Jesus did not say that he came to destroy the Law but to fulfill it," I said.

"He was a Jew all his days. Even the Moslems revere him as a prophet."

Maimonides shook his head, took back the letter he had written to Yemen, and, hugging it to his breast, said gravely: "Perhaps I may one day come to the peak of toleration where you stand, my father. But I cannot forgive so easily now."

"He is right not to forgive," interrupted a harsh voice behind me. Before I could turn about, David strode past me and stared defiantly at both of us. "For once, my elder brother is right."

"He has often led the way for us," I admitted.

Maimonides held up his hand. "Wait, my father," he said quietly, "there is something here I do not understand."

"Yes," David said, a depth of bitterness in his tone that I had never heard before. "There is much you do not understand, Muni."

"Tell me."

"When you took me drugged from Toledo years ago, I did not complain, I kept silence. I have not spoken, all these years, of how you have interfered in my life, in my father's life, in the lives of all of us. You have set yourself up as a prophet, first for the family of Maimon, then for all Jews. Whence comes this mighty wisdom that rules each of our lives?"

"David!" I cried. But he swept on in a torrent of words, long pent up within him. "I have submitted this long only because you saved my life and Yaltah's life at Fez—but even that was at the price of a lie against our faith! I have kept silent because you are older, because you are my father's favorite!"

Maimonides did not move a muscle; his eagle aspect was unchanged. But in the depths of his eyes I saw the glow of agony. "What I have done, I have done," he said slowly.

"I have loved you both," I cried wildly. "What is this sudden madness?"

"And he has loved you more than he has me," Maimonides said to David, his voice rising. "He has done what I have wished only because you were foolish, trying to think with your body, not your mind! He gave me authority because he was weak, because he wished to excuse you in his heart! Ask him, which of us does he love better?"

Maimonides pointed his finger at me like an accusing judge. I felt myself pale, the blood withdrawing from my heart. I looked from one to the other, unable to speak, my throat clogged and my eyes filled with tears.

"Let him alone," growled David, taking a step toward his brother. Maimonides uttered a mirthless laugh.

"You see," he said, "you take his part, you act without thinking. I must think before I do a single act; I must weigh every consideration because I am expected to. Do you not think I have envied you your freedom? You have done as you pleased and I have done as my father expected me to. You have brought sorrow upon him and I have been his staff—yet he loves you better."

"Not true, not true," I said, stifling at the words.

Maimonides drew a deep breath; his head sank to his bosom. "Forgive me, David," he murmured. "I have longed for love as the deer pants for a living stream. You do not compete with our father in what he feels is his own kingdom, that of the mind. You do not threaten to usurp his throne. He admires your body, your muscles, your handsome looks, and so, God help me, do I. You are not a rival to him as I am. Therefore he can love you. But for me are reserved only the crumbs of his contempt."

"Muni," said David hoarsely, "I did not mean this much. I have always been jealous of you, of the closeness of thought between you, of what you were to each other; I have suffered because of my own waywardness and dreams. I ought to have spoken long ago, not spewed it out all in a moment."

"I have often wished to have your strength and skill," Maimonides said simply.

"And I, your genius," David returned.

I rose, trembling with what I had to say. "Will you not realize, my sons, that love is not to be divided like a loaf?" I asked, striving to control my voice. "We make mistakes. Maimonides has been close to apostasy, in Toledo, in Fez, even here, because of his fascination with the subtle thoughts of the Moslem sages. David has been close to the same sin because of his admiration of the feats of the Christians. We have struggled with ourselves and it is only God that gives us the victory. What gulfs there are between our souls are bridged only by our love for each other. We must not diminish it in a world that does not love the Jew nor his children." I held out my shaking arms. "Come to me, come to me, my sons!" I cried. In tears and thanksgiving, I held them to my bosom as they knelt; I knew that I had at last come to the love which passes understanding.

236

Here, after these many weeks in Fostat, I draw near the close of the history of my famous son. I find it good. I have told only what is true, omitting nothing but avoiding what might disturb others. At my age, controversy proves nothing at all and sours the stomach. As Moses spied into the Promised Land with longing, so do I long for the World-to-Come.

I have been a good father. I have had good sons. I trust they will give me grandsons who will be as eminent in medicine and the Law as once I was, as Maimonides is at present. David will supply what is needful in revenue from his business of gem-trading in Cairo. Even at this moment he hastes with the wind aboard a ship in the Red Sea to buy and sell in the marts of India: God give him speed and good· luck and safety.

On and on we have gone, the family of Maimon—never the the family of Mammon, you may be sure—across the world. We have parted with friends and property, with nationality and livelihood, to pursue our God. Perhaps the reward-to-come will be different but, in this world, it has been difficult. We have forgotten so many homes, put them out of our minds; memory does not give me youth as it does other men; thinking only makes me sad. The years close over my head like hanging clouds and the sun vanishes. The days of a life are brief, yet they contain centuries of sorrow and loss. The light shortens and the nights are long. There is no lamp to guide my feet.

Sitting here in the hot courtyard, the afternoon heat dampening my hand with sweat and curling the papyrus while all others sleep, I write as my thoughts drive my pen. Life proceeds in a muddy torrent of good resolutions swept away in evil deeds, whether we will them or not. A Hand hovers over us—if it is God, as we say, or Fate, as the Moslems say, I know not. But we have little to do except to carry out the mitzvot, to perform our small functions in the hope that they will become part of the Perfect. But we doubt, we doubt, all the while.

Like eddies in the stream forming and reforming, we meet our friends and swirl into nothing, parted by life or by death, in all corners of this life. The years roll swiftly on, rumbling across the past like a donkey cart. We find ourselves hurried travelers, limited to no more than a cup of wine, laughter and tears, a few jokes and some solemn sayings; then the young are grown up and bearded and we are as far away as an echo.

The wheel grinds its way around; the circle closes for them as well.

Vanity, vanity: Cold, cold, the year comes to a chill end. The days whirl by like leaves in the wind, rattling scornfully at me; the crickets and locusts make mournful scrapings at the windows and weep shrilly in the fields. The wind increases and stirs the leaves of the vine over my head. The shadows stretch out. Only in dreams do I see those I loved and who have journeyed on before me; only then do I return to life, seeing the faces of Naomi and Rachel bat Abor, of Judah and my friends in Cordova, even now and then the faces of Brujo and Zayd. They light up the dark night like torches in a tomb. When I wake in the early dawn—for no one who is old sleeps late—I go out in the coolness to the gate of woven palm fronds before our dwelling. I watch the carriers pass, bowed under their loads. They cannot understand why I—a white-bearded man without labor—can weep. But my thoughts travel across the world before they can take a single step.

I must put down my pen. There are sounds of a horseman at the gate, the rattle of knocking. The servants have answered, I hear the excited babble of question and answer. Perhaps someone has brought news of David.

END OF BOOK ONE

BOOK II

JOSEPH BEN AKNIN SPEAKS

CHAPTER 14

Standing in the red dust of the road outside the house of the famous Maimonides, humbly waiting permission to enter, I, Joseph ben Aknin, heard a dreadful cry. It sent shivers down my back: the wail of a man utterly bereaved. In a moment it was joined by the cries of women, the bawling of children. The moaning continued, ululating in the shimmering air of the Egyptian winter, but I did not hear that single cry again.

Undecided, I was about to retreat from this house of mysterious grief. Does not the eminent Simeon ben Eleazar say: "Soothe not in the hour of anger, console not in the hour of death, question not in the hour of the vow, seek not to visit in the hour of disgrace"? My intention was interrupted by the abrupt exit of an Arab post-rider from the gate. His dress was still dusty from what must have been a long ride. He strode past me, muttering to himself. "These Jews," he said under his breath, "these Jews! Do they not know what Allah has ordained will happen?"

Seeing my yellow garb and covered head, he hesitated. Then he flung my oiled lovelock a contemptuous glance, frowned, sprang atop his lathered mare and wheeled off at a gallop. His words and scorn decided me: I was a Jew, within were Jews in distress. I clutched my scroll of introduction in my sweating hand. Slowly I entered the courtyard of this small dwelling in the town of Fostat.

I passed between two arbors, each festooned with withered grapevines. I entered the half-open door of the inner court, wincing as I pushed it, and heard the squeal of the socketed hinges. I found myself confronted by a strange scene, almost like a pantomime at Purim. It was the Christian year of 1174. I set eyes for the first time on the great physician and sage of our race.

I recognized him from a scratched sketch of his features upon a bit of whalebone cherished by my father. His face was unmistakable in its sharp outlines. He stood in this inner court

of bright mosaic and sunshine; a bronze fountain leaped for-
lornly in its midst, making music in a tiled pool. Though he
was, I knew, a young man, not yet past forty, his face was
lined and lean. His eagle-like nose and great gray eyes seemed
to brood over what was before him.

At the edge of the pool, stretched out on a low couch, lay
a body. Instantly, by a flash of terrible intuition, I realized this
could be no other than Maimon ben Joseph, the father of
Maimonides.

Beside the couch, alternately kneeling and prostrate, wept
a young woman with disheveled dark hair and a torn robe.
Two other servants, a black man and woman probably of
Abyssinian blood, were on their knees beyond, mourning with
her. Beyond, rigid on a marble bench, was the oddest sight
of all: another woman, older but with the unmistakable family features of Maimonides, seated quietly. Her face was calm
and pale, her eyes unseeing; indeed, a faint smile curled her
lips in this moment of tragedy!

"I beg forgiveness for coming to you at this time," I said
helplessly, extending my hands as a suppliant to Maimonides.

Pale under his swarthy skin, Maimonides stared at me for
a moment without expression. The muscles in his face quivered. I realized the immense emotions under which he labored,
the stronger will that kept them in check. At last he spoke
in a hoarse, uneven voice.

"You are welcome to this house. Who may you be?"

"I come in a time of grief," I said hesitantly, my own tears
rising to my eyes. "Permit me to retire."

Maimonides shook his head slightly. "He who values the
dead more than the living, insults the gift of God," he murmured. But as he spoke I saw the strange sight of tears running down his impassive face, an alien impotent grief that
came from the depths of his soul. He went on more strongly:
"He gives life and He takes it away, blessed be His Name.
Come with me."

He made his way out to the first court and sat down in
the left arbor as if exhausted. I thrust my scroll at him. He
took it with a quivering hand. I sank down on a stool opposite, feeling a surge of admiration for the self-control of such
a man. Maimonides broke the seal and read for what seemed
an unconscionably long time. I could hear the dim sounds of
grief behind us. More to break into that sound of sorrow than
anything else, I said loudly: "Honored sir, my name is Joseph
ben Aknin. By profession, I am a poet and philosopher. My

242

father believes I am in need of additional instruction and he begs you to take me as a pupil."

Maimonides raised his head and let the scroll fly together. "Your father says more," he told me, tapping the parchment. "He says you are a fool."

A flush heated my cheeks. "Perhaps I have not always been the best of sons," I replied, "but my father does not understand me."

Maimonides flashed me an indescribable look. "Nor did I think my father understood me," he said in an unnatural voice. "Now he lies dead within and it is too late to tell him he understood me all too well!"

A single great gasping sob shook his body. He covered his face with his hands for long seconds. When he took them away, they were soaked with tears but his face retained its calm. "Enough, enough," he said. "It will ease my heart if I tell you. My brother, David, is dead; his ship was struck by the winter storms in the Red Sea. Only two sailors survived. Their story was sent by courier from Alexandria and was told my father before I could prevent it. He could not survive the news of his son's death. He has joined him in the World-to-Come. The fortune of our family, a great sum in jewels, was with my brother and is lost with him."

He stood up, his dark face raised toward the sky. "But we are not alone!" he cried. "We are His and He is ours!"

Rising with him, I stood motionless. My own emotions were as exalted as his own. But to my dumfounding, Maimonides whirled and went rapidly into the court where his father lay. With imperious gestures, he motioned out the servants, the weeping woman, the child. Only the figure of the silent woman on the bench remained.

"My sister, Yaltah," Maimonides said to me, speaking rapidly in a low voice. "Out of all that is evil, good must come; I shall take advantage of this moment. For years she has been as silent as an image, never speaking more than a word or two, never making an unnecessary motion. If anything might have touched her heart—as you have seen it pierce the heart of Naomi, David's wife—it might have been her brother's death. More, the death of her father. But she sits there, immobile and aloof. Young Joseph, do you know why?"

He addressed me with such vehemence that I involuntarily stepped back. I did not relish being plunged into the affairs of this unusual family without notice. "No," I managed to say, "I do not."

243

"Because women have eyes turned inward!" Maimonides said savagely. "Avicenna was right! Nothing which does not concern them alone has any effect. The world may collapse, the stars plunge from their orbits, but they remain within the shell of their vanity, turtles in their carapaces! She suffered a shock seven years ago in Morocco in the Maghreb. She has remained so since."

"The Maghreb is my own home," I said quickly, hoping to distract him. "It was to your father that mine in Ceuta sent his message about the apostate Jews, to whom your father wrote his Responsum of consolation in return. My father will tell you I seemed to turn to the Moslem faith but that is not so."

I stopped. Maimonides did not seem to hear me. "Everything has been tried," he said softly. "Medicines and herbs, bleeding and drenches, heat and cold, poultices and salves. It is the mind which controls the body. Shock must be met with a greater shock, the soul must be shaken. Do you wish to be taught by me, Joseph?"

"That is my father's wish, in his wisdom," I said with terror in my heart. I was not at all sure that this formidable person to whom I had been sent was anything but a madman.

"Very well," Maimonides said. "As your teacher, I command you to approach my sister." His voice was deep and ominous.

I made my way across the ornate tiles of the floor and stood beside her. She seemed indeed unseeing, without animation. "Strip off her head-covering," Maimonides said. I hesitated, knowing it for an insult from a stranger; he repeated the command. With misgiving, I did as he said. A convulsive shudder ran over her form. She sat straighter.

"Tear away her tunic!" commanded Maimonides. In dismay I began to protest. He silenced me. "Roughly, roughly!" he cried.

Urged beyond my own will, I did his wish. Her tunic was ripped away, her bosom exposed; it shuddered in the light, firming and lifting. I held my hand as she uncertainly raised her hands and clutched her breasts.

"Her sash!" I knew he meant the sash that supported and half-concealed her nakedness but I could not bring myself to do it.

"I am a stranger in your house," I said falteringly, "I am not a man who attacks the sister of my teacher."

"Obey!" cried Maimonides. "Do you dare to tell me your thoughts? Are you still the fool of your father?"

Stung, almost without thought, I stripped away the sash. It fell to the floor. A strangled cry came from Yaltah. She turned toward me, her eyes glowing with furious life.

"Now!" The voice of Maimonides was like a trumpet. "Tear her skirt from her body!"

Involuntarily my hands went out. As they did, Yaltah uttered a shriek. She sprang to life, a sight as terrible as a woman of stone suddenly given a soul. But she did not run to hide her shame nor to keep me from her. Instead she burst into a torrent of tears, threw her arms wide and staggered to the body of her father. She fell to her knees and threw herself upon it, sobbing, wrenching her body with the tumult of her grief.

Maimonides looked down at her from his lofty eminence. Softly he crossed behind her, touched her hair lightly with a long finger decked with an amethyst ring. He turned to me.

"Come, Joseph," he said in a clear, calm voice. "Let the dead bury their dead. Let Yaltah pour out all the grief and shame she has accumulated for so long."

"Ameen," said a new voice in a low tone. We looked at the door. A handsome middle-aged Moslem stood there, sweeping the floor in a deep salaam. "This is rare medicine," he said in admiration.

"It is the fruit of the study of Avicenna's *Book of Cures*," Maimonides said coldly.

We followed him into the outer court. I shut the door firmly behind us. The stranger and I waited as Maimonides sank slowly down into an arbor seat. Suddenly, rending his gown at the breast, he uttered a long, grief-stricken moan; his face contorted with grief, his eyes became staring and lost. He fell to the ground, rolling in the dust, showering handfuls of it on his head, weeping, crying aloud.

Thus it was I entered the service of Maimonides as his disciple. Here I must confess that I know idolatry is a sin worse than all the rest. It destroys the mind and enslaves the will; it places the creations of man in the cubicle of God. It is as evil to worship another human like myself—a man with senses, thoughts, limbs, and body—as it is to worship the images with which the heathen crowd their temples.

Yet I protest I adore Maimonides outside of the vanished Holy of Holies. He is a man like unto men—no divinity nor

245

supernatural being. He is formed as I am, and he eats, sleeps, bleeds, as I do, but his visions are as far above mine as the sky is over the earth. Did the Torah not forbid it, I would think of him as do the silly Christians of their saints, for if any living being deserves this reverence, it is my master.

I know he has been cursed and reviled—yea, that the precious documents he has written have been burned before a yelping mob of Jews. I also know that sundry such manuscripts in his own hand have been hung up in synagogues with due reverence, almost as if they were a second Law.

I must take arms against both these opinions. Somewhere between the two stands the true, God-inflamed man. I cannot pretend to change a single mind, however: Those who love Maimonides will love him still, those who hate him will denounce him still. Nor do I want to make a god out of a man who is so indubitably a man, nor a man out of one who has approached so near the Seat of Mercy.

Next to those of his own family—and none of these remain, except his sister Yaltah—I know him best. I have been his companion and pupil during the long night hours when he could not rest, through the weary days when he tended his patients, whether rich or poor, as a sacred duty, on the Sabbaths, when he scarcely seemed to breathe, so much he needed to recruit his strength. I have written his words on papyrus, embossed them in my memory despite the fact that he has insisted on inscribing every Responsum with his own hand. I have heard him complain but rarely of himself. I have seen him in health, in sickness, in melancholy, and in his pity for man and his abnegation before God. I have, I confess, written some private verses of my own to celebrate his virtues. I dare not show them to him: He would command me to destroy them, since he is an acute critic of literary style.

On this evening in old Cairo, with the windows showing the bright green blaze of the full moon touching the horizon, I have no more than put down the thick script about Maimonides written by his father before his death. I am horrified. This long struggle between them, the final victory unachieved by either, the despair of Maimon ben Joseph. He did not understand his own son. Perhaps it was ordained by God from the beginning that Maimonides should be a riddle to his family, as he has been to many Jews everywhere.

I know of the hatred, of the powerful enemies he has raised up like serpents from the dust; I know of his reluctance to apply the bastinado of his logic to their foolishness. Not that

246

he is a meek man—far from it; he has castigated all the sins (though rarely the sinners) that rise before him. But he will not stir, even for his own salvation, until he has made sure of his steps, moving from tussock to tussock in the swamps of our world.

You see, he does not feel he is infallible; he knows this is a quality belonging only to God Himself. He knows he is mortal, as Alexander the Great came finally to realize. In his merrier moments—all too rare—he is fond of derisively repeating the jest of the emperor Vespasian, whose son destroyed the Temple: *"Ut puto deus fio"*—"I think I am becoming a god."

What Maimonides wants to do, I truly believe, is the impossible. He wishes to unite all Jews—us, the people of all peoples, who have always enjoyed snarling at each other. Even while Jerusalem was falling, remember, the Jews within the walls killed and calumniated each other. Some of our people work for their own vainglory and split off their followers from the main branches of the tribes like so much kindling; Maimonides will neither say nor do anything (except in defense of sacred precepts) which will alienate a single Jew from God's fold.

I sit here at the precious desk inlaid with ebony and gold which my father sent me as a reward for my studies—sixteen years after my first meeting with my teacher. By the flaring light of burning palm oil in the seven cotton wicks of my lamp, fashioned in brass, I have made a decision. Though Maimonides does not desire it—though he wishes to be remembered only through the writings of his own mind—I shall undertake his cause. Not because it is my desire either to glorify or to disobey him. But since Moses ben Amram, standing alone on the top of Sinai with God, there has been none like Moses ben Maimon. To one it was given to hear the divine Voice and record the laws. To the other came a humbler but no less essential task: to understand the laws and interpret them rightly for the Jews. The story of such a man will not be lost, though it cost me many nights of toil. God give His blessing to such an enterprise!

It is necessary first to remedy some of the omissions in the story of Maimon ben Joseph concerning his son.

Let us return to the dawning of that summer day, in the Christian chronology, the year 1166, when Maimonides, with

David and Yaltah and their father, came into the harbor of Alexandria.

The ship that bore Maimonides and his family passed out of the clashing north waves into the miraculous quiet of the harbor with waters so still that one might see seaweed and anemones of glorious color, flowers of the sea beneath. Accompanied by the so-called sacred dolphins, it anchored at the foot of the quays in the Great Harbor. As they disembarked, Maimonides saw the magnificent ancient buildings, even the sad remains of the great library with its half-million vanished scrolls, burned centuries before by the ignorant fanaticism of the conquering Moslems; and highest of all, the neglected temple of Pan on a pile of rock like a pine cone, from which can be seen the whole of the city.

Proceeding through the immense market place, Maimonides emerged upon the hundred-foot-wide street of Canopus, so straight that for three miles a man can look from the gate by the sea to the gate of Reshid on the other side of the city. He turned eastward to the Jewish quarter (which holds possibly three thousand of our faith) and made his home near the sun-baked lands of the Hippodrome.

What delighted Maimonides in Alexandria was the opportunity for browsing in every pasture of knowledge. What distressed him was the ignorance and the indifference of the Jews to their own faith. What he found intolerable was the mass of the people, who had no regard for anyone in the world. Alexandria was, as it still is today, a town that went mad at festivals, thinking of nothing but feasting, gaming, racing, and musical entertainments with lascivious dancers. None cared, nor indeed knew, what they did on such occasions. Even after such affairs were over, the streets and alleys seethed with excitement for days, like the swells of the sea after a storm.

Nor was there any respect for persons or achievements. The very rulers were given ridiculous nicknames, their faults rhymed and sung in verse; obscene (yet witty) epigrams on various well-known persons were posted everywhere. "They are spiteful, worthless people," Maimonides said to me, "who think of nothing but dress, amusement, eating, and drinking. And when they cannot have these, they while away the time with bloody riots against whoever happens to be in power."

In such a city it behooved the Jews to be careful. They were common butts for the wit and scurrility of the inhabitants. It was not at all what Maimonides had expected to find. He told me on one occasion he had decided to settle in

Egypt, despite the slavery of our race under the Pharaohs, because the Fatimid dynasty—supposedly descended from Fatima, the daughter of Mohammed—was alleged to have Jewish blood in ancient days.

Yet Maimonides found himself, as he told me, more fascinated by the people than despising them; and the surging life of Alexandria and its opportunities for study delighted him. Here, he felt, he could complete the Mishnah commentary and end his days in scholarly seclusion. What complicated his feelings was the state of politics in Egypt. The effeminate Fatimids, despite their tolerance—chiefly made up of lack of interest—could not survive in a world increasingly savage. They were under pressure from the other Moslem leaders. They were suspected (since they had sometimes been allies of the Franks) of treason against religion and state.

None of these considerations weighed as much with Maimonides as his own filial obedience. It was the will of his father, rising in one last effort to dominate his son, which sent him to Fostat. Who can say it was not the will of God? For Maimonides at last had acquired a passion for a woman.

It is understandable why Maimonides wanted to marry. In that year of 1167 he was thirty-two years old. Has it not been said by Judah ben Tema that at five years one is ready for Scripture, at ten for the Mishnah, at thirteen for the Torah, at fifteen for the Talmud, at eighteen for marriage? Is it not the duty of a Jew to be fruitful if he wishes to obey the law and himself be happy?

Maimonides believed—as he later wrote—that the suitable age was the seventeenth year. But his studies and wanderings had given him no time to create his own family. Later, I believe, his secret expectation of the coming of the Messiah influenced him to want to marry. It was important to beget children: The herald of the new world was forbidden to arrive until God had fitted all created souls into their destined earthly bodies.

Finally, perhaps the most important fact of all: Maimonides, man of the mind and philosopher of the soul, fell in love with the things of the body. Rather, he renewed a love that seems to have been in his heart for nearly twenty years.

The way I stumbled upon the story is curious in itself. You must know that Naomi, during the years that David spent abroad selling gems, betrayed an increasingly jealous solicitude for Maimonides. She watched over him as mother and sister—possibly with an affection close to the love of a wife. It was she who came to me one dim evening and opened her heart, telling me what had happened during the early months in Alexandria. It was a tale of romance which Maimonides never mentioned but which I, as a poet, find impossible not to set down.

One afternoon in the great *sooq* (Naomi told me, tears glistening in her eyes at the recollection), she and Maimonides were together, choosing from the first catch of fish for the Sabbath meal. It was necessary to do this at least a day before, for the fishmongers, knowing it was a delicacy for the Jews, would invariably raise the price as the Sabbath approached. As they examined the color of a three-foot *bayad*, prodding it for firmness, an apple dropped at the feet of Maimonides. He picked it up and spied about for its owner but could discover no one.

As they completed their purchase, a page boy in sumptuous clothes came up to Maimonides and presented him with a note wrapped in gold-embroidered silk. He dismissed the child and read the communication with a puzzled frown; Naomi dared not ask him the contents.

That evening before sundown, Maimonides left their house in the Jewish quarter. Without permission—taking much responsibility on herself and driven, I suspect, by a secret jealousy—Naomi veiled herself and followed at a distance. Maimonides stopped at the gate of a spacious house ornamented with marble, well-swept and watered outside, with broad benches before it, the fragrance of attar coming from within. Showing the note to the Abyssinian porter, he was admitted, and Naomi, hurrying after, slipped in without question, the slave thinking, perhaps, she was in attendance.

She passed through a great flower garden lit by the flames of sunset and into the house. Once there, she lost her way. So large it was, the rooms so numerous, she became bewildered, as one in a vast forest. But she heard the sound of a lute, then of voices, and made her way to a great hall, washed with gold and silver, painted with inscriptions from the Koran, with a fountain of alabaster in a marble basin in the center and a canopy of brocade over it. Water flowed gurgling in tiny channels across a mosaic floor of many colors. Nearby was a table set with fruits—preserved and fresh—and candies, sherbets and wines, flowers and sweet herbs.

Beside it, on a cushioned couch, sat a woman of remarkable beauty, of fair skin and blue eyes, with long golden hair;

her figure, like that of the houris of the Moslems, dressed in a tight-fitting bodice of green stones (the Fatimid color) and petticoat-trousers of green gold-starred gauze; gems and gold on her head, a wide collar of gems hollowed and filled with perfumes about her neck. If Maimonides and the woman had not had eyes for none but each other, Naomi would assuredly have been seen; as it was, she slipped behind a pillar.

"You!" Maimonides said in a tone of astonishment.

"Yes," said the fair apparition in ravishing tones. She turned her cheek to him and beckoned him to inspect it. "You may still see the mark, Muni."

"The scar is like a rosebud," he said. "It is charming. So it is really you, Zamira."

"Yes," she said. "This is myself, this is my house—and you are still Muni, handsomer than ever. I dropped the apple from the lattice, where I amuse myself by watching the passers-by, and you read the note."

"It said merely that the sender was ill."

Her eyes sparkled with amusement. "But you are a healer," she protested, "and it is well known that love is a tyrant, melting the body to ruin, causing disease and sighs."

"Then you are in love?"

"I felt the first symptoms of that divine disease when you lifted your head in the market place."

It was a bold declaration and Naomi told me how it distressed her. She said Maimonides started back, but Zamira raised her hand.

"I have hired astrologers to calculate our ascendants and to draw the horoscopes," she told him. "The stars move in our favor."

"Astrology is nonsense."

"I have made a two-bow prayer to seek right guidance."

"God does not heed such prayers."

Zamira sighed and gazed up at the arabesque windows set with colored glass. "Then let us talk of old times," she said. "Since I left Cordova—as you know—I was spared by the Almohades and sold as a slave. I learned how to dance, how to amuse men by music and the feminine arts. I became much in demand. I bought my freedom. Now I am my own mistress and much desired."

"You are much desired indeed," Maimonides echoed in a hollow voice. Zamira laughed.

"You look at me as Solomon looked at Bilkis, the queen of Sheba," she said. "He was wise, setting a pavement of glass

251

over running water with fish. She raised her skirts to wade in it and he saw her legs were hairy as those of an ass. But, see, Muni! Mine are white and naked and hairless!"

She drew up one of the legs of her trousers and, Naomi related sadly, Maimonides did not turn away his head. "Are you wedded?" he asked after a long pause.

"Why do you ask that?"

"I do not mean to be inquisitive."

"No. I have been offered the ceremony many times but it does not appeal to me."

Maimonides, who had been sitting on an ivory stool opposite her, rose and paced the chamber back and forth. Naomi watched him with terror, knowing this was his custom when coming to a decision. At last he stood before Zamira and demanded abruptly: "Once, long ago, we were children and sweethearts, Zamira. Do you remember that?"

"Yes," she said softly.

"Now we have grown up. I, into an ancient man of books; you, into an entrancing vision."

She shook her head but said nothing, watching him intently. Maimonides went on: "I am lonely and it is possible that you are lonely, too."

"Well?" she challenged him.

With an effort, as though the words were difficult to say, Maimonides murmured: "Each of us would be less lonely if we were together."

Zamira smiled. "I like what you say better because it is not, like the Moslem speech, flowery and complicated," she declared. "Are these the words of your heart?"

Maimonides nodded, his glowing eyes fixed upon her face.

"Why do you wish to make me your wife?" asked Zamira lightly.

"Because it is my wish," Maimonides responded. His voice shook.

"You know your belief and mine are different."

"Your belief means nothing to you."

"But it is everything to you."

"You are near the true faith," said Maimonides. "I do not ask more."

"You would not convert me?" Zamira asked mischievously.

Maimonides made no answer but his eyes watched her amazingly expressive face. Zamira said: "You know of everything in the universe—except of women. And of all women, you do not know me."

"I have known you these many years."

"You have not seen me since we were children!"

"In my dreams," Maimonides said gently.

"Do you believe in them?"

"Only when you appear."

"That is very pretty," Zamira said judiciously. "Perhaps you know more of women than I thought."

"I will endeavor to understand you," Maimonides replied earnestly.

Zamira frowned and shook her head. "That shows your ignorance," she said almost angrily. "Would you understand me the way you know religion, astronomy, logic, philosophy, medicine—whatever else it is you know?"

Maimonides reddened and bowed his head. "You make me a proposal," Zamira said. "Even if I were to consent—out of our love as children, only—who should marry us?"

"Moslem or Jew," Maimonides said in a low voice. "It would make no difference."

Zamira arose from the couch and pirouetted with pleasure. "That is better," she said gaily. "So you want me for myself alone!"

"I think that we both struggle in this life for something of happiness," Maimonides returned seriously. "Beneath this there is the truth of God, the same for every belief."

"Now you talk foolishness." Zamira pouted. "This is nothing by which to charm a woman."

"What shall I say?"

"Do you demand a dowry?"

"No."

Zamira cocked her head to one side like a partridge. "But you insult me!" she protested. "I bring my own. I am a rich woman many times over. Would you care to see my jewels?"

"No."

"Would your father allow us to wed?"

"I am the head of the Maimon family."

"But his blessing?" asked Zamira with more than a hint of gravity. "He would refuse it."

"Then we must be married like Jacob, without it."

"Before you choose me," Zamira said softly, "you must see me as I truly am." With this, before Maimonides could answer, she whirled lightly away from him, vanishing into another room. He sat unmoving, his hands folded and his head bent, as Naomi watched breathlessly.

Zamira returned in no more than moments. She had doffed

her tunic and trousers. She wore a veil of cloth-of-gold gauze from head to foot. Through it her body could be seen, white-flushed like a pearl; her hair flowed about her shoulders, a cloud of gold. A thin girdle of precious stones, red and green, held a red silk scarf between her naked breasts; her loins had only a wisp of the same material pinned by a brooch of carved ivory. She walked in sandals made of heron's feathers that caressed her ankles at each step.

Behind her, from the other room, music sounded, the wailing cry of a reed, the rhythm of a tapped gourd. With slow deliberation, Zamira began to dance.

Her slender arms appeared from the veil, beckoning and repelling, thrusting back and forth like twin white serpents, escaping from an invisible lover, first shy, then voluptuous. She seemed to float across the floor in a rhythm of sinuous invitation. The notes of a flute and of tiny bells came to the ears of Naomi; the beat of the dance subtly lifted.

Zamira turned and bent and rose again languorously, her breasts rising and falling, weary and expiring with unreturned love; with half-closed eyes, lost in romantic reverie, she moved toward Maimonides, then away from him. She shivered and her shining body seemed to ripple like the sea with sunlight upon it; her feet traced their tiny steps, obeying mysterious influences outside her body. Her arms and head had one motion, her body another, her feet a third, magically blended into an overpowering emotion of dance.

The music changed once more, now that of a lyre and the light thumping of a drum, faster and faster. Zamira appeared to waken. Her eyes opened wide. She whirled about the room on tiptoe, spinning off the veil, her scarf floating in the air behind her like a red shadow. Jewels Naomi had not seen before, buried in her ghostly, golden hair, sparkled in the light; the colors of her girdle and her flesh seemed to blend into a deep-rosy figure of delight.

Suddenly there was no music. Only the louder, faster, thumping double-beat of the drum echoing in the room. Zamira cast off her white-feathered slippers and twisted frantically about, as if to seek that which was slipping out of her bosom. She hugged her breasts in fright, looking upward, and gradually came to a turning halt before Maimonides on her toes, legs wide apart. Slowly, very slowly, she bent backward; her head touched the floor.

Maimonides sprang to his feet. As if it were a signal, she straightened with a lithe movement, and without looking at him, commenced to circle about him in a frenzied tangle of loveliness, her face alone visible from time to time in the confusing circle of color. The musk of her body was stronger than her perfume; each time her eyes met those of Maimonides, he shuddered as if they burned his flesh. Naomi could see tiny beads of perspiration upon Zamira's body, like tiny pearls.

With a loud thump, the drum beat ceased. At the same moment, Zamira stood before him, arms outspread in invitation, face beaming; her bosom heaving, half-naked and wholly willing. Maimonides hesitated: As he did, there came the sound of a stroked dulcimer and a light clear voice singing (so Naomi thought) as Zamira used to sing, the song of their pleasure long ago in the gardens of Cordova.

Maimonides hesitated no longer. He sprang forward and folded her in his arms. She embraced him with a gasping sigh, her hot moist body melting against him. He bent his head to her mouth but she avoided him, thrusting against his cheek with her fingers.

"I deserve to be punished," she panted. He shook his head. "Yes," Zamira insisted, "I have tempted him who cannot be tempted."

"No," he said. "You have only fulfilled my dream."

She lifted a glance to him full of wickedness. "Once, very long ago," she said softly, "you rescued me from the Almohades who were about to kill me."

"I remember."

"They were about to impale me on a spear."

Maimonides stood speechless.

"Since that time you have changed," Zamira said breathlessly, in a rush, "you have changed."

"No, no!" Maimonides said feverishly.

She put a finger on his lips. "Now," she said impishly, "you wish to impale me on another spear."

"Wretched woman, wretched woman!" cried Maimonides in transports of delight. He bent her body, and his lips touched hers. As they kissed, they brushed the table and the fruit fell rattling to the floor. They parted and, breathlessly, commenced to laugh.

"Muni!" cried Zamira in delight. "Muni, you are laughing!"

"And why should I not laugh?" demanded Maimonides, wiping the tears from his eyes.

"But you were always so solemn!"

He found her lips again and they sank to the divan in a swoon of pleasure.

At this point in her story, Naomi shook her head dolefully. When I urged her to continue, she told me she had stolen away from the place and come home, abashed and confused. "What I have told you, I have told no one else," she said. "What more happened that night, I cannot say."

"Why does this concern you so closely?" I said, fixing her with my gaze.

"I am the sister-in-law of Maimonides," she answered boldly.

"Were you not, first, the wife of David? Are you not his widow?"

Naomi's eyelids fluttered as if she were about to faint; she swayed. "I loved my husband in the flesh," she whispered, "but I worshiped Maimonides. His soul still ravishes me. I cannot sleep when he meditates at midnight, I thrill to his voice when he teaches. He must not yield to worldly things."

"Did David know your feelings?" I asked curiously.

She did not answer directly. "David wanted a child," she responded, in a tone so low I could barely hear it, "but how could I yield to him when my thoughts—my thoughts—"

Her voice broke; she turned, reaching out her hands in a plea for understanding. I sat as hard and still as stone.

"It is fair to assume Maimonides is only a man and a passionate man," I said dryly. To my surprise, she leaped up, eyes blazing; I believe, if I had not been wary, she would have struck me. As it was, she burst into tears and ran out, overwhelmed with sobs.

Not long afterward, in those days long ago, Zamira came, at her own request, to see Maimon ben Joseph. The source of the story of their interview—between them alone—must remain a secret, but it may be imagined. For the first moments it was a joyful reunion with one whom Maimon had never expected to see again after that dreadful night in his garden in Spain, and it was also a welcome reminder of his glorious Cordova.

Soon, however, a sterner note entered their talk. Maimon, already afflicted with the palsy that finally weakened him unto death, addressed her not as a grown woman but almost in the tones he would have used to address the child of so long ago.

"Why do you wish to wed Maimonides?"

"Because he wishes it. Because I wish it. It is none of your affair!" Zamira's eyes snapped in anger.

"You know that he and you are of different beliefs," Maimon said, struggling to retain his composure.

"That is not what he says."

"What does my son say?" Maimon demanded.

She leaned toward him and he could smell the perfume of her body. He swayed back, away from her.

"He says," Zamira said, "that all of us do not see clearly. That beneath all the struggle and confusion, there is always the truth of God that is the same for every belief. That of all beliefs on earth, the Moslem is closest to that of the Jews."

"Are you willing to become a Jewess?"

"No. It is not necessary."

"Does Maimonides say that?"

"He does not deny it."

"You appear to have bewitched him," Maimon said darkly. "As the Fathers said, 'More women, more witchcraft.' "

"More men, more nonsense," Zamira said promptly. "This is a matter in which you have no business. It concerns myself and Maimonides alone."

"It concerns every Jew, everywhere in the world," Maimon told her warmly. "You do not know his fame, how he is looked up to. If he were a Christian, he would be a saint of saints!"

"I can believe that."

"Then you must not consent to his desires."

"Can a saint be denied falling in love?" asked Zamira vehemently. "Is he not a man, after all?"

"But a marriage with a Moslem woman, with one whose name is so—so well known as yours—" Maimon stammered.

Her eyes glinted danger and again Maimon became aware of the magnet of her presence, of the influence which both delighted and frightened him. He could understand at this moment the peculiar, irresistible attraction she exerted over Maimonides. "You object?"

"In the name of our people, I do."

"Does not your law command you to marry?"

"It does—and to be fruitful. But what of such children as you might have? Would they be truly worthy of their father?"

A shadow of sadness came over the face of Zamira. She shook her golden head, the long tresses swaying about it, golden weeds at the bottom of a clear stream. "Children," she said faintly. "Children." But she did not answer his question.

Maimon watched her closely and shook his head. "Listen," he said. "Once, when the great Greek, Socrates, walked with

257

his disciples, he saw a woman of handsome figure and lovely face, and one of his disciples gazed at her. 'Woe is to thee,' said his master, and the disciple replied: 'Not for love nor for desire do I gaze but to see in her the work of the gods.' To him replied Socrates: 'Turn her inside out; then you will understand how ugly she is.' "

Saying this, Maimon rose and feebly left the chamber. Zamira, after a moment's meditation, veiled her face once again and left by another way. Nor was this the end of the connection between her and Maimonides, but that tale must be told in a different place.

CHAPTER 15

Abul Maali, the handsome middle-aged Moslem in rich robes of white inscribed with the Koran in gold, who had entered unexpectedly to witness Maimonides' drastic cure of Yaltah was a constant visitor to the house, I discovered. Compassionately he comforted Maimonides in his fit of grief over the death of Maimon ben Joseph. It surprised me to hear him soothing my master by the name of "Imram Musa ibn Abdallah"; I soon discovered it was the Arabic cognomen of Maimonides.

Afterward, I came to know Maali was a man of learning and political power. Ten years later, he was to be closely bound up with the fortunes of Maimonides; but for the moment, it is enough to know he was the court secretary of the greatest man of our times, Salah al-Din al-Ayyubi, known to the vulgar as the famous Saladin, bearer of the faith.

At this point it should be said that the conditions in our times have been like those in a story by Plato, pupil of the divine Socrates. He wrote a legend of how God created a being called "manwoman," so happy on earth that the Exalted in the skies became jealous. With a lightning bolt the twain were split, one part to be called "man," the other, "woman." Seeking each other ever since, they have been unhappy and, I may add, often unhappy even when successful.

In this half-man, half-woman world of ours, we find no peace. Our rulers uplift rods of impotent flesh in their harems; their commanders raise useless swords of steel on the battle-fields. Usurpers and uproar are everywhere. It is dangerous to swear allegiance to any cause except to that of God in the soul. Do not the Perachot say that, even with the sword on the neck, one does not lose hope of Heaven? In such a miser-able state, the Jew is caught between the hammer of the Christians and the anvil of the Moslems. Our only hope in the midst of our sorrows is Saladin.

The Eruvin says a man's character is recognized by his cup, his anger, and his pocket. By all of these, Saladin must be acknowledged superior. Born on a battleground, raised in the dust and blood of conflict, he was from youth a handsome boy, filled with passion for women and wine. God alone knows where he acquired his many virtues of manhood—from the hands of angels! When he assumed power, Saladin renounced all pleasures but ambition in the name of Allah. He eschewed cloth-of-gold robes and gem-laden turbans, putting on shifts of coarse linen. He drank water instead of rare vintages; he avoided women, remaining chaste as a hermit. It is said of him that he has never missed a time of prayer, that he is scornful of the mighty and pitying toward the poor. On one occasion he was observed reading the Koran between his army and the ranks of the advancing Christians. He is available to all suppliants, gentle with servants, and boundless in liberality.

He gained his first fame in battle at Babain, where the Mos-lem renegade Shawar and his allies were defeated by the genius of Saladin, second-in-command to his uncle Shirkuh. Saladin became governor of Alexandria. Forthwith, the city came under a seventy-five-day siege from the reinforced enemy. Despite the odds, Saladin won fame for his energy and consummate defense. A flank movement toward Cairo by Shirkuh relieved the siege. Peace was restored by both armies' leaving the land, but a Frankish garrison in Cairo remained a thorn in the side of Saladin.

It is supposed by many that the alarms and distractions of the Egyptian wars forced Maimonides to leave Alexandria and turn south one hundred thirty miles up the Nile to Cairo. This is partly true. The clamor of strife was not an existence to be long endured by a scholar; still, it was not the sole cause of his departure.

As a Jew, liable to persecution from both sides, Maimonides

had little interest in the fortunes of war. Nevertheless, he was full of admiration for the immense labors of the soldiers, for the ingenuity of the machines he had seen during the sieges. Arriving at Alexandria in the interval of peace just before the Christian invasion, he often wandered behind the ramparts to see operations that went on by day and night. He told me of immense mines beneath the ground, built with pillars and struts of pine, fired so that the timbers collapsed and brought down the fort; of countermining beneath this, which filled the enemy sappers' galleries with smoke and sulfur fumes. He described steel-pointed rams that gouged out masonry, huge bronze rams' heads swinging on ropes from beneath a tortoise shelter of wooden planks covered with green hides to prevent being set afire. He related that he saw ladders on wheeled platforms and towers of logs, some nearly one hundred feet high, with as many as seven floors; these were loaded with catapults and archers, to sweep the walls until soldiers could crowd over the drawbridges. He talked of tanks of water with hogs' intestines for hoses, used to douse flames; of stones of more than five hundred pounds' weight flung as many yards; of scorpions that were six-foot darts capable of spitting four men at once; of cages of men lifted to attack; of blazing tow and pitch. Once he saw a huge rock crush a dozen men and ministered to them; again he viewed the rotting carcasses of horses and barrels of ordure flung into the city to breed plague and issued medicines against it.

He had marveled at man's inhuman genius to destroy man. He was no less astonished at the triumphant parades, timbrels, fifes, and flutes, huge copper drums, flags of crescented black and green, prancing horsemen with brandished scimitars, lances and feathered trophies, litters of the great, nobles in chains like slaves, heaps of captured goods to be sold in the *sooq*. I asked him his opinion of this worldly folly. He told me: "Like oil and water, swords and books do not mix; one must rise to the top." He shook his head over the glory of conquest: "It is written that man was created last by God so that if he became proud he might remember that a worm came before him."

But the vicissitudes of the siege were as nothing compared to the storm in his own house. Spurred on by Naomi's hatred of Zamira, his father rose for the last time to command his family. Even as the Christian and Moslem war cries resounded outside, Maimon took his son to task.

"You came here," he said sternly, "because it would give you peace to complete your studies."

"I could not foresee the future of wars upon wars."

"I do not speak of the struggles of the body; rather of those of the mind. The Mishnah commentary is unfinished."

"It is a difficult work," Maimonides muttered.

"Are the nights you spend with the fair Zamira equally difficult?"

The eyes of Maimonides flashed. "She is unjustly maligned," he said. "She is a friend from the old times, both yours and mine."

"She was a child in those days in Cordova. Now she is a woman, and a woman is only the fairest among the beasts. Do you make her your wife?"

"She has refused me," Maimonides said slowly.

"For her own reasons," Maimon replied. "For the same reasons that have built her a house of a harlot, filled with gold and gems."

"You shall not say that!"

"Shall I not?" asked Maimon quietly. "Saladin has truly said this is a land without men. She exists to devour men. At this moment she holds communication with Samuel ben Ali of Bagdad, who sent us the wine of death."

"I do not believe it," Maimonides said.

"Yet it is so," the old man said, quivering with sickness and anger. "Do you eat the vomit of a dog?"

Maimonides sprang upright, his hands raised above his head. "And will you strike your father?" asked Maimon quietly. Maimonides abruptly sat down once more on his stool in the small moonlit courtyard of their home where this interview took place. "Everything," Maimon said, "speaks against your association with this woman. There is nothing for it."

"But one reason: We love each other."

"Shall I tell you what is love and what is not? In all your wisdom, has this eluded you?"

"Shall you tell me the difference between your love for Naomi and Rachel bat Abor?" cried Maimonides.

His father flinched. His son had indeed struck him. But his face did not change in its strange white immobility. "The Torah," he said in a strangled tone, "tells you to honor your father to the length of your days."

"I have done so."

"Until this moment. I demand once more implicit obedi-

261

ence. Your duty is to God, not to this woman. I demand you depart from this place of sin. We shall leave for Fostat, the very spot where Moses, blessed be he, prayed to God. There I shall pray for the finishing of your task."

Maimonides rose and bowed. He started to leave the courtyard. A bitter sentence from his father halted him. "I forbid you," said Maimon, "to see Zamira again." Maimonides hesitated, his face hollow in the pale light; then he bowed in acquiescence and disappeared.

A month later, when the Franks withdrew, the Maimon family took ship. They sailed to Fostat with its three thousand families of Jews. Here again they found no peace; the *Siraj*, the *Book of Light*, was finished, ironically, in the midst of the mightiest conflagration of the age.

Amalric and his chivalrous Christian knights attacked and massacred most of the inhabitants, many of them Jews. The people of Fostat, for three hundred years the great city of the land and still the most thickly populated district of Cairo, determined to sacrifice their homes to check the advance of the bloodthirsty infidels. Twenty thousand barrels of naphtha were ignited by ten thousand torches. The city went up in a single huge blaze. It lit up the night skies for weeks on end. Even today, the remains of the homes, the heaps of rubbish stretch for miles.

The Maimon family shared in this common destruction of dwellings. Saving nothing except their beasts and a few coverings, some food and the precious manuscript of the Mishnah commentary, they watched, awed and despairing, the gigantic bonfire of their hopes. Yet, once its fury had subsided, they trod its hot ashes, like the others, to plan another home. Maimonides specified that their house in Fostat should be as the sages had ruled, in memory of the destruction of the Temple: nothing painted nor beamed; surfaces daubed with clay and washed with lime; a space of a square cubit left bare at the entrance. When a meal was ready, one place at table, he decreed, was to be left vacant in readiness for the Messiah. His prayer was always the same: "If I forget thee, O Jerusalem, let my right hand forget her cunning . . . let my tongue cleave to the roof of my mouth, if I remember thee not; if I set not Jerusalem above my chiefest joy."

In truth, during this time, the frustrated love of Maimonides for Zamira appeared to have been replaced with a passion for Palestine. Maimonides was accustomed to say that "Now I have walked in Jerusalem, my sins will be forgiven. I shall be buried in that sacred earth, not in this unclean country." He often asserted he would never have left Palestine except that the famine there was so extreme that "one dinar's worth of wheat was selling for double and there was no way to sustain life." In his later writings, he expressly said it was forbidden to emigrate from Palestine except to study the Law, take a wife, or rescue property. "The greatest of our wise men," he said somberly, "have kissed the stones of the land and rolled themselves in its dust. Are we, then, so much holier than they?" He kept up a continuous correspondence with Japhet, the rabbi of Acre.

His brother, David, accustomed by then to the ways of business, did not share his sentiments. He much preferred living in Egypt, eagerly espousing the cause of the Moslems against the Christians. But he took no part in warlike affairs, kept his counsel, provided his wife Naomi with the necessaries of life, and—when intervals of peace permitted—went on long journeys to buy and sell, to trade the precious stones which formed the family fortune. The Maimons enlarged their home two years later, trusting in the continued successes of Saladin. Maimonides' enthusiasm for that ruler rose to unexampled heights, spurred by the rumored saying of the distinguished potentate: "If Allah gives me Egypt, how much more will He give me Palestine?"

Despite his reputation, gained in Alexandria by treating injured during the siege, Maimonides himself confessed that the first years of his practice as an occasional healer were unrecognized. This cannot be laid to his lack of skill; rather, chiefly, to his infatuation with Zamira; in Fostat, to his dedication to the finishing of the great Mishnah commentary. Occasionally he offered lectures on philosophical subjects to eke out the family income but his purse profited little.

Finished in 1168, his *Book of Light*, the *Siraj*, shows an increased interest in the medical profession, which he had rejected as a youth. In it, he remarks that "A healer should begin with simple treatments, trying to cure by diet before he administers drugs." This same prescription he adheres to in his spiritual writings. In character and habit alien to the disorderly inspiration of the Talmud, Maimonides in the *Mishneh Torah* writes with his usual clarity, terseness, and method. He believes nothing should be added to nor taken away from the Talmud, but he often supplies his own explanations rather than those of tradition. He admits there is profound truth in the rabbinical writings, but argues that it is often hidden behind symbolic allegory to sharpen the understanding. He subtly mixes the Greek way of logic with the ancient thinking of the Jews; he formulates the true creed of the Jews in his "Thirteen Principles," now respected second only to the Torah. And in all of his work, he endeavors to bring all Jews everywhere to a fresh understanding of their heritage of the past and spiritual unity in the present. As for the future, he stoutly proclaims his belief in the resurrection of the soul—an unusual conception which may bring him into much trouble.

Written in Arabic, the *Siraj* has become more popular than the *Mishneh Torah*, written in Hebrew, a language which many Jews do not know. But the *Siraj*, great as it is, does not form the cornerstone of his fame with the masses of Egypt. This was brought into being the following year by an unexpected summons from the caliph himself.

The blubbery black eunuch, nearly seven feet tall, sweated profusely, emitting a peculiar spicy odor. Stalking into the inner court of the Maimon house without warning, he looked down at the startled Maimonides. "Rise, Jew!" he said in a high voice. "I come from the glorious caliph himself!"

Maimonides stood. He salaamed until his forehead touched the table. "To hear is to obey," he murmured. "How can I serve my lord?"

"Not altogether do I speak for the exalted one," grumbled the eunuch in a lower tone. "I have taken much upon myself." He grimaced, showing enormous white teeth; he frowned heavily, looking anxiously about. "I have heard of Moses ben Maimon. It is said you work miracles."

"I do only what nature allows."

"Abul Maali says otherwise. Be that as it may, I have tried all other healers in Cairo," responded the eunuch. "I have received permission to bring you from Fostat to the Palace of the Twin Towers. Woe to me if you fail! Much more woe to you: I shall see you tortured and thrown to the dogs before I am. Come!"

"Allow me time to gather medicines."

"Come! They will not be needed." The command of the *kapu aghasi* was not to be disobeyed. Maimonides touched his forehead in acquiescence and followed the swaying mass of dark flesh into a litter outside his gate. It would take time to reach Cairo from Fostat. As the sunburned white slaves heaved up the poles supporting their burden, the eunuch commenced to explain his predicament.

264

"I have recited this tale many times in the past few days," he began in the rhythmically swaying litter. "I obey the mother of the caliph Al-Adid and the ruler of the harem. She has ordered the *kyahyakadini* that I, the master of the gates, see to preparing the caliph for the royal couch tonight."

"I am a healer, not a lute-player," Maimonides remonstrated.

The eunuch surveyed him balefully. "Do I not know that?" he rasped. "Listen and be wise. Arrangements have been made that the daughter of the ruler of Yemen, far to the south, shall be the bride of the caliph. But it is in the marriage contract that the caliph's mother must be present; she must approve all at the couch-side. She must be sure the marriage is consummated; the representatives of the line of Fatima must be sure that the princess is a virgin. You follow?"

"Yes."

"He must ride an untried filly, eh?"

"Yes."

"He must thread a new needle, put the stick in a fresh kohl pot, eh?"

"I understand."

The massive eunuch chuckled lewdly and nudged Maimonides. "It is your task to stiffen the stick," he said.

"What?" demanded Maimonides, not quite believing what he had heard.

The eunuch chuckled again but did not answer. He lay back against the cushions and went to sleep, snoring with a bubbling sound that sounded as if he were strangling. Maimonides felt himself sweating through his light garments as he rocked back and forth beside him, swamped in the pervasive odor of his companion.

The caliph's bedchamber was immense: slender gilt pillars springing upward, a great arch of blue-tiled bricks, windows opening on rich gardens on every side. Intricate designs in scarlet and gilt scrolled the walls, all descending to a couch at the far end, drowned in pillows. Within the chamber moved restlessly a small anxious crowd of palace attendants in the light gauze costumes of summer. They dispersed at a light clap of the hands of the *kapu aghasi*, leaving him and Maimonides alone.

"The Most High Ruler sleeps after his midday meal," whispered the companion of Maimonides.

"Does he rest in this chamber?" asked Maimonides.

"Stupid, stupid!" hissed the eunuch, his arm a black snake in a gesture of frustration. "He rests among the cushions there!"

Maimonides could see only a colored heap of silk but he imagined he could detect the rise and fall of breathing under the down-stuffing. The eunuch continued in a penetrating whisper: "The All-Powerful One is sunk in despair. He has no will to live. He speaks only of death, of his shame in not being able to perform the ineffable act. He has drunk innumerable potions, he has been subjected to the most powerful charms—but demons work against him, against the consummation of the royal wish. We have brought him musicians and naked houris in play and dance; he has caressed the most lovely maidens in their most vital parts—but he groans with impotence. He is, even as I, no more than a eunuch at this moment."

The *kapu aghasi* sniggered; Maimonides concealed his revulsion and nodded. The eunuch went on: "We know it is important that nothing of his strength be spent before the moment. To this end, we have six maidens of beauty trained to lower the caliph from above, to direct his every movement during the act tonight. But all this will be useless: If there is no arrow to shoot, it is useless to bend the bow, eh?"

A stirring from the midst of the cushions alarmed the eunuch. He put his fat finger to his lips. Maimonides saw a weak eruption of the heap of silk and heard the drowsy voice of the young ruler. "Do you wake me with your whispering? What scheme do you hatch to humiliate me?"

"It is I," said the *kapu aghasi* with an obeisance like a fish flopping. "I come with cheerful news, O Master of the Universe!"

"I am no Master of the Universe," came the petulant reply. "I am not even master of myself. What is this remarkable news, you fool?"

The eunuch drew himself up. "I bring the renowned healer, the Jew Moses ben Maimon, to your aid, O Great One!"

"Who is he?" demanded the feeble voice. "I have never heard of such a fellow!" There was a sudden eruption of cushions. Al-Adid revealed himself—a naked youth of no more than sixteen, his brown body spread in the center of the enormous brightly canopied bed. His body lay unevenly propped up on a series of cushions: head high, stomach depressed, rear elevated, feet depressed. A series of small white cushions, evi-

266

dently filled with gossamer down, supported his long, limp phallus in the middle like a sacred exhibit.

The plump young face stared up at Maimonides as he advanced to stand beside him. The sharp nose of the caliph seemed out of place and awry between the big pupil-less eyes. The full lips trembled. A tear ran down each cheek. "If you have charms, Jew," Al-Adid murmured, "I command you to help me. I am in pain unspeakable. My body throbs with horror when I think of penetrating another woman tonight, no matter how lovely. And they tell me the Yemeni is hardly a delight from Paradise."

"I have no magic charms," Maimonides said with humility, "but I shall do what I can, O Great One!"

"If you succeed," said the young ruler, "your reward shall be great."

"And if you fail," the eunuch said softly in the ear of Maimonides, his foul breath potent, "your reward shall be no less sure."

Maimonides bowed. He bent over the royal instrument. He did not touch the caliph; it would have been a breach of medical etiquette. To his dismay, he saw that the young ruler had not exaggerated his predicament. The circumcised hope of the line of the Fatimids had a black, discolored tip; it appeared bruised and swollen to nearly half again its size. He stepped back in agitation and whispered to the eunuch: "What happened to his highness?"

"Three nights ago," the *kapu aghasi* muttered, "the *effendi huri*, the caliph's favorite, occupied his couch. You must know that if such a one conceives she will receive a magnificent tiara, money and jewels and slaves, a suite of her own, and the praises and blessings of all Egypt. Through excessive greed, this woman became carried away with the moment. The muscles of her cursed loins squeezed much too hard for him, already ailing, to endure."

The eunuch spoke with a mingled ferocity and satisfaction which Maimonides found hard to interpret. He hesitated: There came another petulant groan from the caliph. His black companion drew back as Maimonides again approached the bed. "Do something," said the youthful caliph, his face drawn with pain. "My groin throbs like a war drum, vibrating all my nerves, up to my head. I have no interest in women. Relieve the pain, let me sleep, I shall be satisfied!"

"Your Highness must have an interest in at least this one woman," interposed the *kapu aghasi* respectfully. "Great One, it is not a matter of your feelings. It is an affair of state—and the business of pleasing your mother, as well."

The caliph winced and writhed slightly. "Very well," he said faintly, "but it will be a miracle if I succeed."

Maimonides shook his head over the wounded royal organ; the situation seemed far from ridiculous, rather pathetic. "Can you guarantee that the rod of empire can be thrust into its scabbard?" whispered the eunuch in his ear. The odor of the spiced oil on his body became even more pronounced.

"What are you whispering about?" demanded the caliph. "I shall have you both flogged!"

"We are determining your cure," said the *kapu aghasi* smoothly. "Is it not so, Jew?"

"Is it so?" repeated the quavering voice of the caliph.

"I trust I shall not fail," Maimonides said, his tone exhibiting an optimism not reflected in his heart. "I shall, with your permission, order five different prescriptions for the health of your highness' organ. First, a special extract of the bark of balsam as a salve. This, lightly rubbed on, will draw off the blood. It will reduce the swelling by nightfall. Next, an ointment containing cantharides—made from a small but sexually vigorous fly that lives in fruit. This will communicate its own vigor to your royal member, restoring its ability to assume an erect posture when nature commands it to do so. Third, another unguent, made of the opium poppy, which will relieve your pain and maintain its erection; this will also render it free of discomfort during the performance of its royal duties."

"And the fourth, Jew?" demanded the alert eunuch as Maimonides paused.

Maimonides gave a slight shrug. "That is your concern, if you will," he said. "I suggest the royal encounter with the princess from Yemen be postponed for a single day. This will give time enough for his highness to recover and allow the medicines to provide healing."

"What is the fifth?"

"First let us use all haste to secure the prescriptions."

The eunuch nodded. He clapped his hands three times. Instantly the room was filled with people, issuing silently from every door. The *kapu aghasi* bowed to the young caliph. "Is it your will, O Mighty One," he intoned, "that the directions of this healer should be followed?"

A moan came from Al-Adid. "In the name of Allah, the compassionate and compassionating, let us begin! No matter if it kills me, I can endure my misery no longer!"

268

"Bring music and singers," said Maimonides in a low tone to the eunuch. Without waiting to see if his instructions were followed, he took a few steps to an ebony table on which he had observed a large Koran with golden clasps. He opened it and rapidly flipped the pages. His finger indicated a passage to the craning *kapu aghasi*.

"This verse," Maimonides said, "must be chanted to music, again and again, the caliph joining in, if it be his royal will. It will help soothe his spiritual agonies and lift the black cloud of despair from his mind."

"What must I say?" asked the caliph weakly. "Read the holy words to me."

"The foremost in the race, the foremost in the race,
They will be brought to Paradise, to gardens of delight,
On softest couches, reclining face to face,
There will wait on them immortal youths
Of supremest beauty and obedience;
With bowls and ewers and cups from a pure spring
Wherefrom will come no aching of the head or madness;
And luscious fruits that they prefer,
And flesh of fowls that they desire—
And fair ones with wide, lovely eyes
Like unto hidden pearls.

"Nor shall there be heard vain speaking nor argument,
Naught but peace and peace and, again, peace;
Lovers and friends among the thornless lotus,
With clustered fruit and spreading shade
And water gushing and all in plenty:
Lo, this is certain truth!
Therefore praise the name of Allah, Greatest Allah!"

Maimonides ended his reading, bowed, and replaced the jeweled copy of the Koran on the table. The caliph's eyes had brightened; he had kept time to the sonority of the verses with his fingertips. Maimonides felt a sense of relief.

"Tomorrow," said the *kapu aghasi* meaningfully.

"Tomorrow I shall return," Maimonides agreed. "I beg you to see to it that the ointments are well compounded and applied thoroughly but with gentleness."

Having said this, he did not wait for a reply but backed to the door, bowed again, and went swiftly down the broad marble stairs. At the foot, a soldier confronted him, drawn sword held across his thighs. Maimonides stopped. His face tightened in recognition.

"You know me," said the other. "Do you remember the night at the governor's palace in Almería? Our speech with each other?"

"Musef," said Maimonides. "Yes, I know you."

"I have sworn new allegiance to Saladin against the swine of Christians who befoul the holy places."

"But Spain," Maimonides said in bewilderment, "are you no longer in Spain?"

Musef shook his head. "The kingdom of the Moors is no more in that country," he returned roughly. "We have been driven into the sea. But we shall return. Come with me."

"Where?"

"My commander, the vizier, wishes to see you."

"Who is he?"

"Saladin."

It was a small room, without furniture except for a single chair and some leather stools. Shadows fell swaying across the tiled floor from the palm trees outside; a fountain poured forth a low background murmur. In the chair, in plain robes, sat a man. He seemed only a little older than the moaning caliph in the bedchamber in the other part of the palace. Slight, with a dark, short beard and a sunburned face, he also held a slender scimitar across his lap. He sat without movement, except to raise his head as the guard entered with Maimonides. As they crossed the threshold, the room filled with an extraordinary vitality.

"Here is the one who attended him," said Musef with a deferential salute. "I found him coming from the bedchamber itself. I have known him before in Spain: He is Maimonides, the famous Jew."

"Approach," said the man in the chair. Maimonides, guessing this to be Saladin, salaamed deeply three times. He did not speak, waiting for the other to finish his slow inspection, which seemed penetrating enough to strip flesh from bone.

"You have done a service, I hear, for my royal master," Saladin said at length. His extraordinarily searching eyes, dark in his dark face, were cold; his voice, low and expressionless.

Maimonides bowed again. "If I have been of service, it is sufficient reward," he said. "I ask no more."

"Have you made it possible for young Al-Adid to breed?"

"He is of the line of the Prophet's daughter," Maimonides returned noncommittally. He could not understand where the interview was leading.

"Allah rest her soul!" Saladin murmured, touching lips and forehead. "But her descendants are a kennel of degenerate dogs!"

Maimonides felt a surge of alarm. "If I have offended Your Excellency," he said rapidly, "I am wretched, indeed."

"You have done your duty. But that is not always pleasing to others."

Maimonides felt a light sweat break out on his forehead. He had visions of himself under the executioner's broad ax. "A healer is not always his own man, lord," he murmured. "He cannot mingle with the great."

"Suppose," Saladin said deliberately, "I were to command you to poison this young whelp?"

Maimonides endured a chill that shook him from head to foot. "O Saladin," he said, "you overwhelm the mighty and destroy heroes, you terrify those that stand against you, you inspire fear in the envious and the evil."

"But not in you?" Saladin's tone was sardonic.

"In me, as in all others."

"You have not answered my question, Jew."

Maimonides rose to his feet. He trembled still, but he found courage for the only reply he could make. "I could not mix the poison," he said. "My hands would palsy, my mind would be distracted with the sin."

"Even under torture and death?"

A weight seemed to bow the head of Maimonides. "Even then, Mighty One," he whispered.

Saladin seemed almost amused, though his face remained calm. "You have courage," he declared, "yet you are not a warrior. Whence does it come?"

"From my religion, from my profession. I have skill only in healing, not in slaying. I have studied nothing else. My arts are only for the welfare of my fellow men."

"Observe," Saladin said. He beckoned to Musef. The guard brought a bundle of javelins and placed them with prostrating obedience at the foot of the chair. Saladin suddenly whirled his sword about his head in an explosion of light. The blade clashed down on the javelins. He wrenched it free. "See," he said. Maimonides saw: Half the soft iron shafts of the javelins were severed.

"Even though a dozen necks be made of iron," Saladin said, the gentle tone of his voice contrasting with its intensity, "the steel of my sword will cut them. Not only traitors and infidels and enemies, but the necks of liars and prisoners.

271

What you have spoken, you have spoken. Verily, what you have spoken will be worth more than gold in the scales on the Day of Judgment. I trust in your religion, in your intelligence, in your integrity."

He rapped the hilt of his sword on the hardwood arm of his chair. A door behind opened. A fat, unprepossessing man waddled forward, bowed his head, and stood beside him.

"Al-Alfadhel, as my friend, you will note this Jew. If he says aught to you in reproach of me, do not keep it from me. Direct me on the right path, cure me a perfect cure, of soul, as well as body."

Without another word, Saladin rose. In his characteristic swift, graceful gait, he left the room, followed by Musef. Maimonides and Al-Alfadhel stared at each other. The latter was the first to speak, in a wheezing, wondering voice. "You have spoken boldly," he said. "It has made you a powerful friend."

"I spoke what I must," Maimonides said weakly.

"I shall be your friend also," Al-Alfadhel replied, nodding. He advanced a few steps. "Tell me," he said in a low voice, "will this young rascal of a caliph have children?"

Maimonides pondered. "Perhaps," he said. "But he suffers, in my opinion, from a disease which is incurable, one which devours the organs of reproduction."

"Can you cure it?"

"I do not think so. But am I allowed?"

"Our lord Saladin would not stand in the way of life," responded Al-Alfadhel.

Maimonides shrugged. "He, his disease, and myself are three," he answered. "If he allies himself with me, we may conquer his ill. But if he forsakes me and allies himself with his disease, he will surely die."

"What must he do?"

"He must keep from all intercourse with women for the rest of his life."

Al-Alfadhel gave a great throaty chuckle. "Then," he wheezed, "he is as good as dead."

CHAPTER 16

The opinion of Cadi Al-Alfadhel was correct. Just short of his twentieth year, in 1171, the young caliph died of venereal disease without having bred upon the virgin of Yemen. But Maimonides had done what no one else could do in reviving the ardor of the royal rod, and Al-Alfadhel and the rest of the court (excepting the furiously jealous Moslem physicians) sang his praises. Overnight he became the most sought-after healer in the capital of Cairo.

The very next day, Maimonides told me, he was besieged at the gates of his house in Fostat by a crowd of sick and infirm, clamoring for him to heal them. At that moment he made it the law of his life never to turn away a suppliant. It was from this time—when he was but thirty-six—until the end of his life that he was known as "The Compassionate One."

But he was also stern in his cures. That first day he was confronted by a man whose legs trailed in the dust; he walked on pads of wool attached to his knees.

"Heal me, heal me, mighty doctor!" he whined.

Maimonides, who was not easily duped, examined him. He found no muscles withered, nothing of illness except a curious ability of this man to dislocate his loose joints. He apprehended that this self-made cripple might have been sent to him under bribe by his rivals in medicine to make him ridiculous. He acted accordingly.

"Stretch out your body," he commanded. The fellow had no recourse but to obey. As he lay covered with dust, his yellow face bulging with resentment, Maimonides again made a show of examining him. "Pick up his feet so that the blood flows into his head," he ordered the bystanders. They obeyed with alacrity.

"Give me your staff," Maimonides said to Ramses, his Abyssinian attendant. He took up the stout stick. "Hold up the soles of his feet," he told the crowd. With shouts of joy they

273

followed his prescription while the impostor wriggled in the dust like a worm, praying for mercy.

Maimonides delivered ten blows upon the soles of his calloused feet. He beckoned the nearest of the spectators: "Continue the treatment for half an hour, every hour," he said calmly and walked away. The pretended cripple wrenched himself loose. He ran madly down the street, pelted with clods and jeers from the onlookers.

On another occasion, I am told, Maimonides on the same afternoon examined two men who complained of the same disease. To one, the more wretched of the two, Maimonides said: "Do all and everything that is your desire: food and women and drink," and the man went out rejoicing. For the other, who appeared only indisposed, he forbade women, wine, and prescribed a stringent diet. Those who heard his words were astonished. They asked him his reasons, inquiring if he had made a mistake.

"No mistake," Maimonides said sadly. "The first man is near death. Nothing he does will keep him from appearing before the Seat of Judgment in less than a week. As for the other, he is young and healthy. He will recover, if he but follow my advice."

A third time he was called upon to minister to a fat rich Moslem from Alexandria who fell ill while visiting in Fostat. "Give me nothing that will pain me," said the rich man, his belly quaking in terror. "I cannot stand pain. What remedy can you offer that will be painless?"

"The Romans," Maimonides said calmly, "might recommend hot water."

"Then give me that!"

"It will do no good. The Indians might administer the kernel of *prosper*."

"Then give me that!"

"Again it will do no good. The Moslems might prescribe black *halil*."

"Will that be effective?"

"No," Maimonides said. "But these are all without pain. I can offer you something that will give no pain of body but perhaps much pain of mind."

"That I can endure," said the rich man of Alexandria eagerly.

"Water corrodes the intestines; seeds of *prosper* cause undue moisture; black *halil* softens the belly. But I say to you: When you sit at table, place yourself a half-inch away from the edge. When your sash touches, rise and go away as if demons pursued you, hungry as you may be. Only thus will you cure yourself."

For these and countless other works of good sense and medicine together, Maimonides became famous in the kingdom of Egypt. And in those days it was fitting, profitable, and honorable that a man become a physician. As Job has said, "A man will give his all for his life." Thus a healer—called by the Moslems *tabib* or *hakim* or *mutatabib*, though Maimonides prefered the Hebrew title of *rofe*—was in great demand if considered an honest and competent practitioner. Such titles as "The Totally Successful," "The Thoroughly Accomplished," or "The Always Right" were customary. Maimonides was often addressed as "The Shining Sun of Doctors" and "The Beaming Glory of Physicians." His success inspired one Asad ibn Sina al-Mulk to write doggerel verses in his praise. Maimonides deprecated it but secretly (I believe) relished it. Here is the wretched composition:

> Only the ailing body is cured by Galen's art,
> But Moses Maimon heals both body and the heart;
> His secret knowledge makes him doctor of the age;
> He could cure ignorance and make it sage.
> If the moon, at full, would come down from above,
> He could clear her face of shameful spots of love;
> Relieve her of the pains of monthly menstruate
> And save her from the ills that come on waning date.

Concerning this, Maimonides wryly said to me: "It is no more than I deserve. I cured Al-Mulk of a case of constipation and, as his bowels moved, so did his rhymes."

His constantly increasing success as a *tabib*, however, did not produce universal applause. It is written that the envy of one's associates is the real might of one's enemies. Another poet, high in the regard of the court, wrote a bitter diatribe:

> The Jewish *hakim* tops the heights of hope;
> Aristocrat, no less, with power and scope.
> Our ruler chooses him to make him great.
> Egyptians, change to Jews, for so goes fate!
> It seems, no matter what we Arabs do,
> The very sun itself becomes a Jew.

In such matters there was great danger—not only to Maimonides but also to the colony of Jews, more than ten thousand families, who had settled in Cairo and Alexandria. The Moslems remembered we had been the slaves of the pharaohs; they were not pleased with the high positions to which we attained by merit. But my master had found a friend, a truly invincible barrier against jealousy and spite, in Al-Alfadhel.

I know Maimonides has set his face sternly against the rule of fate in the world. He asserts that the Torah agrees with the philosophy of the Greeks on the existence of free will. "Were a man compelled to act according to the dictates of fate," he says, "then the commands and forbiddings of the Law would become meaningless and false. Man would have no liberty to be either evil or good. Reward and punishment would be sheer injustice. The truth is, every human being may become as righteous as Moses or as wicked as Jeroboam; wise or foolish, merciful or cruel, liberal or miserly. If he wishes to do a thing, he may do it; if he does not wish to do it, he need not. The sinner lashes his own back; he weeps because he has mistreated his soul by his own free will."

Yet I note the master speaks of fate as a force which exists, and there are contradicting statements in the Talmud—in the Mishnah and Midrash—supporting the belief that superhuman energies may overpower our wishes. I can see no other reason for the death of young Al-Adid, which ended the royal line of the Fatimids without issue.

Saladin became sole ruler of Egypt. As a matter of fact, even while the child caliph lay dying, Saladin entered Cairo in pomp. He was vizier of the Shiite sect of the Moslems, who believe that Ali, the cousin of Mohammed (and husband of his daughter, Fatima) is almost divine; like the Jews, they expect a messiah or *mahdi* to arise to lead them to glory. Saladin was also the military front of the power of the Moslems. Like a bazaar juggler, he walked this tightrope of priest and general for the next few years, even fighting off the black Sudanese partisans of the caliph in the very courtyard of the palace.

Saladin had already, the year before, made his first raid on Christian Gaza. It was his first offensive against them, his initial step in the long march which has lasted for many years, and will culminate—as we hope—in the capture of Jerusalem.

But for the first few years, the harvest was among tares. Now that Saladin has reduced Aleppo and Damascus, now that Mecca and Medina have named him protector, few recall how precarious was the truce between his factions. The intermittent raids of the unsubdued Nubians went on for six years.

276

Though Cairo remained peaceful, Saladin himself made secret preparations to take refuge in other lands if he should be driven from Egypt; one of these shelters was Yemen.

Here, with Mecca on the north border, was a land important and powerful from the times of Solomon. It also seethed with unrest. Power lay in the hands of a fanatic mahdi and, as usually happens as a reaction to fanaticism, a Jewish self-styled messiah also rose, to oppose his intolerance to that of the Moslems. It was during this crisis, in which the Jews of Yemen hesitated between apostasy and immolation, that Jacob, the rabbi of Fayum, wrote in 1172 from Yemen to Cairo to seek advice from Maimonides.

It was as much a crisis of state as of religion. I have information indicating that Maimonides took counsel with Saladin himself. Each carried out his part of the secret agreement. On his side, Maimonides wrote the celebrated *Iggeret Teman*, the "Letter to Yemen," denouncing the Jewish pretender—which his father did not understand and criticized, while Maimonides was forced to keep his lips sealed. Saladin, meanwhile, fulfilled his bargain by posting his elder brother to Yemen to put down the revolt of the fanatic mahdi. It was the first time that the power of logic had combined with the power of the sword to restore the Jews in a distant land to sanity and bring them back to their faith. It accounts for those curious passages in the letter which, to this day, are not fully understood by the unknowing, such as Maimonides' advice that, for the good of the Jewish community, the so-called messiah should be "confined in iron chains for a time until the Gentiles learn that he is crazy."

In the troublous times following, through all the vicissitudes of war and peace and politics, Maimonides persisted in his career of healing. His work wove a thread of golden compassion between the scarlet of blood and the black of prejudice.

Naturally, he had no difficulty in gaining a license to practice from the Moslems. He had long ago served his apprenticeship in Toledo and Fez. He complained to me privately about the laxness of ethics such as those of a blind doctor who employed a friend to lead him about, inspect the urine bottles, and assist him in diagnosis. His wisdom was proved when the doctor died in a few months and his ignorant assistant instantly continued his profession. Maimonides quoted Avicenna approvingly on the subject of itinerant eye doctors so commonly found in the sandy dusty countries of the East:

"On no account should they be licensed. They go about attacking instead of healing men's eyes with their lancets and biting salves. There is no honesty nor talent in them."

But, he added, "All the same there is a good deal of harmless pretension necessary in medicine if the patient is to be convinced. Just as the soul is master of the mind, so the mind is master of the body: where it leads, health will follow. In this the astrologers, villains though they be, have a point. The writing of prescriptions in invisible ink, bitter mixtures, nauseous incense—these all have their effect. And the superstitious poor, who are so much more diseased than the sophisticated rich, are even more impressed by mumbo-jumbo."

"Then you use these practices?" I asked.

"I see their usefulness but I never use them," snapped Maimonides. "There is a difference."

"I am a fool," I said remorsefully.

"You are a good son," Maimonides replied. "You agree with your father."

Thus Maimonides had no difficulty in passing the somewhat idiotic examination of the *muhtasib*, chief of the bazaar police. He bled a patient so expertly that not a drop fell to the earth. He took pleasure in the oath of the Greek Hippocrates which forbade doctors knowingly to administer poisonous or unhealthy drugs or to prevent conception in women. He also agreed to the usual stipulations that he would always turn his glances away from the women's quarters, never reveal a confidence, tear aside a veil (after all, I, not he, had done it to Yaltah), or venture upon sexual intercourse with a patient. The *muhtasib* grimly quoted Al-Qais, the poet, to demonstrate what he meant:

"Many the woman like you, many the mother mild.
I've visited at night and made her forget her child;
Whenever he whimpered behind, she turned herself to see
With half her body; the rest, unshifted under me."

"None of that," he said, significantly sweeping a finger across his throat, "none of that."

As we left with the ornate certificate, Maimonides said pensively: "It would have been more to the point if he had recited more of Hippocrates: 'Life is short, art long, opportunity fleeting, experience deceiving, judgment difficult. Not only the healer but also the patient, the nurses, and the circumstances must work together toward the cure.' "

As Maimonides' apprentice, myself versed in medicine, I said, "Is not the curing of the patient, the decision of life and death, a terrible responsibility for a mere man to bear? Aside from the official licensing examination of the physician, what is the true measure of his worth? How can he be trusted to decide the fate of another human being?" My questioning of my master seemed a continuation of the licensing examinations.

Maimonides turned his gaze upon me in silence for minutes, it seemed. In an unforgettable voice he said, "There is a Higher Authority than that of the examiners here. It is to Him that all must go to seek guidance in the cure of the patient."

Maimonides takes care to dress well, in the modest high-collared black jacket that indicates his profession, rather than in robes and turban. He is spotlessly clean (not only because the Talmud demands it of scholars but also because he feels it has a mysterious inhibiting power over disease). He goes agreeably perfumed. His face maintains a calm and pleasing expression, even when confronted with the most shocking cases. He never laughs and rarely smiles, acting without haste, using words that are never despairing but always encouraging. "Small things such as these," he declares, "increase the potency of drugs, enlarge resistance, and promote recovery." He makes it a special point never to argue with the sick nor to rebuke them when they disobey his instructions. "No one must be blamed for an illness which is not his fault," he says.

His habitual procedure at the side of the couch is to inquire what preceded the illness and what and where is the pain. He also asks the patient's opinions, usually of no significance but occasionally revealing. He writes two prescriptions, exactly alike, giving one to the patient and one to the relatives of the sufferer. On his visit the next day, he takes a sample of urine and inspects it by eye and nose and taste, again questioning and issuing a new prescription, continuing this routine daily.

For many diseases Maimonides believes in the traditional dictum of opposites: hot remedies for cold afflictions, moist ones for dry ills. But his prescriptions are not the usual compendium of chemicals and herbs, one of which might center the target. His unusual perception and experience, coupled with his careful examinations, enable him to give precise instructions to the *saydani* who prepare the drugs or the *sharabi*

279

who concoct the cooling sherbets. He does not specialize as a *kallam*, who treats only wounds, nor as a *qudaix*, one who heals only the troubles of the stomach. He is consulted on numerous ailments. He is customarily held to be an authority in all cases, though his sparing use of the useful tonic, the rose-water *maward*, is criticized even by his friends, such as the eminent physician Ibn Jumay, healer extraordinary to the court. He yields to custom sufficiently to subscribe his prescriptions with Moslem cautions: "This will cure you, if Allah wills it," or "To be taken with prayer and Allah's blessing," or "If this helps, thanks are due to God alone."

Not only custom but necessity dictates such postscripts for his own safety. If the patient recovers, the fee is always generous. An honorarium is generally added. If, however, the patient dies, it is a serious matter. The relatives appear before Cairo's chief physician with their copies of the prescriptions. The latter judge from these, and from an interview with the doctor, whether or not he has been negligent. If his work is deemed professional, the verdict runs: "This man's life ended by the will of Allah at the end of his allotted span." If there appears to be negligence, the leading *tabib* advises the relatives: "Your kin was slain through ignorance and lack of skill. Therefore, exact blood-money from this healer." It is, as Maimonides remarks, a salutary check upon charlatans.

Even the lowliest physician has access to the hospitals. Though the first of these were built by the Nestorian Christians in Edessa, those of the Moslems are the most magnificent in the world. Nearly five hundred years ago the first was built at Damascus; then one at Bagdad, the city that is named "the gift of Allah." Indeed, it is said that Bagdad now has some sixty such institutions to serve its two million people. It was from these models that the great hospitals of Cordova in Spain arose.

Yet the most famous and wonderful of all lies in Cairo. Here there is a huge series of buildings devoted to the cures of the children of God, no matter their belief: Christian, Jew, or Moslem. Four fair courtyards are filled with the murmur of the water of fountains. There are special rooms for women and for convalescing patients, isolated rooms for interesting or infectious diseases, chambers for those who are healed but too weak to leave. There are male and female nurses according to the sex of the ill; even orphans are taken care of in one section. All treatments and drugs are given free by order of Saladin. Stimulating or quieting diets are prescribed, prepared in selected kitchens. There is an enormous library of all medical works; there are lecture rooms and places for the sick to beseech their own god for health. For those disturbed of mind, afflicted of Allah, there are hired musicians who play constantly and strolling tellers of tales for diversion.

In one of the remote wards, during the daily tour, I once noticed a niche with an empty couch, bare of draperies. It was dusty and unused, something extraordinary in such a busy hospital. I inquired of Maimonides if there was a particular reason for this. To my surprise, he replied: "It is a request of mine, granted by the vizier, that it shall remain vacant for a period of seven years."

"But why is this?" I persisted in my wonderment.

Maimonides glanced at me and his face changed. He walked wearily to the couch and sat down. His head bowed. "I asked this boon because of my sin," he said bitterly. "To remind me of what I shall answer for in the World-to-Come."

I stood before him, more bewildered than ever. "I do not understand," I said to my master.

"Here," Maimonides said dully, "I killed my brother David."

The shock of what he said numbed my brain. Before I could reply, he went on: "He had gone to India before, he went again. He had returned before; this time he did not return. I know why he did not."

"He died at sea," I faltered.

"It was *here* that he died," Maimonides said dully, "on the day he sailed for India. He had come to say an eternal good-by to me."

"Surely not!" I stammered, my tongue sticking to the roof of my mouth in surprise.

Maimonides waved his hand impatiently. "In spirit only," he said, "not in body. He told me that for him the world had lost its savor. He was weary of the unceasing struggle of the Jew against all others, of the unending series of defeats for our people. He said he no longer wished to survive, despite his family, despite myself. And I rebuked him.

" 'David,' I said, 'perhaps the world is evil, perhaps we are lost when we are born. But it is still God's will that we work with what He has given us, blessed be He, to make it better.'

" 'Speak for yourself, Muni,' he said with a strange and terrible smile, 'but as for me, I am tired, eaten to the bone with the contentions of existence. Nightly I pray your God that he take me hence.'

"I stared at him, my handsome brother possessing health

and wealth and friends. 'You speak a deadly prayer,' I said emphatically.

" 'So be it.'

" 'A man who slays himself is as guilty as one who murders another!' I cried.

" 'Have no fear, Muni,' he replied listlessly. 'Long ago you destroyed in me the will to kill. I shall wait, I shall be patient, to welcome whatever takes my life. Farewell.'

"He turned to go. I sprang after him. 'You shall not go in such a mood,' I said, gripping his sleeve. 'There are ways in which you may be cured of this melancholy. You must learn that God expects us to work with what is real and true.'

"He turned and looked at me. 'When will you learn, Muni," he asked, 'what you have never learned with all your wisdom? Illusion is better than truth, dreams better than the foul fact.'

" 'You are raving,' I said quickly.

" 'Good-by,' David said. I interposed myself, at that very door, between him and the world beyond. Without a word, he circled my waist with his arm and set me aside as if I were nothing. As he went out, I tried to call after him but the words choked in my throat, my feet were fixed to the floor. He took ship, passed down the Nile to Alexandria, and sailed the next day. I never saw him again: I had let him go to his death."

"You have nothing for which to blame yourself," I murmured, not knowing what else to say.

Maimonides looked at me without expression. "While we argued," he said calmly, "the patient I was treating on this couch fell into a fever. He died that night."

"That was the will of God," I mumbled.

Maimonides rose and looked past me, unseeing, into the blank white wall of the hospital. "I have reproached myself bitterly a thousand times," he said, "for bringing death when I should have brought life.

"David, most of all, haunts me in dreams. I seem to hear his pace behind me as I walk at noonday. His death caused me more grief than anything else in my life. In the months since then, I have spent the nights in fever and despair—for was not my brother's death also the cause of my father's death? Am I not a triple murderer?"

"No, no," I said.

Maimonides shook his head. "I still mourn, for there is no consolation; there is no one left to console me. He was my pupil. Joy has changed into darkness. David has gone to his eternal home and left me prostrate in a strange land. Whenever I come across his handwriting or one of his books, my heart grows faint inside me. Surely, the spring is gone out of the year."

During the years that I was the disciple of Maimonides, he harked back many times to that open wound in his soul which was David. "Were not the reading of the Torah my delight, did not the study of philosophy and medicine make me forget for a little," he told me, "I should have succumbed long ago to my grief."

By the year 1176, his famous *Mishneh Torah* was well-launched. His departure from Alexandria had spurred the work; the libraries and sages of Cairo deepened and encouraged his thought. His *Commentary*, written in the running Arabic vernacular, instead of pompous Aramaic or the Hebrew, had already popularized the Mishnah in the common language. The laborer, as well as the learned, could understand what the rabbis of old had meant. Maimonides possesses the genius of condensing whole pages of Talmudic discussion into a few sentences, not losing a whit of sense or logic.

But in these days of ignorance and fear, even to those who cling to the Jewish religion, truth is unknown. As Maimonides writes, "Disasters continually follow one another in our time. The need of the moment sets aside all other considerations. The wisdom of our wise men is lost, the learning of the learned is hidden. All the interpretations which they thought easy of understanding have become unintelligible." Because of this, he said, he would gird up his loins and expound the works of the past "in exact, concise language so that we shall be rid of arguments and counterarguments. My intention is that not many shall have any need to consult any other book on Jewish law."

Yet to how many more does the Jewish religion seem like a series of incantations or senseless rituals, done from memory, without meaning except to the superstitious. It is my task to aid my master in the explanation of what he deems too trivial to warrant notice.

Be it known, then, that our belief is no mere magic or trickery: It is the wisdom of the ages brought together by command of God, to be a pharos like that of Alexandria to all the world. To put it otherwise: It is a forest, the growth of ages, dominated by one mighty ever living tree. It has been

Maimonides' great labor to enter this trackless jungle, to slash away the underbrush (even to cut down some sturdy timber), to create vistas and parks where any Jew may wander and find refreshment.

The mighty tree is the Torah—the word of God given on Sinai to Moses, blessed be his memory—which brought us out of ignorance and bondage. It is known to Christians as the first Five Books of the Bible, the Pentateuch. The rest is composed of the sayings of the Prophets and of sundry Writings. Herein are holy history, laws, poetry, wisdom, inquiry, and philosophy—and the saving promises of our race.

Rabbi Eleazar has said that "the Book and the sword came down from heaven wrapped together. Said the Holy One, blessed be He, 'If you will keep what is written in the Book, you will be safe from the sword; if not, you will be delivered over to it.' " The Moslems call us "the People of the Book" and it is a favorite saying of Maimonides that the study of the Torah is the highest commandment.

Around this tree there has sprung up a lesser circle of growth, which is called the Talmud. This is a mixture of the expositions and the explanations of the wise men of Israel. It is not a code of laws; it contains not only the ultimate decisions of many questions but also the arguments that lead to the conclusions. Before the destruction of the Temple, the Talmud did not exist. In those happy times, the Law was never written but handed down by word of mouth from master to disciple as something too holy to commit to writing. When the Jews were scattered to the four corners of the earth, the ancestor of Maimonides, Judah the Prince, began to put down the precepts of the Oral Law. It grew into an immense compilation, dividing into two parts: one from the wise Jews of Babylon and the other from those who returned to Palestine.

As we know, man is mortal and full of mistakes. What is eternally true may be misunderstood in one time and interpreted wrongly in another. Within the Talmud itself appear many contradictions, dissertations, confutations, and riddles. The language itself is a barrier to understanding.

Thus came into being the Mishnah. With the Mishnah appeared the Gemara, the written code of Oral Law, studies and discussions of the Mishnah. But this seemed still beyond the reach of the ordinary man. So, for their benefit, there appeared expounders of the Torah who formed the Midrash— interpretations of the Torah and the Mishnah and Gemara in

284

story form, in anecdotes, illustrations, even in humorous fantasy. As this final growth grouped about the Torah, the Responsa—the answers given by the great Jewish sages to religious questions—were added. I may say here that Maimonides himself has answered as many as four hundred of these in two days and nights.

It is clear that only someone with supreme courage and knowledge and spiritual inspiration would dare to explore this wilderness, to map all its turnings and byways. His famous *Commentary* was no more, to Maimonides, than an introduction to the *Mishneh Torah*—a total summary and code of biblical and rabbinical law. He went at his work with his usual fearless persistence. In one instance, at least, where the elder rabbis expressed belief in witchcraft and demonology, he flatly states: "These things are all lies. Whoever believes they have any basis in fact is a fool."

Actually, the whole project sprang originally from the Responsa directed to him. With so many queries pouring in, Maimonides found a need for some sort of logical arrangement of authorities. He noted down a list of references in the Torah and Talmud for himself, then determined to give them to the world in expanded form. He catalogued the two hundred forty-eight positive and the three hundred sixty-five negative precepts of tradition in his *Sefer ha-Mitzvot* as a start; then decided, at the last moment, to write his work in Hebrew. "The commentary is sufficient for the ordinary man," he told me, "but I wish to remain a scholar in the eyes of the scholars."

To many Jews such a massive achievement seems a miracle. It is like the legend in the thousand-and-one-nights of the Moslems, where a boy rubs a lamp and wishes for a palace to be built on the instant. It is done for him by djinni. But Maimonides' task took him ten years. It exhausted his vitality and brought on him his father's illness of palsy. What seems so easy and simple to us now was, in truth, the unique imposition of the Greek logic of order upon the tumbled mass of riches to be found in the Talmud.

Countless were the nights that Maimonides spent in pondering the *Mishneh Torah;* that was his favorite time of working, when the stars whispered in his ear. But when the faint signs of dawn appeared, he was always forced to summon Ramses from sleep, mount his mule, and begin his journey to Cairo and his hospital duties. I remonstrated with him over

285

this exhausting life which allowed him to sleep only for a few hours just after sundown.

"When the Temple was destroyed," Maimonides told me, "the lovers of the Law took a vow never to eat meat or drink wine again. The good Rabbi Joshua asked them their reason.

" 'How can we eat the flesh that can no longer be sacrificed?' they lamented. 'How can we drink what can no longer be poured upon the altar?'

" 'Then you must forswear bread, too,' Joshua told them, 'for no sacrifices of flour are possible.'

" 'You are right,' they said. 'We shall eat fruit.'

" 'But the first-fruit offerings are no longer possible.'

" 'True. But we could eat other fruit.'

" 'You must stop drinking water, then,' Joshua said. 'The offering of water for the altar has also been abolished.'

"The lovers of the Law fell silent. Rabbi Joshua shook his head: 'We must grieve at our bitter fate. But too much grief destroys the purpose of life. Let us bear the fate that the Holy One sends us.' "

It was bold of me but I could not help replying. "My master," I said, "there is also the story of the young man who came to the great rabbi and asked to be like him. The rabbi asked him what he had done to be elevated to such an honor.

" 'I go dressed in spotless white like the sages. I drink nothing but water. I have nails in my shoes to mortify my pride, I roll naked in the snow to torment the flesh; daily I am lashed by the shammash to do penance.'

"The rabbi pointed out the window. The young man saw a white horse being led into the snowy yard. It drank from the trough, rolled in the snow, and was soundly beaten by the groom. 'See,' said the rabbi, 'that animal dresses in white, drinks only water, rolls in the snow, has nails in its shoes, and is lashed on the rump. I have only one question: Is it a horse or a saint?' "

Maimonides looked at me with a peculiar expression but did not answer. "I do not mean to offend you," I said, "but to work so hard is not the office of a wise man but that of a horse."

My master now seemed touched and smiled. "You have become more learned than you seem," he said. "Joseph ben Aknin, I love you for your concern."

"Will you take more care of yourself?"

"What would you have me do?"

"Is there not a woman in Alexandria, one named Zamira?"

286

I asked boldly. "Would she turn you away if you stopped at her door?"

Maimonides frowned. But he did not seem displeased. He meditated for minutes, looked out at the stars and sighed. I fumbled in the pouch at my sash and brought out a slip of parchment: I had come well prepared.

"Listen," I said, "to this message from one you love." I read the verses of Judah Halevi in a low voice:

> "Awake, my love, from sleep in bliss
>   To give my heart its due;
> And if, in dreams, you felt a kiss—
>   Awake, to find it true."

"Stop," Maimonides said in a strangled voice. His face shifted from its intense concentration to a vague dreaminess. He passed his hand over his eyes; I saw it tremble. "Stop," he said again, "you tempt me like the demons that assault Heaven."

I said nothing. He looked at me and shook his head. "Did you know," he said gently, "that Moslems believe the falling stars are arrows shot at demons by angel guards to keep them from overhearing the secrets of Heaven?"

I shook my head but he did not notice. I rose and quietly left the chamber with mingled feelings of guilt and rejoicing. I had seen the tears in his eyes. I knew his thoughts were on Zamira and her loveliness.

CHAPTER 17

Never had I seen the *musallim,* my master Maimonides, so happy. It was as if ten years had been stricken from his age. His step was light and quick. His beard was glossy, his eyes shone and—wonder of wonders!—once or twice I heard him laugh in pleasure to himself. Such a sound is rarer than the storied philosopher's stone that changes base metals to gold at a touch. The sound of such merriment enlarged my heart.

"You are happy," I said to him that evening at sunset. We sat on the rooftop of his house, squatting about the low ebony table, inlaid with ivory, which held our evening meal.

"You are perceptive," he replied.

"I am," I admitted. "But will you confess it?"

"Yes," he said. I watched his fingers busy in the saffron rice, toying with bits of stewed fowl. He attacked the gravy, his bread in the practiced fingers of a healer losing not a drop. I thrust some choice bits closer, into his notice.

"I rejoice at your feelings," I said, choosing a bone for myself. "My own mood is one of sorrow. I am wretched. I have not been able to go with you to Cairo to the hospital for the past ten days."

"You do as praiseworthy a work in studying the *Mishneh Torah*," Maimonides declared contentedly, not without an air of pride. "It is a sound work." He wiped his fingers on his napkin of fringed linen. "It is to your credit that you spend so much time with what is holy and good."

"I do not understand it," I complained hollowly. "I have the intuitions of a poet, not the mind of a lawyer."

"Judah Halevi, of blessed memory, who was a physician and poet, was learned in the Torah and taught its laws," Maimonides reproved me. "Its study is the only worthy act of man. Let it be said of you what was said of the great Alfasi by Judah." He stared over my head, collecting his marvelous memory. He recited:

"On Sinai's day, Alfasi, the mountains moved to meet thee;
The angels of the covenant came down to greet thee;
Upon the tablets of thy heart, the Law was scored;
Upon thy head were placed the laurels of the Lord.
And from that day, the Fathers cannot fail to fall
From wisdom's heights—unless they seek thee first of all."

"Alfasi was a glorious teacher," I muttered. "Forgive my foolish words."

"With three crowns was Israel blessed: The crown of the priesthood, to Aaron; that of sovereignty, to David; but the crown of the Torah, given to Moses, is for all Israel. There is no other study like it, none to be compared with it. Is it not said, 'You must sleep on the ground and live hardily while you toil in the study of the Torah'?"

I shifted my knees. I respected my master but he had said such things so many times before. "Yet you are happy after a day in Cairo tending the sick," I could not resist saying meaningfully.

Maimonides nodded. He leaned toward me. His eyes gleamed darkly. "I have seen her," he said to me in a confidential tone.

My heart bounded in my bosom. "Today?" I inquired breathlessly.

"Every day for the last week."

"As long as that? Does she stay in Cairo?"

"She is at the hospital."

"Better and better," I applauded. "There is no scandal in that, that is true love. I shall write a distich of superb rhymes to celebrate it."

"Do you think she loves me?" Maimonides asked slowly.

"Of course!"

"But you have never met her."

"No," I confessed, "but I have heard much of her beauty."

Maimonides shook his head in wonder. "Has it spread everywhere, then?" he mused. "I did not think she was known in Fostat." He took up his favorite silver cup and sipped the sweet citron sherbet as he spoke.

I raised two fingers. "Allow me to select my rhymes," I said airily. "Blonde hair, dark eyes, slender body—is that not correct?"

"Yes, that is all true."

"A low sweet voice."

"Yes."

"A ravishing smile."

"Undoubtedly."

"And her glorious legs that dance and dance and—"

"Dance!" Maimonides interrupted my rhapsody sharply. "She will never dance! What are you speaking of?"

Stung, I retorted: "I speak only of your love, of the famous dancer and singer, Zamira, master!"

Maimonides blinked at me in a luster blended from the moonlight and lamplight. He seemed about to weep. "And I," he murmured, so softly I could barely hear him, "speak of the lovely Frankish child, Joanne, who lies in the hospital at Cairo—who knows not a tune of joy, whose legs will never twinkle in the dance."

I swallowed my surprise as gracefully as I could and instantly begged permission to put aside my study of his *Mishneh Torah*. I pleaded to go with him to Cairo at the next dawning. Maimonides assented: So it was, at the hour before noon, I stood with him next to the couch of the girl Joanne of whom he had spoken the night before.

My taste in beauty is different from that of my master. I prefer a plump short woman who moves like a swan swimming charmingly on the still waters of a fountain-basin. I like a waist which can be spanned with two hands, a navel large enough to hold a vial of perfumed oil, eyes like shadows in a pool, hair which flows like the torrents of spring. I do not forbid the ecstasy of a slightly mustached upper lip above a mouth like Solomon's seal wrought in pomegranate juice and eyebrows arched like willows. I tremble at breasts firm and upright like the hills of Lebanon under snow, legs like columns of marble in petticoat-trousers, small feet, and large hindparts that swing heavy with unfulfilled love. I insist, above all, that such a one be in the prime of her youth, not above the fourteenth year.

I have no hesitation in saying this strange love of Maimonides was entirely unlike the woman of my dreams. At eleven, a trifle young for passion, she was unfitted by intellect and parts for the affection of one of the greatest men in Egypt. True, she had flowing hair the color of coined silver, eyes of dark gray like the luminous dawn. But her breasts were barely formed; her full mouth was a faint pink. And her body and legs, under the silk covering, appeared deformed and ugly.

As we entered, her eyes flashed toward us. She uttered a little laugh. Her pale tiny hands came out like mice from under the quilt and covered her face; I thought I could see the bones, the blood moving in the veins, so clear was her flesh.

"Oh, beware, beware!" she cried in treble. "The Eagle has come, he hovers over me! Beware!"

"You see," Maimonides murmured to me in a delighted undertone, "she calls me the Eagle."

"I noticed that," I said with some acerbity.

To my astonishment, my master promptly extended his arms like wings, smiling down at the child. I swear to you he almost danced about her small couch in this ridiculous fashion, his robe flapping about him.

"I am coming to seize you," he exclaimed in mock menace. "I am swooping down on my Silver Dove."

"I call her my Silver Dove," he whispered to me.

"So I hear," I replied shortly.

The child uncovered her eyes. She gazed up at him with an

290

expression of pure adoration. "If you are going to seize me in your talons," she said, "there is nothing I can do, is there?"

Maimonides ceased his mad prancing and approached her. A smile irradiated his features. I stared at him: a handsome man, in not much more than his fortieth year, with a strong hooked nose, swarthy face, his short curled tawny beard peppered with gray, his height bending over her. "The Eagle descends upon you," he said tenderly. He placed his hand upon her forehead to feel the body heat; he touched her wrist to detect the pulse of her blood.

"Will you devour me?" she asked eagerly.

"Not yet," he said, still smiling.

"Will you lift me up and carry me away?"

"Perhaps, perhaps—if you will drink some medicine and sleep as much as you can," he said, glancing at a nurse in attendance.

The child clapped her hands softly with joy. "And where will you take me?" she demanded imperiously. "The Eagle must tell the Silver Dove where he will take her. That is part of the bargain."

"What is the bargain, little one?" I asked.

She looked at me with suspicious, resentful eyes. She turned with the meekness of deceit toward Maimonides. "The Eagle should not associate with the Vulture," she reprimanded him.

I felt a flush at the insult but, to my indignation, Maimonides laughed aloud. "You see," he said to me in glee, "she names everyone correctly. Each one to his own!"

"I hardly think it to be commended," I replied stiffly.

"Are you angry?" the child asked me.

About to reply with harsh words, the phrases of rebuke hanging on my lips, I saw her huge eyes lift merrily to me. Somehow her happiness communicated itself to my soul; I could not help smiling in return. Her face tinged itself with a blush like that of a summer rosebud. In that moment I saw the sick girl was as beautiful as a princess. "I was wrong," she murmured softly to me. "You are the Hawk, are you not?"

"Thank you, Silver Dove," I returned, touched. "You and I, we shall be friends of the heart and mind."

"I love you," she said promptly, "but I love my old Eagle best of all. He is the one that roosts inside me day and night. I listen to the flapping of his wings and the cooing sounds that comfort me when he is away."

"You have trilled enough yourself, Silver Dove," Maimonides said with authority. "Now you must rest. When you awake, I shall have returned. Give me my medicines, Joseph. There is a potion prepared."

I reached for his pouch but the child Joanne pouted. "I will not go to sleep with your medicine," she replied strongly. "You have not told me where you will carry me in my dreams."

Maimonides sighed, looked at me, then assented to her command. Sitting on the bench by her couch, he took both her hands, burying them in his long palms. "Dear Silver Dove," he said in a tone I had never heard him use before, "I shall tell you of the country where I shall take you in my talons. Here you will run and play and shout—and, perhaps, grow up at last."

"Never!" she told him promptly. "Not unless you are there, so that we can marry and love each other all our lives."

"Softly, softly," Maimonides said. I saw a brightness in his eyes; I felt a smarting in my own. "This, then, is the faraway country.

"There is a land where the sun shines brightly all the day, where the breezes move in procession, and the gnats do not bite but sing songs of gladness. Their tiny voices shake the leaves into spasms of green delight as they listen. In their midst is a great garden, with wide, wide walks and trees heavy with fruit, flowers blazing with colors. If you touch or smell a flower, you fly like a bird among those gorgeous creatures in the sky; if you take but a bite of the fruit, you will live forever; if you drink only a drop of the little streams that wander in delight, in and out of the garden, you will be happy always, as a cloud in the sky.

"There is a magnificent palace of marble and sapphire, radiant and full of majesty, like the house of the sultan but a thousand times more brilliant and golden, full of the murmur of fountains, with all manner of kindly and beautiful women and handsome men who will caress and praise you. There are tables with all the world's fruits and blossoms and sweet-smelling herbs, dainty foods and candy and wine of all sorts; games that can be played forever with pleasure; instruments of music that rise and play by themselves songs that make you laugh until your head is dizzy, songs you remember forever—except when you wake. In a corner of the room there lie heaps of glorious clothes which make a goddess out of a mortal, which shine like the flames of a fire. There are loving slaves to bathe you, to wash your hair in perfumed water, to adorn you with jewels and silks."

"Yes," Joanne said sleepily, "I see it all. I shall be queen over all, shan't I?"

"Yes. Queen of queens."

"And you will be there?"

"Always," Maimonides said with a note of pain in his voice. He reached his hand behind him. I knew what he desired. I uncorked the gugglet and placed it in his palm. He gently lifted it to her lips. She drank obediently. Her head slowly slumped to one side, a slight smile still lingering in the corners of her mouth. She was asleep.

Maimonides stood upright. His face turned black as thunder. He sucked in a deep breath of fury; I was amazed at the change in him.

"What has happened?" I said in fright.

"Look!" Maimonides said in a low furious voice. "Can you believe in the goodness of men, even in the goodness of God, when you see this?"

With a swift motion, he flicked the covering aside. Her naked body lay exposed. I gasped with shock: I saw what he wanted me to see. The child Joanne, that he called Silver Dove, was not deformed. "She was bought at the slave market in Alexandria," Maimonides informed me curtly. "Bought by one Youssef ben Ari, together with other children. He purchased her, he says, out of charity because no one else would touch her. The price was one tenth of a dinar. Her master regretted his moment of pity; he shunned her like death itself when he discovered this."

Maimonides placed his finger lightly on the right knee of the girl. Even in her sleep she twitched with pain at his touch. The knee was grotesque, swollen by an obscene lump into the size of a palm nut. "It is an evil tumor," Maimonides said, his tone expressionless. He took on his accustomed professional manner. "It eats its way every hour, every minute, into her vitals. It cannot be stopped. Nothing known to me nor to any other healer, no herb nor drug, can halt it. Unless I sever her leg at the thigh. Unless I leave her one-legged for life."

"But the Moslems will not allow such—such butchery!" I exclaimed in horror. "They do not allow experiments even on the flesh of dead men!"

"I know," Maimonides said. He paused. "Youssef also discovered the child had been drugged and raped by someone— possibly the slave dealer, perhaps another, unknown, perhaps Youssef himself. My Joseph, this infant is pregnant!"

I had noticed the protuberance of the little belly. I had

thought, from my meager medical knowledge, that it was malnutrition or simple bloating. What my master said stunned me. I could scarcely believe him.

"Could it not be another tumor, excited into life by the one on her knee?" I inquired.

Maimonides shook his head. "Beyond a doubt," he returned somberly, "it is a pregnancy. As normal as one might expect, under the circumstances. Yet I know its desire for growth will unquestionably hasten the growth of the thing which devours her knee."

I grew bold. "In any case," I said, "you cannot allow your own fame and position to be endangered by such operations. Your life is worth ten thousand such as this!"

Maimonides' eyes flashed. "You have turned Moslem," he accused me. "You believe this to be the will of God, that man can do nothing about it. I do not think so. I believe God gave us knowledge and will and compassion! The life of one, no matter what men may think, is no more in His eyes than the life of another!"

I could sense his mind was fixed. "What can you do?" I asked weakly. My knees shivered; this was nothing for me, a novice at such matters, to hear or understand.

"The child must be aborted by the midwives, under my supervision. That will be difficult enough in her condition. Then, as soon as possible, her leg must be cut off."

"This is impossible!"

"No. Averroës once showed me a diagram of such an amputation though he dared not, as a Moslem, put it to the test. Indeed, he performed it upon an ailing horse in Toledo."

"But in her state of weakness!" I argued. "See!" I pointed to her face. Maimonides' own face tightened. He, too, saw the dark lustrous hollows about her eyes, the cheeks pitifully sunken in sleep, the arms which seemed to have only a covering of limpid flesh. "Either one of such procedures as you suppose possible would kill her," I said rapidly.

"That may be true," Maimonides responded slowly. He restored the covering to the child's body with infinitely careful hands. She stirred uneasily at the whispered caress of the silk. "But if such operations are not done—perhaps even if they are—our Silver Dove will be dead within a fortnight."

With that he turned and walked with long strides out of the small whitewashed chamber of the hospital. I followed him, my brain whirling. I had no idea of what was in his mind but I sensed fearful things. Suddenly it occurred to me there

294

was a question which had not been answered. I caught up to Maimonides and pulled at his sleeve. He stopped, his face grim and distraught.

"Forgive me, master," I said, "but you spoke to the child of a bargain?"

"Yes," Maimonides replied. "I told her—I told her if she were good, she would go with me to Paradise. All she wants of the World-to-Come is to be able to run and play, to laugh and have enough to eat, to have sunshine and clear water—and to be free of the black phantom of a man with lust in his eyes."

He pulled away from my grasp. He was about to start down the corridor again when he hesitated. "Joseph, my son," he asked me, almost plaintively, "what does one tell those who are not born unto the Law, who are too young to understand, who can comprehend only small rewards in Heaven and nothing at all about Hell?"

I shook my head woefully. As Maimonides proceeded, as I pattered after him, I found my emotions a mixture of pity and wonder. I knew what he had done in this world to ease the suffering of little Joanne. I had smelled the peculiar pungency of the potion he had administered. Silver Dove would have pleasant dreams: I had recognized the unmistakable odor of hashish liquor.

In a few of my experiments as a disciple in the art of medicine, I have sometimes eaten or drunk hashish. It is made from a certain shaggy plant also employed to make cloth and ropes: a brew of fibers and leaves ground into a greenish-brown mass. It is bittersweet stuff. It may be eaten mixed with honey as a sweetmeat; sipped, heated, with water and butter; or powdered into cold water, as in the case of Joanne, for a murky drink.

It produces curious effects within the mind. In my case, I became obsessed with the vain conviction of my mental brilliance, my ability to spy into the secrets of the universe. I did not hear sounds or feel pain. My sight seemed turned inward for centuries; I contemplated my entrails with consummate delight for eternity. When I fell asleep (as I thought), I had dreams both pleasant and unpleasant; though, in a child such as Joanne—after Maimonides' tale—the visions cannot but be pleasing.

The dreams which ravished me were otherwise: of moving color in long veils, drippings of purple, red, orange, stretching across infinite gulfs of black; then buildings like mosques of the most delicate and ornate architecture, decorated with grotesque human forms that shifted into exquisite tints, trembled, and melted before my inner sight. Occasionally, I was aware of a rat eating his way through my left side, gnawing to the beat of my heart; of a bright-colored parrot which shrieked unspeakable words; of troops of nude women, lovely and voracious, swarming about my bed, forcing me to make love to them until the very act became terror and madness.

This same drug gives its name and power to the sect of the Hashashin of the Moslems, known to the vulgar as the "Assassins." They have a secret and terrible power which lies in nothing more mysterious than their passion to rule by murder. We Jews love the keen but harmless edge of logic which splits hairs; the Assassins cherish poison and the point of a dagger. A wicked old man, the second Mohammed of their tribe, rules over them. He is called the Sheik al-Jabal, the Old Man of the Mountain. When he speaks, his word is the oracle of fate. I have heard, and I believe it to be true, that the Assassins do not believe in the ordinary faith of the Moslems but in the godship of their leader.

They have always despised both Jews and Moslems equally, but the great object of their hatred was always Saladin. It was this which darkened the day on which Maimonides and I were commanded to attend the court of Saladin. The caliph, it was announced, would be there in person, lately returned from a campaign against the Nubian rebels in the south of Egypt. Maimonides fretted. Such an appearance would make impossible his daily hospital visit to Silver Dove. He had become obsessed with the idea of saving the life of the unfortunate child. He was aware that every contraction of her small heart sent creeping death through her veins. Happy as he seemed when she was awake, he became wretched when she slept. He might recall her every gesture and word with a smile; but in seconds he would lapse into a stern hopelessness.

As we left the house in Fostat, he hesitated. Signing to me to wait, he vanished; when he reappeared to step into the litter, he seemed to walk more deliberately. I asked what had caused the delay.

"You are overcurious," he said shortly. "Perhaps I have a forewarning."

"Not of disfavor?" I asked anxiously.

Maimonides shrugged. His shoulders moved in a sluggish manner I did not understand. "Perhaps," he said again.

Thus we proceeded to the sitting of the *darbar*. Saladin had decreed the revival of this ancient Moslem custom, long neglected. In the old good days, the rulers sat morning and evening, twice a week, to hear the pleas of their most lowly subjects; once a week, the caliph sat as supreme judge. In the absence of Saladin, the office had been carried on by Al-Alfadhel. This fat and jolly official, once attached to the Fatimids, had changed both faith and allegiance to become a strict Sunnite of Saladin's persuasion. He remained loyal to his master thereafter. It was he who brought into being justice and order within the kingdom of Egypt, while his master defended and extended her borders.

Streams of pilgrims could be seen going in through the gilded gates of the famous twin palaces, towered and balustraded, surrounded by ever blooming gardens. Under the previous rulers, none who ventured into such heavenly grounds ever again appeared alive—except those who suffered public execution in the *sooq* as an example against trespass. Now, without fear, we joined the procession of our fellows, passing through a series of gloomy ways lined with the benches that the Moslems prefer to chairs, most of the niches filled with suppliants and justice-seekers of all ages, in rich garments or tattered rags. On through glittering doors adorned with carvings and gilt Kufic inscriptions quoting the Koran; past orchards filled with the warbling of birds and the shadows and reflections of running water; through rooms filled with the richest of furniture, hoard of centuries; past cages filled with the rarest of animals from all the corners of the world, miaowing and caterwauling, barking and growling and roaring and hissing behind their golden bars; proceeding through a long hall of unfolding doors guarded by eunuchs richly dressed and tall black soldiers (one company of an African tribe being nearly eight feet high), bearing spears and swords with a vigilant air.

In the days of the Fatimids, I had heard, the door of the audience chamber had been guarded with a purfled veil of cloth-of-gold woven with gems. Here the vizier habitually laid aside all things of metal that might be weapons, prostrated himself three times, to be admitted finally to the inner chamber. In this room sat the Commander of the Faithful, surrounded by his women and the treasures he especially valued: among them a pearl as large and as pure in color as a pigeon's egg; a ruby weighing seventeen Egyptian drachmas; an emerald of choice grass-green color, a palm-and-a-half in length;

a vast collection of porcelain and crystal vases and dishes. Indeed, it was said, if one quaked sufficiently to honor the caliph, the very vibration would break enough fragile ware to ransom a kingdom.

All this had changed. The veil no longer hung in its place. Saladin held court in a farther, less sumptuous, chamber. But the jewels remained on display for the curious—all the rest of the Fatimid treasury having been disbursed to the soldiers of the armies. Maimonides paused beside the guard who stood constantly in watch, day and night, over these priceless objects. His face had a thoughtful cast.

"My father would have rejoiced to see such gems," he murmured. "Once, my Joseph, the Maimon family might have been wealthy with the trade of precious stones. But we lost all, as you know; I have renounced the business and sold the stock which remained. Thus fortune goes, not hesitating to fly away, as the Romans used to say in their stories. Would you have me a great merchant or a humble physician?"

"Healing the body is infinitely better than suiting the vanities of the wealthy," I muttered, alarmed that the guard might overhear.

"Healing the soul with heavenly knowledge is better than both," responded Maimonides, moving onward.

Even though I had expected the famous austerity of Saladin, I was surprised at the simplicity of the throne room. It was no more than a large octagonal place of whitewashed plaster and brick ribbed with brilliant mosaic and the customary gold inscriptions. Arches led to the gardens outside; the air was balmy and fragrant; dozens of caged birds along the wall filled the court with their songs. A high, overarched ceiling, with bricks laid as lightly as a lace pattern, held a huge silver lamp. At one side was a small gallery for the muezzin. In the center, on a dais of cushions, sat Saladin, legs crossed, simply costumed, impassive in his dark majesty. Behind him gathered his courtiers.

Maimonides and I approached and prostrated ourselves before the dais. As we rose from touching the cold tile with our foreheads, Saladin nodded slightly. "Let you and your disciple stand at my left hand and know me as your friend," he said in his low calm voice. "It is pleasant to see those we knew before, whom we trust."

Maimonides bowed and said nothing; I followed his example. We moved to the position that the chamberlain indicated, just below the smile and plump form of Al-Alfadhel.

He bent to speak to us in a whisper. Saladin's voice fore-stalled him.

"Come forth again, son of Maimon," he said. Maimonides and I hurried to obey, again prostrating ourselves.

"I have heard of your good works," the caliph declared. "Your healing arts are devoted to those of all faiths, even as the Prophet would have wished."

"Most powerful Ruler," Maimonides said, "the pleasure in your bosom is also in mine."

Saladin nodded. "There is more to this moment than compliments," he said. "I have a gift for you."

He beckoned with a gesture. A man advanced from the group at the rear of the dais. He was as tall, as distinguished-looking, as Maimonides, but even more impressive in his bearing and appearance. Dressed in snow-white robes and turban, a pure white beard to his waist, his deeply tanned face and hands presented a sharp contrast. To my surprise, he advanced at a rapid pace despite his obvious age; he held his arms wide, a smile on his face.

Maimonides uttered an exclamation in spite of himself. He ran to the stranger and embraced him; they kissed each other again and again. When they parted, I was even more taken aback to see tears shining on the cheeks of my master. "I see you know each other," Saladin said dryly, allowing a slight note of amusement in his voice.

"My old friend!" Maimonides said with emotion. "My old teacher, Averroës!" I started at the name of such fame in the Moslem world.

"My favorite pupil of so many years ago," Averroës said in a deep voice. "None has shown so much promise since. You have become more famous than I."

"Never, never!" Maimonides cried.

"We shall have many a long talk to satisfy our vanity," Averroës returned. "I must see your father."

"Alas," Maimonides said, his brow clouding, "he is dead and you seek him in vain."

Averroës shook his head in sympathy. "Avenzoar also is dead," he replied regretfully, "these many years. I am becoming lonely on this earth. I come here to consult with Ibn Jumay on my way to Bagdad."

"Is Spain still as lovely and blossoming?" asked Maimonides eagerly.

Saladin clapped his hands lightly. "That is sufficient," he told them. "There is business to be done."

Averroës and Maimonides bowed and retreated backward, not too far from Saladin's side, in accordance with his indication. The caliph turned his attention to the long line of his subjects in the doorway and nodded to the guards. The first petitioner—a man in mean clothing but with a proud demeanor, young, dark-fleshed, with features as sharp as the edge of a scimitar and an impudently curling beard—came forward. He prostrated himself and rose to his knees.

"Oh, king and sage of all time," he addressed Saladin in a curiously thick voice, "I bring good news for Egypt and I claim the dress of honor and the gift of *al-basharah!* If I withhold such news, I am born out of wedlock and no true man; command me to deliver it!"

Such a florid speech seemed unusual to me. I scanned the fellow closely. Saladin gave no indication of impatience but said: "And what is your news?"

The court bent its eyes and ears toward the man. He glanced about him in a sort of weird triumph. "Glorious one," he said, "the wise of old have said that fortune is a friend to those who work toward fortune's end." He lowered his voice. He was barely heard by those beyond the dais. Maimonides narrowed his eyes and gave close attention.

"I fear," said the young man, "for the life of your all-conquering self."

Saladin's air of gravity did not shift but his eyes glittered. "Approach," he said, "and inform me."

"I dare not," said the man, "come so near to majesty." But it seemed to me that he mocked

"Let him come," Saladin said impatiently to the guards.

"Fear none but me!" cried the stranger.

On the instant he lunged toward the monarch in his place, propelling himself forward from his knees, up toward Saladin, helpless with crossed legs. At first I thought he sought alms from the lord of Egypt. Too late I saw the gleam of the blade in his fist directed at Saladin's throat.

None moved. Astonishment chained us to our places. Only Maimonides, nearest the dais—in a fashion almost leisurely, as if strolling, but truly lightning-quick—threw himself forward. Yet he did nothing. Nothing except to interpose his body between Saladin and the spring of the unknown petitioner. As he did, he turned his back to the full thrust of the blade.

There was a massive hiss of breath from the court. A shout

rose, then strangled. There was a tinkle as the broken steel of the knife fell to the floor.

The madman shouted with frustrated rage. His contorted limbs made a pattern as he writhed on the shining geometric figures of the tiles. He was seized by a half-dozen guards and held rigid. Only a signal, the raised hand of Saladin, prevented his death at that moment. I knew his fate and I shuddered for it. He had failed in his wild attempt. Now he would be hung upside-down by the legs from the executioner's tripod. He would be chopped to death, blow by blow, through his crotch until the blade reached his vital parts.

Maimonides sank to his knees. It was the hand of Saladin himself which touched him. It was the voice of Saladin himself which first spoke with concern. "Are you injured, good Jew?" he inquired with more alarm than he had shown for his own danger.

"I bring a message!" shouted the demented man. "My master tells you: 'If this fails, there shall be a thousand others! No man can resist his fate if I have doomed him!'"

"Shut his mouth," said Saladin briefly, "and take him away." The man's jaws were crammed with cloth and he was dragged from the room.

But I had no eyes for that. For the first time I saw a blotch of red growing on the white gown of my master. I was unable to move; a quick fainting fear passed over me. The room swam in mist. I was sure Maimonides had been stabbed to the heart. Nor was I the only one: Saladin gave swift orders. The tall Nubian guards bent to support my *musallim*.

But Maimonides regained his feet by himself, from his hands and knees on the dais where he had been driven by the impact. He bowed again to the anxious face of Saladin, to the craning white face of Al-Alfadhel behind him.

"Speak!"

"The physician heals himself," Maimonides said calmly. "A Christian art has saved us both, Most Magnificent."

"I do not understand," Saladin replied, frowning.

"Most gracious Caliph," Maimonides said serenely, "I have used preventive medicine of the best proof."

So saying, he tore away the upper part of his robe. His body was exposed. To my stupefaction he wore a shining, closely woven shirt of chain mail next to his skin. Up to him came Ibn Jumay, summoned too late, with Averroës. With panting gulps and shakings of his head, the court physician inspected the spot. He nodded with relief: The knife point had

301

severed a few of the tough links but the wound was slight. Maimonides would be bruised for days but that was all.

"You said a Christian art?" asked Saladin, his voice level.

The face of Maimonides contracted. "This shirt of steel was once my brother's," he replied. "He is no longer living. Once he desired to be a knight of Spain and spent his youth on such follies."

The ghost of a smile flitted across Saladin's countenance. "My own son, Al-Adil, wishes the same," he murmured. "A fancy of the young." He paused; his voice became brisker. *"Inshallah,"* he said, "it is as Allah wills. See that the Jewish physician receives five thousand dinars of gold and five dresses of honor and this." He took a signet ring from his finger and extended it to Al-Alfadhel, who placed it on the first finger of Maimonides' right hand. As I noticed the prominent scars of burns there, those of which his father had written, I realized for the first time how this might have affected my master.

"There is still the boon which is yours by right," Saladin continued. "What is your wish for *al-basharah,* Moses ben Maimon, dear to our heart?"

Maimonides drew himself up to his full height, as if he were about to launch into the air. His face took on a determined expression, sublime in its defiance of his own misgivings. His lips parted, then closed again. Finally he spoke in a firm tone.

"Great Ruler of the earth," he said, "compassionate to all who seek understanding, I ask for the life of a child."

"A child? What child?"

"A girl of eleven years who lies in the hospital built by your munificence."

"How may I give you her life?"

Maimonides took a deep breath. "She is at the point of death," he said quietly.

"Then her life is in your hands, not mine," replied the puzzled caliph.

"She can be saved only if her leg is severed in mid-thigh," Maimonides said boldly.

Saladin's dark face became stone. There was a buzz of alarm in the courtier group, always eager to destroy a new favorite. Al-Alfadhel blinked in alarm and made a negative sign with his pudgy palms.

"I am a Jew," Maimonides went on rapidly. "This operation I may perform without sullying the tenets of religion."

"Have you done such work before?" asked Saladin coldly.

"No," Maimonides said. He hesitated: "But in Toledo, the eminent Averroës performed such an amputation with success upon a horse's body."

The pale Averroës stepped forth, bowed in assent, and returned to his position. Saladin shook his head slowly. "This I cannot grant," he replied. "It is against the will of the Prophet to meddle in this way with human flesh."

Maimonides slowly lowered his head. As he did, Al-Alfadhel salaamed and whispered in the ear of Saladin. The caliph raised his hand to stop Maimonides' retreat. "Is it true that the girl is Frankish and a slave?" he demanded.

"It is, Mighty One," responded my master.

The court fell silent. Saladin meditated, his eyes not leaving the face of Maimonides. All that was heard was the chirruping of the birds, the sigh of the wind outside. Abruptly Saladin nodded, almost in repugnance.

"A Frank and a slave," he announced. "It is none of our concern. Do what you will with her. But if she dies, your own life will be mine to dispose of."

He waved Maimonides away and nodded to continue the *darbar*. We retreated backward, outside the door, and, turning, continued down the corridor, aside into one of the gardens, where we sank wordlessly on a bench. I had never seen Maimonides' face so taut and unhappy. I did not dare speak to him.

At that moment, Averroës appeared in the gateway, looked about him. He spied us. He came hurriedly to join us, shaking his noble head. "You are a fool, Moses ben Maimon," were his first words. "Today you were made rich and clothed in glory; then you request that which destroys all favor with Saladin. He is not a Fatimid nor an Almohade. The Koran is his life."

"I could not do otherwise," Maimonides muttered through gray lips. "I have promises to keep."

Averroës raised his eyebrows. Then he smiled with extraordinary brightness. "I may not touch a knife nor a saw," he said in a low voice, "but I shall assist you, if you will. I am a healer first, a Moslem second—though you may have my head for repeating it."

Maimonides embraced him silently. They rose together from the bench, I with them, my eyes wet with tears of thankfulness at delivery and annoyance at my master's stubborn obsession. We were joined by a stocky figure bustling into the garden, that of Al-Alfadhel. He shook his finger at Maimonides as he approached.

"I suppose Averroës has already told you, you are a fool," he said, his eyes twinkling. "Still, I admire courage. In time the caliph will come to see what you have done is the act of a brave man. You will regain his favor; fear not, I am always by his side to speak for you."

"My friend," Maimonides said, "how did you know about Joanne, the Silver Dove?"

Al-Alfadhel chuckled. "Do I not have agents everywhere?" he asked. Instantly he became serious. "But you are not to think that the danger is past," he advised. "There is that of which you know not."

"If your honor wishes," said Maimonides inquiringly.

"Saladin himself wears such a shirt. But the blade was aimed at his throat. That is one thing. He is suspicious of you because you once wore armor in his court; it indicates you might have been suspicious of his own exalted self."

"Never!" said Maimonides fervently. Al-Alfadhel made a gesture of dismissal. I did not know if Saladin's associate was trying to save face—for allowing his master to come to such hazard—or was telling the truth.

"Most of all," the vizier said, patting his stomach thoughtfully, "you must beware of visitors, more dangerous than an asp hidden in a date cluster."

Maimonides appeared bewildered. "You must watch those near and loved by you," Al-Alfadhel went on. "These men will come back again and again, in a thousand disguises, bent on the same errand—now against you, since you have saved Saladin."

"I—I don't understand," stammered Maimonides.

"Don't you?" asked Al-Alfadhel slowly. "This man was a Hashashin slave, the servant and messenger of the Old Man of the Mountain. He was an Assassin."

CHAPTER 18

Maimonides gave himself two days, no more. He needed forty-eight hours to nourish Silver Dove, to increase resistance to the blood-letting of an operation. For himself, he needed the time in order to study night and day in preparation for the ordeal.

Every four hours he ordered Joanne filled to brimming with broth of barley and the juice of beef and lamb, and instructed that she eat thin biscuits covered with honey or myrobalan jam. As for himself, he spent sequestered hours in the libraries of Cairo without food or sleep, searching in the books for the procedures he must perforce attain to be successful. Truly, he obeyed the last wise wishes of his father!

On the evening of the second day, he arrived back in the courtyard at Fostat for a much needed rest. He seemed gaunt. He took a little food and some pale wine. He rested on his back and the while insisted on talking to me.. He described how he had studied the books of the unimaginably far East, of Charaka and Susruta, with their fourteen varieties of bandages and their accounts of removing tumors with the knife and applying a dressing of arsenical salve to prevent recurrence. He rose wearily from his mat and demonstrated the surgical operations, drawing them upon a board covered with black wax. He filled gourds with thick wine and showed me the dangers of too much blood issue; he explained how to tap a tumor by using a small leather bag filled with liquid yellow mud. He even punctured the hollow stalks of water lilies to show the feat of lancing blood vessels which he had learned long ago. Finally, filled with enthusiasm, he had the leg of an animal, freshly killed, brought in. At this point he examined the best way of cutting the flesh and cauterizing the wound to stop bleeding. More than once I begged him to stop. My face felt moist and green; my stomach turned. Only continuous swallowing seemed to help me. It was with difficulty that I kept my weak bowels from soiling my garments.

"This is nothing like the study of poetry or philosophy," I groaned.

"It is as much," Maimonides rebuked me, his fingers busy in the entrails of a reeking dead dog brought in from the street. "If no life exists, neither does intelligence nor the will to believe in such things."

"Are you prepared?" asked the deep voice of Averroës, entering the room behind us. I turned gratefully to greet him, but Maimonides offered him only a nod and continued his gory explorations. Averroës ignored me and crossed to his pupil. "Good," he said, his eyes sparkling. "I see you do not depend on theory but on what actually exists. You know, of course, I am permitted to help you only by words and gestures. I must not lift a finger to assist you."

"Yes," Maimonides said impatiently. "It is all upon my shoulders. I accept the burden."

Averroës touched him affectionately. He indicated the high window in the wall. "It is dawn," he said. "It is time to start on the road to Cairo."

I went with them at the express command of my master, for no other reason. They conversed interminably about the mysteries of the human body for the whole three miles. I was forced to close both eyes and ears: The cursed rocking of the litter made me ill. I rejoiced when at last we halted in the courtyard of the hospital El-Mansur and I crawled out from behind the curtains to run after my two mentors. To my surprise, we were met by Yaltah and Naomi; they had gone ahead earlier, at the order of Maimonides, to be ready to assist with what might occur.

Silver Dove's chamber was the same except that it had been sedulously swept and cleaned. A small four-legged stool stood at one side of her couch. She was awake, her shining head cocked to one side so that she did indeed look like a bird. Her expression was both lively and expectant, with not a trace of fear. I noted more color, possibly, and—though it must have been my imagination—more fat upon her body. She had been well nourished under the regimen of Maimonides.

"What are you going to do to me?" asked Silver Dove interestedly. She seemed to view her body as belonging to someone else. Her eyes shone with perfect faith. Her question reflected only childish curiosity, nothing of fear.

Maimonides worked his stiff lips, unable to smile. "I am going to give you a stomach-ache," he managed at last.

Joanne looked puzzled. "But I have one already," she replied. Indeed, she had reason: Her small intestines bulged with broths and the herbal remedies given at Maimonides' direction. It had been the only thing he could do, together with a few rubbed cordial roots, to lift her strength.

"Then I shall make it a little worse," Maimonides said. "But in a moment or two I shall rub your small stomach and it will feel much better."

Enough of a woman at eleven to appreciate this, small Joanne turned her big eyes sidewise at him with a coy expression. "I shall like that," she returned without shyness. "When will you do all this?"

"Now," Maimonides said with decision. Her body lay out-

306

stretched before us on her couch; she had shuddered visibly at the cool touch of my master as she had endured his examination. Now she seemed more relaxed. I raised the thin red silk from her legs, according to the instructions of my master, and dropped the wispy stuff over her face like a veil. It rose and fell slightly with her breathing.

Very gently, Maimonides lifted the small limbs apart, exposing the rosy-tender lips of the vagina. It must have been painful—even with the tumor pillowed with a gossamer cushion—but Silver Dove uttered no sound. My master took from his pouch a small stick of soft willow, peeled and rounded at the end, like a stick used to beat a drum. He carefully smeared it with a soothing unguent of the juices of parsley and dwarf elder mixed with honey and pure hog's fat, cooked until thick. Then, with his fingers, he parted the female opening until the entrance gaped exposed. With infinite care, he inserted the stick, working it in bit by bit, his eyes half-closed as he operated by the most exquisite touch. He ceased, then began again, stopping almost immediately. He left the stick thrust into the tiny vagina and stepped back. His trembling hands betrayed his emotions.

"I believe I have penetrated the sack which holds the unborn thing," he whispered in my ear. "It is a very delicate affair, according to Galen. The stick must be rounded, flexible, soft; it must not thrust its way on through the other side or it will cause almost instant death."

"Are you sure you have not gone too far?" I asked, dry-lipped.

Maimonides glared at me. "No one can be sure of that," he replied. "What was the alternative? To have her dangled and jounced by ropes? To attack her womb with corrosives or give her violent emetics and purges? No, no! This was the only way in her condition."

"Rhazes advises screwing up a bit of paper into the shape of a probe and binding it securely with silk thread; then covering it with ginger and water, inserting it into the uterus. He says it is the best way," Averroës said in a low voice.

"It is much too rough a remedy," Maimonides replied.

"Hot baths and massages," I said. "If she would laugh violently, something might happen. If only the Moslems had court jesters like the Christians."

Maimonides gave me a look of scorn. Averroës went on. "I assume she has been given dishes such as eggs and onion broth, mallows and saffron and oil of almonds and animals' tails with the fat of fowls. The feet of chickens, boiled, are also good."

"Much of this was done," Maimonides replied. "She has also been anointed every hour with warm olive oil, placed more than once in a bath of linseed, fenugreek, and wormwood. Her womb has been softened by pills the size of a bean made of myrtle, wallflower seed, and bitter lupines, ground into meal and molded with rue juice and panax balm."

"Ah!" murmured Silver Dove behind us in a dying voice. As one man, we turned, rushed to her side. She writhed slightly on her couch. Maimonides held her up, sliding a thick cloth beneath her. He watched anxiously. A thin clear liquid oozed forth, slowly becoming bloody, like water in which one has washed after ritual slaughter. Silver Dove cried out again, in pain. Her stomach contorted. Maimonides held her up and motioned to me to take her feet. Between us we placed her cruelly astraddle the stool. Her eyes glazed and her muscles knotted like cords.

Next moment, the convulsions of her abdomen ejected a thick, dark clot of blood. Joanne threw back her head voicelessly, her hair flying in a bright cloud. Her thighs drew together and parted. Between them appeared a bluish-grey object, falling dully into the clay basin below. It was covered with a glistening fluid or membrane—which, I do not know. After it, almost immediately, as Maimonides held her still upon the stool in a grip of iron, came a second slow fall, that of a lump of dark dripping maroon tissue: the afterbirth.

Maimonides lifted Silver Dove lovingly up, placing her back upon her couch. The ordeal was over. Even as my own eyes swam with revulsion, Averroës snatched up the basin. With great strides, he bore it outside, his eyes shining as if he had found a great treasure. I had no doubt he would use the foetus as the object of some sort of wretched experiment.

Maimonides gently rubbed the belly of Silver Dove, forcing her entrails to contract and loosen as he did so, swabbing now and again at the opening between her legs to stifle the flow of blood. She looked up at him with great eyes of worship. "It's better," she said in a whisper. "I can breathe. It's better. I'm not sick. I'm only tired."

"Sleep, Silver Dove," Maimonides murmured again and again in hypnotic tones "Sleep, sleep." Almost immediately, it seemed to me, swaying on my feet beside him, she obeyed his command. I covered her. We tiptoed from the room.

In the courtyard outside, Averroës nodded his approval,

his beard ruffled by the light afternoon breeze. "Very good," he said, "very good. But the most trying moments of all are to come." Maimonides said nothing. We walked in silence down the garden aisles between the fountain-basin mosaics which reflected the brilliance of the sun in the peacock colors of the Moslems.

"I could not use Avicenna's method," Maimonides explained tiredly. "He recommends prolonged baths in cool water, fasting, purgation—these would never do in her condition. Aetius of Mesopotamia advises that such cases should be thrown about by several people or that they should dance violently or lift heavy burdens."

"Absurd," I said vehemently.

"Effective," Averroës murmured.

"Others prescribe tea made of rue, artemisia, ox-gall, eleterium, and violet roots," Maimonides went on.

"It would have killed her," I asserted.

Maimonides paid no heed to me. "Bleeding is mandatory afterward," he said, "in all such cases."

"Very true," I said.

Maimonides glanced at me with an indefinable expression, then at Averroës. His eyes wandered contemptuously back to me. "Don't be an idiot, a parrot," he said without inflection.

My vanity fled inside my bosom; a gorge of pride rose in my throat. Averroës smiled lightly and put out his hand. "Young Joseph," he said, "when you are older and have performed miracles, you will find that even miracle-workers become tired and irritable."

"Forgive me," Maimonides said, but he did not give me time to answer. Instead, he strode forward into the blinding light of the sun.

Less than twenty-four hours later, the hospital attendants were instructed to prepare Silver Dove for the amputation of her leg. They were reluctant to execute these instructions from a Jew, even a renowned healer; but the signet ring of Saladin worked wonders. Just before the middle of the next day, we stood in a second chamber in another part of the hospital, well removed from the wards.

This room, prepared for the operation, still stank of the heavy lime coating Maimonides had insisted be applied to the walls here. By the authority of the ring, he had had enforced his every wish. The place had no windows, only a skylight in the low ceiling and a door so small that all were forced to stoop as they entered. The night before, as Maimonides had demanded, six charcoal braziers no more than a foot above the floor had been lit and had burned until they went out. Since morning the door and the skylight had been opened, shielded by coverings of gauze.

One of the braziers had been refilled and lit again. On this bubbled a pan of oil and pitch; next to it, heating red-hot in the charcoals, were three rods of iron.

"The heat of this room is insupportable," I complained, feeling the sweat start upon my cheeks. "Why was this necessary?"

"It may help the wound to heal, keeping it from suppuration," Maimonides responded curtly.

He had chosen high noon for the time of the operation. The *khamsin*—that hot wind which blows for twenty-five days before and twenty-five days after the spring equinox—had commenced to blow, bringing sand and dust, scorching earth and sky. Maimonides knew the blaze of the overhead sun into the white room was preferable—and possibly more healthy— than the uncertain flickering of lamps. Little else than the clouding brilliance of this light was in the room—except for a waist-high, marble-topped table, a little longer and a little wider than a small body, the burned-out braziers, and some clay amphorae with hot and cold water.

Maimonides raised his quivering hands in a gesture like that of prayer. "I say the cherished words of Halevi," he murmured, "the blessed physician of Toledo and seeker of the Holy City." With this, he recited solemnly:

"Choose Thou alone my medicines of art,
    Whether good or evil, strong or weak;
For it is Thou who makes the healthy heart:
    Thy blessing is the tonic that I seek.
Nothing within my powers brings a cure—
Only Thy healing touch can make it sure."

We stood silent a moment. Maimonides gestured to Averroës. "Honored one," he said, "will you stand there, across the table from me?" Averroës nodded silently and took his place. Maimonides thrust out a finger at me. "You, my Joseph," he said, "will stand beside me here."

"What shall I do?" I faltered.

"See that no perspiration falls from my face," he said sternly, "and try to keep from fainting, as my father once told me."

310

At this moment, Yaltah came in with his medicine pouch, a rolled kit, and a packet of boiled cloths. "My sister," Maimonides said softly, "you and Naomi will wait outside the door. Perhaps you will be of more assistance than you know." Yaltah bowed without response and went out through the gauze curtain.

Maimonides looked appealingly at Averroës. "Remember," the old Moslem said quietly, "that only the soul is eternal and no knife can cut its substance."

Maimonides took in a quick, deep breath and clapped his hands. "Bring in the Frankish girl!" he cried in a loud voice.

"What will I be like?" asked the fearless Silver Dove.

Maimonides grimaced. "You will be like the stork of Egypt," he said, "a beautiful sight."

Joanne smiled contentedly. "I shall fly?" she asked. "Even if I have only one leg?"

"Perhaps," Maimonides said. He signaled to me and I placed the wetted sponge—the remarkable agent carried by every Arabian healer—to her mouth and her lips, squeezing a few drops down her throat. The pungent odor made her heave with coughs. Slowly she subsided, her eyelids falling, her body relaxing. I have often wondered what magic ingredients—hyoscamus, cicuta, mandragora, opium—are soaked into such a sponge to bring this painless sleep. The "sleepmaker," as it is called, may be carried dry in the kit for days; a wetting in spirits of wine and water brings out all its potency.

Maimonides watched Joanne's face until her breathing became soft and regular. His own features hardened: "Now!" he exclaimed.

She lay quiet, supine; the clear flesh of her small body was a pool on the cold marble. Quickly Maimonides, under the direction of Averroës, worked on each leg with utmost care, binding it up with bandages, as tight as they could be drawn. The blood had to be driven to the upper part of her body, he muttered, to save as much of the life fluid as possible. In no more than moments, Silver Dove looked like a half-mummy. At mid-thigh on her left leg, Maimonides left off. Directly in the joint of her groin, he twisted a leather thong tightly, so tightly that it sank out of sight into the tender flesh. I found it hard to bear the sight of this sunken in her thigh, the growing ruddiness of her torso. I tried to turn away. My staring eyes would not tear themselves from the sight of those preparations.

Having completed the preparations, the two elders stepped

back. They waited. It seemed a long time, though it was only minutes; it made me feel as if I wished to shriek. Maimonides beckoned imperiously to me. I made my way unsteadily around the white marble table to his side. Averroës again took his post just opposite. Maimonides drenched his hands in spirits of wine, dried them swiftly on another cloth. He reached out his hand to me, curling his fingers. Automatically, I put the large gleaming bronze knife with a tiny sawlike edge (that he had indicated before) into his palm. He took it. Almost instantly I smothered a cry.

Maimonides paid no heed. He spread the white skin and drew a long cut along the outside of her thigh; another slash, across it in mid-section. He cut again deeply on the inside of her leg, joining the thin red lines. I was amazed at the lack of blood, at the very slight oozing only, which served as a pattern for the work, as a seamstress might mark out a gown. The white-lipped Maimonides flashed a glance toward Averroës. He nodded in silent approval. The Moslem made an imperative gesture toward me. I understood: I took a cloth and wiped the sweat from the brow of my master.

Now, with a hand firm as a rock, he inserted the edge of the knife carefully under the cuts, peeling back the skin as he did; cutting it back and back, skillfully, bit by bit, until he held a whole flap of skin in his left palm. I felt sick. I saw no reason for this. The pink-white meat and muscle of the small leg lay exposed beneath. My stomach began a slow turning; I wiped his forehead, then my own, with a nerveless hand. Within the pink-bleed, tiny white worms seemed to swarm, as if it were already rotten. I turned my head away before I realized these were little white ligaments, cords of the muscles.

Maimonides signaled to me. Averroës corroborated it. I followed my instructions: I lifted Joanne's leg, which was cold and limp. Instantly Maimonides cut underneath, a huge deep cut that rasped on the bone, slicing through muscle and nerve and flesh. My hands grew powerless. I managed only to lower the leg; I wiped my own forehead, then his, with shaking fingers.

Averroës motioned for Maimonides to be quick. My grim master, still holding the flap of flesh, cut across the top of the thigh. The knife disappeared out of sight, grinding and slashing. He turned the leg slightly at the side, then the other side until the whole was like a leg of beef I had seen dangling from a hook in a butcher's shop. My forehead felt cold and wet. I paid no attention except to wipe the drops of sweat from my master's hands and face.

He signaled again with blood-dripping hands. I did what I hoped would be my last duty: I handed him the sharp little saw of iron. His fingers—now that he had laid the flap of flesh back on Joanne's belly—pulled apart the great gash. I saw the bone, its membrane glistening over it. Next to it I saw an opening, large enough to thrust my little finger into. It was the giant blood vessel, the artery he had told me of; he had forgotten it! He dropped the saw. I caught it in mid-air, returned it to the table. Maimonides paid no attention. The artery had commenced gushing blood into the purplish cut. Swiftly Averroës gestured in pantomime. Maimonides seized a bit of string hanging in his belt. With his long fingers mucking recklessly in the wound, he tied off the end of the artery. He spied another under Averroës' vigilant eyes and pointing finger. He stopped the blood there, too; around it oozed clear liquid, the fluid of life.

He took the saw again. My senses began to shiver in my head. My mind and sight reeled but I kept them steady by a titanic effort of will. Through the membrane, the wrenching rough sound of the saw; through the white, white bone; through the red-yellow marrow! The leg! The leg fell away! It rolled on the table! It was I who caught it in my arms without knowing what else I could do. With the bandaged hideous thing in my arms like a baby, I rushed panic-stricken toward the door. I saw the white lintel seemingly descending: I had forgotten to lower my head. The beam struck me a stunning blow. My world spun; I sank to the floor unconscious.

Much later, they told me what happened afterward. How Yaltah dragged me outside by one foot and relieved my senseless self of my burden. How Averroës, despite his religion and his vows, took my place—wiping the oozing of Maimonides' sweat, handing him lint, bandages, compresses, bits of thread, the red-hot irons; bringing the scalding oil and pitch to seal off the great blood vessels in the leg. How they loosened the thong bit by bit and saw where the blood oozed and where it spurted and cautiously cauterized the wound spot by spot with the boiling fluid. How they tenderly folded over the flap of skin at last and sewed it tight. How they gradually loosened the bandages and tourniquets and again watched for the blood to flow, waiting for any sign of hemorrhage.

I came to outside at a corner of the building, dazed and

confused. Then I realized where I was; I sprang to my feet. My legs would not support me and I fell; I crawled back into the room, up to the blood-sticky marble table. None heeded me. I rose like a dog begging, but Averroës and Maimonides ignored me, peering at the small form of Joanne beginning to take on life, coming out of the anesthetic. She stirred, she sighed; her head rolled from side to side. Spittle rose in her mouth, the swallow visible on her glassy throat. She opened her eyes and saw the face of Maimonides.

"Am I better?" she managed to whisper at last, after many attempts.

"Much better," Maimonides said. "You will get well."

"You have dropped me from your talons, old Eagle?" she asked drowsily. Maimonides shook his head. "I shall hold you tight forever," he responded. She smiled a little smile and then, suddenly, she turned and vomited. Averroës placed his big tanned hands like feathers on her head and body, covering her up swiftly with a white silk robe. He nodded to Maimonides. "I shall take care," he said. "You must leave; you will destroy all if you stay."

"But if she calls?"

"I shall summon you instantly."

Maimonides nodded. He went outside with staggering steps, strange for a man who had acted so decisively and bravely seconds before. I managed to get to my feet and follow him out the door. Yaltah waited there, hands clasped, watching with anxious eyes. With an effort, Maimonides nodded inside. "Averroës," he said, "he will need you." Yaltah hurried within.

Even the heat of the sun seemed cool after the stifling room. Maimonides turned his eyes vacantly upward. "She will live," he pronounced, through gray lips, his face sunken in weariness, his shaking hands making me think of his father's palsy.

"She will live!" I cried in weak hosanna.

"We shall make her another leg," Maimonides said with difficulty. "It shall be a leg of the finest ivory, fitted and carved to perfection."

"I shall pay the cost!" I exclaimed, carried away by the rejoicing of the moment.

Maimonides did not seem to hear me. "I shall have it banded in gold," I said exultantly. Maimonides' eyes fixed on me, as if his inner vision were returning from a vast excursion.

"No," he said slowly. "Silver for our Silver Dove."

Upon the words, without warning, his eyes rolled upward and he collapsed, fainting, into my arms.

314

Four months after the operation, it was amply clear that Maimonides' prognosis of Silver Dove's recovery was accurate. She became a lively, inquisitive urchin, impatient with her inability to get about, never for a moment repining about her lost leg. The stump, skin-flap sewed over it, healed slowly. It would be half a year or more before she would be able to tolerate an artificial peg. Even then, the pain of her weight on the bottom of the amputation would be intolerable. Maimonides designed a cup-shaped support in the top of the slender ivory stick so that her weight—when the time arrived —would be borne on the sides of her thigh, high up in the flesh.

Her recovery was a matter of concern to all of us. But Maimonides had yet other cares: He is a man who cultivates worries as the fabulous Greek Hydra grew heads. When one care is cut off, two grow in its place. There was one particular fret which most men find congenial—a growing fame.

Not that Maimonides was a humble man. He knew his own worth; he was capable of defending it. He often spoke to me with mounting pleasure of his high reputation, of the need to sustain it for the honor of all Jews. "Honor and logic compel me to avoid fools," he asserted to me one memorable night.

"The difficulty is to determine who is a fool," I said, intending a philosophic diversion.

"What issues from the mouth determines the taste of character," Maimonides retorted.

I shook my head. "We are all fools in one fashion or another," I replied. "It is in the nature of all men to have some blindness in understanding."

"Yet there are those who are intelligent. I would rather please one intelligent man and displease ten thousand fools at the same time, if necessary."

"You use that word 'fool' too freely," I warned. "It has made more enemies, for a wise man like yourself, than any other word."

"What is true, is true," Maimonides retorted. "Those who believe in such things as witchcraft and demonology, for example. They can be called no other than fools."

"But the Talmud," I protested, "recognizes these as based on fact!"

"Even the Fathers have been mistaken," Maimonides said smugly.

"But *you* are never wrong!" I cried, stung by his assumption of omniscience.

Maimonides transfixed me with a single look. "Do you deign to instruct me?" he asked quietly. I sat silent for a moment in the corner of the upper room. He resumed his work on the *Mishneh Torah*, of which I had read so much—and understood so little. I could not forbear interrupting him once more.

"I beg of you," I said penitently, "to forgive me. I say what I say for your own good. You are the leader of the Jews in all Egypt. Your word is precious coin, passed from hand to hand, from mouth to mouth. Do not sully it by raising enemies against yourself. You, the second Moses, are our only help."

"Everyone must have enemies," Maimonides replied, driving his pen onward without raising his head.

"As few and as weak as possible."

"I have but few."

"No," I said boldly. "There is Yahya-Zuta, who still lives and is listened to."

Maimonides put down his work and leaned back on his stool, rubbing his cramped hand. I thought I spied a glint of amusement on his face by the lamplight.

"So you have heard of that," he said musingly. "It was a long time ago."

"When you arrived in Alexandria," I agreed. "You, a newcomer, took part in Jewish affairs there too soon."

"Yet I deposed him in his pride from his high place. It was I who changed his name from Sar Shalom, as he called himself—the 'Prince of Peace'—to Shor Shalom." Maimonides' face had the glimmer of a smile. "Shor Shalom, the 'Complete Ox.'"

"He has not forgotten," I reminded my master.

"I trust he will remember," Maimonides said.

Perhaps he will, I thought angrily. Perhaps he will devise some vengeance unknown to us. Proud, arrogant, filled with a desire for power over his people surpassing that of the most cruel Gentile tyrant, this madman Zuta had denounced gentle Samuel ben Hanania of Alexandria as a cheat and a criminal. Hanania, an elderly man of great learning, noble in the line of David, was in those days years ago the Nagid, the ruler of the Jews in Egypt. Zuta cunningly aspired to the position. He invented tales of community funds being stolen, of powers misused. Hanania was deposed. Zuta got himself appointed in his place—and perhaps this perfidy might have gone unnoticed except for Maimonides. When the old man was imprisoned for sixty-six days on such charges, the humiliation of one of the ancient lineage of our race aroused the young man

316

just come to Alexandria. He investigated the charges, found them baseless; he aroused public protestations of Hanania's innocence. The clamor—and the bill of facts presented by Maimonides—flung Zuta from power. It reinstated the aged Hanania once more as Nagid.

"But I," said Maimonides, addressing me as if he read my thoughts, "have not consented to become Nagid!"

"No," I said, "and I wonder at it, though it has been offered you many times."

"The Jews need no prince except the precepts of the Torah," Maimonides said. I scented something behind his words.

"And the farther a man climbs up a tree, the more exposed is he behind," I murmured knowingly.

Maimonides nodded pensively. "I confess Zuta sometimes enters my thoughts," he agreed. "But not through fear. Only that a feud with him, helpless as he is today, might cause a clash within our own people."

"Will not the difficult work beneath your hand do that itself?" I asked, presuming upon his softened mood. Maimonides frowned. He leaned back in his chair, a hand rubbing his forehead free of its furrows.

"The *Mishneh Torah* is what its name implies," he murmured, "a repeating, in my own way, of what the Torah says. I swear to you, my Joseph, I do not write this book to gain honor and glory among the Jews. God knows I began it only as a few notes, as a reference for myself. So that I would not be forced to search all of the Talmud for the answers to the letters I constantly receive. It began long, long ago—and then, as time passed, as I amassed an overpowering heap of notes, I decided I should dedicate the labor to the Lord. I saw our nation had no code of laws that could present the decisions of the Fathers without controversy. Errors multiplied with argument. Thus I chose to carry out my plan to the full, for the honor of God."

"It is laudable," I muttered, abashed as always at his flow of words. "But I believe still it can cause nothing but what you say you wish to avoid. If you take argument away from a Jew, you take away his pleasure and recreation."

"Admitted," Maimonides said in the tone he used when he felt he was about to conclude a discussion. "I anticipate that this book will fall into the hands of spiteful fanatics who will tear it to bits. I foresee that it will come to the idiots and fools."

"Again, that word," I interrupted.

317

"Fools," Maimonides repeated firmly. "They will find it an insoluble riddle. Then, too, those who are immature or ignorant will stumble over its passages and its definitions, too slow of understanding to follow my reasoning."

"Still," I declared, "there will be those who are wise and understanding who will praise you."

Maimonides shook his head sadly. "No," he said. "You do not comprehend the pride of which you spoke a moment ago. There is true pride, justified of its works; there is also false pride, born of envy and jealousy. Those who consider themselves wise men will denounce the book on traditional grounds, out of gross spite. They will be worst of all."

"Who would dare do this?" I demanded, aghast.

"Samuel ben Ali of Bagdad, for one," Maimonides said. "He accounts himself the wisest of all the Jews in the world."

Into my mind there flashed a remembrance of the manuscript of Maimon ben Joseph, his father. "He who was your childhood friend?" I asked. Maimonides nodded. "He who sent the bottle of poisoned wine to Fez?" I went on excitedly.

"Perhaps we misjudged him on that occasion," Maimonides said. "But I do not mistake his character in this."

"If he derides your efforts," I inquired painfully, "who will support them?"

"A few," Maimonides replied steadily, "who love fairness and justice above all, who have the wisdom to understand what I propose. I have had letters from scholars in France and Spain; they are pleased with what they have read, they desire me to continue. Some future day, when envy and desire for power vanish, the Jews of all nations will be ready to accept my work."

"But who will defend it now?" I asked. "Who will preserve it for the future?"

Maimonides' face lighted up. He leaned toward me, his cool hand upon my head. "You, dear Joseph," he said quietly, "are first and foremost of them all."

I sprang from my chair, touched at the compliment yet despairing that my master could not see what I had shown him so plainly. Indeed, in regard to his own state, he was peculiarly blind.

"I am grateful for what you say," I said agitatedly, "but it makes me all the more apprehensive. Samuel ben Ali, the most powerful of our race, enthroned in our greatest city of Bagdad; Zuta, the malcontent, still weaving his dark webs in Alexandria. And there are others you will not recognize."

"Others?"

"You will recall what your friend Al-Alfadhel said after you shielded our lord Saladin. Do you not fear the Assassins' vengeance?"

A shadow crossed the features of Maimonides but he did not reply. I went on recklessly: "Even in your own household, my master! Yaltah is restless, unmarried for so long; and Naomi—have you not eyes in your head? She is in love with you herself!"

"Enough!" thundered Maimonides, rising upright. "Have you been intimate with us so long that you dare to say such things?"

A courage I did not know I possessed came to strengthen me. "You write for the glory of God," I said intrepidly. "As for me, I work for the honor and truth of Maimonides."

Maimonides said nothing, staring before him, his passion checked by my reply. I dared one further remark.

"There is one who truly loves you," I said slowly, "and she is the Moorish woman whom you have not seen for years. She is Zamira of Alexandria."

Maimonides turned his head toward me with a terrible look, one I could not understand. It seemed mixed of longing, fury and despair. "Speak not of her to me," he said in a choked tone. "It was one of my father's last commands that I should never see her again. Should I disobey him who gave me not only life but wisdom in this world? As the sages have said, my reverence for him is my fear of Heaven itself."

"Yet your own tongue has said the Fathers have been mistaken," I replied. "Your father once wrote that you would never be a healer, that the very sight of illness made you faint. Yet I have seen otherwise, a few months back."

"You would have me less than the Gentiles," Maimonides responded harshly. "Is it not said by Rabbi Hezekiah, glory to his memory, that a heretic of Ascalon, who was chief among the councils of his people, did not dare to sit upon the stone upon which his father sat? Did he not, when his father died, even worship the stone?"

"I know nothing of it," I said. "I know only that, even as all men—you, as myself—we are prone to error." I bowed deeply. Maimonides paid no attention; my heart hardened. "I say no more," I murmured, "except that a man should keep those who love him as close-bound as his garments; his enemies will come to him without bidding." I paused. Maimonides

319

silently resumed his seat and again began his writing. I went out of the room low in spirit.

There is nothing in the world like a night of full moon from a rooftop in Egypt. Maimonides had once reversed the Sayings of the Fathers in declaring that Jews might settle everywhere in the world—except in hated Egypt. Now he had come to admit their wisdom. Wishing I had mentioned this as well, I stood in the luminous square of light that was the roof of Maimonides' house in Fostat. I looked out at the milky night. It was filled with the glory of the planets, a cloak of loveliness spangled, the stars showing through the fabric. A light mist from the Nile hovered over the land; the breeze was as cool as the touch of a woman's hand. I felt my resentment at Maimonides ebbing. The poetic rising of my spirits from within seemed like a freshet of sweet water in my heart.

It was August. The Nile had turned its customary deep turgid red, the color which often makes me think that Moses —blessed be he—mistook a natural phenomenon for one of the plagues of God. The foul odor of that mighty stream with its unknown burden—not unlike that given off by a gigantic decaying body—pervaded the land. So heavy it was, however, that at night it stayed well down below the first story of the buildings, murky in the streets. It stifled late passers-by in Fostat and torches burned dim, but it was endurable, often unnoticeable on the roof. Even the clouds of gnats and flies which hovered and descended everywhere turned torpid with the evening cool and did not bother the sleepers. Only the chorus of frogs, a hoarse high-pitched chorus like eunuchs' shrill croaking, continued without cessation, noise of an exotic surf upon the beaches of a fantastic sea.

My mind blew clear of its vapors. I thought of what had happened to Maimonides since he had been so successful in his unprecedented operation upon Silver Dove. He had brought her to his home from the hospital weeks ago. Now she lay sighing in sleep, waiting for her stump to heal, roaming far in her delightful dreams about her Eagle. His triumph had been so complete that he had been elevated to the post of assistant court physician to Saladin. By the decree of Saladin's vizier, Al-Alfadhel, his post was next only to Ibn Jumay.

But his fame, I was convinced, had sucked out much of the marrow of his work. His court status—which neither his pride nor his position in medicine allowed him to refuse— demanded his attendance at all functions. It interfered seriously with the completion of his *Mishneh Torah*, on which he had thus far spent eight years of work, night and day. It gave him no time at all for his mathematical and astronomical speculations, sheer recreation to his mind.

Most of all, the tales of his skill gave him a legendary stature among Moslems and Jews, from lowest to highest. From dawn until dusk his house lay under siege by rich and poor with life-and-death requests; sacks of money, offerings of food and drink were placed upon his doorstep as if in worship of a pagan god. I confess Maimonides did often achieve remarkable cures, oddly enough, it seemed, by the faith they had in his abilities. He damned outright Talmudic permissions to carry amulets as charms against disease, but they secretly created ones with his own name upon them. Often he cursed, under his breath, the day that he had saved Silver Dove—but his regrets vanished when he was in her charming company.

All this, one may imagine, left him with little space to administer further duties, such as those of rabbi and dayyan. For Maimonides, as chief of the Egyptian Jews, had risen to be no less than a rival for the favor of his people against the fabled Gaon of Bagdad, his childhood friend, Samuel ben Ali. At first he had attempted to escape this bondage; he flatly refused the title of Nagid. Yet though the title was not his, he could not avoid the labor and the decisions.

One of these was his duty of rescuing Jewish prisoners and slaves. In the terrible wars which swept back and forth across the civilized world like a deadly broom, the Jews suffered most. Slave markets of both sides became glutted with Jewish captives. It clearly became the duty of the Egyptian Jewish community—one of the richest in the world—to set the example for the redemption of captives.

To this end, Maimonides instituted the custom of gifts in the synagogues dedicated to such a purpose. But he found an unexpected resistance: The poor resented being unable to give as much as their more fortunate brothers. I smiled as I recalled very well his remarkable scheme for overcoming this prejudice.

One Sabbath, in the synagogue, he had risen from his seat on the bench at the eastern side and walked into the middle of the foursquare congregation of men. There he raised his hands for silence. He said: "We must provide ransom to the Christians and the Moslems for our enslaved people. We cannot expect them to be set free out of the generosity of the heathen."

321

"How shall it be done?" one voice demanded.

"A tax upon every family," came another voice.

Maimonides shook his head. "God forbid," he said levelly. "This I have thought upon and I would disgrace none, bankrupt none. We shall take from each according to his means, no more."

"This is impossible," sourly objected the first voice.

"There is no way but that it will put the poor to shame and puff up the rich," I added, anxious to register my opinion.

"There is a way," Maimonides said serenely.

"How?" demanded a half-dozen voices.

"To every house, rich and poor," Maimonides responded, "we shall send two locked boxes. The first will hold a sum contributed by myself. With it goes a key, with a note, asking the recipient to open the box and take what he needs, all or part, for ransom of a relative."

"This is folly!"

"There is the second box, empty. There will be a key with it, too."

"This scheme is well for the poor," I ejaculated, "but what of the rich?"

"Those who do not need money shall contribute to the empty box. Both shall pass from family to family, house to house. In this manner, all shall contribute to what is empty and take from what is full. No one shall know the difference between the boxes nor the amount each has contributed or taken, not even myself."

It was the wisdom of a Solomon indeed. That was the plan adopted by acclamation. Not always did it prove enough: Once and again we were forced to pawn the golden utensils of the synagogue or send a speedy messenger to impose taxes upon each congregation. It would not do to delay: Barbarous captors sometimes slit noses or cut off the ears of their prisoners if ransom was slow in coming.

Many times this act of mercy, we discovered, was repaid in full by the ransomed one. So evil men, knowing full well of this policy of Maimonides, often raised the prices of their captives. We Jews paid nearly thirty-five dinars, twice the usual price, for our countrymen; more than once, we groaned under a single payment of one hundred dinars. Sometimes we encountered those of our own who sued each other for sums advanced for ransom. Ultimately, these came to Maimonides for judgment, in his capacity as Ab Bet-Din, the presiding judge of the Great Court.

As for Jews who owned slaves, Maimonides was emphatic in his decrees. "The sages," he said, "have told us it is better to keep as one's servants, poor Jews and orphans rather than any others. He who increases the number of his slaves also increases sin and iniquity in the world from day unto day." This objection to slavery was not because my master thought highly of slaves. He emphasized the responsibilities which lay with the owner: "If a slave is found to be a thief, robber, kidnaper, constant fugitive, glutton, or the like, he cannot be returned to the seller, because all slaves must be expected to possess such traits." Fostat and Cairo were among the leading slave-marts of the world. The difficulties and hatred which Maimonides aroused must have been innumerable, perhaps accounting for his later woes. But he never deviated from his strict regard for what he believed to be justice. He even attempted to forbid the castration of slaves for eunuchs without, however, much success.

I shook my head in the moonlight as I thought of these things. I rejoiced inwardly at my own freedom as a poet. True, I was trapped in the delectable net of philosophy, but I was also young. I had love in gardens and wine in golden goblets and all the world before me: At that moment, into my heart, came the insidious gnat of a desire to travel, to stick my head into all the nooks of the world where there was anything marvelous or outrageous. To that misty night on the roof of Maimonides' house in Fostat I attribute still the ambition for travel which was later to be my salvation.

The sound of voices shouting below drifted up to me, over the sound of the frogs and the far hum of the night in the city. It seemed to come from directly before the house; then a hollow pounding. I ran to the parapet and looked over, down at the gate. I saw two slaves, dressed in fantastic livery. One banged against the door of the courtyard as the other held a lurid torch of reeds, dripping wax, blue and dim in the pestilent vapor from the Nile. Between them stood a small, heavily veiled figure, just emerged from an elaborate litter.

I could not but imagine it was another of Maimonides' patients. Coming to his house at this hour—while he took his much-needed rest—was unpardonable. My anger rose inside me, prickling my skin. I descended the stairs almost at a run, unbarred the door and flung it open—to find the still-thumping fist of the slave brandished before my nose. He mumbled an apology and fell back. The slight figure behind him came up to me. She slowly unveiled.

A woman. Such a woman I had never seen before. Older than I, with a face marked with the dust and weariness of travel, but fairer than a flower, with hair that glistened in the lamplight like a fall of gold. Her eyes that gazed soulfully at me were the most vivid blue I had ever seen; they implored me sweetly.

"Is this not the residence of the great Maimonides?" she asked. The chords of her voice thrilled the strings of my heart like fingers across a lyre.

"Y-yes," I stammered. "You are welcome." I was surprised at what I said; I had meant to turn her away.

Suddenly my dream of beauty was dissolved. A stifled shriek sounded behind me. I half-turned, to see Naomi. Her face was a mask of ugliness. She stared past me at the visitor.

"It is she!" she hissed. "It is she, the witch of Alexandria!"

"What do you say?" I cried.

"Yes," came another voice, calmer and deeper. I looked past Naomi. Maimonides advanced. He went past me and stood before the visitor, gazing at her with a look I could not understand.

"I have come to you for help," she said in a small voice. "I do not know, after such a long time, if I am welcome. I am in need of protection. There is no one else."

She hesitated on a sigh. Her eyes fell away and she blushed deeply. She seemed about to take flight like a bird. I stepped forward to plead for her but Maimonides spoke again. He held out both his hands. She took them with a quick gesture, uttering a small cry of gladness.

"Yes," Maimonides said. "You are welcome, Zamira."

CHAPTER 19

The Moslems tell the story of Mohammed, their Prophet, commanding a distant mountain to approach and worship him. When the mountain refused his invitation, Mohammed calmly accepted the laws of nature. "Very well," he said, "if the mountain will not come to Mohammed, Mohammed will go to the mountain."

So with Maimonides and the arrival of Zamira. If he would not go to her because of his father's pronouncements, he saw no reason why he should not accept her arrival. I taxed him with what I believed to be a fault of logic. He reproved me. "It is forbidden for a friend to act as a judge," he said coldly.

"I do not judge you," I replied. "Is it not written that it is a duty to bring an erring man back to the true path, to continue the admonition even until the erring one assaults his admonisher?"

"Do you wish a dayyan to assault his own disciple?" Maimonides inquired acidly. "Know that a man must never cast judgment behind him: The eyes are set in front, not in back."

I despaired at penetrating the armor of this false reasoning but I made a last effort. "What will the congregation of the Jews think of you, a strange Moorish woman in your house?" I demanded.

Maimonides regarded me contemptuously. "Is it not better to have such a woman in the house and think of God rather than to pretend to have God in the house and think of the woman?" I gaped at the unexpected response. He went on quickly: "Every night for years I have dreamed of Zamira. Now I need dream no longer. Know this, my Joseph: A man may have a wife by purchase—though this is wrong—or by public document or by usus, the embrace of each for the other. Zamira and I have been wedded in the eyes of God. But of this, keep your peace."

He rose and crossed to the linen-lined niche where hung his fringed robe and square black hat with white tassel. "Help me prepare for the sitting of the court," he said curtly. I did his bidding in silence.

For those not versed in our justice, be it made plain that we Jews have by custom established courts of all degree within our nation. First is the Great Sanhedrin, composed of seventy-one elders, the Nagid, as wisest and eldest, being its head. He occupies the traditional seat of Moses of old. On his right hand sits the next in rank, the Ab Bet-Din. This is Maimonides' post (in truth, that of the Nagid, since that seat is now unoccupied). In the days of Jerusalem, there were two lesser tribunals of twenty-three members, each set up in the Temple court and the Temple mount. But these have been dispersed for a thousand years. Courts of twenty-three are set up also in any town with a population of more than a hundred and twenty. In smaller villages courts of three are appointed.

In the Cairo Hall of Justice—despite its many cruel decisions, a most charming place of pure white marble with lace-like carvings and slender pillars, as if built of spun sugar—it is the custom to have three bronze judgment seats upon the dais. One is for the Moslem judge, another for the Jew. The third is occupied occasionally by a visiting potentate to observe the workings of Saladin's justice. It is true that the decrees of this court are subject to appeal to the caliph or his vizier, Al-Alfadhel, but in the majority of the cases, the verdict rendered remains final. Jews, of course, are accustomed to use their own tribunals. But often they appeal to this two-man court (though obnoxious because of its lack of a majority) to achieve an advantage.

From the beginning, Maimonides strove not only to administer righteousness but to persuade his Moslem colleague to a unanimous decision. It was a trying experience in legal diplomacy. My master suffered from increasing headaches and ill health: He was approaching the end of his task of writing the *Mishneh Torah*. At such times his nervous energy alone sustained the frail frame of his body. He went long periods without eating or drinking. But his search for justice was endless. "In our holy tongue," he said to me, "the word for truth is *emet*. It is formed of the first, middle, and last letters of our alphabet. Thus truth must begin, and end, and be maintained."

Despite the complicated mazes of our Jewish law—the Torah, the Talmud, the Responsa, the Midrash, even such things as the Targumim, the Musar, and the Masorah—Maimonides insisted on considering all to judge the particular. His logical thought—though somewhat faulty in private life, as I told him—commonly cut through to the heart of the fact. Nor did he neglect the most important: that of human nature. He was wary of those who came before him. His feeling was, he confided to me, that "All who come to court are equally foolish and guilty. One should think there is no truth in them while they are before the dais. But when they have gone, one should think of them as innocent, in considering their cases with a quiet mind and the evidence before one."

"There is that word 'fool' again," I grumbled, but he gave no response.

I was present during one of his early cases. In this he established his skill both at discovering truth and at frustrating evil designs. It was a case of a rascally Jew accused of a theft by a Moslem. Maimonides was given charge. Boldly, the defendant took advantage of what he believed to be a prejudice in his favor. He demanded the issue be decided not by law but by the chance of drawing lots. Instead of denying the impudent request of this wretch, as all expected, my excellent master allowed it. "I shall place two folded bits of paper in a bowl," he said. "You will select one. If it is marked GUILTY, you will be condemned."

"Who will write upon the bits of paper?" demanded the accused suspiciously. He stared with a roused hatred at his judge.

"I," Maimonides said. Forthwith he wrote upon the two pieces of parchment and folded them tightly. He placed them in a black glass bowl. It was presented to the man before the judgment seat. He hesitated, looked about him blackly, then seized one. Before he could be checked, he thrust it into his mouth and swallowed it.

"Now," he cried triumphantly, "look at the other one! I know your secret heart! You wrote the word GUILTY on both to trap me! But you have sworn to abide by this and I demand the result. Read the other! If it says GUILTY, then the one I have chosen must have said INNOCENT and you must set me free!"

The Moslem judge frowned and began to speak. But Maimonides arose and descended from the dais to confront the prisoner. Without showing the slightest emotion, he unfolded the remaining lot and showed it to the man. The accused read it aloud in a trembling voice. "It says INNOCENT," he faltered. He flew into a rage. "I have been tricked!" he shouted.

"You have indeed," Maimonides said, resuming his seat, "by your own foul nature. You have judged yourself. I wrote the word INNOCENT on both, to try your soul. You stand condemned but I shall reprieve you to stand trial by the law."

Thus the man was held to the charges and proved guilty. After that, none dared attempt to deceive a judge so upright and perceptive. The Moslem hailed his subtle mind. Not long after, Al-Alfadhel, hearing of his friend's skill in reading the mind and heart, sent for Maimonides. "I hear of nothing but your wisdom," he said, smiling, "and I know you will be willing to prove it to me."

"I shall do my poor best," Maimonides said, bowing deeply, fearing the cleverness of the vizier.

"Then tell me," said Al-Alfadhel cunningly, "which is the better religion, yours or mine?"

It was a question worthy of Solomon and Shaitan together. Maimonides bent his head in thought. Afterward, he confessed, his mind fell into a storm of confusion and dismay. "Our faith," he said carefully, "suits us better; it has led us by signs and miracles into a land where we may stand without fear before such mighty men as yourself. But your religion is better for you, since it gives you the power to rule the world."

"And the power to ask such questions?" cried Al-Alfadhel, laughing. He grew serious. "Come, come, my friend," he reproved Maimonides, "this is not a proper answer. It is not worthy of your mind. I appoint you to see me tomorrow and tell me the truth."

All that night Maimonides pondered and prayed. He found no answer. The next day he repaired to the court at the time set and again stood before the cushioned ivory armchair of the vizier. The plump Moslem, who in his master's absence held the powers of life and death, wagged a be-ringed finger at my master.

"Have you the answer?" he asked him.

"I have sought for guidance," Maimonides replied, staring at the sapphires and diamonds of the rings.

"What have you decided?"

Maimonides took a long breath. He spoke almost without thought, he said when he told me the story later.

"This morning, leaving my house," he began, "I suffered a humiliation. I beg you to judge of it before I answer."

"Granted and granted."

"As you know, my father, my brother, and I were formerly dealers in precious gems. One of our customers has two sons. They are jealous of each other and constantly quarrel for precedence. To keep the peace, not long ago he took his two rarest gems—which we had sold him in good faith—and presented one to each of them. This morning the sons appeared at my door. They demanded of me to appraise the gems and tell them which was more valuable."

"What did you tell them?" asked the interested Al-Alfadhel.

"I told them to return to their father. He would give them the true valuation of what they really desired: his love."

"Very good. Go on."

"Then," Maimonides said steadily, "they abused and cursed

me for not rendering a judgment to please one or the other. Tell me, O Great One, do I have a grievance?"

"You have been mistreated without cause!" returned Al-Alfadhel warmly. "Who are these rascals?"

"May your own ears hear your words, merciful vizier!" exclaimed Maimonides. "You have rendered the judgment. You asked me which of these two gems of religion is the better. I can only say we must return to ask Our Father in Heaven before we can tell which is superior!"

Al-Alfadhel, who had asked his riddle only for amusement, shook with laughter and pleasure. But, as Maimonides was leaving, he bent to the ear of my master and asked in a whisper: "Tell me, O wise Jew, without penalty, on my pledge— which is truly preferable?"

Maimonides replied in no less confidential a tone: "Each is better than the other," an answer which pleased the vizier even more. He bestowed many rewards upon Maimonides and increased his favor in his bosom.

Alas, such was not the case outside Saladin's court! In the Christian year of 1180, Maimonides completed the *Mishneh Torah* in fourteen volumes—the only one of his great works which he wrote in Hebrew. He intended it only for the learned. In it, he deals with problems of health, philosophy, ethics, and medicine with enormous good sense. Yet instead of being hailed for the work of genius that it was, it was at first received with indifference. My master took to his bed with disappointment, as I expected. While he lay ill, I assumed the duty of disseminating the work as widely as possible. I ordered two hundred copies made by a dozen of the most skillful copyists. At my own expense, I sent them by messenger to every important congregation of Jews which existed in the world.

I could not foresee that my good intentions would bring down a shower of fire upon Maimonides' head. He complained feebly about my deed, but I believe he was secretly pleased. At least, upon regaining his health, he did not forbid its completion. "God knows my work is not adequate," he mourned. "I have been forced to do so much on my wanderings— aboard ships, in inns, by the roadside, through fire and storm."

Neither of us, however, expected the abuse he received from all sides. Maimonides was accused of trying to write a "new Talmud," of attempting to supplant Moses. Rabbi Abraham ben David of Posquieres, in France, an old friend and a man of wealth and learning, spoke derisively of my master as "that man" who had been totally mistaken in most of his conclusions, even "untrue in statement." He added that he saw "great confusion of thought" in the writing. He wounded Maimonides most deeply when he added that he thought him wholly wrong when he declared God not to be a substantial person. "Better and worthier men than this Maimonides have held the opposite," he wrote—hardly a statement to be made by a friend.

Perhaps the fact that the *Mishneh Torah* tries to be all things to all Jews set off these taunts and attacks. In it, Maimonides promulgates his greatest principle: "A person alone, without connection to any other person, finds his moral laws at rest, without meaning. They cannot offer him the opportunity of perfection. Thus it is the duty of man to associate himself with the community, both for his own and the general good."

Curiously enough, a final blow to my master's hopes for being understood in his ways came from a renowned Moslem healer, Abd al-Latif, who visited him in Fostat soon after his recovery. It was reported to Maimonides (after his guest departed, having stayed more than a week) that Al-Latif had declared his host to be highly ambitious. He said he detected a greed for money and power, and the weakness of pandering to wealthy great ones. It was merely an envious gibe based upon the incomprehension of the aloof character of my master, but it sank deep. He felt the criticism of Al-Latif more keenly because the latter had been so gracious under his roof. He expected the Moslems, I suppose, to be more tolerant than his own people.

Maimonides, to be fair, had anticipated that his opinions—often set down so briefly they seemed arrogant—would not improve his popularity with rabbis who wanted to use their own interpretations. Nor with judges who desired that the laws should remain intricate and confused, enabling them to find somewhere their justifications for a prejudiced verdict. So pained was Maimonides by the great controversy he had raised, that at last, though indirectly, he attempted to prevent the circulation of the *Mishneh Torah*. One Joseph ibn Gabir wrote him from Bagdad, which had become the seat and strength of the sentiment against my master, asking that he make an Arabic version. "If you want to study my work," Maimonides replied cautiously, "you will have to learn Hebrew. I do not intend to produce an Arabic version, as you suggest; to do so would be to lose the real truth of what I have written."

As a result of this vicious campaign, Maimonides became the butt of vile rumors. It was said that he was a *min*, a creature neither Jew nor Gentile. I feared for his anger and further despair at such invective. I was not, at this point, prepared for his extraordinary reaction of amusement.

It came about with the visit of an inquisitive rabbi from Bagdad. He was Pappus ben Kisma, a small man both in mind and body, with a face as yellow as a withered apple. Whether or not he was sent by Samuel ben Ali, we never knew; it was not polite to ask a guest such a delicate question. He came and was welcome. But from the first meal, his suspicions seemed confirmed.

A dish was set before him which appeared to be human hands with bloody stumps. Recalling the widespread reputation of Maimonides as a surgeon, Ben Kisma recoiled from the sight. He refused to eat.

"These are delicious," Maimonides said blandly, helping himself to one of the hands. We ate with gusto. I smacked my lips loudly. Poor Ben Kisma turned green, excusing himself as being listless after his long journey.

"Then you shall have some wine," Maimonides said. He looked at me solemnly. "Peter," he said, "bring the wine and pour it for our guest."

I could scarcely contain my laughter at being christened with a Gentile name, but I did as I was bid. Without surprise, I discovered our visitor shrank from a single sip. "Really," he said shakily, "I don't care to drink. I am not thirsty."

"Very well," Maimonides said genially, waving me away. "We shall have a special feast for you tomorrow. I shall order the cow with calf felled for your pleasure. We shall eat the tender meat of the unborn calf."

At this, Ben Kisma rose and, without excuse, fled from the table. Maimonides looked at me and, though I had never seen it before, I thought I glimpsed an almost imperceptible wink. I stuffed my napkin in my mouth and stumbled from the room. I hoped our guest would not hear my mirth.

That evening I heard Ben Kisma in the chamber next to mine. He was praying loudly and fervently to be delivered from the den of the heretic. I rose and went to his door, knocking lightly; there was no response. I entered without invitation. I found him backed against the bricks of the wall, paralyzed, staring at me with eyes bulged with fright.

"There is nothing to alarm you," I said reassuringly.

"Nothing!" he cried in hysteria. "You eat human hands!

331

You, a Gentile, serve the wine when your master knows such wine handled by an unbeliever is forbidden by law to all Jews! And I a respected rabbi!"

"A moment," I said, but Ben Kisma interrupted me with a torrent of stuttering words. "You expect me to eat meat that is not slaughtered and bled according to ritual!" he squalled.

"My dear friend," came the arresting voice of Maimonides from the doorway, "you disturb the rest of the household with your complaints. May I explain?"

"There is nothing to explain!"

"Indeed there is." Forthwith Maimonides presented him with the silver platter of human hands. "These are nothing more than carved cucumbers with a sauce of red berries. See! Look and taste!"

His commanding mien overcame the scruples of the trembling Ben Kisma. The visitor obeyed and found it to be true.

"You believed my pupil here, Joseph ben Aknin, was a Gentile. He is as good a Jew as either of us, believe me. But do you not know that Peter is an old Jewish name? It may be found in the Gemara, even as the name of a rabbi." He presented the text to the disbelieving Ben Kisma, who read with startled eyes.

"You ran from the thought of fresh meat from the calf, because you assumed it to be not kosher. Know that the calf taken live from a carcass after death need not be slaughtered ritually. It is made kosher with the selfsame benediction given its mother." This, too, he demonstrated by book and verse.

The rabbi from Bagdad commenced to gurgle excuses. Maimonides drew himself up sternly. "I realize who sent you here," he said. "I may guess what the charges are that you and your superior wish to bring against me. I am hated because of your ignorance, not because of my sins, God avert them! Return and tell Samuel ben Ali! Tell him the truth!"

Next morning, after a troubled night's sleep, the rabbi left our house with the most formal farewell. "It was a long way to come, simply to refuse to eat and drink," Maimonides commented.

"Yes," I said. "Longer still, simply to come and not to laugh at the jest."

"Jest?" asked Maimonides severely. "I never jest. I illumine the path of the stubborn and stupid." Yet I could swear I saw once more the slight movement of his eyelid.

"He has no mind of his own," I said. "He is a parrot for

332

Samuel ben Ali. He will not carry back your message but one which will suit the ears of the Gaon."

"Even a mindless parrot," replied Maimonides, "may sometimes speak the truth."

"How can that be?" I wondered.

"There was," Maimonides said, "a man who fancied himself injured by a neighbor. Though his neighbor had done him no ill, he brooded upon his wrongs and planned vengeance. Sitting in his house, day after day, his mind rotting evilly within him, he thought upon his imagined feud. Then, at last, he took his sword and whetted it. He went forth to his neighbor's door with murder in his heart.

"Now the neighbor and his wife and children had left to visit in another quarter of the city. Their dwelling stood closed, its portals barred from within. The only living thing in the house was a parrot in its cage. It was a stupid bird. It had learned to say three words only: 'Who is it?'

"The revengeful man beat upon the door. The parrot, hearing his blows, squawked: 'Who is it?'

"The visitor paused, then slyly replied: 'It is the judgment of God.'

" 'Who is it?' cried the parrot again.

" 'It's the judgment of God, it's the judgment of God!' shouted the roused man.

" 'Who is it?' shrieked the parrot once again.

"The man beat furiously on the locked door. 'It's the judgment of God, it's the judgment of God, it's the judgment of God!' he bellowed. As it happened, so enraged was he that he had a visitation. The blood left his heart, rushing to his head. He fell dead in a fit.

"Then came some passers-by, attracted by the noise of his beating on the door. They found the man dead before the threshold. They looked at each other in astonishment.

" 'Who is it?' one of them asked in bewilderment.

"From within, the cracked voice of the parrot made reply: 'It's the judgment of God.' "

It is not blasphemy to say it was the judgment of God that brought about the crushing of the Christians and upheld the right arm of our lord Saladin in those years. The millstones of the times whirled faster and faster, blurring the eye of history, spraying blood and flesh in every direction. The most powerful matched their might with the art of the most cunning; the odds were no more understood than the cast of knucklebones by children at play. But it was evident from the first that signs and portents had been given to the Moslem hosts of our caliph, to his personal army of mamelukes, to the bands of his emirs. One after another, the designs of a host of enemies of Egypt were destroyed.

The wicked confusion of these times set brother against brother. In Egypt itself, Jews rose against Jews to the sorrow of Maimonides. My master had obeyed the *pidyon shebuim*, the mandate of the Torah concerning the delivery of captive brethren by ransom from the clutches of their captors. Now he found himself forced to free his countrymen from their own inner bondage.

From his first arrival in Fostat, Maimonides had been aware of the rivalry between the two great sects of Jews. The Rabbanites (among whose number he and I counted ourselves) were those who interpreted the precepts of religion in a tolerant fashion. But for three hundred years there had been a growing cult of stiff-necked Jews, the Karaites, led originally by one Anan ben David of Babylon, who clamored for absolute and literal obedience to the Torah without regard for the opinions of the rabbis. The feeling between the two grew so great that a Rabbanite would cross the road to avoid meeting a Karaite. There was neither religious co-operation nor social relations. Business dealings were carried on with a maximum of hypocrisy, even to sharp practices. Marriage, circumcision, eating at the table, even the burial of the dead, were carried on separately. The Rabbanites supported Saladin; the Karaites plotted with the Shiites.

It was a state of affairs fraught with the greatest danger for all Jews. The Christians and Moslems, if persecution came, would not distinguish one from the other. Maimonides observed that "The text of the Torah is eternal, but its spirit must be interpreted by the holy men in each age," and quietly set about to heal the schism. One of his first Responsa, in reply to a fiery Karaite query composed to sound out his feelings, dealt firmly with the problem: "The House of Israel must be one united house. Nothing whatever should create dissension. You are wise and understanding people; you must know how serious are the consequences of discord and to what disasters it may lead." To a similar query from the Rabbanites, he replied: "We must be patient and tolerant with our brothers. We all spring from the seed of Abraham, we all obey the laws of Moses, and we all acknowledge one God."

While thus attempting to heal such open wounds with the

salve of peaceful words, Maimonides found himself confronted with a case in court which became famous as the basis for the conciliation of the controversy. Since it was to be tried according to Jewish law, Maimonides occupied the center bench. Alharizi ibn Adid, the lean-faced Moslem chief justice, sat with folded hands on his right. A visiting chieftain from the Sudan provinces, his dark-shining, delicately molded face in contrast to his white robes, occupied the seat of the observer to the left. It was a worthwhile custom, modeled after that of the old Romans, to have court visitors, and it was used to spread the knowledge of Moslem ways and laws.

Within the alabaster tracery of the hall, the spectators stood at a distance. Red-robed guards with heavy maces, to be used to thwack those who became unruly, herded them together. Before these, just beneath the dais, stood the two who sought a decision.

The first one was an elderly landholder, leader of the Karaites in the divided Jewish community. He called himself Anan ben David, assuming the name of the founder of his sect. He himself was a stooped, sour-faced man with an expression of grim triumph. The other, younger and fatter, was Ehu ben Mishael, a Rabbanite merchant of good standing but inconsiderable estate. His face was pale. He perspired freely as if he had abandoned hope. He kept his eyes fixed imploringly upon Maimonides' face.

The secretary of the court rose briskly from his small ivory-inlaid table. He intoned the articles of the complaint lodged by Ben David. It appeared Ben Mishael had failed to pay him the considerable sum of twenty-five hundred dinars due. He demanded a bankruptcy-and-seizure declaration, enabling him to take the home, goods, and business of the merchant.

Ceasing his drone, the secretary rearranged his robes and sat down. Maimonides cleared his throat. He addressed Ben Mishael. "Are the facts of this accusation true?" he asked.

"Yes, Great Judge," Ben Mishael responded in a barely audible voice.

"Speak more loudly. Will you be left penniless?"

"It will take all I have."

Maimonides pursed his lips, pulling at his beard. "How has it come about that you borrow money which you are unable to repay?"

Painfully, Ben Mishael made response. "I had expected two ships this week," he said. "But they have not been reported,

335

even at Alexandria. I had counted on the ninety days of grace which a true Jew would have granted."

Maimonides turned to the vulturine Ben David. "Is it true you have refused this grace?"

"I am not bound to such a favor," the older man said sharply. "The law is clear. There is no mention of it. It is merely a custom, one in which I have no interest."

"What interests you?"

"I demand from the court my money, in accordance with the law!"

Maimonides nodded. "Was there interest to be added to the whole amount?" he inquired.

The question cracked the face of Ben David into a crooked smile. "O upright Judge," he said, "you try to snare me. I know the law against usury as well as yourself. I asked no interest. The money alone is mine. I ask judgment."

Maimonides considered, mechanically lacing and interlacing his long fingers. "But is it not unnatural for one Jew to suck the blood of another?" he asked. "Perhaps there is some other reason for your demand than the cold letters of the law."

Neither man replied. Their faces seemed to tighten and grow rigid, one despairing, the other waiting in confident disdain. The silence grew until it was almost palpable in the room. Suddenly, from the rear of the crowd, came a confused movement and a voice. One of the guards strode toward the source, his mace lifted threateningly.

Maimonides raised his hand. "If there is anyone who can add to the facts of this hearing," he said, "allow him to come forward."

From among the spectators emerged a haggard young man, his face working under the stress of fear and anger. He advanced and fell prostrate, his thin rump jutting upward through his gown. He rose and burst out: "My name is Ezekiel, son to Anan ben David and I speak only to light a lamp in the darkness."

"Speak," Maimonides said as the young man paused for breath.

"I wished to marry Ruth, daughter of Ehu ben Mishael, and she wishes it and we still desire with all our hearts to be united, to be fruitful for Israel, and yet, as you know, my father and her father forbid it so that we who were once betrothed are now strangers!" The youthful Ezekiel broke into sobs. His emotion was echoed by the tears of a young dark-haired girl who came running heedlessly out of the huddle of spectators to kneel by him.

"This is not part of the task of the court," Maimonides said firmly.

Ezekiel threw back his tear-stained face, the girl's arms about him. "It was part of the bargain!" he shouted passionately. "My father would not grant Ehu ben Mishael the money he needed unless he promised to keep his daughter from marrying me!"

His flood of words ceased as Maimonides raised his hands. An expression of relaxed contentment came over the features of my master, like that on the face of one who has solved an enigma. He turned to Ben Mishael.

"Is this true?" he asked gently. The man nodded, unable to speak.

"Do you love your son?" said Maimonides to Ben David. The elderly man hesitated, then made a grudging bob of his head. "Of course I do," he snapped.

"Do you love him as a Jew?"

"Certainly!"

"Do you know what gives him pain?"

"How should I know that?"

"Only if you know what makes him suffer can you know what it is to love him." Maimonides' voice sharpened and changed. He leaned forward toward those before him. The other judge and the Nubian visitor, engrossed by the scene, leaned with him.

"Is it true you consented to lend this money only on condition that he would not allow his daughter to marry your son?"

"What is wrong with that?"

"You are guilty of usury!"

"Not so, Mighty Judge!" The voice of Ben David rose and splintered. He flapped his arms, winding them together convulsively. "It was but a foolish whim!"

"A whim that tied the sack of money?"

"No, no!"

"Would you have given him the money otherwise?"

Maimonides was merciless. The agitated man was silent. Maimonides turned to the secretary of the court. "Do you have the agreement?" he asked. The secretary nodded and handed up the document. Maimonides scanned it and raised his eyes. He tapped the stiff lettering. "It is written here as a condition," he said coldly. Ben David's face contorted. He sank to his knees.

"The law of the Talmud is clear on the crime of one Jew lending money to another Jew on usury. The court may, if it wills, sell you as a slave to the man you accuse and all you have will become his."

"Mercy, mercy!" moaned Ben David.

"Always it is those who show no mercy who think themselves most deserving of it," Maimonides remarked to his colleague. The Moslem judge nodded somberly; the visitor from Nubia smiled, his teeth a startling white.

"Let me say," Maimonides resumed, "that usury is called *neshech* because he who takes it eats the flesh of his fellow man. He who lends on usury is deemed to be one who has denied the God of Israel."

His even tones were interrupted by wails and the thumping sound of a head being beaten against the tiles as Ben David did penance. Maimonides gestured to a guard to lift him erect.

"But charity is higher than the law. There are eight ways it may be given. The lowest is to give grudgingly; a little higher is to give less than one should; higher, to give enough when asked; higher still, to give without being asked; higher than this, to give without knowing the receiver; higher again, to give with knowledge but without the recipient's knowing of it; better yet, to give without knowing to one unknowing; best of all, is to take up a Jew that has been crushed and to give him a loan or enter into partnership with him—and forget the deed for the glory."

"It shall be forgotten," moaned Ben David in the arms of the guard.

"And the children?"

"May they marry when they please!"

"With your blessing?"

"With my blessing!"

"You may go," Maimonides said and watched Ben David make his way blindly from the court. As he vanished, Ben Mishael stepped forward, his face beaming. "Omniscient Judge," he began and his voice failed. Maimonides had not responded to his grateful smile. The face of my master remained unforgiving.

"Ehu ben Mishael," Maimonides said harshly. "It is equally forbidden to borrow money with the usury of your daughter's happiness as it is to lend it with the usury of a son's happiness. We will now deal with your case."

It was not the last chance Maimonides had to bind together the factions with equal justice, but the case of Ben David against Ben Mishael was the first slender cord tossed across the abyss. Thenceforward his words of advice to all who inquired were always the same: "Respect, honor, kindness, and humility must be shown by all Jews toward each other as long as they are within decent bounds and do not scoff at the Torah or the Mishnah. The Talmud tells us to be friends toward heathen and idolaters; how much more should we be toward those of our own."

Maimonides spoke from the bottom of his heart of friendship for those of alien faith. He never agreed that the Moslems were pagan. He declared to me that they had no trace of idolatry in their hearts: "They confess the unity of God, strictly and unconditionally, unlike many Christians. Perhaps both have pagan symbols in their houses of worship, but their hearts are directed to God, and such symbols are mere relics of an earlier day." Maimonides foresaw the recovery of precious Jerusalem for the Jews by the agency of Saladin; hence every dart directed against the Moslem leader sank into his own breast.

The green crescent of the Moslems expanded to the full and none rejoiced more than Maimonides. In the autumn of the year 1187, I returned to the house from the market place in Fostat, followed by a servant laden with fish for the Sabbath, and discovered my master in the forecourt. Seated on a sandstone bench under the pale withering vine leaves, he stared at the wall, face fixed, eyes immobile. He appeared to have fallen into a fit, but his face was marked with ecstasy.

I knelt in consternation, clasping his knees. At my touch, he stirred. He put his hand upon my head. I felt its quivering warmth. "Three months ago," Maimonides said in a hushed voice, "by the will of God, blessed and glorious be His Name, the forces of the all-conquering Saladin met those of the Christians near defiled Tiberias. Joseph, my son, like the hosts of the Amalekites they were ground into nothingness! The king of Jerusalem, his brother, the masters of the Temple and the Hospital—even the pitiful bits of wood that they call the 'true cross' of their idol, Jesus Christ—were captured! Joseph, Joseph—and now Jerusalem is ours!"

My body went limp. My heart expanded in my bosom until I felt I should suffocate. Without knowing it, I sought relief. I heard myself chanting one of the verses that Judah Halevi

339

had written to his beloved city, throned in the heart of all Jews:

> "To thee, I know, will God return
> At last to take His rest;
> And here, upon His altars, burn
> The sacrificing breast.
>
> "Elect are we who wait to view
> His holy coming home;
> Knowing, as God our faith renews,
> We shall be His alone.
>
> "Here shall the chosen know their peace;
> Here shall we lose our shame;
> Within Thy bosom find our ease—
> And joyful sing Thy name."

In low excited accents, Maimonides commenced to recite what the messenger from the north had announced to Al-Alfadhel. Even as we spoke, we could hear riotous sounds of celebration beginning in Fostat itself.

For more than the lifetime of Maimonides, the government of Jerusalem had been a hollow shell. After the brother and cousin of the great conqueror Godfrey had died, the kingdom had sunk by mere process of inheritance to the rule of a woman, Sybilla. She married Guy of Lusignan, a handsome prince of such low repute that his own brother, Geoffrey, said scornfully: "If they have made him a king, surely I should be made a god!"

Yet for a dozen years supplies came in by sea from the Christian countries to sustain the city, and the Templars and Hospitalers fought well. The occasion for Moslem attack was given when a soldier of fortune, Raynald of Châtillon, married the mistress of Kerak—ancient Kir of Moab—a fortress built to the east of the Dead Sea athwart the Damascus-Egypt caravan route. Raynald, who had been seventeen years a Moslem prisoner, harried the traders and scoured the Red Sea with pirate ships; Saladin was patient, even when the villain harassed pilgrims on the way to Mecca. But when Raynald attacked a caravan in which rode Saladin's sister, the caliph bestirred himself. He called his people to a holy jihad. He took an army of eighty thousand men into Palestine and besieged Tiberias. Guy of Lusignan hastened from Jerusalem to defend it, but his chief vassal, Raymond of Tripoli, had betrayed him by supporting Saladin and by leading him into the desert of Hattin. Here twenty thousand Christians were destroyed. All the knights were executed. Guy and Raynald were captured; the first held to ransom, the other slaughtered by Saladin himself. Three months later, our caliph appeared before the gates of Jerusalem.

"Here," Maimonides said, raising his hands, "the will of Heaven once more intervened. Though sixty thousand people were within the walls, Sybilla shook with fear and the barons and lords quarreled. Most of the populace, I have heard, preferred the just rule of Saladin to the tyranny of the Christians. Within a fortnight, the walls were breached by fifteen cubits, a dozen banners planted in it. Mark the generosity of Saladin! He offered to let the inhabitants remain, if all Franks and Latins left within forty days—giving ten pieces of gold for each man, five for a woman, one for a child."

"This does not seem as generous as profitable to me," I remarked.

Maimonides snorted. "Our noble lord accepted thirty thousand byzants for as many as seven thousand of the poor and dismissed thousands more without ransom! He allowed a year for the caring of the sick and wounded, and most of his treasure was given to the poor!"

"Still," I said obstinately, "his allowing the Christians to go free was wise. They will go to other fortresses, to strain the resources of food and bring discord, as we well know."

"I will not hear treason against our ruler," Maimonides said pointedly. "The sages have said that a king precedes a prophet. We are obliged to follow him as long as he does nothing to conflict with the Torah." I was silenced but not convinced; Maimonides continued.

"With music and banners and joyful shouts did Saladin enter," he exclaimed lyrically. "The great mosque of Omar was cleansed, again consecrated to One God, its walls and floors washed with rose water. Four ivory chests with the images, vases, and relics of the Christians were seized. The golden cross at the summit of the dome was flung down and dragged through the streets!"

"Amen and amen," I murmured. Maimonides thrust me back. He stood up, stretching out his arms.

"The rabbis have said that the sins of him who lives in Palestine are forgiven," he cried in a loud voice. " 'The people that dwell therein shall be forgiven their iniquity,' the holy

Isaiah has declared!" He brought his hands together as if in prayer and said in a low voice:

"This day shall be blessed forever. Joseph, dear to me, assemble the household and our goods. We shall make preparations to return to the land of our fathers!"

CHAPTER 20

Even as Ben Sirach says in Ecclesiasticus, there is a time for every purpose under heaven—and the purpose of Maimonides was not ripe in the womb of time. Saladin decreed—and the mouth of Al-Alfadhel repeated it to my master—that no Jew would be admitted to Jerusalem for the space of two years. Having conquered the citadel at the cost of much blood and treasure, the caliph did not wish to put to chance those uprisings and tumults which might ensue from immigration.

"Curse not the king, even in your thought," Maimonides said to me mechanically. Nevertheless, he was afflicted by the decree. The palsy shook him more often and he fell to speaking of himself shabbily: "An old, infirm man," he said sadly. None of his services to the court was abated. If anything, they increased to such a degree that he found time scarcely to administer admonition and medical treatment to his own people. When Naomi timidly brought him a letter from her father, the rabbi Japhet ben Eliahu of Acre, my master poured out his heart. Japhet spoke of coming to visit him and Maimonides was anxious to dissuade him.

He rebuked him gently for not having communicated with his daughter and himself for so long a space and went on. "Know," he wrote, "before God, that in order to write this to you, I have escaped to a secluded spot, where people would not think to find me, sometimes leaning for support against the wall, sometimes lying down on account of my excessive weakness, for I have grown old and feeble.

"With regard to your wish to come here to me, I confess how greatly your visit would delight me, for I truly long to commune with you. I would anticipate our meeting with even

342

greater joy than you. Yet I must advise you not to expose yourself to the terrible perils of any sea voyage; as for a trip by land, the dangers of the Franks and the Moslems and the wandering bands of savage slaves are even more to be feared. Beyond seeing me and my doing all I might to honor you, you would not derive any advantage from a visit. Do not expect you would be able to confer with me on any scientific subject, even for an hour, either by day or by night; the following is my daily occupation.

"I live at Fostat and the caliph resides at Cairo; these places are a three-mile journey distant from each other. My duties to the caliph are very heavy. I am obliged to visit him or his vizier every day, early in the morning; and when he or any of his children, or any of the inmates of his harem, are indisposed, I dare not quit Cairo but must stay during the greater part of the day in Cairo. It also frequently happens that one or two of the royal officers fall sick. I must attend to their healing also. Hence, as a rule, I repair to Cairo very early in the day and, if nothing unusual happens, I do not return to Fostat until the afternoon. Then I am almost dying with hunger. I find my anteroom filled with people, both Jews and Gentiles, nobles and common people, judges and bailiffs, friends and foes—a mixed multitude who have waited for my return.

"I dismount from my animal, wash my hands, go forth to my patients and entreat them to bear with me while I partake of some slight refreshment, the only meal I take in the twenty-four hours. Then I attend to my patients and write prescriptions for their various ailments. Patients go in and out until nightfall—sometimes, I solemnly assure you, for two hours or more beyond that. I converse and prescribe for them while lying down from sheer fatigue and, when night falls, I am so exhausted I can scarcely speak.

"As a result, no Jew can have any private interview with me except on the Sabbath. On this day the whole congregation, or at least a majority, come to me after the morning service. I instruct them as to their proceedings during the whole week; we study together a little until noon, when they depart. Some of them return and read with me after the afternoon service until evening prayers. In this manner I spend that day.

"I have related to you only part of what you would see if you were to visit me. Now, when you think of visiting me, I beg that you will reconsider, for my time is, as I say, occupied to the full."

His letter to Japhet was a fair summary of what I saw and must acknowledge. I am proud to say it was at my suggestion that he took a larger, finer house on the further side of Fostat for the accommodation of this constant horde of hangers-on and for his own privacy. Here he established proper quarters for the women: Yaltah and Naomi, Zamira and little Silver Dove, and the female Abyssinian slaves. Their rooms, plastered with painted linen bearing bright colored figures (but never the human image), were furnished with luxury. They surrounded a courtyard of two fountains with marble basins, fruit trees and flowers, and seats of ease— much as he remembered his father's grounds in Cordova, Maimonides told me. His own room was a simple cell. It held no more than his mat, a table and two oil lamps. A great wooden cabinet in the corner was filled with manuscripts; there were pegs in a shallow niche for his black turbans and gowns of honor.

It was rare that Maimonides was able to join the rest of his household in the women's quarters, but it was refreshing to him. He delighted in the tinkling fall of water, the odor of the flowers (especially after the first dews had fallen), the silent attendance of his sister and sister-in-law, the dancing and singing of Zamira, the impudent adoration of the little Frankish girl. It was a refuge of quiet, a totally different world from court intrigue, the babble of the streets, and the loneliness of study—even an escape from the customs of our own race.

The faith of the Jew is from everlasting to everlasting like the basalt of the upper cataracts of the Nile; but the Jew himself is like the tiny chameleon of Egypt which suns itself in the crevices. As the shadows of other civilizations sweep over him, the Jew changes, though he remains secure on the rock. So it was with women in the house of Maimonides: Jewish, in what was most like a Moslem harem.

Not that the women of Maimonides were like those of the Moslems. Many are ignorant of the secret influence of such Moslem women in affairs. The female of the harem is often more masterful than the male; she weeps less and quarrels more, making decisions and tyrannizing over her husband. Privately, and behind the lattice, she is commonly powerful enough to shift the base of an empire, clever enough to remain anonymous—and often perverted love binds women together in evil. The Moslems know this yet complain they are powerless, saying that three things devour mankind and are never

344

satisfied: Hell, the grave, and the sexual parts of a woman. Mohammed is supposed to have declared that Satan rejoiced at the creating of Eve, saying: "You are half my armies, the shaft with which I shoot and never miss."

Maimonides did not tolerate the rule of women. Even to Zamira, whom he treated with such tender regard, he was capable of rebuke. Seeing her dressed in an imitation of armor with a jeweled helmet on her head, he declared: "That is not for your beauty, dear Zamira. Adorning yourself with the dress of men is punished, in my faith, with stripes—just as I should be punished if I put on women's garments. Since we are what we are, we obey the law: I cannot, as you see, shave the corners of my head because it was the custom of idolaters." He rewarded her obedience with bright-hued gowns and ornaments of gold and jewels.

Nevertheless, Maimonides agreed with the Moslems in their categories of the seven virtues of women: neither merry nor sad, neither talkative nor musing, neither adorned too much nor neglectful in dress, and at all times master of herself. For who, says the poet, can stem a furious flood or a woman frantic with lust? Mohammed was too lax in detecting their sins; he demanded a witness to see the needle in the kohlpot, as the Moslems so delicately put it. Maimonides trusted his household, though, true to the custom, he forbade their going out alone or unveiled. He quoted with approval a saying of Al-Alfadhel: "If the woman is a jewel, she must be locked up as in a casket, not left about for the covetousness of the world."

Zamira, who had abandoned house and friends in Alexandria forever, stealing away secretly up the Nile to be all things to my master alone, became the model of mistress and wife. She ruled the women of his house by love and fear: the love of Silver Dove and the slaves, the fear and secret hatred of Naomi. Yaltah regarded her as a sister, faithful to her joys and sorrows. I alone know this. In those days, perhaps I was more than a little in love with Yaltah myself, an increasing affection since our startling meeting so many years before. We maintained an intimacy which Maimonides' sister did not share with any other.

With gentle decorum, Zamira celebrated the mo'ed of the Sabbath, Pesshim, Shekalim, Yoma (though she did not comprehend the meaning of Passover), Sukkah, Rosh ha-Shanah, even the Bezah and Hagigah. Maimonides was pleased with her demeanor, with her ability to memorize the harder parts of the rituals. He even translated into Arabic many of the prayers for her use and had them copied into fair books. (Of these, I still have one in her memory, blessed is she among women.) As the consort of a Jew, Zamira strictly observed all ordinances of the Law. She became esteemed in the eyes of Maimonides as much for her piety as her beauty.

One question I desired to ask her privately, because of my inner doubts, in regard to what Naomi had told me that Maimon, father of my master, had said. Had Zamira been mistress to Samuel ben Ali of Bagdad? This I never dared speak about until that final day when all the world changed and our pleasant life broke like the shards of a pottery jar about our heads. Less than twenty months after Zamira arrived, it began to be apparent that God desired a testing of the faith of Maimonides.

At first, it may be guessed, Maimonides had found little time to spend in the women's court. His old habit of studying at night was still with him. During the day he was at the beck of Saladin or Al-Alfadhel or at the courts. Yet after his double disappointment of being excluded from Jerusalem and enduring the sharp criticisms of his *Mishneh Torah*, he seemed to slack in his incessant studying, to enjoy life more for its own sake. It delighted my heart. I was not sorry to see the famed Zamira perform for my master, she who had been so famous in Alexandria and had given up such a life to become the spouse of a humble Jewish physician.

Indeed, she sang and sawed with her small bow across the slender neck of the rabab like an angel possessed. She often repeated the melancholy wailing songs of Spain that transported Maimonides back to his beloved Cordova—then mischievously broke into the swinging, rhythmic common tunes that made him clap his hands. Dancing, she was like a crimson leaf whirling in the early winds of autumn, her garments lifting about her to expose the white limbs that never became hairy like Sheba's or swarthy like those of the Moslem women. Always, Silver Dove danced with her, spinning miraculously on her ivory leg, crying out in dizzy pleasure. At the end, Maimonides never failed to stretch out his arms to them both, to welcome them panting into his loving embrace. I averted my eyes.

More than once I watched Naomi. What I had found long ago to be her secret passion for her husband's brother seemed stronger than ever. Again and again I saw her features convulse with rage or misery as she saw this exhibition of pure

346

love. Nor was I alone in observing this: Yaltah, too, was a witness to Naomi's feelings. Between Yaltah and myself were exchanged those steady looks which are the pledges of friends in confidence; they gave us support and faith in each other.

As a man grows older, he realizes at last that death is his friend, and life his enemy. Still, he wonders what may lie beyond the barrier of soft reposeful darkness. Often, Maimonides and I commenced such discussions only to break them off over wine and music and the glances of Silver Dove and Zamira. Women care little for the soul and what happens after death; to them, their destruction comes with the wasting of their beauty.

I noticed the thought of death gave Maimonides somehow another view of his existence, of its pleasures and how fleeting they were: He abandoned his studies completely for a time and surrendered himself to song and wine with the women. His face took on increased animation; he cut his beard more sharply and his clothes were of richer stuff. When one came posting upstream from Alexandria, telling him that Averroës had left Bagdad under suspicion of heresy for his beliefs (and possibly for his aid in Silver Dove's surgery) but was now forgiven and domiciled at Marrakesh in the Maghreb, Maimonides frowned and said enigmatically: "It is written that God is a devouring fire, but He is not a fire." And when the same messenger related that his old rival, the grossly fat Zuta, had been found dead in the Jewish quarter of the Delta city, a curiously carved dagger thrust into his throat, Maimonides made no comment beyond a murmur: "He that chastiseth nations, is He not right in all His doings?"

With this mood of his came an increasing inclination to discussion rather than writing. I recall one evening that our talk ran to the evidence of God in the world. In these talks Maimonides—like so many great teachers—chose to avoid the flat statements or decrees of principle in favor of stories. I asked him: "Master, how does one find God? He seems so far away, so unreachable for man!"

He considered, his fingers in his graying beard. At length he replied: "A king is in his palace, my son Joseph. Imagine his subjects: part of them in the land, part abroad. Some of those at home go about their business, their backs turned to the king's palace. Others want to seek him in his high dwelling-place but they do not know the road, nor would they recognize the palace if they found it. But some find the way and plod around the walls, looking for the gate; others find it immediately and enter the anteroom; still others succeed in entering into the inmost rooms of the palace, even into the presence of the king himself. But even these do not—immediately upon entering—see the king nor speak to him. For another barrier lies between them and his person before they can hear his words or speak to him. Yet once this is past, there is perfect freedom and happiness. Must I explain what I say?"

"I understand," I replied. "Those afar are those without knowledge of God. Those with their backs turned hold false doctrines about Him and go farther from His presence at every step. Those who seek the palace gate are most of us who follow the Divine Word but are ignorant. Those who perambulate around the walls are those who study but have no conviction. Those who choose to investigate come into the anteroom; only those who have a true knowledge of God come into the inner chambers. But tell me, master, who are those who conquer the last barrier?"

"They are the blessed dead," Maimonides replied.

I considered this. At last I replied: "If there is a road to the palace, master, what is it?"

"It is the road of intellect and faith," Maimonides said. "Those who follow the commandments without thinking are those who build the foundation of the sacred dwelling; those who pray with their lips and mind, while their hearts are occupied elsewhere, erect the structure. Only those whose hearts and minds are entirely occupied with God can enter in and live there forever."

"Can we understand God?"

"There is a boundary. Beyond this, no one can pass. Many things are beyond human understanding. But it is our duty to approach the wall and attempt to peep over it, if God wills."

"Then the road is one which follows the training of the mind?"

"If it is done rightly. One should never start at the end by studying at random and expecting to wake up one day perfect in comprehension. The mind must be tutored and self-taught gradually. An infant fed with wheat bread, wine, and meat will die—not because the food is unfit but because the child is unable to digest it. Thus the truth is revealed bit by bit, unswaddled from its enigmas, paradoxes, and riddlings purposely put about it by the wise men."

I recall this occasion very well: It was the night before the Sabbath upon which arrived a unique visitor. That morning we were chatting drowsily in the cool of the courtyard when Naomi, ordinarily forbidden these moments of masculine relaxation, begged permission to come in.

"Speak," Maimonides said testily to her, "what is it you desire."

"One is outside," Naomi returned with downcast eyes. "He is not willing to go away. He has heard of your fame and wishes to speak to you. But he is a Frank."

"Send him away," Maimonides said peremptorily. "It is the day of rest."

"Wait, my master," I broke in. "He may be interesting. We are bored with our conversation; admit the truth."

Maimonides looked annoyed. He addressed himself again to Naomi. "Is this one noble?" he inquired.

"No. He is a beggar, a one-armed beggar. He claims he has sung as a jongleur in all the courts of Europe and Asia except those of Cathay."

"A beggar!" Maimonides was speechless at this impudence on the Sabbath. I determined to have my way.

"Better and better," I applauded. I leaned to my master. "This a queer rascal, on my head," I murmured. "Why should you not allow yourself a respite from the rigid rules that you observe so well so often? Let us see the fellow. He will amuse you and you need to be amused, so long have you been solemn."

The eyes of Maimonides considered me. "Your curiosity, my Joseph," he murmured, not deceived in the least, "will cause your damnation." He raised his voice to Naomi. "Let him come in, if you wish."

The next moment, it seemed in a bound, the stranger stood before us. His muscular body wore a costume of ragged leather, belted by a rope, with boots of raw animal-skin. He carried nothing except a short-bladed knife and a gittern slung back over his shoulder. His right shoulder-socket showed empty, contrasting with the thick thews of the left arm. He did not look at me. He locked glances with Maimonides.

"You do not know me, eh?" he asked, grinning, showing jagged yellow teeth like a lion.

"No," Maimonides said stiffly.

The man looked at him steadily. He showed no fear, only an arch disdain. He was stocky, of great strength, perhaps more than fifty. His long minstrel's hair, yellow and bleached

from the sun, streamed below his shoulders. His eyes crinkled
in crow's-feet in his tanned face. He stood with his feet wide
apart as he surveyed us. His manner was gay with an inner
delight.

"Do you remember a certain dawn years past at the tournament field in Toledo?" he demanded.

"Toledo?" Maimonides asked, his face puzzled.

"You had a brother and he had a quarrel with a squire,"
the man returned easily.

Recognition came into my master's face. He leaned toward
the man, his hostility vanished. "My brother David is in Abraham's bosom," he said.

"Then he is dead," the other returned, but not in a light
tone. He crossed himself swiftly.

"You," Maimonides continued, "are Noel de Rivière, are
you not?"

The stranger laughed. "I am Noel, the minstrel," he replied. "I sing my way from land to land, seeking what is not,
finding what I do not wish. I heard of you. I told myself that
a song between old friends might not be amiss."

"I do not care for songs," Maimonides said.

"But I do," Silver Dove exclaimed. "Sing one for me!" She
appeared from nowhere, darting out like a bird from the
branches of the massive olive by the north fountain.

"I am charmed by this little one," Noel said. He looked
down at her and his voice warmed with affection. "Joanne,
allow me, great lady: I have not yet finished my devoirs to
your master."

"You know one another?" inquired Maimonides swiftly.

"We met in the street only yesterday," the minstrel said,
ruffling the child's hair as she clung to his waist.

"I listened to him sing," Silver Dove said impetuously. "It
was very pretty. Old Eagle, you need someone to sing to you,
a man, not a woman!"

"It was she who invited me," Noel explained. "Allow me
to accept the blame if she did wrong."

"She is no slave," Maimonides said shortly. "She is free and
mistress of her will."

"Eh?" said Noel musingly. He flung back his long hair and
examined Maimonides with penetrating blue eyes. "You have
become much older," he said.

"And you remain young."

Noel lifted his shoulders expressively. He shook his head.
"I have none of the cares of your position," he told my mas-

350

ter. "I share none of the world except that of music and rejoicing and faraway lands. Turks and Moslems and Christians
—and, now, you see, Jews—welcome me for the pittance of a
verse or two."

"You are welcome for what you are, not for what you
were."

"You are surprised to see me, eh?"

"Yes. But in my soul, there is a feeling of gladness, too.
You come from Spain, after all; and Spain is always in my
thoughts these days."

"Did you think me dead?" inquired Noel.

"Yes," Maimonides said briefly.

Noel shook his head again, his mane flying about him.
"Ah, so might I have been but for your grunting, complaining, compassionate countryman, Avenzoar. He stanched the
bleeding, allowed my arm to become poisoned just enough to
take it off painlessly at the joint. And here I am, healthy and
alive."

"You have become a singer of ditties," Maimonides said
accusingly.

Noel lifted his white eyebrows. "I sing of war, yes. I sing of
love, too. But I sing also of the Holy Cratella, the golden bowl
from which our Savior drinks every year on the night of the
Last Supper, in which His blood is miraculously preserved."

I could scarcely keep my face straight at this superstition,
but Maimonides' countenance was unmoved. "And have you
found it?" he asked.

"Who will ever find the end to a song?" wondered Noel.
Silver Dove hung adoringly about him, her arm around his
waist, looking up and drinking in his words.

"Do you believe in such a thing?" I asked.

"No, my friend," Noel returned amiably. "But it is poetry,
and that is the way a minstrel finds the path to truth."

"Why did you decide to quit the knightly life and become
a wanderer?" asked Maimonides.

"Ah," Noel said slowly, reflectively. "It was your brother
and his clever blow. When he had wounded me unto death,
as I lay on my mat of pain, it was as if, somewhere, a very
small door had opened for me. I could see into the shape of
all things in the world. Do you know what I saw?"

"He is a philosopher," I said amusedly to my master.

"What did you see?" Maimonides inquired.

"That all things are ridiculous, indeed. And beyond that

door there was singing and dancing and golden light and fair things."

"Sometimes," Maimonides returned somberly, "that has seemed so to me. But I see little rejoicing."

"I said to myself, knights are fools, kings are idiots, all men who swink and sweat and slave are blockheads. I shall be different. I shall be a stranger to it all, seeing it from the high place of peace. I shall show my contempt by living on the leavings of fair ladies, on the crumbs of their favor, sucking the blood of noble counts and barons."

"And has it proved profitable?" I asked.

"Nay," Noel responded, "not to the purse. I have not a groat nor a stiver. But it has been meat to my spirit. Now I care for nothing and none cares for me."

"I care for you," Silver Dove whispered at his side. He dropped an indescribable look on her head, as if it were a benediction, but said nothing.

"You play the instrument?"

"My gittern and I are inseparable."

"You have only one arm," I protested.

Noel gave me his friendly grin. Without a word, he reached into his pouch and took out a device of wire and wood. He thrust it firmly onto his chin. "See?" he said. "With my left hand I strum the strings. For the other—since I have nothing else—I use my jaw to fix this bit of wood across the strings, as I need to change the tune. I make a nobly pitiable appearance, I assure you—something between a juggler and a jongleur—but it has won me many gold pieces."

"Show me, show me!" cried Silver Dove. She whirled away from him, pirouetting on her ivory leg. He watched her with admiration and surprise. "Careful," he warned, "or you may fly away!" He broke into a boisterous laugh.

"Sing, sing!" cried Silver Dove. She put her hands together pleadingly. "Sing for me, if they do not want to hear it."

"I cannot resist the plea of a noble lady," Noel said to her, making a magnificent courtly bow. He slung his gittern around and made ready. He tucked it under one arm, his fingers hooked, bending his chin down over the frets.

"First, of war," he said in a stifled voice. He swept the strings. His voice, surprisingly strong and clear, considering his cramped position, rang out:

"Who is for peace? Upon the bend of knee,
Who begs for mercy? Who would see

352

The stretched throat cut for sport—
Aha! 'Tis he of little worth!

"Who will swing his blade in shining arc?
Who will meet it fair, with spark to spark,
And beat him down with armor-clash?
Aha! 'Tis he of choler rash!

"Who will mount the hill that bears the Cross?
Who will mourn a gallant comrade's loss
And fight the better in the slippery blood?
Aha! 'Tis he who knows that strife is good!"

He ceased his rough verses with a clang of strings. He straightened his head proudly. Despite myself, I felt stirred. I involuntarily looked toward Maimonides. The face of my master was stern. That of Silver Dove was disappointed.

"I don't like that," she said softly. "It is too horrible."

"It is for knights," explained Noel to her. "It is for rougher men and hardier times than I trust you will ever know."

"Are there no pretty songs that you know?"

"A thousand, a thousand thousand, dear heart! What would you have me sing?"

"A song," she said hesitantly, her cheeks reddened with the first blush I had ever seen there, "of love."

Noel nodded, readjusted his instrument and twanged the strings reflectively. He broke hoarsely into a surprisingly affecting tune.

"Maiden in the meadow,
    In the meadow lie—
Dappled sun and shade,
Dappled sun and shade—
    In the meadow lie
For a day and aye.

"What does she devour,
    For her goodly food?
The rose and passing hour,
The rose and passing hour—
    For her lover's good.

"Why is she a-dying,
    Dying in her rest?
For her lover's sighing,
For her lover's sighing—
    For her own sweet breast.

"When shall he be true-love,
  When shall he be true?
When roses turn to rue,
When roses turn to rue—
  Then shall he be true.

"Maiden in the meadow,
  In the meadow lie—
Dappled sun and shade,
Dappled sun and shade—
  In the meadow lie
For a day and aye,
For a day and aye."

A melodious chord, very different from the dissonant one
which had concluded his first song, finished it. Silver Dove
stood entranced, her small breasts heaving, her eyes sparkling,
her tongue mute with enchantment.

I must confess it was not good poetry. Nor was it delivered
with finesse or skill; rather a bold gusto which gave it an inimitable flavor. It was this, combined with the gymnastic dexterity of the man in playing, which had provided us with
entertainment. Maimonides and I snapped our fingers in appreciation as a matter of courtesy. Silver Dove hugged him to
her with passion.

"Wonderful!" she cried. "His voice is like that of a seraph!"

Maimonides winced; I covered my mouth. His voice had
been more like the shouting of a commander to his troops.
But Noel took this praise without the slightest sign of annoyance. He bowed and bowed again as Silver Dove spun excitedly around him.

Undoubtedly it was her fascination with the fellow which
prompted Maimonides to offer him lodging for the night.
Carelessly, as if he were conferring a favor by accepting, Noel
granted us the privilege. He went off, his adorer tagging after
him like a sparrow on the hop. Maimonides listened to the
dying fall of their footsteps on the tiles and cocked his eye
at me.

"A fool and his gittern," he said. "He might better have
remained a Christian knight. Then, at least, he was something; now he is nothing, as he admits."

"I do not think he is as disreputable as that," I replied, a
feeling of resentment beginning to burn within me in defense
of my muse.

"He wastes his life," Maimonides said.

354

"Poetry is never waste," I said vehemently. "It is the gift of song from Heaven. That is priceless."

"Are you going to go back to the foolishness which your father reprehended to me?" wondered Maimonides.

I bit my tongue. "You use the word too often and too recklessly," I told him, abandoning even a vestige of courtesy. My voice shook with temper. "This I have said to you before."

"Do you dare defend this vagabond?"

"I defend all poets. It is they who make life beautiful!"

"I see. You have no room for Aristotle, for the holy men of old?"

"I do not criticize them; I say only that poets are the true creators of man's vision! A philosopher or a rabbi is a poet with his gut ripped out!"

Maimonides nodded sardonically. "Thank you for your remarkably vivid description of myself," he said. "You are lost to sense. You have taken the part of nonsense and idiocy, without the gift of thought or reason."

"But with rhyme and music, with dreams and visions, with color and fire and glory!" My words rushed on, almost before I was aware of what I was saying. "It pleases you to speak again and again of what my father wrote," I cried. "Can I not remind you that your own father spoke of Zamira as the whore of Samuel ben Ali, yet you are willing to take her into your house?"

I could have bitten out my tongue the next second. Maimonides gave an inarticulate cry, pulled his robe around him, and shivered, as if cold. He stood up, his face granite. "This we shall talk of hereafter," he said, "or, it may be, never again."

I refused to rise with him or to accompany him from the court. I sat taut with rage, held in my place by an overwhelming desire—for the first time—to be somewhere else than beside my master. At that moment, I understood the fires in Naomi's breast.

This marked the first rupture between myself and Maimonides, one which I was bitterly to regret, for which I now accept the blame with bowed head. Had I known what would come—but what man does!—I should have run after him and kissed his garments to implore forgiveness. But time does not tell until the moment arrives. Human suffering is not to be mitigated by tears before the fact. And these phantoms which

355

rose so unexpectedly from Maimonides' past were to haunt him more and more.

For a week, the household continued as usual. Noel seemed to fit into the pattern of our daily duties very well; in fact, he became almost a nursemaid for Silver Dove. Together they invaded the markets of Fostat, scanned the shops, gossiped in the bazaar. Evening after blue evening he brought her home, laughing on his shoulders, and more than once met Maimonides dismounting at the door (my master forbade me to go with him to Cairo until I had seen the error of my heated talk).

It was an evening of the month of Adet, just as the full moon came into being. Maimonides decided we should have a celebration to greet it as it grew above the horizon—with singing and dancing on the rooftop.

Nothing on earth can equal the pleasure of a night atop one's house in the balmy season of the Egyptian year: lying on one's mat covered by gauze alone, surrounded by stars like a handful of jewel-dust set in canopies of the deepest blue just above one's head. From our isolated spot, one could see other roofs; other shadows rose like ghosts there, also taking their rest in the languorous but still exciting warmth of the breeze from the Nile. It produced a shiver down the spine to hear a lonely dog howl in the distance, to listen to the trickle of music from another rooftop, to see the whiteness of the world in the moonlight, as if a vast heavenly impalpable tunic had been draped around the earth.

Though the hospitality of our race is well known, Maimonides kept all of the fast-days and but few of the feast-days. I secretly raided the larder often to keep body and soul alive. My master sternly excluded all superstitions from the house such as covering bread or knives at prayers, seizing a loaf with all ten fingers, speaking only Hebrew on the Sabbath, wearing amulets, or singing lullabies with mystical sentiments —but he acceded to this custom of joyously blessing the moon. He would not kill a white cock before the fast of the tenth of Tishri, but he allowed the reciting of a psalm before sleep under the moonlight. And he viewed the presence of a guest such as Noel as a sacred obligation to perform such dubious rites.

We squatted about the brass tables with their burden of fruit and meat and rice and bread, passing the goatskin of wine freely from one to the other. Unlike the Moslems, we allowed the women—Zamira and Yaltah and Naomi—to join us in our feasting. I must confess that by the time the moon showed its upper edge on the horizon, my head was heated by drinking. Perhaps my tongue was less responsible than most.

Behind us, I heard the plucking of strings. It was Noel with his grin; beside him, Silver Dove, as he had taught her, placed her fingers in the grooves to coin the different sounds. Silver Dove whispered to Zamira. She, smiling,. assented to the request. She rose and, in the widening light of the moon, commenced one of her graceful dances.

Disturbed by the music, the sleepy swallows flew out of their nests below the roof; they circled about us, twittering and swooping. The long cushions of the roof divan on which we lounged shone softly with the splendor of the moon that beamed across the plains of Egypt below. The chords, languorous at first, became sharper and more insistent; the tempo increased. Zamira, her face grave, matched it with the movements of her body. Her skirt flew out, her trousers clung to her movements, her short brocaded vest flung itself about with abandon. The small silver bells on her cap tinkled madly. Always her face, framed between its coils of yellow hair, brooded over herself with a solemn faraway dreaminess.

How it happened, I do not know. Perhaps Zamira had not danced for an audience for so long. Perhaps the moon has, as they say, the effect of making a person mad. Perhaps it was her Moorish blood, so long pent up by Maimonides and his strictness of living. Or it may have been simply the beat of the music and the atmosphere of the night. Whatever it was, Noel whispered to Silver Dove; the little one giggled. The music changed to a rapid, barbaric beat. Noel began to sing in a hoarse voice, in Spanish patois. Zamira's face took on an inner glow. She flushed. Her body writhed, arm to arm, leg to leg, as she swirled about on the rooftop.

Without warning, she flung off her vest, then her upper garment, revealing her small perfect breasts that trembled unevenly in the white moonlight. As she whirled about us, Maimonides became so startled that he left off clapping, his eyes distended. Zamira flung herself into the improvised figures of the dance without noticing him. She tossed off her red pointed slippers. Then, with a quick movement, she loosed the zone about her waist. Her gauzelike trousers flew to one side.

Naked, alone, spinning on one leg as if in imitation of Silver Dove, her rosy body chalked by the light, she was a picture of delight. Her hands outstretched like a dervish, her very

357

motion was modesty enough, as if her balance on her toes
would keep her beauties concealed forever. In the blur of
twisting flesh, her face—tiny, tense, concentrated—appeared
now and again, flashing its serious inner expression to us,
vanishing.

With a breaking chord that whined its way down into
nothingness, Noel ended. Zamira whirled about thrice more.
She came to a stop facing Maimonides, her hands outflung,
feet wide to keep her wavering balance. I sucked in my breath
at the loveliness of her, a glowing cross against the concave
heavens.

With the swiftness of nightmare, the scene .changed. Directly behind her, on the rooftop across the way, rose a black
formless shadow. Against the moon, it loomed. Shadow
streamed from it, crossing the gulf of the street, striking myself
and Maimonides in the face. Time seemed to slow: I swear I
saw it take an arrow from its belt, nock it, stretch the bow,
but this could not be. I saw a peaked cap, swelling shoulders,
as it bent a bow. It had the strung shaft to its ear but I could
not tell its aim. I uttered a warning cry. Zamira wheeled about
in astonishment. As she did, Maimonides sprang to his feet.
He lunged toward her. Protectively, almost without knowing
it, I thrust out my foot. Maimonides tripped, landing motionless on the roof.

I heard the deep hum of a string, the feathery passage of
the shaft, the thud striking flesh. Noel shouted a Frankish
curse. He vaulted over the low parapet into the street below.
Naomi screamed.

As for Zamira, the love of Maimonides, she seemed untouched except for the long black mark across her bosom,
the quivering shaft. She folded her hands across it. Slowly, in-
explicably, her white nakedness turned. Once, twice, she
stepped with her small bare feet on the prostrate Maimonides,
as if it were some holy ceremony. Then, very slowly, as if
she were tired after her dance, she melted to the rooftop.

Yaltah was first to the side of the stricken. Naomi, blub-
bering and squealing as if she herself were hurt, followed.
Silver Dove plunged at her beloved. All was confusion. I saw
only one thing clearly: Maimonides' dreadful glare at me. He
rolled over and literally crawled on hands and knees to
Zamira's side. I shivered in the warm night, my mind numbed.
Not knowing what I did, I found myself running down to
Maimonides' room to secure his medical instruments, an act so

engrained in my consciousness that I could not do otherwise in an emergency.

Clear fluid like gruel flowed from her breast. It was followed by something like the watery part of the flesh. As she lay half-covered beneath Maimonides' cloak, foamy blood followed. Her breath came with difficulty.

The white skin about the shaft of the arrow began to discolor under the light of the lamp, assuming a purple hue. Maimonides shivered: He knew what this meant. But his movements did not become hurried, nor did his hand have the slightest tremor. He took from his pouch a long forceps, its jaws like that of a bird's beak with saw-toothed edges, tempered darkly. I gave him the salve of dittany and birthwort boiled together with fat and abrotanum; he applied it to the edges of the forceps.

Deep into the wound he thrust the instrument. He gripped the shaft with all his strength. He gave it a quick turn. Pure blood issued forth; Zamira uttered a short, gasping shriek. Her fingers fluttered like white moths about the dark intense face of Maimonides. Her eyes opened for the first time with a long, loving glance.

The time came for the act to be quick, precise, without error. Sweat poured down her forehead, mingling with the liquid from her bulging eyes, but she did not blink. "Muni," she said faintly, "I feel it in my bosom. It is fixed, as if in bone. Do not move it, let me die."

"You must not die," Maimonides said, almost in anguish.

I saw the arrow moving in tiny rhythm with the pulse of her blood. Zamira said, fainter and fainter: "I am so cold in the feet, Muni, in the hands, everywhere—except in my breast, there I am hot as fire."

Without warning, she rose halfway up. Her hands flew to the shaft, pulled weakly at it. Next moment, without a sound, she fell backward. She was dead. Even I, as unversed as I was in such, could see the hand of Azrael passing over her face, whitening and smoothing the flesh.

As if stricken by the stillness of the night and death, no one moved. The silence was broken by a gruff complaint. "There was no one at all on the roof across the street," Noel said plaintively, "no one at all. No one at all."

Slowly Maimonides rose from his knees beside Zamira. His hands showed the darkness of her blood but his face was colorless. He made a slight motion, like that of a man in a daze; as if he wanted to wash his hands but he could not.

"Zamira," he said, a little boy reciting a lesson, "Zamira, dead. She is dead, Zamira."

Sightlessly, rolling on his shoulders, his head turned toward me. His muscles stiffened; I saw a flame of rage light up his eyes.

"You!" he said in deliberate accusation. "I might have taken the arrow in my own body and saved her! You! You killed her!"

Without warning, Noel shot out his enormous fist. He seized me by the throat. He lifted me high above the roof. I saw the moon become a monstrous blaze in heaven. The stars whirled about me, so many sparks about the fire in my head.

"Let him go," I heard Maimonides say, "let him go."

CHAPTER 21

"A poet of Nishapur," I said eagerly, "who died in the reign of Malik Shah."

"Before I was born," Maimonides said dully.

"He has risen to popularity in Damascus and Bagdad today. It is said of fame that she will greet each poet at the other side of his grave, a hundred years from his death. The late caravan to Cairo has brought copies of his verses."

"Does such childish stuff still intrigue you?" Maimonides inquired bitterly.

"It is immortal stuff," I said indignantly. "Have you not said the same of Judah Halevi?"

"He wrote of holy things."

"But his images were of earth, earthly. If you will, listen to what Omar the Tentmaker writes."

"That is a proper trade for poets," Maimonides said, but nevertheless he made an indifferent gesture of assent. I arose and, with appropriate gestures, recited:

"Alas! that the book of years is rolling tight!
And that my purple spring has winter-blight!
That bird of joy, whose name is youth—for shame!
Alas! I know not whence it went or came."

I ceased and, with some trepidation, waited for disdain. I persuaded myself it was my influence which sometimes brought poetics into Maimonides' writing. This, I confess, was little enough conversion of the great man to the pleasures of life. He appreciated only the works of Judah Halevi and those solely which were concerned with the spiritual. For Maimonides, poetry was the plaything of children. So, too, with music. Except for the tunes of Spain, it made him nervous even to hear it; if he paid attention, it bored him, and soon he left for study, out of earshot. If Ibn Gabirol, that great man, had sung the joys of wine, Maimonides only tasted it; eating was only a means of survival. And for him the very act of making love—as far as I could discover—was simply the unaccountable rite visited upon man for his sins, the ridiculous, obscene manner which God had decreed for the propagation of the human race.

But now, to my surprise, there was only silence. At last Maimonides cleared his throat and spoke in a strange, thin voice. "Are there other quatrains?" he asked. Surprised to the point of speechlessness, I managed to speak again:

"The world is but a caravanserai
To lodge the piebald horse of night and day;
A summer court, abandoned by its kings;
A palace, where the graveyard beetle sings."

"Enough, enough!" cried Maimonides in a choked tone. But in my enthusiasm I could not be restrained from another stanza of the divine Khayyam.

"O heart, suppose the world within your grace,
And all within it, as you choose its place—
Why, then, like snow upon the desert lain,
A day or two, you find it all in vain."

Maimonides clapped his hands over his ears and shook his head from side to side like a pony eared with wheat-husk. Tears welled from his eyes; blind with grief, he rose and walked waveringly away, rejecting my assistance. I sank again to my seat in the courtyard, regretting my impetuosity, yet

361

realizing that only by such grief could my master purge himself of what he carried within.

It was clear to me that the death of Zamira had destroyed his peace, perhaps forever. The arrow which had pierced her heart had been like the child's shaft at play which strikes a block and tumbles all. Great had been the events which had followed in our lives.

My master had observed much I had not credited him with seeing; he had known more than I about the intrigues of his household. But to keep the peace, he had never complained. With Zamira dead, however, he no longer felt bound to remain mute. He became an implacable judge, more righteous and less compassionate than he was in the Hall of Justice. For Yaltah, the long-suffering and silent, he had no word of blame. But he demanded Naomi be exiled—back to her home in Acre, to her father, the rabbi Japhet—for her evil tongue and plots against Zamira. Only nights of intercession by Yaltah turned the edge of his verdict. Even so he decreed that Naomi should never stand in his presence again and that he should not hear her voice.

Noel and Silver Dove themselves decided the issue of their fate. It was I who overheard their whisperings in the courtyard one afternoon when they should have been asleep in the cool inner chambers. Restless myself, I strolled past a window overlooking the summer-radiant garden. Their voices came floating up to me.

"Now that Zamira is dead," Silver Dove said sadly, "nothing is left here for me."

"There is the old Jew," responded Noel.

"Yes, I love him and he loves me," she said, "but he is growing old and strange. He will touch my head but he no longer sees me. I have no one like yourself, who loves me, who will listen to my dreams."

"And I am going away," said Noel.

"Yes," Silver Dove sighed. There was a pause, then Noel laughed softly.

"You can journey because you are a man but I cannot, I am only a girl," Silver Dove said sadly.

Noel gave a muffled roar of derision. "I am as badly off as you," he told her. "I am much older. That is much worse, is it not?"

"But I have only one leg to walk on."

"Ah, Joanne, I wot that well. But I—I have no arm whereby to use the plectrum on the gittern, eh?" At this I could not refrain from peering over the sill to where they sat. I saw her clasp his hand as her face brightened. "I have the arm and the hand and the fingers!" she cried.

Noel smiled, a broad contented smile. "That is what I have been trying to tell you, little one," he responded. The warmth of his voice startled me. "You and I, we are different from the rest of the world. We do not belong to whole people. We belong to ourselves."

"What do you mean?"

"Joanne, would you make one whole person out of the pair of us?"

"That is impossible, even for Maimonides!"

"No, I do not mean that. I mean, I shall be your legs and you, you shall be my arm."

"But that also is impossible!" she repeated in an entirely different tone, one which indicated she knew exactly what he meant. Her whole body quivered. Her little ivory leg kicked upward involuntarily.

"Is it thus?" He stood and swung her into the air, seating her astride his broad shoulders. "I shall never know you are there. I shall show you how to finger the plectrum on the strings over my shoulder and I shall sing—"

"And *I* shall sing!"

"We shall sing together, in chorus, and when we sing alone, we shall be jealous of each other!" Noel retorted, laughing. Joanne joined him in gaiety.

"This is wonderful, wonderful!" she cried.

"I shall be your beast and go where you direct," Noel said, turning his head to look up at her. "We shall live together, day and night, taking fortune as it comes. We shall pick up pennies, chant for good and evil, live like the crickets, singing by night in the marshes across the world."

"Who knows what marvelous things we may see?" cried Silver Dove, clapping her hands.

A pang smote my breast, a longing to see such places as she had spoken of. I lingered no longer to hear what they might say but hastened off—talebearer that I had become—to report what they planned to my *musallim*. But Maimonides, Yaltah said, would not receive me; he was deep in meditation in his barred room. My information trembled on the tip of my tongue but resentment sealed my lips. I might have spoken to Yaltah in time to prevent what happened but my temper overcame me. I turned silently aside.

Next day, Silver Dove and Noel were missing. They were

363

reported by the guard at the north gate as having passed through at dawn bound toward the desert—a creature of two-in-one, a silver and a golden head, a beauty mounted on a beast, singing in harmonized voices toward the dawn. Maimonides, with his influence, might have had them pursued and captured; but in his wisdom he forbore. He never afterward inquired of the ungrateful Silver Dove or the minstrel guest, though now and again, through the years, we heard of the twain traveling through strange lands. Once, indeed, I culled the rumor they had spawned a tribe of jongleur children.

I come to myself, last of the once happy household of Maimonides. My master retracted his charge of my killing Zamira, of course; it was he who knocked loose the grip of that villain Noel from my throat. My tripping him as he lunged toward her had been done by instinct, out of my deepest wish to preserve him. This he accepted as well. But he never understood—and never, I think, wholly forgave—my attitude toward Zamira. In truth, I had advised him to visit her only by way of relaxation in Alexandria, as any man might visit a house of pleasure. Welcoming her into his own home, the most sacred Jewish home in all Egypt, was a different matter. To me, at least; not to Maimonides. Logic can be all things to all men, once overruled by passion.

As to the identity of the slayer of Zamira, that was to remain hidden until years later. A peculiar weapon, that deadly arrow: It had no head, rather a dagger lashed to the shaft, bearing a narrow, poisoned blade. Certainly the killer was one of the enemies of Maimonides, I speculated; perhaps one of Zamira's disappointed lovers. It might have been an Assassin sent in revenge from Alamut or Marsayf; it might have been a lunatic adherent of the dead Zuta. My suspicions even went to Samuel ben Ali. But any conjecture was like a twirling signpost in the middle of a vast desert. Surely, as it is written, a host of enemies beset the path of the good man.

For three months or more, Maimonides threw himself into his studies with a terrible energy. Then, as if Heaven punished him for an unknown sin, his phenomenal memory commenced to fail him, as his father had recorded of his youth in Almería. He could not recall the most important incidents, even of yesterday; the pictures on the tablets of his mind grew dim and blank. A wasting melancholy fell upon him, to the point of threatening his life. And I, so much in his disfavor, found myself again the staff he leaned upon.

Outwardly, there was no apparent reason for his continued gloom and dismay. He remained high in the favor of the court of Saladin; his intimate friend was still the vizier, voice of the caliph, Al-Alfadhel. His reputation for healing could not have been higher: Even the famous Ibn Jumay now regarded the gossip that he himself was half-Jewish as a compliment. It was common knowledge that soon he would retire and Maimonides would succeed him in his post as court physician.

Among our own people, the fame of my master grew daily in demonstrations of wisdom, of justice, of learning. His devotion to the welfare of mind and body of all who applied to him, regardless of faith or birth, became a byword in the market place. Yet all this he did with a surpasssing weariness of mind and body. His dwelling was no longer a bower of peace. There was none to whom he could return and find rest. Even the blessed oblivion of sleep escaped him.

Though I could not assign the exact reason for my master's despair, it seemed to me to be akin to one of the many curious beliefs of the Moslems. They declare that on the Day of Resurrection, a terrible veiled figure will be the first to greet the risen soul. It will demand: "Shall I show you my face?" and the soul cannot but signify consent. Whereupon the figure will tear away its veil and show a loathsome, decayed countenance. "Do you wonder at my hideousness?" it will sneer. "I am your evil deeds. You rode upon my back when you were alive; now I shall ride upon your back for eternity!" And this malignant doom is saddled upon the sinner for all time to come.

Something of this dreadful vision seemed to affect Maimonides—and myself, I confess, since I was so closely associated with him in body and spirit. I found my days sinking into despond. I experienced weary awakenings and reluctant nights of lying awake, in terror of the unknown. Thus, in order to dispel the black humors, I became physician for us both. I recalled that his father, Maimon, had written in his script of the long walks they had taken together outside Fez. I reinitiated them; day after day, by dint of persuasion and half-command, I induced Maimonides to take long walks outside the walls of Cairo.

Among the low rocky hills that ran along the eastern side of the city like an enormous grounded brown leviathan, there had come to be an increasing population of strange ascetics, hermits and anchorites. I had heard of such before from

365

Maimonides' stories of the hills outside Jerusalem. These miserable people were much the same. Many were Moslem flagellants; some were of the many religions of Egypt which the rulers tolerated; and a few were Christians. All were given a superstitious respect. They lived on alms and the refuse of the city. They spent days and nights in self-torture, in prayer, and in weird moanings. Occasionally, they chanted songs they composed which sounded like the howling of wild animals.

This region had a peculiar fascination for my master. Despite the fact that I attempted to guide his footsteps elsewhere, I discovered our pilgrimages tended more and more into the lonely wilds of these hills. On the occasion of which I speak, we had ventured further than usual, climbing well into the upper reaches. Here we stopped. We sat silently for a time, regarding the view below.

Here, at a height over Cairo, the city seemed the green hashish dream of a fond people. To our right lay the rude brown rocks of a series of ridges descending to a blue plain, stretching blue into the distance of blue-backed monstrous pyramids, imagined or real, the mountains of the country. The city lay in a crook of the arms of earth, the slow-twisting light-brown Nile winding around it. The terraced houses (some five or six stories high) and the covered streets were indistinguishable in the distance. But the fronts of marble and limestone gleamed whitely. From this place one could see the famous double-towered Fatimid castle on the plain, naked to any enemy. Below us, on this western spur of Mount Mukattam, were the foundations and rising walls of Saladin's own Castle of the Mountain. Far beyond, the lines of the canals extended in all directions, dominated by the threadlike white of minarets and the domes of the mosques.

From afar, the whole seemed a forest of trees and flowering shrubs. Here and there a gilded spire, again the rounded whiteness like a woman's breast where some famous soul had been buried. The fingers of the mosques stroked the sky. The alien traveler might have thought that the inhabitants lived in nothing but gardens. He would be amazed at the number of people, at streets crowded with houses. On such an early morning, with the fresh pure air like a blessing upon our heads, I wondered at the lightness and glory of Cairo from afar.

But, I thought somberly, Cairo was not the peaceful spot for our people that it seemed. Seven thousand Jews lived there, divided still into two congregations: one, with allegiance to the Jerusalem Talmud, the other to the Babylonian version

366

of Bagdad. The latter read a portion of the Law every week, as is done to this day in Spain and Fez. The others divided the whole Law into three parts, reading each once a year. Happily, they agreed to come together on the day of the Rejoicing of the Law and on the day of the Giving of the Law. Thus far the efforts of my master to unite them wholly had been unsuccessful. But he remained head of all our people, bearing the honorary title (given by the caliph) of Hibet Allah ibn al Jami. He appointed all rabbis and officials.

"Let us go on," Maimonides said, rising to his feet and pointing upward.

"We have come far today," I protested. He shook his head and started off upon a narrow, sandal-printed path of sand between towering rocks. I urged Maimonides to turn back again and again. He did not heed me. He paced forward slowly, with a purpose unknown, with the air of a hound questing scent still unidentified. The trail wound up and up. It ended suddenly on a small shelf of rock. Directly behind this, opened a cave, wide and flat; part of nature, partly hollowed by man. In the darkness of the overhang squatted a man, barely discernible to the eye. He wore a single garment of woven reed-fiber, brown and shapeless, three openings for head and arms. His feet showed bare and gnarled. His arms were scarred; his hands bulged with sores. His hair fell long and matted and he peered through it with blank eyes narrowed; his beard flowed in an angry tangle to the girdle of shoddy skin which held his costume together.

As we approached—cautiously, as if we had cornered a wild beast—he chanted tunelessly in a low monotone, betweenwhiles whipping himself, shoulder to shoulder, with a rusty chain. It was Maimonides who first claimed his notice. His shadow loomed across shadow and the man looked up very slowly.

"Who are you that dares to disturb the peace of hell?" he demanded in a voice rusty with disuse. He spoke in the Frankish patois.

"We are passers-by," Maimonides said hesitatingly. "We ask you to forgive us for disturbing your solitude."

"There is no forgiveness, none in Heaven nor earth."

"God is always merciful."

"You lie!" A wide-open cry, nearly a shriek. I recoiled from its violence.

Maimonides seemed undisturbed. "If a man sins all the

367

days of his life," he said, "and asks forgiveness only on the day of his death, it shall be granted him."

"Lies, lies! I have asked and it has not been given." The man dropped the chain by his side. He stood up waveringly, as if he were drunken.

"God knows what we desire and grants it to us when we are truly ready."

"God works in no other way than to punish sin."

"We have all sinned," Maimonides said quietly.

"Aye! Some less, some more. I, more than all the rest!" His voice changed. I saw Maimonides start. At that moment Maimonides' face reflected fear, something near to revulsion. He peered into the tangle of hair before him. "I have heard that voice before," he said. "Speak!"

"You have listened to demons in dreams," retorted the other. His voice changed yet again, taking on something of pride and damnation.

"Sir, will you come into the sun?" Maimonides was pleading, anxious; his tone was one of terrible anticipation.

"Sir? Sir! I have not heard knightly address these many years."

"The light is good," faltered Maimonides. He shook his head from side to side, a man doubting his senses.

"My eyes will not endure it but I shall close them." The anchorite took a shaky step into the sunlight. He shuddered at its impact as if it had been a lash. Maimonides pressed his hand against his forehead. "Your name!" he cried. "Your name!"

"As you may see, I am Guilbert the Damned."

"Sieur Guilbert de Bayonne!"

The miserable soul shook his head. "I have heard the name," he said quaveringly, "but I do not know the man. Is he a friend?"

Maimonides took a quick step forward. He touched the side of the man's head lightly. I saw the other wince as my master stepped back and wrung his hands. "Do you not know me?" Maimonides demanded.

"I who was alive became dead. Being dead, I became alive. Now I am dead once more, to all men!"

"Do you not know me? Tell me!"

"You are sent to torture me," cried the other man, rolling his head and hunching his shoulders. He straightened from his stoop. I saw at once he was uncommonly tall, that his

368

wasted frame must at one time have supported mighty muscles.

"How came you here?" Maimonides asked in a quivering tone.

The hermit shuddered in pain. "Many years ago," he said, "many years ago."

"But how?"

"From Jerusalem, so they tell me. I was a knight, they say, black with sin as armor with rust. A bolt from heaven, a stone flung against my helmet by a pilgrim Jew, directed by God, flung me into Hell whence I was resurrected."

"Who was the Jew?" Maimonides whispered.

"I do not know, how could I know?"

"It was my brother David, I am sure of it!"

The man shook his shaggy head. "Then he was the slinger of God," he said solemnly. "I praise his aim."

The face of Maimonides shifted from stern disdain to an expression both compassionate and concerned. "This is the end of a noble knight, then," he murmured, his voice breaking. He addressed Sieur Guilbert. "I take the blame of my brother upon myself," he said clearly. "His feeling was just but his act was against God."

"I do not know you. It is wicked to have a brother, to have a sister, a wife, a father or mother!"

"I beg your forgiveness," Maimonides said. He sank slowly to his knees before this shabby man. Overcome with surprise, against my will, I imitated his action.

"Mine?" the man asked, bewildered. "Mine? You ask my forgiveness?"

"Can you not open your eyes?" pleaded Maimonides.

"If the night comes, I know it by the cool," the other responded in a voice that grated like an iron door. "Until then I dare not."

"My name is Moses ben Maimon."

"A thrice-damned Jew, one who crucified God!" exclaimed the other. I could not bear it any longer. I sprang to my feet. "Come," I said, urging my master with my hand upon his shoulder, "let us go. This madman is no concern of ours."

Maimonides paid no attention. He kept his gaze riveted upon the stranger. "You are lost," he murmured. "Weak, wandering, lost."

"I am strong in the Lord, to suffer what He suffered!"

Maimonides bowed his head, as if in prayer. I stood by him as the scarecrow advanced totteringly, but I had no need to protect my master. The hermit spoke above both of us, his face raised to the sky. "I see, I see!" he said ecstatically. "Shall I tell you what I see?"

Maimonides said nothing. It was I who responded. "Tell us what you see," I said in a voice I tried to keep calm.

"I see a great mass of rust-colored iron," Guilbert said in a hushed, reverent voice. "On it sits a radiance so bright I cannot set eye upon it. At its foot is a shape all covered with eyes, watching me, nothing like a human form; before this shape is another, that of a boy in a transparent garment—yea, his gender is clear!—and shod with white. On his head pours the splendor, a crown of sparks from the mountaintop. A stream of them, coiling about him like serpents of light, dazzles me; and from the mountain, filled with casements of gold, shine many heads that watch me!"

Guilbert paused. Maimonides waited a moment, then spoke. "What does this mean?" he asked.

Guilbert rolled dull eyes up at him and slowly shook his head. "I do not know," he said, as if in pain. "When I am asked, the vision flees. I cannot speak. My tongue is hung backwards, it clogs my throat."

"Surely the vision will come again," I said timidly. The quondam knight did not hear me. He extended his arms in the form of the cross, his eyes sightless, his dirty white hair streaming in the breeze.

"Where is the gay torchlight now?" he cried. "Where the clapping hands and the dances and the assemblies and the courts and the festivals? Where are the green garlands and the ladies' favors? Where the cry of the town and the cheers of the lists, the flattering lungs of the lookers-on? All that is gone. A wind blew and suddenly cast the leaves and showed me the tree bare, tearing it up by the roots and leaving it stricken. Where now are the friends under the timber whose grain was rent asunder? Where are the pretenders of fashion, the suppers and the feasts, the feats of arms, the hangers-on, the courtiers? Where the strong wine decanted all day long, the cooks and daintily dressed tables, those who wait on greatness, their words and ways to please? They were all of night and of dreaming; now it is day. They are gone. Spring flowers and the spring gone, they have vanished; a shadow traveled beyond; smoke unraveled by the wind; bubbles broken, cobwebs swept away by the handmaids of God."

He sank down once more, his face gaunt and working. Maimonides, his voice shaken, addressed himself once more to the hermit: "Sieur Guilbert," he said.

"Guilbert," interrupted the other harshly.

"What works do you here?"

"I gather the leaves that blow past my door. So many each day, arranged in their various sizes and piles. This I do every day. When the end of the year is come, according to my reckoning, I strike a flame and burn them all together."

"And then?"

"I commence once more. If I am busy, I am haunted by only one devil; if I am idle, multitudes assail me."

"The nights in this lonely spot must be fearful," I said with a shudder, glancing about me.

Guilbert fixed me with eyes like burning embers.

"By night I am not alone," he said.

We stared at him, Maimonides and I, waiting for him to explain. He did not disappoint us. His face became dreamy and soft, filled with an inner ecstasy.

"My lover comes and he lies upon my breast," he said in a singsong chant. "He closes his eyes as I caress him. His fingers cling about my neck and twine themselves in my hair. He lies arm to arm, foot to foot, breast to breast, eye to eye, and lip to lip with me. As the dawn comes, he melts into my being and when I wake, I find him gone and am desolate."

Guilbert gave a yell of inexpressible agony. He turned and rushed inside his cave, his shrieks re-echoing from the rocky walls until they died away in the depths. We dared not follow him. Maimonides and I stepped backward as if in the presence of royalty. We made our faltering way down the mountainside.

We spoke not a word to each other until we had descended to the foot of the hill. Here Maimonides stopped. He raised his hands, fluttering with emotion. "He is holier than I," he said brokenly, "he is holier than I."

"A humility altogether unnecessary," I said in surprised denial. But my master knelt and touched the sand with his forehead solemnly. "He is of the ninth degree of prophets," he said. "One who hears the words and sees the vision, even as Abraham."

"He is a heathen," I said hotly.

"The finger of God touches whomever it pleases," Maimonides said. "It is written that the Lord will make Himself known by a vision, in a dream He will speak to him." Try as I might, I was never able to rid him of this foolish illusion.

Seven months later, as we set out on our usual journey from Fostat to Cairo, a foam-covered Berber courier spurred up to a dirt-flinging halt before our gate. While I spat out the dust and silently cursed the emissary, Maimonides received a curt summons. Saladin had returned from the wars in Palestine. He demanded his presence. Therefore we mounted two jennets and galloped off at speed, with enough bruising of my unaccustomed spine to keep me abed with ointments and heated cloths for days after.

The unusual nature of the call excited my curiosity. Maimonides knew no more about it than myself. It was, therefore, in a spirit of part fear, part expectancy, that we entered the throne room of Saladin. We made our obeisances and advanced. Maimonides, in his new role succeeding Ibn Jumay, took his place among the first rank of those at Saladin's right hand. The caliph himself, thinner and more worn, but still radiating quiet power and steel will, sat immobile on his divan.

Saladin had gradually become less austere in his surroundings—possibly due to the influence of Al-Alfadhel, who had known the luxury of the Fatimids. The room had been freshly painted in gold and scarlet arabesques, and hung with huge green discs inscribed with Koranic sayings. The court stood respectfully about Saladin's divan of black silk, with cashmere rugs of the same color. About it were four pillars of gilded copper studded with topazes, garnets, and emeralds; above it, a silk roof of red and white and green. Long white horsetails hung from golden crescents at each corner. Over Saladin's head was a plate of black marble. Inscribed in gold upon it were the names of Allah, Mohammed, and the first four caliphs—Abu Bekr, Omar, Osman, and Ali. On the far wall, in the gallery, before an open jeweled copy of the Koran on a red marble slab pointing toward Mecca, stood a richly garbed muezzin.

As we entered, he commenced to chant verses from the book in a queer rhythm. His words, I noted, had a strange effect upon a row of meanly clad men before the divan. They wore ragged cloaks and heavy hoods. Their faces were sunken, with owl-like eyes, their noses sharp and hooked. In time to the chanting, they began to shuffle in a circle in front of the throne. Flutes and strings added a high sweet accompaniment to the reading, a mixture of sounds that intoxicated. Eyes gleamed, bare heels smote the floor in unison; they moved quickly and chanted in low voices to themselves. Out of the circle, into the middle, moved one who seemed the leader.

372

He extended his hands like a criminal being crucified in the Roman fashion. He turned slowly on his toes. His gown ballooned. His figure dimmed as he increased his speed.

Suddenly I pulled back, staring at Maimonides. The rite reminded me of nothing so much as the last dance of Zamira on the roof. But the sharp-featured face of my master was fixed on the scene, inscrutable and unmoving. Now another dervish joined the first, like a child's top. A third, a fourth— in seconds, all of them whirled to the beat of the holy chant. All were drawn into self-hypnosis, arms out, head bent tight to the left shoulder, lips parted, eyes closed.

The chant rose to a crescendo and stopped. On the instant, the dervishes collapsed. They rose slowly, as from a trance, and took their places in a smaller circle, two by two. From the crowd, women rushed in religious hysteria, placing their children before the dervishes as they filed out. They stepped on the offerings with ceremony, not sparing the weight. The mothers wept tears of ecstasy at what was apparently Allah's blessing. Two by two, the dervishes vanished down the hall. At last they were gone. The throne room was silent.

"Moses ben Maimon," came Saladin's icy voice. "You have been summoned to answer to the charge of a crime."

Maimonides started. He bowed deeply. "I am conscious of no crime, Caliph of the World," he returned, a vibration in his voice.

"Let the accuser stand forth," said Saladin.

A tall dark man with tight curly hair and a lean frame, eyes gleaming like agates, stepped out. He wore a gown that I recognized instantly, by cut and drape, as one out of my native land, the Maghreb. But I did not know this person. He extended a sinewy bare arm, pointing a finger at my master. Before he spoke, Maimonides burst out in a tone of joy: "Abul Arab ibn Mosa! My friend, friend of my family, savior of us all in Fez! Welcome!"

With a deep sonorous voice, Ibn Mosa replied: "You are the man! I shall say no more!"

For the first time, I saw Maimonides bewildered. "What is this?" he demanded. "Is this old friend my accuser?"

"He has come to Egypt for the first time," Saladin said dryly, almost with an effort. "He has heard of your fame. He has denounced you."

"Denounced me?"

"As a heretic," Saladin said wearily. Maimonides' eyes fluttered, closed, then half-opened. He seemed to be inspecting the caliph more than answering to the charges.

"Have you been a good Moslem all this time and deceiving us as a Jew?" Saladin asked slowly, with a hint of anger.

"I am what I am," Maimonides replied.

Again Ibn Mosa stepped out of the crowd of whispering courtiers. "In Fez, twenty-three years gone," he inquired scornfully, his voice ringing, "did you not say the holy formula of belief in Allah and his only Prophet, Mohammed?"

Maimonides flinched, as if struck. His lips tightened.

"Did you not say the holy formula?"

Maimonides was silent. Ibn Mosa, his eyes gleaming with triumph, advanced a step. His arm lunged out in accusation, his long finger pointing like a javelin toward my master. "Do you deny you repeated the formula?" he demanded once more, his voice ringing out.

"Answer," Saladin said curtly. His voice was cold. All else he could forgive but lies and hypocrisy—the denial of that which was, to him, the One True Faith.

"I did," Maimonides responded firmly. The court gasped. He lifted his head proudly, his countenance shining as if inspired. He turned his eyes to heaven. I clasped my hands in torture.

"Do you know what is the penalty, the only penalty, for a relapsed heretic from the confession in the Moslem faith?" It was Ibn Mosa's insistence, as grinding and implacable as a millstone upon a grain of wheat.

"Yes."

"What is it, Moses ben Maimon? Jew or Moslem, whichever you are, what is the punishment?"

"Death."

"Having said the formula, do you now reject it?"

"I am a Jew," Maimonides said in a slow clear voice, "and a Jew I shall remain, no matter what my God does to me."

The throne room was silent. No one seemed to breathe; only a slight sigh that may have escaped from the lips of Saladin was heard. It appeared to be a signal for the inspiration of Al-Alfadhel. He rolled forward, his eyes serious in his pudgy face.

"O mighty Saladin," he rumbled, "I crave permission to speak."

His master nodded, half-reclining. Not for a moment did he take his agate gaze from the set face of Maimonides. Nor did Maimonides flinch. The threatening form of Ibn Mosa—

may his bones be scattered to the four winds!—retreated. Only the fat form of Al-Alfadhel, my master, and the dark radiance of Saladin remained in my vision.

"If I may ask the healer of the court some questions," Al-Alfadhel said.

"Ask."

He turned to Maimonides. "You confess you spoke the holy formula."

"Yes."

"Was it of free will, a statement of your faith?"

Maimonides slowly shook his head. "No," he said.

There was a stir in the court, a rustling like leaves in autumn. "What force was used?" Al-Alfadhel prodded.

"My brother was being killed, my sister raped," Maimonides said quietly. In the background, I noted a sudden movement. It was that of Abul Maali, who had been a visitor to our house many times since the time he had seen Yaltah recover speech. I had observed him in close conversation with her frequently; she spoke to him only less freely than to myself. In my bosom a spasm of jealousy moved.

"Who were the criminals?" Al-Alfadhel said.

"They were Moslems, in Fez." Maimonides put a peculiar intonation on his words. "My friend, Ibn Mosa, had come to warn me of this."

"They were True Believers?"

"What they believed, they believed. What I spoke was not from your sacred book, the Koran. It was gibberish, intended to halt their madness—the only way one can speak to madmen."

"O great Vizier," came the agitated voice of Maali, "to lose such a one as this, with such powers of healing, will be a blow to the court, to all our nation!"

"If he is false, he shall die," Al-Alfadhel said. With a motion of his hand, he gestured a guard. The court secretary was rudely seized; a hand clamped down over his mouth.

"Is it not written," murmured Al-Alfadhel to Saladin, "that if one is forced to recite what he does not believe, even of our own faith, that the recital is worthless? Have not our own warriors pretended to recite the creed of the Christians and been spared, only to escape and regain safety and a life for Allah and the cause?"

Saladin said nothing, immobile on the divan. Al-Alfadhel paused, then continued with more confidence: "If this is so,

375

as the Prophet has said, then Maimonides' vow is worthless. He remains a Jew."

"I have never pretended otherwise," my master said.

"You injure your own cause," Al-Alfadhel snapped, glaring at him. He turned again to Saladin. "This man has saved many Moslems from untimely death, when it was not the will of Allah that they should perish. He is worth much."

"If he is what he is accused of," Saladin said dryly, "he is worth nothing, though he be a miracle-worker."

Al-Alfadhel was beaten. He bowed until his forehead touched the ground. He moved backward behind the throne. He beckoned two Nubian guards who came forward to stand at either side of Maimonides. They seized his hands, twisting them behind him.

"Wait," Saladin said. His voice was cool, descending as snow from the mountains. "There is another way to settle this, good Al-Alfadhel. This is no light matter, but there are touchstones. One may use them to find the truth, the true metal." He addressed Maimonides.

"Do you believe the dead will rise again?"

I shuddered. It was a fatal question. It was one of the great Moslem principles that resurrection would be sure and just. But there was nothing I knew in our faith like this.

"I do," Maimonides said in a sonorous voice. "I have always believed it."

"That the bodies of the just shall live in Paradise and the evil in Hell?"

"I do believe it."

"Do you say these are mere spirits or substantial bodies?"

"I say they are real bodies. It is part of our wisdom. It is in the Talmud. It is in our prayers and the beliefs of our people. I am not being untrue to my own faith when I say this."

"Some say you mean this merely in the sense of stories told to frighten children."

"That is false! Whoever accuses me of this tells a foul lie!"

"How will this come about?"

"As a miracle, water issued from the rock in the desert for Moses. So will the dead be revived by a marvelous miracle. Whoever believes God has created the world out of nothing must admit miracles; none who can doubt this can think himself a true Jew, a follower of Moses and Abraham."

"Nor a follower of Allah and Mohammed," murmured Saladin almost to himself. He sighed and moved restlessly. As if by magic, the atmosphere of the court changed and lightened. The decision had been made; I felt as if a weight had been lifted from my bosom. I saw Maali openly weeping.

"Come here, Moses ben Maimon," said Saladin. "I am strangely weary. Yet I do not think that Allah has yet granted me my allotted span. Tell me what will cure me."

Maimonides moved forward, falling on his knees beside the caliph. For the first time, I saw his face was wet, his lips moving in prayer. As Saladin extended his hand, the expression of the supreme ruler changed and hardened.

"As for that one," he said, indicating Ibn Mosa, "he shall be taken to the gates of the city. Scourge the false dog thirty times and send him naked into the desert."

CHAPTER 22

In the courtyard, the rays of the dying sun touched the top of the fountain. The heavy drops clustered, hanging there no more than an instant, glittering like jewels. They plunged downward into the shadowed basin. We watched and listened to the plash of the water in its irregular rhythm. Above the tiny noises, I heard Maimonides sigh.

I shook my head slowly from side to side. I knew his thoughts. "You deceived yourself," I said. "Zamira never became one of us, a Jewess. Perhaps she tried and failed."

"Indeed, I am sure she tried."

"Each returns to his own belief—holds it hidden—cherishes it in some obscure corner of the soul. What beckons is a mysterious Hand. None resists the summons," I said sententiously.

Maimonides bowed his head. "What was I to her, then?" he asked in a muffled voice, the master inquiring of the pupil.

"No more," I said soberly, "than a child she loved. She sanctified you, in her heathen way, just before her death. Lost in the ecstasy of the dance, her tiny feet upon your body as the feet of the dervishes upon the children before Saladin."

"Her tiny naked feet upon my body," repeated Maimonides in a dreamy tone. He raised his head with a burst of emotion:

"I would have no other blessing than her touch, whether she thought me child or man!"

"Your mind was too much for her," I said reprovingly. "It is a mighty thing, awesome, far above her."

"Her body, her love, they were enough for me," Maimonides said, his voice shaking. "Could she not understand?"

"There is more to life than thought," I could not help saying, Maimonides looked at me strangely. "Yes," he muttered, "yes, I am beginning to know that is so, that is so." He had taken to repeating himself. I wondered uneasily if he was in truth growing old.

For long moments afterward, we sat in silence. The glow-top of the fountain became incandescent with light, then commenced to fade. In my turn, I sighed and shook my head.

"I know your thought," Maimonides murmured. "You are in error."

"What was my thought?" I challenged.

"That I was wrong to admit so much to the caliph."

"Yes," I confessed. "You might have held him in dispute and won him without so bald a confession."

Maimonides shook his head. "In his youth," he told me, "our ruler was ten years a theology student in Damascus. He knows as much about the intricate ways of philosophy as I."

"Impossible!" I said scornfully.

"He becomes impatient with those who dispute him. In other years, it was a scandal in Syria when he finished an argument with one of the learned doctors. In the very midst of the mosque, he strangled him with his own hands."

I shuddered. "I see," I said. "Perhaps you acted rightly after all."

"Remember," Maimonides said obliquely, "that Saladin, great as he is, has more need of me than I of him." His fingers twisted the signet ring given him by the caliph.

"Should I comprehend what you mean by this?" I asked, irritated at the change of conversation without warning.

"He is a sick man," my master responded.

"Sick? You cannot mean it. He seemed very well when we saw him."

"My Joseph, you have not diagnosed disease as long as I. It takes experience to interpret those hollows about his eyes, the yellow of the skin, the thinness of the frame, the unnatural glitter of his gaze. He has the paludal fever, the disease of the marshes that comes with stagnant water and the insects that live in the scum. It comes and goes, in the midst of good health. Shaking with chill, burning with fever, suddenly vanishing. Over the years, it seems that the blood thins. But there arrives a day when the man is truly ill."

I felt a thrill of shock. "Have you—have you told him this?" I stammered.

"What would be the good of it?" asked Maimonides. "It would not aid his recovery."

"Yes, yes. I see that. But there is no other hope against the Franks and the Christians than Saladin! His arms, the greatness of his name—the soldiers of the Moslems will not fight except that he leads them! Our hopes of Palestine!"

"Perhaps none of us shall see the sacred city of Jerusalem," Maimonides muttered. "You are right. It is my duty to our people, to our God, blessed be He, to keep this man alive. I shall do all I may to heal him yet, I tell you, the disease is of hell. It answers to no herb or mixture that I know."

He ceased to speak. I sat numb with apprehension. I did not know what to say next nor how to broach some subject which might distract my master's mind. Maimonides sat gazing at the fountain, now entirely dark and invisible—only the recurrent sound of the water falling, falling, falling.

Suddenly Maimonides chuckled. "If you knew more," he said abruptly, with his extraordinary twist of humor, "you would endure less. If God has designs for Saladin's death, we shall not stand in His way."

"That is a Moslem creed," I said stiffly.

"What is God's will is God's will," Maimonides said. "It does not mean it is destined. It is my will that you remain and converse with me. It does not mean that you must do so."

"You are not God," I reminded him.

Maimonides did not reply for a long moment. When he did speak, it was in musing accents, as if he had disregarded my very pertinent remark. "This remarkable Saladin splits hairs in theology with as much pleasure as if he were splitting them with his Damascus blade," he said. "Did you know Al-Alfadhel was reproved by his master for speaking in my behalf?"

"Was he angry?" I asked.

"No. Saladin declared it was unnecessary. His mind had been made up to forgive me, no matter what my sin."

"Forgive, in truth!"

"He accused the vizier of being still too much of a Shiite, too addicted to the fancies of the brain."

"He arrogates to himself too much knowledge," I said.

"If I did not love you, Joseph," Maimonides said in a voice

that somehow seemed as cool as the air that descended into the garden, "I might repeat what you say and have your head separated from your shoulders."

"I beg your indulgence," I said.

"Mine would go with it for having listened. You must learn to use your tongue as a man, not as a woman."

It was an opportunity I could not resist. The sunset filled the sky with glory above our heads, shut out from it as we were by the walls of the courtyard. I raised my eyes upward. "I will speak as a man," I told him. "I dare to do this because it has troubled me for a long time."

"What is that?"

"Your sister, Yaltah."

"What of her?"

"She is visited by Abul Maali," I said, growing unsure of myself.

"What concern is that of yours?"

"There is nothing evil in it. But he comes to see her more often than I like," I replied defensively.

Maimonides' face next to me was rosy from the reflected light above. "He is a handsome man, wealthy and well-placed," my master replied calmly. "He is well thought of by those in high offices."

My temper rose. Once more my tongue came unbridled. "Do you intend to sell your only sister for gold and position?" I said acidly.

Maimonides curled his lips. "If I choose," he said in a flat voice. "I look not to my own happiness. That does not lie on earth but in the World-to-Come. I must see to her well-being as my duty—possibly, my one remaining duty."

"Does my well-being enter into it?"

"You are always in my heart, Joseph," Maimonides rejoined, his voice softened.

"Then," I said, taking heart, "is there not one available who is more suitable for Yaltah?"

Maimonides cast me a puzzled look. "She is a lonely woman," he said. "I may not have observed others. Whom do you mean?"

My heart beat loudly in my bosom. I licked my dry lips and drew myself erect on the bench. "I," I said loudly.

Maimonides half-twisted about. "You?" he asked incredulously.

"You are surprised?" I challenged.

"I am amazed," he said candidly. "Have things transpired under my very nose?"

"Why not?" I cried. "Am I not of her blood, of her faith? Do I not have health? Do I not have a mind making me worthy of being your disciple? Am I not wealthy and young?"

"You are young," Maimonides said slowly. "As for wealth, perhaps you will be wealthy when your father dies, God forbid the day. I confess your blood, your belief, and your health are indeed invaluable. But what else is there to offer?" I did not miss the irony in his voice.

I choked back what I was about to say. Words whirled in my head. I chose none of them. To my surprise, what I said came to my lips humbly and simply. "I love her," I said.

Maimonides looked into the fading heavens and sighed again. "You love her," he repeated. "So do I; so does anyone who meets her. So does Abul Maali."

"He!" I exploded. "Has he said as much?"

"He has asked me for her hand," Maimonides said.

I could say nothing. Such a development I had not expected, such a fantastic event: Someone else loved Yaltah, whom I had believed so cloistered from the world!

"Tell me," Maimonides said quietly, "I know a little of what love means. Do you love her from habit, by reason of living in the same house? Or is it with a terrible, irresistible emotion, a passion to share the same house of flesh?"

I got up with dignity in the twilight. "You insult me," I said, my voice quivering.

"Sit down," Maimonides replied sharply. "You are once again the young fool that your father described."

My feelings were in a tumult but I could not help obeying his order. I dropped to the hard bench and stared resentfully before me. I waited for my master to speak once more. I heard nothing. The tide of resentment within me took another turn. It was to twist a sword in his wound that I said what I did.

"You have delivered yourself up to the enemy," I muttered. "In answering Saladin as you did concerning immortality, you abandoned the belief of the Fathers and turned toward Mohammed. All Jews will raise their voices against you."

For a time, my *musallim* did not reply. As the darkness closed about us like the soft folds of a black cloak of camel's hair, I caught a glimpse of his face. It was remote and far-seeing.

381

"Do you believe God has entered into fellowship with our people?" his voice came to me from the gloom.

"Most assuredly," I responded.

"Do you believe, then, that He will desert us after the death of this corrupted body?"

"It does not matter what I believe," I said with heat. I had prepared myself beforehand for such a discussion. I was well fortified in my position. "It is a matter of the faith of the Fathers, a matter of Scripture. Is it not written that he that goes down to the grave shall come up no more?"

"It is also written," Maimonides' sonorous voice said, "that the dust shall return to the earth but the spirit to God who gave it."

" 'We are as water, spilled on the ground, which cannot be gathered up again'!" I quoted quickly.

Maimonides was silent. I gathered courage. "I have many quotations, many more against your belief than in its favor," I told the darkness.

"Shall we determine what is true simply by counting numbers?" asked Maimonides' vague figure. "Is not one righteous statement worth more than a host of wicked lies?"

"You may have taught me to think otherwise," I said indignantly.

"It is useless to hurl Scripture at each other," rejoined the voice of Maimonides. "The writings of the Fathers speak in this sense of the natural. I speak of the spiritual, of the miraculous. I have said what I said before Saladin long before; I repeated the convictions of my youth which my father disdained and which now you disdain. But they have not changed. God, if He will, can raise the very stones into life, even as He created the world out of nothing."

"I suspect you repeat the heathen Greek belief of the intelligence eternal," I said, unappeased. "That is Aristotle, not Torah or Talmud."

"Do you recall what Averroës said as I was about to enter on the operation upon Silver Dove?" Maimonides asked slowly. His use of the name of the runaway child startled me. He had not mentioned it since the hour she had vanished.

"Yes," I replied. " 'Only the soul is eternal.' "

"I have come, in these last days," Maimonides responded, "to believe even more than that. I believe I shall see the child; that I shall see Zamira; my brother, David; my father, Maimon, glorious be his resurrection—all the friends I have known and who have departed—in another life. Is it not said in

382

Daniel that 'Many of them that sleep in the dust of earth shall wake, some to everlasting life, some to reproach and everlasting loathing'?"

"In the body?" I said aghast.

"For a time," the master told me from the shadows. "They will eat and drink and generate offspring as before. They will die as before but after that—as Averroës has said—their immortal souls shall join the soul of the universe."

"You use the Moslem and Greek thought, not the Jewish, to speak this way," I declared to the darkness. "Do you know that which you declared in the court of the caliph only a few months ago has run like wildfire not only within Egypt but also to the lands beyond? That it has made you the target of lampoons ridiculing you?"

"Is this true?" demanded Maimonides. His voice quickened. I rejoiced that I had roused him to a knowledge of his precarious position.

"I shall recite one for your hearing," I said. I addressed his form beside me as I would have spoken to an audience:

> "If those that rise from death must die again
> I shall not long to share their fate—for when
> Their graves, their bones shall twice confine—
> I hope to stay where first they bury mine.

"That," I said triumphantly, "is by the renowned Meir ben Todros Abulafia."

"A rabbi and a scholar, no doubt?"

"He is a poet," I said stiffly.

Maimonides' head turned toward me. I could imagine his wry, sidelong look. "You see to what a pass the art of poetry has brought your master," he murmured.

"Forgive me," I said with dignity, "but I do not believe it is the fault of the inspired one."

"Did you not know that the one who denounced me, Ibn Mosa, was a poet in Fez?"

"I had never heard his verses," I said hastily, "but perhaps he was."

"But for the intervention of good Al-Alfadhel," Maimonides retorted, "his imagination would have brought me torture and death."

I stood up abruptly. "This has nothing to do with the matter," I returned. "A poet is a poet. He is not an informer nor a turncoat simply because he creates rhymes. What Ibn Mosa did was only of his own nature; it was not that given him by divine inspiration."

"Do you argue, then," Maimonides' voice inquired sardonically, "that poetry does not reflect the poet's true nature?"

"Perhaps," I said, struggling in deeper waters than I liked. "But his poems may be beautiful, though he himself is sinful."

"I trust no poets," Maimonides said.

"Then you do not trust me!" I shouted, unable to restrain myself any longer.

There was silence. I could imagine the expression of reproof on the features of Maimonides. "You raise your voice in my presence," he said coldly.

"I regret it," I returned, humbling myself, "but I cannot allow that which proceeds from God to be slandered."

"I slander the Almighty?"

"I did not mean that," I said desperately.

"It is what you said."

"I said only that one, even yourself, should not speak disparagingly of the art practiced by King David and King Solomon, peace unto their souls. By your friend, Judah Halevi; by men of sensibility everywhere," I said tightly.

In his turn, Maimonides stood up. I could see his head tremble in the night. "Even living in my house," he answered, "sharing the food, protected by its roof, you have grown far apart from me. You have not fulfilled the hopes I placed in you."

Not trusting myself to speak again, I bowed to the shadow and went out of the courtyard, venting my emotions by whispers of rage and gestures of derision. What Maimonides may have thought, I do not know.

From that time forth, it was ordained that I would leave Maimonides' house. I could stay no longer: not only because of the cruel words he had said; but bubbling up within me for many seasons had been new desires, fresh urges, the impulse to see the world beyond the fustian-makers of Fostat, beyond the connivings of Cairo, beyond Egypt. The vastness of the horizons called me like the rumble of distant drums: If Maimonides was growing older, was not I also?

But I did not yet dare to leave. It would take more courage than I possessed to face my master and tell him I had had enough of prenticing in philosophy and meddling in medicine. Moreover, in the bottom of my heart, there seemed some dark unfinished business, a warning to wait until the proper moment.

As it happened, three months from that very day, there came corroboration of what I had hinted to Maimonides. Not of the same subject but from another source. The message was from Bagdad. The author was Samuel ben Ali himself.

Delivered by a richly caparisoned courier, the small thick book (representing the vellum from a dozen sheep) showed ivory covers inlaid with gold, intricate jeweled ties. My *musallim* opened it in my presence, his stony face betraying his contempt for such worldly display. Once he commenced to read, his expression changed into one of bitter anger.

It opened with fulsome praise of Maimonides and his work. Samuel ben Ali dared to write that he was "proud to claim Maimonides as a friend" and even reminded him of their boyhood together in Cordova. He added that he had also defended him at one time to the Jews of Yemen who had been opposed to much of the doctrine advanced by my master in his *Mishneh Torah*. Then, Ben Ali wrote smoothly, "as has always been the case with men as great as yourself, those who ascend to the mountaintop sometimes fail to discern what is in the valley."

It was a honeyed introduction, done, no doubt, to render the rest of the poison palatable. Nathaniel ben al-Fayyumi of Yemen—father of the very Jacob to whom Maimonides had written a screed of comfort in his famous "Letter to the South" —had forwarded to Bagdad what he had heard: "The teaching of Maimonides on the resurrection, what he declared before the face of Saladin, has caused great wailing and confusion here. Many people despair of redemption. They have taken to reading heretical writings and again listening to false messiahs. This is grievous to us; there is none but you, great Gaon of Bagdad, to show us the truth."

Yet Samuel ben Ali was clever enough—at the moment— to avoid this topic. Instead, he wrote of a small Responsum my master had written in answer to a technical question. The inquiry concerned the legality of a Jew's traveling on the Tigris or Euphrates rivers during the Sabbath. Maimonides had replied, in his liberal fashion, that no sin was involved.

On this point, Ben Ali took him to task in a hypocritical way. He declared Maimonides had unfortunately erred in his ruling when he said such a law was merely that of the old rabbis, not a scriptural command. He reminded my master of the similarity of what he had said to the pronouncement of that apostate rabbi, Jesus Christ, who had declared that the Sabbath had been made for man, not man for the Sabbath.

In this fashion he inferred that Maimonides was a scholar not only lacking in elementary knowledge of the Talmud but also unversed in the Torah.

At this point, Maimonides stopped reading. His voice choked up with resentment. He flung down the missive and glared at me. "From Yemen!" he exclaimed. "All this from Yemen, the very land I held to my bosom in the time of its distress. They asked me for my opinion and I gave it to them! This they bundled up and sent to Ben Ali in Bagdad—for a greater truth, I suppose!"

"Perhaps they wanted reassurance from everyone," I ventured. "Samuel ben Ali feels it is a great compliment to be asked to comment on your opinion."

"Undoubtedly!" snorted Maimonides. He flexed his fingers as if already writing and went off without another word. That evening, having spent the whole day in his chamber, he brought me his reply. He asked me to read it.

It was a masterpiece. Maimonides took the same deadly polite tone toward his enemy. He declared he had the greatest respect for Ben Ali because of his position and his "infinite knowledge." But, wrote my master, he was aware that the laws of the Sabbath were biblical. Indeed, he had said so in his book of precepts. Perhaps, he added casually, Ben Ali— as astute as he was—had lacked the time to read them carefully. If he had studied the *Mishneh Torah* carefully, he would have found all the details listed. As it was, my master mourned the fact that one so learned as the Gaon of Bagdad had seen fit to indulge in attributing false views to others.

"In regard to traveling on water," Maimonides wrote, "I considered only this, and no more must be inferred from it. Since the rivers mentioned, like the Nile, are wide and deep, it is as permissible to travel on them as it is permitted on the high seas. The fact that the rivers are fresh and the seas salt makes no difference. It makes no difference if some of the worthy Gaonim have prohibited it. They give no reasons for their declaration. We cannot accept it as final. Is it not well known to you, great Ben Ali, that many scholars have traveled on the water on the Sabbath without sin?"

I advised my master to delete the rest of what he said as a precautionary measure. He refused. In it, he flung—like some Christian knight—a challenge directly into the face of Samuel ben Ali. "You seem to place me among those who are sensitive to every word of criticism," he wrote, a noble sentiment which he promptly contradicted by continuing: "You are making a mistake. God has protected me against this weakness. I tell you, in His name, that if the most insignificant scholar, friend or foe, should point out an error to me, I would be grateful for the correction." Thus he delivered a telling lunge of his own against Ben Ali—but it was a mistake.

"This is a gag of wisdom and authority which will silence him," I said as enthusiastically as I could when I finished reading.

"Do you think so?" Maimonides muttered, his usual black fit of reaction coming upon him.

"He will never be able to refute this," I asserted. I could not help adding: "Nevertheless, he has given you a threat upon the subject of your views on immortality. This you may not find so easy to confute."

"He is an ignoramus and a fool!" Maimonides said violently, apparently not hearing what I had said.

"But a learned ignoramus and a powerful fool," I pointed out. Maimonides snatched his reply from my fingers. He walked out rapidly without a word further.

Two days later, he was able to humiliate me. It was my own fault, a trap I might have avoided with the use of the smallest good sense. But I was carried away by the bile of emotions churning in my breast. That morning, as ill luck would have it, I was crossing the courtyard on the way to the market place. I encountered none other than Abul Maali. The handsome, overdressed Moslem court functionary came to Maimonides' house for only one reason: Even when he arrived ostensibly to pay his respects to my master or to deliver a message from Al-Alfadhel, he never failed to visit Yaltah.

On this occasion, as on all others, he bowed courteously and murmured a greeting. I do not know what devil prompted me as he entered briskly. He saw me, smiled and said: "Peace be upon you!"

I scowled and did not reply. His expression became haughty. He turned to pass me. As he did, almost without knowing it, acting from a hatred I could not contain, I spit upon the floor before his foppish red slippers.

He turned convulsively. His hand flew to his sash, where he ordinarily carried a weapon. But he found none. His eyes burned into mine, flaming with fury. I held my ground and gave him look for look. For a long moment, we said nothing.

387

Then, at length, he cleared his throat. His words came out very slowly, in a deep rasp.

"Joseph ben Aknin," he said, "I see before me a head ripe for the sickle. I think already I see the blood between your turban and your shoulders. While your tongue is still in your mouth, before it is torn wriggling from its roots by the executioner's pincers, say, do you wish to speak?"

Under his malignant stare, I remained mute. The air vibrated with our loathing of each other. "Very well," he said at last, "what is destined, is destined. Prepare yourself."

"My very good friend, Abul Maali," interrupted Maimonides sonorously. "I give you greeting and welcome; my house is your house. For what do you prepare my pupil, Joseph?"

"For the executioner's block," Maali said shortly.

Maimonides cast upon me a black look. "What foolishness has he committed?" he inquired.

Without answering, Maali pointed to the tiles before his feet where my spittle still glistened. Maimonides looked from him to me and back once more. Then, before I could prevent him, he stooped and placed his finger in it. He straightened and solemnly rubbed his own forehead with his finger. "Thus," he said, "do I take this affront upon myself. Allow me, my dear friend, to deal with this in my own way. Consider whatever has befallen to have been against me, not against your august self."

Maali's face cleared and became calm. "Because of your great magnanimity," he said, "I do accept this, brother of Yaltah. The incident is closed. It has never happened." Without a backward look at me, they proceeded together to the inner chambers of my master.

The humiliation and despair of this meeting cannot be described. I felt as if my entrails had been torn out of me. Disgraced by my own impetuous feelings, I ran out of the room to my own, where I remained for hours, my robe thrown over my head, tears streaming from my eyes. I was in an agony of frustration and fury, tasting my temper on my tongue, feeling it eat my veins like acid. For a long time, I was able neither to speak nor to eat nor drink—nor even to think about what had happened in that disgraceful instant.

In the evening, Maimonides entered. I did not need to see him. I recognized his footfall and turned away from his presence. I wished to be alone but he would not gratify what he must have known to be my inmost desire.

"Salutations are part of civilization," Maimonides said softly. "Esau ran to meet Jacob and embraced him and fell on his neck and kissed him and wept. The hand touching the ground, then the lips, is another sign; even bowing seven times or striking hands. 'Is it well with thee?' we ask from ancient times. 'Peace to thee and to thy house,' is the greeting of the ancients. The Moslems say: 'Peace upon you,' though such is not to those of our nation. We prostrate ourselves in body before kings, we prostrate ourselves in our hearts before our friends. My son Joseph, so much as I know of courtesy, I have never heard of spitting before a guest being an acceptable greeting to him."

"I hate this man!" I cried.

"Very well," Maimonides said. "Now he hates you. He has the power in high places to tear you from my heart and place your head in jeopardy. Is this sensible?"

"No," I muttered.

"What is the reason for your hatred?"

I could not answer that. "The way he looks, the way he talks," I said. "Anything about him, his gait, his dress—his very presence fouls the air for me."

"He is my friend and a friend of the house. He has done me many favors and will continue them."

"Do you not know why?" I burst out. "Are you so blind? Do you not see that all this is because he wishes to marry Yaltah and is endeavoring to win your favor?"

Maimonides cocked his head and regarded me for a long time with a queer look. "So that is it," he murmured. He rose and shook his head. "Remember, Joseph," he admonished me, "Abul Maali is my guest in my house. I cannot have him insulted. He is important to the well being, not only of myself, but of all Jews in Egypt. When you spit before him, you spit on all your countrymen."

As he turned to leave he said, almost as an afterthought: "There is a packet for you at the gate."

It was from my father. In the letter with it, he congratulated me on the progress of my studies. Wrapped carefully and labeled LINEN was a large sum of money, sufficient for my wants—if I was careful—for years. My father also wrote that the family estates in Aleppo had been liberated from the Christians by Saladin: Our fortunes had been restored.

My grief gave way to exultation. Here was freedom at hand, pulling me toward the unknown, ready to show me the world.

But I realized there was one more act I must perform—one last hope to be expressed—before I could take my leave.

"That is the last of my compositions," I said, putting down the sheet of parchment. "Tell me: What do you think of them?"

It was the afternoon of the next day. We sat in an upper chamber of the house. Yaltah and I, alone: I had begged for an audience with her, excluding all others. I had hired two flute players to perform soft music in a corner of the room as I recited my verses. Now I dismissed them with a wave of my hand and waited for her answer.

Yaltah gazed at me with the great dark eyes of Maimonides that I could never meet except with a thrill of excitement. Slowly she clasped her hands and lowered her head. "I think that you will perhaps be offended with me," she murmured.

My heart sank. "No, no." I reassured her. "You must speak your mind. Poets must learn to bend the knee before the truth."

"Well, then," Yaltah whispered, "the flutes were too strident in their sweetness. They were not suited to the words; the melody distracted me."

My heart bounded. "Well said," I declared. "I know precisely what you mean. But the poetry itself?"

"It is beautiful though it is nothing that I know about."

"Knowledge is nothing, inspiration is all."

"My brother says that knowledge is all."

"He does not include poetry in the arts of the mind," I hastened to tell her. "In verse, it is the liver which swells and responds to the words and music."

"I have tried to say only what I feel," Yaltah said. "You are a generous man, Joseph. Others do not take criticism so well."

"I have trained myself to listen judiciously to everyone," I said. I shuffled the sheets of my verses together, still relishing their tang on my inner palate. "I have faults, no doubt. But I see them. Myself, I am a critic without fear. How, then, can I deny the rights of others? If I have an opinion, I voice it without fear or regard for friend or foe. I wish no less from those that—that love me."

"Of course, the shrillness of the flutes is beloved by the Moslems," Yaltah said. "But perhaps to our Jewish ears it is different."

The conversation was going very well; I approved of the

sentiment. "Let us not talk of either Jews or Moslems," I whispered to her. I extended my hand to touch hers but—at the last moment—I lost courage and withdrew it.

"Shall we talk of ourselves?" she asked. She was utterly without guile. I felt as the serpent must have felt that tempted Eve. "Yes," I said.

"What is there to speak of?"

The simple query threw me into confusion. "Nothing," I said, "yet everything. Dare I call you Yaltah?"

"That is my name. You have called me so for a long time."

"I know, I know," I said hastily, "but that was on different occasions."

"Is this an occasion unlike the others?" she asked naïvely. "We are such good friends, we have talked about so much."

"There is a time to end friendship," I said savagely.

"To end it?" Her eyes became liquid, trembling. I pulled at the neckpiece of my gown and cleared my throat. "My voice bothers me."

"My brother has a remedy. I shall go—"

"No, no!" I interrupted her, taking her by the arm and pulling her down once more to her seat. I sighed and rose, pacing the room as she watched me in bewilderment.

"I remember a mad *madhi* in Yemen who claimed no sword could hurt him. He put his head on the block, and lost it. If it happened to me, perhaps I could speak better," I said impatiently.

"What nonsense!" Yaltah exclaimed in surprise.

"Maimonides says that all poets talk nonsense."

Yaltah smiled suddenly. "He does not care for poetry."

"And you?"

"My opinions are my own."

"Yaltah," I said quickly, decisively, seizing the bull by the horns as the fabled dancers in the labyrinth of Crete once did, "let us talk of love."

Without coyness, Yaltah raised her head. "I do not know what you mean," she said.

"True love, that is what I mean."

"Is there any other kind?"

I smiled sadly, with superior knowledge. "There is almost every other kind," I said.

"There must be one that is real," Yaltah replied promptly, "which makes all the others false."

Her steadfast look made me uneasy. "Now you talk philosophy, like your brother," I chided her.

391

"Do you not believe in a love that will last forever?" she asked me directly.

I felt shaken. "Not in my life, not as yet," I responded. "But I may hope to find it, if it exists."

"You speak of the love between a man and woman?"

"Yes, yes!"

She considered. "Do you think love is no more than the foul things that slaves scribble on the walls of their bath, Joseph?" she asked at last.

"Well," I said judiciously, even before I realized my folly, "I have often deemed it remarkable that the same organs of the body are adapted both to the art of ecstasy and the act of easing ourselves."

Yaltah stiffened. "Perhaps you have done writing of the sort yourself," she said frigidly.

"No, no!" I exclaimed miserably. "It is this wretched philosophical mind in which your brother has trained me so well! True love is nothing like that!"

"Then you believe in true love?"

"I believe in true love, in true philosophy, in true religion —in everything that is true."

"Do you believe in the true hell?" Yaltah asked in a hesitating small voice.

I felt puzzled. "Yes," I said, "it is a tenet of our faith, is it not?"

"I don't know," she responded, "but it need not be in the World-to-Come. I—I have lived in it for many years."

"You!"

Her gaze became intense. "Do you think I enjoy the long hours alone, the hours with the women that chatter like apes, with the slaves?"

"I never dreamed of this," I said wonderingly.

"There must be a world outside the walls, beyond the *sooq* and the stalls. Do you think the same mother and father that gave my brother birth did not give me a brain?"

"Yaltah," I said with difficulty. I sank upon my knees. "If you would be my wife, it shall all be different, different forever!"

I sprang to my feet. Maimonides had entered the room, his face cold and terrible. His presence confounded me like that of an apparition from under the earth. I thought he was away from the house: He had taken to visiting the cave of the hermit Guilbert, known now as Guilbert of the Hill, to meditate, possibly to talk. Whether it was for comfort or to sit by the

392

tomb of Zamira, I did not know. He had buried his beloved there. He sent gifts of food and clothing to the Christian hermit in return for his watch over her resting place. The wild nomads rifled such tombs if they were unwatched, stripping the body, even carrying away the bricks of the monument, if it was a Jewish sepulcher. Maimonides' visits had prompted gossip of heretical discussions; it was an association I abhorred, but Maimonides had cut my tongue off at the roots whenever I mentioned it. He had become haggard and worn with a secret burden I could not share. Now, however, his aspect was terrible in the extreme, disordered and wild eyed.

"Nothing will be different," he said in measured tones.

"We spoke only to each other!" I protested.

"I heard your voices. The master of the house may enter every room at his will. When he is being robbed of a treasure, it is his privilege to protect it."

"I rob no one," I said defiantly. "I have asked Yaltah to be my wife."

"It is not her right to reply," Maimonides said heavily. "I must answer for her." Strangely, he sounded as if he were in pain.

"Listen to me," Yaltah said in a despairing voice. Maimonides wheeled upon her. She shrank back. I sprang to her side but, under his accusing gaze, I refrained from touching her.

"A woman cannot be a witness," my master said, "least of all for herself."

"I shall take her right to ask, as you have taken her right to answer," I replied, not caring any longer that the hostility between us seemed tangible as stone.

"Have you not learned that love is not something you run from but journey toward with joy?" asked Maimonides. He shook his head. "Yaltah considers herself ill-treated. You consider yourself a prisoner. I give you leave to go—but she must remain."

"For what reason?" I cried, my voice breaking.

"I need not reply to that but I shall. Was it not you, Joseph, who tore her garments from her, the first day of your arrival in my house?"

The words were so unexpected that any thought of a reply suffocated me. I could not think; I waved my arms wildly. At last I managed to say: "At your command, at your command!"

"That is true," Maimonides said. "It had been better for

you at this moment if at that time you had thought of her modesty and refused."

Speechless at this incredible unreasonableness from my master, I flung my precious poems on the floor and fairly ran from the room. As I did, Yaltah's sobbing followed me. There was none to comfort her.

Early the next morning, without farewells, I departed from the house of Maimonides. I thought aimlessly of forcing Yaltah to go with me and dismissed the idea. I knew of the prescience of my master's mind, of his unchanging will, of his influence with the officials. I might have stayed, but the place was intolerable to me. I took my own mule and another for my baggage. Sniffing up the dry dust of the road with distaste, I made my way out of Fostat toward the north.

I deny the imputations which have arisen since: that I feared the vengeance of Maali. I had endured enough of the confinement of which Yaltah had spoken; Maimonides had rejected me; I was afire with the desire to see the world. It was my intention to return to Aleppo, there to take up residence with a well-traveled friend of my youth, Zekarya ben Berachal, a scholar and student.

CHAPTER 23

Painful as this is to write, it is true. As the truth, it deserves to be written. Whose fault it was—Maimonides or mine—will not be known. I blame myself. I am sure he, too, blames himself. All that can be said is that my master and I parted in the early months of the Christian year of 1190. For nearly nine years we were not to meet again.

I have one consolation for these years of separation. During this period Maimonides and I myself regretted what had happened to such a degree that we relented in correspondence. Letter after letter—some taking months to deliver—passed between us. I may add, with pride, it was during this time that my master wrote—for me alone—what has become the most famous of all his works, his *Guide for the Perplexed.*

394

As if it were no more than a few hours ago, I clearly recall my journey by lurching camel-back and spine-splitting mule-back, through webs of sandy trails, to Aleppo. My spirits, high and defiant when I left Fostat at dawn, melted to dejection by noon. There is nothing comparable to a continuous jolting at the base of the spine to reduce the brain to numbness—which is why, I suppose, children are punished in that region.

I shall never forget that trip. It was the first I had experienced for long years. I turned northeast to the frontier of Egypt to Ashkelon—or New Ascalon, as it is called (a city I was to see again). I sought my own people. The hundred Karaites there shunned me with averted faces; they had heard of me as the disciple of Maimonides. I repaid them with anathema. I went to seek out the synagogue of the other two hundred Jews of the city, headed by their rabbis, Zemach and Aaron. They gave me a king's welcome; my breast expanded.

Next day I joined a caravan on the great trail to the north. Two and a half days were spent in the journey to Jezreel, then on to Sepphoris with the mountainside graves of the holy teachers, Gamaliel, and Chiyya from Babylon—may they rest in glory! I made a pleasant stop at Tiberias on the river Jordan. The colony of fifty Jews welcomed me. Some took me to bathe in the waters of the hot springs. I was amused by their leader, the famous astronomer, Rabbi Abraham, who braided his long beard about his head so that it would not become wet and defiled. After worshiping in the synagogue built by Caleb ben Jephunneh, I spent two hours meditating on the spot where Maimonides had buried Judah Halevi. I recalled his verses and flung some of them to the ceaseless burning wind:

"Longing for Thee, I sought Thy heavenly trace;
I called on Thee, to meet Thee face to face;
But going out, to find Thee with a prayer—
I looked within—and, lo! I found Thee there!"

As I recited the lines, my heart grew heavy instead of buoyant. I thought of Yaltah, even of Cairo and Fostat, with homesick longing. I stifled the feeling. Two days later I paused for a moment beside the graves of Hillel and Shammai and the sepulchers of their disciples; a day and a half after, I arrived at Dan, to wonder at the small cavern from which the wise maintained that the mighty flood of the Jordan issued.

Two days more of travel: I entered the gates of Damascus. To me, it seemed the fairest city on earth. Full of roses and fruit, of sparkling rills and song, its gardens spread for thirty miles. It appeared to lie at the foot of Mount Hermon, which was covered with a white mantle of snow.

The greatest miracle of Damascus was its huge mosque, called the Dome of Hours. There could be nothing else like it in the whole of the world. Here were chambers plated with gold and glass. If the people walked by, they might see each other through the transparent walls. A thick barrier of crystal worked magic, with apertures according to the days of the year. As the rays of the sun through the dome entered each opening in succession, the hours were told by marked dials.

Again a day's journey: In Gilead I found not the fabled balm but many springs of clear running water with the delicate odor of spice. Still another day and I arrived at solemn, lovely Baalbec, the city built by Solomon's orders. It was a place of massive stones—some twenty cubits long and twelve wide—so tightly placed that not even a knife blade might be pushed into the cracks.

But by far the most marvelous sight I saw was in Fuwared-Der. Here there existed a spring with much water and a strong current. It was called the Spring of the Sabbath. For six days it refused to flow and then, on the Sabbath, it flowed copiously to the rejoicing of the city, accompanied by dancing and music and timbrels.

A day's journey to Hamath, once seized by the Assassins of the Old Man of the Mountain. Here, at the foot of bald Mount Lebanon, by the river Jabbok, an earthquake devoured twenty-five thousand souls in my father's time. More than one hundred thirty of them were Jews. Then, at last, in two and a half more days of travel, my weary body came to rest in the city of Aleppo, called Aram-Zoba, the royal city. The head rabbi, Moses el Constantini, a venerable patriarch who led a congregation of five thousand Jews, gave me welcome.

It was in the synagogue of Aleppo that I first became disquieted at the rumors concerning my master Maimonides. Old El Constantini shook his head dubiously at my request to know the whereabouts of the home of Zekarya.

"He is a strange man," he said in his piping voice.

"He was a boyhood friend," I said.

The rabbi shrugged his shoulders. "Many people change," he murmured. "You may find that he is not as devoted to the blessed *Mishneh Torah* you sent us as some of the rest of the Jews. He is inclined to the word from Bagdad." He would say nothing more. I did not press him. He gave me the directions to my friend's house and I departed.

It was in the very middle of the city. Like many another house in Aleppo, it was windowless and of whitewashed clay brick. As the grinning obsequious slave ushered me in, I felt uneasy. But I regained my calm at seeing a courtyard well planted with all manner of shrubs and trees, fruiting and blossoming, a copper fountain veiled with water in the midst. There was a cry. Zekarya ran out, falling on my bosom and embracing me.

"How well you look!" he exclaimed with tears in his eyes. "After so many years!" I detected a note of reproach in what he said.

"And you," I replied but I lied. He was much changed. He had become a man unhealthy: white-skinned as a woman, fat hanging from his cheeks and thighs, soft-voiced, with red-rimmed eyes set far apart. He had the unctuous manner of a courtier. I swear, from that moment, I could never tell if he was man or woman.

"Welcome, welcome," he said, squeezing my hands between his own pillows of flesh, "you are master here now. Command what you will; even I am your obedient slave."

"So much is not necessary," I hastened to reply. He stepped back and pressed his hands against his cheeks. "You are dusty and famished, in need of ordering yourself," he declared. He clapped his hands over my protest. A gugglet of rose-water sherbet was brought. Behind the servant hastened a frowzy barber with his brass basin to fit about my neck, with his brush and soap and warm water, with his ever dull blade.

"This is different from the hair-tents of the desert," I said, spitting out the soap as he lathered.

"You will be delightful to see," said Zekarya, smiling and cocking his jowls to one side, "once you are yourself."

I endured the torture of being shaved and having my beard trimmed—as well as the incessant meaningless chatter that the barber poured into my ear. By the time he was through scraping my flesh and apologizing, Zekarya's slave had brought in a whole lamb stuffed with rice and almonds. We sat to eat.

"What do you do in Aleppo?" he inquired after gorging himself and wiping his hands on an exquisitely embroidered napkin.

"I come from Cairo," I said. I hesitated.

Zekarya's face took on a secret animation. "Yes?" he said.

"I have been the pupil of Maimonides," I said flatly.

"How unfortunate," said my friend blandly.

I bristled. "I do not believe that," I said. "What does Aleppo know of his teachings?"

"He is not fit to teach swine," Zekarya asserted, "much less a beautiful young man like yourself."

"I want to tell you—" I began, but Zekarya held up a fat white pudgy hand.

"Permit me," he said unctuously, "before you go farther— I have no quarrel whatsoever with your master."

"But—but I have heard—" I stammered and again he interrupted me.

"About me?" he asked. "That I have denounced him?"

"Yes," I said, though I had not heard so much.

"You have been listening to gossip and false rumor," he said. "I swear I wish that God may give him health, wealth, and the blessings of fame, even more than he possesses."

"I am sure he will be grateful," I said, bewildered.

"My prayers will not give it to him, however. It will be his own esteemed character."

"You are too good," I said, quite overcome.

"To preserve his reputation," Zekarya told me, "I would sacrifice my own."

"That is very charitable," I returned, not to be outdone.

"It is much less than he deserves. What shall I say of you, his so-faithful disciple?"

"What would you say?" I asked.

"I would exalt you no less for having endured his teachings for such a length of time," Zekarya told me.

"What does that mean?" I demanded.

"It means only," Zekarya went on smoothly, "that the weight of such learning and wisdom must have been a heavy burden upon your mind."

"Not as heavy as you might think," I responded, beginning to dislike what I heard and surmised.

Zekarya spread his hands. "In truth," he said, "I shall tell you everything. You shall tell me what you like. I am a simple man and like simple things."

"In surroundings such as these?" I said incredulously.

"Mere baubles compared to things of the soul," he told me, rolling his eyes around with evident pleasure, then lifting them toward heaven as if to implore pardon for his pride. "It enables me to forbear asking charity. It puts my thoughts at ease and allows me to turn them to higher things. Once the body is comfortable, how easy it is to approach the Highest, blessed be His Name!"

"You have no love for things of this world?"

"Only inasmuch as they give me a foretaste of the delights to come. But tell me: What evil things have you heard from the refuse of the bazaars?"

"That you reject the *Mishneh Torah,* the teachings of Maimonides, and exalt those of Samuel ben Ali."

"On the contrary," Zekarya said with a show of anger. "I was a pupil of that mighty Gaon. Is it not written one should love one's teacher above even his father?"

"True," I said uncomfortably.

"You cannot ask me to turn against Bagdad. But that does not mean my face is not set toward Fostat with longing, eh?"

"I suppose you are right," I told him, not knowing what else to say. We talked on, turning to our recollections of the Maghreb, of our youth together. I felt stiff and cold by the time Zekarya pushed himself upward from his crossed legs. "You have traveled far," he commented. "You must rest on down tonight. I shall give you my own chamber."

Again I protested, but to no avail. The airy gestures of Zekarya fluttered away all my words. I found myself in a room as rich as that of a houri in the Paradise of Mohammed. I felt a sense of shock at the walls hung with costly draperies and tapestries, the corners filled with cushions of multi-colored silks, the vaguely obscene drawings on panels of linen. The only furniture was a tiny table and lamp. The air was filled with the scent of burning aloes, musk, and ambergris. In one part I dimly saw rows of precious objects—coins from the ancient revolt of Bar Kochba (whom Maimonides always bitterly called "traitor" for his false messiahship), the faces of the Roman emperors overstruck with grapes and lute and vine leaf by Jewish craftsmen; bowls of black glass with gold patterns of the Ark and menorah worked into it. In the midst shone a huge gold plate with the familiar palm tree and shofar, with half-obliterated characters of Hebrew I could not read— and around it were pagan vases, statues, a cabinet of valuable manuscripts. I scanned the codices with reverent admiration. "Are these the Talmud?" I asked, turning to Zekarya.

He laughed, a disagreeable high laugh. "Do you not know," he demanded, "that the Talmud is a load for two mules to carry?" He squinted at me over the bubbles of his cheeks. "I understand Maimonides has it all within his head," he said slyly. "Perhaps he has reduced it all to merely one mule-load."

It was not an auspicious beginning. Despite the luxury of my welcome, I felt unwelcome, almost under surveillance. I spent most of the next morning writing of my experiences to none other than Maimonides himself. My resentment at what I believed to be injustice had not dissolved, but where else could I turn? Now that I had ventured again into the world, the years in which I had been immured at Fostat twisted against me. I was exposed to more emotions than my own, feelings slippery in my mind, which left slimy tracks in my thought. I hired a special messenger for the south and sent him off posthaste.

On my return from the market, Zekarya greeted me with his affable, oily manner. "I have tidings for you," he said, twining his fingers. "An old friend of yours."

"A friend of mine?"

"Perhaps not of yours but of your master, one you should regard as supreme in the realm of thought."

"Only one is such," I said cautiously, my curiosity aroused. Zekarya raised his thin plucked eyebrows. He gestured me before him into the house.

On the cool eastern side of the court's enclosure sat a man in a shabby litter. He seemed very old. The cords in his neck were prominent, the sockets of his eyes deep in his head. I started back as he looked at me: The man was sightless. I hardly observed his rich gown of brocade and the jewels on his shrunken fingers. His blindness and the fact that nowhere on his flesh did he seem to have a single hair riveted my gaze.

"Who is this?" he demanded. I approached hesitatingly. "I can hear a visitor; he is someone new, my nose tells me."

"A friend of a friend," answered Zekarya placatingly. "One whom you knew before you were forced to leave Spain."

"Happy Almería," the other man mumbled in a voice as croaking as that of a raven. "Who may he be?"

"His name is Joseph ben Aknin."

"I do not know it."

"A friend of a friend, I said before. This young man is a mighty scholar and poet." I recognized the sneer in Zekarya's voice but I said nothing.

"We are all scholars here, eh?" said the old man. "Whom does he claim as a friend?"

400

"You have often told me how your magic summoned him," said Zekarya smoothly. "In those days he was scarcely different in age from this tender youngster. The name of the friend is the famous Maimonides, Moses ben Maimon."

To my terror, the face of the blind man writhed as if serpents coiled under the skin. His toothless mouth worked. His be-ringed hands opened and closed convulsively. He leaned toward me from the litter. "Let me feel his face, let me feel his face," he whispered again and again. Zekarya pushed me forward. I resisted, appalled: I could not allow those cold claws to touch my flesh.

After a time, the pale pink flush of anger which had come up into his skin subsided. He sank back. "He is Isaac ben Abraham, Isaac the Blind, the mighty Kabbalist," Zekarya said. He used a loud tone, noting me from a corner of his eye. The title roused the other. He sat upright, nodding to himself. A thread of saliva crept like a worm from the corner of his mouth.

"Young Maimonides was a fool," he said in his hoarse tones, "and I feel nothing against him. But his father, Maimon ben Joseph—he accepted my hospitality and damned me. He made me a fool in the eyes of others. I could not have revenge, he left before I sought him out. But I shall find him. Someone shall thrust him into my grip." His claws curled in the air before him, shaking. "I have saved all my strength for that moment!"

"You will have to descend into the grave," I said, as calmly as I could. "Maimon ben Joseph, may he rest in peace, is long since dead in Egypt, in the House of Souls."

To my surprise, the face of the man commenced to shift and slack. It turned wet with tears. Isaac the Blind began to blubber, but not in sorrow. "To think that I am robbed, robbed," he mourned in a rusty chant. "Are you sure, young sir, are you sure?"

"I was there the day he died. I saw his body with my own eyes."

"Then there is nothing left for me to live for! Ezra and Azriel, my own sweet boys who studied at my feet, left me when the people laughed. They could endure my love, my house; they could not stand laughter—is it not strange? Now they wander everywhere but to my knee, preaching what I taught them as their own. I have no one left."

"You have me," said Zekarya, winking at me. Isaac the

Blind made a horrid grimace. "You!" he growled. "Neither man nor woman! Nothing, nothing is left!"

Unperturbed, as if he were accustomed to such abuse, Zekarya continued: "There is the golem."

"The golem!" Isaac the Blind sat upright in excitement. His crooked hands waved before his sightless eyes. "I had forgotten! That is yet my great work, which shall prove I am right! I shall produce life from the dust!"

I stared at him fearfully and drew back. "A golem?" I inquired in a whisper of Zekarya. He smiled dimly and nodded. "You shall see. Eight days from tomorrow. When the sun has won its proper position in the zodiac."

In our language the word "golem" means that which is embryo, an unborn monster. It is something created out of lifeless, shapeless stuff by the use of special terrible charms—chiefly the *Shem Ha-m'foresh*, the Tetragrammaton of the Ineffable Name.

It seemed to me that if such a one as this Isaac the Blind, so ready with his curses against a man I knew to be righteous, could create dumb servants in the image of human beings—somehow the scheme of creation had gone wrong. Yet the fascination with the feat intrigued me, leaving me sleepless and fearsome. I was not able to resist the invitation of Zekarya to come secretly with him one early morning in the middle of the next week. Nor did I refuse to assist him in the cold dawn in carrying the litter of the mumbling Isaac the Blind —his secret ingredients hugged to his breast—to the synagogue. It was a day when no one would be there, an hour when the streets in Aleppo were clear of their throngs.

We entered fearfully. Gently, noiselessly, we put down the litter in the middle of the floor. Like some great insect, Isaac the Blind crawled out with his unknown chemicals and materials. He spread them by touch on the floor in front of him. One by one he arranged the curiously shaped containers; last of all, he set down a magnificent wide-mouthed Greek vase of glass: rare, colored with swirls of red and white within the substance. Into this (as we watched), grumbling as he worked, feeling his measures by the dip of a finger, his white face hovering over them in the still-heavy shadows of the synagogue like a full moon, Isaac the Blind mixed his golem.

The synagogue, a square room with whitewashed brick walls rising unadorned to the beams above, was extraordinary only in a single feature. It was one which obviously was an imitation of the Moslem Dome of Hours in Damascus. Somewhere had been got a great square of thick glass like those used in the heathen place of worship. With great care, in place of a skylight above, this had been inserted into the south wall. It gave a feeble light indeed. I was at a loss to account for this following of the Moslem practice, until suddenly the sun broke through into the synagogue like a fountain of living light.

Then I understood. This was a loveliness I had never before perceived in such a place. The glory of God hung round about us. Dazzling sheets of color danced like the girls before the throne of mighty Solomon. They quivered and shone—darkest red to brightest orange, deepest purple dye on the walls to the most brilliant yellows and greens on the ceiling—as the sun's rays were refracted through the substance.

The quick illumination was almost a shock. Both Zekarya and I squatted down in awe. Isaac the Blind continued his mumbling over his preparations. He hissed like a serpent.

"See! Charcoal from wood and air!"

"Yes." It was Zekarya's whisper, answering like one charmed.

"Sulfur spirits from the earth!"

"Sulfur."

"The niter from the water!"

"There it is."

"Earth, air, water—what is needed for life is fire!" cried Isaac, rising on his hands and knees. He presented an almost comical figure—were it not for his demented aspect—in his robe of many colors painted by the light of the window that sloped to the south, toward Jerusalem.

"Mix well, mix long," Isaac intoned, stirring the jar's dark contents with a slender smoothed stick. "Gently, because this is life that stirs beneath you. *Adamah* out of which we shall create our own man. We shall seek our own such, over all the earth. With an army of golems, unable to hear or obey anything except their master's voice, who can resist?"

The blind man rose and stretched his arms out to their utmost. His face assumed the most terrible solemnity. I knew he was about to pronounce the unknown name of the Most High. In fear, both Zekarya and myself prostrated our bodies before him. We had no need. Isaac the Blind murmured the word only to himself. He slipped a bit of papyrus into the jar. He flung around, a light of exaltation on his eroded face. "Zekarya, young Joseph, where are you? Come! See the miracle when fire is applied. Show me the route of the sun through the glass that you have described, Zekarya!"

Shaking, Zekarya did as he was obliged, positioning the jar very exactly. Then, in a scutter, he returned to my side. Both of us stared, wide-eyed and awe-stricken, at the old man. He sat motionless before his concoction. "Zekarya," he said softly, "what is the light of the sun like?" Zekarya did not answer. The place was deathly still.

The window of glass filled with the marvelous colors of every hue. It was a magic of light dispersion I could not comprehend. I felt nervous and lightheaded. Zekarya beside me continually wrung his hands in anticipation of some event unknown to me. His fat face betrayed high anxiety. Before us, over the iridescent pot half-filled with its powder, Isaac the Blind squatted again. He mumbled throaty words without ceasing, making peculiar gestures, his white hands fluttering like moths over the top. Slowly the sun crept its way along the floor. I noted a phenomenon. In the middle, there was a spot of light so intense that the eye could not hold it in sight except by looking past it. It moved imperceptibly, holding its inner fire, toward the pot. Indeed, by foreknowledge, Zekarya had placed the container so that it was directly in its path.

We waited. We were silent. In the distance, outside the synagogue, we heard people pass and repass. There were vague colored shadows. I felt we were beneath the sea, buried in the water. My breath caught in my throat. My nerves tingled, my skin itched. I waited. The spot crawled along the floor, a beetle of fire. Closer and closer it came. Isaac must have felt its warmth. His wavings of the hands became frantic; his speech louder, more guttural, echoing in the chamber.

The insect of intense light climbed up the side of the squat vase. It reached the top and touched Isaac's hand. He flinched and jerked back, staggering up once again, his aged face full of extraordinary frenzy. He opened his mouth. He seemed about to shriek out a curse or an imprecation, a charm or chant of praise when the light dipped into the vase.

Instantly, there was a dull roar, unbearably loud. A crash of shards, tinkle of bits. A black-and-white cloud of choking smoke billowed up. It blinded us, even as Isaac was blind. We rose and reeled back. The walls dimmed with the soot of the explosion. We fell to our knees and crawled forward, shaking our heads, dazed, afraid, whimpering like dogs, but impelled to find out what had happened. Zekarya stopped. He tugged at my robe but I went forward.

The smoke lifted a little from the floor. Isaac's enchanted vase had vanished. In its place remained only a small white smudge on the floor, an obscene bloom. Beside it stretched the blind Kabbalist. His limbs jerked, his head turned from side to side. His nerveless hands stretched limp. In his throat—buried deep—with blood springing forth, was a great piece of the striped glass vase.

Crawling to his side, I could not but hear the frightened whisper of Zekarya, awed with his own sophistry: "It is the golem! The golem!"

Indeed the cloud of smoke above us had, for an instant, assumed the shape of a great jinni, menacing and boiling. I had no more time to watch. Kneeling beside Isaac, I threw my weight on his legs to hold him still. I saw that the blood did not spurt. It was purple rather than red. It seemed a miracle from God, praised be He! The glass had missed the great blood tubes. I seized the shard and drew it forth with care. At the same time I compressed the skinny neck tightly with my fingers.

"Zekarya! Zekarya! Quickly! Bring good linen! Pads, soaked in the best hot wine!" With my other hand, I mechanically picked up a burning bit of parchment near his head and snuffed it out, pocketing it.

It was fully half an hour before the dripping dressings were applied. By that time, my fingers were numb. But there had been no more bleeding, nor any foam. Isaac appeared to have fainted, for which I was thankful. I arranged his limbs and kept my other hand pressing upon the pad—always watching the deep irregular breathing of the old man to be sure I did not strangle him. Another hour passed. Still another hour. I had Zekarya renew the pad. At last, cramped and worn, I rose from the floor, having bound his throat securely with a dry bandage. I hoped for the best results, never despairing, according as Maimonides had taught me.

I found myself surrounded by strangers, men of the Aleppo congregation. They watched silently as I spoke to Zekarya, now trembling as if he stood in the blast of a cold wind. "Let the bandage remain," I said, "and take him to your house. He must remain quiet a week or more. Then the bindings may be removed and others placed. Be sure they are dry and touched with the dust of the gall of green pomegranates."

Eyes wide with respect, he nodded. Exhausted, I pushed through the unspeaking throng of onlookers. Old El Constantini, his face stern, shook his white hair in disapproval, watching me over his thick beard.

That night, for the first time in my life, I experienced nightmares. I dreamed I saw Lilith, wife of Azrael, hovering over me. Her dark and beautiful face seemed distorted with her longing for a human life. Behind her, I saw her endless evil hosts. The words of Isaiah—that the night-monster would find her a place of rest—came into my head in illuminated letters. I muttered in agony the names of the three protecting angels— Senoi, Sansenoi, and Sammangelof—those who had spared her from drowning in the sea when she threatened to destroy Adam, howling revenge for his choosing Eve as his mate. *"Lilla abi! Lilla abi!"* I cried wildly. "Begone, Lilith!"

But her hands clutched about my body. I awoke with my hair on end, my flesh bathed in sweat. Next moment my fear turned to revulsion. I heard Zekarya's breathing in my ear. "I am frightened," he whispered, "I am frightened. I have come to you for comfort, do not send me away!" As he spoke, his hands wandered over my breast and thighs.

I thrust him back, beating him unmercifully with my fists. He rolled away and rose and ran whining from the room. Shaking from the nightmare and the reality, I threw on my garments, took up my traveling pouches. I fled that house of evil that very night.

Long after, I heard that, despite my going, Zekarya had obeyed my instructions. Isaac the Blind had survived. But the glass of his last experiment had severed cords in his throat and made him speechless.

Years later I told Maimonides of the ordeal of his ancient acquaintance. He shook his head. He said nothing until he had listened to my account twice more. "Isaac the Blind was meddling with a greater force than he knew," he said at length. "The force must have been the result of the sulfur and charcoal, as you say. I did not know it would explode if contained, but it seems to be true. A devil's invention from the East. I have read of it, but never have I thought of mixing it. There are warnings, there are warnings." He nodded his head sadly.

"Is it the stuff of earth?" I asked wonderingly.

Maimonides nodded. "One can mix it as one pleases," he said, "and I fear that the mad Christian crusaders have discovered the secret."

"Its ingredients?"

"Ground charcoal, for one, as Isaac said. For another, the spirits of sulfur in a fine powder. But the third and special part of it is the white efflorescence on stones, in damp crypts. It comes from death and returns to death. This is scraped and boiled with stale urine. It forms like ice upon the top of the liquid when it is cold. Then it is ground again and mixed with the others."

"Why, if it is this common," I said aghast, "it may kill hundreds of men!"

Maimonides nodded. "The secret is the proportion of the three," he said.

"Do you know it?"

"Without this knowledge, it is useless. Yes, I know it. But I shall never tell you nor anyone. The secret will remain hidden in my bosom."

"No," I said. "Man must find out what he will and control it by the use of his better nature."

Maimonides gazed at me wryly. I fought against the smothering darkness of his eyes. "Of what use is his better nature," he asked softly, "against his desire for slaughter?"

Whatever the explosive compound was, it had disastrous effects. On that night in Aleppo, I was in no wise to consider them. I made my way to the synagogue to spend the rest of the night. I found a single candle burning there, the old rabbi praying beneath it. I prayed beside him. We remained so a long while. When I raised my head, he was waiting; he handed me a letter. He said not a word, leaving the candle behind and passing out of the sanctuary with a slow, dignified gait.

I unsealed the thick missive. It was, as I expected, from my master, Maimonides, in Fostat. He had written me the same day that he had received my own letter. He gave me a loving greeting and praised my magnanimity. My heart melted in peace and joy at the sight of his writing, at his terse, clipped sentiments. He went directly to the point.

Do not listen to the trash of Zekarya's talk. It is worth nothing, fit only to be burned in Gehenna. Others say likewise. For instance—yes, I know it is so!—they say that I am hostile to the Talmud, that I oppose it, that I try, with my writings, to make a new one. I! Of all people, my son Joseph, you know I have devoted my life to its study. At this very moment in Fostat, when I recover from my exhaustion of a day at court, I lecture to stu-

407

dents on its sacred words. I am not the only authority on it—nor do I wish to be considered so. You know this: I am only one of many interpreters of these words. I pray God continually that I may be right.

Have I ever said—to anyone, at any time—that all other books—as many as there are—should be burned and only mine kept? No. On the contrary, my sole object is to further the knowledge of the Talmud among those who do not know it. There are many, too many, ignorant confused people in our race. I wish to make clear and simple what these writings should be to these people.

All this is unnecessary to write you. You, of all people, know me best of all. I have delivered the burden of my soul to you many nights on the rooftops of Cairo or Fostat. Yet hear one thing more: I have been informed from other sources than yourself—though I do not know if it be true—that there is in Bagdad someone who speaks evil against me directly and tries to gain honor by misrepresentation of what I teach. I am glad to hear that you in Aleppo have protested against this and reprimanded the slanderer. For this, you must take my thanks and blessings. But do not do so again. I forgive all who oppose me, such as the one in Bagdad, because of his lack of intelligence—even when by opposing me he seeks his own personal reputation. He does not harm me. When he is pleased, he does not rob me of anything. These, my son, are useless quarrels. Use your time more fitly. I do not need the help of other men, even yourself; people may follow whom they please. I raise a lamp to guide their footsteps. If they do not choose to come into its circle of light, they will not be persuaded by those devoted ones like yourself.

At this point I became aware of a watcher. He was El Constantini, who had silently returned. He stroked his bushy beard thoughtfully as he regarded me in the light of the guttering candle. "You are a fool," he said abruptly.

I started at his use of the familiar, despised term. Before my anger could fuse into words, he spoke again. "Did you not know Zekarya is engaged to be wed to the daughter of Samuel ben Ali of Bagdad?" he demanded.

My mouth opened and closed like that of a stranded fish. All became clear and deadly in my mind. "But he is not a man," I managed to say. The old rabbi nodded agreement. "He is only half a man," he said, "but Sarah is only half a

408

woman. She even teaches the Talmud to students from a window where her face may remain concealed."

"This is sin!" I said.

"Nay," El Constantini reproved me, "there is nothing against it in the Scripture. But it is not the office of a woman. It does Samuel ben Ali little credit, in either office he holds."

"Either office?"

"He is now serving jointly with Ben Hisdai as Exilarch, head of the Jews, as well as Gaon of the Academy."

"It makes no difference," I murmured. "I return to Fostat." I glanced at the rest of the letter. My heart was at peace, I was ready to go back, to spend the rest of my days in Egypt with Maimonides. But I stiffened as I read.

As much as I rejoice to have seen your writing and heard your voice again in my heart, I must tell you that which shall sadden and anger you. I am to be married. I have often longed for children, as you know; once I thought Silver Dove might supply the lack but she fled the cote of my house long ago. Therefore I have made the agreement. The ceremonies shall be performed tomorrow to wed me to Meryem, sister of the court secretary. And there is more: Yaltah is to wed Abul, my best friend. Whatever you have lost in a wife, you have retained and strengthened as a friend. Farewell!

MOSES BEN MAIMON THE SEPHARDI

I crumbled the page in my hand, tough as it was. I looked up at El Constantini, my vision blurred red. "Do you have a camel I may purchase?" I asked, my voice choked with rage.

"I have a female *rahil*. One that is small and will cover a hundred miles a day."

"She shall be mine."

"Her price is high."

"It is no matter."

"She will not endure burdens other than yourself."

"I take only myself."

"Then you set out on your journey to Fostat tonight?" inquired El Constantini curiously.

I shook my head. "I go to Bagdad," I said.

CHAPTER 24

Bagdad is the greatest city in the world. It is the seat of the mightiest government, in the green-succulent bosom of the most populous, the richest region known to man. I, Joseph ben Aknin, say this: I have seen it. Here lives the most mighty caliph, Al Nasir, who aids the religion of their Allah, as his name suggests, to whom even Saladin pays reverence and tribute.

Al Nasir enjoys a double-walled palace, three miles round, with a great park of all varieties of trees, all manner of animals, and all species of fish in a broad lake. He is kind unto Israel. Many Jews are his attendants. The caliph knows all languages, even our holy one. But he is careful of his family, lest they rise against him: Each brother and cousin has luxurious rooms in twenty-three palaces within the city, with the slight addition of guards and iron chains cushioned with velvet. They own and receive tribute from their towns and villages and eat and drink and rejoice all the days of their lives.

Al Nasir maintains marble storehouses, upheld by columns of gold and silver, filled with silken garments, precious stones, stores of valuable furniture and rare goods. Only at the Moslem feast of Ramadan does he issue forth in public. It is a monster celebration. He rides on a mule, clad in gold and silver and fine linen. On his turban, however, covering the jewels of inestimable value, he wears a small black shawl. It is a symbol that all his glory will be covered with darkness on the day of his death. A host of nobles accompany him on his ride as he proceeds from his palace to the great mosque by the Basrah gate. Along the route the walls are hung with silk worked in purple braid. The inhabitants salute him with dancing and song and exultation: "Peace unto thee, our lord the King and Light of Islam!"

My journey to this glorious metropolis took me more than twenty-five days. It might have been much shortened, except that I paused to meditate and worship at the spot near Gizeret where Noah grounded his ark, at the tomb of Jonah near famous Pumbeditha, and at other places. Though I saw many great cities and centers of learning, none dazzled my eyes so much as Bagdad itself.

I took lodging at the academy of the Rabbi Eleazar, whose brethren know how to chant the most ancient melodies of the singers at the time of the First Temple. There, also, to my astonishment, I found two communications from Maimonides —though I did not know he knew I had set out for Bagdad. The mystery was solved when I opened the smaller of the two packets. It was a letter.

IN THE NAME OF GOD, LORD OF THE UNIVERSE, TO JOSEPH (MAY GOD PROTECT HIM), SON OF AKNIN (MAY HIS REPOSE BE IN PARADISE):

My dear pupil, when you first came from a distant country to study under my direction, I thought highly of your thirst for knowledge and your fondness for speculative pursuits—even of your poems. But I thought your desire might exceed your ability. When you had studied astronomy and the other sciences with me, however, I was happy at the keenness of your talents. When you studied mathematics, your aptitude made me sure of your success. Your talents in logic confirmed my opinion.

I had no fears about teaching you the hidden ideas in the Prophetic Books. But here you commenced to be confused. You asked me for further hints—even to teach you the systems of the Moslems, to tell you whether they were right or wrong. I saw you were bewildered and perplexed—yet still you sought solutions to your difficulties.

I sighed. It was true, as he put it in his characteristic blunt manner. Maimonides had noticed that (chiefly because of my despair over Yaltah) I had turned again to writing poetry, indulging in fancy instead of fact. He had urged me to continue my studies systematically. He had recommended this from the first but I had refused.

I lowered my eyes and read again:

I did not want you to discover the truth by mere chance. This is always a mistake. I never refused to explain difficult passages which we happened to study in the Torah or Talmud. And when, by the will of God, we parted and you went your way, I remembered our dis-

411

cussions. The recollection roused in me a resolution dormant a long time. For you and those like you, therefore, I have written this, the first of the treatises I call a *Guide for the Perplexed*.

Last night, in a dream—though I do not diagnose such manifestations in our day as much more than a disturbed stomach—I believed I saw Moses. He declared himself to me. He adjured me to continue with my work, for what I was doing was right and laudable. He admonished me to write to the good Rabbi el Constantini at Aleppo, and he has kept constant watch over you for my sake. The rabbi warned me of your departure for Bagdad by special courier.

Do you continue to remember your teacher, son Joseph. Know that what I have sent you with this letter is the proof of my affections. Farewell!

Moses ben Maimon the Sephardi

Thoughtfully, I opened the second packet. It was bulky indeed. It contained the first of a series of documents which were soon to become famous throughout the world as the *Guide for the Perplexed*, the most remarkable work Maimonides ever composed. As time went on and I received more such manuscripts, I read them with as much eagerness as a thirsty man at the lip of a well. They were couched in three parts: an explanation of the hidden ideas in the books of the Prophets; an examination of the Moslem sect of philosophers, the *muketallim*; and a delving into a mixture of difficult problems of thought.

If it was drink to slake my curiosity, it was also feasting for my mind. I cannot say who had more pleasure, Maimonides in writing, or myself, in reading. He relished the explanation of words and their meanings, of the place of God in the Kalam according to the wise men. He uncovered the mysteries of the *sodot*, especially the *Ma'aseh Bereshit*, the story of creation; and, finally, the most mysterious writing in all the world, the *Ma'aseh Mercabbab*, the description of the divine chariot of Ezekiel. To these he added discussions of the existence of evil, omniscience and providence, temptations for the good man, design and law in nature, and finally, the true worship of God.

What especially fascinated me in the *Guide* was what Maimonides declared about the names of God. My master pointed out that all the names in Scripture are derived from His acts,

412

not His being—all save one. That is the Tetragrammaton, consisting of the Hebrew letters *yod, he, vav*, and *he* and called the *Shem ha-M'foresh*. I recalled the formula which Isaac the Blind had used in his futile effort to call up the golem. I ferreted out of my pouch the slip of papyrus which I had rescued from the floor of the synagogue at Aleppo. I read it again.

Hardly burned by the explosion, it revealed to me a frightening word of forty-two letters, unspeakable and unknowable. Maimonides had scoffed at such "jumbles" of letters, as he called them. I did not agree. I knew its holiness. I knew that this Great Name was never communicated except to a son or disciple and then only once in seven years. It was supposed not to be used at all except in the shrine of the Holy of Holies. Thus I had the parchment fixed within a hollow amulet of gold I ordered made in Bagdad. I wore it about my neck, waking and sleeping.

For more than three years I remained virtually unknown in Bagdad. I had no wish to become prominent by standing forth in the synagogue or teaching the Talmud. I wished for no ostentation of gifts or learning to draw attention to myself. I occupied my days with good works and the practice of medicine—and meditation on the letters of Maimonides.

I wondered much at the greeting concerning my father in his first letter. Finally, I concluded I had misread it. It was not until much later that I learned I had not mistaken the Hebrew characters. My father had died of an apoplexy. All his goods, to the last penny, belonged rightfully to me as the elder son. I might have returned to the Maghreb—indeed, I was on the brink of doing so—except for a strange occurrence which held me anchored in Bagdad.

It grew out of one of my early experiences in tutoring. To eke out the expenses of Bagdad living, since the original money sent by my father had diminished alarmingly, I let it be published in the market place that one Joseph ben Aknin was available—for a price—to instruct the more astute Jewish youth of Bagdad in the mysteries of their own religion. (It is incredible how uninformed and ignorant my people are in such cities, despite their centers of learning.) The young man I finally selected as my disciple was handsome enough, with a shining beard and impeccable dress, but his mind showed a tendency to wander. And he demonstrated an utter incapa-

413

bility to understand, coupled with a desire to ask numbingly stupid questions about the most abstruse matters.

At one point, to give a single instance, it became necessary for me to discuss with him Maimonides' theory about the World-to-Come, the Olam ha-Bah. The ensuing dialogue shook me to the core, like one of those occasional temblors that rocked the city of Bagdad. Because of this shock, I remember it with absolute fidelity.

It happened in a secluded corner of his family garden one afternoon after our habitual midday nap. His face bore that bewildered, knotted look of pain which I am sure he experienced: Poor Yoseh ben Zerorot! Now I can pity him; then, I hated him with all my heart.

"What did you mean," I asked him slowly so that he might comprehend, "when you said you didn't understand about the Olam ha-Bah? It is very simple."

"Me, Rabbi?"

"The doctrine."

"What did I say about it?" he asked.

"A moment ago you said you didn't understand it."

"What?"

"The Olam ha-Bah," I replied, fighting my rising anger.

"Me?"

"We are the only ones in this spot."

He furrowed his forehead. "When?" he said at length.

"When what?" I tried not to be confused.

"When you asked me?" he inquired helpfully.

"I shall ask the questions and you will answer them," I told him. "I am the teacher, you're the student."

"All right."

"What am I here for?"

"To ask questions."

"I'm here to answer them," I said. "What I mean is that I will ask questions about the answers I've already given you."

"I don't understand that," he said. I sighed. "All right," I said. "Be gracious enough to think of me as only asking questions, if you like. Now, what are you here for?"

"To answer questions, isn't that right?"

"That's another question," I reminded him, "but it does not matter."

"Oh. To answer them."

"That's better. Now, what did you mean?"

"I forget what we're talking about," he said. He commenced to weep. "I don't mean to be impudent. I don't know what anything meant. It is more than I can understand. What was it?"

"What?" I said, taken aback.

"Whatever you asked me?"

"You should remember it," I said, struggling to remember it myself.

"I forget."

"I asked you," I said sternly, "what you meant when you said you couldn't understand the Olam ha-Bah."

"Is that bad?" he asked.

"Questions again!" I shouted. I was furious. I was resolved not to be interrupted. He resigned himself to my wrath and rolled his eyes upward.

"I guess I don't understand," he said humbly.

I took a deep breath and I let it out slowly, a procedure for controlling the temper I had learned from Maimonides.

"You have to answer my question," I said.

"How can I answer it?" he asked.

"That's not a proper answer, it's another question," I cried.

"I don't know how to answer it." He was becoming sullen. I decided to try another approach.

"Is there some part you don't understand?"

"No. It's all of it."

"Let's take it part by part."

"How can we do that when I don't understand any of it?" he wanted to know. The tears dripping from his eyes enraged me.

"You're a fool!" I exclaimed.

"No, Rabbi, I'm not a fool," he protested.

"Then I'm a fool!"

"Oh, no, you're not," he said loyally, comforting me. "I don't think so."

"Is that your opinion of me?" I demanded. I jumped to my feet. He watched imploringly while I took a turn about a pomegranate tree and came back.

"I'm trying to say that I want to learn about it," Yoseh told me entreatingly.

"I don't think you do. A thousand devils block your mind. You refuse to cast them out and try to think."

"You hate students in Bagdad because you're from Egypt!" he accused me with a shaking voice.

"All Jews are the same, one race, one people, one God," I said sententiously.

"Why don't you treat me that way, then?"

"Because you insist on arguing with me! No one can learn anything that way!" I flared.

"Didn't you argue with the great Maimonides?" he persisted.

"A little, perhaps," I replied feebly, "but nothing like this."

Yoseh considered. "Maybe it's because there's no God," he said finally.

"You a Jew and you can say that?" I cried, astounded.

"I only thought so. I don't know," he said hastily. "But why not?" he added.

"You're asking questions again," I said sternly.

"I think anyone has a right to think it," Yoseh persisted. "And if there's no God, there can't be any Olam ha-Bah."

"Who told you that?" I wanted to know. The boy had swung me around, as if we were children playing about a pole. Now I was the one who was totally lost.

"I thought it over for myself," he mumbled.

"Which one?" I shouted.

"Both of them."

"God and the Olam ha-Bah?" I asked incredulously.

He nodded seriously. I calmed myself and sat down on the bench before him. "Don't you understand that you can't understand things this way?" I asked him. "Maimonides has always said that one has to go step by step."

"I'm taking my own steps."

"That isn't what I mean. I mean we have to divide anything big into little parts and understand each one of them, and then we can understand the whole of it."

"Can we understand what a flower is, pulling it apart?" asked Yoseh. He snatched up a bloom and gave me an illustration. I sat with my mouth open, holding the denuded stem. It was an argument I had often given Maimonides in Fostat and now I felt helpless.

"We're not talking about flowers and besides that's another question," I said, suddenly exhausted.

"I don't see what we're talking about," he told me.

That was enough. I dismissed him for the day and never went back to his father's house. I gave up my attempts to penetrate the thick skulls of the Jewish youths of Bagdad. Apparently the rote they learned in the traditional academies could make an impression on them, but free inquiry could not.

After this, the business of teaching seemed more than ever distasteful. I decided to fill my purse by working as a healer in the hospital. I was accepted readily enough after a short examination by the chief physician. It was in this fourth year that I experienced another of those curious unforetold events which can change the career of any man. It was no more than a stroll down one of the great streets of Bagdad. I felt a certain protection, an anonymity, which shielded me among half a hundred thousand Jews. On this occasion I ventured through one of the chief *sooqs*, with its brawling, shouting mobs, and saw on the other side a broad avenue lined with imposing buildings.

Strolling down it, my gown held well back and up from my legs, as was the custom to engender coolness, I relished the rising afternoon breeze. No more than a hundred yards had passed when I noted on the left a prominent, low-situated window. It was unusual in that its lattice was gilded. About it stood a small, intent crowd. I could not see nor hear anything which might have attracted them. This, in itself, attracted me.

I crossed slowly, lest I alarm what they were watching. My precautions were needless. I saw by their dress that all were young scholars. They stood attentively about the gilt-latticed window, each with a tablet, industriously scribbling. From time to time, one would ask a respectful question—apparently of the air; then he would fall to writing as furiously as if he would have one scribbled character overrun the other. As I drew near, a guard on the outskirts of the crowd eyed me.

"Are you a scholar, young sir?" he asked.

"I was once the pupil of the chief judge of the Jews of Egypt," I said with dignity. The guard salaamed. Without another word, he made room for me to pass. I joined the group and looked from one to the other in inquiry. None paid me attention. Next moment, I found what held them in thrall: It was a sweet, low voice issuing from behind the lattice—a woman's voice, a girl's voice, I could not tell—repeating the Talmud in Hebrew. Almost instantly, it added a commentary which amazed me by its clarity and profundity. It was like plunging into the depths of a clear pool—an experience vastly refreshing after the brutalizing one I had suffered with young Yoseh.

The short direct sentences of the speaker reminded me of those of Maimonides himself. The thought behind the explanations of the most difficult passages—and nothing seemed to daunt the speaker—was accurate and exquisitely expressed. I edged close to one of the young men, an ill-favored fellow with barely a beard.

417

"Who is this scholar who interprets the sages so well?" I asked in a whisper.

He gave me a look that, if it had been a fist, would have knocked me down. "Are you from the country, fellow?" he snapped. "Do you not know the wisdom and knowledge of Sarah, daughter of the renowned Samuel ben Ali, praised be he?"

What he said surprised me enough to remove all resentment from my breast at his crudity. I stood with my head raised, peering this way and that. I tried to see within the lattice, to discover what kind of a person this Sarah might be, but the lowering sun defeated all my efforts. The voice within, in the midst of a passage, hesitated, faltered, and came to a stop; it resumed, in a firm, even tone, to explicate a reading in the Talmud.

I shook myself and my gown like a man emerging from a dream and turned away. Reluctantly, I admit. This was the most pleasing experience I had undergone since my arrival in Bagdad. The unlettered cannot believe the delight there is in hearing the voice of reason and learning in a desert of stupidity. But I tempered my joy. I assured myself of what I took to be the truth: that God does not give all things to all people. If this wise woman was the daughter of Ben Ali, then she must be—in the nature of things—ugly and misshapen, with a hump and flattened nose, huge lips, a gait like a camel, and a smell like a privy. Nevertheless, I knew, there would be no end of young men like those congregated about her window to sue for her hand—simply to share the fame and wealth and power of her father.

I laughed aloud again and again in derision. Thereby I attracted the attention of the vendors in the bazaar and was forced to fend off their pleadings, ignore their muttered curses, and go my way—but not before I had bought food for thought in what I had experienced. Somehow I was not surprised when a messenger came to the synagogue one evening two weeks later—with the arrogant air which every servant of the Gaon seemed to possess—and proffered me a summons bidding me to the palace of Ben Ali. Despite my misgivings at what might be in store for me, I was glad enough to go.

I entered the massive gates with their notorious black carvings that hung from the stone face like so many creatures struck by magic. I passed through the gardens, lulled by late twilight, the drowsy birds singing carols to the night, the flowers folded into themselves; I went down the long hallway, lit by torches that reflected back from the metaled walls in wild glimmers. At every corner, I passed under the scrutiny of a guard. None stopped me. At what I presumed to be the anteroom, a servant led me in—an old man in rough woolens, with a rheumy nose.

I stood in the center of one of the most glorious and fantastic chambers I had ever seen. Lit by sconces as tall as a man, filled with sheep's-fat candles as thick as my arm, it seemed a realm out of the imaginations of Moslem taletellers. The walls flashed with metals of every kind, interrupted only by rich tapestries; rugs so thick as to hush every footfall were underfoot over the polished marble parquet. There were huge vases of jade, of crystal and ebony; tables inlaid with jewels, and hangings of age and beauty. A faint perfume from the burning candles filled the air.

Before me stood the most magnificent object of all. It was a screen taller than a man, lavishly carved and ornamented with gold upon an ivory base, the whole representing mystic undersea places that Jonah must have seen after he was disgorged by the whale, almost alive in their representation. From the distance tinkled music. I could see, outside, the shadows of the garden shrubs dancing a saraband on the walls.

No one else was in the room. I stood as if glued to the rugs, turning my body this way and that in a ferment of admiration. Then, remembering Maimonides' admonition about the corruption of riches and glory, I came back to myself. I was a stranger in such surroundings. Amid such ostentatious opulence, I had time to meditate as a philosopher on the condition of our people.

More Jews lived in Babylonia and Bagdad than in any other part of the world. The Geonim were their leaders. They had become all-powerful, nearly tyranical—with the Exilarch, chief of the Jews, hovering over their lives. Even the Moslems admitted the Geonim to their circles of power. Rabbi Isaac Gaon had once headed a procession of ninety thousand Jews into the presence of Ali, the fourth caliph. The Rabbi so impressed the caliph that he gave them all privileges denied to them by Mohammed himself, even to witnessing in court against the so-called faithful.

There had been many quarrels between the Geonim and the Exilarch, over the political and religious powers. Exilarch David ben Zakkai had been involved in a great feud with the leaders of the academies, even to riots and murder in the streets. Bribery and kidnaping were not uncommon. There were more denunciations than prayers in the synagogues. Arguments about the calendar, about money and position, marred their history. The Moslems often took advantage of them, extorting funds for their own incessant wars from both sides. At last the Exilarchs left Bagdad to the Geonim, departing for Egypt.

Jewish informers often worked with the Moslems in both countries and played the double agent (to their own advantage) to increase the friction between the two powers in our people. Geonim arose in other countries such as Spain, though those in Bagdad yearly went to Jerusalem to make seven circuits of the Mount of Olives, singing their own compositions as hymns. Meanwhile the Exilarch in Egypt preserved his power in conflict with Babylon. My master, Maimonides, had supported him against the Gaon then ruling in Babylon, who had also claimed the title. This latter circumstance gave me some fear but I put it aside, depending on the law and my own innocence to protect me.

As I stood there, deep in thought, a voice resounded from behind the screen. I stiffened in amazement. It was a sonorous, mellow sound, filled with subtleties of tone.

"You are Joseph ben Aknin, pupil of the scholar Moses ben Maimon of Fostat, who thinks himself a second Moses," it droned. "The eye of Judah has been upon you during your sojourn in Bagdad. You have done nothing to incur our anger but much to deserve our praise. Thus I have sent for you."

I looked about but could not see the speaker. Plucking up my courage, I inquired loudly: "Who is he that addresses me?"

For a moment there was no response. Then, as noiseless as a cat, a man stepped from behind the screen. He stared down at me with a grim smile. He wore heavily embroidered clothes, with huge sleeves that swept the floor; his head was covered with a simple skull cap of white. Tall and slim, giving an impression of towering strength, he appeared as if his sinews had been stretched on a timbered cross. Lean and taut, his face had an expression of superb arrogance. His beard, black and glossy, shone in the light. His fingers were covered with rings, I noted, as he gestured me toward a seat. He took one himself, leaning forward to peer at me through half-closed eyes that bored into my vitals.

"I am Samuel ben Ali," he said in his resonant voice. "I am Chief Gaon and Exilarch, head of all the Jews throughout the world. I am praised by the Geonim and receive rich gifts from the people. I go to the synagogue with trumpets and pipes; I sit in state with a golden canopy over my head. When I speak, all others are as hushed as Moses before God, praised be He. My name is part of the benediction. Never do I leave this palace except in a litter of the caliph's own, with my retinue. Taxes and honor, homage and praise are mine: nothing is lacking. What does your master Maimonides oppose to this?"

I bent my head with the utmost respect. "I have seen you before, noble Samuel ben Ali," I murmured, "but only from a distance. I would not have recognized you."

"The crowds about me are thick," he responded carelessly. "It is difficult."

"It would have been to my credit to have forced my way to make obeisance," I said.

"You are a liar," he said calmly. "You pay respect to no one except your miserable master."

I stiffened upright at the insults to myself and to Maimonides. "I am what I am," I said. "I do not lie. My master is not what you say."

"Take it how you will," Ben Ali said casually, "we are here alone and no one can overhear or see. You may swallow insults as you do your own spittle and no one will be the wiser."

"I came here at your command," I said, not knowing what else to do.

Samuel ben Ali nodded. Lounging in his chair, he surveyed me from head to foot. "You are not much," he said with a laugh. "I had expected more. You are merely a good-looking young man and not at all what I have been told."

"Have—have you been told of me?" I stammered.

"There have been complaints. The parents of Yoseh ben Zerorot, for example. They came to me to seek my assistance in taking you before the court to recover their monies spent on their son. They accused you of being a charlatan."

"That is untrue!" I cried.

"Precisely what I told them," Ben Ali agreed. "You are a highly educated young man. One who will be worth his weight in gems to our people once he has been properly trained."

"I do not understand. I have been trained for many years in Egypt."

Samuel ben Ali threw back his head and laughed, his hairy throat vibrating. He looked at me with an expression of mock reproach. "No, no," he said. "That is training of a sort, but not what I mean."

"What do you mean, gracious Gaon?" I asked with suspicion.

"Maimonides is not the scholar he thinks himself," Samuel ben Ali said obliquely.

"He thinks of himself as a good man who has studied the Torah and the Talmud all his life," I said defensively.

"But in his pride, has he not placed himself in opposition to what the rabbis of old, those quoted in the Talmud, have said?"

"If they were alive today," I answered, "they would agree with him."

"Perhaps, perhaps. I doubt it. In any case, he goes against the whole authority of our people."

"The Torah is forever," I said boldly, "but its interpretation is for each age alone."

"You are very near heresy yourself," he said, regarding me like a hawk. I was silent in fear.

"He that is so emphatic against the belief in witches and demons," resumed Ben Ali, his tone lighter. "Does he not read? Does he not know that the Talmud makes such a belief essential for membership in the Sanhedrin?"

"I do not know," I said sullenly.

"What of the charge that he sets himself up as the sole authority on the Talmud?"

"You have persecuted him!" I cried, stung beyond endurance. To my puzzlement, Ben Ali did not respond at once. Then he stretched and yawned.

"Has Muni got so old that he did not recognize a greeting from an old friend?" he asked with an air of delighted venom.

"A greeting?" I said feebly. "I know of none."

Samuel ben Ali stood. He took two of his long paces toward the other end of the room; then, as if he could not contain himself, he swung about to tower over me. "Let me perhaps recall an evening to you," he said softly. "The blue mist from the Nile, the moon rising. Music on the rooftops, the shadows of the people listening and resting in the warm night. The figure of a dancing woman and the rising of another figure on a rooftop."

"Stop, stop!" I cried, horrified. "Was it you, then? Was it you?"

"I?" inquired Ben Ali, his thin lips curling above his beard. "I? Who was what?" He sounded insanely like Yoseh.

"Was it you who killed Zamira?"

"Zamira, Zamira," he said softly. "I recall a name of that

422

kind, dimly. Long ago. In a country I have not seen since my boyhood days. She was a pretty girl, a playmate. I bit her on the cheek once, as I remember: as if it were a rosy apple I could not resist."

"Tell me!" I cried.

The brow of Ben Ali became like a thundercloud. He came close to me. I could smell the musky perfumes he used, mingled with his sweat. "Tell you what? That I am guilty of a crime? Who but a madman would destroy the life of such as Zamira?"

He shook his head and moved away, lightly, like a dancer. "Not I, not I. I have been her friend—yes, her lover, buying her body like dung in the market; yet none can accuse me of wanting her life. I wanted her to enjoy all she had, as long as she had it."

He paused. "Muni, my old boyhood friend, should have known this. I am sure he would never accuse me as you have accused me."

"I—I know not what to say," I stammered, distraught.

Samuel ben Ali touched my shoulder lightly. His fingers burned with a peculiar heat. "You are forgiven," he said. "I am as distressed as you that she is dead. And atop the very house of Maimonides."

"Did you know that?" I asked, my suspicions flaring up again.

He shrugged his broad shoulders. "I have news from every quarter of the world," he returned. "It is my business to tend to the affairs of the Jews. None are more widely spread in the universe than our people—constantly traveling, always uprooted, forced to move on. I do what I can: I send gifts to all the congregations. The special wine for Passover, for instance. Did not Maimonides and his father, Maimon, receive such a gift from me in Fez, in Morocco?"

I stared at him in horror. At last I commenced to understand this man. My awe grew in proportion to my fear. But still he talked, as if under the compulsion of the whip of conscience that drove him to gloat over what had been.

"Perhaps Maimonides has shown you presents I have sent him," he continued. "Only recently I sent him back again a gift that possibly he had not expected. He had given it to me when we were boys in Cordova, in his father's garden. It was a beautiful thing: a dagger of steel, with a brass handle entwined with a snake whose mouth held a garnet."

I shook my head, indicating ignorance, hoping this inquisition would end. Samuel ben Ali went on. "There is Abraham ben David of France," he told me with satisfaction. "He thinks, and does not hesitate to say to his congregation, that Maimonides is a stupid fool. Cruel to those who do not believe as he does, calling down the most filthy names upon those who disagree, giving himself the appearance of infallibility like Moses ben Amram, blessed be he."

I knew that at least part of this was true. I could not, even in loyalty to my master, disagree. I stood as mute as a statue. The Gaon commenced to take long strides from one end of the great room to the other, his heavy gown making a whispering sound. He did not speak; his head was bowed, his lips moving. Suddenly, without warning, another figure appeared in the room. It gave off a radiance that made my knees quake, as if the appearance were like the angel to Jacob.

There was no need to do combat with the newcomer. Here was only a girl, clad in a dazzling yellow silk robe, a tiny orange turban about jet-black hair that flowed around her shoulders. One look at her—all my previous notions of beauty vanished: Here was the embodiment of dreams. A moon that outshone the sun; her forehead a pearl amidst the dark myrtle-like halo of her hair; her eyebrows as curved as bows, her glances like arrows shot from them; a form as slender and bending as the banyan tree. A mole on her cheek crept like an ant toward the honey of her mouth, over flesh as white as camphor to lips carnelian. Her breasts thrust her gown forward with two deadly strokes toward my heart; her body swayed like a reed in a storm. Her tiny feet in silver sandals hesitated like doves; her hands moved with the grace of swallows swooping toward their nests.

Our glances met. Some spirit passed between us. I do not know its name nor its birth: It was like the invisible energy which crackles the garments in cold desert dawns. My beard stiffened; my hair rose. The eyes in my head burned with tears of love.

My regard startled her, it seemed, as if it were a hot iron directed against her flesh. Her gazelle eyes widened as she felt the same strange attraction as I. Her tiny white hands opened and closed before her. They clung to the intangible cord which had, at the instant we saw one another, bound us together. Slowly a flush rose to her white face. With a abrupt motion, she turned away.

None of this was noted by her self-absorbed father. Samuel ben Ali, taking his huge paces up and down the ornate room, pulling his long fingers through his beard and shaking his head, lifted his eyes to renew his denunciation of my master. He saw our visitor. His visage became cold and hard. "What do you want of me, Sarah?" he demanded. It was the first intimation I had that this was his famous daughter.

"I came as you bade me," she replied. I thrilled at the sound: It was the very voice I had heard behind the gilt lattice in the street! It was she, my unknown tutor, daughter of Ben Ali!

"I had purposed you to stay behind the screen," Ben Ali replied harshly. She bent her head. "I am sorry, my father," she returned. Despite her tone of contrition, I knew with a surge of joy that she was not sorry at all.

The Gaon turned grudgingly to me. "This is Joseph ben Aknin," he said, managing to make it a sneer. "He is the pupil, the only pupil, of the famous Moses ben Maimon."

She turned her face to me and lowered her head. I bowed deeply. When I lifted my gaze again, she had gone. Samuel ben Ali regarded me with the frown of a thunderstorm. "I have four daughters," he said with controlled violence. "They are all spoken to be wed at my pleasure, except one."

"They all must be as beautiful as seraphim," I said impulsively, "if this heavenly one is like the rest."

The Gaon snorted. "I have a long arm and a strong one," he said, slowly and significantly. "Many yearn to lift themselves, to stand above their base position in life. But they shall not, not on my back. Do you understand, son of Judah?"

"I understand," I said, fear shivering along my spine.

His glance fell on the amulet around my neck. With a step he advanced and wrenched it from its chain. With a look of contempt, he opened it and fingered the parchment. He read it. As he did, I saw a terrible change pass over his iron face. It became pale, covered with sweat. His very beard seemed to lose its crispness. He sank to a chair, holding the amulet out to me with a shaking hand. Nothing was said: I restored it to the chain and placed it within my robe. Samuel ben Ali raised his hand to wave me out, then halted it in midair as a sudden thought struck him.

He regarded me with an expression I could not fathom: fear, respect, cunning, doubt were mingled in it. "You carry words of power," he said in a changed voice. "Were these the gift of Maimonides?"

"Yes," I said.

"He has grown mighty in wisdom," Ben Ali said, in obvious disbelief. "I bear him no grudge as the second among the leaders of the Jews." I bowed my head wonderingly, not knowing what to expect.

"Evil people have said that I bear him malice, that I wish him dead."

I said nothing and after a moment's hesitation Ben Ali continued: "You may perhaps have heard that someone tried to poison him."

Again I was silent. He licked his dry lips. "It is true that Maimonides and I have differed on many points of doctrine," he said, his voice now smooth as honey. "But never on essentials, never to the point of hatred or murder. There have been attempts on my life, as well, by knife and poison: Tell him that. But I do not blame him nor do I listen to those who whisper accusations against him. I exile or execute: He might well do the same."

"He would never countenance it," I said, shocked.

Samuel ben Ali nodded. "I believe he is righteous," he said abruptly. "Let him believe the same of me. Before you, I wash my hands of any attempts against his life." He turned to a golden ewer, plunged his hands into it and held them up dripping for me to see, wiping them thoughtfully with a soft napkin. "We are both men of the highest respect among the Jews," he said. "We must be reconciled, in public if not in private! We must work together lest we split our cause and are burned like kindling!"

However I may have disbelieved him before, there was no mistaking his earnestness now. Whether he was lying about his being in danger of his life from some zealous adherent of Maimonides, I had no idea; certainly I guessed he had evaded the facts of what we knew about the wine of Fez, the death of Zayd, and the death of Zamira. But I could not question his present sincerity.

"I shall write him what you say," I murmured.

Samuel struck his two great palms together. "Tell him this," he ordered, "that whatever was between us in the past, from the garden of Cordova to this present moment, shall be as if it never existed. We shall be as brethren; if we disagree, we shall submit ourselves to the authority of the sacred Writings and the measure of wisdom found in friendly discussion."

He stopped: The sly glint I had noted before shone in his eyes. "For your own sake," Samuel ben Ali said, "know that Maimonides has risen too high to be brought down by my shaft; he is out of my range. For if he dies in some fashion which may be attributed to me, he brings me down with his

426

death. Likewise, he depends upon me in Bagdad. What he commands in spiritual influence is mine in temporal power. Still, I know him too well to hope he will join me. Very good: The pillars of the Temple that bear the weight do it best when they are far apart and of equal strength. Tell him that."

"I shall tell him," I said, quick rejoicing springing up in my breast. But Ben Ali dispelled it immediately. He bent his frown upon me. "All this does not mean," he said significantly, "that I shall permit one of my family to be joined to one of his disciples. You are not, as he is, beyond my reach, Joseph; I tell you, your intrigues here are known to me. Beware, despite that amulet of might about your neck: Do not rouse this lion of Judah." Slowly, impressively, without another word, he waved me out.

A week later I received a visit from a member of Samuel ben Ali's intimate household. The slave, a Greek, showed me the greatest respect. He offered me a position, that of teacher in the Gaon Jacob Academy, with monthly recompense of a princely kind. I did not know what it meant; I did not think it wise to refuse. Thus I began, in Bagdad, teaching the Talmud. I was to continue in this capacity for five years, at last to be sufficiently known to be able to think of establishing my own school.

I found I needed some encouragement—and whence could it come but from Maimonides? I wrote him directly, without embarrassment, as one might turn to a father.

> Master [I scribbled], years ago your beloved daughter, Faith, obtained grace and favor in my sight. I wedded her. But soon she left me, though I found no fault with her, and departed from my house. She no longer lets me behold her pleasant face nor hear her sweet voice. I have taken another mistress, named Knowledge.
>
> Perhaps you are the cause of this misconduct. Send Faith back to me, for she will be my staff in my old age. Tell her to be firm and steadfast. As the sages have said: "Blessed is he who restores to the owner his lost property." For my part, I promise, if Faith returns, to reduce to the place of a second wife my present spouse."

I had not long to wait. Within rapid weeks, I received a similar note from Maimonides:

> You, my dear Joseph, accuse me and your wife Faith of disloyalty when, in truth, it is yourself that is to blame

for having neglected her. It is written that "No man can exist without a wife and no woman without a husband." I shall restore her to you if you are more careful in the future. You are right: Knowledge is second to her in this world and in the World-to-Come.

With this as a blessing, I went on to labor. During the five years, I did not speak again to the Gaon, Samuel ben Ali—though I saw him five times from afar on the occasions of his goings-out. Oppositely, I did not see Sarah, his daughter, again; but I spoke to her each week at the lattice, under the guise of questions upon the Scriptures. And occasionally, when such ardor for learning might have aroused suspicion, I submitted the questions to her through the window, on parchment decorated with my kisses. She returned me answers written with her own white fingers.

" 'Kiss me with the kisses of thy mouth,' Solomon said," I wrote. "What does this mean?"

"It is a reference only to the love of Judah for its God," she replied.

"Solomon also wrote: 'Tell me, O thou whom my soul lovest, where thou feedest.' How may this be interpreted?"

"It is meant only as an allegorical figure that Judah seeks its rest in His arms."

" 'He shall lie all night between my breasts,' says Solomon. Is this also allegorical?"

"It is a very obscure passage."

" 'His left hand is under my head and his right hand doth embrace me.' So said Solomon. Does this mean that he was right-handed?"

"There is no record of this; I will do further study on it."

I wrote: " 'Draw me, I shall come after thee.' This is another saying of Solomon's. Does it refer to Judah?"

"Undoubtedly," she replied in her fair, precise characters, "but I am not sure."

" 'Rise up my love, my fair one, and come away,' " I inscribed passionately. To this I got no reply. For months afterward my requests for her interpretations of Scripture dropped unnoticed to the ground. The other young scholars, jealous of the attention paid before to my questions, now smiled scornfully at me.

After this silence, I felt my heart become paralyzed within me. I refused to teach my students. I spent my days alone, in

428

sighing solitude, returning to my old vice of poetry. With different eyes I read again the love verses of Judah Halevi:

> The wedded ones are framed by myrtles;
> The rite perfumes the grove:
> The flowering trees embrace their kirtles
> To share their fragrant love.

Daring greatly, I sent this through the lattice, tossing it in so that it could not fall. To my heart-thumping ecstasy, it was not returned. A week later, I was the first one to appear at the gilded lattice and thrust through it a second poem of wondrous Halevi.

> Sarah finds my tears a rinse
> For all her whims have done;
> And spreads her laundered conscience
> To whiten to my sun.

Almost immediately, it was ejected. I picked it up and went home, angry but content, not knowing that I had been too rash. The next time I approached Sarah's window, the Moslem guard there firmly held me at a distance. After that, whether for fear of Ben Ali or shame for Sarah, I did not return.

I took to brooding. I could no longer make sense out of the world. I had received all of Maimonides' letters; I had carefully preserved and copied all of his *Guide for the Perplexed*, but it left me more perplexed than ever. I could see clearly the differences between my old master and Samuel ben Ali. The Gaon preferred to believe and interpret literally everything in the holy literature, even the fables of the Midrash, taking nothing as allegory or moral fiction. Yet Maimonides—who hated poetry—was a man who interpreted all in the light of symbols, the very lifeblood of poetry!

In the midst of these ponderings, I resolved to leave Bagdad. For what place I did not know. The proceeds of my father's estate, sold by my order, had long since been forwarded to me. I was a fairly wealthy young man, still obsessed by the itch to travel. Perhaps that was the answer to all my inner agonies.

I decided to make a last effort to reach Sarah. I met my old pupil, Yoseh, and collared him for my emissary. I wrote a sealed note, placing it in his hand, to submit at the lattice. It read:

"Jacob was the favorite son of Sarah. Joseph was the favorite grandchild of Sarah. Why was this?"

No answer came back except Yoseh's incredibly stupid countenance; he lifted his eyebrows, shrugged his shoulders, spread his fingers. I went into my rooms, determined to leave, perhaps to the western hills of my childhood. What I found there gave me the last incentive necessary. It was a letter from Maimonides—a plea to my heart to meet him at the city of Ascalon on the borders of Egypt for a reason he did not divulge. I determined to yield to his desire for the last time.

CHAPTER 25

"Samuel ben Ali is a chattering ignoramus," Maimonides said strongly. "He is one of those who will sacrifice all modesty, all shame, when his position is threatened. As I have said to you before, Joseph, the way of honor in such a case is to avoid a fool, not to vanquish him. It is better for me to spend what few years I have left teaching those that are ready and willing to learn, rather than to waste them in winning victory over the stupid."

"He has much the same opinion of you," I said politely.

Maimonides flourished his arms. He acted as I had with my pupil, Yoseh, taking in deep breaths, exhaling them with a snort. He had grown much older; his beard was almost white, his face thinner and more ascetic. His palsy had become more pronounced. But his temper was as fierce as ever; his invective had not lost its sting.

"I shall say no more," he said in a strained tone. "You appear to have been converted to his cause."

"No," said I calmly, "but Ben Ali has more reason on his side than first appears."

Maimonides compressed his lips and looked away. I was secretly delighted with the success of my inspiration: Perhaps I, I thought, would be the one to bring these great leaders of the Jews together! Alas, for my foolishness: I did not know

430

the goodness of my master nor the wickedness of Samuel ben Ali, but this must be told in another place.

"You have not told me why you summoned me here," I said. I spied up about me at the bold ashlar walls of Ascalon which beetled over the small dark-brown tent of Maimonides. "You seem to come as a king, not as a healer or teacher," I added. I smiled and motioned toward the luxurious equipage that lay on the furrows of the palm grove about the fragile walls of woven goat-hair.

"I come at the express command of my caliph, Saladin, at the suggestion of Vizier al-Alfadhel," Maimonides replied coldly. "Saladin himself is ill of his old fever in Cairo. Our friend, Al-Alfadhel, long ago took an oath over the black *kaaba* never to meet a Roumi except with the edge of the sword. Next in dignity, I was chosen as emissary."

"Have you risen so far in Saladin's favor?" I wondered.

Maimonides continued without answering: "I am here to reply in the caliph's name to a message he received from King Richard of England. The king of the Franks himself will be here tomorrow."

He always confounds me, I thought resentfully as the dart of surprise struck into my vitals. I commenced to stutter a question. Maimonides silenced me with a gesture and went inside his tent to take his noon rest. Sullenly I retired. I squatted in the slender shade of three female palms, pondering what his mission might mean. Inevitably, my thoughts turned awefully toward Richard.

What this monarch symbolizes to the world is well known. He has made as deep an impress on the Moslems and Jews as our mighty Saladin has made on the Christians. Within these niches of memory burn forever the offerings of mutual admiration between Christian and Moslem—though the Jew cannot share it in other than fear. Richard's reputation for barbarous madness had become inferior only to Saladin's reputation for magnanimity. Once the ruler of England had been known only to his half-savage subjects, then to the roistering Franks; but his opportune sailing into the harbor of Acre, his rescue of its forts from the engulfing jaws of Saladin's armies, his feats of arms that made other knights seem like children, had made him a living legend. Not without cause did the Moslem mothers admonish their crying children by saying: "What do you fear, foolish one? King Richard is not behind the bush!"

Out of more than curiosity, Saladin's spies had taken his

431

measure from their own gossip and renegade crusaders. Our caliph knew much of this opponent who had thus far single-handedly frustrated his scheme for recovering all of Palestine. The chief weapon of the noble Saladin had become the virtue of patience, which Richard lacked entirely.

Called "Old Yea-and-Nay" from his short, vicious way of speaking, Richard had the strength and mind of a bull. Everything this queer English monarch did was for personal interest or glory. A bully with a scepter, an overgrown child who had the luck to be porphyrogenetically produced. He had drained his own people to their last coin with imposts, levies, ransoms, and feigned auctions. He had the terrible temper of a spoiled infant, the cruelty of an experienced maker of war. Saladin, I felt sure, would never forgive such a one for what I had heard: the cold-blooded butchery of more than twenty-five hundred Moslem warriors at Acre, no more than a year or so before, because of a month's delay in the ransom payment of twenty thousand pieces of gold. The deed had thrown terror into the cowardly hearts of some of the caliph's emirs, but had hardened others to illimitable hate.

The only part of Richard's personality which appealed to me was the rumor I had heard that he was supposed to patronize poets and minstrels. Indeed, it is told that he himself produced passable verses. I doubt this: Probably they were composed by one of his retinue and given to Richard to gain the royal favor. I could not understand why Saladin would treat with such a creature, but I confessed to myself I was ignorant of the plots of high estate.

I roused from my reverie at a blast of trumpets and thumping of nakers which seemed to shake the earth. A quarter-mile off, I saw a long troop of horse and baggage. A tent, gaily striped in red and white, commenced to be staked out. Guards, glinting in armor, advanced to every corner of the compass. Maimonides, unperturbed, emerged blinking from his tent to view the spectacle. People thronged the walls of Ascalon to peer down; one of them fell headlong into the soft earth. He picked himself up unhurt and raced back into the city with laughter and jeers hooting at his heels.

"Come," said Maimonides.

Among the colored shadows flung into the interior of the tent by the sun, Maimonides bowed deeply. I followed his example. When we lifted our heads, the man amongst the cushions—the only person in the tent despite the heavy guard

432

outside—used an enormous square-hilted sword as a lever to lift himself out of the soft trap of cushions and rugs. He stood upright and came toward us, hands on his hips.

A man shorter than I expected, walking with a balanced rolling gait like that of a sailor; a short yellow beard, thick brows, long yellow hair cut (unlike that of the Jews) at the corners. He appeared to be muscled like an ox. His thews forced him to hold his arms out from his body as he advanced, to keep from chafing his flesh. He halted a pace or two away, squinting at us without a word of welcome.

Towering over him, Maimonides gave him back look for look. The English king stared up at him, sparkling blue eyes snapping in his red-burned face. He seemed as calculating as a man about to deal a sword-stroke. Suddenly he spoke, in a voice so high as to be almost comical.

"Are you the Jew healer?"

"I have the honor to serve his exalted majesty Saladin in that capacity."

"You look like a scarecrow."

Maimonides' bow was so deliberate it appeared to be almost an insult. Richard settled into the heels of his long-toed red slippers, rocking back and forth. "I am indeed thin, sire," Maimonides said as the king waited. "My life has been devoted to the service of such as yourself."

Richard grinned, showing teeth like those of a stallion. "There is only one like myself," he said significantly. He surveyed Maimonides from top to toe. Not once had he glanced at me.

"I want you," he said to my master. "Come back to Joppa with me."

"I beg of you, sire, allow me to remain in Egypt," Maimonides returned courteously.

"I want you," Richard repeated like a child demanding a toy. "For my personal healer."

"Alas! I have so many patients untouched in Cairo and Alexandria, so little time to tend them."

"Is not a king more than a filthy Moslem beggar?" demanded Richard. His face commenced to darken with the hue of a prickly choler.

"Indeed he is," Maimonides agreed instantly, "but every man who is sick believes himself a king."

Richard snorted. "You are a queasy Jew," he replied. "You avoid the question."

"But Jesus, whom you call the Christ, did he not say that the last shall be first, sire?"

"He spoke not of kings!" shouted Richard. To my surprise, his face paled. Drops of sweat stood out on his forehead. He swayed where he stood. Hastily Maimonides produced a vial and unstoppered it, holding it under his nostrils. Richard inhaled deeply. His color slowly returned.

"You are a servant to be cherished," he said slowly.

"I am desolated if I offended you unwittingly, sire," Maimonides returned.

Richard swallowed. His truculence began to return. "I came here under truce to see what your master wanted me to see," he told Maimonides. "But my spies can tell me more than my own eyes about his men, his arms, his forts. You are worth more to me than the conquest of a city such as this. In my country, we have no knowledge such as yours. You are the reason for my coming."

"You make me wretched that I have said what I have said."

In a lightning change of humor, Richard chuckled. "Keep your precious head," he returned carelessly. "I would not deprive you of it. I know the habit of Saladin, serving up the topknot of those who displease him on a royal platter."

"He is a merciful ruler," Maimonides said.

The king of England shrugged his massive shoulders. "No matter," he replied. "All good men come to me, soon or late. You will be among them. I shall make you beg my favor on your knees."

"You have much to offer," Maimonides murmured. "I only wish I might accept, sire."

Richard laughed. "I am not a patient man but I am willing to wait for the best healer in the world," he said. "I would not have the ill will of one who might poison me."

"It is too much to boast."

"If we had bred you in England, if only you were an English Jew, eh?"

"Perhaps," Maimonides said with deliberation, "I might have attended your coronation."

To my astonishment, Richard of England burst into a shriek of glee. He choked, hawked, and spat upon the brilliant rug under his feet. He was unable to keep his feet as his face whitened once more; he sank down among the pillows but his unconquerable fit of humor would not be stopped. He waved us out. We made our way backward to the door—a trick

434

which demanded considerable skill to keep from tripping over one's gown—and closed the tent flap behind us. The guards, men-at-arms and pennoned knights, watched us surlily as we rapidly returned through the plowed dirt to our own place. Behind us, Richard's laughter echoed through the cloth of the tent.

"What did you mean?" I asked Maimonides as we hurried off.

He scribbled busily upon a tablet. "Take this," he said, pushing it into my hand. "Give it to an attendant to deliver to Richard. It will relieve him a little of his disease."

"Disease?" I said shrilly. "Disease?"

Maimonides regarded me gravely. "It is difficult to believe," he said in a low voice, "but I am convinced that both Saladin and his enemy suffer from the same mortal ailment, the paludal fever."

I shook my head, not comprehending immediately. "No," I said stupidly, "what did your last remark mean? Why did he go into such a fit of merriment?"

Maimonides slowed his pace. His face lengthened. "My dear Joseph," he said dully, "in England, at the coronation of Richard, more than a thousand Jews were massacred to make him a holiday. He thinks it a joke."

The audacity of it took my breath away. "You dared to beard him to his face like that?" I asked in amazement.

Maimonides grimaced. "He is easily identified as a man of such humors," he informed me. "You have only to look at his coloring, his physical appearance. I was safe at all events."

"Safe?"

"You have heard, have you not, of our women—how, during the persecutions in France and Germany, the rabbis allowed them to wear the dress of men and false beards in order to save their lives and virtue?"

"Yes," I replied uncertainly.

Maimonides sighed at my obtuseness. "It is very simple," he said. "While I was talking to Richard, I was wearing the beard of Saladin."

Long after Richard's noisy, gaily colored train had departed, in the light of the horizon-sun—so yellow that it seemed to be slowly poured like a celestial wine—Maimonides and I talked outside our tent. The Moslem escort waited impatiently for us to finish. I had disobeyed my master: I had only pretended to give his recipe to a guard to be delivered to

Richard. Secretly I had crushed it under my heel, burying it in the ground, hoping the leader of the crusaders would perish in his madness. I had returned to cross my legs in the company of my master for the first time in nearly nine years. It brought a lump to my throat; it was a home-coming to all I had missed.

"Little has changed since you left," Maimonides said.

"Yaltah . . ." I said indistinctly.

"She is happy in her marriage with Abul Maali. I am happy with his sister."

"Do you have children?"

"Maimonides has been punished for some secret sin," my master said, speaking of himself as if he were a stranger. His face sagged in grief. "Maimonides had a daughter—but she died. Maimonides had a son, Abraham, and he lives—but he is so sickly that it requires all the art of Maimonides to keep him alive."

"But he pleases you?" I asked, not without a pang of jealousy. Maimonides glanced at me affectionately.

"He is a delight," he responded, "but you, Joseph, you are my first son. You shall come back with me to Fostat. All shall be as it was before."

His tone could not have been more kindly. My eyes stung with tears; I hesitated and sighed. "I cannot," I said.

"I often go to the top of the ridge of rock where Guilbert once roamed," Maimonides said, his eyes fixed and remote on the darkening horizon. "Guilbert is dead now. He is buried there. So, too, the body of Zamira. I sit on the long slab within the front of the cave and meditate. I long for you to be beside me."

"As I read your *Guide for the Perplexed,* I felt your presence," I said with emotion. Maimonides shook his head. "Only words," he responded. "Nothing more than that. They cannot replace the presence of another. The flesh is more to the spirit than the spirit knows."

He turned toward me with the gaze that no one could deny. "What is the reason for your refusal?" he asked. "Is there still a feeling against me in your heart?"

"There was never that. I was ungrateful and headstrong."

"Yaltah? You are more than a dozen years younger; you would both have been miserable in marriage."

I nodded. I could realize that at the moment with equanimity. Maimonides had been right to refuse his consent. I endeavored to thwart this thrust at me.

"How did the hermit Guilbert die?" I murmured.

"In a trance," Maimonides said, "in my arms."

"Calling on his god?"

"No," Maimonides said slowly, "he called on the name of an old comrade-in-arms, Marquis Armand du Bois, who died long ago in a journey across Hungary."

"Hardly a death for a good man," I muttered.

"Nay," Maimonides said, "he was in delirium, not in an ecstasy. I raised the rock-tomb above him with my own hands."

After that, there was silence. Darkness flowed toward us across the flatland. "You are still headstrong?" Maimonides inquired quietly. The palm-tree shadows stretched to infinity.

I had a flash of inspiration: I should tell the truth and yet disguise it. "I shall return to Bagdad," I said. "There I shall have a school of my own to teach the truths you have taught me, to open to others the mysteries you have shown me."

"In defiance of Samuel ben Ali?"

"If need be."

Maimonides nodded. "It would need be," he affirmed. "Such a venture is foolishness."

The word was like tinder to a torch. "There is a fortune to be made," I said. "Even the Exilarch must pay such teachers a stipend monthly."

"It is better for you to earn a drachma as wages for the honest work of a weaver or tailor or carpenter," Maimonides replied sternly, "than to be dependent upon the hoard of the Exilarch or the Gaons. I myself take nothing for teaching, little for medicine; I have partnered with friends in the jewelry trade once more to support myself—rather than have others pay for the knowledge of God. The sages of the past were sandalmakers, smiths, potters—one discoursed to his pupils from the top of a barrel he had made himself, another had to be summoned from his stone-cutting to teach in the synagogue. Even the apostate rabbi from Nazareth was a carpenter."

"Then I shall teach for nothing," I said.

"Who shall protect you?" Maimonides asked sharply. "The power of Samuel ben Ali is mighty. His revenge is without end."

His words gave me pause. I replied: "I have friends who will shelter me."

Maimonides examined me keenly and rose to take his farewell. "There is more to this than you have told me," he said coldly. "Is there aught more you wish to say?"

"Nothing."

"I hope that God, blessed be He, will bring you to your senses."

I thought he had gone but he lingered in the twilight. "To wash down your folly," Maimonides said softly, "know that Zekarya is the one who is to wed Sarah. He is to become the son-in-law of Samuel ben Ali."

I could not stifle a startled cry. Relentlessly, Maimonides went on. "And remember," he said, "that Saul gave his daughter, Michal, to David willingly, saying, 'I will give him her that she may be a snare to him and that the hands of the Philistines may be against him.'"

I bowed my head. He vanished into his tent and the mounts of the Moslem guard pranced restlessly in anticipation of departure. He knew more of me than I had ever dreamed. He was, as always, right. Not the vision of teaching the Holy Law but the vision of teaching love to the heavenly Sarah filled my inward vision—hopeless as it may have seemed at that terrible moment.

It was strange that Maimonides should have mentioned the scriptural story of David and Saul to me—for that is what came to pass. Even as David had fared, so did I in the years that came to me in the remote corners of the earth. But I was not alone: Sarah was with me as my wife.

How this happened is a story not easily told. I returned to Bagdad, weary, but with my stubbornness unimpaired. I was fixed in my passion for Sarah. I was not disappointed in her. Disapprovingly the synagogue shammash handed me a message. It was unsigned but I recognized the odor of musk. It said simply: "Because Sarah loved Joseph." I sank, half-fainting, onto a seat. I tried to keep my head from whirling. This was the answer I had hoped for to my question of weeks before, yet it put me into a turmoil. Like a slowly unfolding panorama, I began to see my future.

I knew Sarah to be mine for the taking. The thought made my heart bound painfully in my bosom. Its beat slowed. I became cold when I recalled that Samuel ben Ali would be my enemy, that Zekarya would drink my blood with delight. I could not return to Aleppo. I could not remain in Bagdad. My pride would not now permit a return to the Maghreb, least of all to Fostat. I was solitary in the world—with Sarah alone to keep me company.

I reflected on the ruthlessness of the Chief Gaon. He cared for nothing except his own will, despite his protestations of bending the knee before God. He had vast influence, as he had said; more, he cared nothing what others thought. He was arrogant enough to maintain sixty slaves in his household and still be could write letters across the world, to all Jews, begging funds: "Our old scholars sit desolate, our young students sigh in desperation, our teachers complain every hour. We feel bitter for it seems the whole world drives headlong to destruction. We implore you to send of your stores, however humble they be, some contribution for the sake of the academies." I wondered cynically how much of these gifts that poured in to Bagdad reached the schools by way of Ben Ali's treasure chests.

In my desperation, my gorge rose against my own religion. I opened the *Guide for the Perplexed* but it gave me neither guidance nor comfort. I spent a sleepless night. Next morning early, haggard and wild-eyed, I sought the small dwelling of Samuel ben Azariah, the notorious apostate from our faith who had turned Moslem and inscribed the horrifying book, *Silencing the Jews*. So famous was this little wizened, birdlike man with a limp and stabbing light-colored eyes that even Ben Ali did not dare persecute him. He welcomed me. He listened in silence to my woes. He shook his head.

"You have great enemies indeed," he said in his peculiarly deep voice. "You are without a breastplate. Your master Maimonides is right. I have told Samuel ben Ali to his face of the Rambam's doctrines; I have recited what the very sage of sages, Rabbi Sherira ben Hanania, said: 'Things taken from the Midrash and Aggadah are not to be taken literally and never relied on. Only that which agrees with Scripture and is based on logic must be accepted.' As a result, he has threatened me; I count this no more than the bite of a gnat. But you, young man, are unknown. A dagger in your back, a tasteless poison in your cup, a roof tile down upon your head —these would hardly be noticed. Save yourself, for the Jews need such as you. Return to Egypt—alone."

My heart ballooned with rage. I wanted no such advice. I had come for a scheme of my own to employ against Ben Ali. I sprang to my feet. "I shall never return to Egypt!" I shouted, quivering with my own frustration. "I shall live, I shall prosper—and I shall have Sarah! You are a heretic! I should never have come to you!"

Instead of being roused by my anger, Ben Azariah merely looked aside. He shook his head. "As Allah wills," he said regretfully. "I may tell you that the reputation of Maimonides for good works and wisdom in these times exceeds that of the Gaon, even in Bagdad. Nor is the Gaon's logic improved. The Yemenites send many queries to him. One recently asked him to refute Maimonides' opinion on the resurrection of the dead. I saw his reply and I marveled at the legends he had compiled. He pretended to defend Maimonides but he twisted all he had said. Still more strange were the ideas of Ben Ali on philosophy. He told fairy tales, as women do to children, and left all as fantastic and confused as before."

"This is nothing to me."

"Except that his hatred extends to all such as you. He now says there is no need for the Exilarch, only for a spiritual leader of the Jews—and that he who disputes this, disputes Moses himself. And he does not mean Moses ben Maimon, my friend."

Thus ended my interview with Ben Azariah. Thus commenced what we would call an exodus and the Moslems a hegira. But since I write this to tell not my own history but that of Maimonides, I shall put all briefly. I may say only that what happened was in large part a retelling of the story of the pursuit of David by King Saul, even as my master had warned me. The Scriptures gave me the plan whereby I could free Sarah; the lattice offered me opportunity to pass her the message.

One moonless night a trusted slave lowered her in a basket over the wall of the Gaon's palace; left in her bed was a bolster and a date-fringe to imitate her presence. All was prepared. We fled as lovers, into the night, into the teeth of a rising desert storm, with animals and baggage, accompanied only by two slaves and one other. Of all persons, he was the only one I could trust: Yoseh ben Zerorot.

It was further evidence of his stupidity that he was willing to come with me, but my heart had been touched at his simple loyalty to a tutor who had done little for him. That same night, in a village south of Bagdad, a country rabbi married us without ceremony, speaking the words of our joining fearfully between claps of thunder.

Three days later, we could not resist visiting the Tower of

Babel. It was immense: two miles long in foundation, forty cubits wide, two hundred cubits high to its unfinished top. Winding roads curled upward. Sarah and I stood atop and viewed the landscape for twenty miles. Lightning from heaven had undoubtedly destroyed the tower. I myself examined the rocklike masses of bricks which had once been fused together, but were now rent from top to bottom.

We hurried on lest Samuel ben Ali send pursuit. Another day following the flood of the Euphrates (which devours its sandy banks like a lion tearing a lamb), and we came to the tomb of Ezekiel, the prophet. Six days more of forced journeying and we arrived at Sura, where the sages first lived and studied the Torah day and night; we saw many tombs of the princes of David. Eight more days we pressed on. We won to Hillah, where I was forced to make a decision I did not care for. Yoseh, who went alone into the villages to buy what we needed, came back with a garbled story. It seemed orders had come by courier from Bagdad to intercept all couples traveling together, by order of the Chief Gaon. I dared not return to check on what he reported. My questioning was futile.

"I'm sorry," Yoseh said penitently, "I know I'm a fool but I can't do anything about it unless you tell me what I can do."

"If you know you're a fool," I said, "then that is the beginning of wisdom."

Yoseh pondered. "If I am so wise," he inquired, "why do I think I'm a fool?"

"If you listen to what people think of you," I exclaimed, my patience vanishing, "you are surely a fool!"

My own conclusion was almost as stupid as Yoseh's argument. We embarked at twilight upon a long dry arduous journey to the west—across the desert to the land of Yemen. It took twenty-one terrible days. At last we came to that land, surrounded by mountains, where the Jews rule many fortified cities.

But Yemen proved inhospitable. I knew that messengers from Bagdad to this country arrived daily. I chose to double back: We crossed the desert again. Twenty-five days of dry agony to the river Virae, five more days to Basra on the Tigris and Euphrates. We did not stop our flight here but went on down the river two days to the borders of Persia and the sepulcher of Ezra the Scribe. Once beyond the border, I breathed more easily; we no longer traveled day and night. It took us six leisurely days to the half-ruined province of Elam and the capital city of Susa, where there are fourteen synagogues. Sarah regained her beauty lost in the forced marches and I some measure of calm—and Yoseh remained himself.

It was here Yoseh asked me about the art of speaking on the Talmud. I explained again and again the *pasuk* or text, the *kushyah,* or question, and the *terutz,* or answer, but he was unable to keep them in his head. His sample discourses, repeated to me as we jogged along, were entirely disconnected. Finally his mind wandered to other subjects.

"How many Jews are there in Susa?" he asked.

"Seven thousand," I said.

Yoseh became thoughtful. "How many goyim?" he asked at last.

"I don't know," I said. "Certainly more than a hundred thousand."

"Why do we Jews need so many goyim?" Yoseh inquired plaintively.

"To keep us humble," I told him shortly. I goaded my mount and rode ahead but I heard him shout after me: "Surely we could be just as humble with fewer of them, master!"

Fourteen days to Amadia in Kurdistan, the spot where the false messiah, David al-Ro'i, had risen and been exposed later by Maimonides when he came to Palestine. He had used the ineffable Name for many of his works, it was said. I fingered the amulet around my neck uncomfortably. On we went, twenty days to Hamadan and four more to Tabaristan, then seven to Ispahan, the great city with its fifteen thousand Jews. It was here that I received the news of the death of Saladin.

This terrible tragedy came like lightning on a summer day, unexpected and, at first, unbelievable. It happened in Damascus, where our great ruler had gone out on a rainy day to visit the poor, accompanied by Al-Alfadhel. He wore only a light cloak in his customary disregard for the weather. The downpour drenched him. The caliph, already weakened by his long intermittent fevers (which Maimonides warned him were encouraged by his fasts and unceasing labors for his subjects), collapsed. The burly vizier took his master upon his shoulders, thrusting his way through the almost hysterical crowds to the hospital. Messengers were sent to Cairo for Maimonides, directing him to depart posthaste for Damascus. My master obeyed, but he was too late: Halfway to that city, he was intercepted by a messenger in dusty white, the signal of Saladin's death. We Jews had lost our protector; the news, I swear, bowed the heads of more of my own people than of the Moslems.

Knowing that the caliphate of Saladin could not be held together by his sons or his brother, that it would fly apart like flinders, I resolved to stay at Ispahan and make our home there. I settled Sarah and the slaves. With Yoseh, I went hunting for pupils to teach. Yoseh recommended me in the market places in a loud voice; I, with modest dignity, received those who applied. Within a year, we had a small flourishing school and for four years we remained in peace.

At the end of that time, however, the dread warning came. It was poor Yoseh on whom Samuel ben Ali wreaked his vengeance. A strange vendor pressed a bottle of rare wine from Shiraz into his hands, refused payment, and vanished. Such circumstances would have instantly roused my suspicions, but Yoseh trusted all. I found him dying in the courtyard of our home. I sank to my knees in horror, seeing the death-froth was already on his lips. I could do nothing.

Yoseh opened his eyes slowly, painfully. He peeped up at me, agony on his fat wan face. He recognized me as I soothed him. He smiled with effort. "Now I remember," he whispered. "Pasuk: 'It is dark and slippery and the Avenging Angel pursues.' Kushyah: 'But how can he find me if I flee to Ispahan?' Terutz: 'Go anywhere else but there; for in Ispahan he has an appointment with your soul.'"

His body slumped. He was dead. I held his inert form in my arms, saying over and over again the words of the sages: "My son shall not receive his inheritance until he has become foolish." It was Sarah who roused me from my stupor and put me to bed. The next fortnight we left for Ghaznah, seven days journey away.

Our wanderings became a nightmare of unreality. I remember the high forests of Tibet where lived the musk-bearing animals hunted down by trained dogs who make their masters rich; I can visualize again the twenty-eight days we spent journeying to the mountains of Naisabur, being greeted in all kindliness by the Levite prince. Still we fled on. First to the island of Kish, where five hundred Jews do not work but trade only. There was much gossip about us in this clamorous place. Soon we took ship for ten days' journey by sea to Katifa.

Seven days more to Khulam where the people worship the sun. They are descendants of Cush, all black, all honest, but they believe in star-reading. So hot is this place that, from Passover to the New Year, no man goes out of his house after

443

the third hour. They turn night into day to transact their business. We fled toward the east. Twenty-three days by sea to Ibrig, where we found the people to be fire-worshipers.

In this uttermost end of the world we spent years wandering from land to land without peace. We rejoiced we had escaped the knowledge of Samuel ben Ali (though we deceived ourselves): Everywhere we found Jews who bade us welcome. At last we embarked for the land of Zin, a voyage of forty miserable days. Here Sarah became with child. We remained until she was delivered. As I held the small red gurgling thing in my arms, she asked me to name him. "Moses," I said, the word coming to my tongue without thought. Suddenly, at that moment, I became aware of how much my feelings toward my old master had changed. Now I knew without doubt that the only security for us in this world was to return and beseech his protection.

I said nothing to Sarah but when she and the child were ready to travel, we took ship for fifteen days to Al-Gingaleh. After a short stay, we sailed seven days to Chulan, and, finally, a dozen days to Zebid. In all we found a hearty welcome from our people on our arrival and departed amidst a rain of tears. From Zebid we undertook an eight-day caravan journey to India and the land of Aden. We rested there for many months. At last we regained our strength. For the third time, we crossed the desert—this time to Seba on the Nile. From there to Assuan; a dozen days more spent in getting to Heluan. At this city we joined a caravan to pass over the deadly desert of the Sahara. The journey from Heluan to Kuz took thirteen days. Here we found ourselves at last again on the borders of Egypt.

"Fostat is ten days away," I said to Sarah on the night of our arrival at Kuz. She sat silently on the other side of the small fire before our tent, nursing young Moses.

"Then you are determined to return to Maimonides, the enemy of my father?" she said after a long moment.

"Yes."

"Will he welcome you? With me as your wife?"

"I do not know," I said desolately. "I know that here is our only refuge."

"We might return to Bagdad and beg forgiveness."

"Never!"

Sarah rocked the sleeping baby back and forth. Without looking at me, she murmured: "It has been a long, long time, my husband."

444

"Nine years in the wilderness," I said. I sighed. I stood upright, gazing above me at the white sparkle of the stars in the black sky, so brilliant that they seemed to blind me.

"Years in the wilderness of the mind, of the soul, and of the body," I told her. "Though Maimonides once forbade any Jew to settle in Egypt, he came here himself. So shall we, looking for the comfort of our ancestors, even though they were slaves."

Sarah rose beside me. She did not speak but her small lovely face was still and content. "From this night on," she murmured, "my name shall be Ruth."

I frowned down at her. "What do you mean?"

Her smile lighted up her face, even in the darkness, giving it a phantom quality by the glow of the dying coals. "Whithersoever you go, my husband," she said softly, "there shall I go."

CHAPTER 26

The long line, coming and going, bends at last under the weight of time and forms a circle. Ends meet: At last it is impossible to tell the place of their joining. Life turns back and engorges itself like a snake eating its tail. I sit here and write this from the small arbor where Maimon ben Joseph, the father of Maimonides, once watched his son inscribe his noted "Letter to the South," to Yemen—and commenced his own history of my master.

Even as the father did not understand the son, so—I must confess—Maimonides does not understand me. Perhaps that is reasonable. Who is more like a son to a teacher than his pupil? Is it not written that the instructor is more honored than the parent because he partakes of the soul rather than of the flesh?

Well, well: Whatever it is, I write as did the first Moses (blessed be he), being allowed only to see the hinder parts of God. I see what was and what might have been but I do not sorrow for the years that were lost. All ingests its own in the eternity of God, where everything is, was, and shall be—at the same moment.

Were I to follow the rest of Maimonides' life from day to day, it would be superfluous. It would overgo my intention. This is simply to give the essentials of his history, as his father and I knew them. Much has already been written of him. Most of this is unnecessary or foolish, both of which he would declare are evil. But I write to acknowledge the illumination I have acquired from his residence, the guidance from his light. As the poet says of the sea: The cloud showers down rain into it and the sea is enriched but each keeps its own quality.

It is written that man is born with closed hands: He expects to seize the whole world. But he dies, as did Alexander the Great, with his hands open; he can take nothing with him. It is also written that he who runs from fame will find that fame runs after him.

Such were my feelings when I returned to the house of Maimonides after my long self-imposed exile. I had discovered that God, glory to Him, had created the insect before man so that we might be truly humble. I had rid myself of my longing to see the world, that place in which all people look alike—except one's friends; in which every place holds the same disappointments—except home.

Indeed, on our journey to Fostat, I discovered I was already known as Maimonides' pupil—to whom he had so lovingly addressed his *Guide*. I was, for the first time, delighted to stand in his shadow. More and more people recognized me. I found they would walk for miles beside my stirrup simply to admire and chat with me. Even Sarah was impressed, although young Moses expressed his annoyance by continual bawling.

When at last I stood before my master in the familiar courtyard of the house in Fostat, my eyes filled with tears. It was impossible for me to see clearly. But I saw his blurred form advance, felt his arms around me. His patient voice spoke to me with its incomparable resonance:

"Remember, Joseph, my son: A tiny quarrel destroyed Jerusalem. A broken chariot axle devastated the city of Bethar. On account of a single chicken, the city of Tur Malka was laid level with the ground. Let us not imitate history, beloved Joseph. You are my prodigal son returned. Half of all I have is yours. Let us profit by the mistakes of those who have gone before. Let us love one another and let the world pass by."

"With all my heart!" I sobbed blindly. I felt his arms renew

446

their enfolding. The warm drops of his tears fell upon my head. I received them as a sacred blessing. We stepped apart, dashed the moisture from our eyes, and surveyed each other. Maimonides shook his head.

"You have grown thinner," he declared, "and your beard is already flecked with gray."

"Yours is white," I accused him, smiling, "and your head is like the snow on Mount Hermon."

"Which I shall never see again," he said sadly.

"There are many years before us," I told him confidently. I did not truly believe it. He was an old man: His shaking palsy had grown worse. His form was stooped. But the aureole of white about his eagle's face and the huge dark eyes gave him more majesty than a king. My thoughts flamed: Had Moses—Moses ben Amram, the blessed—looked like this, in his last years?

My heart ran over. I embraced him again. Laughing and chaffing each other like youths, we went into the house I knew so well. I spun on my heel. "A moment!" I cried. "I have a wife and a child!"

Maimonides chuckled. "Yaltah and her husband live with me," he said. "Your charming Sarah is already in her apartment and your child being spoiled this instant."

"Yaltah," I said hesitantly.

Maimonides looked at me with an indefinable expression. "She is happy, but her husband is a very dull fellow," he said. I exploded with laughter; nor did we ever mention that subject again. When I met Maali an hour later, I congratulated him with all my heart. I kissed Yaltah on the forehead with the embrace of a brother. I was surprised to see how old they had become; and they, I know, were equally astonished at my appearance. That night, after supping on the roof, Maali made his excuses and hastily disappeared. Maimonides looked at me, his eyes twinkling. "He does not enjoy a good philosophical discourse," he declared.

"Nor I," I said stoutly. "There was no need for you to greet me this morning with your collection of platitudes."

Maimonides smiled. "I have missed your pert tongue and unconventional ideas," he said. "But times have changed. I am no longer a judge, though still a dayyan and rabbi. Nor do I study the books I once studied."

"How is this?" I asked, startled.

"In my youth," Maimonides said musingly, "the Torah was betrothed to me by my father. She continues to hold my heart as the wife of my youth and I find constant delight in her caresses. But there is a strange woman whom I first took into my house as her handmaiden. She has become her rival, sometimes more important than her mistress. Do you know whereof I speak?"

"If I unriddle your conundrum," I ventured cautiously, "I imagine you speak of medicine."

Maimonides laughed in delight and nodded. "But my calling to such a profession is not without holiness," he added. "It is sacred, carrying with it a high religious duty. The preservation and prolongation of life is one of our divine commandments. Our faith believes in healers, even more than philosophers, as agents of God. Is it not written, 'Take exceeding care of your life'?"

"You did not always think so," I said, marveling.

"True," Maimonides replied. "When I was young, driven from one end of the world to the other—you yourself have some knowledge of that—I was troubled by the suffering and exile God had visited on me. I prayed to be relieved of it. I did not see the Hand extended above me, the blessing in another form. Now, in the study of my beloved science, I am happy."

"Others may not think so," I pointed out, popping a ripe fig into my mouth. "You are equally indispensable to the Moslem and the Jew."

"Rabbi Jonathan of Lunel—may his days be filled with contentment—has been good enough to write me on that topic."

"What did he say?"

"That I was a man 'full of divine vision, over whose head the sacred ointment is poured—one who has drawn his people out of the waters of error and sowed the seeds of holiness.' "

"That is true enough," I observed.

Maimonides shook his head. "The excellent man exaggerated, of course," he said. "But I am grateful for his feelings. I am sorry he may be disappointed in my decision. But we must remember when the holy Asa was ill, he sought not God but the healers. Even in the days of the First Temple there were such assigned to the priests."

"This is all very well," I protested, "but I suspect that pride has something to do with your decision."

Maimonides frowned, then his face cleared. "You are too discerning," he said. "I am presently at the height of a medical reputation exceeded by none. The most famous healers

448

from all the quarters of the world do not omit a visit to my house. They ask my advice and solicit my most secret prescriptions, all of which I give freely. I count among my patrons members of the highest nobility. I must say that my income from such sources is not great—they are not very reliable about paying their fees—but the merchants and the better class of citizens pay me gladly. Nor do I neglect the poor—who receive my best efforts and are charged not a dinar."

"There will be those who will hardly be as kind as Jonathan of Lunel," I said. "I can think of one in Bagdad."

Maimonides shrugged. "As you have said at other times, I shall be attacked for pride and arrogance by those who are ignorant. I can even supply their arguments myself. In the Talmud it is written that one should never live in a city whose chief ornament is a physician; it is also said that the best of doctors deserves only the best of hell. But I cannot take these sayings to heart, any more than I can believe the Midrash tales to be more than allegory. Have not the Fathers ordained each town to have at least one healer?"

I was still doubtful. My master, so much older than I, was so much more advanced in his ideas.

"Remember," Maimonides said, "religion prescribes all that is useful and forbids all that is harmful for the next world; medicine indicates what is useful and harmful for this world. As I grow older, I cherish my ability to minister to my fellows. Among a thousand men, only one will die from natural causes. The rest will die early due to irregular and unnatural ways of living. I myself must expect to pay an early price for the travels and privations of my youth."

I looked at him sharply but his face was serene. At first I did not believe that he spoke seriously. Now I realized Maimonides had arrived at a state of perfect calmness on the affairs of life.

"Thus, Joseph," he continued, "I adjure you to remain steadfast in promulgating the faith, to study the Torah—but no longer rely upon my support. I am an old man with white hair, as you have said. Not, perhaps, because of age of intellect but because of my body, which will not do my will."

Despite his obvious failing, however, Maimonides was capable of some extraordinary efforts—especially in the cause of medicine, which he had so firmly espoused. His love for children became more and more evident. He loved to play with his sickly son, young Abraham; he delighted in my sturdier offspring. He spent much of his time playing small games with them, listening sagely to their babble as if he comprehended all nonsense. It seemed to me that he had abandoned his sometimes caustic ways. I told him this was a loss to the world.

"No," Maimonides said slowly, "I have become famous, as you say, but I have learned that praise should come from deeds only. I cannot shame a colleague. I can barely tolerate waiting upon the rich, though I must do it. I am eager to visit the poor and the needful—because this is a virtue above all others."

By the end of that week, he had proved to me the truth of what he said. In the years after the death of Saladin, turmoil had again broken out in Egypt. At first Al-Aziz, one of the great caliph's sons, had succeeded his father. His rule was gradually replaced by the intrigues of Saladin's younger brother and confidant, Al-Adil, or, as the Franks called him, Sapphadin. By the Christian year of 1200, however, the year after Sarah and I returned to Fostat, Egypt had been quieted. Yet the old irritant of the invaders from the West still persisted. It was in response to the caliph's call that Maimonides and I traveled down the Nile to Alexandria, to one of the most extraordinary scenes I have ever witnessed.

We had tied up to the river-slip near the enormous bazaar of the docks, amid a din and bustle and stench which were almost unendurable. Around the central area rose the masts and banners of ships from every nation in the world, a fantastic forest. In the center of the docks, herded in like so many cattle, screeching and praying, were thousands of ragged children.

The messenger from Al-Adil, who had accompanied us with his two Nubian guards, led us to a sheltered corner. In a needfully loud tone of voice he began to tell us of our mission. It appeared, declared the nervous little Moslem, darting glances over his shoulder, that these—ah, here is Yunan, the caliph's chamberlain. He stepped aside. A plainly robed man, tall and gloomy, approached to dismiss the courier who had brought us on the day's rapid journey down the great river. He bowed to us.

"Worthy Maimonides," he said, "you know the story of Abraham, the first man on whom God's will worked to whiten his hair. You put him to shame."

450

"That is a compliment, not a diagnosis," Maimonides said. "What shall I do to aid the great caliph?"

"You come in time," Yunan responded. He nodded his head toward the children. "These wretches call themselves 'crusaders.' There is a madness, in the West which has sent over fifty thousand children running to our land. Their own people do not trust their sons. Hugo Ferreus and William Porlinus, the merchants of Marseilles, betrayed thousands of them and have sold them to the slavers. This is what remains of them."

Maimonides wrinkled his nose at the nauseating odor. I already had bound a perfumed cloth over half my face, wishing I were anywhere else. Yunan went on: "You and your associate are known as workers of wonders in healing. Our master generously wishes to buy these and sell them to anyone who wishes a slave—but he has no desire to cheat the buyers. He asks that you separate the good from the bad."

Maimonides hesitated. I tugged at his sleeve and shook my head, but he gave no sign. He gestured. Yunan bowed, indicating to the guards that they should thrust a passage through the crowd. As we hurried through, Maimonides unexpectedly halted. He reached for the naked swollen abdomen of one of the defiant boys—who was holding aloft a crude cross of sticks lashed together with straw—and deftly prodded. The boy cried out. He swung his cross as a weapon but I warded off the feeble blow.

Maimonides nodded. We resumed our pace. "What is it?" I asked in a low voice, not wishing to be surpassed in medical knowledge.

"The liver and the spleen are enlarged," Maimonides replied in the midst of the hubbub. I frowned. "What does that mean?" I demanded. Maimonides smiled fleetingly. "We shall find out," he responded. I had to be satisfied with that. I felt cheated for I was sure he had guessed something of which I was unaware.

We passed through bedlam. Children clutched at us with filth on their fingers, pleading for food and water, asking for relief from pain. We stepped over others lying flat in puddles of excrement, unable to rise, their glance rolling after us in mute appeal as we hastened on.

At last we managed to gain a small platform in the midst of the assembly. Maimonides produced a vial of aromatic oil. We sprinkled it over our scarves to partially offset the smell. At a sign from Yunan, the guards communicated what appeared to be prearranged orders to a group of Moslem soldiers.

451

They passed among the children, leisurely whacking them with the flat of their scimitars, arranging them into a roughly circular file. Those unable to rise were dragged away, unceremoniously flung into heaps. The sight, the noise, and, above all, the odor of human bodies exuding their incredible liquids, commenced to make me sick. But Maimonides' expression remained lively and interested.

Yunan shouted some indistinguishable words. Soon the children became silent. Their faces looked up at us like a vast discolored mosaic. Suddenly I noted what I had not seen before: Most of them were a bright yellow in color. I had never seen this hue of flesh before. My bewilderment banished my nausea. I leaned to my master.

"They are yellow."

"I know."

"Did you see it before?"

"Yes."

"You didn't tell me."

"You have eyes."

"What is it?" I demanded. "Is it a disease?"

"That we shall discover," Maimonides returned. "I have some hypothesis, as Hippocrates and Aristotle would say—"

"Well," Yunan said at our side, "they are quiet for the moment. What shall we do, eminent healer?"

"Look at their color," Maimonides said. Yunan's eyes widened in fear. "They are afflicted by a djinni!" he muttered hoarsely.

"No, no," Maimonides said impatiently. "This comes from the humor of the body. It does not mean they are mad or possessed by demons."

"What does it mean?" I asked.

Maimonides did not address me but spoke urgently to Yunan. "There are papyri from the ancient Egyptians which I have perused in the great library. They describe this yellow malady. As all-knowing Hippocrates and Galen have shown, this is called 'the yellowing' or 'jaundice.' It is due to an errant condition of the liver. It can be cured in a short time by eating the livers of healthy sheep and cattle."

"Is that all?" demanded Yunan. Maimonides glanced at me. "Never show a fool a secret," he said under his breath, quoting the Talmud. I nodded: "Except the secret of life or death," I added, thinking of Yoseh.

"Take them to the hospital," Maimonides commanded.

"All of them?" Yunan was stupefied.

"Wait," my master said. He turned to me. "Come, Joseph," he said, "we shall pass among them. Do as I do: Discover which of them can be saved and which are beyond hope."

All day we did precisely that, nothing but that. My fingers grew weary from prodding and testing; my lungs filled with fetid odors; my feet trod in slime. I grew to detest my own sweat. I saw the waters of the bay lapping the piles and felt an insane desire to throw myself into it and cleanse my body. Yet before me always moved the tireless figure of Maimonides, his spirit conquering his palsy; he would even speak or joke with the wretched children as he made disposition of their cases to the soldier behind.

Only when a group of the less-diseased broke into barbaric singing about their Lord Jesus Christ did Maimonides pause. A peculiar look crossed his face. He shook his head to his attendants who would have silenced them. The nasal nonsense accompanied us to the end of our tour.

Late that day, our task finished, we took our ease in the royal hamadan-bath. As we sweated out our labors amid the exquisite steam and perfumes, the attendants passing the strigils over our hides, I asked him about the incident.

"Why did you allow them all that bawling about Jesus Christ?" I wondered.

Maimonides ran his fingers through his beard, tossing off drops of sweat. I could see, from his sunken face and shaking muscles, how tired he was. He managed a smile. "I have thought much about the Christians and Moslems," he told me. "The Moslems cannot be regarded as heathen. They ascribe to God His proper perfect unity."

"But the Christians," I said impatiently. "Even these mad young ones mock our religion."

"Nay," Maimonides said. "The teachings of Christ, and of Mohammed who rose after him, tend to bring to perfection all mankind so that we may serve God with one consent. The whole world is thus full of the words of the Messiah, of the Holy Writ, and the Torah. These words have spread to the ends of the earth, even if men deny their binding character. When the Messiah does come, all will return from their error."

"Once you spoke less tolerantly!" I said in amazement, half starting up from my slab of marble.

"As a seed changes and rots, then transforms earth and water into itself, so it is with Christians. They seem to have cast the laws of Moses aside, yet it has changed them. All

453

men, one day, will be the fruit of God's seed when they acknowledge Him. All will become one mighty harvest."

"I do not believe it! What of their Christ—Jesus, the apostate rabbi?"

"The Christians make mention of Jesus but, believe me, Joseph, their thoughts turn toward the true Maker in Heaven and none other."

I rose with vexation, puzzled, confused, and wrapped a linen robe about me. I could think of nothing else to say. As I proceeded toward the cooling-room, I halted and turned. "I suppose," I said bitterly, "we may teach Christians the Law."

To my utter stupefaction, Maimonides nodded. "Yes," he said, "for they admit our Law is divine and preserve it in its entirety."

It had been a hard day but I had never expected it to be a blasphemous one. I was glad to be able to pretend to gasp with the frigid air rather than to gape at Maimonides.

Indeed, my master had changed. He had apparently become meek, like the rabbi from Nazareth, and tractable—toward everyone, except myself. Yet his reputation was illimitable. No one dared offer him other than reverence because of his standing at the court of Al-Adil. His very manner and beneficence won him the same enviable position. At the very time of life when there was little he could not do, there was little he wanted to do.

It was pleasant to live under such protection. Family and friends flourished in esteem. The maledictions of Samuel ben Ali from Bagdad were strangely silenced. Maimonides was able to help countless Jews. He never refused his voice nor his influence except in the most gross cases of wickedness. Nevertheless, he possessed a view of life which had become almost impersonal. In the case of the jaundiced Christian children crusaders, I had been fretted with visions of my own small Moses, of small Abraham, being in the same state. I lay sleepless because we had had to make so many decisions on the sickly ones. When I reproached Maimonides with this, he shook his head: "Death will not be stayed by good intentions," he told me. "We must do all we can but that is all God expects of us. To those children who were dying, we were merciful, not cruel."

As it was, his ministrations and the prompt treatment of the hideous yellow disease cured more than half the afflicted chil-

454

dren. Some few were ransomed, Maimonides raised funds to send more home to their native lands, but many, alas, were sold by the Moslems into slavery.

Somehow the incident mellowed my master yet further. He liked to think of his rescue of the Christian young ones, the tiny crusaders, as a contribution of his own toward hastening the day when all men would see the same light of the one true God. But his work that day in the broiling sun had weakened him noticeably. Despite his severe regimen of diet and sleep, there were increased symptoms (as he himself diagnosed) of the palsy which he had inherited from his father.

This, in turn, shaped his thoughts toward his own youth and his unhappy relationship with his father. He mourned the misunderstandings which had come between them; still, he felt, these might be inevitable between sons and fathers. "It is a balance of nature, I suppose," he said to me, "that when we are strong we are stupid and when we are weak, we are wise. Other than this, the earth might be ruled by brute force or perish because it had become so feeble."

Indeed, Maimonides did penance for his youthful errors in this fashion. He surrendered his days almost wholly to the tending of the sick, an obeisance in soul to the past dedication of his parent. At such times one felt he was communing with the spirit of his father, reconciliation hidden deep in his heart. It was apparent that this was the great satisfaction in my master's life in his declining days, to heal the sick and comfort the despairing. Once I saw him look curiously at his hands, as if they were not his own. "These are the fingers of Maimon ben Joseph," he said softly, half to himself, "and they busy themselves about his arts."

Thus our days passed, in this fruitful autumn of his age, until I lost count of his kindnesses and benefits, bestowed upon me as upon all others. Maimonides had changed much from what he had been; from the fiery youth into the sage of his people and their deliverer, not only from the ills of body but also from the sicknesses of disputation. Yet even as he worked —much more slowly than was his wont—I could perceive he was drifting from this world into another, more bright with welcome than I could imagine. As he labored with the sick, this inner radiance shone often on his face.

It was hardly a surprise to me, therefore, when the time came for Maimonides, my beloved master, to make his farewell to earthly existence. To the last moment, I was with him.

It was a warm day, the twentieth of Tebet, when Maimonides and I sat alone in the courtyard where we had gathered often before. The insects made a pleasing drowsy sound in the barely stirring forenoon air. The sun lay quiet and golden in the doorway like a great tawny cat.

Maimonides stirred, rose stiffly, and came to me. "Let us walk for a while and go to the hill of the tomb of Guilbert and Zamira," he said to me. "I am restless for their company."

I yawned at him and shook my head. "You have not been there for many weeks," I told him. "You are no longer young. The climb will be too much for you."

Without a word, he turned and walked toward the outer gate. I hastily put on my slippers and ran after him, taking his arm. Together we proceeded out of the gate and down the road, slowly and carefully.

Two hours later, we had arrived at the top of the little ridge above the distant palace of Saladin. Maimonides sank down, breathing heavily from his walk, his face beaded with sweat. I watched him with concern. Even a few miles were dangerous for a man of sixty-nine. In his physical condition— even with his strong will—such an expedition might result in an attack of some sort.

He seemed comfortable after a few minutes. His color came back. He closed his eyes and leaned against the wall of the cave. "I wish to write something," he said, "but I am too tired. Will you take it down for me?"

I fumbled in my belt for the case of writing materials I always carried. Suddenly, I saw his body topple and fall. I leaped to his side and caught the leaden weight, raising it, and stretching it out on the slab of stone. I turned to run for help. His weak voice stopped me. "No," he said, "no. Remain with me."

In his low, unreal voice, pausing at each line, Maimonides whispered next to my ear. He repeated one of the poems of Judah Halevi that I had long ago committed to memory:

> "This mortal body hides
> A thing immortal,
> As light hides in the tomb.
> Should flesh not open wide
> To swing the portal
> And let the soul go home?"

He ceased. With great effort, I managed to swing his legs up on the shelf inside the cave. With an evident sigh of relief, Maimonides sank back. I tried to make him more comfortable, but with a quick accession of authority he waved me back.

I took my seat on a stone close to him, my pulse beating with anxiety. I could not rid myself of the feeling of guilt for having allowed him to come so far at his age. Yet he gave so great an impression of strength that such an error was almost unavoidable. Strength that welled up from a source fed by the unceasing energy of the universe.

As I sat there, not daring to stir, I heard the lightest possible rustle on the stone. From beneath the stone slab on which the rigid body of Maimonides rested glided a small black snake. It paused, its beady eyes regarding me, its tongue flickering. I pressed my fingers to my mouth: The incarnation of Azrael, the Angel of Death, said the old tales of the Midrash. I had not believed them before; now my soul was sure. I bowed my head. With a quick movement, the snake vanished.

Maimonides stirred. In a bound, I was at his side, embracing his body. He looked at me with glazed eyes. His beard flowed away from his mouth, moving slightly as he spoke.

"Put my hands upon my heart," Maimonides said faintly. I obeyed.

"Place my feet together," Maimonides whispered. Despite my tears, I obeyed.

"Now," Maimonides said through his pale lips, "take your two fingers and shut my eyes." I touched his cold flesh and did as he bade me.

"Come when you will, Azrael!" cried Maimonides in a voice so strong it surprised me by its echo. "My body is ready! My soul has been ready for lo! these many years!"

With that, his lips closed. He lay motionless upon the slab, his face whiter than the cloth under his head, his feet like snow upon the napkin I took from my breast. I could no longer see his bosom rise and fall. I felt strangled by the grip of the grief in my heart but I could not utter a sob. Nor did I know if what I felt was sorrow at losing a father or rejoicing that such a one was passing to his supreme glory.

I sat alone in the chill of the cave. I waited for some event, I did not know what. I held my head in my hands, pressing back against my temples for fear they would burst with the pounding blood. Through the gloomy murk of my thoughts

457

came creeping a slow gleam of light, a memory of an old tale: the story of how Moses of Sinai had died.

"Come," God had said to the soul of Moses, "it is time for you to return to Me. For a hundred and twenty years you have lived in this body of dust. Now the time has come for you to come back, undefiled, to Paradise."

But the soul said: "I am Yourself and You are myself. At Your command, I left Paradise and entered this body. I was lonely in Paradise and here, for more than a century, I have been companion to the body which has taught Thy truth. I can not come back to Paradise."

"Your earthly days are ended," God said. "Now it is time for you to enjoy Paradise. There you will be in the highest heaven. You will have your place alone, in the shadow of my Divine Majesty."

"Except for Yourself," said the soul of Moses, "will I find any companion there purer and holier than the one I have had on earth? Will I not be lonely for goodness and purity and truth? Forgive me but I beg of you to allow me to stay with Moses."

The heavens brightened as God smiled. The refulgence of His glory illuminated heaven and earth. Slowly the Presence descended to the body of Moses. The lips of God pressed a kiss upon his lips. Upon feeling this divine caress, the soul of Moses could no longer resist; it leaped upward for very joy and flew into Paradise upon the kiss of God.

Alone, I approached Maimonides for the last time. The sounds of the city seemed very far through the rocky walls: rising to us from miles away, the cries, the insults of the vendors, the noises of people passing and speaking. It seemed as if they were assailing Maimonides now, in all vulgarity and ignorance, as they had assaulted him while he lived. An insane desire to shout them down rose within me; but I realized he did not heed them when he lived. He had no interest in their opinions. He had done what he had done, what he had been called to do by God.

The temperature suddenly seemed stifling in the cave. It held me, as in the folds of a wool burnoose. I reached out and touched the folded hands of my master. I started back. They were cold, so cold! He had vanished into some land where I could not follow him any longer. No more by my own will, only by the will of God.

The sun, through the narrow clefts, raised an ark of gold about him. The slanting rafters of the afternoon upheld his

458

invisible covenant with God. I watched his face, like that of a marble statue I had once seen in a Greek home, every line of it clear and noble, eyes shut and pale, cheeks transparent, the high forehead and dominating nose falling back, into his thin white hair, into the wasted muscles of the neck. I wondered what he had been, what he had become—now that he was dead.

If he had been a Christian, he would have been one of their greatest saints. If he had been a Mohammedan, he would have risen to be a prophet. If he had been born among the Chinese Jews or those of Ethiopia—anywhere else in the world—he would have been next to deity. But here: Here he was a man who had done what he believed to be his best. A man who had devoted all his life to the fulfillment of the work he believed God had laid upon him and had remained simple and undefiled to the end.

A slight mist, an exhalation, a scarcely visible cloud, hovered above his lips. I started: Perhaps he was alive! Then I realized it was no more than a deception of my sight. For the moment, it seemed as if Maimonides had been touched with heavenly lips that caressed him while God received his soul.

No, I thought, he was no more than a man. He would never have claimed more than that—a man who had lived and died, who had endured both trials and triumphs with dignity and modesty. A man who had made mistakes and recognized them to his profit, who had outgrown vengeance and become merciful. Was there any more to any existence? In any planet of the skies above was there more than what he had studied so often in his lonely hours? Which was more important, to be holy or happy? Surely he had been the one but the other had fled from his embrace.

No more than a man. But a man of justice and pity, of righteousness and knowledge, of compassion and dreams—of all the strange and wise ingredients which go to make up the best of our clay. Why was I weeping for him, I, who had been closest and most beloved of him during these last years?

He was a man. In this mortal life, he found immortality. In the unholy, he discovered holiness; in the ugly, beauty. From the diseased, he had brought forth the seeds of health. In that which was confused and ignorant, he had brought forth the soul of order and wisdom. For the questions of many, he had produced the answers. Into the darkness he had brought light.

This was his death and his resurrection, the end and the beginning. For I could, in truth, say of him, that of all the men of this time of blood and wickedness, he had been the wisest, the most merciful, the most just, the best.

THE END

NOTE

Oddly enough, in the long list of great Spanish names—from Seneca to Santayana—there is none more illustrious than that of Moses ben Maimon, known as "Maimonides."

Odd, because this speculative and practical genius was most certainly a Jew of Jews, of a line which traced direct descent from King David himself. But Maimonides always thought of Spain as his native land. He invariably signed his letters with a significant postscript: "the Sephardi," which is to say, "the Spaniard."

This Spanish Jew drew upon the Greeks, Arabs, Egyptians, Babylonians—even the Nestorian Christians—for the stuff of his incredible career. Since his day, his work has haunted the philosophic thought of every succeeding civilization—though his towering contribution was essentially to Jewish theology and medicine.

In the twelfth century—the dates of Maimonides are 1135 to 1204—the men of learning in that "Golden Age" were almost driven to be non-specialists. Few names remain from those days which, if notable at all, are not known in more than one field of inquiry. None is more wide-ranging than Maimonides.

In this year following the 760th anniversary of his death, he can boast a reputation in the studies of philosophy, theology, medicine, chemistry, pathology, psychology, jurisprudence, toxicology, sexual mores, politics and diplomacy, education and polemics—to mention a few. In the phrase coined about him in the Middle Ages, "since Moses there has been none like Moses."

Yet though The Rambam—as he is nicknamed from the initials, *R*abbi *M*oses *b*en *M*aimon—holds a classic place in Jewish regard second only to the giver of the Torah, he did not reach the creative inspiration of the first Moses. Maimonides' assets were a gigantic memory, a superlative talent for analysis and organization, a burning ambition to help his people, and

461

—above all—a strangely modern style of writing which remains as simple and direct today as it must have been then to his flowery contemporaries. "I would not write a chapter," he said, "if I could say what should be said in four lines."

His monuments are similar in content but far apart in appeal. One is his *Mishneh Torah*, the enormous and authoritative explication of the Mosaic laws, directed to all Jews. The other is his *Guide for the Perplexed*, a collection of erudite explanations of philosophy and religion affectionately addressed to his favorite disciple, Joseph ben Aknin. A third masterpiece is his *Commentary on the Mishnah;* a fourth is his series of letters to various parts of the world, dealing with Jewish doctrine. Some of his texts, like the *Preservation of Youth* and the *Guide,* are still popularly read today.

It must not be forgotten that during the last fourteen years of his life alone, Maimonides wrote eighteen books on medicine, on such subjects as sex hygiene, poisons, and hemorrhoids, and, in addition, edited the aphorisms of Galen and Hippocrates. In ten years of his youth—between the ages of thirteen and twenty-three—he composed a treatise on the tortuous Jewish calendar, another on logic, and commentaries on the Babylonian Talmud.

The influence of Maimonides on Jewish life then and now remains incalculable. It was he, for example, who first defined the taryag, the 613 mitzvot consisting of 248 positive and 365 negative precepts of Jewish custom. But his influence on Christian ways is almost as strong. His *Guide*—written in Arabic, translated into Hebrew and Latin—was one of the most widely appreciated documents of medieval Europe. And in the Moslem world Maimonides is still revered as a quasi-saint.

As might be expected, not even his massive reputation in his own time served to protect him from denunciation. He was accused by a French rabbi of trying to subvert the old religion; by an Arab poet, of being a renegade Moslem. Brickbats of supposed error and heresy—some dealing with alleged mistakes in grammar—flew about his head. His lifelong enemy was Samuel ben Ali, head of the Jews in Bagdad, and the most powerful religious and political figure of his kind. Nor was Maimonides loath to defend himself. He used every weapon, from invective to logic, from damnation to sweet reason, to defend his theories. The centuries have justified him.

Despite all this, however, Maimonides as a man remains a shadowy figure. Though his father, Maimon, was himself a famous rabbi, physician and judge, prominent in the court of the caliph of Cordova, the mother of Maimonides is unknown. Though Maimonides was twice married (the second time to the sister of the secretary of Saladin's court in Egypt) the identity of his first wife is lost. Even the appearance of Maimonides is uncertain. It seems that he was tall, striking, of imposing dignity. His features were dominated by a boldly aquiline nose that helped give him the soubriquet of "The Eagle."

What is much clearer is the fact that Maimonides devoted his life to his work. It was dedicated to a kind of high slavery no less because of his honors than his toil. Maimonides had to reject the post of Nagid—prince of the Jews of Egypt—because of the pressures inherent in the office. During much of his life he served as one of the supreme judges of that country. Respected as the uncrowned head of the Jews in the Moslem world, he represented them at court, resolved their disputes, set up charitable groups to ransom those seized by pirates or ransom-hungry marauders, brought together warring factions (such as the Karaites and Rabbanites) and conducted an unbelievably heavy correspondence—nearly all in his own handwriting—replying to questions sent him by rabbis and lay Jews throughout the known world.

It was precisely this world which made Maimonides' task so demanding. In the period of the Crusades, that extraordinary ebb and flow between Palestine and Europe, both Christians and Moslems revealed aspects of actual insanity. Between these two factions, as between millstones, the Jews found themselves being ground to bits. But because of their superlative abilities as educated men—as cosmopolitan merchants and world travelers—they were in demand as doctors and teachers, diplomats and stewards. Hardly a court, Christian or Moslem, did not employ them in high positions. Samuel ben Ali rode second only to the caliph in state processions. Maimonides himself was an intimate of Saladin and his prime minister, Al-Alfadhel; and was, at one time, requested as a personal physician by Richard I of England.

The great desire of Maimonides—in common with his people—was to have a homeland. His family was driven from Spain to Morocco, from Morocco to Palestine, and finally—when he was thirty-one—to Egypt, the very spot he had denounced as "unfit for any Jew to live in." Here as well he was buffeted by Christian invasions and Moslem suspicions. Neither party had much scruple about squeezing Jewish purses dry, demanding unheard-of services, then giving the unfortunate over to torture or death. Survival depended wholly upon the ability to make oneself indispensable.

Maimonides all his days walked on such a tightrope, balancing himself by his vast knowledge of medicine. As Saladin's doctor, he was able to avert the forced conversion of Jews, to fend off the attacks of Jewish fanatic "messiahs" within their ranks, to rectify evil. An example is the affair of Yahya-Zuta, a zealot who called himself "Sar Shalom," the "prince of peace"—but whom Maimonides contemptuously designated as "Shor Shalom," the "complete ox." Zuta had denounced a Jewish leader, Samuel ben Hanania, for peculation in office and got him falsely imprisoned for sixty-six days. Because of Maimonides' influence, Samuel was reinstated, but the vengeful Zuta harried his deliverer for the rest of his life.

Nor did Maimonides profit materially from these activities. His most withering rebukes were directed against those rabbis who accepted fees for teaching. He held that exploiting the Torah for personal gain dishonored both teacher and creed. He supported himself, at first, as his father and brother David had, by trafficking in precious stones. He gave this up when he became well-enough known to have a sound medical practice.

But even here Maimonides refused to profit as he might have done. It was not unusual in those times for a brilliant court physician to retire with a fortune equivalent to a dozen millions of dollars in our day. Maimonides left his son, Abraham, in comfortable circumstances, but he was far from wealthy when he died. And the same was true for over two centuries of Maimonides' "physician" descendants.

The sixty-nine years of Maimonides' life divided themselves naturally into two parts: the search for God through law and the finding of God through love. There is a legend that the boy scholar at the age of ten returned from his teacher, Joseph ben Migash, and astounded his father's synagogue with an hour's learned discourse on the Talmud. It may not be an exact fact, but it is certain that great things were expected of the gifted boy. Hs is the only Jewish scion whose exact hour and day of birth have been recorded from those years (one o'clock in the Passover afternoon of the Jewish year 4895—March 30, 1135). Barely out of his teens, he drafted a small book on the Jerusalem Talmud, a more difficult body of work than the Babylonian tractates. His famous "Thirteen Articles of Faith"—to this day fixing the code of Jewish belief but at that time not accepted because it was without sanction from either Scripture or Talmud—were drawn up when he was twenty-three.

The peak of his pilgrimage toward a knowledge of God came in 1180, when he was forty-five. The *Mishneh Torah*, a codified explanation of the numerous Jewish laws, appeared after eleven years of unremitting work. It was, and remains, the most brilliant and daring essay in the whole of rabbinical literature: brilliant because its fourteen books for the first time reduced chaos to coherence; daring because it appeared to set Maimonides up as a rival to the first Moses. Already famous for his letters on the sanctification of the name of God and on apostasy, as well as his thousands of Responsa and the Mishnah commentary of 1168, in this final work he set the high-water mark of his controversial scholarship.

Three years after the *Mishneh Torah*, Maimonides married a second time. By 1186 he had two children. Four years later, he wrote the even more famous *Guide for the Perplexed*. But a different tone pervaded this composition. Where he had been authoritative and didactic, he now reposed in affectionate explanation. He wrote of the highest Scriptural mysteries to Ben Aknin, though that youth's studies had disappointed him. He exorted and pleaded; he no longer thundered or commanded.

For the remainder of his life, as Maimonides admitted, he slowly abandoned the investigation of his faith, serene in its surety: "There are things beyond the human mind inaccessible to human understanding." He devoted himself to the probing of scientific data and the uses of medicine. He relented from his earlier position that Christians were damned by their beliefs and came to the same conclusion as his predecessor—the poet Judah Halevi—that in fact they worshiped the same God. At the end of the *Guide*, Maimonides told his favorite pupil: "God is near to all who call Him if they call Him in truth and turn to Him. He is found by everyone who seeks Him, if he always goes toward Him and never goes astray."

This overflowing of the human vessel was brought about by a full life. The death of his brother David (in 1174) and of his father the same year; the birth of his children, including a daughter who died in infancy, must have brimmed his cup. Nor could he have been stoical about the departure of Ben Aknin, whom he regarded in everything but blood as a son.

More than ever, Maimonides relied upon good works. He rose only to defend fiercely his extraordinary (in the sense of being new) doctrine of personal immortality. His reverence for Moses—and for Aristotle and Averroës next—became part of the bedrock of his personality. He had reached the solution of his private problems—and with them the solution of the problems of most of the Jews for all time.

Maimonides had little liking for poetry and less for music. He had no time for the lighter things of life, such as good food and drink and idle conversation. He lived to study and interpret, to piece together the bits of faith shattered more than a millennium before by the Roman soldiers. His mission, like that of his God, was to bring order out of the abysm.

This was everything needed. Without the cohering touch of his writings, without his healing of body and mind and faction, the Jews of that century surely would have been lost in the boiling cauldron of the Crusades or absorbed by their natural empathy for the Moslem belief. They needed the lash of his harsh, plain prose to see themselves clearly, to regain their heritage.

Still, there are bits of Maimonides' writings that are poetry, others that are music. In speaking of the fits of prophecy, he wrote that "When one continuously dwells upon the great and abstruse themes, having the mind capable of comprehending them; sanctifying himself, withdrawing from the ways of the ordinary men who walk in the obscurity of the times, zealously training himself not to have a single thought of the vanities of the age and its intrigues but keeping his mind disengaged, concentrated on higher things—on such a man the Holy Spirit will promptly descend. He will be changed into another man and will realize that he is not the same as he has been, that he has been exalted." Such a strain compares favorably with the famous monologue of Socrates on the soul.

Other words, no less musical but more humble, are found in his treatise, "The Preservation of Youth," written for the son of Saladin six years before Maimonides died: "Let God lengthen the days of my lord, keep him in health and make him happy both in this world and the World-to-Come, as God has promised His servants and the gathering of His friends. Such is the wish of your servant, Moses ben Maimon the Sephardi."

Still working, still thronged with thoughts that he was now too feeble to put down himself, dictating to his nephew during the still hours of the night that he preferred, on December 13, 1204, Maimonides sighed deeply and lay down on a couch for one of his infrequent rests. In less than an hour he was dead.

His passing was felt throughout Egypt, for the government decreed three days of official mourning. This was observed in mosque and synagogue alike. As had been his wish, his body was transported overland by the grieving Jews of Egypt to be buried—by special permission of the Moslems—in Tiberias, in Palestine. Here, near the tomb of Judah ben Kadosh, his ancestor (and original editor of the Mishnah); near the tomb of the famous Akiba, the rabbi who had singlehandedly resurrected the Jewish faith a thousand years before; and Judah Halevi, the poet-philosopher; Maimonides entered the Olam ha-bah, the World-to-Come.

To him, at the end of his unusually long life—maintained by the domination of his mind over physical ills—all existence must have become a series of illusions except for the last reality. But he must have discovered, too, that every illusion in its place is real. And that only by passing through the reality of the illusions in time could he finally glimpse the reality of the Eternal.

His time—the "Golden Age" of Moslem Renaissance, with its enormous enthusiasm directed toward the absolute ideal and the brutish practical—is almost incomprehensible to modern thought. Our emphasis on the relative utilitarian and pragmatic pity makes the story of Maimonides a difficult one. In this biographical novel, it is interpreted to be intelligible.

The Arabic names have been given English equivalents. Language usages, insofar as possible, have been modernized. The term *ben* has been standardized for Jew, *ibn* for the Moslem. The term "Moslem" has been used throughout for alternatives such as "Mohammedan" or "Mussulman."

In one or two cases—notably that of Judah Halevi, who lived in the same century as Maimonides but earlier—the time sequence has been telescoped. A few characters, of necessity, are fictional—the two Naomis, the woman physician, Rachel, and Zamira. Most of the rest are quite like their real proto-characters.

Certain customs of that time have been used. The reappearance of characters is not fictional coincidence: This is what is recorded in the chronicles of the time. The world was much tighter then; the uproar and transmigrating much more common; the classes to which Maimonides and his peers belonged were much smaller. It was not unusual to meet friends or enemies again and again in different countries under wholly different circumstances. Nor was the psychological swing from bloodletting to asceticism at all uncommon in either men or women. The frequent occurrence of the same name was also part of the times: Originality in naming infants was not then, as now, deemed a virtue.

Finally, concerning the first marriage of Maimonides, Zamira has been invented to fill this gap. It must be emphasized that she was not a concubine in any sense: Maimonides took her for his legal wife by recognized Moslem-Judaic rites (though not with an ornate wedding) and she would everywhere have been recognized as such.

What must be accepted above all is that the novel itself is written from the viewpoint of Maimon ben Joseph and Joseph ben Aknin, respectively father and "son" to Maimonides. This means they had knowledge of facts now esoteric but they were not historically omniscient. Nor did they know many of the items now part of the handy-kits of the historiographers. The story has deliberately kept their knowledge within the bounds of their time in the belief that thereby a greater verisimilitude might be gained. Many of the places, for instance, that Ben Aknin mentions in his flight to the east are no longer in existence or have been renamed. But they indubitably existed then (as witness the contemporary diary of Benjamin of Tudela).

Costumes, customs, ideas—the combination of sentimentality and brute force which was the hallmark of that century—have been held to. On the other hand, the dialogue has been fitted as closely as possible to our own idiom without being ridiculous. As Maimonides remarked: "Who adheres slavishly to the order of words or sentences in the original will meet with much difficulty; his rendering will be faulty and untrustworthy."

In a few cases, the facts have been extended to meet the probabilities. One instance is in the puzzle of Maimonides' "conversion"; another lies in the fact that Richard I asked Maimonides to attend his person and his court. It is a fact that an emissary of Saladin conferred with Richard on the Egyptian border; it is true that Maimonides was sometimes used in confidential missions by Saladin. Ergo: the fictional meeting between Richard and Maimonides.

Beyond these few explanations, one is free to go his way. It need only be added that the whole point of any ritual of historical fiction is to plunge the reader head over heels into the baptismal tank. He should come up dripping and glowing, converted to the delight of being reborn into another life. If the novel does not accomplish this, it is dull, stale, and useless —no matter how expertly oriented and soundly documented.

The authors hope that this effort meets its own standards.

LESTER MORRISON
RICHARD G. HUBLER

Los Angeles, California
Ojai, California
January, 1965